PUCKING AROUND

ALSO BY EMILY RATH

PUCKING AROUND

EMILY RATH

KENSINGTON
PUBLISHING CORP.

kensingtonbooks.com

Tropes: Hockey romance, "why choose," friends to lovers, instalove

Tags: MF, MM, MMF, MFM, MMFM, hockey romance, romantic comedy, instalove, friends to lovers, queer awakening, too much sex, don't poke the bear, golden retriever, everyone has tattoos, baby girl, bend over, daddy, Finnish 101

Content warnings: *Pucking Around* contains some themes that may be distressing to readers including one family's history of receiving harassment, vicious bullying linked to homophobia, and a brief discussion of a family member's attempt to unalive. More than one main character has a history of substance abuse; one went to rehab for treatment (discussed, not shown). A main character also has a history with disordered eating (briefly discussed as part of their past).

This book also contains detailed two-, three-, and four-person sex scenes that include elements of impact play, choking, voyeurism, bondage, double penetration, double vaginal penetration, toy use, degradation, dom/sub, spit play, snowballing, and breeding kink.

To the Jakes everywhere who want to
be loved,

the Calebs everywhere who want
to be seen,

and the Ilmaris everywhere who just
want a place to call home.

Dear Reader,

Wow, to say this year has been a whirlwind is the understatement of a lifetime! In March 2023, I quietly self-published an adorably quirky, unapologetically queer "why choose" hockey romance book. I honestly thought *Pucking Around* would only be read by a handful of people—why choose readers who like hockey

© *Jennifer Catherine Photography*

and hockey readers ready to try their first why choose. Little did I know it would go on to become a "global TikTok sensation" and an international bestseller, topping the charts for over sixteen weeks in multiple countries.

To celebrate you, my dear readers, I am thrilled to announce that I am now partnering with Kensington Books to release all new paperback special editions of *Pucking Around* and *Pucking Wild*. These new editions will include fun bonus content including curated playlists for each book and some hilarious and heartfelt post-game interviews featuring your favorite Rays. Kensington is on board to make us some truly beautiful books to finish out the series.

So, what can you expect with the Jacksonville Rays hockey series? There are five main books of interconnected standalones. Each book follows different players on the fictional Jacksonville Rays NHL team as they fight to win a chance at a "happily ever after." The series is inclusive in every sense of the word, celebrating kink exploration, sex positivity, and ethical non-monogamy. As a queer person myself, a hallmark of this series is highlighting queer joy. The Jacksonville Rays believe hockey is life and love is love.

Are you ready to meet the Rays? Book one, *Pucking Around*, is a spicy MMFM why choose workplace romance. The book opens with Dr. Rachel Price winning an illustrious sports medicine fellowship. Our Rachel gets matched with the NHL's newest expansion team, the Jacksonville Rays. Rachel has less than twenty-four hours to uproot her life and move to sunny Florida.

Once she's in Jacksonville, Rachel instantly gets off on the wrong foot with Caleb, the surly team equipment manager. Things get complicated when Rachel realizes that Caleb's best friend Jake is the Ray's newest hotshot defenseman. . . . He's also the one night stand she's never forgotten. Did I mention there's a stoic Finnish goalie trying to hide an injury? Rachel has ten months to prove herself in this fellowship, so she can't fall for a player . . . let alone three.

Pucking Around is swoony, sexy, and laugh-out-loud funny. You're guaranteed to fall in love with chaotic Rachel, golden retriever Jake, moody Caleb, and quiet Ilmari. And don't let the length scare you! As a why choose romance, this is not a classic girl-meets-boy story. This is essentially four romances in one book. In true "why choose" fashion, I give all four relationships the chance to blossom and grow.

Your support of this series has quite literally changed my life. I couldn't be more grateful that I have this opportunity to tell you more stories and for these stories to reach more excited readers. I hope you love the Rays as much as I do.

HAPPY READING,

Meet the Rays

PLAYERS
Compton, Jake (#42): defenseman
Davidson, Tyler (#65): backup goalie
Gerard, Jean-Luc "J Lo" (#6): defenseman
Hanner, Paul (#24): defenseman
Karlsson, Henrik (#17): forward
Kinnunen, Ilmari "Mars" (#31): goalie
Langley, Ryan (#20): forward
Morrow, Cole (#3): defenseman
Novikov, Lukas "Novy" (#22): defenseman
O'Sullivan, Josh "Sully" (#19): forward
Perry, David "DJ" (#13): forward
Walsh, Cade (#10): forward

COACHES
Andrews, Brody: Assistant Coach
Johnson, Harold "Hodge": Head Coach
Tomlin, Eric: Goalie Coach

TEAM SUPPORT
Gordon, Jerry: Equipment Manager
Sanford, Caleb: Equipment Manager

MEDICAL SUPPORT
Avery, Todd: Director of Physical Therapy
Jacobs, Hillary: Team Nurse
O'Connor, Teddy: PT intern
Price, Rachel: Barkley Fellow
Tyler, Scott: Team Doctor

OPERATIONS/MANAGEMENT
Francis, Vicki: Operations Manager
Ortiz, Claribel: Social Media Manager
St. James, Poppy: Public Relations Director

STAR SIGNS

RACHEL: Cancer (water): intuitive, emotional, guarded
ILMARI: Aries (fire): bold, ambitious, temperamental
JAKE: Taurus (earth): focused, sensual, steadfast
CALEB: Sagittarius (fire): adventurous, adaptable, blunt

Pucking Around Playlist

1. "Let's Fall in Love for the Night," FINNEAS (E)
2. "boyfriend," Ariana Grande, Social House (E)
3. "Beggin'," Måneskin
4. "I Wanna Be Yours," Arctic Monkeys
5. "There's Nothing Holdin' Me Back," Shawn Mendes
6. "Leave Your Lover," Sam Smith
7. "Crush," Campsite Dream
8. "Till We Both Say," Nicotine Dolls
9. "Like You Mean It," Steven Rodriguez (E)
10. "I Don't Wanna Be Your Friend," Rita Ora
11. "TRUSTFALL," P!nk
12. "Magnetic," Phillip Phillips
13. "Fire For You," Cannons
14. "You?," Two Feet
15. "Break My Heart," Dua Lipa

Finnish Words & Phrases

En voi elää ilman sua: I can't live without you
Haluun tätä: I want this
Joo: Yes
Kulta: Sweetie
Leijona: Lioness
Mä haluun sut: I want you
Mä kuulun sulle: I belong to you
Mä rakastan sua: I love you
Mä tuun: I'm coming
Mennään naimisiin: Marry me
Mitä helvettiä: What the hell?
Mitä vittua: What the fuck?
Mun leijona: My lioness
Niin mäkin sua: I love you too
No niin*: *Versatile meanings*
Oon sun: I'm yours
Oot kaunis, rakas: You are beautiful, darling
Rakas: Darling
Saatana: Goddamn it
Suksi vittuun: Get the fuck out (*literally:* ski into a cunt)
Tule tänne: Come here
Vain sun: Only yours
Voi helvetti: Oh, hell

"**R**ACHEL!"

I groan, not ready to open my eyes and face the truth. It's morning. *Again*. And I'm officially going to murder my roommate Tess . . . just as soon as I remember how eyelids work. Why did I let her talk me into going out last night?

Because you're twenty-seven and single, girl. Live your damn life! I can hear her voice echoing in my head along with the steady *thump thump thump* of last night's dance music.

I'm pretty sure there was drinking last night. What else explains why my tongue feels superglued to the roof of my mouth? Oh god—I think I'm gonna be sick. I'm getting too old for this. I can't bounce back like I could when I was eighteen. There's only one solution: I'm just never drinking again. No more dancing. No more bars. Consider this my retirement from night life.

"*RA-CHEL!* Girl, get *up!*"

I roll onto my back, wincing as I gaze up at the blades of my slowly circulating ceiling fan. I think I slept with my contacts in. My eyes itch so bad.

Make a list, Rach. Make a plan.

That's been my mantra for the last two months as I've tried to put the pieces of my shattered life back together.

Hot shower, strong black coffee, maybe some eye drops—

"RACH!" Tess stomps down the hall and stands in the doorway, her wild, red curls spilling around her shoulders. She's a smokin' hot size twenty with a perfect, pear-shaped body. Per usual, she's wearing nothing but a crop top and her undies, a spray of peachy freckles dotting across her chest. The girl sheds clothes around this apartment like a husky sheds hair.

Not that I mind. I'm the daughter of a super famous rock star.

Born in California and raised on a tour bus, I've seen some wild things in my time. A naked Tess doesn't bother me one bit.

"Girl, did you not hear me hollerin' for you?" She pops a hand on her hip and tosses my phone on the bed. "Someone's been trying to call you for like thirty minutes."

I reach blindly for it without turning my head. "Who is it?"

"I don't know. A New York number, I think. And there was a missed call from Doctor H."

I bolt upright, swallowing down the instant wave of nausea that hits me. "Ohmygod, Tess!" I snatch up my phone. "My boss is calling, and you let it just keep ringing?"

"Hey, I've got my own boss breathing down my neck, thank you very much," she says with a huff. "You handle *your* arrogant asshole, I'll handle mine." She flicks her hair over her shoulder as she turns. Her cheeky undies show off her freckled booty as she saunters away.

I roll my eyes, knowing she means well. Tess is just being over-protective because she's never liked Doctor Halla. She doesn't like the way he micromanages me or his cold, aloof manner. I guess it's just never bothered me. He can't help that he's European.

I drag a hand through my tousled hair, checking my text messages while I wait for my brain to warm up. Six texts and a missed call from my twin brother and his husband. I'm pretty sure Somchai is back in Seattle, which means this is early for him.

HARRISON (8:01AM): In NYC for cooking show. Wanna fly up for taping on Sat?

HARRISON (8:04AM): You *skull emoji*??

HARRISON (8:05AM): MISSED CALL

I grin, shaking my head. Just like a twin to give me exactly three minutes to respond to a question before he jumps to rigor mortis in his mind.

HARRISON (8:07AM): Hello *eyes emoji*

SOM (8:12AM): Girl, you better be dead bc your stupid brother just woke me up at 5AM. CALL HIM BACK

SOM (8:14AM): Plz don't actually be dead

HARRISON (8:20AM): I texted Tess and she says you're hungover, not *skull emoji* LMK about Sat

Now I'm laughing. These two are too much. My brother and his husband are rising stars in the culinary world. Apparently, Harrison was asked to be a guest judge on some new cooking show. He's always been more comfortable using our famous father's name and connections. I wouldn't be surprised if he drags him to the taping.

Which means that if I go, I'll be seated in daddy's shadow when the cameras inevitably pan to him for a closeup. Then I'll get three weeks of hassle as the tabloids remember I exist.

Yeah, no thanks.

I type out a quick reply in our group chat.

RACHEL (8:31AM): Not dead. Can't come bc I gotta work. But good luck *kiss face emoji*

Spotlight glare is literally the last thing I need right now because, two months ago, my own career rocket crashed out of the sky. I was in Seattle for Harrison's wedding when I got the news that I lost out on the Barkley Fellowship. The top sports medicine fellowship in the industry, it pairs early career doctors and physical therapists with professional sports teams. The last three residents Doctor Halla put up for it all won. After their ten-month rotations ended, they were all offered permanent positions.

I was supposed to be lucky number four. Doctor Halla was so sure I would win that he confidently started interviewing for my replacement in the residency program. I had to crawl back from Seattle with my tail between my legs and beg him not to give my spot away. He was kind about it, righteously indignant, swearing he'd never recommend a doctor to their sham of a program again.

So that's where I've been for the last two months, back in Cincinnati, going through the motions day to day. When I'm not putting in my residency hours at the hip and knee clinic, I'm working out or hiding out . . . until Tess gets fed up and drags me out.

My therapist might be ready to prescribe Prozac, but Tess has a whole other kind of therapy in mind. Dick therapy. Since I got back from Seattle, she's been on a mission to get me laid. She thinks a wild night with a guy will cure me of my funk. But just the thought of touching another guy has me cringing.

I go still, my phone balanced in my hand.

Another guy. God, I'm such a mess. As if I already have a guy and Mr. Random Hookup would be the *other* guy. I don't have a guy. Not even close. But hey, a girl can dream, right?

In my case, my nightly dreams are full of only one guy. *The* guy. My Mystery Boy. I haven't told anyone about him. Not even Tess. We met on my last night in Seattle. It was the best one-night stand of my life. I've never felt so dialed in to another human soul before. But that's all it could be for me. One perfect night. No names. No numbers. I woke in the morning and quietly packed my bags, leaving him naked in my bed looking like my every dream.

I regret not telling him my name. He asked me to stay. He wanted me like I wanted him . . . *want* him.

I groan, dragging my hand through my messy hair again. I can't think about Mystery Boy right now. I've got to deal with Doctor Halla.

DR. HALLA (8:08AM): Price, call me ASAP

DR. HALLA (8:15AM): MISSED CALL

Taking a deep breath, I lift the phone to my ear and tap the little green call button. The dial tone chirps three times before it connects. "Dr. Halla, sorry I missed your call—"

"Price, are you here? Come to my office," he says in that posh, slightly accented voice.

"I—no, sir. I'm not scheduled to come in until this afternoon."

"Damn. Well, I didn't want to do this over the phone . . ."

I do a quick inventory. A shower is pretty much nonnegotiable.

And I have to put some food in my stomach. And coffee. Lots of coffee. "Umm . . . I can be there in thirty minutes—"

"No. I don't want to keep them waiting."

Them? Why do I feel suddenly on edge? "Sir, what—"

"You got it."

My mind cranks like a pair of rusty gears as I try to puzzle out his meaning. "I—what?"

"The Barkley Fellowship. You got it," he repeats. His delivery is so deadpan that I'm not sure what to say. Is he joking? Because it's not funny. "Price? Did you hear me?"

"Yes." My heart is racing a mile a minute. "I don't understand—"

"I just got off the phone with Dr. Ahmed from the selection committee at the Foundation," he explains. "Apparently, you were first on the waitlist."

"Oh my god." I shove off the bed and stand on wobbly legs, looking helplessly around my room.

"Apparently, one of the fellows made the genius decision to go whitewater rafting and his raft flipped," Dr. Halla goes on. "Broke both his tibia and dislocated his shoulder, so he's out."

"Ohmygod," I gasp, pacing from the bed to the window. "So, what does that—"

"It means you're in," he replies, cutting right to the chase. "Dr. Ahmed called me as a favor. She knows you're my resident. She wanted to make sure you'd be serious about accepting. I told her you were. I hope I didn't overstep," he adds quickly.

"No, sir, I—" I hardly have words to speak. This can't be happening.

"You *are* still serious about it, right?"

"Of course," I all but shout into the phone. "I—this is just the last thing I expected. Didn't the fellowships already begin?"

"They only started this week," he replies. "That was the other reason she was calling. Usually, the fellows get some say in their placement. If not the specific team, then at the very least gender and sport. You'll need to be willing to fill this other fellow's place. It's already set up and it's too late to change it now."

Oddly enough, the total lack of control is giving me a kind of thrill. I feel like I'm skydiving. "Yes," I say. "I'll do it. Whatever it is, I'm in." I'm grinning now.

"Excellent," he replies. "It'll be more of a physical therapy role than primary care, but they're intrigued with your background in both. Dr. Ahmed wanted to check with me to make sure your experience at the clinic will translate well. I told her you're the perfect candidate."

My heart flutters. "Thank you, sir. Thank you so much for your support—"

"Say nothing of that," he says brusquely. He's not big on gushing. One of the residents hugged him at the Christmas party last year, and I thought he might turn to stone. "I believe Dr. Ahmed already tried to call you this morning. Call her back, and formally accept the fellowship. And don't worry about your shift this afternoon," he adds. "I'll apprise Wendy of the situation."

"Thank you," I stammer again.

"This is a great opportunity, Price. I'm pleased for you. Maybe you can get me tickets to a game this season."

His words register and I stop in my pacing. The fellowship started *this* week. Meaning I have to quit my job, pack up my life, and move, and I don't even know where I'm moving!

"Wait—what's the team?" I call out. "What sport? What city? Did she tell you?"

"Yes," he replies. "Your fellowship will be with the Jacksonville Rays."

My mind spins. Jacksonville. Atlantic side of Florida, I know that much. But my mind is drawing a blank at the Rays. The Jaguars are the NFL team . . . baseball maybe? God, if this is a test of my fit for their program, I'm utterly failing.

"I've never heard of the Rays," I admit.

He chuckles. "Well, you wouldn't. The Rays are the newest expansion team for the NHL. I don't think they've even finished the new arena yet."

I all but shriek with excitement, which is completely unprofessional, but I don't care.

Hockey. It's one of the most ruthless, injury-prone sports. The men play with literal knives strapped to their feet. Lots of bone breaks. Lots of shoulder, hip, and knee injuries. Dislocations. Groin pulls.

It's my dream placement. And a new team means all new equipment, new facilities, over-eager fans.

"Sir—" I squeak out, unable to think of any other words.

He just chuckles again. "Have fun, Price. You've earned this." Then he hangs up.

I stand there with the phone in my hand, utterly speechless. I won the Barkley Fellowship.

Tess ducks her head back in my room, green smoothie in hand. "You talk to Dr. H? What—girl, what's that smile? What happened?"

I start laughing, tears brimming in my eyes.

She pushes off the doorframe. "Girl, what—"

"I'm moving to Jacksonville," I blurt out.

"What—*when*?"

I wipe a tear from under my eye, shaking my head in shocked disbelief. "As soon as possible."

2
RACHEL

"**I** don't know what else to tell you, ma'am. I'm looking at the screen, and I'm not seeing any record of your bags," the airline desk clerk drones for the third time.

I let out an exasperated groan, juggling my heavy backpack and purse on my shoulder while I snatch up the receipts on the counter. "Then explain *these*," I say, flapping them in the air. "The guy in Cincy checked all three of my bags. Clearly, they connected somewhere because—*look*—I've got one right here!" I gesture to the bag at my feet. It's one of Tess's old bags. The thing is holding itself together with little more than a prayer.

This is officially a disaster. The two missing bags have pretty much all my essentials. The bag I managed to claim was a last-minute pack job of odds and ends—a few medical textbooks, some bulky winter clothes, two evening gowns, and random workout stuff. I'm gonna look great waltzing into my first day of work tomorrow wearing a custom backless Chanel dress and my spin shoes.

"Can you *please* check again," I say, slapping the receipts back down on the counter.

It's been 32 hours of pure chaos. I'm hungry, I'm exhausted, and I'm feeling totally on edge after a long day dealing with multiple delayed flights. I didn't even sleep last night, too busy packing. I said a tearful goodbye to Tess before I was at the airport by 6:00AM for my first flight.

But a series of mechanical delays means it's now after 5:00pm, and I've only *just* landed in Jacksonville. And now this human gargoyle wearing a button on her vest that says 'I love corgis' is telling me my luggage has disappeared off the face of the earth.

"I don't understand how two bags can just go missing—"

"Oh . . . wait," she murmurs, the screen of the computer glowing in the reflection off her glasses. "Yeeep . . . here they are. I typed the flight number in wrong."

I stay very still. It's easier this way. I don't get a manager called on me this way . . . or a police officer. "Please just find them."

While she starts clicking away, I shift the bags on my shoulder, looking down at my phone. It's been blowing up since I stepped up to the counter. Apparently, it finally decided to wake up from airplane mode. All the messages come flooding in at once.

I'm sure Tess wants updates. There are a few messages in the Price Family group chat too. I also have a few messages from an unknown number. I read those first.

UNKNOWN (5:05PM): Hey, this is Caleb Sanford from the Rays. I'll be picking you up from the airport. I drive a blue Jeep.

UNKNOWN (5:15PM): I'm here. Outside door 2.

UNKNOWN (5:20PM): Can't sit much longer before the guy makes me go around again.

Shit. No one said there would be an airport pickup!

UNKNOWN (5:30PM): MISSED CALL

UNKNOWN (5:45PM): Look, I don't mean to be a dick, but I can't wait much longer. It says your flight arrived 45min ago.

UNKNOWN (5:47PM): This is Dr. Price, right?

"Oh my god," I cry, shifting all my stuff around on my shoulder.

Great, now I look like a total jerk that just ignores calls and texts for an hour, leaving people to wait on me. I need to call this guy back. I need to get out of this damn airport!

"Please," I say over the counter for what feels like the hundredth time. "If the bags aren't here, I can come back, but I can't just keep standing here—"

She raises a hand in my face. "Ma'am, I need you to calm down."

Oh, no she didn't.

"Calm down?" I seethe. "I haven't begun to be *un*-calm. You're the one who said my bags weren't even in the system two seconds ago—" I choke back the rest of my tirade. It's not worth it. "*Please*," I say again. "Just tell me—"

"Got it," she murmurs, her eyes back on the screen. "Looks like two of the bags were misdirected during your connecting flight in Charlotte. We can have them rerouted here sometime tomorrow morning."

I sigh with relief. "Thank god. What do you need from me?"

"Nothing," she replies, sliding the bag receipts back across the counter at me. "We've got all your contact info. Someone will be in touch letting you know when the bags have arrived."

I snatch up the receipts. "Thanks," I mutter, only adding the 'for nothing' inside my own head.

"Welcome to Jacksonville," she deadpans, already waving at the next person in line.

I fight with the strap of my purse, which is now wrapped in my backpack strap and hooked around my metal water bottle. At the same time, I reach down for the handle of my checked bag. It's one of those boxy, black rectangles, lumpy down the front with all the odds and ends I've crammed inside. The thing weighs a ton! Whatever, it rolls. And now I'm on a roll.

I hurry away from the lost baggage desk, dragging my one lonely bag behind me. I've got my purse strapped across my body, so my left hand can be free. I'm already tapping the call button on my phone. It rings and he picks up immediately.

"Hello?" His voice is deep.

"Hi—" *Shit—what was this guy's name?* "This is Rachel Price," I say. "I'm *so* sorry! My bags are lost and then my phone was stuck on airplane mode—it was a whole thing. I'm coming out now!"

"I'm pulling around again," he says. I can hear music rocking in the background. "Blue Jeep." He hangs up.

I race over to the double doors marked with a big number 2 and rush outside. The Florida heat hits me like a slap to the face. I'm used to the dry heat of a California summer, not this swamp. Thank goodness my hair is already up in a knot. I've got to get this hoodie off pronto.

A topless, dark blue Jeep pulls to a stop at the crosswalk about ten yards away. A surfboard is strapped to the top rails, and a dog peeks his head out of the backseat. He's adorable—black pointy ears, with a white snout like a border collie. His pink tongue lolls from his mouth.

I run towards the Jeep, the wheels of my bag rattling against the cement. I lift my hand holding the phone, awkwardly waving the Jeep down. The guy in the driver's seat nods. He's wearing aviators and a ball cap with the brim pulled low.

"Hi," I say, breathless as I stop at the passenger side of the Jeep. "I'm Rachel Price. I'm *so* sorry again! My phone wasn't working, and two of my bags are missing, and I've been up for 36 hours, and I'm just a red-hot mess. But I'm here now, and I'm ready to go and— ohmygod, you are *so* cute—"

The guy in the front seat stiffens, his mouth opening a little in surprise, but I'm not actually paying attention to him. As I spilled my guts, the dog hopped between the seats, popping his face over the edge of the passenger door. He's got gorgeous icy blue eyes, so bright and curious. I'm a huge sucker for animals. I could never have one growing up with the way we always traveled, so now I become painfully awkward in social settings if there is a dog involved.

"Sy, back," his owner commands, cranking the Jeep into park.

The dog wiggles his whole body, his tail flapping in the guy's face before he hops dutifully into the backseat.

"Need help with your bags?"

"Oh, no. I can get it," I say, my eye going back to him.

Oh shit.

Here I am fawning over a cute dog when his owner is even cuter. He slips his aviators off, tucking them into the top of his t-shirt, and I get the full effect of those dark eyes and cheekbones for days. He's got a day or two of stubble along his jaw, and the sexiest bow pout to his lips.

"I—"

Girl, get yourself together.

I snap my mouth shut.

Shit, when did it open?

"I'm fine," I repeat. "Let me just . . ." I don't even bother finishing the sentence. I just duck my head in shame and move around the back of the Jeep.

"Here, let me," he calls out. "The door can get jammed sometimes." That's when he unfolds himself from the driver's seat and—oh my sweet heavens. He's sculpted perfection. I could see the shoulders from the Jeep, but I wasn't betting on the height too.

He's graceful as he moves, turning his back on me to fiddle with the door. Ink covers his right arm from the wrist up, disappearing under the sleeve of his t-shirt. Swirls of color and detailed patterns. He swings the door open, and I step back, ready to heft my bag inside.

"Here, let me get it," he says.

"No, don't bother." Why is my voice coming out so squeaky?

"That looks heavy."

"I'm a big girl," I reply, hefting it by the handle.

Then a few things happen at once. First, the car behind us honks, making me jump and the dog bark. Then the PA system starts blaring about parking in restricted areas. Lastly, as I lift the bag, I snag the edge of the door. This must have been just enough force to fray the ancient bag's last will to live. I hear the fabric tear, and then all hell breaks loose.

And by hell, I mean the contents of my bag. Yep, I stand there, mouth open in horror, watching as all my belongings flood from the shredded canvas, spilling all over the curb at our feet.

Surfer Boy exchanges a wide-eyed look with me before we jolt into action, trying to catch all my falling stuff. I shriek as a book slams down on my exposed toes. This has me knocking back against the open Jeep door. Now the dog is barking in alarm, watching us scramble to keep my stuff from rolling into oncoming traffic.

Once we get the bag to the ground, I drop to my knees, desperate to shove everything back inside.

This is it. I've finally found it.

Hello, limit. I'm Rachel.

I work quickly, stuffing things back inside the broken bag. A few seconds pass when I realize Surfer Boy is just standing there, making no effort to help me. I glance up, my eyes trailing up his bare legs dusted with sand. Did he come straight from the beach? I pass over his board shorts, up his cut torso, to his face.

He's looking down, but he's not looking at me. No, he's looking at the thing in his hands. His expression is frozen on his face, totally unreadable.

And *thing* is right because—

Oh my fucking god.

My heart drops out of my chest. Someone bury me in the earth right here in this airport loading zone. And make sure to dig a hole for Tess right next to me, because I plan to haunt her to death! Surfer Boy is holding a dildo. *My* dildo. It was a gag gift from Tess, and it's most certainly a gag that she packed it for me. It has to be, because the dildo is large and purple and shaped like an octopus tentacle.

3
CALEB

I'm standing in the 'no parking' zone of the Jacksonville airport with a tentacle dildo in my hand. It's electric purple and rubbery, and I can tell from the weight its battery operated.

Holy fucking shit.

How the hell did I get here?

I've been waiting for this woman for almost an hour, getting myself more and more worked up about entitled doctor types who have no consideration for others. I was ready to hate her. Hell, I was ready to drive off and leave her ass here.

But then my phone finally rang, and this walking hurricane of a girl swept through the automatic doors, sucking me into her vortex. She talked at me so fast, I could barely make out the words. All I could do is watch the elegant arch of her throat as it moved. Then Sy had to go bouncing around, distracting us both.

She's gorgeous, I'll give her that. Her curvy body is clad in high-waisted black leggings and a cropped hoodie unzipped to show her cleavage. She did the world a favor by strapping her purse between her breasts and running towards me like a Baywatch model. Once she's close enough, I see the little glint of gold at her nose.

Fuck, she's got a septum piercing.

I'm a sucker for a pierced and tatted girl. Does she have tats too? I can't tell. What I can tell is that the guys are gonna go crazy. She'll be breaking hearts by day's end tomorrow. Coach is gonna have to put up an electric fence around her office. We'll probably have to make the rookies take cold showers before she examines them.

And here I am, still holding her dildo.

She's on her knees, scrambling to gather her shit, cursing under her breath. She looks up at me and I'm still just fucking standing here, like I've been turned to stone. Her dark gaze drops from my face down to my hand and her lips part in an "O."

"Oh my god," she shrieks, launching to her feet. "*Give* me that—"

She all but slaps the dildo out of my hand.

Say something, asshole.

"Just trying to help," I mutter, slipping my hands in the pockets of my board shorts, decidedly *not* helping. I'm afraid to help now. Afraid of what else I might find . . . what else I might touch. Does she actually use that thing or—

"It was a joke gift," she says quickly.

I hope she can't read my thoughts, because I won't deny the moment where I just pictured myself flipping that little switch and turning it on. I'm curious to test the toy's range of motion.

"My roommate's idea of a going away present," she adds, shoving the toy deep inside her bag. "I don't—I've never—*god*, will you just get down here and help me before we get towed?"

I don't bother hiding my smirk. So, she's never used it before?

Don't go breaking my heart, Hurricane.

I bend my good knee, dropping down with a slight wince, and help her shove things back inside the broken bag. The rest of the plunder is innocent enough—books, random chargers, and cables. I pick up a snow boot. "You expecting snow on the beach?"

She huffs and grabs it, shoving it inside the split in the bag. "Always good to be prepared. Thought I might need to pack snow gear for an away game or something."

That's smart. I wouldn't want to be stuck with just my flip-flops in Toronto either.

We finish gathering her stuff quick as we can and team-lift the bag into the back of the Jeep. Whatever wouldn't fit back inside is tossed unceremoniously on top. She tucks her backpack safely in the backseat, keeping her purse with her as she climbs in the front.

I slide in on the driver's side and slip my sunglasses on. "Any preferences on the music?"

"No," she replies, helping herself to my phone charger. "Sorry, my battery is dying."

"Okay, well it's gonna get a bit windy," I say. "You might wanna—"

"I know how Jeeps work," she huffs, clicking her seatbelt on.

We both go still as we sit in the silence of her response.

Then she groans, burying her face in her hands. "Oh, shit—I'm so sorry. That was the bitchiest thing to say ever."

"It's okay—"

"No, I'm *so* sorry, I'm just—*god*—I'm so tired," she says, a note of desperation in her voice. "I think I might be getting a bit delusional."

I swear, if I have to deal with a tentacle dildo *and* tears in the same car ride, I'm gonna ask for a raise. Airport runs already aren't in my job description, but I'm trying to pull my weight, be a team player. Look what I get for my trouble.

"I haven't slept in like two days," she goes on.

Yeah, those are tears in her voice. I am now officially uncomfortable.

"And I'm so hungry. I haven't had anything but a bag of pretzels since this morning. But that's no excuse," she adds quickly. She turns to me, her fingers brushing lightly against the ink on my forearm. "I'm sorry. God, I'm such a mess that I don't even remember your name. I feel like a total bitch. You put it in your text, but I was in such a rush, and I couldn't check it again. And you were waiting for me for so long, and I'm sure you think I'm a total jerk, but I'm not—"

The words only stop because she's out of air. Yeah, this girl is a total swirling vortex of mass chaos.

She closes her eyes and takes a deep breath. Then she opens them, those dark brown pools sucking me in. "Can we start over? *Please*, let us start over." She holds out her hand to me. "I'm Rachel Price. I'm the new Barkley Fellow, and I've had a *really* rough two days."

I look down at her offered hand. She's tugged her hoodie sleeve up a bit and now I can see that she has tattoos.

Be still my cold dead heart.

A pair of hearts outlined on her wrist, a small, detailed sketch of an electric guitar on her forearm. There's a signature alongside the guitar.

Sy chooses this moment to pop his head between the seats, nosing her open palm, which diffuses the tension. She giggles, giving him a pet between the ears. "At least someone wants to give me another chance. I swear I'm not a bitch. No, I'm not," she croons in that sugary sweet talking-to-a-dog voice all people seem to have. "No, I'm not. I'm really nice. Yes, I am."

Sy eats it up, licking her hand as she laughs out loud.

With a groan, I gently push him back and put out my hand, letting her shake it. "I'm Caleb Sanford, Assistant Equipment Manager."

She smiles. "Wow, tough job. You guys work crazy hard."

"Yep." I drop her hand, placing mine back on the wheel.

"And who is this angel?" she asks, turning in her seat to give Sy more attention. "His eyes are *so* gorgeous. I could just eat you with a spoon. Yes, I could," she coos.

The furry idiot is a total chick magnet. Too bad he warms them up only for me to put them right back on ice.

"His name is Poseidon," I reply. "I call him 'Sy' for short."

"Ooo, how regal," she says, her fingers scratching the thick fur of his neck. "You feel a bit salty, Sy. Were you swimming in the ocean with daddy earlier today?"

I go stiff.

Wait—no. My arms—my—*shit*, not my dick. My dick is definitely not going stiff at hearing a gorgeous woman call me 'daddy.'

With a groan, I turn away from her, my eyes firmly on the road as I jerk the Jeep into gear. At the same time, I crank up the radio, blasting the air with my favorite mix of rock music.

She fishes a pair of sunglasses out of her bag and slips them on, leaning back in her seat with a smile the moment we hit that Florida sunshine. Between the wind and the music, it's hard to have a conversation in a Jeep . . . which is one of the reasons I like driving with the top off.

She doesn't seem to mind. In fact, it seems to relax her. Within minutes. she's got one arm propped on the side door, her hand weaving to the beat of the music, as I coast us onto the interstate.

4
RACHEL

"Well, here you are, hon. Home sweet home."

I follow the apartment manager inside the open door of my new apartment. My hands are full with my purse, my apartment paperwork, a drink cup sloshing with crunchy ice, and a bag of leftover tacos. I heft it all onto the kitchen counter, turning to face the view.

This is a fully furnished unit on the fourth floor of a brand-new complex not five miles from the arena. Caleb said the Rays bought out the top three floors of this building to have places to house rotating staff like me, as well as keep units in a constant state of readiness for farm team guys.

"You've got all the amenities," she says. "Dishwasher, stove, microwave are all here. And there's a small washer and dryer stack in your hall bath." She points to an open door.

I step past her into the living room. It's just a one bedroom, but there's a kitchen with a little breakfast bar and a narrow living room capped with a wall of glass that leads out to a balcony. Beyond the balcony, I can see I have a view of woods beyond.

"Bedroom is through here," Loretta calls. "You've got a full bath and the step-in closet."

I follow her into the bedroom, noting the beachy colors everywhere—nautical blue, sand beige, and white. Everything in the unit is accented with wicker and seashells. There's a jute rug in the kitchen. A sand dollar art print is framed over the queen-sized bed. Not a single decorating element is what I would have ever picked for myself. It's coastal chic and I love it.

Okay, I'll get used to it.

Fine, I'm buying a different bedspread at a bare minimum. Anyone who can handle this much sand beige must be part camel.

"It's perfect," I say.

Footsteps behind us have me turning. Caleb is standing in my kitchen, glancing around with a slight frown on his face. "Whoa . . . I forgot they look like this when you first move in."

"Like what?" I say, taking my heavy backpack as he hands it over to me.

He scrunches his nose. "Like aisle four of a Home Goods."

I stifle a laugh. Yeah, I'll be hiding at least a quarter of these decorations in a cabinet.

"Making new friends already?" Loretta calls. "Don't worry, hon. We're not all as surly as this one." She jabs a thumb at him.

Caleb picks up the glass bowl of seashells on my counter with a rattle. "Just curious, Lo, are there any shells actually left on the *beaches* here in Florida, or are they all in these fancy salad bowls?"

"You said something about recycling?" I say over him.

He smirks, setting the bowl back down.

"Yes, we recycle here. There's a laminated list on the counter of what needs to be separated out," Loretta explains. "And if you're caught breaking the rules, there's a $20 fine. The next fine goes up to $50."

"We take ocean conservation very seriously," Caleb chimes.

How the hell did he get around me and into the living room so fast?

"Take only photos, leave only footprints," he intones. At the same time, he's now holding what looks like a dried sea sponge decoration.

I roll my eyes at him. This guy is so hard to figure out. Is he an asshole or is he charming? Maybe he's a charming asshole. I smile, trying to focus on Loretta's long-winded explanation on proper dishwasher usage.

As she talks, I can't help but glance over at him. He's making himself at home on my sofa, moving around the striped pillows. He was so stand-offish at first. Understandable, since he thought I was standing him up . . . which I kind of was, totally inadvertently. Then there was the whole dildo debacle, which he was super cool about and hasn't mentioned again. On the drive he seemed distant. He clearly didn't want to talk, which suited me just fine. Especially since he's got great taste in music.

I thought I had him pegged as the surly asshole loner type. But then, just before we got to the apartment complex, he pulled into a little strip mall and bought me tacos.

"You said you were hungry," he said with an indifferent shrug.

Sure, we ate in silence, but it wasn't an awkward silence. We sat outside at a little metal café table, sharing our chips with a very happy Sy.

Whatever Caleb lacks in charm, his dog more than compensates.

"Oh, no—Sy," I cry, cutting Loretta off. "You can't leave him in the Jeep. Bring him up."

Caleb has his nose buried inside my coffee table book: *Florida's Seashells: A Beachcomber's Guide*. "It's okay," he replies, closing the heavy book and tossing it down. "I dropped him off when I brought up your backpack."

"Dropped him off?"

"Didn't this grumpus tell you?" Loretta laughs.

I glance between him and Loretta. "Tell me what?"

Caleb crosses over to me. "I'm your new neighbor, Doc."

My heart skips a beat. "Neighbor?"

"Yep, he's right next door in unit 403," calls Loretta.

"Why else do you think I was volunteered to pick you up from the airport?"

I gaze up into his dark eyes and feel something in my belly swoop. And no, it's not the tacos. Oh, this is so not happening. No way.

Red alert. Back up, Rachel. Shut it down.

I'm not getting involved with a coworker. I don't care if he's gorgeous and working a smolder so hot it burns.

"So, if you ever need some sugar," he murmurs. "You know who to ask."

5

RACHEL

I sigh with exhaustion, swaying at my kitchen counter as I pour myself a generous glass of chardonnay. I successfully made it to the end of this marathon two days. At this point, I'm not sure which I need more: sleep or air. It's a toss-up, really. As soon as I down this wine, I plan to crash.

Once Caleb left, I unpacked my one ridiculous bag, confirming what I already knew. The only choice in clothes for tomorrow are two evening gowns, a couple bikinis, a white lacy swimsuit coverup, or my winter gear. So, I called for an Uber and made a Target run. Three hours and $600 later, I was back in my apartment with a stocked fridge and pantry, a new comforter on the bed, new pillows on my sofa, and a load of laundry spinning in my mini washer—to include new scrubs and underwear.

Just as soon as the washer buzzes, I'll toss the clothes in the dryer and go to sleep.

I fiddle with my phone, turning on some music. I stripped my leggings off as soon as I got home. Sports bra too. So now I'm wearing nothing but my undies and the softest cropped band tee I found in the junior's section.

Grabbing my phone and my glass of wine, I saunter across my apartment towards the balcony. I'm a snob about making my outside spaces comfortable, and I'm already planning a patio makeover for this weekend—a plush lounger, some cafe string lights, plants for the railing. I could have one just for herbs. Basil and dill, maybe some rosemary. I make a note on my phone, using my elbow to slide the glass door shut behind me.

It's so lovely out here. The humidity from the day has finally cut, so now it's just warm. And so blissfully quiet. My music plays as I scroll mindlessly on my phone, slow sipping my chardonnay. I'm a few pages into my latest monster romance when I hear the loud buzzer on my washer go off. Draining the rest of my wine, I go to open the sliding glass door.

Shunk.

It doesn't budge.

"Oh, you gotta be kidding me," I mutter. I tuck my phone under my arm and give the handle a harder pull.

Shunk. Shunk. Shunk.

"Oh, no. Fuck, fuck, fucking fuck!" I hiss, setting both the phone and the empty wine glass down. "Come on, door. Please, don't do this to me," I whine, trying to see if there's something I'm missing, some lever that need lifting or a latch that needs flipping. But no. Nothing. There is literally nothing on this side of the glass except the handle.

"Oh, come *on!*" I snatch up my phone and go quickly through my contacts, looking for the number to the front office. Of course, I haven't plugged it into my damn phone yet!

"This is just perfect," I mutter, opening my internet to do a google search.

I swear to god, when I get myself out of this, I'm going to bed and I'm never waking up again. I jerk the phone up to my ear, waiting as the dial tone plays some shitty elevator music. After what feels like an eternity, an answering service finally connects.

"Thank you for calling the Silver Shells Maintenance Service. Our office is currently closed. If this is an emergency, please hang up and dial 911—"

I hang up.

Oh god, I am *not* calling the police to come rescue me! I have a sudden image of a firetruck raising up a ladder to my fourth-floor balcony. A handsome fireman reaches out his hands, ready to lift me over the rail like I'm a kitten stuck in a tree. I'm sure all my new neighbors will enjoy watching me shimmy my bare ass over the balcony into a fireman's ladder-bucket-thingy.

I gasp.

I know my new neighbor!

I glance over the edge of my balcony towards Caleb's unit. Less than two feet of space separates our railings. The angle isn't quite right for me to see inside his unit, but I can tell that a light is on.

"Please, oh please," I mutter, pressing the call button on his contact. It rings and rings. No answer.

"No," I whine, dropping the phone to both hands to shoot off a text.

RACHEL (11:04PM): Hey Caleb, this is Rachel. Are you home? I see the light is on. Can you come out onto your balcony?

RACHEL (11:04PM): Right now. It's kind of an emergency.

I wait, desperate to see the three little dots flashing at the bottom or—better yet—hear him open his sliding glass door.
Nothing.

RACHEL (11:06PM): Caleb please! I'm stuck out on my balcony!

I keep waiting.
Nothing.
Oh god, my heart is starting to race with anxiety and now I *really* have to pee!
Going for broke, I take a deep breath and start calling his name. "Caleb Sanford! Hey, Caleb!"
I wait.
"Caaaaaleb!"
Inside his unit, I hear Sy barking.
"Yes, help me, Sy!" I call out like an idiot. "Get daddy's attention for me! CALEB!"
And *whoosh* goes my relief with the sound of his sliding glass door as it opens. Sy hops out, his little black and white head darting between the railing bars as he barks over at me.
"What the—"
"Caleb!" I call again. "Oh, thank god."
"Rachel?" He peeks around the corner at me. He's shirtless, his coppery hair mussed. I can see that his tattoo sleeve goes all the way up his arm, over his shoulder. The rest of him is long and lean, cut with muscle. "What are you—"
"Do you ever check your phone?" I cry, cheeks burning with embarrassment.
He raises a confused brow. "It's in my room. Rachel, what the—"
"I'm locked out," I blurt.
"What?"
"I came out on my balcony, and I shut the door behind me, and apparently it locked!"
He chuckles, dragging a hand through his messy hair. "Oh yeah,

Lo should have warned you. Don't shut the door all the way unless you wanna get locked out."

I deadpan at him. "Yeah, gee, thanks. I think I've learned that lesson. Now, can you *help* me?"

He glances around. "Well . . . did you call the maintenance number?"

"The office is closed. The auto message said to call 911."

"That's probably your best option. They can unlock your unit and get you free."

I whimper, already moments away from doing the pee dance. "But that'll take *ages*."

He smirks. "You got somewhere fancy to be?"

I freeze.

Of fucking course.

If I can see him standing there in nothing but his shorts, he can see me in my thong and cropped Guns N' Roses tee. I cross my arms over my braless tits. No way is he getting more of a show from me today. He's seen my dildo and now he's seen me in my underwear. He's not getting a glimpse of the girls too.

"I can keep you company if you want," he says with a shrug. "While you wait for the police."

I groan again. The last thing I want is to sit up here, possibly for hours, waiting for the police to force entry into my unit and come free me from this balcony prison. If that happens, they're going to find a sobbing mess of a woman sitting in a puddle of her own pee.

And that's when the world's worst, most genius idea slips into my head. "Or . . ."

"Or what?" Caleb replies, one elbow leaning on his rail.

I judge the distance. Not even two feet, with more than enough space where both our balcony railings extend out. Easy peasy. Just don't look down. "Or I could just climb over there."

He blinks at me. "The fuck you say? We're on the fourth floor. You fall, you fall to your death, Doc. Splat."

"I'm not going to fall," I huff. "Look, just extend out your arms and we can better judge the distance—"

"No," he barks, taking a step back. "No fuckin' way. I'm not gonna help you ninja crawl your way over here. How would that even help? You'd still be locked out."

"But you've got a bathroom," I plead. "And if worse comes to worst, maybe I could crash on your couch and maintenance can open the door for me first thing in the morning. That way we don't have to involve the police. *Please*, Caleb—"

"You're fuckin' crazy, Hurricane," he mutters, shaking his head. "I'm not helping you. No is my answer. Don't even ask."

I whimper, hands dropping to my sides. Oh god, I can feel the tears coming. Once the lower lip starts quivering, there's no stopping it. And I'm not a crier. This has just been a ridiculously stressful two days.

"Oh, what is that?" he growls, tone wary.

I sniffle. "Nothing. It's fi-fine."

Oh god, this man is going to *hate* me. Between the way we met and my dildo surprise and now this, I wouldn't blame him if he never speaks to me again. And we have to work together! He was giving me a ride to the arena in the morning.

Now he's standing there like a handsome, bare-chested Hercules, leaning over his railing, looking at me like I'm a three-headed hydra.

"Don't." He shakes his head. "Please don't do that. Don't fuckin' cry. I can't stand when people cry—"

"I can't help it," I snap at him. God, I can't let him watch me fall apart. I duck away from the railing's edge, using our shared wall as a barrier as I fall quietly to pieces.

After a minute, he groans and Sy whimpers. "Come on . . . Rachel?"

"It's f-fine," I garble. "I'll be fine. Just g-go back inside. I'll call the p-police and wait h-here."

I can hear him muttering to the dog. "God—*fuck*—fine!" he shouts over at me. "Rachel, I'll help you."

I go still. "You will?"

"Yes—fuck," he mutters again. "But if you fall and die, I'm telling the police that a crazy woman was trying to break into my apartment."

I wipe my nose with the back of my hand, sniffing back my tears. "That's fair," I call over. "Here—take my phone first." I reappear at the balcony's edge, leaning over with my arm outstretched, phone in hand.

He reaches it easily. See? This is totally gonna work. He takes it and slips it in the pocket of his shorts. His mouth is set in a grim line. "How do you wanna do this, Doc?"

I survey the scene. "Umm . . . I think if I sort of climb up, I can reach out with one hand." I mime as I talk. "Then maybe you can support me as I let go and reach out with the other. Then I'll sort of just jump over, and you reel me in. Thoughts?"

"Yeah, I think this is the stupidest fucking idea ever."

I scowl at him. "Shut up, we're doing it."

"Why can't you just sit over there and wait for the police?"

"Because," I huff, testing out the railing as I shimmy my way up.

"Because why?"

"Because I'm taking back control of my life!" I shout. "In the last 36 hours, I've gone from wallowing in the depths of a depression thinking I didn't win this fellowship to learning that I did." I climb up, using all my yoga balance to cling like a monkey to the bars of my railing.

"I packed up my life, said goodbye to my best friend, moved to a state and a city I don't know, to take a job I'm not sure I can do, with a team I've never met," I go on with a huff, carefully letting go of the wall to reach out my hand towards him.

He's there in an instant, his warm hand wrapping tight around my wrist, providing me balance and support.

"I've survived flight delays and missing bags. I had a stranger fondling my dildo in public—a dildo I totally use, by the way," I add as I fling my other arm out towards him.

"Shit—*fuck*—" he grunts, his hands going from my wrists to just under my ribs as he takes a death grip hold of me. "Wait—seriously?"

"Yeah, I was lying before," I reply. "And before you ask, yes it vibrates and *yes* it feels amazing. And now we are never going to talk about it again. *Ever*. Do you understand me?"

"*Ungh*—yeah—"

We're both panting as I'm now in a kind of stretched-out downward dog pose, with my feet pressed against the top of my balcony railing and my hands gripping tight to his bare shoulders.

He shifts his hold on me and stills. "Uhh . . . Doc?"

"Yeah?" I pant, wiggling my toes and doing my best not to look down.

"My hand is umm . . ."

"Totally grabbing my bare tit?" I finish for him. Because yeah, this crop top is too big, and his hand just slipped right under the bottom hem. He's got a fierce hold on my ribcage, and I can feel his thumb brushing the underside of my boob. "Yeah, I got that Caleb, thanks. Just pull me the fuck over. Ready?"

"Yeah—*shit*—please don't die—"

"Please don't drop me," I echo. "3-2-1-*go!*"

I push off with my toes and his arms snake around me tighter than a vice, pulling me across the void. His skin is hot, and his breath is in my ear, as one arm bands tighter at my shoulders and the other drops down, his strong hand at my waist.

I cry out as my shins whack into his railing, but he gets a hand on my butt and lifts me up and over to safety. He stumbles backwards as I go full koala on him. We're wrapped in an embrace more intimate than what I've shared with some of my former lovers. I don't know where his skin ends and mine begins. We cling to each other, heart's racing, as Sy dances around at our feet.

"Uhh . . . Doc?" Caleb says after a minute, his breathe warm in my ear.

I huff a tight laugh. "Your hand is cupping my bare ass? Yeah, I know. Thanks for the play-by-play, Sanford. Why don't you put me down now."

He grunts, loosening his hold on my bare ass cheek. I un-koala myself, sliding down his front with my whole body as he sets me on my feet. We stand there, both still shaking, my hands on his shoulders and his hands on the bare skin of my waist.

There's an energy sparking between us. It makes me nervous. I haven't felt it since—

No, don't go there.

I can't do this again. I can't let my ridiculous notions about vibes and energy drag me down yet another path to heartache. Mystery Boy was a one-time encounter. Earth-shattering sex? Yes. Soul-shattering to leave the next morning? *Hell,* yes.

Caleb is different. This has to be different. I know him and he knows me. We're about to work together. Heck, my contract is already signed. We *do* work together. This is wrong. This is dangerous. This is not happening.

I inch away from him, my body stiff.

"Are you okay?" he murmurs, his hand raising to brush softly along my jaw.

I close my eyes at the gentle touch. "Don't be nice to me," I murmur. "Please—"

He stills. Then his hand is under my chin, tipping it up. "Look at me, Hurricane."

Hurricane? Is that supposed to be me? Why does the nickname make my pulse flutter?

I open my eyes and glance up at him. The light from his apartment is soft, casting half his face in shadow. He's beautiful. Those sharp cheekbones and dark eyes put me in mind of a fae prince, cold and mysterious. Not to mention those pouty, kissable lips.

"Are you okay?" he repeats.

I nod. Then after a moment, I shake my head.

I don't even know how it happens, but in moments I'm back in his arms, crying against his chest as he holds me, his hand soothing down my back. I cling to him as I let loose all my exhaustion and stress and pain. When nothing is left to feel, only one thought remains.

"You wanna talk about it?" he murmurs.

I let out a soft sigh, my body relaxing against him. "I miss him."

He stiffens slightly. "Miss who? Your boyfriend?"

I shake my head. No. Not my boyfriend. Not my anything.

"Your husband?"

I smile, pushing off his chest. "Nope. Never married."

"Me neither. Brother then?"

I laugh, shaking my head again. "No. He's . . . no one," I reply, even as my heart says the word I really mean.

Someone.

He's my someone. Somewhere out there, he's being a whole person. And I'm here, afraid to let myself give in to the energy sparking between me and this beautiful man. Who knows, maybe this surly equipment manager is meant to be my *new* someone.

But I'm not ready for new. I'm not ready for any of the changes life has suddenly thrown my way. And yet, I have to find a way to fake it until I make it, because my life is happening right now. I've got the throbbing shins to prove it.

"Come on," Caleb says, offering out his hand. "You're dead on your feet, Doc. Let's get you set up on the sofa, huh? Live to fight another day."

Nodding, I take his hand.

6
RACHEL

"**R**eady to go?" Caleb is standing in my doorway holding a travel mug. He's dressed in a Jacksonville Rays tech shirt, a pair of workout pants, and trainers. His coppery brown hair is slightly damp, curling at his nape, and he didn't bother to shave. His five o'clock shadow from yesterday is officially stubble today, and I don't hate it.

"Yeah, just give me a sec," I say, leaving the door open as I dart back in to grab all my stuff off the counter.

I only left his apartment about an hour ago. I spent the night on his couch wearing a pair of his grey sweatpants to hide my bare ass. At some point in the night, Sy joined me. I woke up to my alarm, body sweating, with sixty pounds of dog tangled between my legs.

I slipped out while Caleb was still sleeping and did a barefoot walk of shame down to the leasing office. I was ready and waiting the moment the guy arrived at 7:00AM. He was cool about it, dropping everything to help me get back inside my unit. I barely had time to shower and get dressed before Caleb was knocking on my door, ready to drive me over to the arena.

"Here," I say, hurrying back over.

He holds out his free hand and I give him my spare key. "What the hell is this?" he mutters, looking down at it like it's a live tarantula. "A little forward don't you think, Hurricane?"

"Ha ha," I say drolly, closing the door behind me. "Look, you're literally the only person I know in this city, okay? We work together and now we share a wall. For now, you're my person. The moment I find someone to relieve you of this heavy responsibility, I'll take the key back, thus sparing you the continued horror of being associated with me."

He frowns, closing his hand around the key. "How do you know I won't use my newfound power for evil?"

I snort, snatching the travel mug out of his hand. Of course, the one thing I forgot at Target last night was coffee. I need a fix more than I need air. I take a sip of his and instantly regret it. "*Blegh*—holy shit, that is so sweet." I shove the travel mug back at him while he laughs.

"No one asked you to try it."

Gross! Now I want sandpaper for my tongue to scrub this taste away. "What kind of psycho drinks peppermint mocha in the middle of summer?"

He just keeps laughing, leading the way towards the stairs.

"I take it back," I call.

He pauses, glancing over his shoulder. "What?"

"A guy who drinks peppermint coffee can't be trusted with my key." I hold out my hand. "Give it back, please."

He just keeps walking. "Too late, Hurricane. It's my key now. And if you think I won't use it to go in there and rearrange your seashell collection whenever I want, then you clearly didn't think this through."

"I hate you," I mutter, dropping my hand to zip my backpack.

He just grunts.

I guess this is our new friend language. Insults and grunts.

I sling the backpack on my shoulder, following behind him. His movement pulls my focus from my phone. He's got a definite hitch in his step this morning, favoring his left leg. "Hey—are you—you're limping. You okay?"

His shoulders stiffen and he doesn't turn around. "Yeah, m'fine. Knee is just tight."

I purse my lips, watching him work his way down the first set of stairs. My physical therapist alarm dings as I evaluate his posture and gait. He's in pain. Was he limping yesterday? I don't think so . . .

I gasp. "Oh god, was that from last night? Caleb, did I hurt you? You know we can take the elevator—"

"No," he grunts again. "Leave me alone."

Great, now you've pissed him off.

Apparently, it's going to be one step forward, three steps back with this guy.

We get out to his Jeep and the first thing I notice is that he's got the soft top on it. I'm secretly grateful. I love a windy Jeep ride as much as the next Cali girl, but I was kind of hoping to make a good impression today. And Jeep hair and sex hair make pretty much a perfect circle.

I was ready just in case. My hair is up in a styled high ponytail. Add one more thing to my missing shopping list: contact solution. I'm out, so instead of wearing itchy contacts all day, I had to opt for my glasses. They're cute enough—thick black frames that Tess says make me look like a brunette Elle Woods.

Well, Doctor Elle, because I'm wearing a set of navy scrubs. I'm not sure what the uniform will be, but a doctor can never go wrong with scrubs.

"Any chance we have time to stop for coffee?" I say as we both get in.

"There's coffee at the practice arena," he replies, still acting surly. "Usually, a breakfast spread too. It's for players, but they never eat it all, and no one cares when staff picks at it."

As soon as the Jeep starts rolling backwards, my phone dings with a text. Scott Tyler is the newly appointed team doctor for the Rays. We talked on the phone twice the day I won the fellowship. He's chipper and he used the word 'cool' a lot. A major change from stoic Doctor Halla.

DR. TYLER (8:13AM): Welcome to Jax! My kiddo has a dentist appt this am, so I'll be in a bit later. Have Sanford take you to see Vicki. Then shadow Avery til I get in

I purse my lips, glancing over at Caleb. I'm trying to gauge his lingering level of grumpiness. He seems calm enough, sipping his gross coffee with his eyes on the road.

"Doctor Tyler just texted," I say.

No response.

"He's delayed this morning," I go on. "Says you should take me to see Vicki. Who's Vicki?"

"Operations Manager," he replies. "She's a real ball-buster."

"And who is Avery?"

"Head of PT."

I run down the growing list of names and positions in my head. Right, Todd Avery is his name, I think. "And is he a nice guy?"

"I don't work with him much," Caleb replies. "He's tough. Has a bit of an attitude. Guys don't have much to say about him yet. We don't really have any major injuries yet though, so ask me again in a month."

Right, brand new team. New staff. Clean slate. Everyone is untested, not just me.

"Doc Tyler is popular though," he adds. "He's got great energy. And the first thing he did was make the dietitians up the guys' daily carb intake. That went over well."

I smirk. It's a clever way to gain loyalty. People don't bite the hand that feeds.

I relax back into my seat. "So, what do you think of the team so far? Do we have high hopes for a good first season?"

He shrugs. "First seasons are always rough. The guys have to figure each other out. They can practice all they want, but the only way forward is to just play the game. They need experience. Real experience playing as a team when it counts."

"Hmm, trial by fire," I say. "Or in this case ice."

"Exactly. You can see the arena now," he adds with a point.

I peer out the front windshield, unable to hide my smile as the unmistakable silhouette of a brand-new arena comes into view.

"They're still finishing construction," he says, needlessly pointing to the pair of cranes. "But the practice center is off to the left over there." He points towards another smaller complex. "The center is finished and all the support spaces, the gyms, the offices. First ten games of the season had to be switched to away so they could finish up the new arena. The travel will be brutal, but the tradeoff is then we'll be home for like a month solid. That pretty much never happens."

I sit back again, fighting the buzzing of nerves rising in my stomach. It feels like the first day of school. "So, tell me about the guys. Any divas I should know about? Bad blood? Feuds?"

He glances over at me with a frown. "Did you do *any* research before taking this job?"

"Nope," I reply cheerily. "No time. I was waitlisted for the Barkley Fellowship, and I only found out I was getting off the bench exactly . . ." I check the time on my phone. "Yep, 48 hours ago. In that time, I've been a little preoccupied with packing up my entire life, getting stuck in airports, hunting down bags, getting locked out on my own balcony, and dealing with your grumpy ass," I add with a side glare. "So no, I can honestly say I don't know a damn thing about the Jacksonville Rays. I can't name you a single player. I didn't even know the team existed until they told me I was moving here. But I'm a quick study."

He huffs a laugh. "Jeez. Talk about your trial by fire."

"Right?" I add with a grin. "So, maybe my new key-wielding wall mate can help a girl out . . . give me the deets. What's the skinny? What's the haps? The dirt?"

He groans. "Please stop."

"Talk, or I keep going," I tease. "The 411, the gossip, the—"

"Fuck, *stop*," he growls. "God, you're worse than a chihuahua."

"And I haven't even had caffeine yet," I reply with a smile.

He sighs, his hands flexing on the wheel. "The guys are cool. Some have worked together before, like Karlsson and Langley. They're the first-string wingers. They've got a good rhythm. The goalie is dynamite. He was the first guy the Rays signed. Mars Kinnunen. They call him the Bear."

"Ooo, why do they call him the Bear?"

He smirks. "Meet him and find out."

"And defense?" I know enough about hockey to know how important the defensive players are. They typically work in pairs, and some players can go for years skating with the same guy if the chemistry is good.

"Solid," he replies. "More solid than offense. Today they have an exhibition game."

I nod. We're pulling into the training complex now and I lean forward, excitement humming through me.

"My buddy is on the team," Caleb goes on as we drive into the dark parking garage. "He was the first defenseman they signed."

I glance his way, slipping my sunglasses off and trading them for my regular frames. "That's so cool. And now you get to work together?"

"Well, you asked about divas," he says. "Just know that you've been warned."

"Uh-oh. What's his name?"

"Compton," he replies. "No. 42, Jake Compton. Be sure to give him hell. I guarantee he's earned it."

He pulls into a parking spot and cuts the engine as I laugh. "Okay, will do. Jake Compton is officially on my naughty list."

7

RACHEL

After securing me a cup of coffee, Caleb takes me up in the elevator to the managers' offices on the fourth floor. As we ride up, my phone dings with an automated message. My two missing bags are currently en route to Jacksonville! Who cares if I'm still feeling nervous? I'm holding a coffee, and by the end of the day I'll have a full wardrobe again.

I take a sip of the liquid heaven as the elevator doors open, revealing a long hallway dotted with doors. Skylights let in bright sunshine and the floor has a cool, custom paint job that makes it look like water. The walls are painted in the Rays colors—a teal base with accents of white, navy, and burnt orange.

Caleb shows me through the first doorway on the left that opens into a small waiting room. There's no receptionist, just a series of four more doors that lead to offices.

"This is the Operations Managers' suite," says Caleb. "Vicki is in here." He knocks on the first door to the right.

"Come in!" a woman's voice calls.

Caleb swings the door open. "Hey, Vic."

"Oh, hi honey."

I peek around him to see an older black woman in lipstick and pearls wearing a stylish business suit.

"I have your missing doctor," he says.

"Oh, good gracious," Vicki cries, getting up from behind her desk. "Oh, Doctor Price, you come here, honey. I heard all about your nasty flight delays."

I don't even realize my legs are moving before she's got me in a fierce hug, enveloping me in her floral perfume.

"What a way to welcome you to Jacksonville. I swear, it's almost not worth flying anymore."

I laugh, hugging her back. "Yeah, it was brutal. Two of my bags are still missing. Caleb was great though," I add. "He picked me up from the airport and got me settled at the apartment."

She lets me go, giving him a stern look. "Did he behave?"

He rolls his eyes. Apparently, I had his grump persona pegged.

"He bought me tacos," I reply.

"Good boy," says Vicki, patting his cheek as she moves back towards her desk. "Submit your receipt if you need a reimbursement."

He huffs, hands in his pockets. "I think I can spring for a few tacos, Vic." Then he glances at me. "Well, Doc, you good? I gotta . . ." He gestures with his thumb over his shoulder.

"Of course," I say quickly. "Thanks again, Caleb. Really."

He gives us both a nod and ducks out.

"Well, sit down, honey," says Vicki, shuffling papers on her desk. "We've got a few more things here for you to sign. And I have an update from the dealership. We should have your car ready by this afternoon. They've been playing hardball with me on lease prices. I finally had to sweeten the deal with a few season tickets."

"Oh good," I say with a mix of relief and dread. I hate driving. That's the one drawback to Jacksonville so far. The city is massively spread out, so driving is my only real option.

"And the apartment works for you? No complaints?"

I still, my cup of coffee halfway to my lips. I haven't decided if I want to share my balcony story with anyone yet. Caleb knowing feels like enough of a humiliation. "Umm . . . yes, it's perfect."

"She's here?" comes a loud voice from the hallway.

I glance over my shoulder to see a tiny woman with perfectly styled blonde curls rush through the main door of the office suite. She's got bright blue eyes and a wide smile. Like Vicki, she's dressed in business attire, her stylish black heels clicking as she walks right in, dropping her massive bag to the floor. Okay, *she* has fierce Elle Woods energy, not me.

"Are you our new Barkley Fellow?" She's got a thick southern accent. Georgia maybe? Alabama?

I stand, offering out a hand. "Yes, hi. Doctor Rachel Price."

She looks at my hand and laughs. "Oh sweetie, here in the South we hug."

Before I know it, I'm being squeezed for the second time in as many minutes.

She lets me go. "I'm Poppy St. James, head of PR for the Rays. And can I just say that I am *so* excited to have our team participate in the Fellowship program this year? I mean, who doesn't love good press? And when I learned that *you* were going to be our new Fellow? Well, I just about died!" she adds, placing a hand over her heart as she flashes Vicki a smile.

My own smile begins to falter. I think I know where this is going.

"I mean, it's enough that you're gorgeous and *so deeply talented*," she adds, emphasizing each word. "But then I found out about your family. I mean, nothing goes with hockey quite like rock and roll, right?"

Just wait for it . . .

"Say, do you think your daddy might be interested in coming out for a game this season?"

There it is.

My smile is officially fake. But this is the life of a celebrity's daughter. The second people make the connection, I cease to exist. I become merely a conduit through which people seek to reach him.

"Umm, you know, I'm not really sure of his schedule," I hedge.

"What are you two talking about?" says Vicki, clearly confused.

Poppy glances around me. "Oh, you hadn't heard? Our talented new Barkley Fellow has some added star power. Her daddy is Hal Price from The Ferrymen!"

Vicki blinks. "Is that a band?"

Poppy gasps. "A *band*? Vicki, they're only one of the *biggest* rock bands of *all* time! The Rolling Stones, Aerosmith, Led Zeppelin—they're in the Rock and Roll Hall of Fame for heaven's sake!" She turns back to me, her hand on my arm. "I swear, when I told my brother, he nearly fell out of his chair."

"That's great," I say, still wearing my patient smile.

"Say, does he ever play the National Anthem? You know, like Hendrix? Oh, wouldn't that be amazing, Vic?" She all but squeals with excitement. "The Ferrymen in our arena! Can you imagine?"

"That would be really great," Vicki replies.

"Yeah, you know, I can ask," I say, knowing this won't end until I say something.

Poppy has her eyes on her phone as she reaches inside the massive purse she dropped by the door. "Sorry, I've got like three press events stacked up this morning and I'm trying to hunt down Claribel. I wanted her to get a few pics of Rachel in action—*oh*—do you mind if I call you Rachel?"

"Poppy honey, *breathe*," says Vicki with a chuckle.

Poppy stands still and closes her eyes. She takes a deep, cleansing breath and opens them again. "Thanks, Vic. I needed that. I'm sorry, I'm just a big ole mess these days. It's all this stress leading up to the first game day."

"We're all a little on edge," Vicki assures her.

Poppy smiles, stepping forward with a folder in hand. "I promise I'm not always like this. I can be normal. You'll see. Hopefully once the season starts, we'll all find our rhythm."

"Of course," I reply. My esteem for her is rising again. I can appreciate her for being honest. She's being totally neurotic right now, but at least she knows it and she's sorry.

I take the folder from her. "What's this?"

"That's a schedule for some upcoming public relations events," she explains. "With a new team, we can't leave it to just the players to help put the Rays on the map."

I tug out the top paper and scan it. *Holy shit.* It's a blocked schedule going day-by-day for the next two months showing all kinds of events from a meet and greet at a hospital to something next week called Fin Fest. There's hardly a day not accounted for, including some weekends.

"I'm attending all these events?" I say, glancing up at her over my list.

"Yeah, don't you think it'll be great?" she says with a smile. "We've got the coaches hitting the town too, the players, even staff. Like I said, it's all hands on deck. I really hope you're a team player because we mean to win this game."

"Which game?" I say, returning the paper to my folder.

She finally glances up from her phone. "*The* game. The only one that matters." She narrows her eyes at me, lips pursed. "Sports at this level is never just about the sport, Rachel. It's about everything else. Our most important game this year won't be played on the ice. It's about winning the hearts and minds of the people of Jacksonville. We need to let the hockey world see that the Rays are here to play and we're here to stay."

I f someone told me ten years ago that I would go from being the number three draft pick in the NHL to a glorified blade sharpener, I would have laughed in their face. Hockey is my life. It's always been my life. But *playing* the game, not sitting on the sidelines.

Growing up in Minnesota, I was skating almost as soon as I could walk. I skated my way through high school into a coveted spot as a starting forward for the University of Michigan. My nickname was The Lightning because I was so damn fast. I was the great hope for the Sanford family to make it to the NHL.

And I did . . . for seven minutes.

Seven minutes and thirteen seconds to be exact. That's how long I was on the ice. One bad check into the boards, one brutally broken knee, one career ended before it even began.

Pittsburgh kept me on their injured list for over a year before it was clear my rehab was only going to restore so much function. I just had too many setbacks—unexpected inflammation, nasty infection, a third surgery. I've still got three screws in there holding it all together.

In my life before the injury, everything made sense. I knew exactly what I wanted. I had the drive and the natural talent. I hardly studied in school and still got good grades. If I wanted girls, all I had to do was curl my finger. Parties, drinking, friends—I had it all in the before.

But now I live in the after. The after is a place where I wake up every single day with my knee hurting. The after is a dark place where I'm in my head more than I'm out of it. The after is where the risk of spiraling is always just within reach. Within the span of two years, I went from starting in the NHL with a two-year, multi-million-dollar contract, to waiting tables at a sports bar in Duluth, Minnesota.

It was Jake who saved my life. We grew up playing in the same junior league. Eventually, we both earned starting spots at Michigan. I was the third draft pick our year to join the NHL, he was the thirteenth. We both went to the Penguins.

After the injury, I shut him out like I did everyone else. But he's not the type to let anything or anyone go. I shouldn't have been surprised when he showed up one night during my shift at the bar with a one-way plane ticket in his hand. He'd just been traded to the LA Kings, and he was anxious about moving across the country all alone. He gave me the plane ticket, ordered a burger with fries, and left me a ten-thousand-dollar tip with a note at the bottom of the receipt that said, 'You'll have your own room. Oh, and I signed you up for surfing lessons. You start Monday.'

I didn't think. I just left the bar, packed my life into two bags, and moved across the country into the spare room in his downtown LA apartment. We've never looked back.

Here we are, six years later, and Jake is one of the top-ranked defensemen in the League, notorious for his ability to grind men into the boards. He was one of the first trades Jacksonville made. And he doesn't keep anything from me. I know he's got a five-year contract worth over seven million a year. There was a handsome signing bonus too. Nice enough that he bought a beach house. A gorgeous place one block off the water with great views of the ocean.

More importantly, I know he was responsible for getting me this job as Assistant Equipment Manager. He hasn't said anything, and he won't, but I know. This is the first job I've had in the hockey world in six years. It was time to come home. He knew it and so did I.

So here I stand in the narrow hallway outside the practice arena, sharpening Jake's blades—my best friend, my guide through the crazy, confusing world of the after.

I kill the sharpener, giving the blade a closer look. A few of the guys come shuffling behind me in their brand-new practice uniforms. "Hey guys, lookin' good," I call out.

They both grin. They're young guys, both new recruits. Sully follows close behind them, giving me a pat on the shoulder with his gloved hand. No. 19, Josh O'Sullivan, is a twelve-year veteran of the NHL. I fully expect coach to give him the captaincy. He's a great pick—grounded family man, keeps his nose clean with the press, and apparently, he knows his way around a grill.

"Hey, dinner tonight at Rip's," he says as he passes me. "We're celebrating the end of the preseason. Be there!"

I wave him off, moving in the opposite direction towards the equipment manager's room. Jake's was the last set of blades I needed to sharpen this morning. I bring a load of fresh laundry through into the locker room.

"Hey, Sanny," Morrow calls. He's a defenseman too. "Did you hear about Rip's tonight?"

"Yeah, Sully just told me."

"Cool. You comin'?"

"Probably." I toss him his jersey. "A man's gotta eat."

He stuffs his head into the jersey. "Cool. You bringing the DLP?"

DLP. Domestic life partner. One of the first things the players did once they got traded to the Rays was start a group chat. Not all the guys are on it. In fact, it's a sore subject for some of the more eager rookies that they aren't considered 'in' enough to be added.

When a couple of the guys found out I was added, they lost their shit. The joke spread like wildfire that I had to be added because I'm Compton's domestic life partner. We don't even live together anymore, but the nickname stuck, and now one or both of us use the DLP excuse all the time to get out of plans.

"No idea," I reply. Come to think of it, I haven't seen him all morning. "Where is he?"

Morrow just shrugs. "Don't know. He wasn't at morning meeting."

He shuffles past me as I slip my phone from my pocket and shoot off a text.

CALEB (10:45AM): Where the fuck are you? Exhibition game starts at 11.

Immediately there are dots at the bottom of my screen.

JAKE (10:45AM): Aww, you miss me, baby? Need something pretty to look at?

I snort, shaking my head. But then my mind flashes to images of a face much prettier than his . . . a face with dark eyes, long, dark lashes, and pouty lips. A face framed by walnut brown hair and accented with a little gold septum ring. She took it out this morning. It was the first thing I noticed when she opened the door.

Conjuring up the image of Rachel does more. Now it's like I can feel her all over again, pressed up against me so close we were practically sharing one skin. I feel her heartbeat thumping against my own ribs, feel the smoothness of her skin against my hands—her sides, her bare ass.

Fuck, I almost lost it when I realized she was wearing nothing but a thong, climbing over the balcony like a damn monkey. She's fearless. Crazy. A total hurricane.

I'm not gonna lie, for a moment there I thought she might kiss me. That would have been a huge fucking mistake. After six years of dealing with all my physical and emotional bullshit, I'm still a goddamn mess. I'd be no good for anyone, least of all a coworker with whom I now share a wall.

I raise my phone and snap a picture of J-Lo while he's still got his shirt off. His chest of curly black hair is on full display.

CALEB (10:48AM): Nah, I've got this cuddly bear to keep me warm.

Jake immediately dislikes the message. Moments later my phone pings.

JAKE (10:49AM): If you leave me for J-Lo, I swear I'm gonna walk into oncoming traffic

My phone pings with a photo. It's a closeup of him, hat pulled low over his face. He's scowling. In the background above his head, I can just make out the words on a sign.

CALEB (10:50AM): Why the hell are you at the DMV?

My phone rings and I answer, tucking it under my ear as I start the process of organizing the locker room. It always looks like a tornado blasted through whenever the guys use it.

"Man, don't get me started," Jake mutters.

"What happened?" I nod at Jerry, the other assistant equipment manager. We both get to work straightening things up.

Jake groans. "Apparently, whichever genius helped me the last time messed up my fuckin' ID. Flipped my birthdate around."

"That sucks."

"Yeah, I think Vicki was ready to cancel my contract if I didn't come get it fixed. She's been hounding me for like two weeks. I just kept forgetting."

"Are you missing this game then?"

"Yeah, we all gotta keep Vic happy, right?"

"Totally," I reply, tossing a used banana peel in the trash.

He groans again. "There's still like a thousand people ahead of me in this line. And hey, you never told me what happened with this new doc. What's her name again?"

The group chat has been blowing up for the last hour as news of Rachel's presence spread. Novy was the first in the chat with a 'whoa, hot doc alert.' Since then, the guys have been playing 'hot doc spotted.' I think based on the last ping she's somewhere over in the PT suite.

"Uhhh . . . nothing else happened," I say, lying through my teeth.

I told him about the dildo. I don't know why I'm not telling him about the balcony. There was just something about it . . . her vulnerability at the end. It was funny until it wasn't. I feel protective over her.

"Oh, shit—hey, they just called my number. Gotta go."

"K—hey, are you comin' here today?"

But he hangs up before I even finish the sentence. Asshole. He's always doing that.

"Hey," says Jerry. "What's this I hear about a hot new doc on the block?"

I groan. We're only two hours in to her first day and already the team is buzzing like a hive of damn bees. This can only end in disaster. My plan is to just sit back, grab the popcorn, and watch as she eats them all alive.

9

RACHEL

"So, everything looks great with your records, Price," says Doctor Tyler. He's a lanky older guy with the body of a marathoner. Silver hair, dark eyes. He never seems to stop smiling. It's a major change from Doctor Halla.

He clicks around on his laptop screen. "You've had a great mix of primary care and PT, which I always love to see. It's been a major juggling act here. As we race towards the start of the season, I find myself in serious need of a deeper bench of clowns."

I laugh. "Well, sir, I can juggle with the best of them."

"Looks that way," he replies.

"Please don't ask me to *actually* juggle anything," I add quickly.

He smiles. "I'm not gonna lie, I think you're a better fit for our team than the first Fellow they assigned. I did some research on Doctor Halla's rehab center and I admire the holistic approach he takes with all his preventative therapies. Healing the body before it breaks. Very forward-thinking. I want that kind of innovation for the Rays."

"Well, whatever I can do to bring that kind of care here, I'm ready," I say.

He claps his hands together. "Excellent. Well, right off the bat, we've got a couple guys on our injured list. You'll work with them closely, keep them on track towards recovery."

I nod, slipping my tablet from my backpack, ready to take notes.

"You'll be working with Avery this season. But go gently," he cautions. "He likes to think he knows everything . . . if you know what I mean," he adds with a knowing look.

"Yes, sir."

I've been doing this long enough to read between the lines. And seeing as I just spent an hour with Avery in the rehab center, Tyler's not-so-subtle warning tracks. Avery is a control freak and he'll likely have trouble taking advice from a woman. Maybe I'm wrong, but he's got that vibe.

"All our starting guys are about to go through their last round of physicals," Tyler goes on. "I'd love for you to be in on those," he adds. "You'll be our hip and knee tsar. No player is gonna hit that ice unless he gets *your* approval first."

Nerves flutter in my stomach as I sit forward. "Wow, that's—you haven't even seen me in action yet, sir. You really want to give me power to bench your players?"

"Well, is anything in your records a lie, Price?"

"What? No, of course not—"

"You graduated *summa cum laude* with a degree in kinesiology from USC?"

"Yes—"

"An MD from UCLA specializing in sports medicine, where you completed internships with the LA Lakers and the Galaxy?"

Did he memorize my resume? It feels odd to have it listed out like this. "Yes, but—"

"Most recently you were two years in on a three-year primary care residency program with the Cincinnati Sport Clinic."

"Yes."

"You were working directly under Doctor Benjamin Halla, one of the best in the biz—don't tell him I said that," he adds in a fake whisper.

I'm smiling now. "Yes, sir."

"And while there, you treated athletes, providing physical therapy, primary care, cortisone injections—you've even clocked hours in the operating room," he adds, clearly impressed.

It's all true, but it makes me sound cooler than I am. The operating room isn't my favorite place to be. I prefer to work on athletes before and after the surgeons take their turn. But Doctor Halla demands a holistic education for all his residents, so I clocked hours observing hip and knee replacement surgeries whether I wanted to or not.

"Based on your records, you've worked with everything from

Olympic swimmers to golf pros to—I believe it was *twelve* of the Cincinnati Bengals?"

I sigh, frustrated with myself that I let self-doubt creep in. "Yes, sir."

"Well then, Price, I don't think there's really much else to say," he says with a shrug and that same kindly smile. "You're qualified. Hell, you're *more* than qualified. Our guys are going to be in good hands. And I need everyone pulling their weight. You ready to grab an oar?"

I nod. "Yes, sir. More than ready."

"Perfect. Then let's go. The exhibition game starts at eleven, and I want you to see the guys in action. I'll have Hillary get the players signed up to do physicals with you starting on . . . oh, let's say Monday? Give you the weekend to settle in. Sound fair enough?"

I smile, standing as he stands. "Yes, sir. More than fair."

He groans. "Yeah, and you can nix the 'sir' nonsense. Call me Scott, call me Tyler, anything but 'sir.' It reminds me too much of my father," he adds with a suppressed shiver.

I laugh. "Got it. And you can call me, Rachel."

He leans over his desk, offering out his hands again. "Welcome to the Rays, Rachel. Now, let's go meet the team."

10
RACHEL

The practice arena is buzzing with activity. Tyler takes me through to a restricted section of the stands right on center ice behind the plexiglass. The chill of the ice raises the fine hairs on my arms. A few other people are already seated in this section, tablets and clipboards in hand. We do a quick round of intros, but it's hard to hear over the blasting sound system.

Avery I already know. He's a big guy, built like a linebacker. He keeps his hair shaved close and his brow is furrowed with lines. He's sitting next to a young guy I saw in the PT room earlier. I think he might be an intern. He's super handsome—tall and lanky, with deeply tanned skin dusted with freckles across his face. His eyes are a piercing green and his black hair is thinly locked, pulled away from his face with a sport headband. When he sees us, he gives a smile and a wave at Tyler.

On the far side of the rink, the arena seats are full of excited fans eager to watch the exhibition game. The music thumps through the loudspeakers as the guys skate around.

"Is that the Bear?" I say at Tyler, pointing to the goalie.

Tyler chuckles. "Kinnunen? Heck no. That's Kelso, the third string guy. He's fighting it out with Davidson for a bench seat. Trust me, when Kinnunen is on the ice, you'll know."

I spot Caleb, back bent over a guy's skate, jerking a blade loose. He clicks a new one in, giving the guy's ankle a tap. In moments the player hops the barrier and he's back out on the ice.

Caleb glances around, spotting me, and I wave. He gives me a cool guy nod and turns away. I roll my eyes, but in moments my phone dings.

CALEB (11:03AM): How's the first day going, Hot Doc?

I huff a laugh, glancing towards him, but he's gone.

RACHEL (11:03AM): Hot Doc? Seriously? What happened to Hurricane?

The buzzer goes off and all the guys clear the ice.

CALEB (11:04AM): To me, you're Hurricane. To the rest of the guys, you're Hot Doc.

To my horror, my phone pings with screen shots from a group chat. Apparently, the guys have been tracking my whereabouts for the last hour like I'm an escaped cheetah loose in the building. It's beyond embarrassing.

"Oh god," I groan, tapping out a reply.

RACHEL (11:04AM): How much is it gonna cost me to get you to help me squash the Hot Doc nickname?

My phone is quiet for a few minutes, and I settle in with my tablet, ready to take notes as the guys start hitting the ice to the cheers of the fans. It's just an exhibition, so it's Rays on Rays. Half the guys are wearing white practice jerseys, half are wearing teal. Kelso, the third string goalie is in a white jersey.

The crowd roars as a new goalie takes to the ice wearing teal and my breath catches. He's massive. The goalie pads already make a regular guy look like Optimus Prime. This man could swallow Kelso whole.

"Thaaaat's Kinnunen," Tyler says with a grin. "Two-time Stanley Cup winner, star of the Finnish Liiga. That's the Bear."

"Yeah, I caught that," I reply. My phone dings but I can't take my eyes off him. How can a man that big play goalie? He can't possibly have the agility needed to move fast enough. Right now, he's ambling towards the goal like an unbothered grizzly, twice as big as the next closest guy.

Kinnunen takes up his place in front of the goal, flipping his helmet up to take a drink of water. It's hard to make out much beyond a blond beard.

"Kinnunen is shortlisted for the Finnish Olympic team," says Tyler. "We've got some scouts coming to town to catch a couple games."

"Cool." I sit forward on the bench. "Any of the other guys Olympic hopefuls this year?"

"Not sure," he replies. "I only know about Kinnunen because reps from the Finnish Ice Hockey Association contacted me wanting his medical records."

"And we can do that?"

"With the player's consent, yes. If he consents, we can send his medical records to his mailman."

I laugh again, checking my phone.

CALEB (11:10AM): All the tea in China, Hurricane.

I grin, glancing back down at the bench to see Caleb inside again. He's talking to one of the guys in teal, handing him his helmet as his number is called and the guy skates on.

"No. 19, Josh O'Sullivan," says Tyler, pointing to the player. "Guys call him Sully. Had his fair share of injuries. That left shoulder acts up quite a bit. Watch him like a hawk."

I nod, jotting his number down.

"And the guy in white there, No. 22 is Novy. Lukas Novikov. He's a big jokester. Idiot tripped on the treadmill two days ago on an untied shoelace, went down hard. Check his knee over the next couple days. He says he's fine, but these guys will hide a punctured lung if they think it means time away from the ice."

I jot his name down too.

"I'm sure you know this already, Price, but there's what they *tell* you is wrong, then there's what you see with your own eyes, and lastly there's what your gut tells you," he explains. "You need all three to get to the truth of things."

"Oh, I know," I say. "You ever tried telling a linebacker he can't start with a meniscus tear during the playoffs?"

He chuckles. "Yeah, you get it. It's not always fun playing bad cop, but we're ultimately here to protect them, even from themselves," he adds. "The game only lasts a couple years if they're lucky. Then they get the rest of their lives to deal with the damage."

I watch the guys skate into formation as the puck is dropped. They're playing their own team, so there are no major hits, no violence. The white side offense is constantly taking the puck down the ice. It's obvious they have the stronger line.

I watch Kinnunen carefully. His first couple saves are easy enough. He hardly had to move his blocker or his stick. Two shots just whacked right off his pads, and he tapped the puck away to a waiting defenseman.

He must be well over 6' tall. He's hunched in his stance, his massive body all but blocking access to the top and sides of the net. It's a clever tactic, just putting the biggest guy you can find in front of the net, but his height actually puts him at a disadvantage. He's got a massive hole between his legs. The puck has a wide opening to sail right—

"Whoa," I murmur, eyes wide.

Kinnunen moved so fast, I blinked and missed it. One second, he was casually crouched, the next he was in full butterfly, hips curled in, and knees twisted out, totally flat against the ice. He effectively shut off all access to the net. Another blink and he's on his feet, crouched and casual.

"He's so fast," I murmur. "You'd think with his size—"

"That's he's too big to play?" Tyler says with a laugh. "Nah, Mars Kinnunen is smooth as butter. He won't push too hard for an exhibition game. He'll let a couple sail through just to give the guys an ego boost like—yep—"

The crowd cheers as white scores a goal. But I was watching Kinnunen the whole time. He didn't even try to block it.

"Just wait until the points actually matter," says Tyler. "Then you'll really see the Bear come out to play."

WE'RE only halfway through the exhibition game when a young guy comes up wearing a Ray's polo shirt. "Sorry, Doc," he says at Tyler. "Vicki is asking for Doctor Price."

I cast him an apologetic look, but he shoos me off with a congenial wave. "Go, go. No one keeps Vicki waiting."

I follow the intern through the hallways back towards the office suites.

"There she is," Vicki calls by the main doors leading out to the parking garage. "I just came back from lunch, and I got a call that your rental arrived. I need you to sign the waiver and then I can hand over the keys."

"Oh, great." My hand holding the pen hovers over the signature line as I notice the make and model. "Umm, Vicki? Is this . . . was this my only option in rental?"

She looks up from her phone. "What's that, hon? Oh—yes, we got a great price with the dealership," she explains. "Most of the guys prefer something with a little towing capacity. They've all got boats and sea-doos and Lord knows what else. That won't be a problem, will it? You can drive a truck, right?"

I nod, signing the form. "Yeah, I'm sure it'll be fine."

In reality, I'm terrified. Tess is going to have a big laugh at my expense when I tell her I'm now in possession of an armored tank.

Vicki hands over an electric key fob. "Well, let's head out to the parking garage and I'll show you where you're parked." She slings open one of the double doors, leaving me space to slip through.

She says something else, but I'm not listening. All I can hear is the humming of my body. My brain tries to catch up with the truth that my eyes and my heart already know.

My Mystery Boy is walking right towards me.

11
RACHEL

I can hardly breathe as I watch him walk closer, his eyes on his phone. He's still wearing his sunglasses, his dark hair hidden under a baseball cap. It's a little bit shorter than when I saw him in Seattle, a closer fade at the nape. And he's clean-shaven.

But it's him. There's no doubt in my mind. Those broad shoulders are stretching his NHL tech shirt tight across his chest. His long, muscled legs are wrapped in nothing but a pair of athletic shorts. He's wearing trainers in the Rays colors.

He's a hockey player. Mystery Boy plays defense for the Jacksonville Rays . . . the team I now officially work for . . . as his doctor.

Oh, fuck—fucking—fuck!

I think I'm gonna pass out. But then he dares to look up from his phone and flash us both a panty-melting smile.

I'm dead. Just bury me here.

"Vicki, my goddess, my queen!" he calls out in that deep voice I've heard a thousand times in my dreams.

"Mmhmm," she says, arms crossed. Clearly, she's unimpressed. "You get it done finally?"

"Would I dare defy your direct order?" he replies, slipping his hand into the pocket of his athletic shorts to flash her his driver's license. "All fixed. We're good to go."

"Bring it to my office before close of day so I can make a copy."

As they talk, I just stand here like their own private statue. He sees me, right? He looked right at me. I don't understand what's happening. Why is he pretending not to know me?

"Rachel, this is Jake Compton, and he's trouble with a capital T," Vicki says by way of introduction.

Oh god, his name is Jake. My heart does a little flip. *Jake Compton.*

Caleb's best friend. He turns his gaze fully on me and I swear I can't breathe. Those hazel eyes hook me.

"Jake, this is our new Barkley Fellow, Doctor Rachel Price."

"Hey Doc, nice to meet you," he says holding out his hand, apparently still oblivious.

I can't even believe what I'm doing as I slowly reach a hand out. I've spent the last two months having my every dream revolve around this guy. Now I'm standing here, right in front of him, and he doesn't even recognize me!

12
JAKE

I've had the best morning ever. No early morning workout, no coaches' meeting, no warmups or practice. Instead, I slept in and made myself breakfast. Sure, I had to wait for over an hour at the DMV, but it gave me time to just relax.

The last few months have been crazy. Between Vicki and Poppy, we're having our balls busted every day. If we're not at practice or working out, we're in endless HR meetings, travel meetings, or dealing with press bullshit. I don't even know how many times I've had my picture taken for different promotional stuff.

So yeah, taking a morning off to drink my coffee and go to the DMV has felt pretty damn great.

Luck shines down as I stroll through the parking garage. Vicki is right there, intern in tow. She's always got someone new shadowing her. My phone pings and I glance down.

CALEB (11:45AM): Novy is lookin great. You'll skate well together against Carolina

I sigh with relief. Our starting line is feeling more solid each day. Maybe we actually have a chance at a win this season.

CALEB (11:45AM): Kelso is a mess. Looks like Davidson is in . . . which means I win *stacked money emoji**sushi emoji*

I huff, typing back a quick response. We had a bet on which goalie would come out on top and he won, meaning I'm buying his dinner tonight.

I pull my eyes from my phone, flashing Vicki a winning smile. "Vicki, my goddess, my queen!"

She purses her lips, rolling her eyes at me. I'm always teasing her, but she gives it right back. I knew she was serious about the ID when the teasing stopped. "Mmhmm. You get it done finally?"

"Would I dare defy your direct order?" I say, pulling my ID from my pocket. "All fixed. We're good to go."

"Bring it to my office before close of day so I can make a copy." She turns to her intern. "Rachel, this is Jake Compton, and he's trouble with a capital T."

I let myself look at her intern. Fuck, she's pretty. How the hell did I miss that? The guys have been going on about some hot new doctor roaming the halls today, but I honestly couldn't care less. There's only one doctor I want.

Wow, this girl looks a lot like my Mystery Girl—

"Jake, this is our new Barkley Fellow, Doctor Rachel Price," Vicki goes on.

Wait—she's a doctor? The pretty girl I dismissed with a glance isn't an intern, she's a doctor. The doctor who looks like *my* doctor is a doctor . . .

And then my brain explodes. I can't think, can't breathe. Somehow, my hand is sticking out and I'm pretty sure I've said something. Did my mouth just make words? I have no idea. I'm just standing here, waiting for my body to catch up with my brain. And I have no heart to beat because it just went splat on the floor.

She's looking at me like I've got two heads. Doctor Rachel Price. The new team doctor. *My* doctor. Doctor Mystery Girl. It all clicks into place, and I blurt out, "Oh my god!"

"Oh *my* god," she cries, tears in her eyes.

Holy fuck. Oh god, it's happening. She's here. She's standing right in front of me. My Mystery Girl. Only she's not a mystery anymore. She has a name.

Rachel.

Fuck, just saying it in my head is gonna give me a heart attack . . . or a hard on. Both. I've thought of this moment so many times. I've given her so many names in my mind. Maybe she was a Rachel once. Now no other name exists.

Rachel Price.

I smile. Mystery solved. But wait—*shit*—why is she looking at me like that? Why is Vicki still fucking here? Why aren't we kissing? Why are our clothes on?

"Am I missing something?" says Vicki, glancing between us. "Do you two already know each other?"

I look to Rachel, ready to take her lead. She's so fucking smart. She'll know what to do, what to say.

"We met a couple months ago," she murmurs. "We *umm* . . . sat together on the plane."

I glance at Vicki. Shit, is she buying it?

Vicki lets out a little laugh. "Huh, small world, isn't it? You know, I once sat in first class with Denzel Washington?"

Neither of us make any reply. I still can't breathe, and it looks like Rachel is trying very hard to perfect the power of teleportation. My girl would clearly rather be anywhere else but here.

Fuck, I'm messing this all up. I don't know how, but I am. I need to talk to her. I need Vicki to be the one to teleport somewhere else.

"Well, hon, let's give your key fob a try," says Vicki. "Yours should be one of those," she adds, pointing to a row of white trucks parked near the back of the garage.

Rachel fumbles with the key in her hand, her gaze glued to it as she gives the fob a squeeze. The truck at the end flashes its lights as the doors unlock.

"And there you go," says Vicki. "You let me know if you need anything else, okay? And you," she says, glaring at me. "Bring me that ID or you'll be flying to all the away games this season tied to the wing of the jet!"

With that she gives Rachel's shoulder a squeeze and walks off, back through the doors into the building.

Rachel and I stand there, looking at each other, not speaking. Both our brains are broken.

I move first, reaching for her. "I—"

"I can't do this," she whispers, darting away from my outstretched hand.

"What? Wait—*whoa*—hold on!" I spin around, chasing after her. "Rachel!"

She stills, her whole body stiff as I catch up, standing close behind her.

I can't help it; I'm smiling like a lovestruck idiot. "Rachel," I say again, just because I can. I put everything I'm feeling into the word. Fuck, it's a pretty name.

"Don't," she murmurs, her voice catching.

"Hey," I say gently, my hand reaching out and stroking her arm. It's the barest of touches. "Baby, turn around. Look at me."

She sucks in a breath, turning around. "Baby?"

Oooh, shit. She looks mad.

"I'm not your baby," she snaps. "You didn't even recognize me!" She spins away, stomping off towards her truck.

Her words punch all the air out of my chest. "What—Yes, I did! Get back here!" I shout, chasing her down. "Rachel, *stop*—"

She makes it to her truck and tugs on the driver's side door. I shove my weight against it, shutting it. She gasps, spinning around, her back pressed against the door. I've effectively boxed her in, my hands on either side of her head.

Fuck, my body is on fire. What she does to me—I can't explain it. I've never had anyone else make me feel this way. I'm trembling like a fifteen-year-old kid about to get his first kiss.

"Stop running," I beg. "Rachel, *talk* to me. What the hell is going on in your head right now? You're freakin' out. I know you are 'cause I am too, and that's okay. Let's just . . . let's freak out together, okay? And let's use *words*—"

"Oh, you want words? I was standing right in front of you for five freaking minutes, and you didn't even *see* me!" she snaps. "Am I that forgettable to you? *God*—"

She drags her fingers through her hair, pushing the loose strands back from her face. I wanna slap her hand away for doing my job. I'm the one who brushes her hair back. *I'm* the one who takes care of her. That's my fucking job, and I swear to god, no one is gonna do it better than me. Not even her. She's *mine*.

"I was distracted," I say. "It's been a crazy day, and I wasn't expecting to see you here and—and you look . . . different," I admit, scrunching up my nose.

She scowls at me, those perfect lips pursed in annoyance. "Different?"

I shrug. "Yeah, you know like . . . your makeup is all different, and you're not wearing the nose ring, and you've got glasses on—"

"Ohmygod," she cries, trying to shove her way out from under me. "You're worse than a Disney prince! What, the girl puts on glasses, and suddenly she's unrecognizable to you?"

"Hey, it was for like *five* seconds," I counter. "And you know I get hit in the head for a living! I was minding my own damn business, walking into work. I never in my wildest dreams expected to see you in my parking garage, so I didn't. I didn't see you, Rachel . . . until I did."

She shakes her head, her bottom lip quivering like she's about to cry.

"What is this really about?" I murmur, inching closer. I reach out a hand and gently tip her face up to look at me. "This isn't about me not recognizing you because you know I did. I *do*. You think I forgot about you . . . you think I left that hotel room and moved on?"

She closes her eyes. "Please . . ."

I brush my fingers featherlight down the line of her jaw. "You really think I could forget my Seattle Girl? Baby, you're *all* I think about."

"Don't," she begs.

I frown, frustrated. "You left *me* in that bed, remember? I'm the one who should be stomping around. I wanted your name. Hell, we could have been two months deeper into something by now instead of starting fresh—"

"No," she gasps, pulling away. Her arms are wrapped around her middle so tight, a pathetic excuse for armor. "Jake, we can't do this."

Oh, fuck me. My name on her lips is stronger than a shot from cupid's bow straight to my dick. "Say it again."

She looks up at me. "We can't do this."

"No." I shake my head. "Say my name."

"Don't," she murmurs. "Please, don't."

"Don't what?" I reply, inching closer, my hand cupping her cheek. She smells so fucking good. She left me her perfume in Seattle, but it's nothing like smelling the combination of that scent on her skin mixed with her hair products and her detergent and just . . . *her*.

I want to wrap her in my arms and never let go. I want to wear her t-shirts to bed like a lovesick fool. Okay, so there's no way they'll fit me, but I could take two and cut them up and sew them back together. Or Caleb can do it for me. He's good with sewing machines and—

Oh shit, *Caleb*. Rachel and Caleb. Rachel is the hot doctor Caleb picked up from the airport yesterday. The doctor with the kinky dildo who now shares a wall with him. The hot doctor he drove in to work this morning.

I was about to find him and grill him for more details because I *know* something else happened last night. He was being too cagey about it. Now my pulse is racing, and my tongue feels too big for my mouth. Do I want to know what happened? I don't know if I can take it. We've shared the occasional bunny in college, but this is totally different. Rachel is—she's *everything*.

"Please look at me," I murmur.

She glances up, her hand wrapping around my wrist as I cup her face. "We can't do this," she whispers. "I work for the team now. I just signed a hundred pages worth of contracts. I'm your doctor."

"No."

"You're my patient. I can't cross that line—*we* can't—"

"No," I growl again, pressing in with my hips.

She gasps. Yeah, my girl is mad for me. I can feel it. I lower my hand from her jaw, wrapping my fingers gently around her throat, my fingertips brushing against her racing pulse. She whimpers, her neck arching. She can't help it. She loves my hands on her.

We're both on fire, trembling with need. I have never been so turned on by another person in my life. She breathes near me, and I'm ready to fucking go. I have her in my hands again, and I can't wait a moment longer to taste her. Lowering my face, I press my lips to hers.

Boom.

Like kerosine tossed on a bonfire, we ignite. We're pressed so tight, my hands racing down her sides to grab her ass and lift her, wrapping her legs around my hips so our heights match. I slam her up against the side of her truck. She hisses in my mouth, our tongues chasing, hands desperate.

Fuck, she's the girl I want to kiss for the rest of my life. I don't care how crazy that sounds. She's ravenous, whimpering as I pin her with my hips, my hardness right there. If we were naked, I'd be inside her. Fuck, I'd be pounding her into the side of this truck.

Her groping hands knock my hat off and her fingernails drag over my scalp. It makes my whole body shudder as my dick twitches. I need to be inside her. Need to bury myself in her and never resurface.

But then she's gasping, her body squirming in my hold. "Jake," she whines. "*Please—*"

And I know what she's saying without saying it because that's just the way we are together. *Please, put me down. Please, stop.* And then my heart is breaking into pieces.

I loosen my hold on her and she slides down my body back to the floor of the parking garage. We're both shaking, need hammering through us. What we have is volcanic. She knows it too. I can't do this. I can't *not* be with her. She's in my city, on my team, in my fucking arms . . . and she's saying no.

"Don't push me away again," I plead, my heart shredding. "I can't do this twice, Rachel. Don't ask me to pretend that we're nothing. I don't care about the damn contract."

Her chin lifts in defiance, lips glistening with my kisses, teary eyes dark and dangerous. "Well, *I* care. This is my life, Jake. This is *my* chance," she says with such determination. "This fellowship, this team. It's my whole career on the line. You don't have to care about breaking the rules, but *I* do."

She's closing off, shutting me out. Goddamn it, she did the same thing in Seattle. "No," I growl. "Rachel, *please—*" Am I begging? Fuck, I have no pride when it comes to this girl. No chill. No game. I'm lost to her. I was from the moment she turned around on that barstool. "Don't do this. Don't push me away."

But I see the resolve shining in her eyes. "My contract lasts the whole season," she says, voice tight. "We can be friends. We can be colleagues . . . but nothing more."

I drop my hands away from her, our connection broken, and we both take a gasping breath.

My Mystery Girl is putting me on ice. She wants to focus on her career, and I can respect that. I'm a career addict too. You don't get to my level of sport and not be obsessive over your job.

I swallow, heart racing out of control. "Ten months," I say, my gaze locked on her. "Ride out your contract. I'll play nice." I lean in. "But the second it's over, you're mine, Seattle. You're not leaving me again."

13
RACHEL

I walk on jelly legs back inside the building, Mystery Boy striding silently at my side. *Jake.* His name is Jake Compton, and he's not a mystery. Jake Compton, starting defenseman of the Jacksonville Rays.

And I didn't imagine our chemistry. Over the last two months, I've downplayed it in my mind. The sex wasn't that good. Our connection wasn't that deep. I was tipsy. I was lost in the moment. Now I know the truth. It was real. All of it. Our connection, our heat, the instant passion, the way he reads me, the way I read him. What's worse, he knows it too. He knows I can't resist him.

Can I really survive ten months of this?

Make a list, Rach. Make a plan. I repeat the mantra in my head.

"I'm through here," Jake mutters, pointing towards an open hallway that I think leads to the gym.

I nod, looking at my feet.

"I don't know how to do this," he says. "I can't—" He groans, tugging on the bill of his hat. "I'm a shitty liar, Rach. The guys don't even let me play poker anymore because they say it's like taking candy from a baby. I'll try," he adds. "I'll . . . I won't say anything about us. But I'm not a good liar."

"Okay." I don't know what else there is to say.

"At the very least, Caleb is gonna see right through me," he adds. "We don't have secrets, Rachel."

I glance up at him. There's something in his tone—worry, jealousy, pain. He's right, he wears every emotion on his sleeve. But why is he jealous? "Just ask me," I say, desperate to relieve that look of pain.

He glances up and down the empty hallway before blurting, "Did you fuck Caleb?"

My eyes go wide. "What?"

"Last night, did you—" He groans again. "Fuck, I think I can take it. Just say it. Rip the band-aid off."

"Jake, no," I say, placing my hand on his arm. But then my indignation rises. "Did *he* tell you that we did—"

"No," he says quickly. "No, he didn't tell me anything about what happened last night . . . but something *did* happen between you," he adds. "Didn't it?"

I sigh, dropping my hand from his arm. "I'll leave it to him to give you the humiliating details, but no, Jake. I did not have sex with Caleb last night. I slept on his couch with the dog."

His hazel eyes go wide. "You—*why*—"

"Despite what you may think, I don't go around having one-night stands with every handsome man I meet," I add, my temper rising.

Jake's dark brows pinch together. "So, you admit that he's handsome."

I grit my teeth, ready to tell him off, but then I see the hint of a smirk on his face. He's in pain, he's not happy with the conditions I've set for us, but he's trying. I breathe a little sigh of relief. "I don't know how to do this either," I admit. "Let's just . . . one foot in front of the other, okay?"

He nods, his face carrying such a look of a hurt puppy that I want to wrap him in my arms. But I hold back. I have to stay strong for the both of us. It's easy for him to say he doesn't care, but he could get in trouble same as me. He signed non-fraternization contracts too.

"I'll see you around, Seattle Girl," he murmurs, his eyes touching me in all the ways his hands can't.

I don't even try to suppress my shiver of want, even as I glower at him. "Seriously, Compton?"

He smirks. "Oh baby, just you wait. I've got the next ten months to slow burn the fuck out of this." He brightens a little at the thought. Then he straight up laughs. "Oh, shit. This is about to become my new favorite game."

I raise a wary brow. "What game?"

He grins, lowering his face closer to mine. "Operation Unravel Rachel. I may not be able to touch you, but by god I can look," he says with a wink that I feel like a slap to my needy pussy.

Oh, fuck him. This is not happening. I'm not going to spend the next ten months getting edged by Jake Compton. I give him my best, bitchiest look. "Don't you dare do what I think you're gonna do."

"Too late, Seattle," he says with a laugh. "I'll be seeing you around. All day. Every day. For the next ten months."

I groan, watching him walk away with a new spring in his step.

I am so toast.

14
ILMARI

*S*he's watching me. That new doctor won't take her eyes off me. The guys have been blowing up the group chat about her all morning. One more reason why I hate group chats. They usually use it to make fantasy football trades and roast each other's golf scores. I keep leaving, but they always add me back in.

Focus.

I track the puck down the ice, relaxed in my stance. This is just an exhibition game. No need to hurt myself saving a rookie's sloppy shot. The guy with the puck has good footwork, I'll admit, but he's too obvious with his hands. He'll go for my glove side.

High or low?

My glove is already in the air before he shoots. I catch the puck easily. I didn't even move my feet. The crowd cheers as if I made some great save. I'm making it look effortless because this is taking no effort. He should go back to the minors where he belongs.

The game continues down ice until Novikov takes the puck. I perk up a little. He's a defender with great offense capability. I don't hold it against him that he's Russian. Well, Russo-Canadian.

I track him as he races down the ice in a breakaway. Novikov is unpredictable. I'm curious to see what happens if I put up a real defense. I square off in my stance, my eyes locked on the puck, as I instinctively measure his distance to me. He's moving fast, cutting left. He's going to pass the puck across. Inside pass to Fielder. I need to drop. I sink into the butterfly, one push with my right skate, and the puck hits my pad.

Blocked.

Pivot. Double push to guard the other post. They're skating around for a rebound. Puck is passed to Novikov. Right leg extends as I stretch out. The puck hits my pad again, and I fish it out with my stick and pass to a defender who shoots it down the ice to a waiting winger.

Saved.

But it cost me. I groan, getting up as fast as I can. The push followed by a full extension stretched my groin muscle tight. Pain lances through my right hip. I shouldn't have done that. Should have just let it in.

The puck is down at the other end of the ice, so I take a moment to stand, bringing my legs together. It was a mistake to dress for this game. I'll skip the next one. I'll make any excuse.

The truth I've tried ignoring for weeks sinks deep into my chest: the pain is getting worse. And damn if the doctor isn't still watching me. I noticed her in the stands sitting next to Doctor Tyler. Now she's standing right at the plexiglass in my eye line, arms crossed, mouth set in a firm line.

Coach Tomlin comes up to stand next to her and I watch them shake hands. She finally looks away from me and I realize with a pang of curiosity that I don't like it. Eric has all her attention now as he makes her laugh. What is he saying to her?

"Saatana," I curse as I nearly take a puck to the face. It whacks off the crossbar and hits my shoulder before dropping into the net. White scores because I was too busy watching my coach flirt with the pretty doctor to guard my damn goal.

"Head in the game, Mars!" Sully barks at me.

I shake my head. What the hell just happened? Was I bewitched? Nothing breaks my concentration on the ice. Anger bubbles in my chest. I don't like that I was distracted.

Focus.

The buzzer echoes all around, ending the game, and I relax. Even with that last goal I let in, white still loses 3-6.

Sully skates up, sliding to a stop. "You alright there, big guy?"

"Yeah," I say through the mask. "Fine."

He skates off, following the others off the ice.

I snatch up my water bottle and turn. "Voi helvetti," I mutter, skating over to where Coach Tomlin waits with the doctor.

"Fallin' asleep out there, eh, Mars?" calls Coach. "You nearly took a facer."

"Game was over," I mutter. "Fielder needed the goal more than I needed the save."

He just chuckles, gesturing to the doctor. "Mars, this is Doctor Rachel Price."

I let myself look at her openly. She's standing with her arms crossed tight around her middle. She's cold. Not used to the rink then. She has dark eyes hidden behind thick, rectangular-framed glasses. Her hair is up, with a few pieces framing her face. She's beautiful.

And she's still looking at me. Her gaze roves unashamedly, taking me in from my skates to my helmet. I tower over her in my full kit. We're like the kitten and the gorilla. Slowly, I take my helmet off, holding her gaze without the cage in the way.

"Doctor Price, this is Mars Kinnunen," Coach says. "He's the best damn goalie in the League."

I hand my helmet over to coach and tuck my stick into my knee pad. Then I tug off my blocker, offering out my right hand. It's sweaty, but if the new doc has a problem with that, she's in the wrong business.

She leans over the boards with a smile and takes it. "Really great to meet you, Mars," she says.

I want to know what she's thinking. Did she see my save? Did she see my slow recovery? Coach was distracted trying to make her laugh. I nearly missed the block because I'm too afraid to do a full right-side extension. Too afraid I'll pull the groin muscle worse.

I've been doing all I can to rehab it on my own. It's not my first pull and it won't be my last. I just need some more ice, massages, and a better stretching routine. The scouts from the FIHA are coming to watch me play, so I can't be sitting the bench with a groin pull.

I want to make this Olympic team more than I've ever wanted anything. It's my legacy. My grandfather played for Finland in the Oslo Olympics in 1952. Father was in Lake Placid in 1980. This is my time. Father's team placed fourth. I mean to make the podium. The Leijonat are good enough. I know who else they're scouting. They can do it. They can win. I want to be in the net when they do.

"You feeling ready for the start of the season?" says Doctor Price. Her voice is deeper than I expected, smooth like honey.

I nod, dropping her hand as Coach slaps my shoulder pad. "Mars was born ready. He's in the best shape of his life."

"Great," she says. "Then you should sail through your physical no problem. Just let Hillary know his training schedule and I'll be happy to work around it," she says at Coach.

"Can do," he replies.

I'm just standing here on the ice as she turns to walk away. "Wait—"

She glances over her shoulder, one dark brow raised.

"What physical?"

She smiles again. Americans always do that—smile when they don't mean it. I suppose it's meant to put people at ease, and it works on most other Americans. To me, it always comes off as disingenuous. Don't smile unless you mean it. And I don't want *her* fake smiles. I want to earn them.

"All the starting players have their final physicals next week," she replies. "I'm new to the team, so I'm playing a bit of catch-up here, but I promise I'll be thorough. We don't want to miss anything with the eyes of the hockey world focused on the Rays."

"We appreciate it, Doc," Eric replies.

Sure, he can smile. He's not the one under inspection. Meanwhile, my heart stops. "What was your specialty?" I call after her.

"Knees," she replies. "Hips and knees. I imagine that means you and I will become good buddies this season." With another nod, she turns and leaves.

Goddamn it.

15
RACHEL

Mars Kinnunen might just be the most intimidating man I've ever seen. I thought the man looked big from across the ice. In person, he's a giant. Then he took that mask off, and my stomach flipped.

Jake and Caleb are pretty boys—perfect jaws, cheekbones for days, the floppy jock hair. All-American athletes. But Mars is . . . wild. He looks like the toughest guy on a hockey team had sex with a Viking and made a super baby.

He's got a full blond beard an inch long, trimmed longer under the chin. The rest of his hair is shaved to the skin around his nape, leaving a full head of unruly blond hair at his crown long enough to pull back into a messy knot.

His features are rugged too—his nose sits a little crooked at the bridge, likely from a break; his left brow is scarred in two places. But he has the most beautiful ocean blue eyes, piercing in their intensity. I felt like he was staring into my soul as he scowled at me.

I shake my head with a soft laugh. This has certainly been an interesting first day.

I catch up with Tyler in his office to grab my backpack and he introduces me to Hillary, the team nurse. She's a lovely, older lady with curly grey hair and kind eyes. She'll be responsible for scheduling my appointments.

"We've got an office ready for you down here," she says, leading me towards the gym. "It's easiest to catch the guys during their strength and condition time, so we have a few exam rooms set up right off the floor. It's a bit like herding sheep," she adds with a chuckle. "Sometimes you just gotta stick your crook out and snag one. I've found the easiest way to get them to come willingly is to catch them on the treadmill. You show me a hockey player who likes the treadmill, and I'll show you a liar."

I laugh. "Strong treadmill avoidance. Got it."

I can already hear the clank and jangle of workout equipment over the boom of loud rock music.

"They're usually good about turning it down if you can't hear yourself think," she calls over the music, pulling open a glass door.

"Wow," I murmur, stepping inside.

The facility is amazing. You wouldn't know it from the somewhat nondescript hallway, but the room opens into a gymnasium-like space spread over two levels. There's the main floor which is all for weightlifting. Several guys are milling around, doing reps and spotting each other. Most are players, but the guys in polos must be the strength and conditioning team.

A wall of glass lined with treadmills to my right lets the guys look down on the main practice rink. It's already been cleared from the exhibition game, and it looks like figure skating lessons are happening now. Upstairs is a running track.

"All the therapy equipment is through there," Hillary says, pointing to a large set of open doors to the left. "We've got hot and cold tubs, massage tables and chairs, all the PT equipment you could want, space for stretching. And our corner of the world is right here," she finishes with a wave of her hand at a set of three doors along the wall.

She opens the first door and stands back. I peek my head in. It's just a windowless broom closet with a desk and a chair. Frankly, I've worked in smaller spaces. Behind us, there's hooting and clamoring as someone cuts the music.

"Whoa—"

"Guys!"

"Hey Jacobs, is this the new doc?"

"Hot Doc spotted!"

"New doc on the block!"

All the guys are shouting and laughing as they abandon their equipment.

Hillary rolls her eyes at me. "Ignore them. They go after new staff like dogs with a bone."

One of the guys shoots straight for me, his face a sweaty mess. He looks young, bright eyed and friendly. "Hey, Doc," he says, holding out his hand. "Ryan Langley, forward."

"Yes, you are," Hillary says. "Get back, before you soak us with your sweat."

I just laugh, taking his sweaty hand and giving it a shake. "Rachel Price."

"Rachel," he calls over his shoulder.

"Her name's Rachel," a guy echoes, and then all the guys are saying it.

"Price," Hillary corrects them. "Her name is *Doctor* Price to you."

A big guy with a shaved head elbows Langley out of the way. "Cole Morrow, Doc. Best damn defenseman in the League."

The guys all laugh as I shake his hand next.

"Yeah, you wish Coley. What's your EA ranking now?" someone shouts.

Morrow scowls at him, giving his shoulder a good-natured slug.

The guy laughs and I can't help but smile to see his two missing front teeth. Hockey truly is a brutal sport. "I'm Gerard," he says.

"Hey, J-Lo, get outta the way!"

I smirk up at him with a raised brow. "J-Lo?"

He just shrugs. "My name is Jean-Luc, and the guys are assholes."

"Oh, don't get salty, J-Lo. You know we love you!"

"Alright, enough," calls one of the surlier looking strength and conditioning coaches. "Leave the doc alone, and get back to your reps. *Now.*"

"Welcome to the team, Doc," the cute blond says with a cocky grin.

They all amble away, still laughing and shoving each other. I just smile, shaking my head. Boys may grow into men, but they never really grow up.

"How long will the hazing last?" I say, glancing at Hillary.

She purses her lips. "With how pretty you are? My guess is forever."

"Great," I mutter.

This is going to be the longest ten months of my life.

As if I needed direct confirmation of that statement, my phone pings with a message. Then another.

CALEB (2:07PM): I had nothing to do with this. Asshole took my phone

UNKNOWN (2:07PM): And now I have your number. Just face it, we're inevitable, Seattle

That message is followed up with a picture of Jake giving 'fuck me' eyes. Then a second of him with Caleb in a headlock.

I groan. Just slather me with butter and jam because I am so fucking toast.

16
RACHEL

"So . . . wait. You're saying you met this guy in Seattle at Harrison's wedding?" Tess is incredulous, her thick brow raised behind her glasses on the phone screen.

It's Sunday night, and I've avoided Jake all weekend. I was invited out to Rip's on Friday night to celebrate the end of the preseason, but I declined. I still had my bags to fetch from the airport and I just needed a minute to breathe and recalibrate.

I hid out all day yesterday, only making a run to IKEA to trick out my balcony, which included getting a stopper for the sliding glass door because I am *never* getting stuck out here in my thong again.

I spent today exploring the city on my own, picked up some flowers, and now I'm nestled in the corner of my new mini sectional. A row of freshly potted flowers and ferns hang along the railing. I added an outdoor rug, some electric candles, and a little reed basket for my yoga equipment. Two sets of patio lights are strung from the ceiling, letting off a soft golden glow.

All in all, I'm proud of myself for this flip job.

I take a sip of my wine, holding Tess's gaze in the phone. "Yeah, we met in Seattle."

She blinks at me, then there's a shuffle as she sits forward on her bed. "Oh, girl—wait. When you say 'meet' . . . did you *meet* meet him?"

I nod and she shrieks through the phone.

"Oh god, that is amazing!" she cackles. "You dirty little horndog. You hooked up with an NHL player at your brother's wedding—"

"Not *at* the wedding," I correct. "And I didn't know he played for the NHL. I didn't know anything about him. We didn't do names."

Tess laughs. "God, you are *wild*, girl."

"It didn't feel very wild in the moment," I admit. "It felt . . . right.

He felt right. It was . . ." I struggle to find the words to explain what Seattle meant to me. "Cosmic," I say. "We had a cosmic connection . . . have," I add softly.

Tess heaves a dramatic sigh. "But now you've signed on to his team, and you're twisting yourself up because you're a doctor and he's a player and you've gotta keep your horny little horndog hands to yourself, right? Is that the problem?"

"Of course, it's the problem," I say. "Tess, I can't—" I groan, setting my wine glass aside with a clink. "I can't start something with him again. I can't mess up this chance. The last three Barkley Fellows from the Clinic were all offered permanent positions when their fellowships ended. This could be the start of my new career."

Tess is pensive, lips pursed as she nods. "Yeah . . . or it could be the start of the rest of your life with Magic Boy—"

"Mystery Boy."

She sighs again. "Look, Rach. You know I love you. You know that, right?"

"Yeeeah."

"Okay, well you have this thing you do where you sabotage all your relationships. You don't give them the legs to stand before you cut them off at the knees. And now you're telling me you have a cosmic connection with Magic Boy—"

"Mystery Boy," I correct again.

"Whatever." She waves her hand. "We're talking about planets aligning, stars shining, and you're sitting alone on a Sunday night, talking to *me*? Rach, you're living in the same city as this Magic Boy and—*wait*—I'm assuming the sex was good? Oh, please tell me it was good. Tell me he's got a gorgeous, nine-inch member that vibrates."

I all but whimper as the memories flood me, swallowing a gulp my wine. "Tess, I—I'm actually speechless. I have no words."

She's squealing again. "God, I'm *so* jealous. I need a decent fuck like I need a good detangling spray," she says, fluffing her bouncy red curls with her fingers. "Has he tried to contact you at all?"

Has he tried? I flip open my messaging app and click his name. A long string of messages over the past two days fills my phone. Most are from yesterday.

JAKE (7:37AM:) Good morning, Seattle Girl. Another beautiful day in Jax. Perfect for a walk on the beach *wave emoji**palm tree emoji**sun emoji*

He followed that up with a shot of him shirtless on the beach looking like a goddamn snack.

JAKE (9:45AM): Hey, how do you take your coffee? We never got to compare morning routines

JAKE (9:46AM): Wait—do you drink coffee? Please don't tell me you drink kombucha or some frufru shit with foam

JAKE (9:48AM): Cay drinks peppermint mochas like some kind of weird Christmas elf. I swear, if I didn't love the jerk, our friendship would be over

I was in the potting soil aisle of the garden store when that message came through and I snorted on a sip of my perfectly normal americano with cream and two sugars.

JAKE (12:37PM): I love cheat day!

Then he sent a photo of a massive plate of colorful sushi.

JAKE (5:50PM): What's your favorite color? Mine is *blue heart emoji*

JAKE (9:45PM): Night, beautiful. FYI, I go to sleep pretty early

JAKE (9:45PM): Unless you're in my bed, obvs

The last thing he sent on Saturday was a picture of him, shirtless in the dark, stretched out on his bed. He had a sleepy smile on his face, one hand tousling his hair.
I can't stop smiling.

"Girl, what?" Tess says with a grin. "What is that face? He's been texting you, hasn't he! Omg, what is he saying?"

"Nothing," I reply, tapping her screen to hide his messages.

"You little liar," she teases. "You practically have hearts in your eyes. Is it dirty stuff? Text him back."

"No—"

"Oh god, please text him a dirty pic. Do it now—"

"Tess!" I cry, setting my wine aside again.

"Your tits!" she shouts. "Text him a sexy picture of your tits. You've got great boobies, girl. Share the love. Please, Rach. Do it for me."

"What kind of example in restraint am I setting if I go from leaving him on read all weekend to texting him a shot of my boobs?"

"Hey, two can play his game," she says with a shrug. "He can look, but he can't touch. Drive him wild."

My heart flutters at the idea. "I think that would qualify as torture in like at least thirty countries. Cruel and unusual punishment."

Tess just rolls her eyes. "Trust me when I say that no straight man on this earth would consider it a punishment to get an unsolicited tit pic from Rachel Price."

I grin, snatching up my glass of wine and taking a sip. "If I'm sending one, you're sending one too."

She chokes on a laugh. "What—to Magic Boy? Honey, the majesty of my titties would end his sweet little life."

"No," I say, all but snorting on my wine. "Not to him. Surely you have someone whose soul you'd like to see ascend to a higher plane of existence?"

She smirks. "There might be someone."

I'm grinning now too. This is the world's most terrible idea, but I'm two glasses of chardonnay in, and he's been blowing up my phone all weekend. Two can play his game. "I'm doing it."

Tess hoots with delight. "Yaaass, get it, girl! Make him sweat! And call me tomorrow!" She hangs up before I can reply.

As soon as she's gone, my confidence falters. Rachel Price does *not* send nude pictures of herself to men. I'm suddenly nervous. Snatching up my wine and my phone, I go inside.

I really shouldn't do this. I don't want to lead him on.

But you really want an orgasm.

I shiver at the thought, my mouth quirking into a smile. Yeah, just picturing Jake's face when his phone dings is enough to have me hot. And there's literally *no* way he won't respond. If I'm not careful, I might have him breaking the laws of traffic, racing over here to handle business in person.

Would that be so bad?

I groan, setting down my glass of wine. I strip off my ratty Ferrymen sweatshirt, tossing it to the bottom of the bed. Now I'm standing in just my silky pajama shorts. No way am I sending a picture of my coochie. I'm not even going to let him see my full tits.

I crawl onto the bed, sitting back against the pillows. I cross my right arm over the girls, squeezing them together a bit and giving them a lift. The lighting is good, just a soft glow from my side lamp. And if I angle the shot right, I get just my neck and chest. Everything is covered and the angle ends at my hips.

Before I lose my nerve, I take the photo. This is crazy, but I have a plan. I send the picture and wait.

11
JAKE

After a long day of practice, it feels good to unwind with the guys. A few of us are out exploring a new bar tonight, eating our weight in chicken wings and salad. The food is crap, and the music is too loud, but we've got a great view of the ocean.

Caleb sits next to me, reading out the stats from the other NHL teams' exhibition games. Morrow and Novy sit across from us, elbows bumping at this narrow table.

"Oy, boys," says Novy with a laugh. "Look who we have here."

Caleb and I glance over our shoulders.

"Apparently that asshole thinks he's too good to sit with us," Novy says with a huff.

That's when I see him. Mars Kinnunen is a giant. He's sitting by himself at the bar, glancing down at his phone while he eats his dinner. If he's noticed us sitting fifteen feet away, he's not letting on.

"He hates me," Novy adds, snatching up his beer and taking a swig.

"He likes you fine, Nov," says Caleb, turning back around.

"No, he's Finnish," Novy counters. "When we first met, he tried to speak to me in Russian and I just stared at him. The only Russian I know are my grandpa's curse words. He rolled his eyes and walked off."

"Nah, he's okay," says Morrow. "Great player. Goalies are always weird, eh?"

"Have you tried talking to him?" Caleb asks me.

I shrug too. There hasn't been a ton of opportunity. The goalies always have slightly different schedules. They've got their own coaches, their own practice times. I mean, I've seen him around, and we talk on the ice when we have to, but I couldn't tell you a single thing about him outside his stats.

Caleb gives me a hard shove.

"What the hell?" I growl, as the other guys laugh.

"Go talk to him. Go say hi."

"*You* go talk to him," I huff.

"I talk to him all the time," Caleb replies. "He's a cool guy. Yeah, he's quiet, but you try looking like that and see how easy it is to have people approach you first."

I glance back over towards the giant Finn. Caleb is right, even in this crowded bar, there's an aura around him. The guy gives off serious 'don't fuck with me' energy. I once saw footage of him in a fight on the ice. He knocked the guy out with one punch.

"Do it," Novy jeers.

"Yeah, tell him to get over here," Morrow adds. "We can pull up a chair."

I groan as Caleb gives me another shove. He's right. It's the polite thing to do. I wander towards the bar. "Hey, man," I call out, patting his shoulder.

Mars stiffens under my hand. He's got an awesome full-back tattoo that creeps up the back of his neck. I can see the ink peeking out the top of his t-shirt. I know from seeing it in the locker room that they're the feathered tips of a raven's spread wings.

Slowly, he turns to face me. I'm 6'3", but even sitting on the stool he's taller than me. "What?" he mutters.

"Saw you over here," I call over the music. "Just wanted to say hi."

He just blinks at me.

Great. This is already going so awesome.

"Umm . . . so how do you like the food?"

He glances down at his half-eaten salmon and baked potato. "It's terrible."

I huff a laugh. "Yeah, wings are pretty bad too."

He waits for me to keep speaking.

My courage is starting to falter. "So uhh . . . what brings you here?"

"I was hungry."

Fuck, this is painful. Abort mission.

I rub the back of my neck. "Great, yeah . . . well, me and some of the guys are over there," I say, pointing out our ocean view table.

Novy and Morrow wave like a pair of idiots.

Mars gives them a curt nod.

"Wanna join us?"

He glances back at me. "No."

Mayday. Mayday. Prepare to crash and burn.

I shift my weight, hands tucked in my pockets. "Cool, umm . . . well—"

You know what? Fuck it. I'm trying to be nice, and he's being a total dick right now. I'm not gonna tiptoe around his ass all season.

"Can I ask why you won't come sit with us?"

He just looks at me with that expressionless gaze. "I'm on the last chapter of my book," he explains, tapping his phone screen. It lights up to display his e-book. "It would be rude to read at a shared table. I don't want to be rude."

I blink at him, mouth slightly open in surprise.

Well, now I'm the asshole.

I can't help but laugh. I thought this guy was being a dick, but really, he's just trying to *not* be a dick. Go figure. Finns are so weird.

"Sure, umm . . . well, okay then," I say, backing away. "Have a good night, Kinnunen."

He gives me a nod of dismissal, turning back to his phone.

I wander back to the table. Why do I feel like I just tried to hit on a girl and got shot down?

"No dice?" calls Caleb.

"Told you. He hates us," says Novy, tearing into another chicken wing.

As I sink down onto my chair, my phone buzzes in my pocket.

Caleb slides his basket of fries over to me. "Here, you've earned these."

But I can't think about fries. I can't think about anything. Because after two days of shooting my shot and getting nothing but radio silence, I'm looking down at a topless picture of my Seattle Girl.

I shift on the bed, feeling a little self-conscious, but then my phone dings.

JAKE (8:15PM): Holy shit. Warn a guy next time. Caleb is sitting right next to me

I smile down at my phone. Why does the idea of Caleb seeing my picture on Jake's phone give me a secret thrill? I lay on my back and type a reply.

RACHEL (8:16PM): Well, then angle the phone away *wink emoji*

My smile widens as I raise my camera and take a new picture from another angle. This time my hand with the star tattoos is cupping my breast, fingers splayed in a nice side-boob shot. You still can't see anything, and only he would know it's me because of the tattoos on display. I send it. Immediately, I see three dancing dots.

JAKE (8:18PM): Fucking hell. Seattle, I'm in public. Hold on—

It only takes a minute or two before the phone is ringing. Of course, it's him. Taking a breath, I answer. "Hello?"

Wherever Jake is, it's loud. He sighs into the phone. "What the hell are you doing to me, Seattle?"

"I'm answering your many many texts," I reply. "Why, did you not want me to?"

"I'm out with the guys. I almost fell out of my chair and just shuffled to the bathroom sporting a semi."

"Where are you?" I say, stretching out on the bed. Just the sound of his voice is soothing me, even as it spins me up tighter.

"I don't know. Some beach bar. Seattle, why do I have a topless photo of you on my phone?"

"You've been sending me topless photos all weekend. I thought it only fair I reciprocated."

He's quiet for a moment. "This is a trick. This is . . . I don't know where the trap door is, but you're about to pull some lever, aren't you?"

I laugh. "No tricks. No trap doors. Consider this my apology."

"Apology?"

"Mmhmm," I shamelessly let my free hand roam over my bare chest. Knowing I have him all to myself is making me so wet and needy.

"Why are you apologizing? Wait—" He growls his frustration. "Seattle, what the hell are you doing?"

I sigh as I slide my fingers under the top of my panties. "Touching myself."

"Oh, fuck. Switch to video."

I swirl my fingers over my clit. "No."

"Baby, what are you doing? Talk to me."

"I have my hand in my panties," I reply. "I'm touching myself. Jake, I'm so wet," I whimper, my fingertip dipping inside my pussy.

The gravelly sound in his groan is like a slap straight to the clit. I arch my back on a sigh, sinking a finger deeper inside.

"Baby girl, you gotta talk to me. Tell me what's happening."

"I'm—I—" I huff with frustration. I've never been good at dirty talking on a phone. If I ever worked for a phone sex hotline, the guys would probably ask for a refund. "Hold on." I shimmy out of my silky sleep shorts and my underwear.

"You're killing me here, baby—"

"Hold *on*," I say again, tapping the icon on the phone to switch to video.

"Oh, fuck yes—" His words cut off as the call switches.

I hold my phone out with one hand, so my face is in view. His camera flicks on and I see his beautiful face close in on the screen. It's dark. There's a heavily graffitied wall behind him. "Where are you?" I murmur.

"Fuck if I know," he replies. "Some bathroom in a shitty beach bar. I've locked the door, but I can't camp out in here. Now, you called me for a reason."

"Yes," I reply, spreading my legs and letting my fingers explore again. I can't help it. Seeing him and feeling so turned on, I can't *not* touch myself.

"You called me to apologize," he presses.

"Mmhmm," I say, circling my clit again. I'm biting my bottom lip to keep in my moan.

"And why are you apologizing?"

I still my hand, holding his dark gaze. "I don't want to hurt you," I reply. "I *never* wanted to hurt you."

He nods, dragging a hand through his hair. "Well, it is what it is, right?"

I shake my head. "No. This is real, Jake. What we have . . ." If I try to put it into words, I'll cry. And I don't want to cry tonight. I just want to feel good. I want to make him feel good too. "I left you in Seattle. You didn't get to say goodbye."

"Yeah, that sucked," he mutters.

I take a deep breath, letting it out. "So, now's your chance."

He raises a dark brow. "What?"

"Say goodbye."

"Seattle, what are you—"

"I robbed you of the chance to have me one last time," I explain. "I knew if you did, I wouldn't be able to walk away. I would have stayed. I would have told you my name. Well, now the game has changed. Neither of us can walk away. And you know my name anyway. The reasons I slipped out don't matter anymore. So here I am. I'm naked and I'm saying yes to anything you want for the next . . ." I tap my screen to check the time. "Five minutes."

He groans, dragging a hand through his hair. "Five minutes? What the hell?"

"Hey, I've got a plane to catch, remember?" I tease. "Say goodbye, Jake."

"You are in so much trouble."

"Clock is ticking, angel. Are you going to make me come?"

"So hard you see stars," he replies, spinning to lean against the wall of the bathroom. "Touch yourself. Touch your breasts. And show me," he adds, his voice harsh with command.

I angle the phone down a bit until my boobs are in the shot. I cup each one for him, pinching each nipple tight until I'm shivering with need.

"Good girl. You look so beautiful," he croons. "So fuckable. You know if I was there, I'd be flicking those tits with my tongue, biting until I leave teeth marks, branding them. You're fucking *mine*, Seattle."

"Mmhmm . . . for four more minutes," I tease. "You gonna hurry this along?"

"Take your panties off," he orders. "Spread your legs."

I smile, shifting the phone up to show my face. "Way ahead of you." I raise the phone up a bit and flip the camera so it's panning over my naked body.

"Oh, fucking hell," he groans. "Kill a man, why don't you. Spread those legs, baby. Touch yourself. Use your fingers. Two in the pussy, thumb on your clit."

I rush to comply, loving the feel of taking orders from him. My fingers sink inside my tight wet center, and I let my thumb rub little circles on my clit. "Oh god," I whimper. "Jake, are you hard for me?"

"As fucking steel, baby. You have no idea."

I suck in a breath, feeling that glorious spiral of a looming orgasm low in my gut. That warm feeling is spreading. "I'm close," I pant. "Get your cock out. Come with me."

He groans again. I can't even see him at this angle, but I can hear him, I can hear his want for me. "Do you have a vibe? Not that tentacle thing. You're not using that unless I'm there to hold it for you."

I gasp, my fingers stilling inside me. "He told you about that?"

"Of course, he told me," he says with a low laugh. "But can we not talk about Cay while I've got my hand on my dick? Get a vibrator. I wanna watch you ride a toy and pretend its me."

I roll over, opening the drawer of my bedside table. I pull out my trusty pink vibe with a clit stimulator. The thing comes with like fifteen settings, but I only like one. High voltage buzz. Ruins me every time. I hold it up for him and smile, turning it on.

"Oh, fuck yes. Put it in nice and slow. Ride it for me and let me watch. Fuck—I'm so fucking close. Gonna come in this shitty fucking bathroom watching you shatter, baby."

I slip it in, adjusting it on my clit with a soft gasp. It vibes so good, hitting me inside and out. I move the camera angle so he can watch as I give the toy a few little wiggles, my hips arching.

"Oh god—I'm so close, Jake," I whisper.

"So am I. Fuck, you're so beautiful. So perfect. Come for me, baby girl."

Between his voice and the vibrations, I crest my high so hard and so fast. I come apart, crying out for him, convulsing with each wave of my orgasm. I clench around the toy, strangling it with my pussy, as it buzzes against my clit. I'm hot all over and then I'm shaking, jerking it loose and tossing it on the bed next to me.

I sink back against the pillows, flipping the camera to look at him. He's breathing hard too, his eyes glassy. We came together. Even through the phone, our bodies are so in sync with each other. We may be separated by circumstance, but this man holds a piece of my soul.

I lick my parched lips, waiting for him to look up at me. When he does, I see the relaxation there. "Better?" I murmur.

"Much," he replies.

"I can't offer you more right now, Jake."

He nods. "I know."

"But at least you got to say goodbye."

"That was a goodbye to who we were in Seattle. Two strangers lost and alone." He looks straight at me, his eyes burning with intensity. "But we're not strangers anymore. My name is Jake Compton, and I'm the starting defenseman for the Jacksonville Rays. I like sushi and the color blue, and I drink my coffee black. I have a twin sister, and I hate all flavors of sparkling water. And I am not going *anywhere*, Rachel."

"Jake . . ."

"You give me a chance, and I'll be so damn good to you. I'll treat you so right, baby. You're it for me."

I sit up, eyes wide. "Jake—what?"

He chuckles. "Easy, I'm not out here about to propose. I'm not *that* crazy. I'm just saying I'm in. You want a friend, you got one. A boyfriend, great. A fuck buddy, I'm there. You just name the time and the place. Because we are *not* strangers, Rachel. And I refuse to act like it. I'm not gonna tiptoe around my life pretending you're not in it when you are. And if you don't like it then . . . well that's just too damn bad. You made a choice for both of us in Seattle, now I'm making this choice."

I smile, settling back against the pillows. "Relax, Jake. I like it too. We're friends."

He raises a dark brow. "With benefits?"

I purse my lips. "Friends."

"Right, friends working on the conditions of their friendship, to include a provision about benefits."

I laugh, rolling my eyes. "You better get back to your table."

"I guarantee you they left without me. I bet they think I ducked out to avoid paying the bill."

Just then I hear a thundering pound at the door. "Jake! Jeez, man, you die in there?"

"Hold on!" Jake bellows.

I snort. "Goodnight, Jake."

"Night, Seattle. See you tomorrow, bright and early."

I raise a brow. "Bright and early?"

He flashes me a devilish grin. "Didn't you check your schedule? You're doing physicals tomorrow."

"Yeah . . ."

"Well, I'm your first patient."

I groan.

"Better get in that beauty sleep, Seattle Girl. I can be quite a handful in the morning. And I'm nothing compared to the rest of the guys."

"Oh god. They're gonna start hazing me tomorrow, aren't they?"

He laughs. "You know it." Then he hangs up, leaving me blissed out on my bed with a buzzing vibrator.

19
CALEB

"**C**ome on man, poop already," I mutter.

Sy is taking his sweet fuckin' time this morning. Usually, we try to get over to the beach and do a sunrise walk, or he roams around while I surf. But I've got an earlier start than usual today. This dog needs to hurry up and make so I can bring him back upstairs.

I check my phone, tapping the message thread for Jake. Last night was weird. He disappeared into the bathroom for like twenty minutes. When he came out, he looked all flushed and glassy eyed. If I didn't know any better, I'd swear to god he was hooking up in there. But I was right there when the door opened, and he came out alone.

I asked him about it on the drive home and he got all cagey, changing the subject. Something is up. I hate thinking he's hiding something from me. That's not how we are together. Or at least it wasn't . . . but he's been weird for a few months now.

I blame his Seattle Girl.

Jake went out to Seattle to meet up with Amy before training camp. He was so excited about it too. For weeks, it was all he could talk about. I mean, I don't blame him. Amy is awesome. But then I got a desperate call from him that Amy's flight was cancelled, and he was alone. Jake *hates* being alone. I talked him down and he promised to call me back after he got his flights changed.

Next thing I know, I don't hear from the asshole for *two* fucking days. I was ready to call the Seattle police and start a manhunt. Then he shows up back in Jax with stars in his eyes, talking about his precious Seattle Girl. Best sex of his life, his every dream come true. Blah, blah, blah.

If she was so great, why did she ghost him? She snuck out before sunrise without leaving her name or her number. I'm not out here trying to rain on my best friend's parade, but it doesn't sound like the start to any love story I know.

For the past two months, I've watched him change. He's gotten quieter, moodier. I mean, it's all relative, so we're talking Jake's version of quiet. The man has no filter, no shame, and no 'off' switch. He used to drop everything and call me if he saw an interesting bird while driving. He can't eat a meal unless he sends me a picture of it first. Now he's doing fishy shit in the bathroom and hiding it from me.

I think the start of the season is coming at just the right time. We'll get back on the road, and he can vent his frustrations over his lost Seattle Girl with a few bunnies. Not gonna lie, I'm squirming a bit just thinking about it. After a few bad experiences in college, the luster of the puck bunny life faded fast for me.

It took losing everything with my knee injury to face the truth I hid from everyone, including myself: I'm queer. Growing up in men's locker rooms, I found ways to dissociate with that part of myself. If you'd tried telling twenty-year-old me that he liked sex with men, he would have laughed in your face.

When the burden of being an NHL star was suddenly yanked from my shoulders, I took my first unrestricted queer breath. I was free to explore what I'd kept buried all those years. A few drunken hookups in the back of bars revealed the surprising truth. Turns out I really like the feel of a dick in my mouth.

Not that I indulge very often. In fact, I haven't gotten laid in like a year. I'm over the emptiness of bar hookups. I can take care of the urge with my hand. What I crave is something . . . deeper. I want connection and intimacy. Someone who challenges me. Someone who just . . . gets me.

If I can't have that, I think I'd rather be alone.

I give Sy's leash a little tug, turning to head back towards the apartment building. As I turn, I spot Rachel hopping down the stairs, phone in one hand, travel coffee mug in the other. Her dark hair is twisted up in a knot.

She doesn't notice me or Sy as she heads over to her truck. I watch her slide to halt in front of the driver's side door. She just stands there, looking at the handle. After a minute, she gets inside and shuts the door, but she doesn't take off.

Curious, I wait. She turns the truck on, and it roars to life. She all but jumps in her seat at the sound and I smirk. What is this girl doing driving so much truck? She just sits there, both hands clutching to the top of the wheel, engine running.

Goddamn it.

I wander over, giving Sy's leash another soft tug. He trots along happily. I step up to her window and tap.

She jumps, one hand flying to her chest, as she rolls down the window. "Ohmygod, you scared me half to death! Don't you know you're not supposed to sneak up on a woman in a parking lot?"

"I was right here the whole time," I reply with a shrug. "You just weren't paying attention to your surroundings."

"Still," she mutters, her hand going back on the wheel.

"Sooo . . . what are you doing in there, Hurricane?"

She narrows her dark eyes at me. "If I tell you, you'll just mock me."

I raise both hands, one wrist wrapped up in Sy's leash. "I wouldn't dream of it."

She sighs. "Fine. I'm hyping myself up."

I raise a brow. "What?"

"I may be a little bit nervous about driving this truck," she admits. "I'm just not used to it yet," she adds quickly.

"Why did you pick something so big if—"

"I didn't," she huffs. "I—it was the only option, apparently. Vicki said they got a deal."

"You *do* know how to drive, right? Like, you're legally licensed to operate a motorized vehicle?"

"Yes, Caleb," she says with a roll of her eyes. "I'm a grown woman, a full medical doctor, and I have a driver's license, okay? I just—" She goes silent, both hands still clutching the wheel.

"You just . . . what?"

"Ugh, *fine!* I'm just not a very confident driver, okay? I hate driving, and I'm not good at it. Some people are good drivers and I'm just— I'm not. The gene totally skipped me," she adds under her breath with a sniff.

Oh shit, is she about to fucking cry again?

"I'm sure you're fine," I say, shifting on my feet. I should walk away now. She's clearly got this under control. Nothing to see here, folks.

She laughs, but it sounds weird. It's too high and squeaky. "Oh yeah, I'm great. Super safe and reliable. I only failed my driver's test *three* times!"

"You—*three* times? How is that even possible—"

"Hey, I *aced* my MCAT, thank you very much!" she snaps. "Driving is hard for some people. And I never had to learn growing up."

"Where the hell did you live that you didn't need to drive?"

"I always had a driver," she says with a shrug.

I put the pieces together and grin. "Oh . . . shit. Hurricane, are you a silver spoon girl?"

She glances sharply over at me before dropping her gaze back to the wheel. "More like multi-platinum."

"Rachel—"

"I'm fine, Caleb. I'm a big girl with a big freakin' truck. I'd just maybe wait a few minutes before following me on the road," she adds. "You know, for your own safety."

Making the decision I should have made three minutes go, I shrug. "Why don't I just drive you to work?"

Her gaze darts back over to me. "No."

"Why not? We're going to the same place. It's better this way. More eco-friendly."

"I don't need to be driven around like some spoiled little rich girl. And I don't want to upset Vicki either," she adds. "The team is paying for me to have a truck as part of my fellowship. I can't just not drive it. I'm fine, really," she says again.

I shake my head with a laugh, patting my pockets. This girl is so damn stubborn. I've already got my keys and my wallet. I jerk open her car door.

She shrieks. "Caleb—what—"

"Move over."

"What the hell are you doing?"

"You won't let me drive you in my car, so I'm gonna drive this one. Unlike you, I love to drive, and I'm excellent at it. Now, move over."

"God, this is so embarrassing," she mumbles, unbuckling her seatbelt and climbing over the center console. I get a nice shot of her ass as she scrambles across.

"Sy, up," I say, patting the seat.

He leaps into the driver's seat, and she gasps with delight. "Oh my goodness. Is he coming with us?" She's already got both hands out, rubbing his ears. The little traitor has his tail wagging in my face. I try to slap it down.

"Yeah—Sy, *over*," I direct with a snap of my fingers.

Sy hops the seats into her lap.

"You're such a cutie patootie. Yes, you are. Ugh, I'm obsessed with his eyes," she coos, wrapping both arms around him as he straddles her lap and licks her face. "You're coming to work with me. Daddy gets to see you all the time. Yes, he does. I'm never letting you go ever." She kisses his face, and he eats it up like a total ham.

Lucky jerk.

I huff to myself. I have no idea where that thought came from. Sure, she's gorgeous, but she's also neurotic and kind of annoying. I smile to myself. She and Jake would be perfect for each other. My smile falls as I go still, my hand on the truck door.

Rachel and Jake. Why does the thought of them together turn me on as much as it terrifies me? I glance over at her, watching her buckle in as she talks nonsense to my dog. If this gorgeous, sophisticated, slightly neurotic doctor ever decided to give Jake Compton the time of day, it would be game over. She'd have him as her shadow for the rest of her natural life.

And then I'd lose him.

A reformed puck bunny-turned-kindergarten teacher I could compete with no problem. But Hurricane? Hell, no. She'd sweep him off his feet and drag him out to sea.

Shit, why do I suddenly feel like I'm sweating?

He took her number out of my phone the other day. Said he wanted it to haze her. He and Novy have taken it upon themselves to haze all the new staff, so I didn't think much about it in the moment. Now I'm thinking I was a fucking idiot.

But her quiet confession from our first night together still simmers in the back of my mind. I held her on the balcony, her bare skin like heated silk under my fingertips. *I miss him,* she said, tears in her eyes. She's already got a guy she's totally hung up on. For the moment at least, Jake is safe.

20
RACHEL

*C*aleb and I part ways at the coffee cart in the lobby. After swearing on his life to let me and Sy have another sleepover soon, he and the dog wander off towards the locker rooms. I find my way to the gym, only taking a wrong turn once.

Am I embarrassed about what happened? I mean, yeah. At this point, I'm just keeping a mental list. If there's an embarrassing moment to be had, odds are Caleb Sanford is going to find a way to witness it. I really hope the cosmic wheel finds a way to balance this relationship soon. I'd love to feel like I was the one helping him for once.

I step into the gym to find the weight-lifting floor packed and the music pumping. There has to be twenty guys in here already. Several of them wave and call out hellos to me as I weave between the equipment.

"Morning, Doc!" calls the cute, boyish blond.

I spent some time yesterday going through the roster to try and put as many names to faces. His name is Langley, and he's on my list for a physical today. "Morning, Langley," I reply with an awkward wave, still juggling all my crap.

He beams at me, his chest puffed out like I just gave him a gold star on his homework. "You remembered my name."

"Of course," I reply brightly.

Good thing most of the guys go by their last names. Between first names, last names, and the hordes of nicknames they give each other, I expect I'll be confused for a while.

I shuffle into my tiny office. I barely have a chance to set my stuff down before I feel him. I spin around in my swivel chair, whacking my elbow against the wall. "Ow—shit—" I rub at it, looking up to take in the massive frame of Jake Compton.

He's smiling at me and I feel it all the way down to my toes. "Good morning, Doctor Price."

I roll my eyes, snatching up my travel cup. "Okay, champ, dial it back a little."

"What? I can't call you Doctor Price?"

"No, you can call me Doctor Price," I say, taking a sip of my coffee. "I meant dial back the eyes."

He leans against my doorway, arms crossed. "My eyes?"

"Yeah, they give you away."

"Oh, yeah? And what are my eyes saying this morning?" He flutters his lashes like a total flirt.

I get up from my chair, which does very little to make me feel like I'm taking back my space. He still stands head and shoulders taller than me. "They're saying they watched me come last night."

He feigns a gasp. "Why, Doc, I have no idea what you're talking about. My eyes were with me all night. You can ask Caleb. He'll tell you that at no point did I watch you ride a toy to climax."

I stand right in front of him, clutching my coffee and my tablet. "You gonna move?"

"Huh?"

"You make a better door than my actual door, Jake. Move your body."

"Oh—" He laughs, stepping out of my doorway.

"Hey, Doc, if Compton gives you a hard time, you let us know!" one of the guys shouts. "We'll set him straight!"

Some of the other guys laugh and shout too, the noises layering with the thumping music.

I open the exam room door and he winks as he walks past, turning to hop dutifully up onto the exam table. This room is a much better size, with enough space for a small sink and cupboard, an exam table. There are a few pieces of equipment I can use to test flexibility and range of motion too.

I set my coffee on the counter by the sink and wake up my tablet. I lean against the wall by the open door and pull up his electronic medical files. "So . . . let's see what we've got here."

Jake crosses his arms over his broad chest, still giving me the I've-seen-you-naked eyes. I wish they weren't so damn pretty. They're a caramel brown at the outside, fading to apple green at his iris. "You gonna shut the door, Seattle?"

I glance up over the tablet. "Hmm?" My gaze darts to the open door. "I don't think we need the door shut for this exam. It's not like I'll have you taking off any clothing. This is more of a formality. I'm just gonna poke and prod at your knees a bit."

"Yeah, well, I'm a pretty shy guy," he says with a shrug and that sultry grin. "I prefer to know my doctor-patient confidentiality can't be breached by some nosy rookie. These guys look for weaknesses, like sharks chasing chum in the water."

I pause in my skimming to look up at him again. "If I close that door, are you gonna behave?"

He nods, raising the two fingers of his right hand. "Scout's honor."

Oh, goddamn it. He did that cutesy little move in Seattle too . . . right before he fucked me bare and made me scream with my ankles on his shoulders. I can tell from the look on his face right now that he's picturing it too.

"Compton, I swear to god—"

He barks out a laugh, raising both hands in surrender. "Alright, alright, I'll behave. Look, I'm totally behaving. Ask your questions, Doc. This is about hips and knees, right? No word of a lie, I'm in the best shape of my life. I had some issues with my meniscus about two years ago. Had a minor surgery. I've been playing great since."

I narrow my eyes at him. "Mmhmm. Did you know I have a magic talent?"

He raises a brow. "Making a man hard with just a look?"

I shake my head. "Nope. I'm basically a human lie detector. So, I'm gonna review this file, and I *will* do an exam, and I *will* ask you questions, Compton. And if I think you're lying to me, I'll ask more questions. I'll do *more* exams. I will poke and prod and X-ray and scan until your records are thick as a phone book."

His cocky smile falters a bit. There's nothing pro athletes hate worse than the threat of medical testing. And I bet you any money Jake Compton is afraid of needles. I'll be giving him an orange juice after he passes out and whacks his head on my table.

"You should know that Doctor Tyler has given me the power to approve your final preseason review," I add. "You wanna play next week?"

He nods. "Yeah, of course I do."

"Good. Then get rid of that dirty look in your eyes. I'm not Seattle right now. I'm Doctor Price. So, tell me, how long was your post-op recovery after your meniscus surgery? What was on your regimen of care? And do try not to leave anything out." I pluck the stylus off the side of my tablet, glancing up at him, and wait.

He sighs, his shoulders relaxing a bit. "Fine, Doc. We'll do this your way."

JAKE was a perfect gentleman for the rest of the exam. He answered my questions, performed all the range of motion tests I requested, and only groaned once when I did a quick check of his hip joints, my fingers prodding the muscles, checking for tightness or tenderness. I let him go with a smile and a quick promise that his starting position was safe.

My morning hurries along as I work down my list of guaranteed starters. All these guys are head coach approved for the active roster. So long as they pass my exam, they'll be suiting up for the first game.

After Jake, I meet Lukas Novikov. He's another defenseman. Tall and burly, he has a face that looks like it's taken more than a few hits. But he's kind and flirty. He seems fine from his treadmill tumble the other day, and I leave him with a tease to make sure he's double-knotting his shoelaces.

Next in the door is Jean-Luc Gerard, the one the guys call J-Lo. The first thing I notice when he wanders in—besides the missing teeth in his smile—is the wedding ring on his finger.

"You married?" I say as I massage his knee cap.

"Yeah, Doc. Six years and counting."

"That's nice. You got any kids?"

The rest of the exam goes quick as he flips through his phone, showing me endless photos of his two little girls, who apparently spend every waking moment in princess crowns and tiaras. I snort at the one of him in the middle, toothless grin spread wide, with big circles of red rouge colored on his cheeks. Yeah, all the athletes I've met are tough guys until their daughters are born. Then they melt like butter. I bet he can name more Disney princesses than me.

He shakes my hand as he leaves, and I check my list.

"Kinnunen, you're up next!" I call out to the crowded weight room, my eyes on my tablet as I close out Gerard's file.

After a minute or two, I glance up, looking around the gym. No sign of Kinnunen. The man would be impossible to miss. I walk over to Novikov who's about to get on a treadmill. "Hey, you seen Kinnunen this morning?"

He just shrugs, glancing over his shoulder to scan the room. "Maybe his practice ran long. I'd just skip him, Doc. He'll show up eventually."

I sigh, checking my list. "Langley! You're up!"

I hear a clang from close by and turn around. "Great. Yeah, Doc. I'll be right there!" Blondie gets up from his weight rack, smiling like he's the star of a bubblegum commercial.

"Why don't you head into the room," I say. "I'm just gonna check something in the office."

We part ways at the doors, him for the exam room, me for the stand-ing-room-only office. I snatch up my phone, looking to see if I have any missed messages from Kinnunen or the goalie coach. Nothing.

I move through into the exam room, tablet tucked under my arm, as I text out a message to Hillary to get Kinnunen rescheduled. Tucking the phone in my pocket, I turn back to the tablet. "Alright, Langley. Let's get star—*ohmygod*—what the hell are you doing?"

He jumps up to attention, eyes wide as his gym shorts slink to the floor. He's standing by the table in nothing but his junk-hugging briefs, socks, and trainers. "What—I didn't see one of those paper gown thingies."

My eyes go wide as I hug the tablet to my chest. This guy is cut. There is not a single ounce of fat on him. And he was in the middle of a workout, so his perfect pecs are shiny with sweat. "Why the hell are you getting naked, Langley?"

Now he's looking at me like *I'm* the crazy one. "This is a physi-cal . . . isn't it?"

I gape at him. "This—I'm a *knee* specialist, Langley. You were al-ready wearing shorts." I gesture to the pile of polyester at his feet.

His face blanches whiter than an almond. "But the other guys all said—" He pauses, and we just stare at each other. Then his cheeks go from white to red. "Oh, fuck those guys! I'm gonna kill Novy." Then he's dropping to his knees to snatch up the shorts.

I can't hide my smile as I shake my head. "Just put your clothes back on. I'll wait outside."

The second I step out, the gym explodes with laughter. All the guys were apparently waiting to see what might happen. Jake is standing by Novikov, his arm around his shoulder. The pair of them are wearing matching shit-eating grins.

"See somethin' you like in there, Doc?" Novikov teases.

"Who are you hazing here, him or me?" I call back.

"Both!" shouts a guy—I think is named Karlsson. He's Swedish and very GQ-looking.

Langley appears at my shoulder, fully dressed, and the guys all hoot and howl again. "Fuck you, Novy! You guys are all jerks!" he shouts before disappearing back inside the room.

"Please tell me he stripped totally naked," says Novikov, tears in his eyes.

"No, he didn't," I reply. "And just for future reference," I call out. "The first guy who gets naked in my exam room is gonna get benched for a week. Bad idea to piss off the person who signs your medical releases," I add, shooting daggers at Novikov and Jake.

"What's wrong, Doc? Can't appreciate the male form?" jeers Novikov.

"Oh, I appreciate the hell out of a fine male form," I reply. "I just like to have finished my damn coffee first."

"So, you *would* want to see us naked . . . just later in the day," says Jake. "After you've finished your coffee."

"Yeah, it's all a matter of timing," Novikov adds with a nod.

"Noted, Doc," Jake says with a grin.

"We could try again after lunch!" someone calls. At the same time, a guy starts singing 'Afternoon Delight' and the guys all fall to pieces again.

"You're all twelve," I grumble, turning back to go inside the exam room.

"And you love our dumb asses!"

I snap the door shut, drowning out their laughter, as I face a mollified Langley.

"Let's just get this over with, eh Doc?"

21
RACHEL

I finish my last physical of the morning with Josh O'Sullivan, the forward who was just made Captain of the Rays. He's a sweet guy with a body that he's keeping in fighting shape with little more than a hope and a prayer. My guess is that his knees might just be seeing their last season. Of all my guys this morning, he'll need the most preventative care.

As soon as he's gone, I wander over to the PT wing to compare my notes with Avery. He's in the middle of some stretching reps with a young guy with black curly hair who has his knee artfully wrapped in athletic tape.

"You really need a babysitter to double-check your work, Price?" Avery says with a huff. "Are you that incompetent that you can't do a few basic range of motion tests?"

The athlete he's working on goes still, trying hard to pretend he's not listening.

I don't know Avery well enough yet to tell if he's just having a bad day, or if he actually is the world's biggest fucking asshole. "I wasn't asking you to babysit me," I reply, keeping my tone professional. "I was just hoping to confer with a colleague. You know the guys better at this point and—"

"Well, I have to finish up with Jonesy here first," he says, giving the kid a pat on the shoulder. "Can't drop everything to do my job and yours."

"That's fine," I say. "I'll just grab some lunch and come back."

He waves me away and Jones gives me an apologetic look.

I leave the PT wing and let out a shaky breath. No way am I going to let one jerk drag me down. He's going to have to try a lot harder than that to hurt my feelings. Pushing all thoughts of him from my mind, I let my nose follow the tantalizing smell of hot dogs, leading me down the long hallway.

This practice complex is technically for the Rays, but the rinks can be rented out for other purposes—junior hockey, figure skating lessons, even just a free skate session open to the public. When a rink is open to the public, they open a small concession stand too.

I stand in line and order a hotdog, a bag of BBQ chips, and a Diet Coke. Taking my lunch with me, I wander between the rinks until I find some of the guys doing drills. I sit on the bench, quietly eating my lunch, watching as they skate lightning fast through some cones, moving the puck down the ice towards the goal. The swish of their skates and the click of the puck against their sticks is almost hypnotic.

These men are sharks on the ice. They each take a shot on the goal boxed in with a fake goalie. It's like one of those ski ball games with holes cut out for the five pockets. Each puck sails through a hole, hitting the back of the net flawlessly.

"Your footwork is sloppy, Walsh! And choke up on your stick, you're not playing mini golf."

I glance sharply to the left to see Caleb standing at the boards. He's got his arms crossed, his full tattoo sleeve on display. I was studying it in the truck on the drive in. It's a mess of individual tats that have been woven together with a consistent pattern of ocean waves and geometric honeycombing to make a sleeve effect.

The guy he was shouting at skates up to the boards, sliding to a stop. "What am I doin' wrong, boss?"

I pop a chip into my mouth and crunch it, watching as Caleb tears into him about his form and puck handling. "Do another rep," he says. "And try not to suck this time."

The guy nods, as if Caleb is a coach and not an equipment manager, skating off into the middle of the rink to flick a fresh puck off the pile. I watch as he does a circle to pick up some speed. Then he's flying between the cones, his blades slicing left and right, as he works the puck. He blasts out the end of the cones and takes a shot on goal, aiming for the five-hole. The puck whacks the board instead, ricocheting away.

"You're trying too hard to control the puck," Caleb shouts. "It's all in your stick, Walsh. Get outta your own head."

One of the other guys is taking a breather against the boards, water bottle in hand. "Can you believe this joker gets to start next week?" he says, squirting some of the water on his head until it's running down his neck into his pads.

Caleb just shakes his head. "He thinks his flashy footwork is gonna compensate for sloppy stick handling. My bet is they bench him after game two."

He says this loud enough for Walsh to hear as he skates up to the boards. The poor guy looks crestfallen. He does know he's an NHL player, right? Maybe with all this criticism he's forgotten.

I scowl at Caleb. "Jeez, Sanford," I call, drawing their attention. "Who died and made you head coach? If it's so easy, you put on some skates and show him how it's done."

The second the words are out of my mouth, I know I've said something wrong. Caleb's glare turns murderous. At the same time, the two guys share a nervous look.

I glance between them, confused. "What—"

"See you boys around," Caleb mutters at the other two, turning on his heel and stomping away.

I watch him go, feeling suddenly guilty.

"Yeesh," Walsh mutters. "That was harsh, Doc."

"Yeah, going' in for the kill," says the guy with dark hair.

"Clearly, I just stepped in something," I say, slipping off the bench and walking over to the boards.

"Eh, Sanny'll be alright," says dark-haired guy. He skates off, ready to do another drill.

I look to Walsh. "Will he?"

He shrugs. "Yeah, probably. But maybe you should google him. And cut him some slack," he adds as he sets his water bottle aside. "It can't be easy for him." With that he skates off, leaving me with my head spinning.

THE second I get back to my office, I shut the door and whip out my phone. I google 'Caleb Sanford hockey' and after the most cursory of glances down the search result page, I'm ready to crawl inside a hole.

He was a player. A forward, just like Walsh. The articles are a mix of his college stats and interviews, glowing reviews of his speed and scoring ability. I read the press release announcing him as the number three draft pick for the NHL. He signed with the Pittsburgh Penguins before he was even out of college.

But then there's the articles . . . and videos. They're almost too awful to watch. He was taken out game one of his first season in the NHL. A brutal hit from behind smashed him into the boards. The defenseman was twice his size. He went down and he didn't get back up again, writhing in pain, his mouth open on a scream you can't hear as the camera feed cuts away.

One article has me frozen, eyes glued to the phone. It includes a photo from earlier in that first game. Caleb is skating towards the camera with his arm slung around the shoulders of a smiling No. 42.

Jake.

They were both signed to the Penguins. For one shining moment, their shared NHL dreams came true. But then Jake watched his best friend go down. He had to watch him be carried off the ice, his dreams shattered with his leg.

I set the phone aside, tears in my eyes. That's why Caleb was limping the other day. He never recovered from his career-ending hockey injury. He can't play anymore, certainly not at the level required for the NHL. So now, Jake lives out their dream alone, while Caleb gets to watch guys like Walsh who have less talent than him, skate down the ice with sloppy stick handling.

Yeah, I'm a total jerk.

I have to say something. I have to apologize. I leave my office and go in search of him. I don't know the back side of the rinks very well. This is an all-in-one facility—laundry, loading docks, food service, maintenance. I ask a few guys as I pass the locker rooms and they point me towards a stairwell that opens below into a wide hallway.

Sy pops out of a doorway, and I smile, knowing I must be in the right place. He comes running over, tail wagging. He's such a sweetheart. He's got the coloring of a border collie, but a body more like a pointer—longer in the legs, with the spotting of black under his white fur. My favorite feature is his blue eyes.

Like ice, I realize with a smile. His eyes are the same white-blue glossy color of fresh ice on a hockey rink.

"Where's daddy, huh? Is he down here?" I murmur, giving him a pet.

I walk down the hall, taking a deep breath before I peek into the open doorway. Inside the bright room is a wall of industrial size washers and dryers. A table is set in the middle for folding and ironing. A massive stack of white towels sits on the end of the table, all but concealing Caleb from view. He's standing, quietly folding more.

Sy goes prancing in, sniffing the floor as he snakes behind Caleb.

Pulling on my big girl pants, I step in. "Hey," I call.

Caleb glances up, his expression carefully veiled. His gaze falls right back to his work. "Hey."

Great start.

I cross the room, coming around the stack of towels. "Listen, I'm sorry. I didn't know."

He stills, not looking at me. "Who told you?"

"Google."

He just goes on folding.

I take a step closer. "I didn't know, but that's no excuse. I didn't understand the context of what was happening, and I shoved my foot in my mouth. I'm new to this team and to this world. I'll make mistakes, but I'll learn. And I *am* sorry, Caleb—"

"It's fine," he says, grabbing a stack of towels and turning away. He loads them in a massive laundry cart big enough to hold three grown men.

I should leave him alone. He clearly doesn't want to see me or speak to me. I should go. But I don't. Instead, my feet are moving. Before I know it, my hand is on his tatted forearm. "Hey . . . can you at least look at me?"

He stills, his gaze dropping to my hand on his arm. "Take your hand off me, Rachel," he says quietly, his voice cold as ice.

I drop it to my side, my stomach doing a little flip acknowledging the strength of his command. I don't like him using my real name. I want to be Hurricane again. "Caleb—"

"Just *stop*," he growls, turning to look at me. His eyes are so dark, almost obsidian. It's a beautiful combination with his reddish-brown hair. Mix in his cheekbones, his pouty lips, and the fuck-all-the-way-off energy oozing from his pores, and I'm ready to fight a whimper as he leans in. "You see what you're doing here? You're making it worse. Just *go*."

He turns away from me, stalking off back over to the table to snatch up more towels.

I spin around, heart racing, following right on his heels. "How am I making things worse by apologizing?"

He turns again, his shoulder almost knocking into me. His hand goes under my chin, tipping my face up sharply. Our chests are almost touching as he glares down at me. "See that look in your eyes right now? That pitying look. 'Poor Caleb can't play anymore. I'll go pat him on the hand and make him feel better.' I hate that *fucking* look."

"I didn't—"

"You think you know what happened?" he growls, leaning closer. "You think you have *any* idea what I've lost? Or how I've picked up the pieces? You don't know anything, Doc. You don't know me."

He's right. Of course, he's right. We've known each other all of a week. I don't know him. But I can't focus on that. My mind is humming. *Oh god, he's so close.* I can feel the heat of his skin. I can smell his aftershave. It's crisp and clean, with soft notes of citrus. I can also all but taste his burning resentment on my tongue.

I raise a hand, wrapping it gently around his wrist. "I don't pity you," I murmur, holding his dark gaze. "Empathy and pity are not the same."

"They are to me," he mutters, trying to pull away.

"No," I say, holding him still. "Pity implies that I feel sorry for you. Poor, sad sack Caleb got a raw deal, right? Well, we both know that's bullshit."

He glances sharply up at me, his dark brows narrowing.

"You knew what you were doing," I explain. "You were at the very top of your game in a dangerous sport. You were a forward, a damn good one from your records, which made you a target. But you knew the risks." My fingertips brush the inside of his wrist. "Why would I pity you for doing your job and taking the hit you always knew might come?"

He softens slightly. He lowers his gaze to my lips, and I fight the urge to lick them. My mouth feels suddenly dry.

"You're not the first athlete I've known with a career-ending injury,

Caleb. And you certainly won't be the last," I go on. "And I saw that hit. I saw the video, and I *empathize* with your pain—"

"Oh, you do?" he huffs, trying to pull away again, but I tighten my hold on his tatted wrist.

"Yes, I do. I may not have seen your chart, but I can only imagine how you fought in your rehab to regain the level of function you have now." I'm determined to get through to him, to set this right. "But I think that's who you are. You're a fighter. You're fighting me now," I add, gesturing to the way he's pulling back. "So no, Caleb. I don't pity you. I would *never* pity you. I admire strength and determination. I admire resiliency. Which means I admire you." With that, I drop my hand away.

His gaze lifts again and those dark eyes pierce me, holding me captive. Something is shifting between us. I'm sure he must feel it too. The darkness in his eyes changes from vehemence to something warmer. I can hardly believe when he adjusts his hand under my chin. Suddenly, his thumb is brushing gently over my lips.

Oh god, he's going to kiss me.

The thought ricochets inside my head as my lips part. He dares to give my bottom lip the slightest tug, wetting the tip of his thumb against my teeth. My breath catches and I'm leaning in. He's so close. I want him to do it. I want to know what his lips feel like against mine. I want to chase each kiss. I want—

"Thank you," he murmurs. Then he's dropping his hand away from me and stepping back.

I'm left standing there, swaying slightly with my lips parted, heart racing, wholly unkissed.

He's already turned away, reaching for another towel to fold. "Oh, and hey—" He reaches in his pocket and tosses something at me.

I catch it on reflex, clutching my key fob to my chest.

"I'm getting a ride with Jake. Think you can drive home in one piece?"

I nod, slipping the key into my pocket.

I don't know what the hell just happened here. His signals are all over the place. They have been since we met. He's burning hot, then he's ice cold. He's grumpy, he's funny, he's sexy, he's sad. It's like he's a walking mood ring.

I turn around and stomp out. Sy follows me at a jog until I reach the stairs.

These boys are going to be the death of me. I've already got one hockey player in my bed—well, okay, he *was* in my bed. Now he's . . . god, I don't even know what to call my not-a-relationship with Jake. He's still texting me. He's been burning up my phone all day. Random stuff like a picture of his lunch and something he's calling 'pelican watch.' Apparently, a pelican keeps landing on the railing of his deck. That's it. That's pelican watch. It lands, and he takes a picture, and sends it to me.

So, I have Jake talking me to orgasm through the phone and sending pictures of pelicans. I have Caleb helping me climb balconies and edging me without even trying. Did I mention they're best friends?

This is a disaster. I need some space. I need some uncomplicated dick.

No! Bad Rachel.

I pause in the stairwell, hand clutching the railing. No more dicks. No more drama kings. I need to do my job. And my job is physicals. Which means I need to go find my missing goalie.

22
RACHEL

Kinnunen is a no-show for the rest of the day. I finally hear from his coach as I'm about to head out for the afternoon. Something about extra video review sessions with the second and third string guys. Whatever, it's fine. We've still got plenty of time.

I shoot a text off to Coach Tomlin and we get Kinnunen rescheduled for tomorrow. Now that the roster is set, I'll need to add Davidson to my list too. He'll be suiting up as goalie with Kinnunen for the first two games.

My first official day as a Ray went well enough. Aside from the hazing this morning with Langley, the guys were all perfect gentlemen. Jake blew up my phone a couple more times. A picture of a hotdog with mustard he must have snagged from the concession stand. A picture of him with Sy asking which face was more handsome. That got a reply out of me. I said the dog. And he's continued his game of twenty questions that for now I'm leaving unanswered.

Caleb, on the other hand, remained totally MIA. If he was somewhere in this sports complex, I didn't see him. Didn't even catch wind of him. Or Sy. I was hoping maybe he'd change his mind about the driving thing. Not because I don't want to drive—which, okay fine, I don't. I was just hoping maybe it might be a sign of him thawing.

I apologized. I meant it. We had our second confusing almost-kiss moment. I don't want this guy to hate me or be weird around me. We share a team and a wall. We'll be traveling with each other to 41 away games, here for 41 home games. That's a lot of togetherness.

Whatever. If he doesn't want to accept my apology, if he's determined to think everyone looks down on him and pities him, fine. I can't change his bad attitude. I huff, slinging my backpack over my shoulder, as I walk out to the parking garage.

Maybe I'll go to the beach tonight. I've been in Jacksonville for almost a week, and I haven't even seen the ocean—

I still. An odd sensation prickles on the back of my neck, a feeling of being watched. I glance around the parking garage. It's a bright, sunny day, so the garage is well-lit. I don't see or hear anyone. I hurry along over to my truck, clicking the key fob to unlock the doors. The big truck beeps in the eerie quiet, taillights flashing.

I rush over and jerk open the driver's side door. That's when I let out a scream.

My soul leaves my body as a flood of colorful balls comes pouring out the open door, spilling around me in a cacophony of sound. Red, yellow, blue, green—they're small and plastic, like from a kid's play gym.

Someone filled the inside of my truck with a ball pit's worth of balls!

I shriek, stumbling back. That's where I hear it. Howls of laughter. I spin around to see ten guys standing a row of cars away with their phones out filming me, including Jake and Caleb. Sy is inside the back of a fancy Mercedes, his head poking out the window as he barks.

"You guys are jerks!" I cry, stumbling over the balls as I come out from between the cars, hands on my hips.

"Welcome to the Rays, Doc!" Novikov shouts.

"I had *nothing* to do with this," Langley adds, looking almost nervous to be included in the prank.

"Oh, I know *exactly* who did this," I reply. My gaze levels on Caleb, the guy who had my keys all morning.

Caleb says nothing, that sexy little smirk his only tell.

"How long have you all been waiting out here for me?" I say, watching the balls freewheel across the floor.

"Only about an hour," Jake replies with a shrug.

"J-Lo snagged us some beers to drink while we waited," Novy adds, crunching his empty can.

"And we made Porter wait in the gym to tell us when you were comin' out," says Morrow.

I just roll my eyes. Quite the elaborate prank for the two seconds of fun they got to enjoy.

Jake steps forward. "Come on, Doc. We're all going to dinner." He wraps an arm around me, pulling me away from the truck.

I stiffen. "Well, I—"

"Nope, we're not taking no for an answer," he says, cutting off my protest. "We tricked you twice today, and that can't go unanswered. We're taking you to dinner, and you get to order the most expensive thing on the menu. Novy's buying."

"Hey—"

I smile as all the guys start moving towards their cars. "Well—wait," I call, gesturing around. "We have to clean up this mess!"

There are easily a thousand colored balls rolling across the floor of the garage.

"Don't worry about it," Jake laughs, his arm leaving my shoulder as he kicks a few balls away from his car.

"Walsh and Perry are on cleanup," Caleb adds, stepping in behind me.

I glance over my shoulder to see the two forwards from the ice this afternoon already scooping the balls into big plastic bags. Ah, to be a rookie. I can only imagine how long it will take them to wrangle every ball.

"Come on, Hurricane," Caleb mutters, gesturing to the passenger side of Jake's car.

I don't know which sensation I like more: the warm glow of his tacit forgiveness, his soft use of my nickname, or the brush of his fingers at the small of my back as he opens my car door.

23
ILMARI

The worst part about being a professional hockey player? The constant travel. People my size were never meant to live on airplanes. So, you tell me why I picked a career that has me traveling on a plane for a third of the year.

I move down the aisle, checking the seat numbers as I go. There are no assigned seats, but we all have our routines. Some might even call them superstitions. I'm a goalie, of course I have them. One of my habits is that I like to sit on the right side, window seat, row 20. Don't ask me why. But this is flight one. I have to stake my claim, so the guys know not to take my seat.

My eyes narrow and I feel a growl rise in my throat. Someone is already sitting in my seat. It's none other than the new doctor. Of course, she's traveling with us. We always have our own medical staff at away games. Did she know this was my seat? How would she know?

I've avoided her all week. She's been hounding me to complete my physical. She wants to check my range of motion, put me through stretches and balance tests. I heard from the other guys that she's thorough. Just my damn luck that the team hires an eager new doctor that specializes in hips and knees when I'm doing everything in my power to keep this pain from getting worse. As soon as she starts jabbing her fingers at my joints, she'll figure me out.

She hasn't noticed me yet. Her eyes are downcast, fingers typing away on her phone. I have two options: give up my seat or draw her attention by asking her to move. I glance around. There are some empty seats further back. Or I could sit on the opposite side of the aisle. But Compton is already seated there with the equipment manager. I'd have to make them both move.

Goddamn it.

My palms are itching just thinking about sitting in a seat other than the window of row 20. Sucking in a breath, I clear my throat.

She glances up, her face flashing with a flurry of emotions before she settles firmly on annoyance. "Well, look at that, you *are* alive. I couldn't be sure from the way you've been ghosting me all week."

I grunt, putting my bag in the overhead compartment. "That's my seat."

She blinks up at me, lips parting slightly. "Excuse me?"

"You're in my seat," I repeat.

"There are no assigned seats, Ilmari," she murmurs, her gaze dropping back to her phone.

Her use of my name takes me aback slightly. No one calls me by my name here in the States. It's not a difficult name to pronounce, Americans are just lazy. The only time I hear my real name spoken is when the announcers shout it out at the start of each game.

I loosen my tie a bit. Surely, we can be reasonable about this. "There are other seats."

"Great, go sit in one," she mutters, not looking at me.

Why is she making this so difficult? A player would have moved already, no questions asked. I groan, looking around again. I'm officially holding up the line. Langley is behind me, peeking over my shoulder.

"I . . . can't," I admit.

She glances up at me, those pretty brown eyes narrowed. "You can't go sit in another seat? You have to sit in *this* exact seat? The one I'm already sitting in?"

"Yes."

"I'm not in the mood for more hazing, Kinnunen. And if this is you doing some kind of weird flirting, save your breath," she adds, looking back down at her phone.

"I . . ." Wait—flirting? She thinks I'm *flirting* with her? "Mitä helvettiä," I grumble. "I *need* this seat."

"Ohmygod, Kinnunen, what is your damage?" Now she's glaring at me.

"Everything okay?" Compton says from my left hip, shrugging his headphones off.

"Apparently, I'm in Kinnunen's seat," she says with a wave of her hand. "He's telling me I have to move."

"What's goin' on?" Langley calls from behind me.

Great, let's all have a conversation about this.

Compton glances up at me. "You need that seat, man?"

I give him a curt nod.

To my surprise, he leans around me. "Sorry, Doc. Goalie says move, you move."

Her eyes go wide, lips parted in surprise. "What?"

Compton shrugs. "Hey, I don't make the rules, but I sure as hell follow them. Rule number one in hockey: never touch the goalie. Rule number two: never piss him off. He says that's his seat, it's his seat. You gotta move."

"Unbelievable," she mutters, unbuckling her seatbelt and shoving her soda bottle and her phone back in her bag.

I step back, letting her out.

"Here, Ilmari. Here's your precious seat. You could have said 'please,' you know. Or used more than five words to explain why you needed me to move," she adds.

She brushes against me as she slides out, the floral scent of her shampoo wafting up my nose.

"Thanks," I mutter, sliding into the pair of seats and sitting down.

The moment I settle, she takes the aisle seat next to me.

"What are you doing?"

She shoves her bag under the seat in front of her, phone in hand again. "I'm sitting down. Or what—you need this seat too?"

I groan. *Yes.*

A few players and staff file past as I build up the courage to tell her to move again. I'm a big guy. I don't like sharing a row. Taking a breath, I let it out. "Doc . . ."

She glances over at me, one brow quirked up. "Oh god, you *do* need this seat. You want me to move again. You want that seat *and* this one."

"Yes."

We hold each other's gaze for a long moment. Slowly, she crosses her arms. "Give me *one* good reason why I should respect you, when you clearly have no respect for me."

"What?"

"You ghosted me *four* times this week, Kinnunen," she snaps. "I worked with Tomlin to get you scheduled for a physical, and each time you were a no-show. You show up on time for every team meeting, every workout, every practice, every press event." She ticks them off on her fingers. "Notice a pattern yet? You respect everybody else's time on this team except mine. And I can't help but wonder why that might be." She's staring daggers at me.

"Doctor Price—"

"Is it because I'm a woman?"

"What—no! How can you think that?"

"Is it because you think I'm too young to be a doctor?"

"No—"

"Too unqualified?"

I groan, fists clenching on my knees. "No."

"Then what, Kinnunen? Why are you ghosting me? I'm not moving until you tell me, And it better not be some bullshit answer about extra practices."

Before I can reply, a flight attendant leans down. "Ma'am, you need to fasten your seatbelt. We're about to push back."

Doctor Price glances up at her. "Hold on. Apparently, I'm moving seats. *Again.*"

"No, ma'am, you're gonna have to stay in your seat," the attendant replies. "We've closed the cabin door. You can move once we've reached cruising altitude."

I groan.

"Would either of you like anything to drink?"

"No," we say in unison, and the flight attendant shuffles off.

"I need that seat," I mutter hopelessly.

"Too damn bad, Kinnunen," Price replies. "I'm the barnacle on your butt for the rest of this flight. And until you give me what I want and do your physical, I'm gonna be sitting in this seat for *every* flight from now until the Rays win the Stanley Cup. So, either get in my exam room, or get comfortable with me hogging all your air." With that, her arm stretches over our heads, and she angles my air vent in her direction with an irritated huff.

As the plane begins to roll back, I consider my options. Let this doctor examine me, and most likely bench me for half the season . . . or let her sit next to me, shattering the comfort of my long-established routines and throwing off all my concentration with that wonderful way she smells.

Fuck.

A shutout! The Jacksonville Rays beat the Carolina Hurricanes 4-0 in their first game of the season. The guys were on fire tonight. Even as the away team, the mood in the arena was electric, with all the fans excited to see a new NHL team hit the ice. Sure, they booed each time the Rays scored, but Kinnunen made a few truly spectacular saves that had the Carolina fans screaming in their seats with frustration and awe.

And I had a front row seat for it all. Well, technically I was standing *behind* the front row. I tried to make myself small as possible, wedged in the corner of the player's bench, watching as the guys passed the puck and slammed the other team into the boards.

Not gonna lie, it did unholy things to my lady parts to watch Jake Compton on the ice. He was laughing and joking all through the warm-ups, flashing me those hazel 'fuck me' eyes. But the moment that warm-up jersey came off, and he skated out under the music and the lights, it's like he became a different person. He wasn't my fun-loving Mystery Boy. He was No. 42, Jake Compton, and he was lethal.

When I wasn't watching the guys on the ice, my gaze kept trailing to the other end of the player's bench where Caleb was hard at work. He and Jerry were on a constant rotation—passing out sticks, changing blades, handing over water bottles and towels. It made me feel guilty for my role, which was to stand in the corner, taking up as little space as possible, and just praying I wouldn't be needed.

Seconds before the final buzzer, the Rays erupt with cheers, the puck sliding forgotten along the ice. The Carolina fans clap for us and our first ever team victory in the NHL.

The bench clears out as the guys book it back to the locker room. We've got a tight schedule and they all know their roles. Most of the team will hurry up and shower, shedding their uniforms quick so the EMs can finish packing everything. The guys in need of medical treatment or therapies will get it, while at least a couple guys have to go with the coaches to the press briefing.

"Well, Seattle Girl?" Jake said with a wide grin, his face wet with sweat. "How'd you like your first NHL game?"

"You were amazing, Jake. Really incredible," I say, smiling up at him.

He leans in, his body twice as large as usual in his full kit. "Fuck— god, I wanna kiss you so bad right now."

I lean away with a laugh. "Fat chance, 42. You smell like a half-dead badger."

"You looked gorgeous tonight, baby."

"Uh-huh." I'm trying to stop my stupid stomach from fluttering.

"What's it gonna take to get you to wear my jersey to a game?" he asks, eyes scanning my Rays polo. "Of course, you'll have to keep your little charge paddles handy 'cause seeing a big 42 across your back might just kill me dead."

Okay, he's not allowed to be so good at flirting.

"I couldn't keep my eyes off you. You're gonna have to wear a paper bag on your head so you don't distract me at the next game."

I roll my eyes. "You seemed pretty dialed in to me."

"I'm an excellent multitasker," he replies. "How about we continue this conversation over a drink later? Maybe you sit on my lap naked and tell me more about how amazing I looked out there tonight."

I give him a shove. "*Go*, 42. Shower, before you attract vultures."

"I'm not giving up on us, Seattle. We're inevitable."

"Yeah, yeah. Change, before you make Caleb mad."

That has his smile falling. "Oh, shit—yeah. And I'm up for press tonight. See you on the bus!"

He hurries into the locker room, and I move down the hall to the room set aside for PT. It's got a nice setup inside with a hot and cold tank, massage tables, stretching equipment, exercise bikes. Walsh and Karlsson come through showered and powder fresh. They both head straight to the massage tables for leg massages. A few more guys filter in and hop on the bikes and start pumping their legs, breaking down their lactic acid buildup. One or two just want a space to do some stretching.

Then Kinnunen comes through, talking low with Coach Tomlin. He looks so different out of his kit. He's still a bear of a man, but he looks more approachable now, more human. The only time I saw him today was on the plane, and goodness gracious but does that man look fine in a suit. I mean, all the boys look great, but Ilmari rocks a sexy Viking mafia boss vibe that would melt anyone like butter. Too bad he has to be such a dick all the time.

Now he's wearing the Rays warmup gear of shorts, tech shirt, and trainers. His hair is still wet from his shower, tied up in a top knot.

Setting my annoyance aside, I call out. "Hey Kinnunen, great game."

"That last save torqued his left knee," says Tomlin.

My eyes narrow immediately to his legs. His quads muscles are thick and well defined, wrapping around the top of his knees. I've already read his files thoroughly. Like most of these guys, his knees have taken a beating in his career. Several pulls in his hamstrings and ligaments. I wouldn't be surprised if he has issues with his meniscus. You can't do the constant range of motion a goalie does and not shred your meniscus bare.

"What's the problem?"

"I dropped down too fast," Kinnunen explains. "My angle was off, and my knee twisted."

"Let's take a look."

He hops on the table, and I get to work, starting with a visual exam. No defined redness or swelling in either knee. I palpate his right knee first, looking for any tenderness or excessive heat. "Does this hurt?" I murmur, dropping to one knee as I glance up at him.

"No."

I switch to the other knee and don't see or feel any difference. I do a few standard range of motion tests on both knees and he doesn't seem to be in any pain. "On a scale of 1-10, how bad was your pain out on the ice?"

"Six."

I glance up again. "And now?"

"Three."

I raise a brow. "And what's your resting level of pain in these knees?"

His blue eyes flash but he conceals whatever he's thinking. "Three," he mutters. "I'm fine."

I sigh, getting to my feet. "Well, I'm not feeling any obvious damage. Your range of motion is good. No heat or swelling yet, but we'll keep a close eye on it," I add for Tomlin, who is standing over his shoulder like a nervous mother hen. "If pain persists, we might need to get some scans—"

"No scans," Kinnunen says. "I'll ice it at the hotel. Coach is just overreacting."

"We all just want you healthy and as pain free as possible," I reply. "I don't know if you know this, but you're kind of a big deal."

His face twitches into something that could almost be an emotion before he's walking off. The press is chomping to hear a word from him about his shutout game.

IT'S nearly eleven by the time we get to the airport and all settle onto the flight. I wouldn't call my knee check a proper physical, but it was better than nothing. And I'm feeling generous, so I leave Ilmari to his precious seats in row 20, finding a seat a bit farther back next to Morrow, who is already dozing against the window.

I've got my head down, phone in hand, texting Tess photos from the game.

"What are you doing?"

I glance up sharply to see Kinnunen looking like a Viking billionaire, staring down at me. "What?"

"You have to sit with me."

I swear to god, the only reason I believe he said those words out loud is because I watched his lips move. "Ilmari, what the—"

"Come," he mutters, turning away.

"No thanks," I call after him.

He turns, glaring at me. "This is your fault. You have to come. Quickly, before they make us sit for takeoff."

My eyes widen as I glance from a confused Morrow back to the massive goalie. "What the hell are you talking about? You literally made me move on the last flight. You said row 20 is yours. You said I couldn't sit next to you. So *now* what's your damage?"

"You're his lucky charm," says Langley from across the narrow aisle, his eyes on his Nintendo Switch.

"His what?"

"Oh, shit—yeah," says Morrow, shifting in his window seat. "Doc, you gotta go. Mars needs you."

I cross my arms with a huff. "Will someone please explain this madness with the seats before I swear off sitting and stand for the whole dang flight?"

"You break it, you buy it, Doc," says Langley with a shrug.

"Break *what*?"

"His pattern," Morrow replies. "You broke his pattern by taking his seat and sitting in his row. No one sits with Mars. Not at meals, not on the bus. Definitely not on the plane. It's his thing. Keeps him in the zone. You sat with him. You broke his pattern. And tonight, he played a shutout game."

"So now he's gotta know," adds Langley, eyes still on his Mario Kart.

"Know what?"

"Maybe the shutout was a combo of his skill and bad shots on goal," says Morrow.

"But maybe it was luck," Langley adds.

"Maybe it was *you* breaking his pattern."

I finally catch up with a tired groan. "Oh god, so this is like a can't-wash-my-socks thing?" I glance up at Ilmari who is still just standing there, a frown on his handsome face.

"Pretty much," Morrow replies. "Mars needs to know if you're lucky. You gotta go sit with him."

"Whoa—wait," I say, holding up a hand. "What happens if we win tomorrow?" I look back up at Kinnunen. "What if it's not a shutout? What if we lose? Then you're gonna blame me, won't you? It'll be all my fault, your rotten, not-a-good-luck charm, right?"

"Pretty much," says Langley. "You're tough, Doc. You can handle it."

"But you can't sit here," Morrow adds, giving me a little shove. "Sorry, Doc. Gotta keep the goalies happy."

Muttering to myself, I snatch up my stuff again, rising out of my seat. I shuffle my way down the aisle towards Kinnunen. "Say, when I jump from this plane for you, will my backpack have a parachute? Just wanna know my chances of survival."

He doesn't reply, but I swear I see the faintest flicker of movement at the corner of his mouth as he turns away. I think that was Ilmari's version of laughing.

I follow him down the aisle and we settle into row 20. Jake and Caleb are in their same seats too. Caleb already has his eyes closed, resting against the window, but Jake perks up. "Hey, Seattle. What are you—" His gaze darts between us as Mr. Surly next to me buckles himself in. "Ohhh." He snorts. "So, you're his lucky charm now, eh?"

I groan again, burying my tired face in my hands. Stupid superstitious hockey players!

25
RACHEL

Another shutout! Game six of the season, and the Washington Capitals didn't know what hit them. The Rays played amazing. Sully and his offensive line kept the puck in the zone, bringing the fight to the Capitals' goalie all night. The first period he fought them off hard, keeping the score 0-0. But he couldn't make the saves in the second period, letting in two back-to-back goals by Karlsson.

By third period, the Capitals were hungry for a goal. They were vicious, throwing elbows and slamming the guys into the boards. Penalties increased. I had to treat Langley for a busted brow, and Sully took a seriously hard hit from an ogre of a D-man that put him on the bench for the rest of the game. I'm surprised he didn't crack any ribs.

But Kinnunen was king of the ice. He owned the net, furiously guarding his posts. I watched in awe as Jake and the other defensemen came to his aid again and again, working the puck out of the corners, and shooting it down the ice. It was a horrible grind, but the Rays pulled it out, keeping the score locked at 2-0 and earning Kinnunen a beer shower in the locker room.

Head Coach Johnson is off giving the post-game interview with Kinnunen and Karlsson while the rest of the guys finish getting changed. We're spending another night here in D.C. Our flight home leaves first thing in the morning.

"Right, so I've made a reservation at Club 7 for 11:00pm! The VIP area is all set up!" Poppy calls into the locker room. Her hand is over her eyes like she's afraid of what she'll see. God, she's precious. We've gotten to know each other a little bit better over the last few weeks. She's pretty funny when she's caught her breath, and she's sweet as pie.

"You only need to stay for an hour, but I want a good showing of guys there," she calls, her other hand on her hip. She's all business in a sleek suit coat and pencil skirt with three-inch heels. "First round of drinks is on the house. And don't forget to snap those pics!"

I watch her do her thing with my arms crossed as I lean against the wall in the outer hallway. As soon as Sully gets showered and changed, I need to check him. And Langley will probably need a butterfly bandage over that nasty cut on his brow.

"Are you going out with the team tonight?" Poppy says, spinning around. Her shadow, Claribel, is at her shoulder, eyes on her phone, thumbs flying as she taps away.

Claribel is the new social media manager for the Rays. She's got a hot goth girl vibe going, so at odds with the preppy, All-American look of an NHL team. Her hair is dyed inky black, violet at the tips. She wears thick, black eye makeup, and her bottom lip is double pierced. To see her in a Rays polo shirt tucked into her khakis is a bit jarring.

"Oh, *please* say you'll go," says Poppy, grabbing my arm. "Claribel is underage, so she can't get in."

"I told you it's not a problem," Claribel mutters, eyes still on her phone.

"We are *not* breaking any laws, Miss Naughty," Poppy counters with a glare. "And I don't want Sanford to be the only other sensible adult there. *Please*, Rachel," she begs. "Please come with me. Please, *please*—"

"Alright, fine," I say with a laugh, shoving her hand away.

"Hey, Doc!" calls Langley, coming out of the changing room in his sweats. He points to his shiny red cut.

"Yeah, coming!" I say with a wave.

"Be ready at 10:30pm in the lobby," Poppy shouts at my back. "And look unobtainable! We've got a brand to build!"

I smile to myself. I may or may not have packed a special outfit for this trip. You know . . . just in case I needed it.

26
JAKE

Hoooooly fucking shit.

I'm standing in the lobby of the hotel with some of the guys when the elevator doors open and out walks my Seattle Girl. She's wearing the outfit. *The* outfit. The one that's been haunting my dreams for almost three fucking months. It's a sexy black jumpsuit with a low-cut "V" in the front and absolutely no back. She wore it the night we met.

This girl, I swear to god. For weeks I've been out here playing checkers with my stupid photos of tacos and my endless questions, just trying to get something out of her. *Anything.* She leaves me on read ninety percent of the time. I'd say it doesn't hurt, but that's a lie. I'm shredded by this distance. I'm not sleeping well, not eating. I'm distracted on and off the ice. Caleb has totally noticed. He keeps asking me what's wrong and I hate lying to him.

But here comes my girl, floating out of the elevator, and with a flick of her hair, I know she's playing chess. She wants me to keep chasing her. That's the only reason she's wearing this outfit. It's not for her. It's definitely not for some random guy she might meet at the club tonight—god, the thought alone has me seeing red. No, it's all for me.

Fuck, she's so gorgeous. Her dark hair is down and curled, sorta golden at the tips. And she's wearing a mix of gold jewelry, including her little septum ring. I haven't seen her wear it since she arrived in Jax. *I missed you, beautiful,* I want to say to that twisted ring of metal.

I've never really liked face piercings, but on her I'm ready to drop to my knees. My dick twitches in desperation. I'm riding the high of our win, and I need some goddamn relief tonight. And I know she knows *exactly* what she's doing to me. She's winding me up, waiting for me to explode.

Well, tick, tick, boom, baby girl.

A few of the guys let out wolf whistles and clap. It's only then that my vision refocuses, and I see she's not alone. Poppy St. James is walking at her side looking like a fun-sized snack in a curve-hugging blue dress. I mean, she's gorgeous too. Fine, whatever. I don't care. I only care about Seattle. If any of the guys even *look* at her sideways tonight, I might be knocking out some teeth. I'm already at her side before I realize I was moving.

"Hey, Compton," she says with those red-painted lips. I want that color smeared on my dick tonight. "Lookin' good," she adds.

Of course, I look good. I'm a guy in peak physical condition wearing Armani pants. But I don't care about me. I'm not going out tonight to wheel any bunnies. I already wheeled my girl. The *only* girl. I'm going out because if I have to breathe air tonight, it's gonna be Rachel's air.

I offer out my arm and she takes it, shifting her little clutch to her other hand. I'm actually fighting the urge to offer to hold it for her. God, I am so fucking whipped for this girl.

Novy's right behind me, offering out his arm to Poppy. The group heads out the doors to the trio of waiting Ubers and we all pile in. I practically shove Langley out of the way to be the next in the van behind Rachel. I'm too big to fit a third person in the last row of seats, so we have it to ourselves. Poppy and Novy take the middle two pilot seats and Langley rides shotgun. Our van drives off, and Langley starts blasting some tunes.

I feel like everything is moving in slow motion. Rachel is next to me, the scent of her perfume taunting me. Our legs are touching from hip to knee as she leans forward, laughing and saying something to Poppy over the music.

Her bare back is on full display for me. She's got that shoulder tat of three lines of coordinates. I never asked her what they're for. My guess is her parents and her brother. Since he's her twin, it'll be for her too.

She's got another one under her ribs disappearing along the side of her top. I can't see it, but I know it's there. My hand drops off the back of the seat until I'm brushing my fingertips over it. Her ribs give a little shiver, but she doesn't break her conversation with Poppy.

I smile. Yeah, she wants me. She's leaning in now, her arm on my leg. To anyone else, she's just leaning forward to chat with her friend. But I know what she's doing.

It's so dark in this van and the seats are in the way. Poppy can't see a damn thing, and Novy is on his phone. I let my hand snake around a little more until I'm brushing the edge of her top with my fingertips. A little wiggle and I'm under the hem, my fingers smoothing along the outer curve of her breast.

I shift in my seat, my dick screaming, and then I let my hand slip all the way in, cupping her full breast. Fuck, I love the weight of it. So heavy and full. I want to strip off her top right now and suck on her dusky pink nipples. I want to flick them with my tongue until she's moaning, pinch them with my teeth until she digs her fingers into my hair and pulls me off.

I let my first and middle finger drift up, pinching her raised nipple until she clamps her arm down on mine, digging her elbow into my quad. Smiling, I back off, letting my hand drift out of her top and back to her side just as the driver pulls up outside the club.

The door glides open and Langley, Novy, and Poppy all get out.

"You gonna get out of the van, Compton?" Rachel says in that sultry voice. "Or do you need a minute first?"

I hold her gaze. This chemistry we have is otherworldly. "You like knowing my dick is hard for you, baby girl?"

She swallows, her teeth rolling her bottom lip inward on a little bite.

I lean in, brushing her hair off her shoulder as I whisper in her ear. "Tell me you're not wet for me right now, and I'll get out."

She shivers again and it has my dick throbbing. "Jake—"

"Lie to me," I growl.

She leans back, holding my gaze. "I'm not wet for you."

Then my vixen damn near makes my cock explode as she takes my hand and puts it between her legs, clamping down on me with her thighs. Oh goddamn, I can feel her heat. She's radiating with it.

"I don't melt for you, Jake Compton," she murmurs, holding my gaze. "I *burn*."

With that, she slips over my knee and darts out of the van.

Oh, baby girl, the chase is so fucking on.

27
RACHEL

This club is packed. It's modern and sleek, with a main floor for dancing and some reserved booths. The second floor creates a U-shape, and it holds all the VIP areas. A stage at the front has a DJ spinning tracks while people in a series of cages dance, silhouetted by a curtain like something out of *Moulin Rouge*.

It's not quite my preference for dance music, but the energy is great, and I'm in the mood to move. As soon as we order drinks, most of the Rays make their way up to the VIP area. But I weave my fingers in with Jake's, pulling him out onto the dance floor. I don't even know if he likes dancing, but there's no way he's not following me.

I hate keeping him at arms-length all the time. Not that he's very good at staying away. Most guys might interpret a girl's radio silence as disinterest, but I think it just spurs Jake on. He texts me all day, every day, and sometimes calls. He's sneaky about it too, usually including offers to get food or he makes it clear other people will be there too. And hey, a girl's gotta eat.

If we don't slow down, people are going to catch on that we're more than just colleagues. But I'll worry about that tomorrow. Tonight, I just want to dance. Taking a sip of my mojito, I lead him behind me. The music is pumping, and the energy is primal as Jake and I weave our way around the edge of the dance floor. His hand is on my hip, his fingers slipping so easily inside the edge of the fabric.

We duck into the dark corner under the lip of the upper balcony and his hand goes to my waist, his other hand holding his beer. He pulls me against him, my ass bumping against his hips. He's still rock hard, his cock angled up, tucked into the belt of his slim-fit charcoal dress pants. He looks like a dream in a short-sleeved white button up undone at the neck. The shirt fits his muscles just right, giving him shapely biceps I want to lick.

Pull it together, girl.

He keeps his hand on my hip as we start to sway with the press of the other human bodies. I keep my ass tucked against his hardness as we dance, my arm lifting up to wrap around his neck. He trails his fingers up and down my bare side, rocking into me with the beat. We're practically fucking with our clothes on.

I totally lied in the van. If he put his hand inside my panties, he'd feel how wet I am for him. I'm fighting the urge to drag him to the bathroom. I want him on his knees. I want him drowning in my pussy, and I want to scream his name as I come apart.

It wouldn't even be a question. If I ask, he's saying yes. Hell, he'd probably toss me over his shoulder like a caveman and use his defense skills to body check people out of his way. I smile picturing it.

God, what I wouldn't give to have him toss me around a bit in his uniform. I've never gotten a full show of the guys getting all their gear on. I'm curious to know how all the pieces work . . . how they all come off . . .

"Yo, Compton!"

I gasp, pulled from my dirty thoughts as Langley elbows his way towards us.

Jake is on edge, his arm still at my waist. "What?"

"Aspen Alert," Langley calls, pointing up to the far side of the balcony.

Jake goes from turned on to pissed off in the blink of an eye. "What?" he barks, spinning around. His eyes narrow as he peers over the purple and blue strobing lights of the dance floor.

I turn too. "What's happening?"

"Oh, fuck no. This is *not* fuckin' happening!"

"She clocked him, man. Went right for him," says Langley. "She had to know he was here. Total bunny move."

"What are we talking about?" I shout, still trying to see through the flashing lights.

"Succubus sighting," Langley yells in my ear.

"Two o'clock," adds Jake. "Rays VIP. The blonde talking to Caleb."

And then I see her. Tall and leggy in a black, sparkly body-con dress. She's got a long, sleek ponytail. As I watch, she flips it over her shoulder, smiling as she talks to Caleb. I cringe inside as my first emotion is jealousy. Here I am, practically riding Jake's cock through my clothes, and I'm feeling territorial that another woman would dare talk to Caleb?

"Who is she?" I ask.

"Caleb's toxic ex," Jake replies. "Come on. I gotta go save his ass."

He weaves our fingers together and pulls me off the dance floor. We follow Langley along the edge of the main floor, heading for the stairs. The bouncer checks our stamps and lets us pass.

It's quieter on the stairs so I say, "What's going on?"

"The busted bunny talking to Caleb is Aspen Albright," Jake replies. "They dated for over a year in college. She was his girlfriend when we both graduated and moved to Pittsburgh to start training with the Penguins. He broke his knee game one and she didn't even wait two weeks before she was riding another player's dick."

"She's a total bunny, man," says Langley. "They only see green."

"She dumped him?" I ask.

"Yeah, while he was still in the fuckin' hospital," Jake replies.

We round the top of the stairs, and I can see the Rays VIP area better. Caleb is no longer standing. He's sitting in a club chair, a glass of what looks like a vodka tonic in his hands. But I've learned in the last few weeks that he doesn't drink.

Bunny Barbie is standing in front of him, talking with her hands, laughing and smiling like a beauty queen. I've met enough groupies and celebrity chasers to know *exactly* what she's doing. She doesn't want Caleb. She's just using him. She's standing above him to keep herself on display. Who she's really performing for is the table *behind* him. The table of Rays. I see Morrow and Novy and Karlsson. Even J-Lo and Sully are there. Both guys are happily married, but I'm sure she's not picky.

"How the hell did she even get up here?" Jake growls. He's surging forward, ready to go drop her over the side of the balcony.

I grab his arm. "Hey—*wait*—" My mind is spinning out an idea and I slowly smile.

He turns around, glaring at me. "What?"

"Let me deal with her," I say. For a month I've been waiting for the chance to right the epically unbalanced cosmic scales between Caleb and me. This seems like the perfect opportunity. Low-hanging fruit, really. I can banish groupies in my sleep.

"What are you gonna do?" Jake says with a raised brow.

I take a sip of my mojito. "Just a simple bunny extraction." I hold out my mojito. "Langley, hold my drink."

"Oh, shit," he says, taking the mojito with a wide, boyish grin. "No way am I missing this."

Jake's eyes flash with such a look of hunger that I swear I'm probably pregnant now. Yeah, I thought he'd like me sticking up for his best friend.

"Watch and learn, boys," I say, sauntering off.

"Don't hurt 'em, Doc!" Langley calls after me.

As I approach, Bunny Barbie leans down and brushes her hand over Caleb's shoulder. I watch him flinch, his face a tight grimace. He's so uncomfortable it makes my heart hurt. He clearly just wants her to leave him alone.

Enter Rachel.

28
CALEB

A spen Fucking Albright. As if this night can't get any goddamn worse. I didn't even want to come out tonight. I'm exhausted and I hate big crowds. Jake made me come, and then the asshole abandoned me the second Hurricane came waltzing out of that elevator.

Fuck, that outfit she's wearing should be illegal. I mean, I guess it covers everything. It's more fabric than most of the bunnies' entire wardrobes. And yet it leaves nothing to the imagination. Her body is dynamite. I'm not surprised Jake was all but tripping over himself to get to be the one to take her arm.

They've got great chemistry and they're not even trying to hide it. They're like a pair of magnets. He moves when she moves. I'm happy for him if chasing Rachel means he'll move on from his Seattle Girl. I don't want him hung up waiting for a ghost.

And yet, I can't help the feeling of jealousy growing in the pit of my stomach. He could have picked anyone. Why did it have to be Hurricane? I watch them down on the dance floor all but fuck with their clothes on. They're hypnotic. I can't look away.

I don't know what the fuck is happening to me. Rachel Price is so far out of my league. Girls like her don't fall for sulking, washed up, former pro athletes with bad knees and a drinking problem. No, she falls for guys like Jake. All-American hockey stars at the top of their game, rolling in the money and the accolades.

Power couple; that's the term, right?

I've drained my glass of club soda twice, praying it might miraculously turn to vodka. And then Aspen flounces up.

I can't believe I wasted a year of my life on her. Jake tried to warn me, but I was a stupid kid. I was so busy with hockey and going to class that I missed all the signs . . . or I just chose not to see them. We never had much in common, honestly. She was extroverted and fun and so damn sexy. Not to mention she sucked my cock like a hoover vacuum. What else could a nineteen-year-old kid want?

"What are you doing here, Aspen?" I mutter, pulling my gaze away from Rachel and Jake. My hard-on is shriveling up like a worm on a hot sidewalk now that Aspen's blocking my view.

"I can't believe you're here, Cay. You work with the Rays now? How are you?" She's talking so damn loud.

"Tired."

"You're such an old grandpa, Cay," she teases. "Hey, you wanna dance?"

"I'm good," I say, swirling the ice in my drink.

I hate that she's using my nickname. We're not dating anymore. We're not even friends. We're nothing. I don't want her saying it.

She flicks her ponytail over her shoulder again. "So, why don't you introduce me to your friends?"

I glare up at her. "I'm good."

Before she can reply, a new voice has us both turning. "*There* you are! God, I've been looking everywhere for you, baby."

My eyes go wide as Hurricane comes striding up, that low cut in her top showing off a dainty little sternum tattoo. I don't even register her words before she's swooping forward, all but knocking over Aspen as she sinks down onto my lap. Her arm goes around my shoulders and then she leans in, kissing my temple with those fire engine red lips.

Behind us, the guys hoot and holler.

"Yeah, Sanny!"

"Get a room!"

"Kiss her good, Sanford!"

My arm wraps around her waist on instinct, holding her in place on my lap. I'm faintly aware that this outfit has no back. We're skin on skin, my fingers brushing her lower ribs.

She laughs. "Oops. Sorry, babe." She dips her thumb in my club soda and rubs my temple, wiping away the mark of her lipstick.

Holy fuck.

"Uhh . . . who are you?"

We both glance up to see Aspen standing there, one hand on her hip.

Hurricane shifts, her half-exposed boob all but in my face. The softly floral scent of her perfume is warm against her skin and she's holding me so close. Shit, I'm gonna get hard if she keeps this up.

"I'm sorry?" Rachel says, one dark brow raised.

No, she's not. She's a fuckin' hellcat. I glance over in the direction she came from to see Jake and Langley standing there, Langley holding a beer and a cocktail. He's grinning like an idiot. But Jake's look is shuttered, impossible to read.

"I said who are you," Aspen repeats, her smile falling.

"I'm Rachel," Hurricane replies, holding out a hand. "Caleb's girl. Who the fuck are you?"

I don't know who's more surprised—Aspen or me. I work quickly to school my emotions.

Aspen crosses her arms under her boobs. "Oh, yeah? And how did you two meet—no, wait—let me guess," she says with simpering sweetness. "You were his nurse? Or maybe his physical therapist?"

Not missing a beat, Rachel laughs, flicking her dark hair over her shoulder in a mirror move to Aspen. "I'm a doctor actually. Sports medicine. But Caleb has never been my patient. Well, except for sometimes when we're in the mood for a little role play. Right, Snuffy?" she says, nuzzling her nose against mine with a sultry little laugh. "But the physicals we give each other would *definitely* be unethical," she adds with a wink up at Aspen. "I mean, not that I'm complaining. The man is great with his hands," she says in a fake whisper.

Then my soul leaves my body as she wiggles around on my lap, straddling me with her ass pressed against my crotch. She takes my hands by the wrists, splaying my palms over her hips, weaving our fingers together.

With the way we're sitting now, it's nothing for me to brush my lips against her bare shoulder. I feel the way she tenses, and it's not in hesitation. Oh god, what the hell are we doing? I shift my arm, pulling her a little closer, until her back is brushing fully against my front.

Aspen scoffs. "Oh please, you can drop the act, honey. I know you're not his girlfriend."

Rachel narrows her eyes, her fingers brushing lightly down my tatted forearm. "Oh yeah? And how do you know that?"

Aspen purses her lips. "Because I know Cay. We've been friends for years."

False. We were casually dating until I broke my knee. Then she was fucking my teammate before I signed the hospital discharge papers.

"And I follow him on all his social media accounts," she adds.

News to me. I blocked her years ago. Besides, I never use social media.

"I'd know if he was dating some mystery doctor girl." She narrows her gaze at me. "Whose girlfriend is she really, Cay? Compton's? Novy's? It's sweet of them to loan her out to you so you don't have to look pathetic in front of your ex. But really, honey, I got that message a long time ago."

Rachel goes impossibly still in my lap. One might think she was just turned to stone, but I know the truth. Hurricane just went full cobra mode, and she's about to fucking strike. Her hands tense on my arm, even as she doesn't let the smile drop from her face.

"What was your name again? Apple?"

"Aspen—"

"Yeah, whatever." She waves her hand in dismissal. "Look sweetheart, this is just sad, okay? We all know you didn't wiggle your way past the bouncer by offering him a handy just to come up here and reconnect with your old college flame."

Aspen snarls. "Bitch, you don't know me—"

"I *do* know you, Asphalt. I've known girls like you all my life. Caleb broke his knee, and you took him out with the trash. Well, lucky for him, hitting your curb is the best thing that could have ever happened to him. Because now he has me."

She leans forward, which presses her ass even harder against my crotch. "You had your chance with a great guy, and you blew it, Asteroid. He's gone, and he's not coming back. You're so far off his radar now, you may as well be lost in space. And don't for one second think he's going to waste his breath introducing you to any of the great guys sitting behind us either," she adds "My advice? Go orbit another VIP section. This one is private. Rays only."

Aspen's cheeks burn pink, her eyes flashing with rage. "You're a rotten bitch!"

Hurricane just laughs, her hands stroking down my arms. "Yeah, I am. A well satisfied one. Right, Snuffy?" She twists on my lap, kissing the tip of my nose.

"Control your girl, Cay," Aspen snaps. "She needs a muzzle and a leash!"

Feeling a lightness in my chest, I brush Rachel's hair back, laughing against the warm skin of her shoulder. "That's not a bad idea. You'd look good with a leash, Hurricane. Something with spikes."

She flashes me a sultry smile. "Oh, daddy, don't tease me."

"God, you're both psycho!" Aspen shouts, storming off in her mile-high heels.

"Bye, Avocado!" Rachel calls after her, waving like a total bitch.

It only takes 2.7 seconds before the booth behind us explodes. The guys whoop and cheer, slamming their fists on the table. Several shout and wave bye to Aspen.

"Later, Alligator!"

"Bye, Asteroid!"

"No bunnies allowed!"

Langley comes rushing forward, sloshing Rachel's drink as he hands it over. "Hoooly shit! That was the single hottest thing I've ever seen. That was like an Animal Planet shark attack, but with heels and hair flipping—"

"You destroyed her!" Novy jeers.

"We bow to the master," says Morrow with a fake bow.

Novy elbows him. "It's *mistress*, jackass."

They exchange a few more punches as Gerard steps around them. "Sanford, marry her, or I will," he says, patting my shoulder.

Sully slaps him in the chest. "J-Lo, dude. You're already married."

"Right? That's what I mean. That's how much I am serious," Gerard replies in that French Canadian accent, his eyes wide with innocence as he shrugs.

The guys settle back down, waving down a waitress to pay their tabs, and Rachel leans in. "Sorry about all that," she murmurs over the music. "Jake thought you might need the save."

I glance sharply to my left to see Jake still standing there, leaning on the edge of the low wall that boxes in our VIP section. He's got his arms crossed and he's just watching us.

She's still on my lap. I like the feel of her in my arms. I like her scent. I like the way she's touching me, the way she sticks up for me. Sure, she and Jake have some kind of magnetic chemistry. But she and I have . . . *something*. I don't know what it is, but it's something more than nothing.

Before I can ponder it any longer, Jake crosses over to us, his gaze carefully veiled. "Wanna dance?" He offers out a hand to Rachel. It's such a dick move. He's taking her away from me, making her choose him in front of me.

I knew they were flirting, but this feels different. This is territorial. Man, he has it bad. The idiot has fallen for the team doctor, and it's barely been a month. What the hell is he doing? First his Seattle Girl, now Hurricane?

She glances back at me, hesitation in her eyes. There's a question there too. I sit perfectly still, offering nothing.

Your move, Hurricane.

The devastation is coming either way.

She takes his hand, letting him pull her up off my lap, and I exhale. Fair enough. He's the better choice. Hell, I'd choose him too. Hotshot NHL star. Rich, handsome, shining in his golden spotlight. I'm just the guy with a limp who changes his blades.

But then she surprises the hell out of me as she immediately turns, offering out her other hand. "Come on, Snuffy," she says with a smile. "Come dance with us."

My eyes flash to Jake. He's just as surprised as I am. He glares down at me, his emotions roiling. He's always been so easy to read. He wears everything right there on his damn sleeve. Frustration, hunger, jealousy, need. I see it all.

Slowly, his shoulders relax, and he huffs a laugh. "Snuffy . . . that's the kind of shit that sticks."

Rachel laughs too. Snatching my hand off my knee, she gives it a pull, bringing me to my feet. One hand on Jake's shoulder, her other linked with mine, Rachel calls out to Novy, "Hey! Keep an eye on Poppy! Switch her to Shirley Temple's at midnight!"

Novy nods, his eagle eyes already on the PR manager cutting loose down on the dance floor.

Jake leads the way towards the stairs and Rachel brings me along behind them. My heart is racing. I have no idea what the fuck I'm doing. I don't dance. I *especially* don't dance with Jake fucking Compton. I may be queer, but I'm more of a blowjobs-in-the-bathroom queer. Secretly-pines-after-his-best-friend-but-will-never-admit-it queer.

But Hurricane has me by the hand, and there's no way in hell I'm letting go.

"Bust a move, Sanford!" Morrow calls after us.

"Have fun, Snuffy!" Langley adds.

The other guys all laugh.

And that's fine. I'll give them tonight to laugh it up. But I swear to fuck, the first guy to call me 'Snuffy' tomorrow is gonna get his bag conveniently 'lost' on every flight for the rest of the season.

What the heck am I doing? I've got my hand on Jake's shoulder as he leads us to the stairs and I'm pulling Caleb along behind us. Am I seriously about to be the ham in a hockey player sandwich?

They both look so gorgeous tonight. Caleb may not play anymore, but damn is he still fit. Jake is like my angel in charcoal and white while Caleb is my devil rocking all black in a fitted polo and cuffed dress pants.

Jake turns the corner, grabbing my hand off his shoulder and pulling me forward into the dark stairwell. He doesn't get four steps down before he's turning. I hardly have time to catch myself before he's cupping my face and kissing me senseless. Two steps separate us, so I'm practically level with his face. My hands go to his shoulders, and I hold tight as he spins me, coming up a step to press me against the wall.

I sigh into his fevered kisses, chasing him with abandon, as his hands slide up my jaw and into my hair. His hips press in, and then I feel him. *All* of him. His need, his hunger, the power he's keeping in check. He wants to unleash himself on me. I've been teasing him all night. For weeks this has been building. This is Jake at the edge of his limit.

I break our kiss, sucking in air. The side of his face glows purple pink in the flashing lights from the dance floor below, reflecting along the line of his jaw. His lips are wet with my kisses.

His gaze darts to the right and I turn too. Caleb is there, mere inches away. He watched us kiss. His expression is impossible to read.

My body is buzzing like I'm drunk, but I've only had half a mojito. It's them. Their strength, their presence. They consume me. Even when Caleb is being a grumpy asshole, I'm pulled to him. At the practice rink I'm always looking for him, waiting for him to give me his cool guy nod of acceptance. He's flawless in his work—organized and efficient. You wouldn't think there'd be a lot of grace in sharpening blades and handling broken sticks, but everything about Caleb is graceful.

I want to ruffle his feathers. I want to shake him up. I want to be his Hurricane. Grabbing him by the front of his polo, I pull him down a step. At the same time, I step up. He's not going to make the first move. It has to be me. Whatever this energy is between us—between the *three* of us—I'm letting it sweep me under.

Our lips collide and his mouth opens on a soft groan. The music pulses as we stand in the dark, pouring our pent-up need into each other. His tatted arm goes around my waist as he cups my face, bending me back with the force of his eager kiss.

Jake's kisses are like molten lava, melting me from the inside out. The passion I feel for him is white-hot and uncontrollable. Kissing Caleb is electric. My skin crackles with energy as he teases with his tongue, flicking and owning before he bites down on my bottom lip.

I gasp, pulling away, and raise a shaky hand to my lips, brushing over them as I glance from Caleb to Jake. They're standing shoulder to shoulder, boxing me in, Jake two steps lower. Both men look like they're going to eat me alive. If Jake is angry at me for kissing Caleb, he's not letting on. In fact, all I sense from him is that he's *turned* on.

Fuck it. I'm calling an audible. I fist the front of his white button-down, one hand holding onto each of them, claiming them. My angel and my devil. Let's see how well they share. I pull him forward with a smile, my lips parting to meet his in another fierce kiss. Jake grabs me by the hair, fisting tight enough to make me wince. The sharp pain shoots straight to my core. I moan like a desperate creature, melting against him.

But then I give my devil a little tug. Is he willing to play? We haven't talked about this. He can always walk away—

Boom.

Fireworks go off inside my chest as he presses in, flicking my hair off my shoulder, and sinking his mouth onto my neck. I arch into him, lifting up on my toes as they both crowd me. The heat of Caleb's mouth on my pulse point zaps straight to my clit, and now I'm humming with need. I want this. I want them both.

I break my kiss with Jake. Digging my fingers into Caleb's hair, I jerk him off me and bury my tongue in his mouth, my lips still wet from Jake's kisses. He chases me, his hand slipping inside the back of my low-cut jumpsuit to palm my ass cheek.

"God," I gasp, breaking for air. "Oh, god—"

"HEY!"

We all stiffen, heads twisting to look down the stairs.

"Up or down, lovebirds," barks the bouncer. He's standing at the bottom, guarding the velvet rope keeping the stairs private.

Oh god, it wouldn't have taken much for someone to stand at that rope and look up. Then they would have seen us. At least it's dark. But phone cameras have flashes. Jake is already in protector mode, moving down a step to block me from the bouncer's view.

"Fuck," Caleb mutters.

Jake grabs my hand. "Come on."

He leads me down behind him, the fingers of my other hand entwined with Caleb's. We slip past the bouncer and hit the dance floor. The bass of the music hammers through me, rattling my bones as the strobe lights go off. Blasts of pink, blue, and green blind me.

The boys box me in, sticking tight to my front and back, as Jake leads the way across the floor. His size means I can hide myself close at his back and move through the crowd, keeping my head down. If anyone snaps a picture now, they'll just get the curtain of my dark hair.

Jake pulls us down a dark hallway that leads to the bathrooms. Several women mill along the wall, waiting to get inside. I turn my face away from them, stumbling in the dark in my heels. He grabs the handle of a door marked 'EMPLOYEES ONLY' and jerks it open, swinging the door inward to reveal a crowded storage room—stacked chairs, a shelf of cleaning supplies, cases of beer and liquor piled in tipsy towers to the ceiling.

"In," he growls.

I've barely stepped in before I reach the shelf and turn around, just as he closes the door. The effect is instant, dulling the music to a muted roar rather than a full sensory assault. He leans against it, turning the lock with a click. Caleb stands between us, his dark eyes molten with hunger.

"What is this?" says Jake.

"I don't know," I admit, heart still racing from the thrill of being in their arms. God, these men just have to breathe in my general direction, and apparently that's enough to make me forget everything. Our positions. Our signed contracts. My career aspirations. Their reputations.

Someone could have snapped a picture of Jake and I dancing earlier. Sure, we can shrug that off. Poppy will spin it easy. Two colleagues cutting loose, having fun, celebrating a win. But the three of us tongue-fucking in a stairwell?

"Rachel . . . what do you want to have happen here?" Jake presses. "Do you want me?"

His words cut through the swirling torrent of my thoughts. Every part of me softens at the look in his eyes. Oh, my sweet Mystery Boy, always doubting himself. "Jake, *yes*," I say, crossing over to him. I cup his face, tipping up on my toes to kiss him once, twice. "I want you," I murmur against his lips. "I want you. You *know* I do."

He holds me by the elbows. "But you want him too . . . don't you?" He doesn't sound angry or hurt. He just needs to know.

Oh god, is this possible? Have they done this before? Jake didn't strike me as the sharing type. Caleb is the wild card, always so difficult to read. He stands there in his all-black, those dark eyes burning like coals as he waits for me to decide his fate. What we have is new and certainly much different from my connection with Jake.

I turn in Jake's arms, leveling my gaze at his best friend. This is the kind of moment where the best approach is the most direct. Heart in my throat, I part my lips and say those four little words. "Do you want me?"

30
RACHEL

*C*aleb holds my gaze, not looking at his best friend. "Yes."

Jake's hands brush down my sides and around to frame my hips. He tucks me in against him and leans down, kissing my shoulder. "Tell us what you want, baby. What happens next?"

My eyes are still on Caleb. He's watching us together, watching Jake's hands roam. His hunger is making me desperate. A glimmer of awareness prickles in the back of my mind. "I want you both," I admit. "I want you at the same time."

"You know I'm clean," Jake says, his hand slipping inside the stretchy fabric of my halter top to cup my breast. He weighs it in his hand, kissing my neck and flicking my nipple until I'm arching against him. He pauses, his hand on my tit, and looks over my shoulder at his best friend. "Cay? You clean?"

Caleb gives us a curt nod.

"You broken over there?" Jake teases.

Caleb shakes his head. "No."

Jake huffs a laugh. "Well, I'm not leaving this room until she comes. So, get over here and help me, or get out." As if to prove his willingness to share, he tugs on the fabric of my halter top, stretching it wide enough to expose my bare tits to his best friend.

"Shit," Caleb mutters. He crosses the few feet of space separating us and smashes his mouth against mine, pressing me against Jake, who is already up against the door.

I sigh into Caleb's kiss, arching my back into the cup of his hands on my breasts.

Jake works his fingers under my hair at my nape, fumbling with the halter top. It comes loose and the two triangular pieces drop down to hang at my waist, leaving me topless. Caleb breaks our kiss, his mouth trailing down my neck and collarbone to my breast. He sucks and nibbles, driving me wild.

Jake's hand slips between us, diving inside my pants. His fingertips brush the silk of my undies, just over my clit. "Fuck, you're such a little liar," he growls in my ear. "You're soaked, baby girl. Tell us what you want. Unless Cay is a kinky freak, I doubt we have lube."

"No lube," Caleb mutters. He cups my cheek, glancing from me to Jake over my shoulder. "But you might wanna see what I'm working with before you invite me to play," he admits.

I still, my back pressed against Jake. "What?"

In answer, Caleb unbuckles his belt and unzips his fly. Taking my hand, he slips me right inside, letting me feel his hard cock. His—

"Oh my fucking god," I say on a breath, my smile spreading. "Holy shit, Caleb." I stroke him from root to tip and he groans, one hand going to my shoulder. My hand is wrapped around his dick. His *pierced* dick. Four times pierced. I brush my thumb over four stiff, metal rods with barbells at either end.

"What is it?" Jake says, clearly concerned. "You have an accident or something, man?"

I snort, my smile spreading. "Oh no," I reply. "He's just fine." My eyes lock on Caleb as I give him another stroke, running my thumb over his tip. He twitches in my hand. I want him in my mouth. "You'll have to try a lot harder than this to scare off a Hurricane."

"Well, I'm scared," says Jake.

Caleb's smile mirrors mine as he leans in. "Why don't you take it out? Show Jake."

I've never been with a man with a pierced cock before. My pussy is already clenching with nervous excitement. I drop my hands to his hips and shimmy his pants down a few inches, exposing his gorgeous dick. The piercings are perfectly aligned.

Jake shifts to my side. "What are you—oh—*fuck*—" He gasps, his hand going to his mouth like a Southern Baptist church lady. "When the *fuck* did you do that? How did you do that? *Why* did you do that?" His gaze darts up to Caleb's face.

"You wanna get into all that now? Or you want to fuck our girl before the staff kick us out of here?" Caleb deadpans back.

"Well . . . both," Jake admits. "I mean, does it help?"

I snort again. "Help what? His balance? I doubt it."

Jake rolls his eyes at me. "I meant like, with sex. Is it . . . does it make the sex crazy good or something?" I can practically see his competitiveness bubbling right beneath the surface. He doesn't want to be bested by Caleb and his pierced wonder cock.

I turn around, wrapping my hands around his neck. "You think you can't make me feel good, angel? You worried I'll fake my orgasm? Chant your name while I'm dreaming of his ribbed dick?"

Behind me, Caleb laughs, his hands brushing over my bare shoulders.

Jake scowls at us both. "No."

But his eyes give him away. *Yes.*

I purse my lips, trying hard not to smile. "Tell you what, angel," I say, flashing Caleb a heated look over my shoulder. "Caleb is going to stand back with his fancy dick in his hand and watch us. Show him how good you make me feel." I run my hands down his chest to the top of his pants. "He doesn't touch me until you've had your fill."

Behind me, Caleb is practically growling, stepping closer.

Now it's Jake smiling. "Oh, baby, you have no idea what you just started."

I glance between them. "What?"

"Cay likes to watch," he replies. "He likes to boss me around—or at least he did in college. We haven't fooled around with a girl in a long time."

I turn in Jake's arms, fisting Caleb's polo shirt and pulling him closer. That sense in the back of my mind flickers like the flame of a little candle. "Is that right, handsome? You want to watch him take me? Want to watch him fuck my mouth?"

"Yes."

I smile, pushing his shoulders until he steps back. "I'll let you boss me around. I'm already wet just thinking about you bossing him. But *I'm* bossy too," I add, pushing him again until his back hits the supply shelf with a rattle. I drop my hands to his belt and jerk it loose.

He grunts, his hard dick still sticking out the top of his pants. "What do you want, Hurricane?"

"I want you aching for me," I reply, grabbing both his wrists.

"Done."

But I shake my head with a tsk. "You don't know the meaning of the word. Not yet." With that, I slap his belt around his wrists and raise them up over his head.

He lets me, relaxing his arms to rest atop his head. He's so tall, I can't reach much higher.

"Oh shit—baby girl, what are you doing?" Jake says from behind me.

"He can look, but he can't touch," I reply, arching up on my toes to tie him loosely to the supply shelf.

Caleb smiles at me like the snake to the rabbit and I fight a hungry shiver. This man has layers. A little light bondage is only the beginning, I can tell. It would take nothing for him to tug his hands free, but I know he won't.

"He can boss us around," I say, running my hands down his chest. "Until his hands come down, we do whatever he says." My rules stated, I give his tip a little rub with my thumb, making him twitch. "Do you consent, Caleb?"

He nods.

I glance to Jake, one brow raised in question.

"You kidding me? Fuck, yes. I'm dyin' over here." His eyes heat as he looks to Caleb too, waiting for his first direction. He's my good little hockey player, used to taking orders from coach. And he clearly loves a game. I have a sneaking suspicion these men will ruin me.

Caleb is standing there, tied to the shelf with his own belt, pants open and down around his hips, dick out and hard. The lights flicker over our head. This is rough and dirty, and I can hardly wait to see what he does. Those dark eyes smolder. "Kiss her. Those perfect lips, her tits. Make her moan."

My core clenches with excitement as Jake wraps me in his arms, doing as he's told. The thrill of his submission to Caleb has me ready to come and no one has even started touching my clit.

Jake pours himself into me, leaving nothing unsaid with his hands, his eager lips. God, he's such a good kisser. How did I go without this for months? How did I walk away from him in Seattle?

"Touch her clit," Caleb orders. "Feel how wet she is."

With an eager groan, Jake slips his hand back inside the front of my pants, never breaking our kiss. His large fingers part my pussy lips and then he's sliding through my wetness, so slick and warm, so ready for him. We both groan with longing as he drags that middle finger over my clit, circling it with his fingertip.

"Is she wet?" asks Caleb.

"So fuckin' wet," Jake replies, breaking our kiss with a panting breath. He leans back to watch me as he sinks a finger inside me.

"Show me," Caleb growls.

I whine with loss as Jake pulls out. He flashes his glistening fingers in Caleb's face.

"Taste."

Jake doesn't hesitate to suck his wet fingers into his mouth, letting out a satisfied groan.

"Good boy."

Ohmygod. I shiver as Jake shivers. We're both so turned on by this, we might orgasm without any stimulation.

"Face me, Hurricane," Caleb directs. "Hands on me. Look at me while he fucks you with his fingers. Jake, don't stop until she comes."

Jake turns me and I all but stumble forward, my hands going to Caleb's chest. Jake is right there, bracing me with his body as he slips one hand back inside my pants, fingering me until I'm a trembling mess. His other hand tweaks my nipples, teasing me. He kisses me— my neck, my shoulder, my earlobe. All the while he grinds with his hips, letting me know how hard he is for me.

And Caleb watches, that dark gaze so hot and heavy as he breathes through parted lips. I hold his gaze as I come with a long moan, Jake's fingers in my cunt and his thumb on my clit, his hot breath against my ear. "What a good fucking girl. You're squeezing me so tight."

"Fuck, get inside her," Caleb growls. His arms flexing, testing the hold of the belt. "I need to watch you fuck her. Hurricane, don't you dare look away."

I smile. He's losing his cool. I swear I'll break this man.

Jake is behind me, working his pants and then mine, dropping my jumpsuit to my ankles. I'm standing between them, still riding the high from my orgasm in nothing but my thong and high heels. Jake smooths his hands over my ass, his fingers curling under the string of my thong. He gives an almighty jerk, tearing them clean off me. Reaching around, he stuffs them in Caleb's pocket.

"Spread for me, baby," he murmurs.

I shuffle my feet wider as he puts pressure on my back, bending me forward a bit. The angle brings me that much closer to Caleb's face.

"You're so beautiful," Jake says, reaching between my legs to sink his fingers into me. I know what he's doing—he's using my wetness to lube his cock. I'm so ready to go again. I want this man inside me. I want Caleb to watch. "God, you make we wild, baby," he pants.

"Stop talking and do it," Caleb growls, his eyes still on me.

"You want me to stop talking too?" I tease. "Why don't you put my mouth to work."

"Don't mouth off, and you'll get exactly what you want," he replies, his eyes molten.

"Hold still," Jake pants. "Fuck—baby—" He's got his hand and his dick between my legs, his tip rubbing at my entrance, before I spread a bit more and he's able to notch in.

I gasp, sinking down on his tip. "Oh, right there—"

"Fuck—hold still—" Jake slips his hand out, bending his knees, and then he's lifting up and in at once, impaling me on his cock. The fullness slams through me, lifting me up on my toes. I cry out, biting my lip to swallow the sound, my nails digging into Caleb's shoulders. Behind me, Jake shudders, both hands on my hips as he starts moving, rocking into me.

Feeling him around me and in me, I can't help the swell of emotion in my chest. My Mystery Boy. My Jake. Oh god, he's *mine*. I ride the spiraling of my next orgasm, feeling the flood of heat course through my body. "Oh, please," I'm saying again and again. I'm begging, but I don't know for what.

Then Jake's hand is in my hair, tightening to a fist as he jerks my head back, bending my neck. I cry out, back arching as he pounds into me. I'm going to come. I can't hold it off.

"Please, Cay," Jake pants behind me, his hips slapping against my ass as he fucks me so good. I love being between them. I just wish—

"Suck my cock, Hurricane."

Dead.

My second orgasm shatters me as Jake grunts out his approval, shifting back even as he pushes down on my head, his hand still twisted in my hair. He wants this too. He wants to see me on Caleb. He wants us all in. I love the way he dominates me, even as he submits to Caleb, bending me forward until I'm able to wrap my eager mouth around Caleb's tip.

Holding Caleb by the hips, I sink my hot mouth around his shaft, taking him deep. The metal of each piercing clicks over my bottom teeth as I swallow him, sucking him until he's crying out.

My pussy strangles Jake's cock as I suck on Caleb, loving this feeling of fullness. Caleb's tart cum coats my tongue and I know he's at the edge of release. I slip my hand inside his pants, cupping his balls.

"Fuck—*shit*—" He jerks on the belt, his hands coming free. Then he's dropping them to my head, the belt still wrapped around his tatted wrist. He buries his fingers in my hair, taking over for Jake. He gags me on his cock, tapping the back of my throat as I choke, loving every second. The shelf behind him rattles as his hips hit it. The barbells of his piercings roll over my tongue. I can only imagine what they'd feel like in my pussy.

"Oh, baby, I'm gonna—" Jake pants from behind me.

I moan in approval around Caleb's dick, giving them both my consent. We're not stopping until we've all chased our release. I want them undone.

"Fuck—you're so tight—so goddamn perfect—" Jake slams his hips against mine twice more and then he's crying out, his warm release filling me.

I suck on Caleb and he lets loose too, his cum filling my mouth. I swallow him down, pulling back to gasp for air. Just when I think I'm shattered beyond repair, Jake snakes his hand around and flicks at my clit, setting off one last little shuddering tremor of release. It's an echo of my other orgasms, an aftershock, an unraveling.

I slump forward, my forehead pressed against Caleb's abdomen. Behind me, Jake works his way out from between my legs. The emptiness I feel leaves me both hollow and full. It's such a strange sensation. I have Caleb's taste in my mouth, Jake's cum between my legs. I love it. There's nothing that compares to the feeling of being used by two men at once.

My adrenaline is cooling, my blood going from fire to ice. I shiver, all my limbs suddenly boneless. *This* is the feeling I crave almost as much as the orgasm. This feeling of being hollowed out and filled up in one. It doesn't last long. I need to savor every second.

Caleb lifts me gently under the arms, holding my weight, wrapping me in his embrace. It feels strange to be naked while they're both fully clothed. The next time we do this, I want them both stripped bare. They're too gorgeous to hide all that perfect skin away from me.

Jake drops to one knee, shimmying my jumpsuit up my legs, covering me. When it gets to my hips, he zips me up.

"Come on," Caleb murmurs, lifting me away until I'm swaying on my feet. He gives me an appraising look before he lifts both his hands brushing his thumbs lightly under my eyes. I can only imagine what I must look like—my hair tousled from their hands, my makeup streaked with tears from choking on his cock. But I don't care. He's looking at me like I'm his reason, and in this moment, I want to be.

The sound of the club crescendos again beyond the door. The very walls hum with it. Loud voices in the hall. Thumping bass music I feel in my chest.

I'm losing it. That feeling of emptiness.

Behind me, Jake carefully flips the pieces of my halter top up, moving my hair so he can hook the straps. My clothes feel like armor. They also represent reality setting in. I'm alone with one of my players and the equipment manager in the storage room of a busy club. We just fucked. All three of us. *Together*. My resolve to keep Jake at bay lasted all of a month.

Oh god, this is hopeless.

I can't deny them. Can't escape.

"Come on, beautiful," Caleb murmurs, tucking his belt back through its loops.

"We'll take you back to the hotel," Jake adds.

Glancing between them, the resounding truth sets in. I want Jake Compton. And I want Caleb Sanford. Separately. Together. I want them both. I'll be counting down the hours until this can happen again.

31
JAKE

We barely make it half a mile in the Uber before I'm crawling out of my skin with the need to say something. Our driver's upbeat, Korean pop music is pulsing in the speakers, the surprisingly fitting soundtrack to my chaotic thoughts. Every moment of the last two hours flashes in my mind like one of those old school slide projector things. The images are spinning, spinning—

"What does this mean?" I blurt out.

Next to me, Rachel goes stiff, and I hear Caleb's muttered 'fuck's sake'. What? Do they actually expect me to have a threesome in a mop closet and have no comment? Have they even *met* me?

"Get over yourself, Cay. We had sex, and I wanna talk about it."

"Maybe wait until we're in private, asshole," Caleb mutters.

"I won't say anything," our driver calls from the front seat in a sing-song voice.

"Yeah, see? Melanie won't say anything," I say with a wave of my hand.

Rachel's gaze flashes from me to the driver, her mouth opening in horror. "You *know* her?"

"What—*no*—her name is right fucking there." I point to the hot pink laminated sign she's taped up on her dash that says 'Hi, I'm Melanie' in five languages.

Rachel groans, and now I'm officially starting to panic. She regrets it. She's pulling back again. God, I can't win with this girl! It's always one step forward and five steps back.

I mean, sure, Caleb is a bit of a surprise. He's been such a surly asshole since his accident that I was starting to wonder if he'd just sworn off romance altogether. I'm not surprised that he's interested in her because she's totally his type. And I'm not surprised at all that she's interested in him because, again, he's kind of totally her type—

And that's when my heart drops out of my chest.

Jake Compton, you're a fucking idiot.

I'm gonna remember this moment forever, sitting in the back of an Uber with my best friend and the love of my fucking life while "So Hot" by the Wonder Girls plays on the radio. This is the moment I realized it's me. I'm the problem. They don't want to talk about the possibility of more because they both want less. One *person* less.

Heart in fucking pieces, I glance over at them. I didn't even notice that Caleb took her hand. Their fingers are entwined atop his knee.

"Yeah, alright," I say. "It's fine. I get it."

I'm not gonna give them the benefit of seeing me fall apart in this fucking Uber. As soon as I get back to my hotel room, I'm calling my sister Amy. A tough guy can cry to his twin without any fear of judgement.

And in the morning, I'll reach out to my agent. Surely, there's some team in the League open to a mid-season trade. Because one thing is for damn sure: it was hard enough leaving Seattle knowing I would never see Rachel again. No way in hell am I going to live in the same city, play on the same team, and have her always just out of my reach. Fuck being friends. I want all or nothing. If she doesn't want my all, then I have to be strong enough to live with nothing.

32
RACHEL

I glance sharply over at Jake, noting the way his entire demeanor has suddenly changed. "What's wrong?" I say, placing my hand on his knee. He stiffens. "Jake—"

"Don't," he mutters. "Please—just—" He removes my hand from his knee and I feel it like a punch to the gut.

"What the hell is going on?" I press. "You just said 'it's fine.' What does that mean?"

"You don't want this," he replies, still not looking at me. "You don't want me. He's the better fit, I get it."

My gaze darts open-mouthed over to Caleb and he groans. "Jake, you're a fuckin' idiot—"

"Say it again when we get out of this car," Jake snaps, his shoulders now suddenly twice as broad. He leans across me, pointing a finger in his face. "Don't fuckin' push me, Cay."

"Whoa—*stop*—" I throw both my hands out to either side.

"What's that?" the Uber driver calls. "Stop here?"

"No," the three of us say at once.

"Actually, yeah," says Jake. "Let me out. I'll walk the rest of the way."

"Okie-dokie," the sweet blonde says, pulling over.

"Jake, no," I cry. "This is crazy—"

He's out before I can even snatch for his shoulders, slamming the car door in my face. Caleb already has his side open, following him out.

"Jeez, he's pretty upset," the driver murmurs, eyes wide as she watches Jake storming off, Caleb jogging after him. "Want me to wait? Or take just you back to the hotel?"

"No," I reply. "I have to deal with this."

I slide out Caleb's open door, following after them.

It's nearly one in the morning. All the restaurants and businesses on this street are closed. A few have glowing signs—Chinese takeout, a laundromat, a dive bar. Rock music filters out an open door as I rush past, chasing after my hockey players.

My heels click on the sidewalk. God, my feet are killing me. I'm within an inch of flinging these heels off and running barefoot.

"You've got it totally backwards, man!" Caleb calls after Jake.

"Don't tell me what I see with my own fucking eyes."

Caleb catches up, grabbing Jake by the shoulders. "Don't do this. Don't close off. You want to talk, so let's talk—"

"I *don't* wanna talk," Jake growls. "I can't do this here. Not now."

I catch up, panting. "Jake, talk to me before I scream. What the hell was that back there?" I gesture to where our Uber is still parked down the street. "One minute we're all blissed out from a three-way orgasm, and now you're running like a ghost is chasing you. Make it make sense."

He holds my gaze, those gorgeous hazel eyes full of so much pain. "Rachel, I can't do this anymore."

My breath catches as Caleb's dark brows narrow in confusion. "Do what?" he says, glancing between us.

Jake looks to me, waiting for my permission. Even now, he's willing to keep us a secret. Or maybe this is a test? He wants to know what our secret is worth to me. Am I willing to tell Caleb the truth? The pain on his face has me stepping forward, grabbing his hand. "I know this has been hard for you. It's been hard for me too. I *never* expected this. Neither of us did."

"Expected what?" Caleb says, his obsidian gaze darting between us. "How long has this been going on between you two?"

"Almost four months," I reply, my eyes still locked on Jake.

I wait for Caleb to catch up. There's no way Jake didn't tell him about me. I'm waiting all of five seconds before Caleb is cursing under his breath. "Oh, fucking hell," he mutters. He glares at Jake. "You kidding me right now, asshole? *She's* your Seattle Girl?"

Slowly, Jake nods, his eyes still on me.

"Oh, fuck," Caleb says again, dragging his hands through his tousled hair. "Why didn't either of you say anything?"

"She told me not to," Jake replies, his tone flat.

Caleb punches his arm. "Yeah, well I'm your best fucking friend. And I'm pretty sure secrets go out the window when you invite me to face fuck your dream girl in a closet!"

"She didn't want anyone to know," says Jake, glaring in my direction.

"Why the hell not?"

Jake shrugs. "You'd have to ask her. Rachel gets to call all the shots, apparently. But my guess is that she's ashamed of me."

His words knock out all my air. I gasp, hand to my chest. "Jake—what the *fuck*? Are you serious right now? You tell me if you're serious, before I cry right here in front of Mr. Chen's!"

A half-lit dumpling sign flickers behind his head as he crosses his arms. "Tell me I'm wrong."

"You're wrong!"

"You said we can't be together because of the contracts you signed," he says, leveling a finger in my face. "But I talked to Vicki, and she said we just have to sign a 'we're together' form and I can't see you as my doctor."

My eyes go wide. "You asked Vicki about me? When?"

"The day you showed up in my goddamn parking garage! It's not a big deal, Rachel. With the shredding of one document and the signing of another, we can be together. And I think you know that," he adds. "You just don't want me."

How did I not realize the extent to which I was hurting him? He's always in such a good mood—always smiling, always teasing and laughing and texting me pictures of tacos and pelicans and every cup of coffee he consumes. But this whole time he's been masking his pain.

"Jake, I'm sorry."

He stiffens, his last hope shattering.

"Wait—*no*—" I lunge after him, grabbing his arm. "I didn't mean—Jake, I'm sorry for hurting you. For not realizing how difficult this was for you."

"Difficult?" he growls. "This has been fucking *unbearable*, Rachel. Do you know how hard it was to wake up and find you gone in Seattle? Do you know what I felt seeing you again? How I've suffered knowing you're in my city, in my goddamn ice rink, on my bus, in my gym, on my plane—you're fucking *everywhere*. All day. *Every* day. And

I can't fucking touch you! Can't kiss you. Can't feel this heart beating under my hands." He splays his hand over my chest.

"I'm not eating, Rachel. Not sleeping. I can't concentrate on or off the ice. Ask Cay, he knows," he adds. "He's been bugging me for weeks wanting to know what's wrong. *You're* what's wrong."

I raise a hand, wrapping it around his wrist. "Jake—"

"I'm in love with you, Rachel. And you can say that's crazy, but I'm not some lovestruck fool that falls for any girl at the first flick of her lashes. You turned around on that barstool in Seattle, and I just knew. You're the one."

I'm crying now, my head shaking. "Jake, you don't even know me—"

"I *do* know you," he counters, cupping my face with both hands. "I know you and you know me. We proved that in Seattle. I may not know the name of your high school or your favorite salad dressing, but I can learn. I *want* to learn them. Give me a chance, baby, please."

My hands go back to his wrists, pulling his hands from my face. "Jake, you don't want me," I say with a shake of my head.

"Don't," he growls. "Don't push me away again."

"I can't let you be with me," I say. "Not in public anyway."

"Why the hell not?"

"Not in public?" Caleb adds, arms crossed as he glares at me. "What are you, Hurricane? A fuckin' geisha?"

I fight back the tears that want so desperately to keep falling. "I can't be with you in public because it would ruin your life," I admit at last. "*I* would ruin your life . . . the way I've already ruined mine."

33
CALEB

My mind is racing. An hour ago, I had this girl on my lap, dazzling me with her show of friendship. Thirty minutes later, I was fucking her hot mouth, coming down her throat while I watched Jake pound into her from behind. They were both goddamn perfection.

I wanted to ride back to the hotel and go for round two. I wanted this gorgeous girl riding my cock, slamming those curvy hips down—

Fuck, concentrate.

Now I'm standing on some random street corner, connecting the dots I should have seen a month ago. Rachel Price is Jake's Seattle Girl.

"Rach, what do you mean your life is ruined?" Jake says. "You're a hotshot doctor. Your career is on the rise—"

"I'm flying just under the radar, always only one more indiscretion away from total ruination," she replies. "I can't put that on you, Jake. I can't drag you down with me."

"Drag me down?" He glances sharply to me. "I don't understand."

Movement in the alley a few storefronts down has me on edge. "We should get off the street," I mutter.

We move down the sidewalk a few more blocks, ducking into a narrow, 24-hour diner that is all but empty except for a small group of frat guys slamming pancakes at the counter.

"Sit anywhere, hons!" the waitress calls. "Be there in a sec!"

Jake leads the way to the booth in the corner by the window. Rachel sits down first. Jake surprises me when he sits across from her. I slide in next to him.

The waitress bustles over clutching a pair of coffee pots. "Caf or decaf, honeys?"

We all order decaf, and she fills our plain white mugs to the brim.

"Y'all eating anything tonight?"

"Just the coffee," I say. As soon as the waitress leaves, I lean across Jake, snatching up the dish of creamers. "Alright, Hurricane. Spill."

She takes a creamer too, adding it to her coffee and stirring it with a spoon. "Neither of you have googled me, have you?"

We glance at each other. I sure as hell haven't. Googling a person you like feels like such a puck bunny thing to do. "No," I reply for both of us.

She holds her mug with both hands. "I can't believe I did that tonight. Anyone could have snapped a picture of us kissing in that stairwell. Or coming out of the closet. It was reckless, and I'm never reckless. But you both just—*god*—you make me so crazy," she says, taking a sip of her coffee.

"Why are you so worried about some pictures?" Jake presses.

She sets her cup down on the sea-foam green Formica tabletop. "Because it wouldn't be my first indiscretion," she admits softly. "And the press is ruthless. They would have splashed it everywhere. They would have said the most awful things—" She catches her words, snatching up her coffee again.

Jake and I share a wary glance. "The press?" he says.

I raise a brow at her. "Are you some secret princess or something?"

She shrugs and gives a little laugh. "Sort of . . . in a way, I guess."

"For fuck's sake, drop the veil already," I growl.

She drums her fingers on her mug. "Do either of you know the name Halston Price?"

My mind buzzes.

"Halston Price?" Jake repeats. "Wait—oh, shit—*wait*—" He gasps, leaning forward, elbows on the rickety table. "Halston Price as in *Hal Price*? Like, Hal Price, lead singer of The Ferrymen?"

Rachel nods, taking another sip of her coffee.

"Oh my god!" Jake cries.

"Easy," I mutter, glancing over towards the counter. The frat boys are looking our way.

"What?" he says with a laugh. "I'm sorry, but this is crazy. The Ferrymen are one of my all-time favorite bands." He turns to Rachel, grinning. "I saw them in concert in Amsterdam with Amy. Hal Price is a fucking legend. He's rock royalty!"

"Yep, that's daddy."

Jake laughs again. "Oh god, she calls Hal Price 'daddy.' I'm dead." He snatches up his mug with both hands, taking a big gulp.

Now it all makes sense. Her wanting to keep her anonymity in Seattle, all the sexy little tour t-shirts I've seen her wearing when she runs, her silver-spoon life with a hired driver, the electric guitar tattooed on her forearm. I bet you anything the signature is Hal's.

My eyes narrow on her. "So, Daddy Hal is a rock god, and you've lived in his spotlight all your life? Is that your deep dark damage, Hurricane?"

She nods, her expression solemn. "My family has been torn apart again and again by the press. Daddy cheated on my mom when we were little. He regretted it and wanted her back. But there was picture proof, and it was the 90s, when divorce was still taboo. It ruined him for a while. He took the heat for his infidelity ten times over."

"I'm sorry," Jake says, reaching across the table to hold her hand.

She looks up at us both, tears thick in her eyes. "The constant press scrutiny almost lost us Harrison."

"Oh, shit," Jake mutters.

I glance at him, a question in my eyes.

"Her twin brother," he replies.

Seriously? I shake my head, taking a sip of my shitty coffee. Of course, they're both fraternal twins. They probably bonded over it when they first met in Seattle. Maybe that's why he and Rachel have the vibe of magnets.

"What happened?" I say.

She looks sharply at me. "The press outed him to the world."

"Holy shit," Jake mutters. "Babe, that's awful."

"You don't know the half of it," she replies. "A few assholes at his prep school hid a camera in his room and caught him with another boy. They sold the video to the tabloids." She pauses, her eyes locked on her coffee cup. "My parents found out he was gay when his first porn tape went viral. It went on for like two years before we won the injunction to get it all taken down."

"I'm so sorry, baby girl," Jake murmurs. "What happened to Harrison?"

"The harassment was so bad at his school that he tried to kill himself. Took a medicine cabinet shelf's worth of pills. They had to pump his stomach. He was unconscious in the hospital for days. We thought he might not make it," she finishes, tears falling.

"Where do you fit in?" I say.

She picks up her coffee mug. "Me?"

"Yeah. Daddy Hal is the rock god with an infidelity problem. Brother is an outed gay man. What did the press do to you?"

"They hounded me worse than Harrison. Girls always get it worse," she adds. "And I was a bit of a seeker in my youth. I was in a lot of denial about how the fame affected me. So, I acted out. I made a lot of bad choices. And the press was there for every one of them. Just google me, and you'll see."

"We're not gonna google you," I say gently.

"Rachel, we all have a past," Jake adds. "I don't care if you were some spoiled rock star princess getting high and screwing douchey boys in your daddy's tour vans."

"More like getting high, screwing boys, and wrecking a three-million-dollar yacht off the Amalfi coast. Or getting drunk and puking all over myself at the White House Easter Egg Hunt. I was eleven for that one," she adds.

Shit. When I was eleven, I was already living to play hockey.

"I wasted three years trying to make it as a model when it made me miserable every second—starving myself, losing sleep, losing friends. That led to rebelling and getting myself engaged to a fashion photographer twenty years my senior. Daddy had to fly to Paris and physically drag me home."

She sets her empty cup down, sliding it away. "But it all worked out in the end. He put me in rehab, and I finally snapped out of it. One of the other women was an alcoholic heart surgeon. We bonded and she told me I'd make a great doctor. I had all the drive and the smarts, I just lacked direction. So, I finished rehab and went to college. I've never looked back. I graduated with my degree in kinesiology, secured a great residency, won the Barkley Fellowship. I've been Doctor Rachel Price for three years . . . and the press didn't report on *any* of it. They only ever cared about watching me fail. That's what they want for me and from all celebrities' kids. They want the train wreck, the drunken mess, the pill-popping anorexic model. I won't give them what they want anymore, so they leave me alone."

Jake and I are silent. I have no idea what to say. She's certainly lived a different life than a pair of hockey boys.

"Do you think being with me will bring you bad press?" Jake says with a raised brow.

She shakes her head. "No, angel. I think being with *me* would bring *you* bad press," she corrects. "Especially if we get caught doing what we were doing tonight," she adds.

And fuck it if I don't know she's right. We were so damn reckless. We could have cost Jake everything.

But Jake is shaking his head. "No. We could make it work."

She leans over the table on her elbows, eyes narrowed. "You think they shredded Harrison over being gay? What would they do to this?" she says, gesturing between the three of us. "You really think your NHL fans would accept you being with a rock star's train wreck of a daughter who likes getting face-fucked by your friend while you watch? Because I'm here to tell you that they would bury you alive, Jake. The sports press is just as brutal as the celebrity press."

"It's not their business who I spend my free time with," Jake growls.

"Poppy would disagree," she counters. "Call your agent. I'm sure they would too." As she speaks, she tugs her phone out of her pocket, tapping the screen a couple times. Then she sets it down on the table. "You're a public figure now, Jake. If you pulled me under your spotlight, it would shine on me *and* my two decades of baggage. You think it would play well for us that barely a month into my new job I'm already fucking my patient *and* his equipment manager—"

"Four months," Jake growls. "And we met when I wasn't your patient."

"You mean when we hooked up in a hotel bar? We knew each other for all of five minutes before we were tongue-fucking in an elevator. You want to tell the press that story? Would that help our image, do you think?"

"It wasn't like that, and you know it," he snaps.

"Oh, and you think the press cares about the correct story? You think they'll want to fact check the details with us before they print their salacious gossip?"

"Then we get out in front of it," he counters, getting more agitated. "We tell the story *our* way, control the narrative."

"No such thing. They will twist every single word to paint the story how they want to see it. And when it comes to Rachel Price and the press, the only story is mayhem—"

"I don't care about the fucking press!" Jake barks, slamming his fist on the table and rattling all our cups and silverware.

The guys over at the counter all turn to face us, brows raised in curiosity.

"Keep your shit together," I mutter at Jake.

He huffs, shaking his head.

Hurricane taps her phone and holds it up, showing us the screen. "Fifty-three seconds," she murmurs, the stopwatch app flashing the numbers in bright red. "It took me fifty-three seconds to unravel you, Jake."

"I'm not unraveled, I'm just pissed—"

"Yeah, and I get it," she says. "Look, I've been dealing with this bullshit all my life. For twenty-seven years it has been the Price Family against the world. We've finally learned the best way to survive the press is to just keep our heads down. We keep each other's secrets. No drama. No sharing the spotlight with other celebrities . . . or public figures," she adds gently.

Him. She means Jake. No sharing a spotlight with an NHL star if it could bring him negative press. He groans, sitting back and crossing his arms tight over his chest.

"*Please* believe me that I'm protecting you, Jake. I don't want to hurt you. And I don't want to be the reason you get hurt."

"She's right, buddy," I add. "The press would have a field day if any pictures of us at the club leaked. We gotta be more careful. You could lose your starting position. Hell, you could lose your contract. Careers have tanked for less."

"So where does that leave me then?" he asks, his gaze locked on her. "Is this over, Rachel? I tell you 'I love you' in front of a Mr. Chen's takeout, my cum still sticky between your legs, and you're gonna sit here and tell me that it's over? I can just take my love and choke on it, I guess."

An idea simmers in my mind. And because, apparently, I have no filter when it comes to these two, the words come tumbling out of my mouth. "I think you should move in together."

Jake chokes on his coffee, snorting it up his nose with a cough. "Fuck—ouch—"

Rachel turns slowly to look at me, her dark eye makeup still messy from gagging on my dick earlier. Her full lips part in surprise. "What did you say?"

"Hurricane, you should move in with Jake."

34
RACHEL

"**M**ove in?" I cry, pulse echoing in my ears as I lean over the table. "Did you not listen to a word of my speech for the last half hour?"

"Yeah, I did," Caleb replies. "I also listened to Jake. You guys really messed this up bad," he says, glancing from Jake back to me. "You put the cart *waaay* out before the horse, and then you fucked that cart. Without condoms, apparently, which, dude—" He punches Jake in the arm. "You're a fuckin' psycho. No rubber, no ride, remember?"

"*Ouch*—fucker," Jake growls, punching him back. "I said that in Seattle, but she was all like, 'condoms are less effective' and then she felt so good bare that I—"

"*Shhh*," I hiss, my eyes darting behind their shoulders.

"More coffee, hons?" calls the waitress, not waiting for our answer before she's pouring the decaf. "Let me know if you need anything else," she says over her shoulder.

"Anyway," Caleb mutters, peeling back the lid of a creamer and dumping it into his coffee. "You both messed this up, and now you gotta backtrack. Cool off and just get to know each other outside the pressures of the job."

I scoff. "Yeah, and you think moving in together is how we 'cool off'? Whatever happened to no-strings-attached casual dating or— oh, I don't know—just hanging out?" I snatch for a creamer from Caleb's clutch, and he practically snorts at me like a dragon. "Give me one, you greedy monster."

"I need them," he mutters, pouring his third creamer into a coffee that is now a sickly beige color Sherwin Williams would probably discontinue.

"Fuck—*here*—" Jake twists around, using his long arms to snatch the dish of creamers off the table behind us. He slides it across our table at me, away from Caleb's reach. "He's not gonna share, and you'll get a fork in the hand if you snatch at him again."

"Surly ass," I mutter.

Caleb just stirs his cream-hold-the-coffee with a rattle of his spoon.

I hold my warm cup between my hands, taking a deep breath. "Look guys, I'm happy for the first time in my life, okay? I've got a job that I love, and I've got this amazing opportunity to make a big move with my career. And I'm making all of this happen without trading on my dad's name or his fame. Do you know how much that means to me? Can you even imagine what it's like to have the specter of being Hal Price's kid haunting you night and day?"

"But the MCAT didn't care that I was Hal Price's daughter," I go on. "Neither does the Barkley Fellowship. The only thing that got me here is *my* talent. *My* hard work. And frankly, I don't want my work overshadowed by a relationship right now," I admit. "Do I wish I could see you more and laugh with you more and just exist where you are? Of course, I do. I've loved every minute we've spent together," I say, taking one of each of their hands. Caleb stiffens, but Jake quickly laces our fingers together.

"And would I like to have more sex?" I add with a smile. "Hell, yes. You two drive me wild and I—*god*—I can hardly think around you."

"The feeling is mutual, Seattle," Jake murmurs.

"But does that mean I'm ready to flip my life inside out and put you before my career—or risk hurting yours?" I add. "No way. I'm not ready to brave the chaos of the press." I reach for my coffee, taking another sip. "So, I'm sorry, Cay. But I think moving in with Jake is literally the *worst* idea ever. I would only end up hurting him . . . and I've done enough of that already."

Resting my case, I sit back, content to finish my coffee and head back to the hotel.

Both guys are pensive, their shoulders turned in slightly as they exchange pointed looks. I've heard the other guys refer to them as DLPs. Domestic life partners. Caleb would make a much better wife for Jake than I ever could—

I go impossibly still, glancing between them, reading their body language. That's when it hits me. All my niggling feelings of curiosity and confusion suddenly make sense. They behave like domestic life partners. They behave like lovers. Like soul mates.

I suck in a breath, feeling rattled by my revelation.

"I mean, we could," Jake mutters.

Caleb frowns. "But would you . . ."

Jake shrugs. "Better than nothing, right?"

"Fine," says Caleb. "It's your call, man."

Then they both turn to me.

Jake pierces me with this gorgeous hazel eyes. "Seattle, I want you to move in."

Now it's my turn to sit there stupidly with a surprised look on my face. Recovering my wits, I choke out. "What the *actual* fuck?"

35
RACHEL

"**W**ell?" I say, my voice coming out all high and squeaky. "I *literally* just said moving in would be the worst idea—"

"You'd have your own room," Jake says quickly. "Own bathroom and everything, and it locks, and you can see the ocean from your window."

"It's a block off the beach," Caleb adds. "Gorgeous. You'll love it, Hurricane."

"And there's off street parking for your truck," says Jake. "And I've got a home gym and a rooftop terrace to watch the sunset. You can cook anything you want. Or don't cook. During the season I have a company make all my meals so I stay on track with my diet. But there's a second fridge, and you can fill it with whatever you want."

I feel like I've entered some bizarro dimension where my words come out, but I'm not understood. "Jake, you're not listening. I can't play house with you. I just said—"

"Cay's gonna come too," he adds, jabbing a thumb at his friend.

I sit back, hands pressed flat against the sticky Formica tabletop. "What?"

"Yeah, you said you want more of both of us," Jake presses. "Not a relationship if that freaks you out," he adds. "But I can't keep doing this, Seattle. I can't have you in my city and on my team and not be closer to you. I need more. And I'll take anything I can get. You wanna fuck me? You just name the time and place. You want him?" He jabs his thumb at Caleb again. "Have him. With me there, without me, me watching from the side holding some electrolyte water. I guarantee you, he's not saying no, and neither am I."

I look to Caleb, and he gazes unflinchingly back.

"But this isn't just sex for me, Rachel," Jake adds, his face solemn. "Hell, at this point, I'll settle for just breathing your air. I'll rub your feet on the couch after a long day. I'll do your laundry. I'll hold your purse while you shop for trail mix. That's how crazy I am about you. I have to be me, and this is who I am. This is how I feel. Move in and be with me. With *us*. Whatever that looks like to you, we'll figure it out. Just give me more than this nothing. I can't bear another second of the nothing."

Girl, hold it together.

This man is so damn earnest. He loves me. He doesn't know me yet, but he loves me all the same. I glance between them. "I don't understand the rush to move in. We can do all those things, Jake. We can hang out and get groceries and explore the city. We can cook at your place or mine and—what?"

Caleb snorts as Jake just shakes his head.

"What am I missing?"

"Jake's a pro hockey player, Hurricane," Caleb replies.

"Yeah . . ."

"And I'm an equipment manager. And you're the team doc. And the season has already started . . ."

I raise a brow. "Yeah? So?"

He tugs out his phone. "Dude, show her your schedule," he mutters at Jake.

Jake pulls out his phone too and they both flash me their calendars for the coming week. It's madness as I take in all the dots and colored bars denoting activities. On Jake's calendar alone there's a complicated matrix of practice, workouts, PT, travel, games, PR, video meetings. Caleb's calendar is just as jam-packed.

"I bet yours doesn't look any prettier," says Caleb, tucking his phone back in his pocket. "You want a pro hockey player in your life while he's in season? You gotta live with him. You'll never see him otherwise."

I look to Caleb. "So . . . what? You're gonna move in with Jake too?"

He shrugs. "We've lived together before. It's not a big deal."

I narrow my eyes at him. "Yeah, domestic life partners, right?"

"God, that nickname haunts us," Jake mutters, still messing with his phone.

But Caleb holds my gaze. "Something like that," he says softly.

"And what's your endgame here, Snuffy? You're just gonna move into Jake's house with your cute dog and your surfboard and . . . what? Rub our feet and buy us trail mix?"

"Hey, don't knock it, Seattle," says Jake. "Cay gives excellent foot rubs. Better than me, actually. But I'm the better cook. We can only trust him not to mess up breakfast. He's strictly an eggs, bacon, and toast guy." He leans forward, elbows on the table. "You come to me if you want pasta carbonara with seared pancetta, grilled jumbo shrimp with coconut rice . . . or, you know, help in the shower."

I shake my head. "You two are crazy. This is so beyond crazy."

"Yeah, crazy smart. Come on, Seattle. Make me the happiest man on earth and move in with me . . . and Caleb . . . and Poseidon. We can't forget the world's greatest doggo," he adds with a grin.

Shit, I forgot about the dog. Oh my god, this is so not happening. Has the lure of unlimited dog snuggles really just tipped the scales in the boys' favor? "Fine," I hear myself say.

They blink at me like a pair of sexy owls. Then Jake all but chokes. "Wait—did you just say *fine?*"

"She just said fine," Caleb mutters.

"Oh, god. Okay. Breathe, everyone," Jake says, hands flat on the table, wide smile on his face. "We're so fucking doing this. You're moving in. You're *both* moving in. Tomorrow."

Caleb slips out of the booth, holding out a hand to me. "Three platonic fuck buddies and a hyperactive dog. What could possibly go wrong?"

36
RACHEL

I stand in line at the bottom of the stairs, shifting the strap of the bag on my shoulder. It's barely seven in the morning, and the whole team is shuffling around the tarmac waiting to board the plane. My phone buzzes in my hand.

JAKE (7:04AM): Hey roomie *wave emoji* What time should I come by to help get you packed up?

JAKE (7:04AM): The coffee on this plane sucks btw

JAKE (7:04AM): Just FYI, I'm tryna do my part to conserve water, so we'll need to assign shower buddies

I can't help but smile as I shoot back a reply.

RACHEL (7:05AM): I call dibs on Poseidon! You and Mr. Peppermint Mocha have fun *shower emoji**eggplant emoji**soap emoji*

I glance over to see Caleb hard at work with the other equipment guys, getting the bags loaded. He's focused on the job, not looking my way. I can't help but take in the sharp lines of his back as his muscles stretch under his Rays tech shirt—

"Hello? Earth to Doc," Langley laughs, giving me a gentle nudge.

"Hmm?" I jolt, nearly dropping my phone.

"Line's moving, Doc."

I hurry forward, mentally kicking myself. Why do I have zero chill when it comes to that damn equipment manager? I grab the metal railing with one hand and hoist up my wheelie bag with the other. Then I'm rushing up the stairs and onto the plane.

The flight attendants greet me as I shift past them. I'm not really paying attention, trying to stuff my phone in my pocket, as I feel my bag slam into something. I nearly topple over, but a firm hand wraps around my shoulder, keeping me from going ass over tits.

"Shit—sorry, Doc," Sully mutters, retracting his huge foot from the aisle without taking his eyes off his Nintendo Switch.

I gasp, clutching my bags as I glance behind me. Ilmari is there in his cosplay of Thor at the Oscars. His topknot is as messy as ever, a few strands framing his face. He's wearing a maroon three-piece suit. I can see the black ink peeking up at his neck. I haven't gotten a good look at where that ink goes yet.

"Thanks," I murmur.

His gaze trails down the length of his arm to his hand and he raises a brow, as if he's surprised to see it there. He lets me loose.

I sway, clearing my throat before I shift further down the aisle. Ilmari is still doing his whole 'sit with me if you want to live' routine, so I head straight for row 20. Jake is already in the opposite aisle seat, headphones on, eyes locked on his own Nintendo. I learned quick that most of the guys play endless games of Mario Kart on every flight. It's adorable, really. You can tell when things are getting heated because they all curse and groan up and down the plane.

Spying an open overhead bin, I bend over to grab my bag.

"Leave it," Ilmari mutters, still just behind me.

I glance over my shoulder again. "What?"

"Leave the bag."

"I'm a big girl, Mars. I can lift my own bag—hey—"

He steps in close, reaching around me to grab the handle of my wheelie bag. He lifts it one-handed into the overhead, lifting his own at the same time, sliding them both long ways into the bin.

I step back with a sigh, gesturing to our pair of seats. "After you."

"Hold on."

He strips out of his suit jacket. Carefully folding it inside out, he lays it on top of our bags in the bin. Standing so close to him, I catch the soft whiff of his cologne and fight a groan. This man smells as good as he looks. I can't quite place this scent. It's woodsy and crisp.

It makes me think of fall nights on our family ranch up in Montana. Daddy bought it as a place to escape the world. I picture myself wrapped up in a knit sweater and faded jeans, head tilted back, looking up at the blanket of stars.

Peace. The word comes to my mind unbidden. That's what Ilmari smells like: the peace and quiet of Montana nights, the quiet cool of autumn—

"Excuse me," he mutters, shifting into the seat.

I blink, sucking in a breath. Whoa, how can one scent be so powerful? I didn't even notice that Ilmari stripped out of his button-up too. Seeing Ilmari Kinnunen in nothing but a sleeveless undershirt is giving me heart palpitations.

Holy Bulging Biceps, Batman!

And I'm sorry, but does this man have a full back tattoo?! As he turns and slides into the seat, the thin white fabric stretches to reveal a dark shadow down the whole length of his back. The ink peeks out the sides of his exposed shoulders and up the top at his neck. I can see more of the top design now. It's bird's wings.

Clearing my throat, I sit down, brushing up against the bare skin of Ilmari's toned arm as I buckle myself in. I tuck my earpods and kindle into the seat pocket and cross my arms, trying to avoid glancing over at him.

Tattoos are art. They're meant to be seen and appreciated. He had to commit to several sessions—base color, fill-ins, touch-ups. A piece that size must be steeped in purpose and meaning for him and, goddamn it, I want to see it.

"Can I see your tattoo?" I blurt.

He stills, glancing up from his phone. "What?"

Oh, shit. Well, I've said it now.

"Your back tattoo," I say. "Can I see it?"

He raises a brow at me. "We're on a plane."

"Yeah? And?"

"You're asking me to strip my clothing off on a plane."

Now I'm laughing. "I'm sorry, but hasn't pretty much every guy on this plane already seen you bare ass naked like a thousand times? In the shower, in the locker room—"

"You're not my teammate, and this isn't a shower," he deadpans.

Well, shit. Why am I now picturing it?

Because you're a horny little horndog, comes Tess's teasing voice in my head.

Oh god, I want to crawl under the seat and hide with my inflatable life vest. "Fine," I murmur. "Forget I asked."

The flight attendant comes by and offers us drinks. I order a Diet Coke and Ilmari orders milk. No cereal, no side of cookies. Just a glass of milk. I can't remember the last time I drank a plain glass of milk. The only dairy I consume comes in ice cream or cheese form.

We settle into our seats with our drinks and the flight attendants start their safety demonstrations as the plane pushes back. In no time at all, we're in the air, and I'm ready to settle into my routine of reading quietly and pretending not to exist. After all, Ilmari doesn't want me here, he just can't *not* have me here.

I glance to the right and smile. Yep, Caleb is already asleep, his face smushed against the window, lips parted slightly on a soft snore that I can't hear over the roar of the plane. He looks like a little kid when he sleeps, his tousled hair a mess, his defenses wholly down.

Next to him, Jake has his thumbs working furiously on his game controller, his little green Yoshi flying down the colorful track.

If Caleb is a Rubik's Cube, Jake is a Bop It. And I don't mean that in a bad way. He's just exactly who he is. There's no artifice with Jake. No complication. He's fun and funny and he makes me feel good.

I want to live with them.

The quiet honesty of the thought settles my churning emotions. I want this. Is it the right thing? The smart thing? Hell if I know. But you only live once, and they make me happy, so I'm doing it. I'm moving into Jake Compton's beach house.

I'll tell Tess as soon as we land and make it official. Carpe diem. I'm seizing the shit out of this day. And you know what? Fuck Ilmari Kinnunen and his weirdness. I'm not gonna sit here like a houseplant and freshen up his air for nothing. I snatch up my Diet Coke and turn to face him. "So, tell me about yourself, Kinnunen."

31
ILMARI

My phone is in my hands, but I'm not looking at it. I can't concentrate. I can't stop reliving moments from last night's game.
It was another shutout, but just barely. Each save cost me. I was in
butterfly more than I was out. It hurt every time I dropped down.

Prior to getting signed by the Rays, I already had one of the highest shutout rates in the League. My size helps, and my skill. I wouldn't
be in the NHL if I wasn't skilled. But shutouts aren't only about the
goalie doing *his* job. I need my team. But they're not a team yet. These
first several games have proven that. We need more time on the ice,
more time playing when it counts. And I can't carry all the weight
alone—

"So, tell me about yourself, Kinnunen."

I blink, glancing over. She's sitting next to me. Doctor Price. *Rachel.*
I like her name. There's a music to it. In Finnish we would say it
Raakel. It's so close to Rakas. My love. My darling. So soft, so sweetly
feminine.

But there's nothing sweet about the woman sitting next to me.
My mind floods with images from last night—her striding across
the hotel lobby like she owned it. Her perfect breasts swayed in that
black outfit, and those cherry lips parted in a sexy smile as Compton
rushed forward to take her arm. I watched the whole thing from my
seat at the hotel bar.

Not much can hold my attention outside of hockey or a good
book, but *she* can. And I don't like it. I don't like that she's sitting next
to me. I really don't like that I can smell the soft notes of her perfume
each time she leans up to adjust the air. She overwhelms me. I feel
out of control. Why did I go to her? Why did I make her sit with me?
Why do I dread the idea of her sitting anywhere else?

Damn it, she's still looking at me. She's not wearing her nose ring.

She was wearing it last night. It was the first thing I noticed. That and the tattoo inching down between her full breasts.

"What?" I know exactly what she said.

She purses her lips. She knows too. "I said tell me about yourself," she repeats, taking a sip of her cola.

I reach for my drink too, wanting something to do with my hands. "You know enough."

She scoffs. "I know your name: Ilmari Kinnunen. I know you're Finnish. You're a goalie in the NHL. I know your stats. But I don't know *you*."

I've never been good at this. Small talk. If there was a trophy for the smallest talk, I would win that every time. I talk so little that most guys assume I don't understand English. Ignorant Americans. My English is better than theirs.

As if she can read my mind, the next words out of her mouth are, "You don't like talking very much, do you?"

"No," I reply.

She lets out a little laugh, tucking a strand of dark hair behind her ear. "Okay, tell me the truth—how often do you pretend not to speak English just to get out of talking to people?"

I smirk, crossing my arms. "Often."

I watch the motion of her throat as she swallows another sip of her drink. "Okay, so new game."

"Game?"

"Yep." She turns her shoulders, her dark eyes locked on me. They're walnut brown with flecks of gold near the iris. "You have to ask me three questions."

"I need to concentrate," I mutter, dropping my gaze back to my phone.

"Ohhh, no you don't." She reaches out, covering my phone with her hand. "I'm not buying your 'I gotta stay in the zone' bullshit, Kinnunen. You played another shutout. Which was awesome, by the way," she adds, nudging my shoulder. "I can respect that in the lead-up to your games you need to be in the zone. But now we're flying home, and you won't have another game for five whole days. You can stand to human with me for a bit."

My mouth quirks. "Are you implying that I'm not human?"

She narrows those pretty brown eyes at me. "Undecided. Which is why I want you to ask me questions. Ask me anything you want, and I'll answer."

"I don't have questions."

Her smile falls and I suddenly feel like kicking myself. I was making her smile and now she's not smiling anymore. "Can you not pretend that you care about anyone or anything other than hockey for five minutes?"

Her words sting. It's not the first time someone has accused me of being too focused on my game. But you don't get to my level by being complacent. Obsession is a necessity. Drive. Tenacity. They're almost more important than natural skill on the ice.

"I've been watching you, you know," she goes on. "You always keep to yourself."

"Goalies have a different schedule."

"You don't go to their dinners either. You don't participate in their group chats. There's more to being a hockey player than the game, Mars."

"And how would you know? You're not in the group chat."

"Hockey players are notoriously a chatty bunch. Present company excluded," she adds. "They want to know you, Ilmari. Whether you like it or not, you're part of this team. For the next few years, Jax is your home, and so are the Rays. Throw them a bone. Every once in a while, say yes to dinner."

I sigh, rubbing the back of my neck, my elbow hitting the bulkhead. "Is this an official medical recommendation from my doctor?"

She laughs, taking another sip of her cola. "You know what, yeah, it is, actually. Because I think it's unhealthy the way you keep yourself so isolated from the rest of the guys. Hockey is a team sport, Mars. And you don't have to be a goalie all the time either," she adds. "You're so busy keeping pucks out of nets that I don't think you realize you're keeping everyone else out too. It might be nice for you to think of letting some of us in occasionally. Put down your stick, take off your blocker, and let us be nice to you . . . let us get to know you."

"I'm a private person," I reply. "I don't know any other way."

"I can appreciate that. I'm protective of my family, my private life. But I can't just sit here trapped in your silence all season, Mars. I'm a chatty person, and I can't sleep on planes. And I didn't ask for this," she adds, gesturing between us. "You're making me sit here, even though you'd clearly prefer that I leap out the side—"

"I don't want that," I say quickly. My pulse races at the very idea of harm coming to her. I watched her trip down the aisle earlier and I acted without thought.

She stares at me. "Well . . . thanks for not wanting me to plummet to my death."

I'm ruining this. Somehow, I'm making her madder at me.

"Here's the deal, Kinnunen. Ask me three questions, alright? I'll answer the questions, and then I'll leave you alone for the rest of the flight. Deal?"

My heart is in my throat. I'm afraid to ask her questions. Talking seems to be making this worse, not better. Besides, my mind is a total blank. "And if I don't?"

Her frown deepens. "Well, if you can't show me the bare minimum of interest, then I'm moving seats. It's too awkward for me, okay? I can't just *sit* here, Mars. I feel . . . chained to you. Or like I somehow lose agency each time I feed into your tic by sitting here like a house plant, purifying your air of bad juju."

"Joo-joo?"

She waves her hand. "Nevermind. Will you just ask me a damn question before I get totally stressed and chug your glass of milk?"

I let out a slow exhale, my mind a humming blank room of nothing. How long can two people sit on a plane, staring at each other, saying no words?

Think of a question, Ilmari.

Why don't you wear your nose ring all the time?

No, too invasive. You can't ask a woman about her body. And she's not just any woman, she's your doctor.

What is your brand of perfume?

Damn it, no. You want her to know that you sniff her now too?

"I . . ." Nothing else comes out.

"Great," she mutters. "I'll see ya." She reaches for the buckle of her seatbelt with both hands and my own hand flashes out.

"No—*please*—" I don't want her to leave.

She just stares, those brown eyes locked on me. "Hey, Mars?" she murmurs. Her voice is so soft. Her eyes are luring me in deeper, like two dark pools I want to swim inside.

"Hmm?"

"Take your hand off my crotch."

I glance down to see that I've got my hand pressed flat over her seatbelt, which means my hand is pressed in her lap—

"Mitä vittua," I curse, jerking my hand away.

Now she's laughing. "You okay there, big guy? You gonna make it?"

I huff, dropping my hand to my lap.

"I'll show mercy, okay?" she teases. "Two questions. Just ask me two lil ole questions and I'll leave you alone for the rest of the flight."

I shake my head, letting myself glance back over at her. "Do you . . . always drink diet cola?"

Her smile falls and she rolls her eyes. I'm ready for her disappointment. "Seriously, Kinnunen? You can ask me anything, and that's your question? No, I don't always drink diet cola. In fact, you've been sitting right next to me as I've ordered an array of beverages to include coffee, water, and ginger ale."

She's right. Of course, she is.

"We'll call that your warm-up question, okay? Try again," she says more gently. As if she knows this is difficult for me, she adds, "You can do this, Ilmari. If it helps, just think of me as a doctor. Free medical advice can be yours, my friend. Or we could talk books, music, movies, food—"

Medical advice.

My heart beats faster and my hands clench into fists on my knees. Could it be this easy? Could I finally get the help I've been too afraid to ask for?

"Or we could talk about—"

"What is the most effective way to treat a groin pull?"

38
RACHEL

I blink, the words 'pop culture' dying on my lips. "Oh—*umm*—yeah, sure. We can talk about groin pulls if you want." I tuck my hair behind my ear. "Are you . . ." I glance down. Big mistake. Now I'm looking at Ilmari Kinnunen's groin. I clear my throat, eyes darting back up to his face. "Do you—are you worried you might have one?"

"I've had several in the past," he replies. "It's one of the most common injuries in hockey."

"Especially for goalies," I add.

I've been doing my research since the moment I was first offered the Barkley Fellowship. All the major joints take a beating in ice hockey. For goalies especially, it's the hips and knees that end careers. Meniscus and ACL tears, strain on the hip flexors, groin pulls. It's brutal.

"So . . . how would you treat one?" he murmurs.

I know I'm pushing him out of his comfort zone by making him talk to me. But it struck me as I've watched him over the past several weeks that I might just be the *only* one pushing Ilmari Kinnunen. The coaches push him in practice, sure, but it's also clear they think the sun rises and sets out of his ass. Hard to argue the point when he makes a shutout look as easy as breathing.

"So, groin pulls," I begin. "You say you've had them before?"

He nods.

"How bad?"

"With one, the whole inside of my groin and upper thigh turned black and blue, tender to the touch for weeks. I lost almost three months of my season before they cleared me to skate again."

"Yeah, that sounds like a bad one. Unless there's a total tearing of the muscle that requires surgery, it just has to clear up on its own. I always hate feeling like my hands are tied, but it's really on the athlete to put in the work—or in this case *not* work—and let the body heal itself."

He nods, listening intently.

"What did your team doc prescribe at the time?" I ask. "What was your treatment plan?"

"I was benched," he replies. "Ice for twenty minutes every four hours for the first week until the inflammation went down, compression bandage on my thigh during the day."

I take a sip of my Diet Coke. "Yeah, that sounds about right. Do you have a good stretching and core strengthening regime in place? You like the work Doctor Avery is doing with you?"

He goes still, his expression turning placid, wholly unbothered. I have a feeling this might be an Ilmari-ism. Something about Avery or this line of questioning is bothering him.

I glance around. Most of the guys wear big, noise-canceling headphones and either sleep or play games on their phones. No one is paying attention to us. "Do you wanna talk about it?" I murmur, leaning closer.

"No."

"Mars—"

"I said no," he repeats, his expression now cold as ice. "Avery is fine. Everything is fine."

"Ilmari, you don't have to—"

"You made me do this," he growls, pointing a finger in my face. "*You* made me ask you a question, and now we're finished. Move seats if you must."

I know what he's doing. He's in full goalie mode, shutting me out. But I'm not a puck he can just bat away with a flick of his wrist. Oh no, I am soooo much worse. I'm Doctor Rachel Watch-me-beat-this-dead-horse Price. And this conversation is not finished. Not even close.

WE'VE got a pretty good system in place for when we return from away games. We all mingle in the big multipurpose room that doubles as a sort of cafeteria. The chef service preps a big brunch for all the players and staff with egg bake casseroles, fresh fruit, and pancakes by the stack. It's cheat day for the guys, so they stuff their faces with double and triple helpings of everything.

Meanwhile, PT and medical staff stay on hand to do check-ins. We've set up in the corner with a massage station. Several of the guys start a rowdy soccer circle close by, and more than once I'm forced to duck from a flyaway ball.

"Oops—sorry, Doc!" Langley yells, chasing after the ball with one of J-Lo's little girls hard on his heels.

I try to keep my eye on Ilmari as I examine a few bruised knees and help the PT intern strap an ice pack to Karlsson's shoulder. "Yeah, just like that," I murmur, holding the end of the bandage down as Teddy winds it around. My gaze darts left as I watch Ilmari slip out of the room. "Yeah, then just tape it down—hey, you cool to finish up?"

"I think so," Teddy mutters, all his concentration on his wrap job. He's not quite over the starry-eyed, I-get-to-touch-professional-athletes magic of the job.

I pat his shoulder. "You'll do great. Karlsson, Teddy's gonna begin the amputation now, okay? Just breath it out."

"What?" Teddy squawks as Karlsson huffs a laugh.

I wander off, trying to avoid making it look like I'm stalking Kinnunen. I snatch some grapes off the buffet table before slipping out the same door he went through. This is a massive practice complex. He could be anywhere. I snoop around, slowly working my way back towards the gym.

The soft hum of music has my ears pricking up in interest. I follow the sound as it gets louder. God, it's intense, some kind of death metal. They're shredding the guitars as a man with a deep voice growls and shrieks into his mic.

I turn the corner into the stretching studio and pause in the doorway. Only one row of lights is on, giving the room a dark, cozy feel. It's framed in with mirrors on three sides, and a range of stretching tools are stacked on racks by the door—balance balls of various sizes, rubber bands, weighted medicine balls, straps, rollers.

But my eyes focus on the man in the middle of the room. Ilmari is alone on the mats, down on all fours, hips pulsing to the beat of the music. I know what he's doing, it's a groin muscle strengthening exercise. All the players do it. But I'm not gonna lie, watching Ilmari Kinnunen doing it alone in the dark feels almost pornographic.

He glances up and our gazes catch in the mirror. "Mitä helvettiä," he curses, pausing the music as he pops up to his knees. "What are you doing in here?"

His back is to me, so I'm holding his stormy gaze in the mirror. The silence between us is deafening. "Looking for you," I admit.

"You found me," he mutters. "But I would like my privacy."

I nod, crossing my arms as I lean against the open doorway, not leaving. "Show me."

He raises a brow. "What?"

"Your stretching routine. Show it to me."

"You're not my physical therapist."

My mouth curves into a smile. "Maybe not . . . but I am *a* physical therapist. I have degrees in kinesiology and sports medicine, an M.D., and a license to practice physical therapy. I specialize in sports injuries to the hip and knee, and I've spent the last two years working at one of the top private sport rehab centers in the country. I'm not asking to watch you hump the mats because it turns me on, Kinnunen. I'm telling you, as a trained doctor paid by this team to protect the players to show me your damn stretching routine."

Our stand-off continues as his reflection glares at me in the mirror.

I inch further into the room, kicking the door wedge out. The glass door whooshes softly shut behind me. His eyes track my movement. "I'm going to ask a few questions now," I murmur. "You answer if you feel like it, okay?"

He makes no reply. He's wearing a Rays tech shirt and a pair of Nike shorts. His trainers are the team style with his number embroidered on the heel: No. 31. He's acting like prey, but we both know that's not true. He's all predator all the time. Three times my size and nothing but muscle. And I've cornered him. The fox has the bear on his guard. One wrong step, and he'll eat me alive.

"On a scale from 0-10, what is your current pain level?"

He swallows, his eyes darkening. "Four."

I nod. "And during your last game . . . what was your pain level then?"

"Eight."

"Is the pain isolated to any specific spot?"

"Yes."

I drop down cross-legged to the mats behind him. I let my eye trace the broad roundness of his shoulder, down his cut back to his hips. "Which side is it?"

Slowly, he shifts his hand, his palm splaying over his right hip.

I nod. I knew it had to be the hip. He wouldn't be so casually perched on his knees if he was having meniscus or ACL pain at an eight. "How long?" I say, holding his reflection's gaze.

"A while."

"Goddamn it," I mutter. "Have you told anyone? Or have you just been lying and compensating on your own?"

He says nothing, which is answer enough.

"Will you let me examine you?"

"No."

I grit my teeth, frustration flashing across my expression in the mirror. "Mars, you—"

"I said no," he snaps, snatching up his phone and getting to his feet. "I'm fine, and this conversation never happened."

I scramble to my feet. "Oh, no you don't!" I snatch for his arm as he dares to brush past me. "You're gonna stay in this room, and you're gonna talk to me."

"No, I'm not," he mutters, moving towards the door.

I chase after him. "Mars!"

He reaches for the door handle. Without thinking, I leap.

"Saatana—paska—fuck—" he grunts. "Let me go—"

"No," I grunt, my arms around his neck as I lock my legs around his waist. Jeez, this man is a tree of solid muscle.

He pries at my legs with his iron fingers, and I squirm, practically choking him as I wrap my legs tighter. "Get off—"

"You walk outta here, you're gonna have to explain to everyone why you're wearing me as a koala," I grunt.

"You're a mad woman—"

He turns, knocking my hip into the rack of weighted exercise balls. They quickly go tumbling across the mats, rolling in every direction.

"Ouch—*shit*—I'm tryna *help* you, asshole!"

"I don't need your help—"

"You're injured, you idiot! Stop fighting me!"

He stills, chest heaving like an angry bull.

I look at us in the mirror and can't help but burst out laughing. He's got one hand at my arms around his neck and one on my ankle where he was trying to pry my legs apart . . . my legs that are currently wrapped all the way around him tighter than bark on a tree.

"You need help," I pant. "Let me help you. Let me do my job."

He closes his eyes. "I can't," he whispers, shaking his head. "I can't do this. The pressure is too high. Everything I wanted . . . everything I've worked for . . . I can't let you take it all away."

He sounds so deeply broken. He's not an angry bear ready to maul me. And he's not an immortal athlete, untouchable in his pads and his face mask. He's just a man. And he's scared.

Tears spring to my eyes. "Oh, Mars." My grip on him softens. "I swear to you . . . hey, look at me," I plead.

Slowly, he locks his steely gaze on my reflection.

"I will do everything in my power to help you . . . but you have to let me. You have to *trust* me. Give me a chance?"

*D*octor Price is wrapped around me, the curve of her thighs tucked above my hip bones. The weight of her pressed so close has me wholly distracted. Her warm breath fans across the back of my neck. I'm fighting the urge to throw her across the room . . . or flip her down to the mats and tuck her under me and—

I groan, shaking my head. If we stay like this much longer, I won't be able to hide the effect she has on me. I relax my body and she relaxes hers. Slowly, I loosen my grip on her arms and she slides herself down my back, dropping down to the mats.

She steps away from me, leaving me swaying on my feet. I rub my face with my hand, smoothing it over my beard with a soft groan.

"So," she says, breathless. "Umm . . . is that a yes? Will you let me help you?"

I turn around, meeting her gaze for the first time without the crutch of the mirror. "You have no idea the pressure I'm under."

"I know about the Olympic scouts," she replies, crossing her arms under her breasts. She's wearing a teal Rays polo with black leggings, her hair up in a knot like mine. A few dark tendrils frame her face. I want to brush them back. My hand twitches with it. I curl it into a fist, holding it at my side.

It's not like playing injured never happens. You could ask any player on this team, and they'll point to at least one part of their body causing them pain. It's all about balance. How injured can you be and still perform? I've played with broken fingers, a bruised rib, a mild concussion—

"Ilmari," she murmurs, her hand brushing my forearm. "Hockey isn't the only thing that matters, you know."

I jerk away from her. "I'm nothing if I can't play."

"It's just a game—"

"You don't understand." I turn away from her.

She huffs. "You think I don't understand the pressure to perform? I'm a *doctor*, Mars. Lives are literally at risk in my job. I've stood at the operating table over a person cut open from groin to hip, their bones exposed. Can you say the same?"

I glare down at her. "I carry the weight of the entire game on my shoulders. Which means I carry *everyone*—my team, my coaches, you, the people selling tickets, the men serving hotdogs. Tens of thousands of people, every game, every night. I'm the goalie. *It's all on me.*" I emphasize every word of that last sentence, leaning down closer to her face.

Her hand presses lightly against my chest. "You're not alone, Ilmari."

"I *am* alone! That's what it means to be a goalie. One man in the net, and it's me. I have to be able to play—"

"No, you don't actually. You have to be able to *live*. Are you really content to grind your body into the ground, doing what is likely irreparable harm? That's pain and damage you may have to live with forever—"

"Nothing is worse than the pain of not playing," I snap. "Hockey is the only thing that matters to me!"

She leans away, eyes wide, shaking her head in disbelief. "I swear to god, you guys are worse than addicts! You think there's nothing more to life than chasing that thrill you think you can only find on the ice. But here's a newsflash for your, Kinnunen: hockey careers are *short*. Life is long!"

I don't want to hear this now. I *can't* hear this now.

"You've had an impressive career for a goalie," she goes on. "You're already thirty. I'm guessing you've got maybe two years left before they force you out. Four if you're lucky." She leans in, tone flat. "But we both know that at the rate you're grinding down those hips and knees, you won't be one of the lucky ones."

I turn away, desperate to block out her cutting words.

"They'll bench you," she threatens. "You'll have to watch as a younger, clumsier man takes your place. They won't force your retirement right away because you're Mars Kinnunen, NHL darling, first player to sign on to the Jacksonville Rays. You're their shiny star.

You'll help sell so many tickets . . . all while you collect dust on the bench—"

"Stop it," I growl.

"Washed up duster—"

"Stop bloody talking!"

"Then stop hiding your head in the sand! What will you do when your two years are up? Hmm? Who will Ilmari Kinnunen be when he's thirty-two and retired? Do you want to be the forty-year-old getting a double hip replacement? Do you want to live in a first-floor condo because you just can't bear to take the stairs?"

"I won't let them bench me," I declare, knowing full well the power isn't in my hands. "The scouts have to see me play. This means *everything* to me! My entire life has been building to this moment. My family legacy is to play for the Finnish National Team. My grandfather played, my father. Now, it's my turn. It's all I've ever wanted. The timing has never been right before, but this is my chance. My *last* chance. Please, Rachel—"

This calms her down, this raw truth exposed. I hate laying myself bare to this stranger, but she won't stop needling me, splitting me open.

"Help me," I plead, holding her gaze. "Help me stay on the ice, and I'll do anything you say."

She huffs, glancing around the dark studio. Finally, she faces me, her hands back on her hips. "If you expect me to help you stay on the ice, doing everything I say starts right now. There can be no in-between here, Mars. You're taking a risk by playing injured, and I'm taking a risk by helping you hide it."

I nod, the weight of this secret lifting slightly from my chest. I told someone. Rachel knows. I don't have to carry this alone anymore. "Tell me what to do."

"Well, first thing is an exam. You know, the one you've been ducking away from for the last month?" she adds with a pointed look. "I assume that's the real reason our schedules became utterly incompatible, right? You were avoiding me?"

I nod again. I should feel ashamed, but I don't. I'm a desperate man. I'll do anything to stay on that ice, even hide from my own doctor in a utility closet . . . which I did last week . . . *twice.*

She lets out a slow breath. "This is fucking crazy. I don't even know how to do this. We need scans—"

"No scans," I growl. "Scans make it official."

She makes a strangled sound. "Well, how the fuck do you expect me to do this without scans? You're having groin pain, right?"

I nod for a third time.

"Yeah, the problem is that there's easily fifty things that can present as groin pain," she replies. "You may have a muscle strain, or you may not. It could be *so* much worse than that, Mars. We could be dealing with hip flexor pulls, a labral tear, bursitis. You could need surgery—"

"Okay," I soothe, placing my hand on her shoulder. "Just breathe."

She jerks away. "Just *breathe*? Are you kidding? You're trying to calm me down when you're the one with an injury you won't let me properly treat!"

"It doesn't hurt off the ice," I say. "And I've been compensating in the net, not using butterfly as much. Too wide a stretch with my right leg hurts, so I've been gravitating to my left post. That way I can push off with my left to reach the right post. I think it's working. It's—"

"It's madness," she snaps. "You can't just guard *half* your damn net and hope nobody notices."

We both go quiet. Her seething. Me waiting.

Slowly, she takes another calming breath. "Okay, I can't deal with this right now. I'm starving and I need caffeine. Here's what we'll do." She points a finger at me. "You're gonna take me to lunch somewhere away from prying eyes and ears. You're gonna feed me, and get me some caffeine, and then we're gonna come up with a plan."

"Okay."

"Good. Because I'm not gonna let you do this alone for another minute. Do you hear me? Everyone in this building gets to care about the game first, including you. But I don't. *You* are my priority, Mars. Your health. Your wellbeing. We're gonna figure this out."

I watch her walk away, my gaze on the gentle sway of her hips. My roiling emotions are shredding me open. No doctor has ever put me first. It's always about the needs of the game. You're in this business too long, you start to feel like a cog in a big machine, utterly replaceable.

With one impassioned speech, this doctor has ripped me from the machine and put me in the safety of her hand. She's fierce. My dark-haired lioness.

"Leijona," I mutter under my breath.

I have no choice but to trust her now. And she's taking a risk too. She's as much in the safety of my hand as I am in hers. I'll tell her everything. I'll keep her safe. I vow it now: Rachel Price won't regret helping me.

"Rachel," I call after her.

She turns at the door, one hand on the push bar.

"Thank you," I say softly, feeling my breath coming easier for the first time in weeks.

Her eyes narrow at me. "You better not make me regret this, Kinnunen. Now, let's go. I'm about to scarf down the biggest plate of chicken wings you've ever seen."

Mun leijona. I follow her with a smile.

40
RACHEL

True to his word, Ilmari takes me to a bar and grill down on the water that serves chicken wings and sweet potato waffle fries. Apparently, this man doesn't understand the concept of 'cheat day' because, while I order my weight in chicken wings, fries, and celery with blue cheese dressing, he orders a grilled salmon fillet with steamed broccoli and a side of island rice. He doesn't even order a beer. What hockey player doesn't drink beer on cheat day? Instead, he drinks water with lemon like it's his job.

We stay at the bar for almost two hours. The weather is lovely, and we're seated outside. The ocean breeze ruffles my hair as I interrogate him on every aspect of his pain and self-medication strategy. He's finally forthcoming, answering every question I ask with more than nods and one-syllable words.

We leave the restaurant and head back to the exam room at the practice arena. I shut the door. "Why don't you lie down. I'll do an exam and test your range of motion a bit, okay?"

He says nothing, which I'm learning is Ilmari for consent. By the time I turn around, the big bear of a man is lying on my exam table. He relaxes back, one arm slung over his face as he takes a few deep breaths.

I rub my hands together to warm my palms. "Do you have any visible bruising in the area?"

"I didn't this morning."

I purse my lips, my gaze clinical as I take in the thick cut of his muscular thighs. "Bruising can sometimes take a day or two to come to the surface. If you had any muscle tearing in last night's game, we may not see immediate proof. Can I check for any swelling or discoloration?"

He nods.

He's only wearing a pair of athletic shorts. This will be easy to navigate. I clear my throat. "I'll need to . . . work around your shorts a bit. Is that—"

Before I can finish my sentence, he drops both hands to his shorts and gives them a tug.

"Oh, no—Mars, you don't need—"

But it's too late. Ilmari slips his shorts down his hips with one hand while doing his best to cover himself with the other. The man has huge hands, but I can still see some of what he's working with.

Sweet baby Jesus.

I step up to the table and complete a quick visual inspection of the skin around his groin and upper thigh. No bruising. No swelling. "Does this hurt?" I gently palpate the crease of his groin with my fingers.

"No," he says, body stiff.

"Try to relax for me."

He grunts, muttering something in Finnish. He does that a lot. I can only imagine it's a curse of some kind . . . probably directed at me.

I shift my fingers over, running down the line of his adductor muscles. "How about this?"

"No."

"What's your pain level right now?"

"Three. I'm always at a three," he clarifies.

"You can pull your shorts back up." As he does, I add, "I don't see any discoloration, but that doesn't mean we won't in a day or so. The area feels slightly hot to the touch, which can be a sign of a strain. So definitely do the ice routine like we discussed."

He nods, taking a deep breath, his gaze on anything but me. Am I making him uncomfortable? Typically, I'd ask if they want another person present for this kind of exam, but seeing as I'm the only one he's trusting with this, I imagine his answer is a big fat no.

"I'd like to do some range of motion tests to narrow down if your pain center is really your groin, or if it lies deeper in your hip joint," I explain.

"Do anything, Doc."

I do a few basic range of motion exercises, telling him to stop me when he feels pain. I've seen his range of motion on the ice. He can do a full split. "Let's do a five-second squeeze test."

Before I can explain, he's already shifting his knees up off the table and placing his feet flat. The motion has his athletic shorts sliding down into his crotch, exposing the whole length of his bare, tree-trunk thighs.

I smirk down at him.

"This isn't my first cow show," he says.

I snort, the sound turning into a choked laugh as he frowns up at me.

"What?"

I shake my head. "It's 'rodeo.' This isn't my first rodeo."

"Right," he murmurs. "Well, it's not. You can fist me, Doc. I don't mind."

And now my professionalism has officially left the building. I'm crying I'm laughing so hard.

Ilmari sits up. Scowling at me. "What did I say now? That is the five-second squeeze test, yes? You put your fist between my knees, and I squeeze. I've done it a hundred times."

Oh my god, and now he's pouting. He doesn't like being teased. I clear my throat. "Yeah, champ, that's how the squeeze test goes. Now, lie back and let me fist you." I snort again, because, apparently, I'm twelve.

He lays back down and then goes still. "It's something sexual, isn't it?"

I chuckle, tapping his knees. He lifts them for me, bringing his feet flat once more. "Yeah, Mars. It's sexual."

He raises a brow at me. "Will you tell me?"

"No way," I reply with a laugh, positioning my fist between his knees. "Consider it homework. Hey, that could be your contribution to the group chat this week—ask the guys to explain fisting to you. Go ahead and squeeze," I add.

He rolls his eyes, placing enormous pressure on my fist as he squeezes as tight as he can. "It's not hard to imagine what it means. I assume it's when you take your fist and place it inside the—"

"Ooooookay, and that's five seconds," I say over him, tapping his knee again. "How was that?"

"Maybe a four."

I nod, taking more mental notes. "Okay, you can get up. We're done for now."

He sits up but doesn't get off the table. "Well?"

"I don't want to engage in wild speculation."

"Is it wild speculation when you're a hip and knee expert? You must have an opinion."

I glance over at him. "Okay, well . . . first impressions? I don't actually think it's a groin pull."

His hopeful expression falls. "You think it's something worse."

"No, not necessarily worse, just . . . different," I reply. "I think the problem is deeper inside your hip. I think it might be your labrum. It's a common injury in ice hockey and soccer given your constant overextension. And you're likely to feel it like a groin pull, but not actually have outward symptoms of a pull," I add.

"Does it require surgery?"

"Not always."

"But sometimes?"

I nod. "But then so do some groin pulls," I add. "I've seen cases of both. If any tear gets bad enough, it'll require surgery to fix it. That's what we need to ward against from here on out. If your labral tear isn't too bad, we can rehab it, and get you on a strict strength and conditioning regime to get those hips as strong as possible."

"I'll do whatever you say, Doc," he replies.

I smile. "I don't want you to worry, okay? We've got a plan. And you played great this week. Go home and rest. And you're gonna call in sick for your Monday practice, right?"

He nods, his expression darkening.

"I'll speak to your strength and conditioning team and say you're working with me. Then Wednesday is the travel day up to Pennsylvania, so you can rest then too," I add, ticking the days off on my fingers. "Friday and Sunday are game days. I really wish you'd skip the first one—"

"No," he mutters.

"Davidson suits up for a reason, you know. He's a damn fine goalie—"

"He's a sieve—"

"He's your teammate!"

Ilmari crosses his arms, glaring at me. "I have to start."

I just shake my head. "On your head be it then."

He nods, his gaze falling to his hands folded in his lap.

"Hey," I murmur, stepping closer.

He glances up sharply, his stormy blue eyes narrowed.

"I'll be watching, okay? You're not alone, Mars. I've got your back."

He holds my gaze for a moment. He has nothing of the pretty boy looks of Jake or a sweet puppy like Langley. No, Mars Kinnunen is all man. He's rugged and sharp-edged and not my type at all. And yet, I feel inexplicably drawn to him.

Then he slips off the table and suddenly the air in the room seems to vanish. He's a whole foot taller than me. His chart reads 6'5". Closing the space between us, he surprises me by wrapping me in a tight embrace.

I go stiff, his scent filling my senses as he wraps his strong arms around my shoulders, his chin dropping to rest on the crown of my head. Recovering from my surprise, I wrap my arms loosely around him, hugging him back.

"Thank you, Rachel," he says for the second time today. Then he's pulling back, leaving me chasing his warmth and his scent that smells like my every dream of home.

41
RACHEL

By the time I get back to my apartment, it's nearly five o'clock at night. I drop my bags down in the kitchen, glancing around my tiny space. Jake buzzed my phone a few times this afternoon. And I had a missed call from Caleb by the time I finished up Ilmari's physical exam.

I know I owe them answers about today, but I can't give them. Ilmari is trusting me not to say anything. The guys will just have to understand.

Moving over to my little breakfast bar, I sit on the stool, pulling my phone from the high waistband of my leggings. I'm desperate for a shower, but I need to make a call first. I'm in over my head with this whole situation. I'm the only person Ilmari has trusted with his secret. I need to call the only person I can trust with mine. He'll know what to do.

Flipping through my contacts, I pull up his name and take a deep breath before tapping the call button. To my eternal surprise, he actually answers his phone.

"Price? This is unexpected," comes his deep voice.

"Hi, Doctor Halla. So sorry to call like this but . . ." I really wasn't planning to speak to him directly. I had a voicemail all planned out in my head.

"Is something wrong?"

I clear my voice. "Umm . . . I need your advice on a course of treatment, actually. It's . . . well it's a complicated situation. Do you have a few minutes to chat?"

He's quiet for a second. "Of course," comes his reply. "Walk me through the case."

I take a deep breath. "Well . . . where to begin?"

An hour later, I step out of my shower, wrapping a towel around my hair. Then I slip into a silky, emerald green cami and a pair of matching sleep shorts. The heat of the shower helped relax my muscles. I can't wait to sink onto Jake's couch with a glass of wine. Maybe he'll give me one of those foot rubs he promised.

I'm not planning to move all my stuff over at once. I decided that in the shower. I'm too damn tired to deal with it all tonight. I'll go over there, apologize for ghosting them all day, and hopefully scrounge up something to eat.

I snatch my phone off the vanity, checking my messages. Jake sent me his address earlier . . . and a picture of his cheat day sushi lunch. I think, in another life, Jake *was* sushi. I smile at the thought as I tap out a quick message, moving through my bedroom towards the kitchen.

RACHEL (6:17PM): Hey, leaving here in ten. Plz tell me you have something to eat.

My stomach may be empty, but screw it. Mama needs a glass of wine after this marathon of a week. I step into the kitchen and promptly scream, phone clattering from my hand to the floor. "What the fuck, Caleb!"

The asshole is standing in my kitchen, leaning against the stove with his arms crossed. "So, you *are* alive. Good to know."

I bend down and snatch up my phone, checking for damage. Jake is already responding.

JAKE (6:18PM): YAY!!!! *confetti emoji*

JAKE (6:18PM): Pizza good? Preheating oven now

JAKE (6:18PM): Hey, I think Caleb was still over that way too. Maybe ride together

Heart racing, I glare at Caleb. "You breaking into women's apartments now? How did you even get in here?"

He raises a dark brow, arms still crossed. "Seriously? You *gave* me a key, remember?"

Wow, I totally did. That feels like a lifetime ago instead of only a few weeks. I scoff, jerking open my fridge to take out my bottle of chilled chardonnay. "Yeah, but that was for emergencies. What's the emergency, Caleb?"

"I was out of seashells," he mutters, gesturing to the glass bowl on my breakfast bar.

I open the cabinet and pull down a wine glass, helping myself to a generous pour. "So, why all the cloak and dagger?" I say, taking a sip.

He's still giving me that level look, arms crossed. "You've changed your mind."

I pause, glass of wine halfway to my lips. "Is that what you think?"

He nods, his fuck-all-the-way-off energy simmering at a low boil. After the day I've had, Dragon Rachel feels ready to come out and dance a little. Jake would never give me the fight she craves, but Caleb is a whole other story. There's a darkness in me that I see mirrored in him. Two jaded coulda-beens used to standing in the shadows of other people's spotlights. Only we've both found we prefer the dark over anything we ever had sharing their light.

I set my drink down on the counter. I'm still wearing my towel wrapped on my head. My silky cami and shorts leave nothing to the imagination. I'm sure he can see all my curves. And he's looking. I'm watching him do it, his gaze heating.

I cross my arms under my breasts, leaning against the counter. "So, you think I changed my mind? It took me less than twelve hours to decide living with two hockey bros might not be the best life choice. That's what you wanna think, right?"

"I don't *want* to think that," he corrects. "I'm just not surprised that you have. It's a lot for anyone. Jake is a lot. But I'm here to see if you'll reconsider."

I raise a brow. "Oh yeah? And what are you gonna offer me, Caleb?"

He takes a deep breath, dropping his hands to his sides. "I'll bow out."

There it is. Like clockwork.

Snatching up my glass of wine, I take another sip, saying nothing. Best to give them as much rope as possible when they're determined to get tangled up in it. And Caleb loves a little bondage. He wants this. I bet he's getting hard right now, high on his own bullshit martyrdom.

"Look . . . this is all a lot," he goes on, rubbing the back of his neck. "Jake doesn't need the distraction at the start of a new season with a brand-new team. And you certainly don't need the added complication. I mean, you've been on the fence from the beginning. You tried to ghost Jake in Seattle, so I know you have your doubts. I just don't want to add to them."

Oh Caleb, you sweet, scared mess.

"Mhmm," I say, taking another sip. "So . . . you've decided that if I mean to cut and run, best I do it with only Jake to hurt, right?"

"No," he growls. "I don't want Jake hurt."

"Are you sure this is about Jake? Sounds like you're ending this before it begins to keep *you* safe. Sparing yourself the pain of getting left behind. That's your fear, right?"

"No—I—fuck, this isn't coming out right," he mutters, lowering his gaze.

"No, you're doin' great," I deadpan. "Let's get all this bullshit out on the table now."

His gaze flashes, his eyes molten. "You think this is funny?"

"Not at all," I reply. "I also don't think this is actually about me and *my* loyalty issues," I add. "It's certainly not about Jake. Look up 'constancy' in the dictionary, and you'll see a picture of Jake Compton giving a thumbs-up."

He shakes his head, dragging a hand through his messy, dark auburn hair.

"By the way, I already texted him and told him I was on the way over," I add. "That's what I was doing when you scared me half to death just now."

His brow scrunches as he looks at my buzzing phone on the counter. "You did?"

"Yep, Caleb, I did. I had no intention of ghosting either of you today. Work just got in the way. I handled it as quickly as I could, and

I was ready to head over. But now that you're standing in my kitchen, we can have this out here and now."

His eyes narrow. "Have what out?"

I scoff, setting my wine aside again. "You really expect me to believe you used my key for the first time to come in here and tell me you're bowing out? You're not even the teeniest bit curious to see where this might go?"

"It can't go anywhere. You said so yourself."

"I said it can't be public," I correct. "For a whole mess of reasons, we all need to keep this quiet. But there's a lot of room to dance in the dark, Caleb. For you especially."

His frown deepens. "What the hell are you talking about?"

I shrug one shoulder. "Well, you've got a chance to see all your dreams come true here."

His arms tighten over his chest. "I don't follow."

"You don't? Let me spell it out for you then." I take a step closer. "Your best friend found the love of his life. So, now you're reeling. You don't know what to do. Because she's not some blonde puck bunny named Kelsey who wants to marry him and have his 2.5 babies that she'll dress in Gucci onesies."

The corner of his mouth twitches. "She's not?"

I tug the towel off my head and drop it to the floor. My mess of damp hair falls around my shoulders. "Nope. She's a Thai-food eating, scrubs-wearing, curses-like-a-sailor hot mess of a doctor. A born and bred rock'n'roller who grew up dropping acid behind the amps at her daddy's sold-out shows."

I take another step closer, watching the way he tenses. He's fighting himself now more than me. He's got his own monster chained up tight.

Come play with me, baby.

There's barely an arm's length between us now. I reach out a hand, brushing my fingertips lightly down his chest. He stiffens at my touch, his hands going back to grip the stove.

"Jake's new girl has battled addiction, depression, *and* dysmorphia . . . all before she turned eighteen," I go on. "We both know she's all wrong for him . . . and all right too." I close the space between us, my hand still splayed on his chest. "She's strong. She doesn't take his bullshit. And his shine doesn't blind her the way it has other women. She can handle him, protect him, and more than match him in strength."

I lean in closer, counting the freckles dusting his tanned cheeks, and whisper, "And do you wanna know the best part about Jake's new girl?"

His jaw clenches as he looks down at me, his dark eyes flashing. "What?"

I smile. "She's Caleb's girl too."

He goes impossibly still as I slip my thumbs into the top of my silky sleep shorts and tug them down, letting them drop to the floor. I stand before him, naked from the waist down.

"Your girl likes to be shared, Cay. She likes to be fucked. Separately, together. She wants you both to devour her."

"Fuck, Rachel," he mutters, gripping to the stove so tight I'm surprised he's not bending the metal.

"Nuh-uh," I say, putting a finger over his pouty lips. "When we're alone, you don't get to call me that." I hold his gaze, waiting.

"Hurricane," he says, voice low.

My insides light up as I raise my hand, brushing the hair off his brow.

He closes his eyes, as if my touch is physically hurting him.

"You want an emergency exit because you're afraid," I say. "Afraid to want. Afraid to be wanted."

He flinches at my words, his jaw clenched tight. "You don't know me."

"I know enough."

He shakes his head.

"Jake loves you, and I trust Jake," I say simply. "And *you* love Jake," I add. "Can I trust you to keep loving him? Can you ever learn to share him with me, Cay? He's got a lot of love to give. Enough to sustain us both, I think."

"I'm no good for you," he mutters. "Either of you. I'll break this— I'll—" He bites back the rest of his words.

"Caleb—"

"I'll ruin it," he says. "Let me go. Let me walk away now, before . . ." He fades into heartbreaking silence.

Words won't get through to Caleb. I need to rely on a little action to show him what we could be. I hold his gaze as I take him by the tattooed wrist and guide his hand between my legs. I suck in a breath, shivering with relief at his touch. We both drop our gaze to our shared point of connection.

"Fuck," he says on a breath, his fingers finding my center and plunging in, lifting me up on my toes. His other hand curls around my waist, holding me still.

"Jake is our angel," I say on a breath, my hands tightening on his shoulders as he moves his fingers slowly in and out. "He makes us both feel bright and shiny. He sees us for all that we are."

I cup his stubbled cheek, holding his gaze once more. Caleb's fingers go still inside me.

"But I think you might just see me for all that I hide," I whisper. "You're in this, Cay. With me. With *us*. Be my devil. Come dance with me in the dark."

He pulls his fingers from my pussy, leaving me empty and aching for more. Slowly, he lifts his wet fingers and traces them over my parted lips. "Is that what you need, Hurricane? You want a taste of my shadows?"

I fist the middle of his shirt. "Just a taste? Baby, you better make me drown—"

He's kissing me before I finish the words. His hands delve into my damp hair, fingers digging in tight, as he jerks my neck back, owning my mouth. I open eagerly, moaning out my need as my hands drop to his waist, fingers hooking into his belt loops.

He spins us around, pressing my bare ass against the handle of the stove. His jeans are rough against my skin as his hard cock presses at my center. I press right back. His hips hold me pinned as his hands roam, the calloused pads of his fingers setting my skin on fire. He brushes down my neck, over my collarbones, until his fingers snag on the silky little straps of my cami. With his tongue in my mouth, cock pressed hard against me, he fists the little strands of silk and jerks, tearing them loose.

I gasp as the cami slips down around my hips. Then his hands are cupping my breasts, pinching my nipples tight until I cry out, breaking our kiss. I love mixing pain with my pleasure. It keeps my nerves firing faster and my core coiling tighter. I'm on fire, body humming with need.

Reaching for the hem of his shirt with both hands, I give it a tug. "Take it off."

He breaks our kiss with a grunt, pulling his shirt off one-handed. Tossing it aside, he ducks down, his hot mouth closing around my peaked nipple. He flicks and sucks, driving me straight to that edge.

I smooth my hands over his shoulders. His muscles are lean and hard over his broad frame. I can practically feel the lingering warmth of the sun on his tanned skin. I dig my fingers into his surfer boy hair and rake his nape with my nails until he groans.

"Fuck," he pants against my flushed skin.

He drops a hand back between my legs and I open for him, not caring that the stove is digging into my ass. He works my clit with his thumb, two fingers buried in my wet center. Then he pops off my breast with a sucking sound, righting himself to hold my gaze. His other hand cups my cheek, holding me still, watching my expression change as he finger fucks me.

I'm falling to pieces in his arms, knees trembling. "Baby, I'm so close," I pant, feeling desperate and weak.

He smiles, his dark eyes flashing. "I've thought of this moment since I first saw you. Thought of the sounds you'd make for me, how you'd taste on my tongue." His hand softens, smoothing down the column of my neck.

I arch into his touch, panting through parted lips, as I feel my release coil tighter. "Please—"

"You swept into my life like a swirling storm of chaos. You've shattered everything. I'm in fucking free fall. No parachute. No one to catch me."

I cup his face with both hands, my body aching with need. "Cay . . . look at me, baby."

His obsidian gaze locks on me, shattering my last shred of control.

"I'll catch you," I say on a breath. "Let me catch you. Fall into me. Never stop—"

And then we're kissing again, both our hands dropping to the front of his pants. We fight for the button, jerking it open. He tugs his tattered jeans off his hips to the floor.

I slip my hand inside his boxer briefs, wrapping my fist around his hard cock. He's long and lean, with less girth than Jake, but fuck if those piercings don't already have me salivating. His tip leaks, the wetness slicking the palm of my hand. I can't help the eager sound that escapes my lips as I tease his lips, our tongues tangling.

"Fuck—stop," he growls.

Chest heaving, I watch him tug his briefs down his thighs freeing his cock. I'm literally desperate to come, but now I don't want to until he's inside me.

He pinches his tip, staving off his own release, as he buries his free hand back in my wet hair. "Tell me what you want," he says, nipping my chin.

"I want you to fuck me," I reply, holding tight to his hips. "Cay, make me yours. Please, baby—*ah*—" I gasp as his free hand circles my neck.

"I'm not your baby," he growls, squeezing my throat. "You're my twisted fucking Hurricane. Chaos in a brunette bottle. Who am I? Who waits for you in the dark?"

I wince, even as I smile. The monster in him is finally coming out to play. I swallow against his hand, loving that exquisite tightness of breath. Meanwhile, my pussy is desperate for some more attention.

"Please, daddy," I whimper, loving the way his eyes flash with hunger and triumph. Oh yeah, Cay screams daddy dom kink. My control freak. Mr. Fixes Everything. "I need you. Fuck me so good. Own this pussy before I scream—"

I shriek as he grabs me, hoisting me up his body as he turns. He shuffles forward two steps and sets me down roughly on the edge of the only part of the counter free of overhead cabinets—my little breakfast bar. I gasp, hands falling back to catch myself. My elbow hits the big glass bowl of seashells, sending it teetering over the edge. It shatters on the floor, seashells spilling everywhere, as Caleb parts my legs, notches the tip of his cock at my entrance, and drives into the hilt with a single thrust.

I scream, body convulsing with a spasm as I instantly shatter. My pussy clenches down on his cock and then he's moving, pounding into me. "Oh—*god*—"

I feel all four of Caleb's piercings like the world's most luxurious ribbed condom. I swear, my soul has to be floating somewhere above my body. Having a pierced dick isn't enough to accomplish what Caleb is currently doing to me. This man is fucking me with everything he's got. The ribbed sensation is just a delightfully kinky bonus to what would be some otherwise mind-blowing sex.

"Oh my *fucking* god," I cry out, holding on to whatever piece of him I can reach. I can't even think because he's holding my hips tight enough to bruise as he absolutely destroys my greedy pussy, slamming into the hilt again and again until I feel another wave of release hit me, cresting off the first that never really stopped.

"God—you feel amazing," he groans. "So wet and tight. Gonna fuck this pussy every damn day."

"*Yes*—"

"Gonna own you, sweet girl. Bend you over and spear you on my cock. Jake's cock too. You'll take us both together. In this pussy, in your ass. You'll be begging us to stop even as you scream for more."

"Do it," I plead, my body trembling from the aftershock of my double orgasm—and he's not done.

With a desperate groan, he pulls out of me and jerks me off the edge of the counter. I all but fall into his arms, sagging against him as he turns me roughly around. "Bend over. Show me this perfect ass."

I gladly fall to my elbows on the counter, a smile on my face as he buries his hand between my legs. His other hand massages my ass cheek, giving it a sharp slap that I feel straight through to my clit.

"You're gonna take me deep," he orders, pressing in with his hips, his cock wet with my release as he slides it between my legs.

"Please," I whimper.

"You want me to come inside you, don't you?" he teases, softly nipping the lobe of my ear. "You're a needy girl who wants to be filled with cum. I bet you'd take two dicks at once, wouldn't you, Hurricane? You want me and Jake stuffing this cunt together?"

"Yes," I pant, loving the feel of my hips wedged tight against the counter. The hard edge is cutting into me, but I don't care. "Finish with me, Cay. Take everything."

With a growl, he pushes down on the small of my back and notches himself at my entrance. "Tell me you want it."

"I do," I cry. "I want *you*. Please—*god*—fuck me 'til there's nothing left."

And then he does. He slams home once more, the new angle with his piercings on my G-spot making me see stars. I'm a shaky, mewling mess as he pounds me against the counter, my hips getting cut in half with each thrust, but I don't care. He's ruining me in the best possible way.

I'm lying palms-flat on the counter, my sensitive nipples pressed against the cold surface. I lift up, arching my back, mouth open on a slowly building moan, as he fucks me so hard, I think my hips might crack.

We both cry out our ecstasy as I clench tight around him, strangling his cock. My legs clench around him too, begging without words for him to stay buried deep. I feel the warmth of his release as he groans, his sweat-slicked body folding over mine.

I don't know how long we hold onto that moment of our shared release. Time becomes meaningless as my body unravels from its high and I'm left with nothing but the exquisite aftershocks.

Eventually, his grip softens and then he's slipping out, his hands framing me in as he pushes off the counter. I lay there, body trembling. The counter feels like ice against my burning skin. I shift back, wincing at the pain in my hips.

Caleb's breath is warm against my neck as he bends over and wraps me in his arms, lifting and turning me off the counter. I curl up against his chest letting him hold most of my weight. We're both shaking. He brushes my hair back from my face, kissing my brow.

"Don't pull away from me," I murmur. "From us. Please stay."

The hand petting circles on my back stills. "I'm not going anywhere," he replies.

Letting out a relieved exhale, I smile against his warm skin. "Take me home, Cay. Jake is waiting for us."

42
RACHEL

"**W**hoa," I murmur, peering out the windshield of Caleb's Jeep as we pull up to a sexy, modern beach house. It's tall and narrow, with an industrial vibe of metal and glass. "It's gorgeous."

Poseidon pops his head between the seats, panting with his hot doggy breath in my face. I grin, giving him a pet under his neck.

Caleb cranks the Jeep into park outside the two-car garage. "There are some off-street spots round the block. We can carpool whenever it works for our schedules, otherwise I can plan to park there, and you can park your monster truck here in the drive."

I groan. I really hate that damn truck. I can't mention it around Jake, that's for sure. He seems like the type to engage in extravagant gift giving.

Caleb hops out of the car, Poseidon following after him. The dog races around the front of the Jeep and up the walkway to the front door, letting out an excited bark.

I can't help but laugh, slipping the strap of my overnight bag onto my shoulder. "He seems happy to be here."

Caleb grunts, shouldering his own bag. "He's a furry little traitor."

"Jake mentioned you both in Seattle," I say, shutting my door. "You know . . . the night we met."

"Oh, yeah?"

"Yeah, he said Sy liked him better than you." I mean it to be teasing, but as soon as I say it, I realize I've done wrong.

Caleb's smile falls and he turns pensive. "He likes everyone better than me," he mutters.

Stepping forward, I loop my arm around his waist, tucking myself in against him. "Hey." I pull him to a stop. "Look at me, Cay."

He glances down, those dark eyes black in this light. His hair is tousled, and his tanned cheeks have a soft flush. He really does have beautiful bone structure. I can't help but think of a fae from a fantasy book. The dark stubble gives him an edge and ages him up a bit.

"How old are you?"

"Twenty-eight," he replies. "You?"

"Twenty-seven. How old is Jake?"

"Same as you. His birthday is the end of April."

We keep walking towards the door.

"Yeah, our bull-headed diva," I say with a laugh.

"God, he's such a Taurus," Caleb replies, his arm slung casually around my waist.

"Wait—when's *your* birthday? What's your sign?"

He purses those pouty lips, eyes narrowing. "I don't wanna say."

I sigh. "I swear to god, if you're a Virgo, I may have to walk away. I can't pinball between a Taurus and a Virgo."

"I'm not a Virgo," he replies.

I gasp, pulling him to a stop. My eyes go wide as I smile like a loon. I slip his arm off from around me, holding it by the wrist as I turn it over.

"What are you—"

"Aha!" I cry in triumph. I trace my thumb over the tattoo on the inside of his forearm. It's a bow and arrow. "You're a Sagittarius, aren't you?"

"No," he says, tugging his arm away.

"Yes, you are," I croon. "You're a moody, temperamental, emotional mess of a Sagittarius. Ohmygod, this explains everything. You are *such* a Sagittarius."

"Stop," he grunts.

"I bet you're artistic too, aren't you?" I tease. "So, what's your pleasure, daddy? Watercolors? Music? Oh, *please* tell me it's poetry—"

"I will pay you to stop," he growls.

"Aren't you going to ask me what my sign is?"

"Nope," he replies, walking off towards the front door.

"Oh, come on! Ask me!"

"I already know," he calls over his shoulder.

I follow him. "How?"

He stops at the front door, glancing back at me. "You've got the

Cancer constellation tattooed on the back of your arm, just above your elbow."

"What—" I snatch at my own arm, trying to twist it to see. "Oh, shit—I *totally* forgot about that one! God, that was done when I was like fifteen. Harrison and I got them to match."

He steps up to the front door, which has a fancy keypad lock. He taps in the digits to unlock the door and swings it open, letting Poseidon bolt inside with an excited yip. "After you," he mutters. "Home sweet home."

I step past him into the house, and I'm instantly greeted by an industrial layout of warm wood, dark metal, and glass. The entryway has a set of open stairs that zigzag up to all three levels.

Caleb shuts the door behind us, taking my bag off my shoulder.

"Hey!" comes Jake's call from deeper in the house.

I step through the entryway and the floor plan opens into a huge great room—comfortable living room with a big sectional, the TV is on the sports channel; dining area framed in on two sides by floor-to-ceiling glass featuring a beautiful wooden table that has an almost driftwood vibe; and a massive kitchen that is like something out of master chef.

My gaze is immediately drawn to the double fridge because standing right in front of it is Jake. He's wearing nothing but a pair of low-slung grey sweatpants, his dark hair messy, like he just woke up from a nap. His muscles are like carved marble, a six-pack leading down to a cut "V" that has me eager to touch.

"There you are," he calls. "Jeez, you said you were on the way like two hours ago. I was about to call in a search party and—*hoooly* shit—you two fucked." He glances between us, his smile falling as his eyes narrow.

I go still.

"That's why you're so late, isn't it? Yeah . . . I see it all over Cay's guilty face and—oh, fuck me—he fucked you with his android cock, didn't he?"

"Easy," Caleb growls.

But Jake's eyes go wide as he slips his hands into the pockets of his sweatpants that are leaving absolutely *nothing* to the imagination. "Well, how was it?"

I glance over my shoulder at Caleb. This is new territory for all of us. "Umm . . . do you really want to know details?"

"Of course, I wanna know," Jake cries. "Oh god, it was amazing, wasn't it?" He groans, rubbing his hand over his face. "It's not fair. He's got all the smarts, and that weird surfer vampire vibe, *and* a kinky ribbed cock. How's a guy supposed to compete with a surfing, sun-kissed Edward Cullen?"

Now Caleb and I are both choking on our laughter, Poseidon dancing at our feet.

Jake's petulance only fuels my giddiness. "You think this is funny, Seattle? You think you're gonna cast me aside for Caleb and his weird Klingon cock?"

I have tears in my eyes as I prop my hands on my hips. "Well, what are you gonna do about it, handsome?"

With a feral growl, he lunges forward, grabbing me around the middle and swinging me up over his shoulder. I'm caught totally by surprise, my tender hips screaming in pain, as he takes off with me towards the stairs, giving my ass a swat for good measure.

"Jake—put me down—"

"Not a chance," he replies, hurrying for the stairs as Poseidon chases after us. "Cay, take the pizza out of the oven!" he calls over his shoulder.

"Sweet, thanks for warming it up for me!"

"Eat it and you're dead, asshole!" Jake barks back. He hurries us up the stairs, every bounce of the steps murder on my hips.

"Nice place," I pant, my hands pressed against his back.

"I'll give you a tour later," he replies, taking me straight down the hall to what I can only assume is his room. He slips me off his shoulder and leaves me swaying on my feet. "Out, Sy!"

Poseidon skitters away back down the hall and Jake slams the door.

I do a quick turn, taking it all in. The only light comes from the bedside lamp. It's a beautiful room done in a style to match the rest of the house—masculine, warm woods and cool metals. His bed looks mussed, like he really was napping this afternoon. His sheets are bright white, in sharp contrast to the soft grey of his comforter.

He steps in behind me, wrapping me in his arms, his face dropping to the crook of my neck to breathe me in. "I missed you," he murmurs against my skin.

I shiver in his hold as his lips tease my pulse point. "You saw me a few hours ago." My hands curl around his forearms.

"It's not the same," he replies, cupping my breasts as he flips to the other side, giving my neck more soft kisses. "I've missed you so much, baby. For weeks. Months. Needed you. God, it feels so right to have you here with me."

I lean against him, closing my eyes, and let myself feel everything. His aura is everywhere in this room, his scent; that soft, woodsy smell that acts like my pussynip. I want to bottle it. If he's got body wash, I'm stealing it. I want this scent lingering on my skin always.

"I need you," he whispers. "But I don't know how this works. With Cay, I—"

We both go still. Slowly, I turn in his arms. I place my hands flat on his bare chest and hold his gaze. "Ask me anything," I say.

"How does this work? Is it like . . . dibs?"

I raise a brow. "Dibs?"

"Yeah, like he had you tonight, so now I can't? Or do I have to wait or something?"

I snort. "What, like waiting thirty minutes after you eat to go swimming?"

"Well, I don't know," he says, dragging a hand through his hair. "I'm trying to be, like, respectful, when really, I'm freaking the fuck out because all I can think is, 'Holy fuck, she's here! She's in my room! Why am I not inside her yet?' And I'm trying to make that voice shut up and focus and have 'the talk' or whatever this is," he says, gesturing between us. "But it's just . . . I've just missed you so goddamn much. And I don't want to miss you anymore."

I cup his face. "I'm right here, angel. And there are no rules when it comes to timing or dibs, at least not for me. But if it makes you uncomfortable to think I was with Caleb earlier . . . if *you* want to wait, or if you want me to shower first—" I bite off my words, my hands lowering as I feel my cheeks go a little warm.

Jake's gaze drifts to my black, high-waisted leggings. "Did he take you bare?"

I nod.

He lets out another low groan. "God, why does that turn me on so much?" He leans in, one arm at my waist as he brushes his lips along my temple. "Are you dripping with my best friend's cum right now, Seattle Girl?"

"Maybe a little."

His hands tangle in my hair as he pulls me forward, tipping my head back to kiss me. "So fucking hot."

I sigh into his mouth, loving the feel of his lips on mine. Both the boys are excellent kissers. I don't care that they got this good through years of practice with puck bunnies because I'm reaping the benefits now. I wrap my hands around his waist, my fingers slipping inside the top of his sweats to cup his ass. Jake Compton has an ass that literally doesn't quit.

"Wait—wait," he murmurs, pulling back.

I suck in a breath, blinking up at him.

"Babe, you're fired," he says.

"What?"

He grins. "I gotta fire you. You're not my doctor anymore. I'll see one of the other docs. Hell, I'll buy another doctor, and ship them to every practice and game."

"Jake—"

"I'm serious, baby. I'm not messing this up for me or for you. Do we need to sign the form thing?"

My heart flips. "What?"

"We don't have to tell a soul outside of Caleb and HR," he adds. "No one has to know if that's really what you want. But I want this all above board. I don't want this biting you in the ass later. I'm the only one who gets to do that," he adds with another wolfish grin.

I let out a breath, my mind racing. Signing a form feels so official. Hell, you sign a marriage license. The look of hope in his eyes is tearing down all my walls. He's laying me bare. Slowly, I cup his cheek and nod. "Okay."

His eyes go wide. "Wait—seriously?"

"Yeah, okay. We'll sign the forms. We'll tell Vicki."

He grins like a loon, wrapping me in his arms. "Oh, you are so fucking fired. I'm not your patient anymore, Doc. I'm not gonna go to you for so much as a hangnail. Never again." His hands are all over me as he murmurs in my ear. "I'm gonna be so professional. People will give us an award for 'most collegial.'"

I snort, my body arching into his hands, craving more.

But then he cups my cheek, jerking my face up to hold his gaze. "But when we come home, all bets are fucking off. No colleagues. *Say it.*"

"No colleagues," I reply on a breath.

"No ghosting me."

I shake my head. "No ghosting."

His gaze softens as he smiles. "We're gonna have so much amazing sex, you'll think you've died and gone to pussy heaven. I'm gonna treat you so good, baby. And we'll cook and go to the beach and do couples shit too. You're mine."

"Yours."

We seal it with a kiss, his hands softening on me, slipping down to my shoulders. "Tell me the truth," he mutters against my mouth. "What's the deal with the pierced cock?"

I huff out another laugh, pulling back. "Are you really that curious? I guarantee you he'd let you play with it. You could have all the firsthand knowledge you want—"

"Seattle," he growls. "I'm dying over here."

I bite my lip, trying to think of how to sensitively phrase my first experience of mind-blowing fuck-me-all-better sex with Caleb and his magically ribbed dick. My hips still have a heartbeat from being bent over and pulverized against the counter. "Umm . . ."

"Oh, fuck that." Jake snatches me up again, marching me across his room into the bathroom.

"Jake—what are you doing—"

"We've gotta remind this pussy what an all-natural man can do." He gives my ass another stinging slap before setting me on my feet in his massive, dark-tiled bathroom. He's got a deep soaking tub. It's big enough to fit two people easily. The shower is huge too, with a double rainfall shower head.

Jake jerks the dials, sending water cascading down, filling the room with the sound of a waterfall. "Take your clothes off, Seattle."

"Oh, yeah?" I say, arms crossed. "What'll happen if I do?"

He drops his grey sweats to the floor. It's the only piece of clothing he's wearing. So now I'm standing with a perfectly naked Jake

Compton. God, he's got a gorgeous cock. I'm one of those women that actually finds cocks beautiful. Jake's just does something to me. I'm salivating, desperate for more of this man.

He steps forward, fisting that pretty cock, his gaze molten. "You're gonna get in my shower, Seattle. And I'm gonna press you up against the wall and tongue fuck you til you scream. Once you've come on my face, I'm gonna remind you how good we are together, how much you like *this* cock. You know you crave me like I crave you. Now take off your fucking clothes."

I'm only pretending to be a cool customer. Inside, I'm a molten volcano. Slowly, I strip off my tank top, dropping it to the floor. He watches me, his hooded gaze calm and confident. He knows there's no universe in which I'm not getting in that shower. He's my magnet. We're meant to collide.

I kick off my little slip-on tennis shoes and dip my thumbs into the top of my leggings and undies together, pulling them down. I shimmy out of both and right myself.

"Baby—what—" Jake's lazy smile disappears in a blink as he steps forward. "What happened?"

My own smile falls as I glance down. Standing naked in front of your lover, the last thing you want to hear them say is 'what happened?'

His hands ghost over my hips, his thumbs barely brushing the skin.

"What?" I say, trying to look down.

He spins me around, so I see myself in the mirror.

"Oh...shit," I murmur. I've got bruises growing on my hips from where Cay slammed me up against the counter.

"What did you do? Are you hurt?" says Jake, his voice so earnest as he looks at my naked reflection in the mirror, his hands feather-light on my hips.

"No," I say quickly. "I, umm . . . it's fine."

His eyes narrow. "Oh . . ." I see the moment it clicks for him. *Snap* goes his control. "Oh, no he fucking didn't. I'll *kill* him—CAY!"

"Jake, no!" I spin around, grabbing his arm as he tries to stalk off naked and hunt Caleb down. I honestly don't know who could take who in an ass-kicking contest. Sure, Jake is in NHL-ready shape, but Caleb might secretly take cage-fighting lessons. "Jake, I'm fine—"

"You look like he tried to saw you in half!"

"I *asked* for it," I admit, placing a soothing hand on his chest. "It was a moment for us. We had some stuff to iron out. We did, and now we're good, and we're both here." My hand drifts up to cup his face. "Look at me, angel."

His gaze softens as he takes me in. His hand raises to wrap around my wrist.

"In Seattle, I packed up my stuff in tears," I whisper, giving him all my truth. "I left that hotel room . . . I left *you* . . . and the moment the door shut, I slid down the wall to the floor and I cried. I wanted to go back in so badly. I left both the room keys so I couldn't. Not without waking you—"

"You should have," he mutters. "I wasn't done. One night wasn't enough. It'll *never* be enough for me."

"I think you think you've been alone in missing me," I go on. "You think this is one-sided . . . don't you?"

His silence is answer enough.

"Cay might have swept in and shook our foundations, but everything we are, everything we had, it's still right *here*." I take his hand, splaying it over my heart like I did all those months ago in Seattle. "I'm right here, Jake. Whatever this is, wherever it goes, I'm here. We'll make our own rules, okay? We'll define happiness on *our* terms. But I want you both. And there is no winning here. There is no first or second place. No trophies and no choosing. I am not a prize to be won."

Slowly he nods. Oh god, can this be happening? Is he in this too? Are we giving this a real shot?

He holds my gaze. "But you can't keep me away anymore, Rach. I can't handle it. I need you with me, okay? You gotta answer my texts. No more leaving me on read. Your silence tears my heart out. Call me clingy, I don't care. I have to be me—"

"I *want* you to be you," I say, brushing my thumb along his cheek. "My Jake," I murmur. "You're mine." I brush my fingers over his mouth. "These lips . . . this chin . . ." I trail my fingers down. "This strong heart . . ." I splay my hand over his chest. "I want it all. Be mine, Jake."

He wraps me in his embrace, his forehead dropping to mine as he breathes me in. "I'm yours, baby. I was yours the moment you turned around on that bar stool."

I wrap my arms around his shoulders, lifting up on my toes. His hard cock is angled up between us, pressed against the bruise on my hip. The pain centers me. Jake has been living in pain too. His bruises aren't visible, but they're there. I put them there.

Taking him by the hand, I lead him into the shower. I step under the hot spray and turn, my hands going back to his shoulders. "I want to make you feel so good. No more worry. No more missed tomorrows. Come back to me. Find me again like you did in Seattle—"

He silences my request with a kiss, his hands roving my body with eagerness as we just melt into each other. Our bodies seem to have memorized each other. I know how to fit him. And he knows me. We kiss as we tease, my hand around his cock giving slow pulls. Just enough pressure, with a sweep of my thumb at his sensitive tip.

He groans into my touch, pressing in with his hips. His hand delves between my legs, his fingers finding my center slick with my own wetness and Caleb's release. The shower washes it away as we stay breathing each other's air.

Then he's walking me backwards until my butt hits the cold tiled wall. He doesn't wait a beat before he's dropping to his knees. His hands are gentle at my hips as he places a few open-mouthed kisses over my bruised skin. His lips trail lower, kissing my bare pussy, giving it little teasing licks. He moans his eagerness and I feel the vibration right on my clit.

My whole body is a live wire. I'm crackling like I have electricity under my skin. He nuzzles his face against me, his hands tightening a bit as he groans again. "Fuck, I missed you so much."

I can't help but laugh, my body relaxing against the wall, as I realize he's not actually talking to me. "You think she missed you too?" I tease.

"I know she did," he replies with confidence, parting me open and flicking his tongue against my clit. "Mmm, this pretty pink pussy is all fucking mine. I swear, you have the prettiest pussy I've ever seen."

My laugh dies in my throat as he latches on with his mouth, his hands circling around to fist my ass cheeks. "Please," I murmur, spreading my legs a bit. I want Jake eating my pussy like it's his last meal.

My hands dig into his wet hair, and I shift my weight as he tugs on my left leg, flipping it over his shoulder. Then he goes all in. He's ravenous, his tongue and lips showing me just how much he's missed me. It takes nothing to have me spiraling right out to that edge of release.

The moment he sinks his fingers inside me, I'm coming, the walls of my cunt clenching tight around him. He rides it out with me, sucking my clit and flicking it with his tongue until I stop pulsing around his fingers. He gives my pussy a few more soft kisses, pulling his fingers out and licking them clean as he stands.

I lead him over to the tiled bench seat, passing under the shower's hot spray, and push down on his shoulders. He sinks down bare-assed, his hands trailing up my sides to cup my breasts. I gently climb onto his lap, straddling him with my knees on the hard tile of the bench. Jake helps position me, lifting me under the ribs as I notch his cock at my entrance and sink slowly down, taking his full length inside me on a soft exhale.

His gaze overflows with such longing as he looks up and down my body, helping me rock on his lap. His perfect cock fills me so full. I feel him everywhere. We sink into each other, two souls woven together as one, as we chase our releases. My thrusting gets faster, my fingers digging into the muscles of his shoulders as my back arches and my head tips back on a low moan.

"Jake, I'm so close—"

"Me too, baby. Fuck, you're so beautiful," he murmurs. "I don't know how to stop wanting you. I love you so much. I'm gonna be so good to you—"

His sweet words catapult me over the edge, and I'm coming again. I've lost count of my orgasms tonight. I'm wrecked. Utterly ruined. My body falls against Jake, my forehead pressed into his neck as I feel him slamming up with his hips, crying out his own release so deep inside me.

We hold to each other, breathing in sync, as we spiral down. The steam feels so good in my lungs, opening my chest. I push gently off his shoulders to look at him. "How do you feel about eating pizza in bed?"

He smiles. "Best idea you've ever had."

43
JAKE

"**C**ome on," I tease. "It'll be fun." I follow Caleb around the kitchen island as he snatches up his keys, fills his travel mug with coffee, and snags a banana off the hook. Poseidon dances at my feet.

"Dude, no," Caleb huffs, slipping the banana in his pocket.

We're all on totally different schedules this week. Rachel has already been gone for over an hour. She's doing some kind of PT training down at the hospital. Cay is ducking out now, and I bet I won't see him again until after dinner. Meanwhile, I have the day off. Only problem is that everyone I like is busy. Novy is at the dentist and Morrow had to drive down to Orlando to help his mom move. The married guys never want to hang out on off days. I guess I'm alone with Sy.

Fuck, I'm already bored.

If Caleb would just agree to play the game, I could set my mind to coming up with my plan. "Why don't you want to play?"

"Because it's not a game," he says. "She's not some trophy, Jake."

"I know that, asshole," I huff. "It's just for fun. Come on, we each pick a night this week to take her out and show her a good time. Points for each time she breaks her rule about no PDA. What are we thinking? Maybe one point for a kiss, five for a handy, ten for a BJ?"

He stills. "And what's the point value for sex?"

I laugh. "You really think you can get Rachel to have sex with you in public?"

He shrugs. "I just think it needs to have a point value."

"Fine," I say. "Fifty points for full P-in-V sex."

This is all wishful thinking, of course, because our girl was crystal clear. There will be no funny business of any kind outside the four walls of this house. No fuck me eyes. No kissing. No tender embraces. Nothing. We all have to be totally cool and professional at all times.

Which is fine for around the Rays. But I feel like her rules are a little strict for the general public. I mean, no kissing? Like, at *all*? Not even on a nature hike where only the trees can see us? No hand jobs in a parked car as we watch the sunset?

Of course, Caleb is on board. Mr. No PDA will have no problem following the rules. In all our years of friendship, the only time I've ever seen him intimate with a person was when I was in the room. I think that's why their moment at the club shook me so deep. He let her show him off. It melted his brain a little, but I could see the truth there too. He liked it. Loved it. Fucking craved more of it. He wanted her to claim him in front of the guys like that, in front of Aspen. He definitely wanted her doing it in front of me.

Our Cay may think he doesn't like PDA, but I know better. Which is why I thought up this game. There's nothing Caleb likes more than a little competition. And there's nothing I want more than to ruffle Rachel's feathers. I'm thinking, between the two of us, we can break her. I want that girl ravenous to kiss me. I want her all over me— hand in my pants, lips on mine, moaning my name as a little old lady rushes past us in the cereal aisle.

Okay, so maybe we won't get freaky in a Publix. But still, she can't possibly mean no PDA *ever* . . . right?

"Jake, you need to cool it," Cay warns, giving me one of his serious stares. "She set her limits, and we need to respect them."

I scoff. "You just know you'll lose."

He rolls his eyes and walks off towards the front door. "See you later, asshole."

"Come on," I call after him. "Just play the game!"

"Why would I bother playing the game when I know you've got no game?" he teases, slipping his feet into his shoes.

"Oh, you wanna bet?"

He huffs again.

"I bet you ten thousand dollars that she'll sleep in *my* bed to- night," I say, jabbing my thumb at my bare chest with a cocky grin. "And I'll be shutting the fucking door. You can just lie in your own bed hearing us moan as she comes all over my dick."

We haven't quite figured out our sharing arrangements yet. It's been pretty much open door on my end. If he wants to join, he can.

But when he's had her in his room, the door shuts. Let's see how he likes it.

"I'm not betting with you, Jake—"

"Yeah, because you don't have the money," I tease, folding my arms across my chest.

Caleb pauses, hands on his shoelaces. Tying the knot, he slowly stands. "And on that note . . ." He steps around me.

Then the world comes crashing down as my brain catches up with my dumb fucking mouth. "Cay—wait! I'm sorry!" I throw myself at the front door, slamming it shut as he pulls it open.

"Move, Jake," he mutters, not looking at me.

"Shit—no," I pant, one hand on his shoulder.

He shrugs me off.

"Cay, I didn't mean it. You know I sometimes say shit without thinking. I'm sorry. I *swear* I didn't mean it like that. I'm totally done. No more betting."

"Move," he mutters again.

"Not until you look at me," I plead, desperate to feel his eyes on me. "Not until you forgive me. I'm sorry—"

With a growl, Caleb turns and points his finger in my face. "You and I both know I don't need the money or the flashy cars or the big fucking beach house to steal her right out from under you."

I snort, trying to pretend I'm not intimidated by his vampire death glare. "Shows what you know. She likes it on top—"

Yep, it's too late. The words are out my certifiably stupid mouth. Oh my god, he's gonna kill me. Or leave me. I don't know which would be worse. He's reaching for the door again.

"No!" I squawk, throwing myself harder against it. "Fuck—god-damn it—please don't take her from me!" I beg.

Caleb stills, glancing over at me. "Are you seriously worried that I will?"

"Of course, I am! You're both so fucking smart. She's a doctor and you were a chemistry major in college. You won all those awards," I say with a wave of my hand. "You have way more in common with her than I do, Cay. The minute you set your tough guy bullshit aside and actually try for her, she'll fall in love with you. Hard. And then

I'll lose her. She'll walk away right into your kinky daddy dom arms. I'll be the ring bearer at your wedding."

That asshole has the confidence to smirk at me. "Let that be the fun thing you do on your day off today. Sit in this awful fucking feeling of knowing how fragile your position really is. You can't win this girl with flashy spending. She's not a bunny, Jake."

"I know—"

"She doesn't want us playing games either, putting her in the middle." He levels his dark stare at me.

"I know. Totally. It was a dumb idea."

"And I'm allowed time to figure out what the fuck I'm doing here," he adds. "I'm allowed to shut the door and keep her to myself for a few hours."

"I know," I say again, nodding.

"If that's too fucking hard for you, or you feel like you need to throw it in my face that I'm trying here—I'm *trying* to build intimacy with her, Jake—"

"I know!"

"You two already had your kismet moment in Seattle. And you've got the weird twin thing. You even breathe in sync, like you're a pair of damn aqua lungs. You practically finish each other's sentences. You think you're the only one dealing with feelings of being on the outside? To be in a room with you both is to be on the outside, Jake."

His confession tears at me. I had no idea. He's such a damn closed book. "Cay—"

"You're already locked all the way in," he goes on. "She's never letting you go. Stop worrying and stop trying to control this. It'll happen how it happens. I'm doing this my way. I'm taking my time, and I'm figuring this out. And if you don't like it, then I can have my shit out by the end of the day—"

"No!" I say, grabbing his shoulder. "Cay, I'm sorry. I was being a dick. Let's start over. Let's forget the bet."

"Good idea," he deadpans.

"Say you forgive me," I beg. "Please, Cay."

He huffs, shaking his head. "Forgiven."

I sigh with relief.

But that's when he leans in, dark eyes flashing. "But unless you want me to test the limits of your nightmares, you'll watch your fucking mouth when you talk to me. Understood?"

"I will," I say with a determined nod. "I'll watch it so hard. I won't say anything to piss you off ever again, Cay, I swear. Scout's honor," I add, holding up two fingers.

Rolling his eyes, Caleb jerks the door open and leaves.

Fuck, he's not gonna let this go. Cay forgives, but he doesn't forget. And he can be diabolical when he wants to be. I don't know how, but he's gonna find a way to make me pay for my smart mouth. And fuck if I won't deserve it.

44
RACHEL

This has been one heck of a week. Between all the game day travel, and the series of PT workshops hosted by the community college that Poppy oh-so-generously volunteered me to help run, I am absolutely beat. The boys are too. Honestly, I've hardly seen them this week. It seems like the only time we're all in the house on non-travel days are between the hours of 9:00pm and 6:00am. Poor Jake is usually so tired he just crashes out asleep.

Which is why I'm surprised they said they wanted to go out tonight. I got the text from Caleb while I was finishing up my last hour of the PT training course. We're going to Riptide's Bar & Grill. I've already heard from Poppy that she's going too. And some of the other guys—Novy, Langley, Sully and his wife Shelby.

I finish up with Fiona, the program coordinator, and she helps me drag my equipment bags out to the parking lot. As we walk out the automatic doors, Caleb's Jeep pulls up to the curb. Both guys are in the front seats, shades on, hats flipped backwards. Caleb's surfboard is strapped to the top rails.

"We're lookin' for a hurricane," he calls. "Either of you ladies seen one around?"

I snort, rolling my eyes at his cheesy line.

Fiona glances around, confused. "No, umm—I mean, it's clear skies today. Rain this weekend though—"

"It's okay, Fiona," I say. "He's just teasing you. He's my ride."

"Ohhh," she says with a little laugh. "Are you both players then?"

"He is," says Caleb, jabbing a thumb over his shoulder at Jake.

"Wow. You know, Doctor Price was such a great addition to our program." she says. "You're really lucky to have her."

"Oh, we know," Jake calls with a smile.

"We're so grateful this could work out," she adds, turning to me. "Maybe we could do it again next semester?"

"Sure," I reply. It's a cool program, offering college students hands-on experience they wouldn't expect to see until residency.

While we say our goodbyes, Jake slips out of the Jeep and takes the bags, loading them into the back. Then he opens my car door, letting me slide in the back seat. As soon as Fiona is safely back inside, Caleb cranks the Jeep into gear and we're off.

"So, party at Rip's, huh?" I call over the roar of the wind and the radio.

"Yep!" Jake shouts. "It's cheat day and I wanna eat my weight in sliders and fries!"

A$ we pull up to the big, sprawling beach bar, I sense a mood shift in Jake.

"Wait—what day is it today?" he says, his hand frozen on the strap of his seatbelt.

"Thursday," I reply. We'll be on the road again tomorrow for a game. "Why?"

"Oh . . . shit," he mutters. He glances over at Cay. "Man, don't do this. I swear I learned my lesson. You said you forgave me."

Meanwhile, Caleb just smiles, casually putting the Jeep in park. "I did. But sometimes we need a reminder before the lesson can really sink in."

Jake's eyes go wide. "What do I have to do to make this stop?"

"What am I missing?" I say, popping my head between the seats. "Why are you two being weird?"

Caleb smirks. "It's nothing, Hurricane. Jake here is just learning an important lesson in memorizing the days of the week."

On that cryptic note, both guys slip out of the Jeep, their doors slamming shut in unison. I have no choice but to follow after them.

Live music floats through the autumn beachy air. A crowd of people is spread out across the many umbrella-clad tables. There's a whole building of inside seating, but the charm of Rip's is the outdoor bar area. People can walk up right off the beach and order food and drinks. Surfers, families with sandy-faced kids, couples on an evening stroll.

Nestled in its own cabana near the bar is a covered stage. A band is all set up playing cover music. As we turn the corner, I freeze. The woman at the mic singing this particular rendition of Shania Twain's "That Don't Impress Me Much" is none other than the Rays' own Shelby O'Sullivan.

I gasp, eyes wide with excitement, as I snatch at Jake's arm. "Wait—is it karaoke night?"

He sighs, looking nothing like his usually perky self. "Yep. And it was nice knowing you, Seattle."

"What—"

I follow after him, my words cut off as the rest of the team notices us and hails us over. We make a huge show of cheering for Shelby as she finishes. Then she comes prancing back over to sit on Sully's lap.

The Rays have snagged a few tables together, and there's already a wide spread of salads, wings, fried pickles, and something I think might be gator tail bites. Jake and I settle down at the free end of Sully and Shelby's table, while Caleb goes to shake hands with Novy and Langley.

"Hey, Doc!" Shelby calls to me with a wave. "You look like you came straight from work."

"Yeah, I was stuck doing a training event downtown," I explain, snatching a fried pickle out of the basket. "The guys picked me up on the way over."

"That was nice of them," she says, glancing their way.

"Parking can be a pain," Jake mutters, helping himself to the pitcher of water. "Easier to take one car."

Whether she buys our lame excuse or not, she's quickly distracted by the arrival of Poppy and two more players.

"I better see the same turnout for our hospital benefit this weekend," Poppy calls to the boys with narrowed eyes as she takes her seat.

Damn, that's right. She hasn't been subtle with her repeated nudges that we're all expected to attend this fancy dinner and silent auction the day after we get back from Boston. These public relations events literally never end. I don't know how Poppy finds the energy to do so much. It would run me ragged.

Pretty soon, the Rays have taken over half of Rip's. The cover band is cranking out the tunes, as more people take their turn at the mic. Novy loses a coin toss with Langley and chooses to sing a terrible cover of a Backstreet Boys song. Then Poppy does a pretty great "Jolene" that has the whole bar whooping and cheering.

Glancing down the table at Jake, I see he's still brooding, both hands wrapped around his second beer. I slide over and nudge his shoulder. "What are you doing, angel?"

"Contemplating the consequences of my actions," he replies.

"What—"

"Hey, Hot Doc!" Langley calls from a table over. "You're gonna sing, right? Daughter of a rock'n'roll legend, you gotta get up there and sing!"

"Yeah, sing," Sully and Shelby cheer.

"Sing!"

"Oh no," I call, raising both hands. "The gene totally skipped me. Believe me, if I get up there and sing, you'll all need immediate medical attention."

Most of the group laughs.

Before Langley can reply, the guitarist takes the mic. He's a big guy, shaved head, maybe late forties. "Hey everyone, how y'all doin' tonight?" he calls into the mic.

The crowd hoots and clinks beer glasses.

"Welcome to Riptide's Bar & Grill," he says to more cheers. "If you hadn't noticed, this here is karaoke night at Rip's, and we're the Jacksonville 5," he adds, waving at the band. "We're gonna be up here playing for the next hour or so. The sign-up list is over at the end of the bar by Stacey—Stac, give the people a wave."

A pretty blonde behind the bar gives a big smile and wave, holding up a tablet.

"But first—" He shields his eyes with his hand. "I'm told we've got Caleb Sanford in the house tonight."

The Rays pound the tables.

"Yeah, Sanny!"

"Get it, Sanford!"

I go still, watching as even some of the regulars in the crowd go wild cheering for Caleb. Next to me, Jake groans.

"Sanford, come on up here," the guitarist calls. "Come hold this for me while I chat up the pretty redhead at the bar."

The bar crowd goes nuts as a lady in her mid-forties with red hair blushes. Meanwhile, our tables are still cheering for Caleb.

"Sanford! Sanford!"

"Get it Sanny!"

"Freebird!"

Caleb looks at me before leveling his eyes at Jake. Something is happening right now. The guys are in the middle of some contest. I can only assume it's about me. I can tell by Caleb's confidence and Jake's spanked puppy look that Cay is winning. Slowly, he gets up from the table and the whole crowd cheers again. He weaves between our tables, patting Jake's shoulder as he passes. Jake groans again.

Am I going to have to get in this middle of this?

"What's wrong with you?" I say, giving Jake another nudge.

"I'm learning my lesson," Jake replies. While the crowd is distracted, he turns to me, dropping his hand down to rest on my thigh. "Seattle, let's go. Let's get out of here."

"What?" I cry. "We can't just leave—"

"I will give you ten thousand dollars to leave with me right now," he presses.

I roll my eyes at him. "Can he even play the guitar?" I say, distracted as I watch Caleb climb the stage and shake the guitarist's hand before taking his guitar.

"Caleb Sanford, everybody!" the guitarist calls into the mic to more cheers.

Caleb tunes the guitar for a minute, his back turned to the crowd as he talks to the band. His dark coppery hair is messy and wind-blown from the Jeep. He's wearing a black t-shirt, ripped jeans, his bare feet dusted with sand. I can't help the little flutter in my stomach as I watch him step up to the mic. Oh yeah, this is working for Rachel.

He lowers his mouth to the mic, his voice deep as he says, "On behalf of the Jacksonville Rays, who are in the house tonight havin' a great time . . ."

Our guys all hoot and clap.

"I'd like to dedicate this next song . . . to the hottest doc in the NHL." Caleb looks right at me, and the Rays go wild.

"Yeah! Doc Price!"

"Hot Doc!"

"Don't hurt 'em, Doc!"

"Rachel Price," Caleb calls over the noise. "This one is for you."

My heart does a flip, and the Rays lose their minds as Caleb takes a deep breath and starts singing with no backup, both hands gently cradling the mic. I recognize the song instantly. The crowd screams as the band comes in. Caleb strums the guitar, the drummer pounds away, and they launch into an epically good cover of Måneskin's Beggin.

My mouth opens in shock, and I swear my pussy bursts into flames. His voice is so hot—gravelly and low, sinful even. And the boy can play. He works the guitar, moving his shoulders as he strums. He looks right at me, extending his hand as he sings.

Holy fuck. I teased him about this the other night, and it turns out my moody Sagittarius is a musician. We've been dancing around each other for days, trying to find a way past our volcanic physical connection towards something deeper. I want to *know* him. I want to see inside his walls, see behind his hurt. He's so much more than his trauma. He knows it too; he just doesn't know how to let me in.

Well, now he's on that stage using the lyrics to bare his soul. He wants me to stay. He wants me to keep trying to find him. I smile as he plays, using whatever mind power I possess to send him a clear message.

I'm not going anywhere.

My pulse hums as his fingers strum the guitar. He's so talented, standing up there looking like my perfect, broody, rocker boy fantasy. I know I laid down the law when it comes to PDA, but I swear to god, if this man drags me into the bar bathroom later, all laws will be broken.

45
RACHEL

"Oh my good gravy," Poppy gasps. "Rachel, you look stunning, girl!"

I smile, smoothing my hands down the front of my Chanel gown. It's a piece I've had for years and worn easily a dozen times. Champagne colored silk comes to two points, at my collarbones, with thin straps trailing over my shoulders and down the fully open back. The silk flows loose around my ankles, giving the dress beautiful movement. It's easily one of my favorite things I own.

"Thank you," I say with a smile. "You look gorgeous too."

And she really does. She's wearing a show-stopping red gown with a thigh slit that could stop traffic. Her makeup is darker tonight, edgier, and her hair is in a slicked back high pony. She looks sinful, all 5'2" of her.

I glance around the art museum gallery. "Everything looks beautiful, Poppy."

"Oh well," she says with a hurried wave. "I'm sure you've been to more than your fair share of these kinds of events."

I just smile, making no reply. I literally can't count the number of times I've attended a charity benefit. All I'm thinking about right now is how I'm starving, my feet hurt, and I forgot to pack my Spanx. Things were so hectic today that I did my hair and makeup in the ladies' restroom before driving straight here.

I'm dressed to impress, but I'm not the focus tonight. The players are the real draw. The attendees don't care about a plated salmon dinner or winning a silent auction trip to a winery. They just want to brush shoulders with two-time Stanley Cup winner Ilmari Kinnunen. They want to get up close and friendly with Canadian Olympian Head Coach Hodge Johnson.

Speaking of Kinnunen . . . I smirk as I spot him over in the corner, his huge frame bent over the silent auction table. He was my last patient of the day. We spent over an hour working on some hip strengthening exercises as part of his new PT regime.

I've learned to read him better over the past few weeks. For how easily he stands out in a crowd, he's a very subtle person. His movements are small, his opinions understated, his actions deliberate. It's as if his aura takes up so much space all on its own that he compensates by making the other pieces of himself smaller. I think I'd like to see Mars Kinnunen unleashed. What does he look like off the ice trying to dominate a situation?

Well, sweet heavens. Now I'm thinking about Mars Kinnunen dominating things.

Rein it in, psycho.

I blame the tuxedo. He looks hot enough to pour on pancakes. That tailored jacket fits him like a glove. Rachel approves.

Down, girl.

A few people stand behind him, whispering, watching him like a curious animal in an exhibit. People do that to him a lot. His size is certainly intimidating, and there's that fuck-all-the-way off aura. He's perhaps one of the least approachable people I've ever met.

So, of course, I waltz right up, snagging a bacon-wrapped shrimp skewer off a tray as I go. "Hey, Mars."

He turns to look at me, his blue eyes taking me in. "You look different," he mutters.

I snort, chewing on my shrimp. Is that a compliment? It's impossible to tell with his deadpan delivery. "Yeah, it's the concealer. Does me wonders, huh?"

"What?"

"Nothing," I reply, taking a glass of red wine from a waiter. "You bidding on something?"

He gestures wordlessly down at the paper.

I lean in a little closer, unable to avoid taking in a whiff of his intoxicating cologne. I hold my breath, reading the top of the paper. "I—Mars—what the hell is this?" I set my glass aside. "These items are up for auction. Do you understand? You're not guessing what you think the organization is worth. In this case, they're asking you to donate the amount of your bid to the organization. It's like a sponsorship."

"I know," he replies.

"You—" I gape at him, glancing back down at the paper. "Mars, you want to donate half a million dollars to a sea turtle conservation fund?"

"Yes." This is a joke, right? He's joking. His face says he's not joking. I don't think Mars Kinnunen knows how to make a joke.

"I—well, that's a big investment, Mars. Have you done any research into this organization?"

"Ms. St. James vetted them, yes?"

"Well, I—" My honest answer is yes. Poppy is ruthless. I'm sure all of these auction items have been thoroughly vetted. But that's not what's confusing me.

"I'm sorry—the other guys are over there eating their weight in free appetizers," I say, pointing to where Sully, Hanner, and J-Lo are all loading up tiny plates. "And you're just casually over here donating five hundred thousand dollars to sea turtle conservation?"

"Is that not the point of this evening?" he says.

"Well . . . yeah," I reply, snatching up my glass of wine. "But I mean, you could win the bid by donating like *five* thousand dollars."

"And how long do you think such a paltry amount will last the organization?" he counters. "Would it not be better to give them funds they can use to actually plan for the future?"

"Well . . . yeah," I say again, sounding like a total broken record.

"And if I am in a position to help this organization, should I not help them? I have the money, I'm willing to part with it, and I'm intrigued by the cause. Should I not donate?"

"Of course, you should," I say quickly. Weirdly, I think he's relieved to hear my answer. Does he care what I think about this? "Can I ask . . . why sea turtles?"

He just shrugs. "Why not sea turtles?"

"You could've picked anything." I wave my hand at the table. "A children's hospital, a burn center, an after-school sports program for underprivileged youth. And yet you picked to give the largest donation of the night to a bunch of sea turtles. Tell me why."

His gaze traces my features and I fight my blush. "You'll judge me for my answer," he says.

I go still. "I promise, I won't."

He shrugs again. "I make millions as a professional athlete. It comes at a cost that I will never pay."

"What do you mean?" I step in closer.

"I mean to say that I uphold an industry that thrives on the dec-imation of the environment. I spend a third of my life traveling and living as unsustainably as possible. I play in arenas that create moun-tains of waste. Every day. Every game. For the whole of my life, this has been my life. I do harm, Rachel. Active harm."

"Oh, Mars," I murmur. "So, you're donating to the sea turtles. You're protecting them . . . from you."

He nods. "This amount is utterly insignificant. But I've jotted down the name of the contact at the organization," he adds. "If I like their business model, I intend to become a patron. I will fund them in their entirety."

I sigh, shaking my head. *Of course.* Mars Kinnunen, ladies and gentlemen. Devastatingly handsome, rich, talented, environmentally conscious, and self-deprecating to a fault. Yeah, I'm gonna have to walk away now.

"Are you bidding on anything tonight?" he says as I turn away.

I huff a laugh, still trying to unscramble my brain. "Umm, well I was hoping to maybe bid on a yacht trip to the Caribbean or a month of free salsa dancing lessons."

Before he can reply, Poppy comes hurrying over. She may be the only staff member on the Rays besides me who is wholly unafraid of this man. "Mars, you can't hide in the corner all night, honey. We gotta get you mingling. Oh and, Rachel, can you track down the other fellas and corral them back this way?"

"Sure thing, Pop," I say with a smile, watching as she drags a re-luctant Mars away by the arm. She wastes no time introducing him to a group of silver haired ladies that all 'Ooo' at his approach.

I dart away before I'm the next one pulled in, ducking around the corner, moving deeper into the museum. I walk up behind Langley and Novy, each chowing down on appetizers.

"I'm telling you, it's art," Langley says.

"No way," Novy replies. "This is not art."

"It's hanging in an *art* museum, asshole."

I peek around them to see what they're looking at. It looks like a blank canvas. I smirk as I see that the plaque next to it actually reads 'Blank Canvas.'

"Hey, Doc," Langley says in greeting. "Whoa . . . you look really pretty."

I smile. I can't help myself. Langley is just so sweet and sincere. "Thank you, Langley. You look nice too." He totally does. All these guys are knockouts in their fancy duds.

Langley points at the art behind them. "Hey—is this art?"

I step closer, stealing a mini quiche off his plate. "Well, how does it make you feel?"

"Uhh . . . confused?" he says with a shrug.

"Bored," Novy adds.

"Like I'm a little out of my depth here," Langley adds, glancing around.

I laugh. "I think, at its heart, art is just supposed to make us feel something. It sounds like you're both feeling plenty."

"Whoa," Langley mutters, eyes wide as he looks back at the blank canvas. "Trippy."

"Hey, Poppy was looking for you," I say.

"What?" Novy huffs. "Me—why?"

I give him a curious look. "No . . . not *just* you, Nov. She wants all of you to stay in close. I'm supposed to be rounding you up. Any more of you back this way?" I add, glancing around.

"I think Compton wandered off," Langley replies, pointing towards an archway.

I walk in the direction Langley pointed. I was hoping to catch Jake here. Between karaoke night and the game day travel, we haven't really gotten a moment alone together. My heels click on the wooden floor as I walk through the modern art exhibit room into a room of more Neoclassical work.

My heart skips a beat as I see Jake. He holds a drink in one hand, the other in the pocket of his tux. He's gazing up at a large painting with a serious look on his face. He looks gorgeous—that dark hair sweeping over his brow. He should always wear a tuxedo. No more grey sweats, no more hockey uniform. Just all tux, all the time.

"Hey, angel," I say softly.

He glances at me quickly, then back to the painting, his frown deepening.

"What's wrong?"

"It's this horse."

I step next to him and gaze up at the painting. It's large, nestled in a gaudy gold frame. It depicts what is quite possibly the ugliest man I've ever seen riding what I have to assume is a horse. But the face looks possessed . . . and sort of squished.

"I feel like it's following me," he murmurs, swaying a bit. "When I move, the eyes move. It freaks me out."

I snort, stepping closer to the plaque to read. "Apparently the painting is called 'The Ugly Knight and His Uglier Horse'—well, that's not a very nice title," I add with a laugh. "Painted by Lord George Corbin in 1804."

"Well, Corbin sucked." Jake takes a sip of his drink.

I turn to face him. "Jake . . . are we gonna talk about it?"

"About what?"

I sigh. "Cay told me about your argument the other day."

"Yeah, well, he should keep his mouth shut," he mutters, swirling the ice in his glass.

I step forward, placing a gentle hand on his arm. "Hey, this isn't you. My Jake doesn't hide in the back of art galleries or pout his way through karaoke night. And my Jake looks at me when I talk to him," I murmur, giving his arm a squeeze. "He takes one look at me in a dress like this and tries to convince me to take it off."

The corner of his mouth twitches as his gaze darts to me.

"I can't have you two fighting," I say. "Not over me. Your friendship means too much to risk it. And you both mean too much for me to get in the middle—"

"We're fine," he says quickly. "It wasn't about you, really. I was the one being a jerk. I was pushing him. I've been all in my head 'cause I said some shit I didn't mean. I'm just . . . I get in my head about Cay. And sometimes I speak without thinking . . ."

"I know," I say gently, rubbing his forearm. "He forgives you."

He huffs. "Is that why he decided to show off at karaoke?"

"He's trying, Jake," I reply. "It's been just you in his heart for so long. Making room for me hasn't been easy. But he wants to," I add. "We can all feel it. You know what we have together is special, right? Not just between you and me but the three of us."

"Yeah," he murmurs, swirling his drink again. "Yeah, it's special."

He looks at me again, his gaze settling longer this time, roving me up and down. There's an appreciative twinkle growing there.

I smile, knowing him so well. "Is that what you need? You need a little physical reassurance? Want me to take you into the stairwell and blow you?"

"Don't tease me," he says, taking a sip of his drink.

"Who's teasing?" I reply. "You're *mine*, Jake. Mine to care for, mine to love. Right now, you're upset. And I intend to make it better. I feel like I haven't seen you in days."

"I know," he sighs. "How is it possible to miss you when you're standing right in front of me? But I do. I miss you, baby. I can't stop. I feel like we still have this distance and I fucking hate it."

"Well, then close it."

"Close what?"

"The distance."

He frowns, gesturing around. "We're in public, Rachel. No public displays of affection, remember?"

"I hate when you guys call me that," I murmur.

"What—your name?"

"I don't want to be Rachel in your eyes." I step closer. "I want to be your Seattle Girl," I say, brushing my fingers down the fabric of his lapel. "Your baby girl . . . yours."

He sighs, closing his eyes. "I'm barely holding on here."

"Then let go," I whisper. "Jake, just let go."

He opens his eyes, his gaze molten.

"I want you, Jake," I say on a breath. "I need you. Find me again. Please, come find me—"

He silences me with a kiss, his free hand pulling me closer. I open to him, my head tipping back as I taste the alcohol on his tongue. In moments, he's breaking away with a groan.

"Fuck, I can't do this here," he mutters, his lips brushing against my temple.

"Why? What's wrong?"

"It's . . . I feel like the horse is watching me," he admits, glancing back up to the painting.

With a laugh, I grab his free hand. "Come on."

"What are you doing?" he says, following after me.

My heels click across the floor as I pull him into the stairwell, letting the door shut behind us with a clang. There's no way to secure it, so we'll just have to risk it. "Cay said your game was to try and break my PDA ban," I say, taking his drink from his hand and setting it down on the steps with mine.

"Yeah, listen—I'm sorry, Seattle. I was being a competitive jerk. This is all new to me, and I was worried about what I said to Cay, and missing you, and I was being an asshole—"

I step forward, placing my fingers against his lips. "I'm breaking my ban," I declare. "If I don't have you right fucking now, I'm gonna scream. So, you just tell me what the point system is, and I'll make sure you leave this stairwell winning. Agreed?"

He smirks down at me. "What did you do with Cay in the bathroom of Rip's? Don't think I didn't notice you both disappear for fifteen minutes."

I smile back at him, unashamed. That was a fun night. "He ate me out on the sink," I reply, my body responding as Jake stares me down, his hands stroking my hips. "And then I sucked him off."

His brows lower as he does the math. "So . . . I think that's twenty points. Ten points for each mouth action."

I gaze up at him. "Okay, well you've got exactly three minutes to claim the top score. What are we doing here, angel?"

He presses me back against the wall by the door. "For fifty points, I'm gonna rail you hard and fast," he breathes, his lips brushing mine. "Your sweet pussy is gonna come all over my dick. And then we're gonna walk back out to that boring party with me dripping down your thighs."

Oh yeah, this is my Jake. Back in the game. *Finally*.

"Do you worst," I tease. "Just cover my mouth when I scream."

He growls, his hands dropping to his pants. "Take your undies off and slip them in my pocket. Every time I look at you tonight, you're gonna squeeze those thighs, understood?"

I fist the skirt of my gown with both hands, hiking it up. "Too bad for you, angel. I'm not wearing underwear."

He goes still, one hand on his dick. With a groan, he steps in, cupping my face with his free hand. "You are my every fucking dream."

"I know," I say with a smile, my hand wrapping around his on his dick. "Now get inside me."

"BABE."

Someone is jostling me. Is it in my dream? No—wait—am I dreaming? "Baby, wake up."

I shift with a sleepy groan and blink my eyes open, trying to orient myself. I'm lying naked in the world's most comfortable bed. Jake is here, his hand nudging my shoulder. He brushes my hair back from my face and kisses my brow.

"Babe, look. He's here. I didn't want you to miss it." The tone in his voice is so bright and eager. He jostles me fully awake as he slips off the side of the bed.

God, what time is it? Last night we stumbled home from the benefit to find Caleb crashed out with the dog on the couch. We all but fell into his bed and went straight to sleep. I'm not even sure I took my contacts out.

His room looks so different in the daylight. The room is bathed in beachy white light. I watch, lips pursed, as a very naked Jake tiptoes over to the wall of glass with his phone in hand. The glass has a door inset into it, which leads out to a balcony.

Jake glances over his shoulder at me, grinning like a little kid, then points out through the glass. There, sitting on the deck railing, is a massive pelican. The thing is so ugly, it's cute, with drab brown feathers and beady eyes. Jake raises his phone, his bare butt mooning me as he snaps pictures.

Watching him, I'm overcome with a wave of such emotion that it literally takes my breath away. I swallow, tears in my eyes. "Hey," I call softly.

"Hmm?" he says, eyes on his phone.

"I love you."

"What?" he squawks, spinning around. The combination of his movement and his voice must scare the pelican because it flaps away. "Oh—shit—" He spins back to watch it fly off. "Man, he's never come that close before."

I snort, my heart overflowing as I watch my sweet angel pout over his pelican playing hard to get.

"Wait—what the hell did you just say?" He crosses the room, tossing his phone down on the end of the bed.

"You heard me," I reply, fully aware that the sheets are pooled at my waist and my bare breasts are on display.

He crawls up the bed. "I'm gonna need you to say it again."

I go to squirm away, but it's hopeless. He pounces on top of me, pinning me down under the sheets.

"Say it," he growls, burying his face at my neck as he breathes me in.

I run my hands down his back, giving both his booty cheeks a playful slap.

He clenches, his face buried between my breasts. "Come on, Seattle. *Please*, say it again? Say it, or I'll climb the railing and jump off."

I dig my fingers into his hair and pull his head back until I catch his gaze. "I love you, Jake."

He pops up on his elbows with a smile that could power the whole city. "Baby, I am so fucking in love with you. I swear to god, you're it for me. I love you more than I love sushi. More than I love coffee."

"More than you love hockey?" I tease, laying back as he peppers my breasts with kisses. His morning stubble feels rough on my skin, but I don't care.

"Fuck—would you accept the truth that I don't wanna pick? I want both. I want a hockey and Rachel sandwich every day for the rest of forever."

I laugh. "Fair enough." I arch back with a contented sigh as he latches onto my peaked nipple, giving it a little suck.

He's barely started teasing me before he stops. "Come on, babe. Today is cheat day, and I'm starving. Your stomach is growling too."

I fight the urge to pout. I was about to have a very fortifying meal. A 6'3" professional hockey player was on the menu . . . hopefully with a side of equipment manager. "What did you have in mind?"

"We're gonna go find the biggest, most ridiculous stack of banana pancakes and order a whole tower of bacon on the side. And coffee," he adds, rolling off me. "Lots and lots of coffee."

I laugh, stretching out like a lazy house cat. "Make them bananas foster pancakes, and I'm in."

He launches off the bed. "Awesome. Get ready. I'll go tell Cay!"

46
RACHEL

Game night. Jacksonville Rays versus the Pittsburgh Penguins. Puck drops in twenty minutes and shit just keeps hitting the fan. First, Walsh tripped on a poorly placed electrical cord heading out to practice and busted his knee. The damn thing is still swelling. I've got him nursing an ice pack in the locker room.

Meanwhile, J-Lo has some kind of stomach bug. He's been puking his guts out for the last hour. And now Karlsson is worried he overextended his finger. Not to mention these guys are all a bunch of raccoons who like to raid the medical bags. All my athletic tape is missing.

"Hey—Avery," I say, catching him in the hall. "Do you have any athletic tape?"

He huffs, brushing past me. "It's not my job to chase after you, holding your first aid kit, Price. I've got my own job to do."

"I'm not asking you to follow me around, Avery. I just need some tape—"

He spins around, getting up in my face. I hate that my natural reaction is to flinch away. He sees it and smirks. "Listen, Princess. I don't know whose dick you sucked to win your fellowship, and frankly I don't care. But I'm not gonna let your constant incompetence affect the way I run my PT program. Do your job, or I'll find someone else who will." With that he stomps away.

I'm so shocked, I can't even muster a reply. Did Avery really just accuse me of performing sexual favors to win my fellowship? Over the past several weeks, I've given that asshole every chance to prove he's not a sexist pig. But now I'm done. I am so *fucking* done. He comes at me again, I'm going there. Full spider monkey.

Rushing to the end of the hall, I'm fuming as I dive into the backup medical bag. I'm so frustrated with Avery. And I'm starving. And I have to pee.

"Hey, Hurricane."

I glance over my shoulder to see Caleb standing there with a box of blades in his hands.

"You're looking extra twisty today," he says. Clearly, he can read the 'fuck off' sign I've got hanging around my neck.

"Either help me or get lost, Cay," I say, digging through the bag.

"Ooo, twisty *and* salty. Like a sexy, mean pretzel," he teases. "My favorite kind."

"God *damn* it," I snap, zipping the bag shut. "Where the hell is all the athletic tape?"

He huffs a laugh. "The guys stealing your stuff?"

I brush my hair back off my face. "It's nothing I can't handle." As I say it, I know I'm thinking more about Avery than the missing tape.

His dark eyes narrow at me. "When's the last time you had something to drink? Or eat? You're looking feral—"

"I'm fine," I snap.

Now he's smirking, and it makes me want to nut punch him. "You're hangry."

"I'm not hangry, Cay. I'm just busy. I'm *working*. And all you guys are making it freaking impossible today!" I take a shaky breath, glancing around. "I gotta go hunt down some tape," I mutter. Apparently, I'll pee when I'm dead.

I move to brush past him, but he sticks out his hand. "Whoa, whoa. Hold on there, killer. Where are you going?"

"I'm going to find an EMT, and I'll ask to raid their bag—"

"Nope. Come on," he says, pulling me down the hall.

"Caleb, let go," I huff. "I know how to do my damn job. Are *you* a doctor?"

"Nope," He hands off his box of blades to Jerry as we pass him. "But I was a hockey player for twenty years, and now I'm the equipment manager on an NHL team. Do you know what that means, Hurricane?"

"What?" I say with a sigh, letting him lead me towards the locker room.

"It means I manage equipment," he says with a wink.

He pulls me into the busy locker room. Rock music is blasting as the guys get themselves pumped up for the game. The room is

crowded and noisy and buzzing with excitement. Jake sees us immediately and flashes us a smile.

"Novy, cut the music!" Caleb shouts.

Novikov snatches up his phone and the volume of the rock music
cuts in half.

"What's up, Sanny?" one of the guys calls.

"Whoa, Hot Doc in the lock!" another shouts, and then the room
is full of hoots and hollers.

I roll my eyes. It's so close to game time that they're all wearing
layers of moisture-wicking undershirts, jocks, kneepads, hockey shorts,
socks, chest protectors, jerseys. The only peep show I'm getting is their
fingers—and even some of those are already stuffed into gloves.

"What's up, Doc?" Sully calls, which makes half the guys burst
into more laughter.

Caleb snatches up a plastic box and calls out, "Alright, everyone
pay up! Give the Doc back her athletic tape. *Now.*"

Grumbles and groans filter around the room as the guys shift.

"Do it, or I won't wash your practice towels for a week," he barks.
"Things are about to get really musty up in here, fellas!"

As one, the room moves, the guys digging in their bags or reaching
on their shelves to grab their athletic tape. Caleb does a circuit of the
room, letting the stolen tape rattle into the plastic bin. I shake my head,
lips pursed in annoyance, as even Jake shrugs and tosses a roll of tape
in. It seems the only one who *didn't* steal from my bag is Ilmari.

Caleb brings me the bin with a smirk. "And that's how it's done.
Got anything to add, Doc?"

I glance at him, and he gestures with his eyes over his shoulder at
the crowded locker room.

Oh, right. Establish dominance. Hockey boys follow strong leadership.

Clearing my throat, I snatch the bin from Caleb. "Right, so listen
up! The next guy who steals from my medical bag is gonna get a courtesy tape job. Teddy here is gonna mummify your cash and prizes with
any tape you steal," I say, jerking my thumb at the wide-eyed intern.
"Your girls can have fun helping you rip it off after the game!"

The guys go wild, laughing and ribbing Teddy, whose cheeks
promptly turns an adorable shade of salmon pink.

Caleb grins, wrapping an arm around my shoulder. "Come on,

Hurricane. Lemme show you something." He leads me out of the locker room and across the hall into equipment manager HQ. "This is a secret, okay? You tell any of the guys, and we'll get a load of trash pandas in here stealing from us too."

I raise a brow. "Not even Jake?"

"Especially not that asshole. I'd never get him out of here." He points out a small black box labeled FIGURE SKATES.

I give him a scathing look but he just grins.

"Open it."

I pop off the lid and gasp with delight. It's packed full of snacks, and none of it is dietician approved: chocolate-dipped granola bars, teriyaki jerky sticks, candy bars, oatmeal pies. I'm legit about to cry. "Ohmygod."

"Go crazy," Caleb says, giving my shoulder a squeeze. "See you out there."

WE'RE four minutes from the end of the second period and I've already dealt with a bleeding lip, and two gruesome body checks that took the guys down to the ice. They're both okay, but they'll be feeling it in the morning.

My eye can't help but follow Jake as he darts up and down that ice. He's a machine, working the puck out of the Rays' defensive zone and shooting it down the ice. He's been on the line with Novy a lot and they seem to work well together. Each time his shift is over, he sprints to the bench, barreling over the boards to rest and rehydrate.

I may as well be invisible to him right now, and I don't mind. I love watching him in his element. His intensity is magnetic. He's just so beautiful inside and out—

"No, *no*—cover him!" Jake yells, launching to his feet.

Oh shit. The Penguins are working the puck in front of the net. Ilmari drops down, pads flat against the ice. He's sliding left and right as the players fight in front of him.

"Get it out!"

"Get the puck out!"

The whole bench is shouting as the Rays fight to get control of the puck. It's madness. Snow is spraying in Ilmari's face.

Shot on goal.

It hits Ilmari's knee pad and ricochets off, but the Penguins rebound. "Come oooon!"

Heart in my throat, I watch as Ilmari and the defense fight it out. The Penguins are feral. They want this goal and they're ready to bleed for it.

"Get it out of the slot!"

The bench is going nuts and so is the crowd. The whole arena is on its feet, screaming for the Penguins to make this goal. Jake and Novy both already have one leg over the boards, ready to leap back into play, but they have to wait for this dogfight to end. Morrow and Hanner are on their own. It's pandemonium.

All the while, I only see Ilmari. He's in full butterfly, guarding his net with everything he's got. Playing the game means everything to him. But what will be the ultimate cost?

I swallow, heart racing as he gets a reprieve. The Rays worked the puck away from the net. No goal. The Penguins fans are screaming their outrage, booing as the puck moves down ice.

Morrow and Hanner race to the bench as Jake and Novy go flying off to join the fray. Morrow promptly puts his head between his knees and throws up. It's nothing but electrolyte water. He'll recover and be demanding to get back on the ice when Jake's shift is over.

I take a breath, turning my focus back to Ilmari. He clambers up to his skates and a zing of knowing rattles me to my core. He's not okay.

"Get him off the ice," I whisper, knowing no one can hear me.

The crowd is going crazy. They wanted a goal before intermission.

My gaze darts up to the jumbotron. Less than a minute left. But the Penguins have the puck, and they're racing down the ice. Ilmari gets into his stance.

The Rays catch up, and it's a tussle in the slot to clear the puck. Ilmari darts left, following the forward, but then the winger shoots the puck through Jake's legs to the guy waiting on the other side.

Shot on goal.

Buzzer.

Ilmari is too far left. The puck sails into the unguarded corner of the net and the cherry lights up, siren wailing, as the whole arena erupts with boisterous cheers.

The period is over, and the Rays are officially down 0-1. The players all clear the bench for intermission, their spirits shaken. I wait, watching as No. 31 collects his water bottle and ambles across the ice, pushing with only his left skate.

He lifts his mask up as he skates closer, and I see the simmering anger on his face. At himself. At his defense. Goalies can get deep in their own heads, taking each goal so personally.

Tomlin flips the door open for him to step through. "Alright, it's alright," he says, patting him on the padded shoulder. "You were working the rebounds. We just gotta get the defense to clear the puck better and there's still a whole third period—"

Tomlin keeps rambling, but Ilmari isn't listening. He's too deep in his head. The jumbotron could drop from the rafters and he wouldn't flinch. Tomlin slips in front of him, leading the way back towards the locker room.

"Hey!" I call out, rushing to Ilmari's side. I put my hand on his arm.

He spins around, nearly whacking me in the face with the end of his stick. He's pouring sweat, his pupils blown black.

"Oh . . ." I whisper. It's worse than I thought. "Ilmari—"

"I'm fine," he mutters, jerking away and stomping off.

"Don't walk away from me!" I shout, chasing after him. "Mars!"

He ducks around the corner into the tunnel, under the halo of jeering Penguins fans and the few diehard Rays fans. They call out his name. He ignores them all.

I race after him, grabbing for his arm again as soon as we're under the cover of darkness. The sounds of the arena echo behind us, but we're alone in this narrow hallway, suspended in the dark between the rink and the locker room. Gear litters either side of us—row after row of colorful sticks, water bottles.

"Hey—hold on. Talk to me!"

He's massive in his full kit. The skates add inches he doesn't need, so he absolutely towers over me. The broad shoulders, the padded hockey shorts, the huge leg blockers. The only piece of him I can see inside his thick armor is his face and even that is now cast in deep shadow.

I step in closer, one hand on his blocker. "What's your pain level?"

"Six," he mutters.

"And if you're not trying to put on a brave face for me so you can stay on that ice? What is it then?"

He jerks his blocker free but doesn't move away. "Eight."

"Oh, Mars . . . let me help you," I plead.

"You are helping me."

"No, let me *really* help you. Let me get you scans—"

"No."

"We can't keep doing this! I need to know what's wrong. And I have an idea—"

"I said *no*," he growls.

I take a breath. He's in fight mode. Well, I'm a fighter too. I pop my hands on my hips and lift my chin. "Well, I'm saying *yes*."

He scoffs, turning away.

"Walk away from me, Kinnunen, and just see what happens."

He stomps forward, crowding me. "Are you threatening me, Doctor Price?"

"You're damn right I am," I growl right back. "I don't think you understand the position you're in here, Mars. You're skating around like *you* call the shots. But *I'm* in charge," I say, jabbing a thumb at my chest. "Did you forget that I sign your medical release forms? The FIHA wants your records, Mars. *I'm* the one that gets to fax them over. What I write on those forms depends on you. So, do you have a labral tear that will require emergent surgery, benching you for the rest of the season? Or do you have a mild groin pull and you're sitting out for two weeks as a simple precaution?"

"You can't bench me. I have to play—"

"No, you idiot. You have to *live*," I cry, fisting his jersey with both hands. "You may look like a hockey Thor, but you're not a god, Ilmari. You're flesh and blood and you're grinding yourself into that ice. And I won't allow it."

"What does that mean?" he growls.

I hold his gaze, letting the hammer fall. "It means you're done. You're benched, Mars—"

"No!"

"For the rest of this game *and* your Tuesday game at a bare minimum," I add.

"Saatana," he curses, punching the concrete wall. I doubt he feels it through the blocker. "I trusted you. I came to you for help."

"And this *is* me helping," I counter, not giving him a single inch.

"You said you would keep me on the ice—"

"I said I would try," I correct. "You get to think about the game first. Every single person in this arena right now is thinking about the damn game. I'm thinking about *you*—"

The words are barely out of my mouth when he slings his massive, padded arm around my shoulders, pulling me against him. He crouches down in one swoop, pressing me closer, and then he's kissing me. The stubble of his beard tickles my mouth. He tastes like salt and sweat, and something sweetly spiced, honey and menthol.

Oh, holy fuck—I'm kissing him back.

Yep, my lips are definitely moving. I'm tasting him. My fingers are clutching to his jersey. One minute we were standing in the dark, shouting at each other, and now we're kissing. I gasp, slapping at his pads as I tilt my head back, breaking our kiss. He lets me go and I dart back a step. "What the fuck was that?"

He's panting too, eyes locked on me.

I feel like the stupid fox who wanders into a sleeping bear's den.

Don't poke the bear, Rachel. Don't poke the desperately attractive, sexual magnet of a man-bear.

"I'm sorry," he mutters.

I let out a shaky breath, my fingers brushing over my lips. "Do that again, and my official medical opinion will lean towards amputation . . . and castration," I add with a level glare.

He closes his mouth, jaw clenched tight, and gives me a curt nod.

"We're doing this *my* way, Mars. No games. No practice. We're going to get scans, and we're going to get answers. And I promise I will do everything in my power to have you back on the ice in time for the Olympic scouts."

He shakes his head.

"Hey, I made a promise, and I'm keeping it," I say. "I will protect you, Ilmari. Even if that means I'm protecting you from yourself. Hate me if you want, but I'm putting you first. You're done with this game."

Not giving him a chance to contradict me—or throw me up against the wall and kiss me breathless again—I slip past him and head straight for the locker room. The coaches aren't going to like it either, but I've made my decision.

47
JAKE

We lost. 1-4. I shouldn't be surprised. Mars was benched at intermission, leaving us with Davidson in the net. He's not bad, but he's no Kinnunen. J-Lo was back in the locker room puking his guts out all game. And Karlsson was out with a finger sprain. *Seriously*. A fucking finger sprain. In junior league, I played a whole tourney with two broken fingers and didn't complain.

Not to mention Novy got a bullshit charging penalty at the beginning of the third that put him in the box for five fucking minutes. The Penguins scored on us twice while he was in there.

I shouldn't be making such a big deal about this. I've lost plenty of games before. And the Rays will lose again. I just hate fucking losing. Oddly, I think it makes the team feel more real to me. It makes what we're fighting for feel more real too.

We've got to start playing better as a team. We're leaving too much weight on the goalies' shoulders. Mars is one of the best in the League, and we ran him ragged. He's on the bench right now because we couldn't stop the puck from coming to his front door. We couldn't protect him.

I blame myself. I'm a D-man, I can't help it. And whatever, maybe I've got some baggage about guys getting hurt on my watch. I try not to think about it. You can't let the losses get to you. We play so many games that you have to be able to shrug it off and move on. If you carry that shit, you could ruin tomorrow's game.

I groan, shifting the ice pack off my knee as my phone timer goes off. That's twenty minutes. Time to switch knees. Fuck, I'm getting old. Pretty soon I'll be cruising the fiber supplement aisle looking for sales and asking Cay to pick me up some denture cream.

I sit up, moving my ice pack over to my other knee, when there's a soft knock at the door. I tap the screen of my phone. No missed messages. Usually, the guys text ahead before they come to your room. We've all learned too many hard lessons about puck bunny stalking. And I didn't order any room service . . .

Tap. Tap. Tap.

"Jake, open up," comes Caleb's voice.

I toss the ice pack aside and swing my legs off the bed, hurrying barefoot over to the door. I undo the chain and lock and swing it open to find both Caleb and Rachel standing in the hallway. He's wearing a grey sweatsuit with the zipper only half-zipped, his chest bare underneath. His hair is still wet at the nape. He must have just returned from the arena.

My gaze drops to Rachel. She's balancing a bright pink box in her hands with a bag slung over her shoulder. She's wearing a pair of black yoga pants and a grey half-zip to match Caleb. Her hair is up in a messy bun, and she put her septum ring back in.

"Let us in. We have contraband," she says with a wide grin.

I step back in an instant, holding the door open. I lock it behind them as they make themselves at home. Caleb unzips his hoodie and tosses it on top of my suitcase. Then he flips off his sandals and flops down onto the bed with a groan.

"You said you have contraband?" I say, moving over to Rachel and wrapping her in my arms. God, it's like just seeing them again has my serotonin kicking in. I already feel more relaxed. I'm happier. I nuzzle my face in her hair, breathing her in.

She laughs softly, tilting her neck to let me kiss her pulse point. I brush my fingers over it, then my lips. She knows I like kissing her here. I like the mingling scents of her shampoo and perfume. Fuck if it doesn't make my dick twitch. I haven't had her in two days because of our game and travel schedule. Not since the night of the gala. My fatigue is quickly ebbing away, replaced with interest.

She flips open her bag. "First things first. And this was all Cay's idea," she adds. "He said it's your favorite." She pulls out the nectar of the gods: an icy cold bottle of chocolate milk.

I gasp, snatching it from her hand. I don't technically get another cheat day until Sunday, but I will literally murder the person who tries to take this from me. I have the cap off in seconds, taking a long swig. Fuck, it's so delicious I could cry.

"And these were my idea," she goes on, picking up the pink box and popping the lid.

Nestled inside is an assortment of six different cookie sandwiches stuffed with frosting. One is rolled in chocolate chips. I smirk. Chocolate chips are like heroin to Caleb. If I touch that one, I'm getting my hand chewed off. Another is dusted in rainbow sprinkles.

"Oh, fuck yeah," I murmur, pulling out the rainbow sprinkle one.

"Cay, you said you wanted the chocolate chip one, right?" she calls.

"Yes," we say at the same time.

I roll my eyes as Caleb sits up to claim his double-stuffed chocolate chip cookie sandwich.

"How about you give me a swig," he says, nodding at my chocolate milk.

"How about you go die," I reply, draining it in two more gulps. I crunch the bottle and toss it into the trashcan.

Rachel fishes out a cookie for herself. "How are the knees tonight? Did you ice them?"

"Rough," I reply, my mouth full of soft cookie and enough buttercream frosting to cover a cake. "Don't think I don't know what you're doing," I add, picking a sprinkle off my chin.

She raises a dark brow at me, daring to look all innocent. "Oh, yeah? What's that, angel?"

"I know pity food when I see it, guys." I stuff the rest of my cookie in my mouth. "I'd get petulant about it, but these cookies are orgasmic," I add, licking my fingers clean of frosting.

Rachel watches me, her own cookie ignored in her hand.

"What?"

"Hmm? Oh, nothing," she replies, setting her cookie back in the box. "I just had something else for you. But seeing as you've got sore knees, and you just orgasmed over your cookie, I doubt you'll be very interested."

I perk up. "What? No, I'm interested. What else did you bring me?"

Over on the bed, Caleb chuckles. "I don't know if he can handle it, Hurricane."

My gaze darts between them. "What is it? Tell me. It's not fair if he knows and I don't."

Rachel shrugs. "Alright. Just know you asked for this." She reaches inside her shoulder bag and pulls something out. Turning slowly, she shows it to me.

Be still my kinky fucking heart.

My girl is standing in my hotel room holding a massive purple dildo shaped like a squid tentacle.

48
JAKE

My mouth falls open as I stare at the massive toy in Rachel's hands. It's easily like a foot long. It's tapered at one end, getting bigger at the base. We're talking Pringles can. Shit, if she sat on that thing, it would tickle her damn tonsils.

"Are you fucking serious right now?" I say, my gaze darting between her and Caleb.

She's still grinning. "You too tired to play, angel? You can always watch."

I sweep forward, cupping her face, and kiss her senseless. I've needed my girl like I need air. The travel and the weird schedule are the worst part about hockey life. I just want to be in my bed every night, with her warm pussy making a nice home for my dick.

She shifts between us, dropping the squid cock onto the desk, her hands going back to fist my shirt. She pulls it off over my head, her hands going to my chest, smoothing over my muscles.

"Cay, come here," I call.

She smiles up at me, her dark gaze warm and sensual. I love the pout of her lips. I brush over it with my thumb as Cay slips off the bed and steps around behind her.

"What's the game plan here, baby girl?" I say brushing the loose tendrils back from her face.

She turns her face into my hand and kisses my palm. "I have some ideas."

"Wanna share with the team?"

She reaches behind herself for Caleb's hands, pulling him closer as she places his hands around her, helping his fingers find the zipper of her hoodie. Her hands go back to my chest as he unzips her.

I look down to see her sports bra has a front zip too. "One more, Cay."

His hands drift back up, finding the zipper, pulling it down. He pops the two pieces of zipper free, and the stretchy fabric gives, Rachel's bare breasts dropping with their natural weight.

"Fuck, they're so perfect," I mutter as I cup one. I love their size, their fullness, the dark pink of her sensitive nipples.

She arches into my hand, smiling and tipping her head back as Caleb sheds her of both pieces of clothing, her topless tatted skin on full display.

"What do you want?" I say again.

Her gaze is hooded with lust. "I want you," she replies. "Jake, I have to have you." Her hands trail down my chest, fingertips brushing my abs, as she lands on the waist of my shorts.

My cock is so hard already. I'm a mess for this girl. For Cay too. I want him here. The idea of sharing her, of having two cocks to drive her wild, it just does something to me. It's blowing my mind, because outside of sharing her with Cay, I feel feral at the idea of another man even looking twice at her. But Caleb coming in her mouth while I fuck her pussy? Apparently, that gets me harder than steel every time.

She slips my shorts down my hips, letting my dick spring free. Her hand is ready to wrap around it, her skin soft as she gives me a stroke that has me groaning. I watch as Caleb steps into her, brushing her hair aside to kiss her neck in the same place I like.

"Get on your knees, Hurricane," he murmurs in her ear. "Show him how much you like his pretty boy cock," he adds with a wink at me.

Oh shit, how do I always almost forget what he's packing in his pants? I still can't believe he did that. Perks of not being a pro player who has to stuff his dick into a jock six days a week. Is it a perk? I'm still undecided. And Rachel is cagey as fuck about it.

She smiles up at me, as if she's waiting for my consent.

My heart is in my throat. Everything feels more sensitive with Caleb here to watch. I nod and she sinks against me with a satisfied little sound. She takes her time, kissing down my chest, my cock still in her hand. Then she drops to her knees between us and looks up at me. Damn, and she accuses *me* of having fuck-me eyes.

She leans in letting her warm breath fan over my tip. It has me twitching in her hand. Then she gives it a teasing lick. Slowly, she parts those bowed lips and takes just the tip, swirling it with her warm tongue until I'm groaning.

"Cay," she murmurs, glancing over her shoulder at him.

They've come a long way in these past weeks. As if he just knows what she wants, he steps in, digging his hands into her hair. She relaxes into his hold and opens her mouth, letting his touch guide her back onto my dick.

Oh, fuck.

My hands drop to her shoulders, while Cay keeps his hands on her head.

"That's it," he croons, moving her mouth further onto my dick. "Relax your throat and take him all the way in. Feel him deep. Such a good girl. Suck him harder."

"Fuck, you can't dirty talk or I'm not gonna last," I pant, already feeling that spiraling sensation growing tighter.

Rachel sucks on me, her talented tongue working my tip as Caleb moves her.

"Baby, I'm gonna—*shit*—" I hiss, pushing her shoulders until she's off me. My breathing is ragged after a two-minute blowjob? Yeah, I'm officially a mess. I pull her up standing and jerk her leggings down, helping her shimmy out of them. "Time to show us your toy, baby girl. Get on that bed and spread your legs for us."

She tips up on her toes and kisses me, her tongue flicking my bottom lip, before she's turning, her hand smoothing down Caleb's chest as she kisses him too. "You gonna join the party, devil?" she asks him. Then she slips from between us and saunters over to the bed.

I watch, heart in my throat, as she crawls onto the bed, flashing us that round ass. "Does her magic bag have any lube?"

Cay snatches up the toy and hands it to me as he shoves his hand in her bag.

"I'm waiting," she calls.

Both our gazes dart back over to her. Rachel is perched up on her elbows, knees bent. With our gazes on her, she holds that soft smile and drops her legs open, exposing her glistening pussy.

"Oh, fuck that," I growl, tossing the toy back to Caleb. I cross the room and dive onto the bed, burying my face in her cunt.

She cries out, her thighs locking around my head until she relaxes, letting herself fall open. Then I straight up devour her. Apparently, not all guys like the taste of pussy. A lot of locker room talk makes it seem like this is a chore. Fuck, I would live on my knees for a good pussy. And Rachel tastes so fucking good. Sweet and feminine. I want to roll her over. I want her straddling my face. I want to drown.

But then the mattress sinks, and Caleb is crawling up the bed next to me, tossing the dildo and a bottle of lube onto the comforter. I've got two fingers inside her, stretching her out, feeling her inner wall for that spot that'll make her toes curl. She's arching into my touch, her eyes open as she takes us both in.

"Taste her, Cay," I say, scooting back. "Taste our girl."

With a hungry groan, he drops down to his elbow, wedging himself in next to me as he closes his mouth around her pussy.

"Oh—" She arches into him.

With his left hand, he takes two fingers and opens her, exposing her clit. She shivers under his touch, one arm going up over her eyes. "Spit on her clit," he orders. "Get her wet."

She moans at his words.

I lean forward on my elbows and spit, letting it drip down onto her glistening clit. With a satisfied grunt, Caleb rubs it in. I watch him take my saliva and bring her to the edge. It's captivating. While his fingers still massage her clit, I lean forward and spit again, watching it run between his fingers and drip down onto her pussy. I don't even have to touch her. I'm gonna lose it just watching.

"Fuck," he mutters, dropping his mouth to taste it, sucking on her clit slicked with my spit until she's practically grinding against his mouth. Then he pops off. "Jake, make her come while I lube up the toy."

He doesn't have to tell me fucking twice. I shift her over, burying my face back in that sweet cunt, spearing my tongue inside her.

"Oh, Jake—"

Her hand grips my hair as she works my head, her hips grinding against my chin. And just like that, I'm within an inch of blowing my load again. God, this is the best kind of torture. I shift my weight and shove three fingers inside her, curling them along her inner wall. I move my mouth up to her clit and suck hard. I'm making obscene noises, but I don't care, because in moments my girl is shattering, her cunt strangling my fingers as she orgasms.

There's nothing better than this feeling. This exact moment right here, feeling her free fall against my mouth. The female orgasm is a beautiful thing. I like to earn it. It's the sportsman in me. I want to learn Rachel's rules and play to win.

Score one, Jake Compton.

She's breathless, one hand on her heart as she recovers.

"We're just getting started, Hurricane," Caleb teases. "I've been wanting to do this since the day we met," he says, holding up the massive squid dildo. He flicks something on the bottom and suddenly the toy is alive, buzzing and wiggling in his hand.

My dick twitches with interest, and he and I share a wicked grin.

Oh, this is going to be so much fun.

49
CALEB

The tentacle dildo vibrates in my hand as the top moves in a swirling motion. I lower my gaze to Rachel. "Do you have a favorite setting?"

She looks like a depraved queen of heartbreak, lying spread-eagle on the bed for us, the shine of her first orgasm still glowing in her eyes. She blows a puff of air to move the tendrils of her dark hair off her forehead. "Number three," she admits, giving me a knowing smile.

"At the airport she told me she'd never used it," I explain to Jake. "But later that night, as she climbed our balconies like a lemur, she told me she lied." I glance back at her. "So, what's gonna happen when I press the button two more times? What sound does it make?"

She purses her lips, holding my gaze. I know I'm being an ass, but I don't care. I want her to tell me everything she likes about this toy. "It's a high buzz," she replies. "And the tip doesn't swirl, it sorta goes back and forth."

"There she is," I murmur with a smile. I press the button twice more and, true to her description, the tentacle is now buzzing on high, and the tip has gone from hula-hooping to zigzagging.

"Oh shit," Jake mutters, his eyes on the toy.

"Wanna do the honors?" I say, holding it out.

He rolls up to his hands and knees and takes the toy from me. "You ready, baby girl?"

She lets out a short breath and nods.

Jake holds the tentacle at the base and brings it to her pussy, letting it buzz and vibrate against her lips and clit.

She shivers, biting back a whimper of anticipation. Watching them together has me so damn hard. Jake notches the tip at her entrance and slides it in. "Breathe out and relax, baby." He holds the toy still, letting her get used to it before he presses it in deeper. Four inches are inside her pussy, with plenty more to go.

"Stretch her out nice and slow," I warn him. "Ease into it, Hurricane. If you're a good girl, and you take the toy, you can have both our cocks at once."

"Oh, god," she whimpers.

"Would you like that? Do you wanna feel me and Jake fucking this sweet pussy at the same time? Want us buried in you together?"

"Yes," she says on a hiss, her back arching.

"You'll strangle us so beautifully, Hurricane. You were made to take us. You're *ours*."

"Yours," she pants, breathing through the sensation as Jake presses the toy in deeper.

"You'll sit on my cock, Hurricane. All the way to the hilt. Then we'll let Jake be the one to stretch you out. He'll push his way in, his cock fucking us both at once."

"Fucking hell, Cay," Jake mutters. I can tell he's turned all the way on.

"Oh—*yes*—" she pants, throwing both her arms up over her head, which puts her full breasts on display, nipples peaked.

I can't help it. I have to taste. I crawl up alongside her, lifting up on my elbow as I close my mouth around her nipple, sucking and biting as I feel her moving with the toy that Jake is pressing in deeper.

"Oh," she cries, her voice a mewling broken sound that makes me feel wild. She digs one hand in my hair, holding me to her breast as she moves her hips with the toy, chasing her own pleasure.

All my senses are firing. She makes me feel alive. Fuck, she makes me feel loved. I drop my hand between her legs, working her clit as Jake moves the toy, angling it inside her until she's practically levitating.

"Oh—*oh*—god—"

"Come for us, baby. Fucking shatter," he orders, twisting the toy. "You're taking this toy so well. Ride it like you'll ride our cocks."

She shouts out her release and we watch her whole body jerk with her second orgasm. It's so much stronger than the first. She's curling over the toy, bearing down on it as Jake holds it steady.

"Yes—yes," she pants through clenched teeth, the orgasm still tearing through her. "*Ahh*—" She falls back, squirming to get off the toy.

Jake pulls it out and tosses it to me, his mouth dropping down to lap at her release. He's loving in his touch, his hands bracing tenderly against her thighs. She relaxes completely, her body going limp on the bed.

He rolls to his side and stretches out alongside her. Cupping her face, he kisses her. She sighs, her hand fluttering as she reaches for him. They're like works of art. And they're *mine*.

I click off the toy and toss it to the side, snatching up the lube. We need to move quick while her body is relaxed. "Help me, Jake. Shift her over." I flop down on the bed next to her and snatch up all the pillows, making a sort of back rest for myself. "Come on, Hurricane. Grand finale."

She rolls over, totally blissed out from her orgasms. She's so loopy, she doesn't even connect with my command. She just pops up on her elbows and takes my cock into her mouth. Fuck, she's such a good girl. I've never had a more eager sexual partner. I'm biting my tongue to stop from slipping into degradation play. The things I want to say to her, the way I want to watch her squirm. I know she'll be into it, but that's not our vibe tonight.

I let her tease my tip until I'm hard and aching. "Come on, be a good girl. Get on my cock and face Jake." I help her sit up and turn her until she's straddling me reverse-cowgirl.

Jake shifts down the bed and gets on his knees between my spread legs.

"Help her," I direct. "Guide her down."

She's recovering quick, her senses sharpening by the second. She takes over as Jake helps her arch forward.

"You need to be able to spread her legs," I say. "Like she's sitting in a chair. You won't get the right angle otherwise."

He nods, helping her unpretzel her legs. Then he's holding her weight as she notches herself on the tip of my cock.

"There—right there," I mutter. I take a deep breath, readying myself for the sensation of her taking me to the hilt.

Holy god.

Nothing prepares you for that first slide home. Fucking magic every time. I take another deep breath, supporting her weight against my chest as she whimpers, wanting to move her hips. Her perfect ass is smashed against my groin. I'm buried all the way inside her.

"Caleb," she whimpers, bracing the bed with her palms. "You feel so good, baby. Love you inside me."

I smile, heat blooming in my chest. "Spread your legs open, Hurricane. Let Jake see us like this. Let him see how well you take me."

Her legs fall open as I hold her steady.

"Fucking hell," Jake mutters. "Guys, I've never done this," he admits, his gaze darting to me.

"Do you want to?" I ask, heart in my throat. Please let him say yes. I want him. Need to feel him.

He raises a dark brow and laughs. "You kidding? *Look* at me," he says, gesturing to his hard dick. "I'm about to lose it right fucking now."

Rachel whimpers, reaching out for him. "Jake, we need you."

"Go slow," I caution. "She's stretched out from the toy. But if this hurts you, Hurricane, or you wanna stop, we stop," I add, kissing her shoulder. "No questions asked, okay?"

She nods. "Do it, Jake. Please, baby. I want to feel you both inside me."

Jake leans forward on his knees, claiming her lips in a searing kiss. Then he's shifting closer.

"Lean back, Hurricane," I murmur. "Give him a better angle."

She trust falls against my chest.

My cock is desperate for that first squeeze of Jake pushing his way in. "Take your time," I say. "Work the tip in, just like anal."

He lets out a slow breath as he inches closer, his cock in hand. "You ready, baby girl?"

She nods, her body elastic in my arms. "Mhmm."

We both tense as we feel him prodding at her entrance. His knuckles brush against my cock as he feels her out with his tip, looking for space to press in.

"Relax, Hurricane," I soothe. "Deep breaths. Let him in."

She lets out a shaky breath, moaning as he prods again. "Oh—Jake, there—"

I'm gonna die. I can feel him. His tip is pushing in, gliding against my slick cock.

"Oh—oh," she whines. "Oh god, yes—"

Jake is holding his breath, working his hips to get his tip in further. "Fuck—Cay, you okay?"

"So fucking good," I mutter, dropping my head back.

"You're so tight, baby girl. God, you both feel so amazing. I'm gonna lose it."

"Move your hips," I say. "Fuck us both. Take control."

He shifts forward, his angle changing as he dips down with his hips. He slides another inch inside along my shaft and I'm ready to come. When he starts moving his hips in earnest, my soul just leaves the whole fucking building.

"Holy fuck. Cay, I feel you your ribbed dick," he groans. "Oh my god. Nobody fucking move." He doubles down, grabbing her by the hips as he thrusts in. We're falling apart at the seams as he barks out, "Come. Both of you come. *Now*."

My good boy wants to dom me? I'm so fucking here for it. I cry out my release as Rachel does the same between us. We flood her cunt with our cum. The pressure of her orgasm on our cocks has me seeing stars. I lose all sense of control as the three of us spiral through the cosmos, our bodies taking control as we just ride the wave of a three-way release. It's a magic unlike anything I've ever felt before.

I don't know how long we lie there before Jake is pulling out. His body is boneless as he fumbles his way over my leg and crawls up the bed to flop down at my side. I shift slightly, rolling towards him to let Rachel slide off me. She flops to the bed between us, halfway on Jake. I scoot over, giving her more room, but then her hand is reaching blindly for me, pulling me closer. I curl up next to her, her body tucked against me. She weaves our fingers together and pulls my arm around her, holding it between her breasts. Then she tangles her legs in with Jake's.

"*God*," he puffs, totally breathless. He flops his arm over both of us, giving an exhausted groan. "That was the best sex of my fucking life. Go team." He slaps my ass, then hers.

Rachel is coherent enough to snort. "Next time it better be one of you with the tentacle," she warns.

And now I'm picturing Jake on all fours, Rachel lubing up his ass so I can slide the wiggling dildo up inside him. Shit, I can't get hard again. I'm totally spent. We're too exhausted.

Maybe when we get home . . .

Next to me, Rachel lets out a soft little sound of contentment. "I love you guys," she murmurs, lifting our joined hands to kiss my knuckle.

Jake rolls on his side towards us, his hand slipping under the covers to stretch over us both. His calloused fingertips brush the bare skin of my hip, lighting a fire that spreads. "Love you," he replies.

And just like that, I can't breathe. I don't know if he meant it just for her, or if love for me is also implied, but I'll fucking take it.

50
ILMARI

For all the things I dislike about living in America, I'll give them this: they have really good bad television. Every show is worse than the last. Already this morning I've watched an episode of a children's cooking show where adults yell at the children, forcing them to make a four-course meal. Then there was a house hunting show where a woman turned down twelve houses because she didn't like the paint colors.

I've settled on watching a show where a man buys storage units and people bid on them, not knowing what's inside. One of the units had a taxidermied alligator and a vintage Harley motorcycle.

This is rock bottom. I'm benched with a groin pull, icing my crotch every two hours and popping pain relievers like they're candy.

At least Rachel told a white lie to the coaches. She downplayed the injury for me. Damn it, she's still trying to protect me, even when I crossed the line. I was so angry. I blamed her because it was easier than blaming myself.

And that kiss . . .

I'd be lying if I said I hadn't thought about doing it for weeks. She's beautiful. Smart. Strong. But she's all wrong for me. I'm wrong for her. I need to apologize. That's the professional thing to do. I'm not sorry, but that's beside the point. I need to say the words, then distance myself. I'll request to work with another PT. I'll think clearer if my doctor's exams don't have me milking my cock in the shower after—

Stop.

I take a deep breath. That happened once. I got it out of my system. It's done. Rachel Price is not to be touched again. I don't want her. I *hate* her. She's derailing my career. She's inserting herself into my business and pretending to care. No one works for the players in this business. It's all about the team, the game.

Rachel talks a good talk. *I care about you.* Her sultry voice plays on repeat in my head. The heat of her gaze. The way she kissed me back— *No, she didn't.*

I groan, shifting the ice pack off my crotch. The cold is doing nothing to cool the fire in my blood. I look down. Saatana, I'm getting hard. Why does she keep getting me hard? I have better control than this.

My phone chirps. It's been going crazy for the last half hour. The group chats I always leave are buzzing with activity. Apparently, all the guys are meeting up at the beach this morning. They're coordinating food, drinks, and games.

I move to silence my phone when I see the name flashing on my lock screen. I snatch it up.

DR. PRICE (10:14AM): Hey, Mars. A bunch of us are hanging out at the beach today. You should come.

A second message pings. A GPS map with the location.

Absolutely not. The last thing I want to do is spend my morning standing around at the beach watching the guys kick a football. That's all they do. We play hockey or they stand around in a circle kicking a football.

DR. PRICE (10:16AM): I'm sure you've decided you're not coming, but we really need to talk. I have a plan to get you scans. Come to the beach, and I'll explain.

With a groan, I tap out a reply.

KINNUNEN (10:17AM): Explain via text

DR. PRICE (10:17AM): No way. This is nonnegotiable. I'm still your doctor, remember? I call the shots, and today I'm prescribing vitamin T. Get over here.

I scrunch my nose as I think through all my years of taking supplements.

KINNUNEN (10:18AM): Vitamin T?

DR. PRICE (10:18AM): Yeah, Vitamin Team. You're on one, Mars. Act like it. Come to the beach and have fun.

KINNUNEN (10:19AM): The beach is not fun

DR. PRICE (10:19AM): Then come to the beach and have no fun, you crusty ole crab *crab emoji**frown emoji*

I grunt. She can't make me, can she? I'll ignore this. My plan still holds. Monday, I'm cutting ties with Rachel Price.

My phone chirps again. It's already open and in my hand so I check the message. It's the damn team group chat.

NOVIKOV (10:21AM): Whoa, hot doc spotted!

I sit forward on the sofa, eyes narrowing on my phone as the asshole sends a picture. It's Rachel, standing in the surf in a sunhat and large sunglasses. She's wearing a blue bikini. Her perfect breasts are on full display. She's curvy in all the right places. She has enough to hold, enough to sink between and—

"Saatana," I mutter, stroking my hand down over my beard.

My cock twitches in my shorts as I breathe hard through my nose, clutching the phone.

Another photo pings in from one of the other guys. A different angle. She's wearing some kind of sheer shirt that flutters open around her thighs. She's smiling, mid-sentence, talking to some other woman with red hair.

The guys all start chirping, wanting to know the name of her friend. Compton cusses Novikov out and tells him to stop taking pictures. Compton is right. She's not some puck bunny asking to be used for his entertainment. She's a doctor. The team's doctor. My doctor. My—

Fuck.

Why am I standing?

Why have I moved towards the door?

Why are my keys in my hand?

Because you're going to the beach.

51
RACHEL

Tess takes a sip from her big tumbler of iced tea. She's rocking a red, high-waisted bikini to go with her crazy mane of sunset red curls. "Okay, girl, you gotta walk me through it again."

We're standing in the surf, far away from the boys, who are busy setting up beach base camp. Jake sent a message through the group chat and now my casual idea to go for a walk with Tess has turned into an all-out Sunday morning beach party. Half the team is already here, and the other half is likely on the way.

I glance back over my shoulder. Jake and Caleb are fighting with Novy, kicking sand at him, and throwing soccer balls at his head. He runs off jeering, beer dripping down his hand. Behind them, Langley helps Sully and Shelby set up a big beach awning. Sully's three kids are already in the surf with buckets and shovels, digging in the sand while Poseidon bounces around them.

I sigh, looking back out at the water. "His fears aren't unfounded. I've seen the way teams can treat players. Physical care takes priority, but the emotional care is often forgotten in the equation. We have to be able to treat the whole person, and that's what I'm trying to do."

"So . . . you wanna take this guy up to Cincinnati for super-secret scans? And Dr. H is willing to help you?"

I roll my eyes behind my sunglasses. "There's no reason to sound so incredulous. You don't know Dr. Halla like I do. He's a good person, Tess. He understands better than anyone how the players get caught between a rock and a hard place. We're both just trying to cushion the blow for him."

She nods. "Yeah, makes sense. And your goalie is willing?"

I bite my bottom lip. "Umm . . ."

"Oh god, girl." She laughs. "You set it all up with Dr. H without clearing it with the goalie first?"

"I wanted it to be as easy as possible to say yes," I reply defensively. "If it's all set up and all he has to do is get on a plane, he'll do it, right?"

"I mean, I would, but I'm not a pro athlete. We've got no idea what he's thinking or how he deals with this kind of stress." She steps forward, looping her arm in with mine. "But enough about work, I wanna talk about your juicy steamy love life." She tugs me forward and we walk in the wet sand, the surf lapping at our ankles.

"Oh god, where to begin?" I mutter.

"How about you start with the little handy session I stumbled upon in the kitchen this morning?"

"Tess!" I cry, smacking her arm as she cackles. "I thought you were asleep upstairs!"

It didn't go too far past PG-13 . . . I don't think. Caleb was at the counter making his gross coffee and he looked so edible, his hair all tousled. I couldn't help but wrap my arms around him and tease him a little, my hand slipping inside his sweats. Jake came in and joined us, pressing in behind me. No clothes came off. We didn't even kiss. But it was still a slow-burning, three-way orgasm. I worked both of them at once while Jake worked me, Caleb's hands pressed flat against the counter. We all just eased our way to climax, breathing as one. It was amazing. Just thinking about it has me wanting to drag them behind the Hawaiian ice stand and do it again.

"Girl, you are in *so* much trouble," Tess says with a laugh. "This is already serious. Especially for you," she adds, giving me one of her all-knowing Tess stares.

"We're just having fun," I say. "Exploring what this might look like. With the season in session, it's easiest to just live together," I deflect with a shrug.

"What this *looks* like is you waltzing down the aisle of every hockey girl's greatest fantasy," she replies. "Those boys worship you, Rachel. You've got them hooked on your top-shelf kitty cat, and now they're gonna follow you wherever you go."

"Tess . . ."

"Hey, you'll get no judgement here," she adds. "If you're happy, Tess is happy."

"But can we really be happy?" I say, letting my truths out now that I'm alone with my best friend. "How do I maintain this if I want it to stay private? They won't be happy being my dirty little secrets forever. It's not fair to them."

"Hmm . . . well, what do *they* want? Do they want the world to know you're a fearsome threesome? Are they ready to brave the media storm that comes with the Rachel Price experience?"

"I think we're all happy with things as they are right now. Maybe we'll get through the season and . . ." I sigh. "I don't even know. I don't know what the hell I'm doing. I just can't seem to stop."

"What you're doing is falling in love with two men at the same time, Rach. And they are most definitely in love with you," she adds.

I spin to look at her. "You've been around them for all of *two* seconds!"

"That's all it takes to see how crazy they are about you," she says with a laugh. "Plus, none of you were really trying very hard to hide it from me. I mean, you picked me up from the airport and drove me to your lover's house, and he met you at the door with a kiss, while your other lover cooked us dinner and made moon eyes at you all night."

I glance back over my shoulder. "Are we being that obvious now?"

Before Tess can reply, we're both shrieking as a rogue soccer ball whacks her in the back of the head. She spins around, her iced tea sloshing out of her cup. "Hey, watch it!"

Langley comes running over, a horrified look on his face. "Whoops. Sorry, ma'am."

Tess gives him a level stare, nostrils flaring as she massages the back of her head.

"Langley, you did *not* just call her ma'am," I tease.

He ducks down for the ball before it floats off with the surf. As he straightens, he turns to face her. "Whoa," he says on a breath.

Tess and I both smirk as Langley glances at me. "Doc, who is this?"

"She's right in front of you, Langley. Ask her yourself."

He shakes his head. "I wouldn't dare."

Tess tips her head to the side, her wild red curls blowing in the sea breeze.

"Why not?" I laugh.

"Because no mere mortal would dare speak to such a goddess," he replies. He barely gets the words out before he's flashing her an All-American smile.

"Ooo, that's a good line," Tess hums, batting her lashes.

Next to her I groan, rolling my eyes.

"You like that one?" he says with that boyish grin.

"Mhmm."

"What am I? A troll under a bridge?" I mutter.

"Nah, you know you're still our Hot Doc," he replies, tucking the soccer ball under his arm. "But you're like, way off limits. And waaaay out of my league. Both of you are."

Tess pops a hand on her hip. "What's your name, Cutie?"

"Langley—umm—Ryan," he adds, raking a hand through his sandy blond curls. "What's yours?"

"Cuteness, you can call me whatever you want, so long as you call me for dinner," she teases with a wink.

His smile falls as he blinks, dazed by her brilliance. I'm not surprised, she's a ten and a half. In her plunging, high-waisted red bikini, she's a fifteen. His gaze darts to me. "Wait—can we do that? Is that—she's off limits, right?"

"What are you lookin' at her for?" Tess huffs, both hands on her curvy hips. "Rachel isn't my mother. You wanna ask me to dinner, you ask *me*."

He looks like a kid on Christmas as he blurts. "I—dyouwannagotodinnerwithme?"

Now I'm laughing. "Tess, I think you broke his brain."

Tess snorts, crossing her arms under her full breasts. She knows exactly what she's doing, drawing his eye down.

"Langley!"

"Langers!"

"You got the ball, man!"

The guys all shout for him, and he waves, turning around to chuck the ball towards them. He looks back at us, his eyes on Tess. "Nice to meet you, Tess. Later, Doc," he adds at me. Then he's running off, those cut back muscles glistening in the sun.

"Okay," Tess says, tipping down her sunglasses to watch him run away. "Yeah, no I'm not mad about that. He's cute, right? Like a cute lil puppy at the beach. Maybe he needs to find a new owner . . ."

"Hands off," I say, giving her my best level stare.

She snorts. "Why?"

"Because you're a goddess of epic proportions who would eat him alive."

"All goddesses gotta eat," she replies. "I bet he tastes yummy."

"Langley is like twenty years old. He's an infant, Tess."

"That just means he's got stamina," she murmurs, watching the guys kick the soccer ball. "You've seen him workout. I bet he runs a five-minute mile without breaking a sweat. Mmm . . . I like a runner."

Now I'm laughing, my tension easing. "You are the worst. And you're *not* getting involved with a Ray this weekend."

She scoffs, flipping her hair back. "How can I, when you've already got them all locked down in the Price Pussy Palace?" As she says it, she kicks water at me.

I squeal, splashing her back.

"Rachel!" Jake calls over with a wave. "You want one hotdog or two?"

My face falls as Tess howls with laughter. Covering my mouth with her hand like we're twelve, she shouts back, "She wants two!"

52
RACHEL

Beach day is a huge success. Practically the whole team is here, which is great, because it means I'm finally meeting more of the wives, girlfriends, and families. A few guys brought their dogs, so Poseidon is having a huge time running and playing.

Tess is busy making the rounds, flirting up a storm with any single guy who looks twice at her. Which is all of them. They're *all* looking twice. Langley is still wandering around like he's been zapped by an electric fence.

"So . . . our Hurricane has a Tornado for a friend," Caleb muses, handing me a sparkling water from the cooler by his chair.

I roll my eyes. "Don't get me started."

He just smirks, taking a sip of his own lime water. "Holy shit," he mutters, tipping his glasses down as he peers over my shoulder.

"What?"

"Mars is here."

I spin around, my gaze narrowing on him immediately. He's impossible to miss. He's wearing a pair of dark Ray-Bans and a white t-shirt with athletic shorts.

"He never comes to anything," Caleb says, taking a sip of his drink.

"Maybe he just wants to be part of the team," I offer. I hate feeling like I'm lying to him.

"What's the deal there?" he says.

I turn around to face him. "What deal where?"

"With you and Mars. Did you invite him?"

I fiddle with my sunglasses. "There is no me and Mars."

He nods, glancing back over my shoulder. "Does he know that?"

"Caleb, I—"

Just then, Tess drops down at my side, a wild grin on her face. "Girl, who is *that*?"

I look around. "Who?"

"Who?" she cries, incredulous. "*Him*, Rach. The hot as sin Ragnar Lothbrok lookalike!"

"Scuse me." Caleb unfolds himself from his beach chair and walks off.

I sigh, rolling my eyes as Tess snags his chair. "Thanks for that," I mutter.

"For what?" she replies, digging in the cooler for a soda.

"Never mind."

"So, spill. Who is he?" she presses, slurping the top of her Diet Coke can.

"That's Mars Kinnunen."

"The goalie?" She gasps. "Oh—*wait*—like . . . *the* goalie? The one you . . ." She twirls her finger, leaving the rest silent.

As of now, Tess is the only other soul who knows about the kiss in the hallway. I don't know why I told her, but I did. I just felt like I had to say something to someone. It meant nothing. He was mad and deflecting it all on me. That's all.

"Girl, he's looking at you like you're a damn snack," Tess murmurs.

I go stiff. "He is not."

"I mean, he's standing over there. But in spirit, he's right behind you dripping an ice cube down your neck."

"Stop," I hiss, sitting forward in my chair. "You're crazy, Tess."

"Am I? Is Tess Owens known to be wrong about these things?" She leans over, elbow on the arm of her chair. "Let's recap, shall we? Exhibit A: I told you that nurse at the clinic was way into you, and you ignored me, and then he tried to stalk you into our building. Remember how fun that was?"

"Tess—"

"Exhibit B, Your Honor," she says over me. "I said the guy at Trader Joe's was flirting with you, and you didn't believe me, and then he wrote his number on your receipt."

I laugh, shaking my head.

"And the guy at the bar with the tattoos and the lip ring? I said he was going to try to take you home and you said 'no, I think he's gay,' and then he cornered you by the bathroom, and you made out with him in a stall. You remember that one?"

"Okay, fine," I mutter. "I will admit that you do sometimes . . . on rare occasions...and usually fueled by alcohol . . . make educated guesses about men's intentions where I'm concerned."

"This is all I'm saying," she replies, settling back into her chair. "So, what's the deal there?"

"There is no *there* there," I reply for the second time.

"Uh-huh . . . then why are you blushing? Do the boys know? Do they not want to share—oooohmigod, three-way sharing." She slaps her forehead, mouth open in awe. "I don't even—how would that work? I guess we have three holes . . . but I don't see how that would—"

"Tess," I hiss, slapping her arm. "Will you *shut up* about orgies? This is a family fun day at the beach. Emphasis on *family*." I point to the many little faces dotting the sand in front of us.

She just laughs. "Girl, better you than me. I don't know if I would enjoy being made into a human Twinkie, I don't care how good the books make it seem. When I'm with a man, I want to give him *allll* my attention. And you better believe I want all his attention on me."

I follow her gaze with a frown on my face. "Tess," I say in warning. "This is not the humane society. Stop looking at that puppy right now. He is not up for adoption."

She snorts, dragging her eye away from Langley. "Hey, if you get to juggle three hot dogs at once, I'm allowed to take an All-American cheeseburger out for one little dinner."

"And on that note," I say, getting up out of my chair.

"Yeah, go get him," she teases. "Go invite him on a whirlwind get-away to charming Cincinnati!"

I roll my eyes, crossing over the sand towards where Ilmari stands watching some of the guys play volleyball. "Don't feel like playing?" I say, standing next to him.

"Can't," he replies. "Don't want to risk it."

I nod, taking a sip of my drink. I can't even offer him one to break the tension because he's already holding a bottled water. "Come meet my friend Tess," I say.

He follows next to me as we go over to the rainbow striped beach umbrella. Tess is now stretched out on a beach towel. Her eyes are closed, but she's got a little smile on her face. I know the faker was watching me talk to him.

"Hey, Tess," I call. "Meet Mars."

She sits up, one hand holding onto her hat. "Well, helloooo, handsome," she sings. "My, you're a tall drink of water, aren't you?"

He glances at me.

"I'm sorry for your pain and suffering," I say by way of explanation.

"Come have a seat, Mars," she coos.

He sits down on the beach chair Tess was just in, and I take up my seat again.

"Why don't you take your shirt off and stay awhile," she says, perched up on her elbows. The angle does great things for her curves.

"Can't," he replies.

I share a quick look with Tess, who asks the question both of us are thinking. "You can't take off your shirt at the beach?"

"I have a tattoo. Sun is bad for it," he explains, taking a sip of his water.

"Well, good thing you're in the shade," she teases, pointing up to the rainbow umbrella.

"Tess, will you leave the man alone? Mars, you don't have to—"

Too late. He sets his water bottle aside and tugs it off one-handed, tucking it in to the top of his shorts. I'm trying really hard not to look but Tess makes no such effort. She ogles him shamelessly, her mouth tipping up appreciatively.

"I don't get it, handsome. I don't see a tattoo."

"It's on my back," he replies.

I can see it. Well, part of it. And I was right, it's practically a total blackout.

Tess being Tess, she crawls around the side of his chair and pushes on his shoulder, a silent request for him to lean forward. "Oh, holy fuckballs! Mars, this is *gorgeous*. Rach, look at this. What am I even looking at?"

I look. I can't help myself. His entire back from the base of his neck, across his shoulders, down to his waist is blacked out in a full-back tattoo. It's incredibly intricate, with multiple scenes playing out.

It's like some kind of creepy, death-themed fantasyscape—skulls, wolves, an open-mouthed, rabid-looking bear, a demon king, a raven in flight at the top. Those are the wingtips you can see even when his shirt is on.

"What is it?" I say.

"Stories from the *Kalevala*," he replies.

"The kale-what-a?" says Tess.

"The *Kalevala*," he repeats. "It's the Finnish book of folklore. Our mythology. The making of the world, Ilmarinen and the forging of Ukko's hammer, mighty Otso guarding his forest, the death god on his throne."

"It's beautiful," I murmur, fighting the urge to reach out and touch it. For some reason, it's making me emotional. This means something to him. It matters so much, he doesn't want sun to touch it. He doesn't like sharing it either. It's art not meant for consumption. It's a piece of his soul he wears on his skin.

And I suddenly know without doubt that he didn't show it to us because Tess teased him to take his shirt off. He's showing it to us because he knew *I* wanted to see it that day on the plane.

He *wants* me to see it. He didn't before. Now he does.

Fuck, I am in so much trouble.

53
RACHEL

"You want me to go to Cincinnati?" Ilmari is standing in the beach parking lot next to his big blue truck, arms crossed over his barrel chest. I followed him over here, leaving the rest of the group behind. This has been our only chance to get a real moment alone all afternoon.

I wrap the ends of my white sweater tighter around myself. "I have a specialist at my residency clinic in Cincinnati. You and I go, we get our scans, we keep it private. It will be off the NHL's radar. Off the FIHA's radar too, which matters more to you, I think."

He gives a curt nod.

"Please," I beg. "I'm asking you trust me here. Just come to Cincinnati with me." I hold out my hand, waiting to see if he'll take it.

Slowly, he unfolds his arms, dropping them to his sides. Then he raises his right hand and shakes my hand. "I trust you."

I sigh with relief. "Thank you, Mars. God, I was so afraid you'd say no. Okay, well it's all set up. We'll leave tomorrow, yeah? Our flight goes out in the morning, and we'll go straight to the clinic. If the scans are clear, and you respond well to rehab, you should be back on the ice for the week the FIHA scouts come."

He's quiet for a moment, his expression still unreadable. I go to drop my hand, but he holds onto it. "Rachel . . . Doctor Price," he corrects. "I'm sorry."

I gaze up into his rugged face. *Oh, shit.* He's talking about the kiss. I can't see his eyes behind his sunglasses. My gaze darts down to our joined hands. "It's fine—"

"No, it was unpardonably rude," he says. "It won't happen again."

I nod, trying to control the confused fluttering of my heart. Unpardonable is such a strange word choice. Passionate. Possessive.

Those words better describe our kiss. Maybe it really meant nothing to him . . .

Yesterday I would have believed that. Today, I'm not so sure.

"*SO,* you're going to Cincinnati . . . with Mars Kinnunen?" says Jake, setting his fork down atop his massive bowl of spaghetti. Beach day is long over, and Jake, Caleb, and I are eating take-out spaghetti in the kitchen. Caleb and I sit at stools, while Jake stands across the island, waiting while a few more pieces of garlic bread reheat in the oven.

Tess is out for the night. A friend from college just picked her up and they took themselves down to St. Augustine for dinner and a ghost walking tour. I'm sure booze will be involved. I imagine she'll call around midnight expecting a ride home from one of us.

"Mhmm," I say, taking a bite of my salad.

"What's in Cincinnati?" says Caleb.

I pause, looking down at my food. I don't have permission to discuss Ilmari's medical history with his teammate.

"Oh, shit," Jake murmurs, getting there on his own. "This is about his groin pull, right? Is he gonna be out for rest of the season? Does it need surgery? Did it happen during the last game?"

"Stop," I plead. "Jake, I can't discuss his medical status—"

"What about your relationship status?" Caleb presses. "Are we allowed to know about that? Or is that confidential too?"

My gaze shoots over to him. "Okay, that's the second time you've made a snarky comment about me and Mars. Just ask me what you want to ask."

"Fine." He rattles his fork down. "Are you fucking him?"

My eyes go wide. "What? *No!*"

"Do you want to?" he presses.

"Caleb—"

"Because he sure as hell wants to fuck you," he adds.

I cross my arms over my chest. "What makes you think Mars Kinnunen wants to fuck me?"

He glances over at Jake and back to me. "Seriously? You're serious right now? You want us to list it out for you? We've got a running list of like ten things. Your list is shorter than his, but it grows longer every day too."

"Wait—you're *both* keeping a list? Are you in on this?" I cry, looking at Jake.

"Well, yeah. We only talk about it all the time," he says with a shrug.

"Look, guys. I've been helping him manage an injury, and that's all. I want to take him to Cincinnati to see Dr. Halla. He's a hip expert, and he can get us scans off the record. Scans that won't have to go into any official NHL files."

The guys share a long look, a novel's worth of words passing between them.

It's Jake who speaks first. "You're helping him *off* the record? Isn't that, like, illegal?"

I huff. "No one is going to jail for giving Ilmari an MRI."

"But it's not policy," Caleb clarifies. "You're hiding it from the team, from the *coaches*, which could get you in serious trouble. It could get you fired, Rachel. It could get Mars released from his contract."

I shrug. "Sometimes what's in the best interest of the team isn't always in the best interest of the player."

Jake nods, his face solemn, while Caleb just gives me a look like he's chewing on glass.

"Look, I swore to Mars that I would help him," I explain. "No matter whether it's the right thing for the team, *he's* my patient. I don't want his career ending before it has to."

"Why do you care so much about Mars Kinnunen and his damn career?" Caleb says.

"Because I'm a *damn* doctor," I snap back at him. "Do you really think for one second I wouldn't have moved heaven and earth to help *you* if you were the injured player on my table? Or you?" I add, spinning around to glare at Jake.

"How bad is it?" Jake murmurs.

I shake my head, setting my fork down, appetite gone. "We don't know yet," I admit. "Right now, it's presenting like a groin pull. But I can't treat him properly without scans, and he's terrified to get them with the Finnish Olympic scouts on their way. This is his dream, guys," I add, glancing between them. "Playing for Finland in the Olympics. His grandfather played, his father. This is his shot. I'm just trying to help him take it. Is my way the right way? Hell, if I know. But I'm following my heart here, and I'd *really* appreciate if you guys would back me up instead of tear me down."

Slowly, Jake nods. "It's good that you're helping him, Seattle. Go to Cincy and get your scans."

I smile at him with relief.

But next to me, a storm is still brewing. "That still doesn't address the other thing," Caleb mutters.

"What other thing?"

"The 'Mars Kinnunen wants to fuck you with his Viking cock' thing," Jake supplies.

I suck in a breath, trying to control my spiraling emotions.

"Look, Seattle, you just gotta *tell* us," Jake urges. "What the hell is going on with you and Mars? I mean, you sit next to him on every flight, every bus ride."

"Yeah, because he *makes* me," I counter. "You all made me move, remember?"

"When the team is on the ice, your eyes are on him half the time," Caleb adds, his gaze obsidian.

"Because he's been playing injured, and I've been terrified he'll make it worse!"

Caleb shoves off his stool and moves away, circling around the other side of the island. Each step he takes is a chasm opening between us, tearing at my heart.

"He talks to you," Jake goes on.

"He talks to Tomlin too! And Davidson and Coach Johnson. He talks to *you* on the ice all the time, Jake. And you, Cay."

Jake shakes his head. "That's the job. When the job is done, he's a total closed book. He opens for you, Seattle. Only you."

"Are you seriously gonna sit here and tell us there's nothing between you two?" Caleb jabs, arms crossed over his chest.

They're both standing across from me now, my angel and my devil. Jake is in a white t-shirt, Caleb in black. Jake looks wary. Caleb is pissed.

"Oh god," I groan, dropping my elbows onto the counter and

burying my face in my hands. "I don't know!" I lift my face, shaking my head as I give them the only truth I have. "I don't know, okay? I don't know what's happening to me. I don't—look around us!" I cry, waving my hand around Jake's kitchen. "This is all fucking crazy! What are we doing here, guys? What *is* this? Where is this going?"

"I thought it was pretty obvious," Jake replies, crossing his arms over his chest again.

I laugh. It's a little, choked sound caught in my throat. "Obvious? Nothing about this screams obvious, Jake. We've all been dancing around this for weeks, not saying anything. We live together! We buy groceries and cook like a happily married throuple. We fuck like crazy. I've only slept in my room twice since I moved in. And yet there is *nothing* but walls up between us. Things we're not saying, feelings we're not acting on, truths we won't let out. It's a goddamn obstacle course in here, and we're all stumbling around it in the dark, and it's driving me crazy."

My speech over, I realize I'm standing too, hands gripping to the white granite countertop.

Now both boys have their arms crossed, glaring between me and each other.

"Well then let's have it out," Jake says. "Sudden death. Let's leave it all on the ice."

54
RACHEL

I take a shaky breath, glancing between the boys. *Sudden death.* We're leaving it all on the ice.

Jake looks to Caleb. "Cay? Sudden death?"

His jaw clenched tight, Caleb nods.

"Great . . . well, who goes first?" Jake tucks his hands in the pockets of his grey sweats. "Do we flip for it or—"

"I kissed Mars," I say. "Well, technically, he kissed me but—"

"When?" Jake growls, his expression darkening. "Where?"

"Penguins game. He was coming off the ice and I held him back to tell him I was pulling him. I think he did it just to shut me up," I add. "He was angry, and he took it out on me. He apologized. But now, between you guys ribbing me, and Tess, I . . . I think he meant to do it. I think he wanted to—"

"Of course, he did," Caleb jabs. "He wants to fuck you, Rachel. Our question is does he get to. Is this three-way about to become a four-way? Because we'd kind of like a say in that."

Sudden death. Nowhere to hide.

"I don't know yet, and that's my honest answer."

Both boys fold their arms tight again. They share wonderfully well together, but the idea of sharing with someone else is clearly a non-starter.

"How would that work?" says Jake. "Mars is a goalie. They're not team players, you know what I mean? No way would he be cool sharing you. Does he even know about us yet?"

"No, of course, he doesn't. Up until that kiss, everything has been strictly professional. Even with that kiss, I really think part of it was him just not knowing how else to handle his frustration."

Jake narrows his hazel eyes. "And what happens when he finally sweeps you off your feet with his Viking charm and his monster cock?

What do you do when he tells you to choose—him or us? How soon should we expect you to pack your bags, Seattle?"

I push off from the island. "Okay, so let's get this clear right now." I point a level finger at him. "You do not own me, Jake Compton. And you don't own me either, Cay. I'm not his and I'm not yours, I'm *mine*. I am my own person, and I will decide the bounds of my own happiness. I wouldn't be here if I didn't want you. *Both* of you. And my love is not finite, Jake. Loving you has nothing to do with my loving him," I say, jabbing a thumb at Caleb. "And I *do*," I press. "I love you both. It's crazy to say it out loud, because we've only known each other for a short time, but I mean, am I crazy?" I gesture between the three of us. "Does this feel crazy to you guys? Or does it feel so right it scares you?"

"I'm afraid to lose you," Jake admits. "Cay is such a better fit for you, babe. He's smart like you and weird like you. I lift right out. Even between the three of us, I know I'm the weakest link."

"Jake," I whisper, my heart breaking.

"You add Mars into the mix with his European charm and his stupid, sexy manbun—to say nothing about his huge cock—and I just know there's gonna be nowhere left for me," he finishes with a shrug, his face a mask of tortured pain.

I can't help the smile quirking my lips. "You spend a lot of time looking at his cock then, angel?"

He glares at me, while next to him Caleb gives me a warning look. "You've seen it too."

"I'm an equipment manager, Hurricane. I set up and tear down locker rooms for a living. We've all seen the monster between Kinnunen's legs."

Now is absolutely not the moment to ask for details. Instead, I move around the island towards Jake. He goes still at my approach. He dropped his shields and shared his truth. He's not as okay with sharing me as he's been letting on. Not because he doesn't like it, but because he doesn't want to get left out.

I reach for him, brushing my hands down his bare arms. "Jake . . . look at me, angel," I murmur, stroking his jaw. "Don't you ever doubt what you mean to me again," I say, voice low with emotion. "Jake, I've been telling you almost since the moment we met that you're my soulmate. Can you really forget what we shared in Seattle? The universe tied us together that night. I live with a rope around my heart now, woven through my ribs, and it connects me to you."

Slowly, he raises his hands, wrapping them around my wrists.

"I love you, Jake Compton. I love that you text me incessantly. I love your pictures of pelicans and sushi and tacos. I love that you give me a weather report every morning, even though I literally have a weather app saved on my lock screen," I add with a soft smile. "You make me laugh. You make me happy. You make me hopeful for the future. You make life fun, Jake. And you make the living of it less lonely. And you might find someone else too—"

"Not possible," he says with an ardent shake of his head. "You're it for me, baby. I don't need anyone else."

"Don't say that," I say, too afraid to look over his shoulder and see the hurt on Caleb's face. "You have no idea what the universe has in store for you," I say instead. "We never dreamed we'd find each other, but we did. Whoever else comes through your life, I'll be here, Jake. I *want* to be here. I won't restrain you or deny you any of the love or joy you deserve. Stop doubting yourself and your place in my heart."

I lean in, still holding his face gently in my hands. "I'm not good at labels and cages," I admit. "The idea of being someone's girlfriend or their wife terrifies me. Sometimes I think I was just wired wrong. Everyone wants to get married, right? People want the normalcy of monogamy and the 2.5 kids. The dog and the white picket fence. But I've never wanted that life," I say with a shake of my head.

"What *do* you want, Rachel?" he asks.

"I want the world," I reply. "I want to sail around Phuket Island, topless on a yacht. I want to fuck in the gardens at Versailles and get chased out by French police. I want to eat pizza by the hour and drink wine straight from the bottle, stumbling around the streets of Rome at two in the morning. I want to dance in a fountain, Jake. I want to be a doctor and travel the country watching men at the top of their game play hazardous sports. I want to feel their sweat and smell their blood on the ice. I want to *live*. And I never want to turn an opportunity down out of fear that I'm not conforming to that dream of normal. Because I'm *not* normal, Jake. *We're* not normal. We're extraordinary. Be extraordinary with me."

Slowly, he lets out a breath, his body curling around mine, until our foreheads are touching. He drops his hands from my wrists, wrapping them around my waist, as he breathes me in. His perfect, woodsy scent fills my senses, and I sink into his embrace.

"I love you so much, Seattle." He lifts his head away so he can gaze down at me. "I don't want to cage you. I'm a mess sometimes, and I can get in my own head—Cay can tell you. I overthink shit . . . or underthink it, with no real in between. But I don't want to over-think this, Rachel. You love me—"

"I do. I love you, Jake. I'm so damn crazy about you."

"Good," he says with a sigh.

Biting my lip, I ask the question eating me alive. "But I have to know . . . does sharing me with Caleb hurt you?"

He leans away, eyes wide. "What? *No*," he growls. "Fuck no. He's my best fucking friend. I need him in my life. And sharing you with him is literally the best sex I've ever had. There is not a single bone in my body that regrets turning this twosome into a threesome, Seattle. I mean, you feel the same, right Cay?" He glances over his shoulder, and I finally let myself look at Caleb.

My dark-eyed, fae prince stands there in all black, watching us confess our love to each other, and I see the pieces of himself he still hides in the shadows breaking. It's his turn for sudden death. How much truth he reveals is up to him.

"The sex is good," he mutters.

"It's good for you, but it could be great," I say. "If you'd stop hold-ing back on us."

Jake looks down at me. "What do you mean, Seattle?"

"I mean that Caleb has been playing it safe. He's afraid to show us what he really wants, afraid to ask for it, afraid we'll run. But really, it just makes *him* the coward."

His jaw clenches tighter as he glares at me.

"Is that true, Cay?" asks Jake. "Look man, I'm new at this group thing. If there's something I'm doing or not doing, you just gotta tell me."

I see the flicker of shadows in Caleb's eyes and an idea blooms in my mind. Sudden death, remember? Caleb is better at doing than saying. With a firm hand, I push back on Jake's chest. "Step back, angel."

He lets me push him back against the counter. "What are you doing?"

Caleb is wondering the same, his dark eyes narrowing on me.

"Sudden death," I reply. "It's Caleb's turn."

Caleb crosses his arms over his chest. "Sorry to disappoint, but I don't have any deep dark secrets. I like the sex. I like living here. You can fuck whoever you want, Hurricane. It's not my business. You want someone rubbing lotion on your tits on that boat in Thailand, I'm your man. When you're done fucking me, you just let me know."

His words sting. Of course, they do. He wants them to. "You know, for a Sagittarius, you make a really great Scorpio," I deadpan. "Too bad for you, I'm a double Cancer. It would take a deep-sea oil drill to pierce through my shell. So, how about we cut the shit, and get back to sudden death?"

His eyes flash. "I just said I've got nothing to offer."

"Tell me you love me."

He goes impossibly still, his gaze darting from Jake back over to me.

"Don't look at him," I snap. "He can't help you right now. This is between you and me, Cay. You look at me, and you tell me the truth. Sudden death. Do you love me?"

"I can't do this," he mutters, taking a step back.

"You can't what?" I challenge. "You can't love me? Or you can't admit it? Because they're two completely different things."

He says nothing, jaw clenched tight.

"You wear your anger like a shield," I say, taking a step closer. "You're angry at the world for your lost chances, at the man who hit you after the play for crushing all your dreams, at yourself for not seeing it coming." Tears sting my eyes. "You're full of so much anger, Cay. You need an outlet for it. You can't bear it all alone, so stop trying. Let me help."

He shakes his head.

I swallow my nerves, holding my ground. "I love you, Caleb Sanford, and I am not afraid of your darkness. You'd have to do a lot more than break a knee and become an alcoholic to dance all night with *my* devils. I dare you to let me in," I challenge. "Or if you won't . . . then let *him* out. I'd like to meet him. I think Jake should meet him too."

His eyes flash again as I see him warring inside.

"Let who out?" Jake rasps, his gaze locked on us prowling across his kitchen at each other.

"You don't know what you're asking," says Caleb, his voice low.

My heart races as my core tightens with need, the anticipation of a fight building. Moving fast, I snatch up Jake's half-eaten bowl of spaghetti and fling it at Caleb's head. He ducks it easily, and the bowl goes smashing against the cabinet, china shattering, spaghetti flopping from the counter to the floor.

"Whoa—" Jake cries. "Seattle, what the hell?"

"Don't fucking push me, Rachel," Caleb barks, pointing a finger at me.

I don't turn around. Jake's not my priority right now. Caleb is the one in the net for this round of sudden death, and I'm taking my shot. Stripping off my ratty band t-shirt, I drop it to the floor and move topless across the kitchen towards him.

"Don't," Caleb growls.

I grab him by the neck with both hands and press myself against him, latching onto his mouth to pour everything I have into him. His hands wrap around me, smoothing up the bare skin of my back. I jump and he catches me, my legs wrapping around his hips as he turns us, setting me on the edge of the island.

My pussy presses up against his crotch as I kiss him breathless, chasing each kiss and flick of his tongue with a tease of my own. We're moaning into each other's mouths like starving animals. Then I'm breaking the kiss, pushing hard against his shoulders to shove him back.

He leans away, his hands at my hips. I'm still locked tight around his waist, my ankles crossed against his firm ass. I gaze up at him. His lips are pink and swollen with my kisses, his eyes dilated almost black.

"Do you love me, Caleb?" I murmur, searching his face. I need to know. This can't happen without me knowing first. I can't handle it otherwise.

"You know I do," he mutters.

Sucking in a sharp breath, I raise a hand and slap his face. *Hard*.

He reels with a grunt, his gaze jerking back to glare at me, his eyes now two burning coals.

"Good," I pant. "Then fuck me like you hate me."

55
RACHEL

Caleb digs his fingers into the hair at my nape and jerks hard, pulling my head back. "What did you just say to me?"

I smile. "I said fuck me like you hate me. Come on, daddy. You know you want to tear me apart," I tease. "Make Jake watch. Show us both who runs our shit—"

He silences me with a fierce kiss, his mouth dominating mine, his tongue burying itself deep. His hands cup my breasts and I arch into him, desperate for more. He goes from kneading me to pinching my nipples, clamping down with finger and thumb and twisting until I hiss and slap his hands off. The cool air stings and I shiver, goosebumps breaking out down my arms.

Jake steps forward. "Guys, what are you—"

"Shut up," Caleb barks, breaking our kiss to glare at him. "You wanna stay?"

Jake glances from me back to Caleb, jaw clenched. He nods.

"Good. Stand right here next to me, and don't say a goddamn word," Caleb commands, pointing to a spot on the floor.

I raise a brow, curious to see what happens next.

Slowly, Jake steps forward, gaze heated as he watches us. I can feel the protective energy simmering across every inch of his skin. I have a feeling he's either going to love this or hate it. We'll quickly find out which judging by how soon he pulls Caleb off me and slugs him in the jaw.

I refocus all my attention on Caleb. "Go on then, daddy." Dropping my hand between us, I cup his hard cock and give it a squeeze. "Do your worst."

He grabs me by the hair and pulls me off the counter. I gasp, bracing against him as I find my feet. He jerks me forward, our noses brushing, his warm breath fanning over my mouth. "On your knees,

Hurricane. Whores who like to get fucked get on their knees and beg for it."

Oh, thank god.

His demon wants to play. My pussy does a little dance as I drop eagerly to my knees. Bratting is over. I'm going to be so good for him. And in return, he'll lower these damn walls and finally let me in.

"What do you want?" he growls.

"I want to please you," I reply, gazing up at him from my place at his feet. "I want your cock. Please, daddy."

He huffs a mirthless laugh. "You think you get my cock just because you want it? That's not how this is gonna work, you greedy little slut. Besides, you don't want my cock. You just want something to choke on. Open your mouth."

My heart is hammering a mile a minute, my core clenching with need, as I part my lips for him.

He shoves two fingers in my mouth. "Suck."

A soft moan escapes me as I suck his fingers, using my tongue and teeth to tease him. He inserts a third finger and I take it, saliva dripping down my chin as he pumps his hand to his own rhythm. Grabbing my hair with his free hand, he holds my head steady and pushes his fingers in deeper until I gag, eyes watering.

"Good fucking girl," he murmurs. "Your mouth is so warm, so wet. How about your cunt? Are you wet for me, Hurricane?"

I nod, blinking back my tears. He's calling me 'Hurricane' and I hold onto that. I will break down all his walls. Let my winds blow, let the rains pour. This man is *mine*. I will pull him into the eye of my storm.

My throat gags on his fingers as he forces my mouth open. He quickly pulls his hand free, and I pant, catching my breath. My endorphins are rushing through my veins, leaving me with that buzzing, humming feeling. I'm drunk on his domination.

"Jake, get on your knees and check her cunt," he demands. "See if she's dripping for us."

My stomach does an excited flip as Jake drops to his knees, his gaze searching my face. I give him a reassuring smile. "Please, baby," I murmur, parting my legs wider for him.

I'm still wearing my sleep shorts and a pair of panties, but Jake works around them easily, dipping his hand inside the top, his fingertips brushing over my bare pussy as he seeks out my wet center. I can't contain my moan as he dips his fingers inside me, dragging them up to gently circle my clit.

"Well?" Caleb growls.

"She's wet," Jake replies, voice hoarse.

"How wet? Show me."

Jake pulls his fingers free of my shorts and holds them up for Caleb to see. They glisten in the bright lights of the kitchen.

"Let me taste," Caleb orders.

Jake lifts his arm up higher, and I watch, mesmerized, as Caleb takes Jake's fingers into his mouth, sucking them clean.

"Fuck," Jake mutters. Caleb lets him go and Jake drops his hand down to his side, his gaze glassy with unchecked arousal.

"Stand up, Jake. Take out your cock."

Holding my gaze, Jake stands. I give him another reassuring nod and his hands go to his grey sweats, tugging them down his hips. His hard cock springs free in my face.

"See, look at you," Caleb growls at me, giving my hair a tug to reclaim my attention. "Look at the way you're salivating for a taste of his cock. I bet this mouth will fuck anything." His thumb brushes against my bottom lip.

I breathe slow and steady, my knees starting to ache from the hard kitchen tiles.

Caleb leans down. "You want to choke on something bigger than a pair of fingers?"

I nod.

"Speak."

"Yes," I whisper.

"Yes, what?"

"Yes, I want his cock. Please, daddy. I need more."

His nostrils flair as he glances over at Jake. "She's asking for a cock to choke on. Are you gonna give it to her?"

Slowly, Jake nods.

"Damn it, not you too," Caleb growls. "Speak words, Compton."

"Yes," he mutters. "I wanna give it to her."

Caleb smiles, clearly loving this feeling of control we're both giving him. Has Jake ever played these games before? I doubt it. Not at this level.

Caleb directs my head towards Jake's crotch. "Suck Jake's cock, Hurricane. Show him how much you love to be filled. Such a good whore for us. Take him deep."

I eagerly comply, my eyes on Jake as I open my mouth and taste his tip, teasing with my tongue before I go deeper. Caleb keeps his hand on my hair, guiding my pace. With a groan, Jake drops his hands to my shoulders, his thumbs brushing up the sensitive skin of my neck.

"How does she feel, Jake?"

"Like fucking heaven," he mutters, eyes closed, head tipped back.

"Hurricane, you like sucking his cock, right?"

I hum and nod, my mouth still around his cock.

"That's enough," Caleb growls, jerking me backwards.

Jake's eyes flash open as he glares at Caleb, his glistening cock twitching with need. My pussy is aching for it. The delayed gratification is the hardest part of this kind of play, but it makes the eventual release all the sweeter. I have a feeling Caleb is the king of edging. I don't know if my pussy can take it.

"Look at you on your knees," Caleb croons, stroking my face. "So damn beautiful. You want more?"

I nod. "Please, daddy. I want your cock. Wanna make you feel so good."

"Then get it out."

I reach up without hesitation, pulling on his athletic shorts and dropping them to the floor around his ankles. His gorgeous cock is in my face, hard and proud. The silver barbells on the bottom catch the light of the kitchen.

He fists himself, holding his own base as he steps in. "Open. Show me what that smart mouth can do."

I open my mouth, gazing up at him as he pushes his tip between my lips. I tease him with my tongue, letting it slide over his piercings. Even against my tongue, the ribbing feels too good. I suppress a shiver as my core clenches on nothing. This feeling of emptiness is driving me mad. I'm not going to last much longer.

Caleb groans, his hand softening in my hair. "What a good fucking girl."

Next to him, Jake mutters a curse under his breath.

Caleb tenses, pulling me off. "You got something to say?" he asks with a raised brow.

Jake shakes his head.

"I think you have a praise kink," Caleb teases, his voice dark and edged. "Every time I call her a good girl, you squirm in your damn skin. Are you jealous, *angel*?"

"Fuck," Jake mutters, his cock twitching as he fights every urge to touch it.

Caleb is practically crowing as he reaches out a hand and grabs Jake by the hair, tugging him closer. "Maybe you want a taste of her medicine. Is that it? You wanna sub for me too, Jake? We both know you love taking direction. You could be such a good fucking boy for me," he purrs, and now Jake and I are both squirming messes. "Wanna earn your O for once in your spoiled goddamn life?"

Slowly, Jake nods, and my pussy is ready to burst into flames.

Caleb smiles like the devil incarnate. "Good. Then get on your fucking knees."

"Oh god," Jake mutters, dropping to his knees beside me.

Caleb keeps a hand on each of our heads, his fingers dragging through our hair. "Kiss," he orders. "Jake, get your fingers in her cunt, but don't you dare let her come. Shove them in there and hold. If she squirms even an inch, you pull out, understood?"

I whimper with frustration as Jake holds my gaze, his expression volcanic with heat. With one hand, Jake cups the back of my neck and pulls me closer, kissing me senseless. God, my boys are such good kissers. His other hand delves inside my shorts and he's thrusting two thick fingers up inside me. He holds them still, just like he was told, offering me nothing. It's the most perfect kind of torture.

But his tongue doesn't hold back. He's as ravenous as me, claiming all the passion he won't give my pussy with his desperate mouth. Our hands rove as we cling to each other. All the while, Caleb keeps his hands on our heads, holding onto us. Just as it begins to heat up, he's pulling us apart by the hair. Our kiss breaks and we're both panting.

Jake is so hard, the tip of his cock leaking. There's a bead of precum about to drop to the floor and I whimper, biting my lip with need.

Missing nothing, Caleb's hand tightens in my hair. "Catch it, pet. Now, before it's wasted."

I go to put my mouth on Jake, but Caleb holds me still. I reach out a hand instead, brushing my finger over Jake's tip, his cum slick on my fingertip. I raise the finger to my mouth and wince as Caleb's grip tightens again in my hair.

"What do you think you're doing?" he growls. "That's not yours. You haven't earned our cum yet, greedy girl. Give it to me."

My heart flips as I lift my hand in the air. Jake watches as I feed Caleb a drop of his cum. Caleb hums around my finger, sucking it clean. "Mmm, you don't know what you're missing, Hurricane."

Now it's Jake squirming, his hand wrapping around the base of his own dick, unable to keep from touching it.

"Are you getting antsy, angel?" Caleb teases. "Do you want more?"

"Yes," he says on a breath. "Please," he adds, and I think Caleb may have just died and gone to heaven.

"Then be my perfect good boy and suck my dick."

Oh god, this is it. The moment of reckoning. Whatever we've been doing before now, *this* is the real sudden death moment. I wait, watching Jake decide what he's going to do. He glances at me, desperate for guidance. He looks so nervous, so innocent, when I know he's anything but.

But this is new territory for him. I don't even have to ask. Jake has never sucked a dick before in his life. Never wanted to . . . until now.

"I'm right here, angel," I murmur, offering him my consent, though he doesn't need it.

"Fucking hell." He shifts slightly, turning to face Caleb a little more, as he reaches out with both hands, tentatively placing them on Caleb's hips. Caleb's hard cock is right in his face, his tip leaking.

I glance up, seeing the desperation in Caleb's eyes, the longing, the raw need.

Jake groans, his head tipping up. "I've never done this before, Cay. I don't—"

And that's when my heart grows two more sizes. He doesn't want to do it wrong. He wants this to be good for his best friend. I reach up and wrap my hand around Caleb's wrist, silently making my demand. He's so in tune with me, reading my body language. He lets me go, his hand dropping to his side.

"Let me show you, angel," I say, shifting forward, wrapping my arm around Jake's waist. I kiss his shoulder, smiling up at him. "We'll take him together. Teamwork, right?" I add with a little wink.

"Yeah . . . teamwork."

Caleb's chest is heaving as he stands still, watching us on our knees before him.

"Hold him at the base," I direct with a nod.

Jake slides his right hand off Caleb's hip and wraps it around the base of Caleb's cock.

Caleb groans and I smile. How quickly the tables have turned for him. But he's about to get one of the best orgasms of his life, so he better not complain. I guess I just can't help but top, even from the bottom.

"You want to start with a tease," I explain. "Lick the tip, then give it a suck. Like this." Then I'm demonstrating, sucking on the tip of Caleb's pierced dick while Jake holds it steady for me. I pop off him with a smile, leaning in to kiss the corner of Jake's mouth. "Now you try, angel. Drive our Cay wild."

He grins, wrapping his free hand around my waist. Then he's turning to Caleb and sucking his dick into his mouth.

56
CALEB

Jake's mouth is around my dick and I'm dead. This is death, and I've died. It must be heaven because Rachel is here too. They're both on their knees, and she's coaching him through how to suck me like a champion.

This fucking woman. This goddess. She's topping me—topping us *both*. From her fucking knees. And now I'm dead all over again. This is it. I'm done. I'll follow her anywhere. Just call me Reddi, 'cause I'm fucking whipped.

"That's so good, angel," she murmurs at Jake, her hand around his cock, stroking him as he sucks me. His tongue is warm and wet and it's all I can do to stay standing. "Take him deeper," she croons, her other hand in his hair, soothing him like she knows he needs. "Relax your throat and let him slide over your tongue. Mmm . . . just like that."

Oh my fucking god. She has to stop narrating, or I'm gonna blow. I cannot let my first blowjob from Jake Compton be over in sixty seconds. I have to slow this down. I have to last.

"You're doing so good," she says. "Look at you taking my Cay. Cup his balls, baby. You know how you like it. Give him a little squeeze."

Oh, god—I can't—oh, fuck—

And then his hand is right fucking there. Jake Compton is cupping my sack while his mouth is fully sucking my dick.

"He's losing control," she teases, her free hand brushing down my bare thigh. "If you're not careful, he's going to blow his hot load down your throat."

"Fuck, yes I am," I growl, finding my words at last. "And my good boy is gonna swallow it all. I'm gonna fill you up so fucking full."

"No, you're not," she counters. She leans in, murmuring softly in Jake's ear. "You're gonna let him blow in your mouth, angel. But you're not going to swallow. Nod that you agree."

Jake groans, the vibration humming down my shaft, and I swear to fuck I can't stand this much longer. He's nodding around my dick, and that's it. I'm so fucking done. I dig my hand into his hair and thrust once with my hips. He growls around my cock, glaring up at me, not liking the intrusion, but I thrust again. He grabs me by the hips, his fingers tight as iron, as he controls the pace so I can't choke him the way I want. Fine by me. He can do anything he wants so long as he lets me come in his mouth.

"You're such a good fucking boy," I mutter, giving him the praise he's earned. "Look at you on your knees for me. So fucking beautiful, so powerful. You're sucking me like a dream, baby. God, you're so talented."

He's groaning around my cock, and I want this feeling to last forever.

"You own me right now," I say. "You've got all the control. I'm yours, Jake. Fucking finish me. Take it all. Take everything."

With a grunt, he reaches around and slaps my ass and—*holy fucking god*—I'm coming so hard I see stars. I cry out, my every sense swimming as Jake Compton lets his mouth fill with my hot cum, gagging as he fights the urge to swallow.

I'm a shaking mess, my hand trembling in his hair as I unload. I open my eyes and glance down to see both my loves on their knees before me. Rachel is looking up at me with tears in her eyes. She made this happen for me. She hasn't outed me yet, but she knows what I want, and she knows Jake well enough to believe I might just be able to have it.

Never in my wildest dreams did I think I'd be standing naked in Jake's kitchen, my hands on *two* loves of my life, watching as they please me. I can't make sense of it. I can't—

"Oh, fuck," I mutter, because Jake is pushing off me, his chest heaving, eyes dilated black as he turns to Rachel. My cum drips down his chin.

"Spit it into my mouth, angel," she murmurs, brushing her hand along his cheek. "And then stand up and let me suck you with his cum."

Is it possible to die when you're already dead? Because I just took another arrow through the fucking chest.

Jake morphs into some kind of feral beast as he grabs her by the hair and presses his mouth to hers. I watch, dumbfounded, as Jake spits my cum into her mouth. He breaks away from her, gasping for air, wiping his mouth with the back of his hand, as he stumbles to his feet. His hand reaches out, bracing on my forearm for balance. He stays holding onto me as she looks up at both of us, naked and gorgeous, her confidence overflowing.

The awesome truth hits me all over again: I would follow this woman off a cliff. She wants to go sailing around Phuket? I'll build the fucking boat. She wants to dance naked in a fountain? I'll shut down a city block of Rome and hand her a pool noodle. My Rachel gets whatever she wants. She wants Mars Kinnunen to fuck her with his dragon dick? I mean, I'm gonna watch, because holy fuck, if that guy has even the slightest idea of what to do with that equipment, he's gonna shred her alive. And I want to see it. I'll jerk off to it. I'll be in her ass while he takes her cunt, that monster cock making her so tight I can hardly breathe.

The sobering truth is that I really don't care. She can fuck Mars. Hell, she can fuck the whole damn team. That's her choice. Either way, she's mine. Jake is mine. They're not going anywhere, and neither am I. I have everything I'll ever want or need right here in this kitchen.

I watch as Rachel shifts forward on her knees, hands bracing Jake's hips as she sucks him deep.

"Oh, baby. Fuck yeah," he groans, his hands in her hair, lovingly holding her as she glides up and down his shaft, my cum acting as her lubricant.

"Look at you both," I murmur, my heart breaking open. "I love you," I say, the words pouring out of me without conscious thought. "I love you both so goddamn much. I'll die without you." I step in closer, my hands on each of their shoulders. "Don't ever leave me behind," I whisper, taking the shot I never expected to take. Sudden death, right? Holy shit, this stuff is heady. "Be extraordinary together, take on the world, only let me come too."

Rachel whimpers around Jake's cock, her left hand leaving his hip to brace mine instead. Jake loosens his hold on her hair, his hand sliding around me to graze down my back. With the three of us touching, Jake tips his head back and blows in her mouth, his hand gripping sharp to my shoulder as he shudders.

Rachel slips her mouth off Jake's cock. Slowly, she stands. She's naked and breathtaking. Strong inside and out. We all know who really runs our shit. Standing there like a queen, her eyes glassy with lust, she breathes heavily through her nose. Raising both hands, she snaps her fingers and points to the floor in silent command.

Jake and I drop like rocks to our knees. I have to compensate, only touching down with my left knee, my right knee bent like I'm in a football kneel.

She takes hold of our chins and tips them up, the silent command in her eyes. I don't fucking hesitate. I open my mouth and she leans over with a smile, spitting the mixture of our cum into my mouth. I swallow with a groan, letting the salty taste coat my tongue. It's me and it's Jake. It's her. It's the three of us together. The start of something completely new.

She turns to Jake with a smile, and he doesn't hesitate either, opening his mouth as she hovers over him, letting the cum dribble down onto his waiting lips. Jake swallows, licking his lips with a soft groan. She swallows the rest. Then she brushes a hand through our hair at the same time and smiles. "What good fucking boys," she coos. "So pretty on your knees for me."

The surprise must be evident on my face because she does a little laugh and smiles, a queen triumphant. When we started this scene, I was in control. Now I'm on my fucking knees and loving it, ready to beg for more.

She brushes her fingers down my cheek, mirroring the motion on Jake. "Now . . . who's going to be the first to take me upstairs and fuck my ass til I scream?"

We can't scramble to our feet fast enough.

57
RACHEL

It turns out traveling under the radar with Mars Kinnunen is more difficult than it seems. The man is a 6'5" tatted, bearded, Viking. He sticks out in any crowd, regardless of his pro athlete status. As we move through the airport, people don't have to know he's one of the NHL's top goalies for all eyes to turn our way.

And apparently, his idea of a Clark Kent disguise is wearing sunglasses with his hair down. I've never seen him wear it down before. It's thick and textured, a blond lion's mane hanging just above his shoulders. He finishes the look with a pair of black dress pants cuffed at the ankle and a crisp, grey t-shirt that hugs all his muscles. The man oozes effortless wealth and sophistication.

Meanwhile, I'm all but jogging at his side in my uniform of high-waisted yoga pants, crop top, and black $5 flip-flops. Whatever, it's the airport. I didn't know the dress code for the trip was GQ casual. I grip tighter to the strap of my overnight bag. "Do I know why we're rushing?"

He glances down at me, slowing to a halt. I can't see his eyes behind his dark Ray-Bans. "What?"

I puff out a breath, flipping the messy tendrils of dark hair off my face. People glide past us at a more casual pace, wheeling bags and chasing kids. "Is there a fire or something I don't know about? You rushing to the bathroom before you have an accident?"

His blond brows raise behind his sunglass frames. "What?"

"God—*slow down*, Mars," I huff, dropping the jokes. "I can't keep up with you. We look like a miniature pony chasing after a Clydesdale."

"What?" he says for a third time, his lips pursed in confusion.

I snort a laugh. "Just forget it," I say, waving him off. "As you were, Kinnunen. We've got our own tickets anyway. I'll just see you at the gate."

"You want me to walk without you?"

"Well, it's kind of inevitable if you're gonna walk so damn fast!"

I can see that it finally clicks. "Oh," he says. "My apologies."

Jeezus. We got there in the end, I guess.

"I was just walking," he adds.

"Yeah, well, keep walking," I say, gesturing down the terminal. "Don't worry about me, Mars. You go on, and I'll catch up."

"But I want to walk with you."

He says it so softly, I could also imagine he didn't say it at all. Before I can reply, a trio of guys press in from behind us, wheeling their bags.

"Shit, fellas, what'd I say?" calls the big guy in front. "It *is* Mars Kinnunen. Yo, man. You're amazing!"

Ilmari goes stiff for the briefest of moments before he transforms. It's like who he just was with me steps inside a closet for a quick change and out comes Mars the NHL Goalie. He puts on a weird, fake smile that doesn't meet his eyes and thanks the guys, signing something for each of them and letting them take a picture with him.

All the while, he doesn't let me move from within arms-reach of him. I tried twice, but both times he just stuck his hand out, wrapping it around my upper arm to keep me close. He shoos them politely away and his hold on my arm relaxes.

"That's why I must walk fast," he mutters. "They don't stop me when I walk fast."

I nod, understanding his dilemma. How many times have I all but run through an airport at my dad's side, our coats pulled up over our heads to block a paparazzi shot? I snatch up my bag and sling the strap over my shoulder. "Alright then, big guy. Let's do it."

We take off, him speed-walking on his giraffe legs, me jogging at his side.

BY the time we get to the gate, they've already begun boarding. Mars checks his ticket, flipping his sunglasses up on top of his head.

"Now boarding all rows, all passengers, for flight 1647 with service to Cincinnati, leaving out of Gate C5," comes the gate agent's alert over the intercom.

"That's us," I say, tugging my own ticket out of the front pocket of my bag.

He leads the way over to the counter and we get checked in. It doesn't escape my attention the way people milling around the gate openly stare. A few people raise up their phones, snapping pictures while his back is turned. I take an instinctual step back, keeping my gaze averted from any camera lenses.

The gate agent takes his ticket, scanning him in. "Thank you, Mr. Kinnunen. You're in seat 2A."

He mutters a word of thanks and moves past her towards the jet bridge.

She scans my ticket next. "And Ms. Price, you're in 17B."

"Thanks," I murmur. "All good," I say at Mars, joining him at the door.

We move down the jet bridge onto the plane. He gets to his row in first class, sliding into the window seat.

"See you when we land," I say cheerily, already slipping a pod into my left ear.

"Wait—what?" he growls. "Rachel!"

I pause, glancing over my shoulder at him. "Yeah?"

"Where are you going?" He's looking at me like I'm crazy.

The feeling is mutual as I look right back at him. "To my seat, Mars. It's kinda the thing on airplanes," I add. "Come on, you should know that better than anyone."

He doesn't return my smile. No, in fact, he looks pissed. His blond brows narrow over his deep blue eyes. "Why aren't you sitting in first class?"

"Because I bought these tickets at the literal last minute. We'll touch down in like 90 minutes," I add with an indifferent shrug. "Hardly time to even get comfortable."

At his look of supreme annoyance, I can't help but roll my eyes. He wants me to sit next to him on this flight too. *Really?* "You can't pull your goalie card on a commercial flight, Kinnunen. And it's not a big deal, okay? I'll see you in a bit."

People are piling up behind me, so I hurry down the aisle, not giving him a chance to respond as I go find my seat.

58
ILMARI

Not a big deal, she says. This is a very big deal. My palms are sweating knowing that she's on this plane and not next to me. I want Rachel next to me. I want Rachel.

2B is still empty. Why can't she move up here? I'll gladly pay. As I reach for the flight attendant call button, a man comes around the corner and I know he's about to sit in the empty seat. He's a businessman—golf shirt, slicked back hair, Rolex watch.

He looks right at me, dismissing me as he drops into Rachel's seat. "Uh-huh. No—Chuck—I said, tell Danny I sent the specs on Friday."

He's on his phone, talking loudly into his earpiece. Meanwhile, I feel like I'm crawling out of my skin. Once they close that door, and we push back, there's nothing I can do.

"I told you they'd go for it. Uh-huh." My seat mate wordlessly accepts a mimosa from the flight attendant, not even looking up at her.

I politely wave her away.

"Well, just tell Danny that I'll take care of it when I get back."

With a groan, I lean in. "Excuse me."

"Yeah—" He turns to look at me, dark brows lowered in annoyance at being interrupted. "Yeah—hold on, Chuck. No—hold on, Chuck. Can I help you?" he says at me.

"My travel companion and I got separated," I explain. "Would you be willing to switch seats with her?"

He glances around. "Is she in first class?"

"No."

"Then no, pal—Yeah, Chuck, I'm still here—" He chatters into his phone as I feel my anxiety mounting.

"I'll pay you $500 to move," I say, interrupting his call again.

"Hold on, Chuck," he growls. "Dude, what's your problem?" he says at me.

"I said I'll pay you to switch seats with her," I repeat. "$500 cash."

He scoffs. "Look, guy, I make $500 an hour. It's a short flight. Finger your girl in the bathroom if you're that hard up."

My shoulders tense. I don't like him talking about Rachel that way. If he was a player, he would have just earned himself a punch to the jaw. But this isn't hockey. I have to speak the language he understands.

The flight attendant asks him for the second time to hang up his call. I'm running out of time. Any moment they'll say we're pushing back.

"I'll give you $1,000 to move," I offer, talking over him for a third time.

"Jesus—*no*, asshole," he snaps. "Keep harassing me, and I'll have you booted from this flight."

Swallowing my growl of frustration, I snatch up my bag from under the seat. "Then move."

"What?"

"Let me out. *Move.*"

"Look, I gotta call you when I land, Chuck. The guy next to me is being a total dick." He unbuckles his seatbelt and stands.

"Sir, you need to sit down. We're about to push back," calls the flight attendant.

"Tell that to this guy," he says, jabbing a thumb in my direction.

"Sirs, you *both* need to sit down," she repeats.

But I'm not listening. I slip past the asshole and move down the aisle into coach, my eyes scanning the seats looking for Rachel.

The flight attendant follows behind me. "Sir, you have to return to your seat—"

I spot Rachel. She's looking down at her phone, probably texting her pushy red-headed friend.

"Sir, I said you need to sit—*sir!*"

I approach Rachel's row and she spots me, eyes going wide. "Mars, what are you doing?"

There's a young man sitting next to her. He's wearing a backwards baseball hat and a Buffalo Sabres t-shirt. His eyes go just as wide as Rachel's as he sees me approach. "Whoa—holy shit," he cries, grinning like a fool. "Mars Kinnunen? For real?"

Rachel groans.

"Hello," I say at her seat mate. "Would you like to sit in first class?"

"Mars, this is ridiculous," Rachel cries at the same time that the kid just glances between us and says, "Uhhh . . ."

"Sir, please take your seat," the flight attendant says again. "Now. Or you'll be removed from the flight."

"This is my seat," I say, pointing to the kid. "He's going up to 2A."

"Oh my god," Rachel mutters, shaking her head.

"I mean . . . yeah sure," says the kid, unbuckling his seatbelt. "Hey—can I get a picture with you really quick?"

"Sirs, find your seats *now*," the flight attendant orders.

The kid climbs out of the narrow seat, unafraid of the flight attendant's threats as he pulls out his phone and leans in, snapping a selfie with me.

I sit down, folding my large frame into the impossibly narrow space.

"Jesus, Mars," Rachel mutters. "Are you happy now?"

I am happier, yes.

"Ouch—*god*—hold on, you big tree." She elbows me sharply as she shimmies the armrest up between us. It buys us two spare inches. "This is why I got you the first class seat. Professional hockey players aren't meant to fly coach."

I reach for the end of my seatbelt.

"Mars, stop grabbing my ass."

"Then get off my seatbelt," I mutter, tugging it loose from under her thigh. I do my best not to elbow her too aggressively in the process.

"God, we're only an hour into this trip, and you're already determined to drive me crazy," she mutters, leaning away from me as I get the buckle fastened.

The plane starts to move, and the flight attendants begin their safety demonstration. I settle into my seat, letting out a low breath.

"Mars, why the hell did you do that?" Rachel murmurs, her dark brown eyes gazing up at me, all flecked with gold.

"Because I wanted to sit next to you," I reply. Taking her hand, I weave our fingers together, balancing them on my knee. "No one sits next to you but me, Rakas."

"Rakas?" she repeats with a raised brow. "What—is that Finnish for Rachel or something?"

"No."

She hasn't tried to take her hand away, which I'm taking as a good sign. I have no idea what the hell I'm doing. Ilmari Kinnunen is methodical. I watch and I wait. I weigh my options. But with Rachel Price, there is no plan. I just do.

Right now, the thing I'm doing is holding her hand. And it feels fucking good.

She's looking up at me, those dark eyes searching me, knowing me. I can't get this woman out of my head. I've been trying for days. Weeks. Everything in me is telling me to walk away. She's my doctor. To ask for more would be unprofessional. And I am not unprofessional. I do my job. I put in the work. I leave it all out on the ice. I don't let emotion cloud my thinking.

Yet, here I am, flying on a plane on my off day, because she asked me to. Traveling to a strange city to meet a doctor I don't know because she trusts them to help me. Offering a man $1,000 to move seats because I can't be in the place where she is and not be by her side.

And now I'm holding her hand and she's letting me. I don't dare look down. I don't move. I just breathe. Next to her. Her hand is so small in mine. I fight the urge to lean in, dropping my face to that place at her neck where I know she'll smell sweetest.

What is this perfume she wears? The scent is soft and warm. It makes me think of lichen on rocks warming in the sun on a summer's day. You put your hand on it and feel a heat that doesn't burn. But it seeps through your skin, warming you all the same.

"Mars?" she says again, her free hand brushing down the bare skin of my arm. "You alright?"

"No," I reply, giving her the honest truth.

I'm not alright. Nothing is alright. I'm at war with myself. Part of me wants to jerk my hand free and move away. No more Rachel Price. How many times have I said it? This needs to be finished. I need to put distance between us. But the idea of distance aches like a physical pain. No more distance. I want closer. I want touch. I want to drag her down the aisle of this plane and fuck her in the galley. I want us to sink to the floor, utterly spent, my cum sticky between her legs. I'll wrap her in my arms and hold her tight, blocking out the rest of the world.

She sighs, leaning back against her seat. "Yeah . . . I'm nervous too," she admits, giving my hand a little squeeze. "But it's okay. We'll get through this together, yeah?"

She thinks I'm worried about the scans. She thinks I'm worried they'll be bad, that I'll be out for the season and lose my chance at the Winter Olympics. I am worried. Of course, I am. But what's wrong with me that now I'm *more* worried the scans will be clear?

Without this to bind us together, we have nothing. Without her caring about my physical health, I have no point of connection to Rachel Price. No reason to call, no reason to seek her out. I'll have to watch her drift away, giving her full attention to other players.

Saatana, it makes me angry just thinking about it. I can't watch her laugh with another man or share her smiles as he shamelessly flirts with her. I'm already within an inch of flattening Compton. He looks at her like he's seen her naked. I've watched them together. He's so obvious with his intentions, the way he finds excuses to touch her as he brushes past. He wants her too.

I finally let myself glance down at our joined hands. She hasn't tried to pull away. Not once. At this angle, I can see the tattoos on the inside of her forearm. One is an electric guitar with a signature tattooed along the neck. She likes tattoos. She likes talking about them. Maybe she'll talk to me . . .

"What does this one mean?" I mutter, the finger of my free hand brushing over the signature.

She glances down, and I don't miss the way she shivers slightly at my touch. "Oh, um . . . okay, well this is my dad's favorite model of Gibson Les Paul," she explains. "And this is his signature," she adds, tracing over the jagged script.

"Is he a musician?"

She fights a smile. "Yeah, Mars. He's a musician." She turns to face me more squarely. "Actually, my father is Halston Price. He's the lead singer of—"

"The Ferrymen," I finish for her.

Her smile curls up on one side. "Yeah . . . you know them?"

Know them? The Ferrymen are my favorite rock band. I grew up working out to their music. I've seen them in concert in different venues across Europe over a dozen times. Rachel Price is Hal Price's daughter. How did I never put that together?

"Listen, Mars." She shifts in her seat. "There's something else I've been meaning to tell you. Something I think it's only right that you know before we—before we land," she finishes.

We both know that's not how she ended that sentence in her mind.

"Tell me," I say, not letting go of her hand.

"I'm with Jake Compton," she says on a breath, her dark eyes wide and hopeful and she gazes up at me. "We're together, Mars."

Her fingers go like ice in my hand as I pull away, leaving her open hand resting atop my knee. She's with Compton. They're together. And now everything makes sense. He laughs with her, teases her, looks at her like he's seen her naked . . . because he has. Jake Compton kisses Rachel. He fucks my Rachel. And suddenly my world is crashing down. She's taken. Of course, she is. She was never going to be mine. I was deluding myself.

"Mars—"

"It's fine." I drag a calloused hand over my face, stroking my beard. "It's not my business. Please, let's not discuss it."

"I think it *is* your business," she replies. "You deserve the truth, Mars. I don't want to hide anything from you or lead you on when I can't offer you what you want."

Why the hell is she still talking?

"And Jake and Caleb agree with me," she goes on. "You deserve to have all the facts. If you really think you're interested in me, you better know what the heck you're walking into. Because I can't offer you exclusivity, and the guys are pretty sure that'll be a deal-breaker for you. You know, because of the whole 'goalies work alone' thing—"

"Caleb?" I say, cutting her off. "The equipment manager? You and Compton spoke to him about me?"

She nods, biting her bottom lip as she holds my gaze. "Yeah . . . cause that's the other thing. I'm sort of with Caleb too."

59
RACHEL

This is a disaster. Oh god, why did I do this? Why did I try to have this conversation now in the middle of a crowded airplane?

Because if you didn't pump the breaks, you were gonna start snogging him right here in the seat, comes the snarky voice in my head.

She doesn't know anything. I'm totally in control. It's not like I've been sitting here, heart racing, memorizing the shape of Ilmari's mouth as he speaks. I'm not holding his hand, our legs brushing from knee to hip, wondering if he'll notice if I just rest my cheek on his shoulder and breathe him in.

Yes, you are.

Oh, god-fucking-damn it. I totally am. I don't know what it is about this man, but he completely unravels me. His strength inspires me, his calm quiet makes me curious. What happens behind his thick outer walls? Who is Ilmari inside the defenses he wears? The man is a living, breathing goalie, and he's quite literally never off the clock. He keeps out everyone and everything all the time. It must be exhausting. And lonely.

Maybe it's just my damn stubborn streak, but I want to take a shot on his goal. But the more contact we have, the more I learn about him, the more hesitant I am to take my shot. Because I have a strong feeling that, if I *do* get inside this man's net, there'll be no getting out again.

Caleb is calling this a recon operation. I have questions, and I need answers. Is this just about physical attraction? Or is it more? I think he and Jake still see Mars as the quirky goalie. They see his silence and his tics, and they believe this is only about sex for him. He wants me, and I want him, and we'll both feel better when we get it out of our systems. One wild night.

Now I'm not so sure.

But I had to tell him. The boys and I agreed. I couldn't take a step forward with Ilmari unless he knew the truth about us. It wouldn't be fair to him or them. At least he'll be discreet. If there is one single person on the Rays I can trust to know our secret and not go blabbing it around, it's Ilmari Kinnunen. He won't tell a soul.

But now the look on his face has me wanting to press rewind. He's pulling away, stacking the bricks of his thick walls a mile high. I guess this is answer enough. He's not interested in sharing. They said he wouldn't be. I should have known better than to hope.

Or . . .

Maybe his hesitancy is more about civility. There are unspoken rules in hockey, after all. Sacred rules. Like how you don't go after another teammate's girl. Or his sister. In Ilmari's eyes, Jake has already staked his claim. He has no choice but to bow out.

"I'm sure you have questions," I murmur, watching him tense at hearing my voice.

"I don't."

"Mars—"

He rounds on me, his blue eyes depthless as the sea. "Fuck whoever you want, Doctor Price. Leave me out of it."

His words are so cold, his tone so unfeeling. I sink back in my seat away from him. "So . . . I'm Doctor Price again? That's convenient."

He crosses his arms, trying to minimize our points of contact. "I will call you Doctor Price, because that is who you are," he counters. "And when we return to Jacksonville, I believe our professional relationship will need to end. I'll seek out an alternative medical care provider."

Thank god the lady next to me in the window seat is zonked out asleep, because I really don't want an audience when I start to cry. I look down at my knees, blinking back the tears I refuse to shed. "How did we get here?" I murmur. "One minute, you're racing down the aisle, desperate for the chance to just hold my hand. The next, you're cold as ice, severing all ties as if that's so easy for you to do." I glance up, trying to search his face in profile. "I have a life, Mars. I live it, and I'll not apologize to you for that."

"I never said you had to," he replies, still so cold.

"Yes, but you're judging me for it. I can only imagine what you're calling me in your mind right now. I'm sure it's not 'doctor' or what-ever that word was in Finnish. I'm only trying to be open with you. I won't lie, and I won't lead you on—"

He glares down at me, the look in his eyes halting my words. "I get it. You've told me, and now I know. My English is proficient enough to understand your full meaning, Rachel," he all but growls. "You are with Compton and his DVP. Which means there is nothing left to be said."

I flinch, the sting of his words hitting me like a slap. Somewhere behind his walls, he's churning, seas bubbling, as a dormant volcano deep in his ocean floor begins to heat. I've always preferred fire to ice.

"Okay, Mr. English Major," I say, leaning in with a matching glare. "First, the term is DLP, domestic life partner. And yes, I'm with them both. I love them both, and they are *mine*. But they don't own me, and I don't own them. And my interest in you has nothing to do with them . . . unless you want it to," I add with a teasing smile. "Which brings me to my second point." I flash two fingers in his face. "DVP means double vaginal penetration, Mars. Do you know what that is?"

He glares at me, the muscle in his neck twitching.

Fuck it. I'm poking this bear.

I lean in closer, lowering my voice. "Imagine your cock buried to the hilt inside my cunt, Mars. Then Caleb slides in with his pierced dick, edging you to the point of euphoria. That's when my pussy will strangle you both, and we all come together in a shaking, sweating pile of arms and legs and dripping cum. *That's* DVP."

I cross my arms as we glare at each other. He shifts in his seat with a soft grunt, and I glance down, my mouth tipping into a smile. The reason he's suddenly so uncomfortable is unmistakable. He's hard. Getting harder.

I slowly raise my gaze back to his face to see him smoldering, his jaw clenched tight under his blond beard. "You alright there, Kinnunen? Things feeling a little tight back here in coach. You had your chance to sit in first class. You gave it up to sit with me. And if you'll remember, *you* kissed *me* in that hallway, not the other way around. You started this, Mars. Do us both a favor and just admit it: you want me too—"

Before I finish speaking the words, his right hand comes up and grabs me by the jaw, tipping my face sharply up. I suck in a breath, eyes wide, as he leans down, turning my head away. I arch my neck for him, waiting . . . hoping.

His breath is warm on my skin as he hovers his face over my ear, the tip of his nose brushing featherlight against my lobe. Then he slowly breathes me in, filling his lungs, breathing out against my skin as I suppress a shiver of want.

"Careful, Rakas," he murmurs in my ear, the growl in his voice sending a shock straight through my chest and down to my aching core. "I am not the kind of man who appreciates being teased . . . or managed." He rests his forehead along my temple, his hand still holding tight to my jaw. "You're trying to handle me," he adds. "You think if you bend me to your will, you'll feel less like the ground is shifting beneath your feet."

My breath hitches as I turn to hold his piercing gaze. He thinks he knows me so well?

"You like control," he adds, his gaze boring into my soul. "I'm sure you've done this before. I'm sure men fall to their knees for you. I'm sure you lead Compton and Sanford by their cocks, and they follow you gladly, your pretty pink cunt taking them so sweetly."

As he speaks, his left hand curls around my leg, just above the knee, and he slides it up my thigh. I fight a whimper as his other hand moves down my neck to circle my throat. He applies no pressure, but his hand rests there, his fingertips brushing against the racing of my pulse.

"But know this, Rakas," he says, voice low. "I do not bend. I do not get on my knees. And I do not share what is *mine*. I started this and clearly that was a mistake. I'm finishing it. Here. Now. There is nothing left." With that, he lets me go, leaving me reeling in my seat as he shifts away.

60
ILMARI

You want me too. Her words echo around inside my head for the rest of the flight. She wants me. By her own words, she admits it. She wants me, but she wants Compton and Sanford too. She's already in a relationship with them.

Yet still, she seeks me out.

And they both know.

That's the part in all of this that confuses me most. Compton knows his woman wants me. Does the man have no pride? Does he care so little about her fidelity? He must not, because she brazenly admits to having a relationship with Sanford as well. Can it be possible they enjoy sharing her in such a way? Can they really bear to let another man kiss her or touch her?

The concept is wholly foreign to me. Even just thinking of their hands on her has me shifting in my seat, desperate to get away. I can't sit here and feel her presence so close to me while I'm thinking of other men touching her. Other men making her moan. Making her come.

And not just any men. Compton is my teammate. We're on the ice together every day. He's my sword and my shield. He's a damn good player. To add insult to injury, he's a good person. He's just . . . nice. He always tries to include me in things. I know it's him who keeps adding me back in to the group chat. Novikov told me. Compton always has a kind word when I fail to block a save. He encourages me.

But he's fucking my Rachel. And he knows that she wants me. They talk about it.

I press my head back against the seat, eyes shut tight, breathing through the feeling of deep, aching need coursing across my chest.

I can't do this. I can't indulge her curiosity. She wants to fuck me, that's all. She doesn't want *me*. Why would she when she has Compton and Sanford? She's offering me a taste and nothing more. But what mortal could ever stop at just a mere sip of ambrosia? If I can't have all of her, I will have none. I'll let her go. I'll walk away. Not a single drop of her essence will pass my lips again.

Resolved, I cross my arms and keep my eyes shut, pretending to sleep until we land.

"*DAMMIT,*" she mutters, eyes on her phone as she walks at my side through the airport towards baggage claim.

"What?" I say, trying to let her set the pace. Walking this slow feels odd.

"Oh, it just looks like we'll have to get a taxi over to the clinic," she replies, eyes still on her phone as she taps out a message. "My friend Tess was going to pick us up, but she's having some kind of crisis at work." She sighs, looking up from her phone. "You good to head straight to the clinic? Or do you want to check into your hotel first?"

She's as casual as can be, strolling at my side as if we're discussing the weather, not the potential demise of my two-decade-long hockey career. But my mind snags on something else she just said. "*My* hotel?"

"Uh-huh. I booked you a room at the Cincinnatian," she says, eyes back on her phone as she leads us onto the airport tram. "It's really nice. I've stayed there before. And it's just a few blocks up the street from the clinic."

The tram starts to move, jolting us forward. I grab for the metal pole. She just leans into it with her shoulder, eyes still on her phone. Is this another tactic? A game? Why won't she look at me?

"Where are you staying?" I mutter, feeling increasingly irritated.

"With Tess," she replies. "Before I moved down to Jax, we rented an apartment together. She turned my room into a guest room."

So, she'll take me to the clinic, let her doctor run their tests, and then leave me at my hotel? That's what I want, right? Distance. I want to be alone. I want away from her cloying presence. Before I do something I regret . . . like grab her by the hair and kiss her senseless on this tram.

"Fine," I say. "Clinic first."

We walk out to the taxi stand and the businessman from first class is waiting at the curb. He's on his phone again, talking with his hands.

"Yeah, Chuck. I'm on the way right now and—yeah, hold on—Hey," he says, spotting us standing behind him. He flashes me an American smile as he taps his earpiece, ending his call. "The kid told me who you were. Big NHL goalie, huh? That's cool, man. My buddy plays for the Bengals." His gaze darts to Rachel and I fight the urge to step in front of her, wanting her blocked from his view. "Wanna sign something for my kid?" he adds, patting his pockets like he's looking for a spare piece of paper.

"No," I reply, feeling Rachel tense next to me.

His eyes narrow under dark brows. "You won't sign something for a kid? That's a pretty shitty move. The kinda move that could get you in trouble," he adds, making it clear he means to threaten me.

"Do it," I say. "Report me to the League. See if they care that one asshole couldn't get an autograph."

"Mars," Rachel murmurs, her hand wrapping around my wrist.

His gaze darts back down to her and he smirks appreciatively, taking in her curves. "Nice," he says. "I see why you wanted to pay me. You should listen to your girl, man."

"Suksi vittuun," I curse, squaring my shoulders at him. I'm 6'5" and nothing but muscle. This man is maybe 5'8". He'll back down or get flattened into jelly.

"Sir, your taxi is here!" calls the stand attendant.

Mr. Business glares at me for another moment before he turns away with a muttered, "fucking asshole prick." Then he gets into his taxi and drives off as another pulls up.

"You know that guy?" Rachel murmurs, her hand still on my wrist.

"I was sitting next to him in first class." I step forward to open the taxi door for her, taking her bag from her shoulder. The attendant helps me get them into the trunk, and then I move around to the other side and slide in. Rachel is already giving the driver the address.

Rachel shifts, crossing her right leg over her left, her body angled a little closer in towards mine. "What did he mean about you paying him?"

"Nothing," I mutter, turning my gaze to look out the window.

"Did you—" She falls silent.

Silence fills the void between us. Uncomfortable silence. I can't help it. I have to look over.

She's looking up at me, her expression soft. "You tried to pay him to move, didn't you? So you could sit by me in first class?" At my silence she nods. "But he wouldn't take your money."

"It doesn't matter," I say.

"How much did you offer him?"

"I said it doesn't matter."

"Mars—"

"A thousand dollars," I reply, my gaze on the green interstate signs.

She lets out a soft breath. "Oh, Mars . . ."

We're silent for a few minutes.

"What did you say to him?"

I glance over again. "Hmm?"

"In Finnish. You said something to him. It didn't sound very nice," she adds with a small smile.

"It wasn't," I reply. "I told him to fuck off."

She huffs. "Yeah, he seemed like a jerk. Say it again."

I raise a brow. "Why?"

She rolls her eyes at me. "Obviously because I want to hear you speak Finnish. I like hearing you talk. And it's a pretty language."

"I was cursing at him, Rakas. I can say nicer things in Finnish."

"Oh, don't hold back on me now," she says, smiling wider. "Give me a little of both. Sugar and spice. Say the curse again."

"Suksi vittuun," I repeat.

"Sooksy vi—what?"

"Vittuun," I say again, unable to control my smile.

Her dark brows raise as she unscrews the cap to her diet soda. She's always drinking either diet soda or coffee. Does the woman ever drink water? "What? Why are you smiling? Did I say it wrong?"

"No, you're correct. Your pronunciation is good. But what you are saying is 'ski into a cunt.'"

She snorts her diet soda, choking and laughing. "Ohmygod— ouch—Seriously? 'Suksi vittuun' means 'ski into a cunt'?"

"Literally, yes. But the meaning is to go fuck off."

She laughs again. "Okay, I like that one. Suksi vittuun. Now give me something nicer." She's more relaxed now. She likes talking. It eases her nerves.

I've never liked talking, but it feels easier with her. It definitely feels easier in Finnish. Using her ignorance as a shield, I let myself gaze at the bold features of her face and say the words I feel. "Oot kaunis, Rakas." I let my gaze drop to the bow of her lips, wanting to trace them with my fingers, my tongue. "Mun leijona . . . Mä kuulun sulle."

She blushes, biting the inside corner of her lip like she does sometimes. Her hand with the hearts tattoo lifts as she tucks her hair behind her ear. "And . . . what does that mean?" she murmurs, all but breathless. Some things don't need to be translated.

I look back out the window, avoiding her gaze. "It means 'you're beautiful,'" I reply, giving her at least part of the truth.

"Thank you," she says softly. After a minute she adds, "I think you're beautiful too, Mars . . . for whatever that's worth to you."

What is it worth to me?

Everything.

WE arrive outside the clinic and Rachel has transformed before my eyes. As the taxi drove, she changed her shoes to something more professional with a closed toe and a heel. Then she slipped out of her zipped, hooded sweatshirt and tugged on a sheer, silky white blouse with a collar and buttons. It fits her loose, cuffed at the wrists to expose some gold bracelets on both wrists.

I watch her shimmy in the seat, tucking her shirt into the front of her black leggings. Lastly, she pulls her hair down out of its bun. Adding a flick of red color to her lips, she looks like a different person as we pull up.

"Right, so we'll do the physical exam first, and then the scans. The team here is great, so you don't need to worry about that," she says, going into full doctor mode.

I get out of the taxi, taking both our bags from the driver, as Rachel waits on the curb. The sounds of the city echo all around us.

It's an overcast day, much cooler from the tropical climate in Florida. I don't mind it. In fact, I prefer the cold.

"I just texted Doctor Halla, so he knows we've arrived," she goes on, her heels clicking on the sidewalk as she leads me over to the front door and pulls it open.

I'm distracted, watching the gentle sway of her hips as she walks. I'm passing through the door when I register her words. A sinking feeling settles in my chest, and I pause just inside the doorway of a bright clinic waiting room. "Wait—Rachel—what name did you say?"

"I said—*ah*—Doctor Halla!" She hurries forward, thrusting out a hand to greet a tall man wearing a set of navy-blue scrubs. "Thank you so much for agreeing to do this," she says, shaking his hand with both of her own. "You have no idea how grateful we both are, sir."

But he's not looking at Rachel. I'm not looking at Rachel either. I'm looking at him. This has to be a joke. A cruel, cosmic joke. Is she in on it? Does she know? How the hell would she know?

Rachel drops his hand and turns, one brow raised in confusion. She doesn't understand my coldness. "Doctor Halla, this is my friend, Ilmari Kinnunen, goalie for the Jacksonville Rays. Mars, this is Doctor Benjamin Halla."

I don't move. This can't happen. Not here. Not now.

Slowly, he sighs, clearly sensing the war I'm waging with myself. "Hello, son," he says in Finnish. "It's good to see you again."

61
RACHEL

Something's wrong. It's written all over Ilmari's face. He's white as a sheet. It only lasts a moment before he's burying himself so deep behind his thick walls. It's like I watch him disappear, his whole body icing over. And then he's gone, his face a blank mask.

Doctor Halla is speaking. It takes me a moment to realize why I'm confused. He's not speaking English. Ilmari answers him in what I can only assume is Finnish, his voice low, his words clipped.

I knew Doctor Halla was European, but I never knew from where. Honestly, I never thought to ask. It's not like we swapped life stories. If we weren't talking about patient care, we weren't really talking. I doubt he knows a thing about me other than that I like cheesy bagels and require a coffee IV drip to make it through a night shift.

"You two know each other?" I say, glancing between them.

And that's when my heart drops from my chest. Doctor Halla is a tall man, broad-shouldered. He has short blond hair, peppered with grey at his temples, and deep blue eyes. My gaze darts from Ilmari to Doctor Halla and back. It's the bridge of their noses that seals my suspicions. The slight downturned crease in the outside corner of their eyes. The thin set of their lips as they exchange clipped sentences in Finnish. "Are you two related?" I say over them, knowing I'm right.

"No," Ilmari replies at the same time Doctor Halla says, "Yes."

Ilmari is hard as stone, giving nothing away.

"I'm his father," Halla explains.

"You are not my father," Ilmari snaps. "You are nothing to me and never have been."

As the men stare each other down, my brain is still mid-seizure. "I don't understand," I manage to say, looking at Mars. "I thought you said your father was a hockey player. Isn't that the point in all of this?" I add, gesturing around. "You said the Olympics was your family's legacy—"

"It's the Kinnunen legacy," says Halla with a decided frown. "Ilmari is not a Kinnunen."

"Yes, I am," Ilmari counters. He steps forward, his eyes blazing with heat. "My father is Juhani Kinnunen. What else do you call the man who raised me? You are nothing to me, Halla—"

"Because your mother never gave me a chance—"

Ilmari cuts Halla off with a string of vehement sentences spat in Finnish that I can only assume are colorful curses designed to let Doctor Halla know exactly where he can go. And then Halla is replying, his tone more measured, like he's refusing to rise to Ilmari's obvious bating.

Sensing the rising tension, I step between them. "Okay—" I lift a hand up in each of their directions. "I forgot my universal translator back on the *Enterprise*, so I'm gonna need you both to switch to English, okay? I'm sure we can figure this out—"

"No. I'm done," says Ilmari. "This is done."

"Son, don't be a fool. You need these scans," Doctor Halla replies. "Let me help you—"

"I don't want your help," Ilmari snaps. "I don't want anything from you."

And that's when the truth I've been missing up to this point hits me on the head like an anvil. This isn't some wacky coincidence. Doctor Halla knew what he was doing. From the moment I said Ilmari's name on the phone, he knew I was talking about his son. He wanted me to bring him here. He used me to get to Ilmari.

And one look at Ilmari tells me how much this has hurt him. He has no relationship with this man, and I have to assume that's on purpose. I trust Ilmari. I trust his reasons. My protective instincts flare.

Ilmari snatches the bags up off the floor and turns away like he means to leave.

"Ilmari, wait," I call after him.

"Price, this wasn't our agreement," Doctor Halla's cheeks are reddening with embarrassment as Joanne, the nurse at the front desk, watches all of this unfold. "You said you could get him here. You said he would see me."

My mind is spinning. "I—"

Ilmari turns slowly back around, and now he's staring daggers at me. "You said what?" He takes a half-step towards me. "You did this on purpose? You brought me to him?"

"Well, yes—but only to *help* you—"

"Did you know?" he says, looking at me like I'm a hydra with ten heads. "Did he tell you?"

"What?" I cry. "Mars—*Jeezus*—does this look like the face of a person in the know?" I say, gesturing to what I hope is a look of utter shock on my stupid, surprised face.

"You said you would get him here," Halla challenges. "You promised me a dinner with my son."

I see Ilmari's face fall and then he's turning away.

"What the—oh, come on, Mars—wait!" I call after him. "Mars—"

"Price, get him back here," Doctor Halla barks at me. Then he shouts something in Finnish at Ilmari.

Ilmari snaps something back as he shoves his shoulder against the glass front door and leaves. Meanwhile, I'm halfway between Doctor Halla and the door, my senses spinning, heart racing.

I spin around, angry tears stinging my eyes. "Are you fucking serious right now? What the *hell* were you thinking? This is so unethical in like a hundred different ways!"

"Price—"

"Oh, don't *Price* me," I snap. "You *knew* what you were doing. You played me, asshole. I called you because that man is terrified," I cry, pointing towards the front door. "He's alone, and he's scared, and he trusted me to help him. And I trusted *you*. And you just shit all over that trust!"

"Careful, Price," Halla growls. Clearly, he dislikes being reprimanded by a resident in his own clinic. But I don't fucking care. I spin away from him, slinging my purse back onto my shoulder. "Price, where are you going?"

"I have to go after him! I have to find him and apologize and try to mend the damage from the emotional grenade you just lobbed at us!"

"Talk him down," he pleads, following me to the door. "Reason with him. He needs to do these scans. I can help, Price—"

I huff, shrugging away from him. "You really think I'll get him back in here now? Have you met Ilmari Kinnunen? There's no making that man do anything he doesn't want to do."

"He'll do it for you," he calls at my back as I push on the door. "It's clear he cares about you, Price. Use that."

I spin around again. "Don't you fucking dare," I growl at him. "You're a sports injury specialist, not a goddamn couple's therapist. Stay *out* of our business."

He smirks like I've just given him a compliment. "So, I was right. You're together, yes?" He nods like he already knows he's right. "You're good for him, Price. You're evenly matched in stubbornness."

"Don't pretend to know me. Or him. I don't know what you did to that man, but his sentiment seemed pretty clear. And I think I'll have to echo it. You can go ski into a cunt!"

Not waiting for his response, I turn on my heel and shove on the door, racing out into the crisp October afternoon in search of my wayward goalie.

62
RACHEL

"**M**ars!" I race down the sidewalk in my heels.

I spot him almost instantly. He's marching in the direction of the hotel, still gripping tight to both our bags. I should take it as a good sign that he hasn't lobbed my bag into incoming traffic or hurled it down a dark alley.

"Ilmari, come on! Stop walking so damn fast!"

Of course, he doesn't slow down. I hurry after him, regretting immensely my decision to change out of my flip-flops. Idiot Rachel of fifteen minutes ago thought it mattered to look professional. I wanted Doctor Halla to see me as a colleague, not his lowly resident. Yeah, well, this is what you get for trying: blisters on every toe.

I catch up to Ilmari in front of a dry cleaners. "Mars, stop!"

"Go away."

"No—"

"I need to be alone," he snaps. "Give me space—"

"Not until I've had my say." I hold tight to his wrist and all but dig my literal heels into the sidewalk. "God, you are being such an Aries right now. You are literally dragging me! Will you *stop*?!"

With a growl, he spins around, towering over me as he glares down. "What? What message does he bid you bring me now?"

I blink, eyes wide, lips parted as I pant from the exertion of sprinting in heels. "What—*no*—" I hold tighter to his wrist. "Mars, fuck him. I just told him to go ski into a cunt. I don't care about him."

His expression flickers. "You did?"

"Of course, I did. Look, Mars, *please* believe me," I say. "I had no idea. I swear to god, I reached out to him in good faith. We worked together for two years, but I didn't even know he was Finnish. The man is a total closed book. That and the bridge of your nose might be the only things you have in common," I add, gesturing to his nose with my free hand.

Ilmari just frowns at me. "Halla is Finnish, Rachel."

I flap my free arm helplessly, still holding to his wrist in case he decides to bolt. "Well, you know Mars, I'm not exactly a walking lexicon of Finnish surnames. So, you'll have to forgive me for missing that Scooby-Doo clue, okay?"

He just holds onto our bags, staring stoically down at me. But he's not ranting in Finnish or running away, so I'll take it as a win.

I inch closer, relaxing my hold on his wrist. "I swear to you, Ilmari. I brought you here because the Cincinnati Sport Clinic is one of the best in the nation for pro athlete hip injuries. Hate him if you want, but Doctor Halla is one of the best too. And I did *not* know he was your father. How could I?" I add with another helpless shrug. "If I did, I would have *never* consented to this, Mars. I wouldn't have even made you the offer. This is all kinds of unethical, and he knows it."

Mars just shakes his head. "You're saying he tricked you."

"Yes."

"He used you to get to me."

"Yes. And he can go fuck himself. *Hard*. With a sandpaper dildo."

The corner of his mouth twitches and I have to take my chance. I have to beg the universe to let him hear me. I step in a little closer, my hand sliding up his forearm.

"Mars, I would *never* intentionally hurt you. And it's not just because I'm a doctor and I took an oath," I add, glancing up to hold his deep blue gaze. "I care about you, Ilmari. I don't want to see you hurt. But whatever your history is with that man, he's hurt you. Which means I'd like to see him torn apart. I don't care that he helps other athletes on the regular. Your blood spilled is my blood spilled, and I will not let him hurt you again. *Never* again."

He lets out a soft exhale, shoulders relaxing slightly. "But you want me to go back. That's what you're not saying."

"This isn't about what I want, Mars," I say, dropping my hand away. "And this *definitely* isn't about what that conniving jerk wants," I add, jabbing my thumb over my shoulder. "If he wanted to reconcile with you, there are a million more ethical ways to go about it. Fuck him."

He raises a blond brow at me. "But?"

"But we're already here," I say, gesturing around. "And he *can* help you. And you have something he wants. I say use *him*. Use his fancy machines and all his big, important knowledge and experience, and get yourself the answers you need. That's all that matters here, Mars. *You*." I take a step back. "But this is your decision."

He narrows his eyes at me. "My decision?"

I fold my arms across my chest. "Yep. You're in charge, mister. I'm gonna stand right here and wait until you make up your mind. You wanna go get your hip scanned? Just say the word. Wanna go back to the hotel and get drunk on tequila shots? Then that's what we'll do. You choose, Mars." I wait, glancing up at the blond giant in front of me.

Slowly, the corner of his mouth tips into a smile.

I raise a brow. "You've made your decision? That was quick."

"Easiest decision of my life."

"Well? What's the plan, Mars? What do you want?"

"I want you to kiss me."

63
ILMARI

"**K**iss me," I say again, my body humming with need.

The flash of want in Rachel's eyes is quickly replaced with surprise as they grow wider, dark pools I want to sink inside. "What?"

I caught her off guard. I love that she wasn't expecting this. "You asked me what I want," I explain. "I want you to kiss me like you'll die if you don't. Kiss me, and I'll go back in there. Kiss me, and I'll do the scans."

She huffs like she's indignant, but I see the fire burning inside her. "You're extorting your doctor for sexual favors, Mars? Not a great look."

"I'm past caring."

"We're in the street," she reasons, gesturing around.

"I don't care."

"Well . . . a kiss to save my life wouldn't be very PG," she adds, one dark brow raised as she smiles.

"Show me."

My body is already reacting to hers, and she hasn't even touched me yet. We both know she will. We've been dying for a second kiss. She was surprised the first time. She didn't ask for it. She was afraid to reciprocate, afraid of getting caught. Now I'm placing the power in her hands. She's going to kiss me, and she'll see it coming. She'll be the one to start it.

I know the moment she's made her decision. I'm ready for her, dropping our bags at my feet. She drops her purse at the same time. Her hands go to my shoulders as she jumps. I catch her easily, her legs wrapping around my waist as her arms do the same at my neck.

And then we're kissing. Rachel presses in close, her lips parting as she hums her need into my mouth. Her lips are so soft, her tongue warm as she flicks and teases.

I have my left arm wrapped under her ass, supporting her weight, as my right arm bands around her shoulders. I'm not letting go. Fuck what I said on the plane. Nothing is finished between us. We're only just getting started. This woman is *mine*.

Her grip relaxes around my neck, knowing I won't let her fall. Then she's bringing them around to frame my face, her fingers brushing over my beard. I groan as she bites my bottom lip, my cock growing harder by the second. We're both panting, needing breath, even as we're desperate to keep kissing. Her hands are in my hair, sweeping it back from my face.

Someone wolf whistles and we both go still. Rachel pulls away, her lips parted as she huffs, gazing into my eyes. Her dark eyes flecked with gold pierce through my walls. I want her like I haven't wanted anything.

She pushes against my shoulders, and I loosen my hold on her, letting her slide down my body to the ground. We stand there, her hands on my chest, my hands at her hips, as the city moves around us.

"There," she murmurs. "You got what you wanted, right?"

I nod, incapable of words.

"Good. Now grab those bags, and let's go. There's an X-ray machine waiting with your name on it."

"**YOU** came back," says Halla, glancing between me and Rachel.

"As you see," I reply, grateful to have her quiet strength as she stands beside me.

We stopped by the hotel first, leaving our bags at the front desk. Then she made us run by a coffee shop. She said if she had to face Halla again without caffeine reinforcements, she might be spending the night in jail.

"Here's how this will go," she says, her eyes narrowed at him, travel cup of coffee firmly in hand. "You'll perform a physical exam. And we want X-rays and an MRI. If we confirm it's a labral tear, I want—"

"You expect me to administer a cortisone shot to ease pain in the joint," he says, clearly annoyed. "I know, Price. This is *my* practice, remember?" He glances to me. "What do I get in return?"

She inches in front of me, shoulders squared at her former boss. "You get the warm and fuzzy feeling of knowing you weren't a total fucking asshole to my injured patient," she replies for me.

The corner of his mouth quirks like he's impressed. I'm not surprised. She's a lioness. And she's *mine*. I don't even bother fighting the urge to inch closer to her.

"And the dinner you promised?" he says, glancing between us.

She scoffs. "Oh my god, will you stop saying it like that? I never promised you a dinner with Ilmari. You were the one who suggested it. I just thought you were trying to be a nice fucking person. I didn't know a seafood dinner would come with so many strings attached."

"We will go to dinner," I say, my fingers brushing down the small of her back. I really don't want to have to pry her off him when she decides to scratch his eyes out.

She relaxes slightly, flexing her shoulders. She takes the smallest of steps back towards me, her shoulder brushing against my chest.

He glances between us, his smile spreading. "Fine. We are agreed."

WE spend the rest of the afternoon at the clinic. Halla performs a full physical exam, including stress tests and range of motion exercises. He has me walk and run on a treadmill before I show him my pre-game stretching routine. When I attempt a full split, the pain in my right hip is enough to have me groaning.

"Okay, that's enough," says Rachel, stepping in. "We don't want to make any tears worse."

"Agreed," Halla mutters. "I've ordered the additional tests."

Hours later, I've survived a series of X-rays and a kind of MRI that involved inserting dye into my hip joint. It's nearly five o'clock by the time Halla returns. "His scans are ready," he says, his eyes on Rachel. "Would you like to consult with me, Doctor Price?"

She bolts out of her chair, setting her bag of pretzels and diet soda aside. "Yes, sir. Thank you."

"I want to see them too," I say, rising to my feet.

"You're not a doctor, son," he says in Finnish.

"It's my body," I reply. "And I'm not your son."

"English," she interjects, giving me a scowl.

"Fine. Come with me, both of you," he says in English.

He leads us down the hall to an imaging room and shows Rachel scans of my hip. They talk quietly, pointing to various parts of the black and white images. They don't seem concerned. Rachel just nods as he talks, her dark brows narrowed in concentration.

"Here's what you need to see," he says gesturing to a new image on the screen.

"There it is," she murmurs, sighing with relief as she leans in, her finger tracing over the ball joint of my hip. "Mars, come here." She takes my hand to pull me closer. "Look here. See this dark spot? That's the tear in your labrum."

I narrow my eyes, noticing a little black dot in a strip of white that coats the ball of my hip joint. I've been in this sport long enough to know the dangers of a labral tear. It's a common injury for goalies, but it's a first for me.

"It's small," Halla adds. "I don't think it needs surgery to repair it. Not yet, at least."

"I agree," she murmurs. "Will you do the cortisone injection?"

"Yes, that should give him some relief." He turns to me. "Your hip is already on its own way to recovery. And I don't like doing procedures when I don't have to. You need to moderate your physical activity while you heal. Do nothing to risk that hip. Compensate on the ice as much as possible. I trust Price to supervise."

She nods, the look of determination on her face telling me there'll be no escaping her now.

"You should sit out at least a week of practice and games if you can," he adds. "If the corticosteroid gives you relief, and your pain feels managed, you can play. If it gets worse, get more scans. We may need to go in arthroscopically and do the repair."

"How long would that take me off the ice?" I say, my gaze still fixed on that tiny black dot on my scan.

"That really depends on the extent of the injury, but a safe window would be four months. Maybe six," he adds. "I'll go prepare the cortisone shot."

He leaves and I'm left alone with Rachel. She glances up at me, her face relaxed. She's still holding my hand. "Now we know," she murmurs, raising a hand to push my hair back behind my ear. "Doesn't it feel so much better to know for certain? Now we can make a plan. We can fix this, Mars."

I fight the urge to lean into her hand. Yes, now I know. But I'm not thinking about the injury right now. My mind is spinning over the details of an entirely different kind of plan.

64
RACHEL

This is a nice restaurant. Situated on the water's edge, a view of the skyline blinks before us all yellow, white, and orange. There's a light rain, making the lights look hazy through the glass. A live jazz group plays in the corner while a woman sings. I've got an expensive glass of red wine in my hand, and a beautiful man sits at my side.

I should be feeling light as air, relaxed to finally have the answers I've been craving for weeks. But I'm not. How can I be, when the tension between Ilmari and Doctor Halla sits heavier than a lead balloon?

I clear my throat, taking a sip of my wine. Apparently, Finns are comfortable sitting in the world's most awkward silences. Neither of them has spoken for a whole three minutes. That may not seem like a long time, but sit perfectly still for three minutes across from another person and see how quickly the tension sets in.

Maybe I'm the only one who feels it. Am I the only one squirming in my chair?

"I find it hard to believe you were so surprised to see me today," Doctor Halla says at last, his gaze locked on Ilmari.

"I can't see why," Ilmari replies.

Halla purses his lips in slight annoyance, setting aside his wine. He ordered the bottle for the table. I'm not surprised when Ilmari drinks only water. "You were traveling to Cincinnati to see a hip and knee specialist," Halla says. "You truly didn't consider whether it would be me?"

It's a fair point. I'm curious myself. I glance over at Mars.

"I would have to consider you at all," Ilmari replies. "And I don't."

The chill in the air is enough to give us all frostbite.

Doctor Halla clears his throat. "Not even when you're going to see a specialist? You never thought to ask for the doctor's name?" He turns slowly to look at me. "You didn't think it important to inform your patient of who they were seeing?"

"I trusted my doctor," Ilmari says for me. "And the last I heard, you were in San Francisco."

"That was five years ago," Halla replies, taking a sip of his wine. "I've made contact since then. Christmas cards, birthdays. And I'm told you received my gift when you signed with the Rays."

"I don't need your money and never have," Ilmari counters, seeming almost bored with the whole conversation. "I donated it all to a local charity. Your generous gift is now preserving sea turtle habitats."

I fight my smile, hiding it behind my wine glass. Mars and his sea turtles.

"Good," Halla murmurs. "The money was yours to do with as you wished. I'm glad you made use of it for such a noble cause."

I glance between them, surprised Halla was able to turn that around so smoothly. Clearly, Ilmari is annoyed. He wanted it to sting more than it did.

"How is your mother?" says Halla.

At that question, Ilmari freezes, his hand reaching for his water glass. He snatches it off the table, taking a sip. "Dead," he replies, setting it back down with a hard clink.

Doctor Halla and I both shift uncomfortably. "How?" he murmurs. "When?"

Ilmari glares at him. "Cancer. Thirteen years ago."

I do the math quickly. I know he's thirty years old, meaning he was still a boy when she died, only seventeen. His own father didn't know about his mother's death? Ilmari has been alone for thirteen years?

"Do you have any siblings, Mars?" I ask.

"No."

"Other family?"

"I have the Kinnunen's," he replies. "Juhani took me in and paid for my hockey."

Across the table, Doctor Halla grunts, his gaze darkening. "*I* paid for your hockey. I sent money to you both every month, double what was required. I never missed a month."

"And we never wanted or needed it," Ilmari says again. "Mother didn't keep a single euro. I owe you nothing. There is nothing between us."

I see the way his words hurt Halla. Even though I'm pissed at him for tricking me, I feel a twinge of sympathy for him. Maybe he was just desperate. Ilmari doesn't make getting close to him very easy.

"You are determined to see the worst in me," Halla mutters with a tired shake of his head. "There is no room for grace in you, Ilmari. There never has been."

Ilmari's hand curls into a fist on the table. "You left us—"

"I left *her*," Halla corrects, his blue eyes narrowed at his son. "It was never my intention to leave *you*. But sometimes people disappoint us, Ilmari. They make mistakes. They act selfishly. How long will you punish me for my sins? Are we never to reach a point of equilibrium where you can accept that, while I may be flawed, I am still your father?"

Ilmari says nothing, but I can sense the tension roiling in him.

Halla shakes his head again. "Now I see my lack of perfection is an unforgivable sin in your eyes. After twenty-three years of trying, you may have finally convinced me to give up on ever having a relationship with my only child."

"Good," Ilmari mutters.

He's playing it cool, but I sense his pain. I can't imagine what it must feel like to be so alone. As a twin, the idea of living in a world without Harrison leaves me with a physical ache.

"Mars," I murmur, unable to help myself. My hand brushes his thigh, and he tenses.

"Will you treat her the same?" Halla asks, gesturing at me.

Ilmari goes still. "What?"

"When she disappoints you," Halla presses. "When she makes a mistake, when she proves to you that she can't be perfect. Maybe she's done it already," he adds. "Lord knows she's got a foul temper—"

"Don't talk about her like that," Ilmari growls, valiantly defending my honor.

It's enough to make me let out a little laugh. Now my hand really is on his thigh, giving it a squeeze. "It's fine, Mars. Doctor Halla is right. I'm a foul-tempered, potty-mouthed disaster. And I'm sure my past would have you running for the hills."

Neither man laughs at my poor attempt at levity. I bury my soft groan behind my wine glass as the waiter comes with our salads, cracking pepper atop them and refreshing Ilmari's lemon water.

As soon as the waiter leaves, Doctor Halla is glancing between us again, a look of sadness on his face. It stirs something deep in me. He's lonely too. Damn it, I wanted to hate him for the stunt he pulled on us today. Why is he making me feel sympathy? I shift in my chair, wanting him to look away.

"Don't treat her like you've treated me, Ilmari," he says, a note of tenderness in his voice.

Ilmari stills, salad fork in hand, not looking up at either of us.

"It's cold in the harsh winter of your hatred," his father goes on. "I can take it, but then I'm a Finn. She is not."

Slowly, Ilmari raises his gaze to look at his father. Doctor Halla switches to Finnish, asking him a question. I can't understand it, but god I wish I could. Ilmari is quiet for a long moment before he finally responds with one word, spoken so softly. "Joo."

OUR Uber pulls up outside the Cincinnatian Hotel and I let go of Ilmari's hand. It's still raining—more like a soft mist. I open my door as Ilmari opens his. He's around the back of the car in moments, stepping in next to me as we duck out of the misting rain. We move quickly through the doors into the sparkly hotel lobby, my heels clicking on the tiles.

"I just need to get my bag," I murmur, phone in hand. Since it's raining, I'll hop in another Uber to head over to Tess's apartment. I've been sending her and the boys updates when I can. They're all frothing for more details of the soap opera reveal that Doctor H is Ilmari's long-lost father.

Meanwhile, tension sits heavy between Ilmari and I. He's so difficult to read. I can't tell what he wants from me, what he's feeling. The rest of the dinner was bearable, but only just.

We walk up to the front desk, and I find a smile for the clerk. "Hello, we should have a pair of bags on hold back there. Last name is Kinnunen."

"Okay, just let me check," she says brightly, flashing Ilmari a winning smile as she ducks away through an open door.

I just roll my eyes. If I summoned up the energy to get annoyed any time a woman looked appreciatively at one of my men, I would live in a constant state of triggered. No one has time for that. Ilmari is gorgeous in a totally unobtainable, I'll-eat-you-for-breakfast kind of way. He doesn't even try. He just breathes. She can look all she wants.

The clerk comes back empty-handed. "I'm sorry, Mrs. Kinnunen. It doesn't look like I have any bags back here. Are you sure you didn't have them taken up to your room already?"

I sigh. We don't have time to unpack her calling me 'Mrs. Kinnunen' in front of a moody, possessive goalie. She may as well have just stripped me out of a big trench coat to reveal me wearing his jersey . . . and nothing else.

I glance over my shoulder to see he's standing two steps closer, his expression hungry. "Mars, did you send our bags up to your room?"

"It seemed prudent," he replies with a shrug. "You may have valuables."

Of course. I let out another breath, turning back to the desk clerk. "Thank you."

"No worries," she says. "If you get up to your room, and they're not there, call down, okay?" Her cheeriness is so at odds with our mutual, slow-burning heat.

"Great," I say, pushing off the counter and stomping towards the elevators. Ilmari follows close behind me. Once we have distance between us and the desk clerk, I turn. "Will you go get my bag while I call another Uber?"

Ilmari's gaze drops away from my face to trace my body. The man is undressing me with his eyes, and there's nothing I can do about it. I hold still, heart in my throat. I don't want him to see that I'm nervous. His gaze levels on me again as he smolders. "No."

I gasp. "What? You're seriously going to hoard my bag? You need contact solution and a pair of fuzzy panda sleep socks?"

"No."

I cross my arms, giving him my best glare. "Don't one-word-answer me, Mars. I'm not in the mood. Is this a manners thing? *Please* go get my bag."

Stepping into my space, he raises his hand and brushes his thumb over my parted lips. "If you want it . . . come and get it." Not waiting for me to respond, he turns on his heel and stalks off towards the elevators.

65
RACHEL

The elevator dings and the doors slide open. Mars steps inside, not looking back to see if I'm following. Of course, I am. He steps to the back of the elevator and turns, folding his arms across his chest, watching me stand at the threshold with an unreadable look on his face.

Heart in my throat, I step inside and turn quickly around. "What floor?"

"Three."

I press the number three with my thumb, and it glows white. The car instantly starts moving. I close my eyes counting my heartbeats as Mars steps in behind me, his presence overwhelming me. He doesn't touch me, but he leans in, his breath warm against my skin.

I feel him everywhere, my every sense prickling. I bite my lip, fighting the urge to lean back against him. The elevator dings and the doors open. I all but stumble out, breaking the connection between us. He shifts past me and moves off down the carpeted hall. I hurry after him, taking in the cut of his athletic body in his grey fitted t-shirt and slim black dress pants rolled up at the cuff.

His hand is in his pocket, fishing out his key, and then he's opening the door to his room. I follow behind, watching as he walks right past our pair of bags on the floor by the closet. He walks all the way to the back of the room and slowly turns, holding to the edges of the desk as he leans against it, watching me, waiting.

I step inside the doorway, one hand holding the door open, the other curled around the strap of my purse on my shoulder. It's a comfortable room with a king-sized bed along one wall, minibar under the large, flat-screen TV. My weekender bag is far enough inside the room that I'll have to take another step to reach it. And unless I want to look like a total idiot holding onto the door and stretching my body out, I'll have to let the door shut behind me.

Mars watches me, his expression totally unreadable. He's not going to help me out here. This is my choice. If this door shuts behind me, we both know what will happen. God, I want it. I want him. I've wanted him for weeks.

Sudden death, Rachel. Take this shot and live with the consequences.

And I know what the consequences will be. If I reach out my hand, he's taking it. Decision made, I take another step inside and drop my right hand away from the door. It swings shut behind me, settling into the latch with an ominous click.

The room is dark and moody, lit only by a single lamp in the corner. Ilmari leans against the edge of the desk with all the casual calm of a leopard on the hunt. As I watch him, he slips his hand in his pocket and pulls something out. Then both his hands are raising as he sweeps his hair back and up into a high knot on top of his head. His biceps bulge as he bends his arms, his fingers flexing around the elastic as he secures his hair. The move shows off the deep fade he has going up both sides of his head to his crown. The shave continues around the nape of his neck.

All the while, he watches me, his blue eyes blown black with desire. His eyes are the only thing giving him away. That and the tension in the room that now sits so thick you could cut it with a knife.

My pulse hammers as I take in the strength and elegance of his powerful form. "How are you feeling?" I murmur. "No pain from the cortisone shot?"

"No pain," he mutters. Then he's kicking off his shoes.

"You might have some stiffness in the hip for a day or two," I stammer. "Some . . . umm . . . swelling. But that's normal."

"I don't want to talk about my hip." His hands drop to the hem of his shirt.

"Ilmari . . ." I say on a breath. There's nothing else to be said.

We hold each other's gaze. The only sound is the gentle hum of the AC unit. The heat of his gaze is going to burn me to ash.

"Tell me to stop," he says.

Fighting a shiver, I whisper, "No."

He pulls off the shirt, dropping it to the floor, and sweet baby

Jesus. My eyes widen appreciatively. He looks almost ethereal in the soft golden light of the lamp. This man is beyond fit. Broad shoulders carry heavy muscle. He has well-defined pecs and an eight-pack that leads to a sharp V at his hips. My gaze follows the angle downwards, ending at the top of his pants. His hands are already resting there.

He can't tear his gaze from me either. "Rachel, tell me to stop."

I drop my purse to the floor, kicking off my shoes. "No."

As he works the top of his pants open, I tug at the buttons of my white, silky blouse, untucking it from the top of my pants and stripping it off. It flutters to the floor at the same time that he slips his pants down, leaving him in nothing but a pair of fitted black boxer briefs.

I don't hesitate, stripping off my black crop top and tossing it aside, exposing my bare breasts. My skin prickles with nerves, goosebumps spreading down my arms as my nipples harden into sharp peaks.

My leggings go next. I shimmy out of them, holding Ilmari's molten gaze as I drop them to the floor. Now we're standing feet apart wearing nothing but our underwear. Mine are a pair of blush pink panties.

He scans me from head to toe, nodding appreciatively as he takes in all my curves. "You're beautiful, Rakas," he murmurs.

"So are you," I reply.

He holds my gaze, his chest expanding with each deep, steady breath. "Tell me to stop," he says one last time.

"No," I whisper, sealed to my fate. It barely takes a tug, and my panties slip down, dropping to my ankles. I step out of them, standing wholly naked before him.

With a low growl, he's shoving off from the desk and crossing the room. I'm ready for him, my body melting against the warmth of his chest as he all but bends me back, stealing my breath with a desperate kiss. I sigh into him, my fingers brushing over the buzzed hair at his nape before I'm cupping his bearded cheeks.

I open fully to him, holding nothing back, and he reciprocates. He smells like heaven—that cologne that makes me think of cool summer nights on my family's Montana ranch. In his arms, I feel like starlight and firelight mixed in one, cold and hot, distant and so very present. I'm experiencing everything at once, alive in my skin and burning with need.

Ilmari's calloused hands rove. They take in the curve of my shoulders, sliding down to brush along each rib. I love the feel of his hands on me, exploring me, learning me. He cups my breasts with a groan, weighing them in his hands. I shiver with want as he pinches my nipples with thumb and forefinger. The burst of need coils deep in my core.

"Say it," he growls, breaking our kiss.

My mind can't form thoughts. "Please, Ilmari," I whine against his lips.

"Say it," he says again, his mouth dropping to my neck. He drives me wild as he sucks at my pulse point, his hands curving around to cup my ass and pull me tight against him. I feel the thick bulge in his briefs grinding against my hip.

"*Ah*—I want you," I say, my hands holding tight to his shoulders as his face drops down, his mouth teasing my breast. His tongue starts flicking the tip of my nipple, sending rippling waves of desire straight to my aching pussy. Then he's biting down with his teeth until I gasp.

He straightens, cupping my face with both hands as he stares into my soul. "Say it."

I hold his gaze, my hand dropping down to cup his cock and— oh my fucking god—Caleb and Jake were right. Ilmari has a monster between his legs. Thick and long, I feel out its shape as he grunts, pressing back into my hand, craving more pressure. I burst open, saying all the things I'm feeling. "I want you, Mars. *God*—I have to have you. I've wanted you for so long. I'm aching for you . . . so wet for you . . . desperate for you."

"Oon sun," he whispers, his forehead pressed against mine, groaning as I slip my hand inside his briefs and fist his bare cock. "Say it, Rakas," he begs one more time, and now I know what he wants to hear, though I can only guess at its meaning.

"Oon sun," I repeat, trying to match his pronunciation.

He groans, fisting my hair and tipping my head back. "You're mine."

"Oon sun," I say again. "I'm yours."

"Mä kuulun sulle," he murmurs, brushing my hair back. Then he's dropping a hand to cup my bare pussy. "Haluun tätä." His voice is little more than a groan. "I want this."

I sigh with relief that my wait is finally over and press my hips into his hand. "It's yours. Take me. Fuck me, Mars. And don't hold back. God—*please*—just stop holding back. Let me in out of the cold," I whisper, one hand still on his cock, the other smoothing down his chest. "I want in, Mars. Please, just let me in—"

His body crackles with electricity as he cups my chin hard, jerking my face up, holding my gaze. No one does intense like Ilmari Kinnunen. "I will not be gentle," he growls.

"Good." My pussy is already desperate.

As if to prove his point, he shoves two fingers inside me, sliding so easily through my wetness. I cry out, that first shudder of excitement at being filled zapping me down to my toes. He thrusts in and out, letting me adjust to his thick fingers.

"I will not wear a condom," he adds. "This is a claiming, Rakas. I want to see my cum dripping from all your holes."

"Yes," I say on a breath, my heart fluttering like a wild bird trapped in a cage. I grin, still riding his fingers as I stroke my fist up and down his length, my thumb swirling at the top of his thick head, gathering his warm precum and spreading it down his shaft. "Enough talking. *Do* it, Mars. I'll be so good for you. Show me what you like, and I'll make all your dreams come true."

He leans his face closer. "Bend over. Grab your ankles."

My pussy screams as I turn in his arms. I press my ass against the bulge in his briefs and he growls, smacking my ass cheek hard enough to sting. I gasp, feeling the heat of that slap echoing deep in my core. At the same time, he wraps a hand around my throat and pulls me against him, whispering in my ear. "Do what you're told, Rakas. Show me how well you bend."

I smile. This man would die before hurting me. I know I'm safe. I know he'll respect my limits. And he thrives on using his intuition. I want to see if he can read me as well as he reads the puck. Raising a hand, I tap his wrist. He immediately drops his hand away from my throat, shifting it down to the curve of my hip.

I bend forward, dropping into a yoga pose as I grab my ankles, my bare ass and pussy on full display for him.

"Perfect," he murmurs, both hands smoothing over the round curves of my ass. "Wider."

He supports my hips as I adjust my stance. Then he's dropping his briefs to the floor, fisting himself one-handed before bending his knees and notching his tip at my tight entrance.

"Breathe," he says, his hands on my hips as he makes a few thrusts, working his huge cock inside my tight pussy, made all the tighter by this angle.

"Oh, please," I whisper, loving the feel of him pressing in deeper. "More."

"You want more?" he says, his right hand smoothing over my ass.

"Yes," I beg.

In an instant I'm crying out as he does two things at once. His left hand grips tight to my hip, holding me still, as he pounds in with his hips, burying his monster cock inches deeper inside me. At the same time, his right hand slaps my ass. *Hard.* I love this feeling of being so full. I'm getting dizzy from the blood draining to my head.

"Fuck me," I whimper. "Mars, please—"

And then he unleashes himself. Holding me tight by the hips, he pounds into me, his hips slapping against my ass as my orgasm spirals tight and fast. I'm coming before I can even warn him, my moaned words unintelligible as my pussy grips tight to his dick, pulsing around him.

Abruptly, he's pulling out, leaving me empty. "Up," he orders. "Get up."

I suck in a breath, rising up from my forward bend. Slowly, I turn in his arms. "Mars—"

"Get on the bed," he orders. "On your back. Spread your legs."

Curious to keep playing his game, I do as I'm told, crawling onto the bed, and flopping down onto my side before rolling onto my back. As he watches me, I let my legs drop open, exposing my pussy to him once more.

Then he's crawling up the bed, wasting no time as he drops his mouth onto my clit and sucks. Once he starts mixing in his tongue, I know I'm a goner. I'm fisting the covers, knees bent open as Mars Kinnunen devours me. His beard tickles, but I'm not here to complain. I can't focus on that when he's fucking me so good with that powerful tongue. He doesn't stop until I'm crying out again, legs shaking, body bowing on the bed around his face in a half-curl.

"Oh my god," I pant, flopping back onto the bed as he lifts his face away. I take a few deep breaths, my whole body humming.

He's on his elbows between my legs, looking at me like he's starving. "I'm just getting started, Rakas."

With a dizzy smile, I stretch out on the bed. "Show me."

Ilmari growls, crawling up my body to reach my mouth. We kiss, our tongues teasing as I taste my sweetness on his lips. I love the feel of his weight pressed on top of me, my hips cradling him as his thick cock grinds against my bare pussy. I rake my nails down his nape and across his shoulders, as he arches into me.

"Fuck yes," I pant, shifting my hips under him. "Mars, you feel so good—"

His right hand slips around my thigh to spread me open and then he's shoving his huge cock back inside me, burying himself to the hilt. I moan, clinging to him as he begins to pump with his hips, hammering me into the bed.

"Don't stop," I beg. "God, you're so deep. Please don't stop—"

He grunts, dropping his face to the crook of my neck as we move together. My hands hold to his shoulders. I arch back, letting the deep pressure of his fullness bring me back to the edge of ecstasy. Then his hand slips between us and he starts working my clit. "Come again," he growls.

"I'm so close—"

He pounds into me, shifting his angle by lifting my left leg. "Take me, Rakas. Come all over my cock again. Need to feel it."

My orgasm spirals tighter. I feel it ready to break like waves crashing on rocks. "I'm right there—"

"Come for me," he commands. "Oot niin timmi, Rakas. So tight. *Come.*"

"Come with me," I moan, hips writhing as he works my clit, pressing down with his thumb. "Oh god—" I cry out, my whole body spasming with a heavy orgasm. My cunt squeezes him as tight as it can, pulsing with my release over and over. It's all I can do to hold on, stars flashing in my vision.

"Fuck—" His tempo hitches as he slams into me and holds me on that edge, his own release filling me. He groans, burying his face back at my shoulder, his massive body shuddering on top of me.

I float downward, my entire body boneless. I sigh, my hands smoothing over his broad shoulders, my fingers brushing the black ink trailing up his neck—the delicate feathers of a raven's wing.

With a grunt, he pulls out of me and slips down the bed. "Spread your legs," he growls. "Show me, Rakas."

"Mars," I pant, lifting up on my elbows. I watch Ilmari gaze at my spent pussy with such longing in his eyes.

"So beautiful." He peppers my inner thigh with kisses, his beard bristling against my sensitive skin. His hand smooths over my bare pussy, settling just over my pubic bone. "Squeeze for me, Rakas. Show me how well you've taken me."

I fight the racing of my heart as I squeeze the muscles of my dick-drunk pussy. At the same time, Ilmari presses down gently, just above my pubic bone. "Ilmari," I whimper, gasping as I feel his warm cum leaking out of me. It's obscene and dirty and so fucking hot. His gaze heats and I can't help but tease. "Like what you see, baby?"

He's speechless, his fingers dipping into the mess between my legs, pumping it back into my quivering pussy. "You're dripping, Rakas."

"It's yours," I say on a sigh, stretching out on the bed.

It turns out my quiet goalie has a breeding kink, and I couldn't be happier. If he likes me dripping after one round, I can only imagine how he'd feel seeing me used by three men at once. I don't bother fighting my well-satisfied smile. Maybe there's hope for him yet.

"Roll over," he says, breaking through the happy pink bubble of my thoughts of a four-way lovefest.

"Hmm?"

"Hands and knees, Rakas."

I let out a little laugh, my breasts jiggling as I glance up at him. He's already shifting off the bed to stand. "Are you serious? You don't need a little breather?" My gaze follows down the center line of his chest to where his hand is slowly pumping his hard cock.

Oh, sweet heavens.

"Do I look serious?" he says, his face a grim mask of determination. "We're not done. Edge of the bed. Hands and knees. Now."

66
RACHEL

"Oh god," I whisper, sitting up. I can't look away from the proud length of his cock. "Yeah, you are ready," I say, my smile growing. "Haven't you ever heard of a refractory period, Kinnunen?"

He just stares down at me, the heat of his gaze breaking me open, melting me inside and out. Total marshmallow goo. "You will tire long before I do, Rakas. Now, I won't say it again. Come to the edge of the bed."

I fight the urge to tremble as I do what I'm told. I'm getting the feeling I'm in way over my head here. "What are you going to do?" I murmur, turning around at the bed's edge and dropping down to my hands and knees. I glance back over my shoulder. "Mars?"

He's gazing down at me, taking in the lines of my shoulders, my hips, my ass. It's almost unsettling to feel the way he covets me without touching. I need his touch. But then suddenly he's turning away, leaving me on the bed.

I don't mind. It gives me a chance to breathe. It also gives me an unobstructed view of his gorgeous back tattoo. It spreads across the entire surface of his muscled skin, stretching down his lower back and ending at his ass.

"Mars, what . . ."

He says nothing, dropping down to one knee to get something from his bag. Then he comes back over to the bed, a travel-sized bottle of lube in hand.

"Well, aren't you Mr. Prepared," I say with a grin.

"I want this." His right hand raises up to cup my ass cheek. Then his thumb grazes down my crack, pressing in at my hole.

I gasp, clenching on instinct. "Mars—"

He drops down to one knee, tossing the bottle of lube on the bed as he spreads my cheeks wide, his hot mouth covering my hole as he teases me with his tongue.

"Oh—*fuck*—god—" I'm a shaking mess, falling forward to my elbows when he adds two fingers in my still-dripping cunt.

"Do you consent?" he mutters, his thumb rimming me, making me squirm.

"Mars—I—"

"Say stop, and it stops," he says, lifting both hands away. "If you can't handle me, Rakas—"

"Don't you dare fucking stop," I pant. "I just—will it fit?" I know it's a stupid thing to ask, but it's the best my dick-drunk brain can manage. I'm legitimately concerned.

He smirks as he stands, reaching for the little bottle of lube. "It will fit."

I've never taken such a big cock in my ass before. Jake has serious girth and length, but it's like comparing a big, delicious bratwurst with a two-pound salami. No way will this fit. My insides already feel rearranged. But I must be crazy, because apparently, I'm nodding. "Do it," I murmur. "Mars, take me."

He works me slow, taking his sweet time to play and stretch me out. It becomes a whole new round of foreplay as he trades off between working his fingers into my ass and strumming my clit with his free hand, dipping his fingers into my cum-filled cunt to own me with both hands.

I'm squirming, desperate to come again by the time he's notching his fat cock head at my back door, telling me to breathe and relax as he pushes in. I'm slick with lube, but it's still a tight fit.

"You take me so well," he murmurs appreciatively. His hands soften on my hips as he works himself in deeper.

"Please," I whimper. "Go harder, Mars. I need you to go harder."

He doesn't need telling twice. Now that he's in, he means to claim me. He starts moving his hips in earnest, my rounded ass slapping against his thighs as we fuck, his monster cock buried deep in my ass. I'm a moaning mess, loving the feel of my next orgasm building in my core and spreading across my chest, all the way down to my fingertips.

I need more. I need to feel connected to him in all ways. I arch up, changing our angle as my right arm reaches blindly to wrap around his neck and pull him closer to me. Keeping my ass pressed tight against his hips, I arch my back and glance over my shoulder, taking in the features of his rugged face. "Kiss me—Ilmari, please—"

One hand cups my face as the other wraps around me to fondle my breast. Then he's kissing me, pouring his passion into me with his entire body. We rock together, sharing air, moving as one.

"I'm gonna come again," I whine against his lips. "Don't stop, I'm—" My words die as I ride out another orgasm. This one is deep and packed with pulsing waves that have my whole body trembling. I squeeze him with everything I've got, desperate for him to come with me again.

In moments he's groaning, his hips jerking against me, lost in the spasm of his release. "Mä tuun," he grunts. "Rakas—" I feel it hot and wet in my ass, filling me.

After a moment of suspended euphoria, we fall in slow motion down to the bed. He's only partially on top of me, but that's enough to feel his sinking weight. The man is a tree.

"Roll over," he mutters, lifting off me enough that I can flop like a fish, rolling to my side to face him. Then his left hand is dipping between my legs, his fingers swiping the entrance of my pussy. He raises a pair of glistening fingers to my lips, coated in a mix of our releases. "Taste."

I suck his fingers into my mouth with a soft sigh, savoring the taste of pure sex on my tongue.

He's looking at me with such tenderness. I can hardly believe it's Ilmari Kinnunen naked in my arms. "Now your body knows mine," he intones. "My cum has claimed all your holes, Rakas. You're mine."

I smile up at his beautiful face, feeling so at ease in his arms. So safe and content. For so long I've felt like a small boat set adrift on a perilous sea. Ilmari Kinnunen came skating into my life as this closed-off, moody bear of a goalie. I smile, knowing with such clarity how he fits with us. He's my safe harbor.

Jake is my joy. Caleb is my comfort. Ilmari is my rest. I want them all. *Need* them all. Please, god, let him want this too.

"I'm yours," I echo, my hand brushing down the planes of his chest. "Oon sun."

He smiles, tucking my hair back behind my ear.

"But I'm Jake's too," I say, watching his smile fall. "And I'm Caleb's. Nothing has changed for me when it comes to them. I *love* them, Mars. I intend to keep loving them. But my love isn't finite. There's room for you in my life, in my heart . . . if you want to be there."

He rolls away, one arm still pinned under me, staring up at the ceiling.

I bite my tongue, letting him process his swirling thoughts and emotions.

"I don't know how I feel about this," he admits at last. "The idea of them touching you . . . loving you . . . I can't get perspective." He drags a hand over his face with a groan. "I've never done this before, Rakas."

"None of us have," I say. "There are no rules, Ilmari. Other than honesty," I add quickly. "We're all figuring it out as we go. Jake and Caleb are on their own journey. I'll support them, come what may. And this doesn't need to be about competition. You make me happy. Jake and Caleb make me happy too. They make each other happy. Separately. Together. And it's not just about sex," I add. "It's a whole life we share, Mars. We live together."

"What?" he growls, his head turning to face me. "You live with Compton and Sanford?"

"And Poseidon," I add. "You can't forget about the dog."

He grunts, turning away again. "The dog I can tolerate. It's Compton and Sanford I want to push off a cliff."

"Push them away, and you'll push me right along with them," I warn. "And this isn't some kind of 'they came first' situation," I add. "Even if you came first, this is just who I am, Mars. I'm . . . complicated." I wish there was a better way to describe me, but now the word is out, and I'm going with it.

"There are so many facets of Rachel Price," I go on. "The idea that one person could satisfy all of them and be my perfect match . . . I just don't think that's possible. You make me happy, Mars. Caleb makes a different part of me happy. It's not more or less happiness; it's just different. By feeling such happiness with all three of you, I get to be the fullest, best version of myself. Am I making any sense?"

His face is stoic as he breathes quietly next to me, saying nothing.

"It's a lot," I admit. "And I understand if you need this to be a one-night only thing. I mean—it's fine—if that's all this can be for you. I can accept that—"

He rolls to his side, placing three fingers over my mouth to quiet me. "Rachel . . ."

"Hmm?" I say behind my muzzle.

His gaze softens somewhat. "I'm not going anywhere."

Heart in my throat, I push up on one elbow, studying his expression. "You're sure?"

He gives a curt nod and I sigh.

"This is kind of a big moment, Mars. I'm gonna need more than a nod."

He's quiet for another long moment, looking for the right words, before he finally speaks. "I'm willing to admit I'm curious. I think I need to see you with Compton and Sanford. I need to understand what this is, what you have with them, and where I fit."

My eyes go wide. "See us together as in like . . . *see?*"

He growls low, pulling me against him and twining our legs together. "I'm not talking about sex, Rakas. I don't want to think about their puny cocks poking anywhere near you."

I can't help but snort a laugh. "No one's going to make you do anything you're uncomfortable with," I say more diplomatically.

He's still tense, his gaze locked on the ceiling. "But you are with them in that way."

"Yes," I reply. "Separately and together. They love sharing . . . and I love being shared," I admit. "And I think maybe you should also know that Caleb is queer. He likes men and women. He's been in relationships with both. And Jake is currently exploring his own bi-curiousity," I say with a soft smile.

"Bicuriousity?" he repeats.

"Yeah . . . I think Jake's in love with Caleb," I admit, my stomach filled with warm fuzzy thoughts as I remember the way Caleb gazed down at him with such wonder in his eyes, Jake on his knees. "He just doesn't know it yet. But he's on the path."

"So, they are with you *and* each other?"

"Jake's not quite there yet. But I think it's on their horizon."

"And would they . . ." He doesn't finish the thought, but I know where he's going with his question.

"Mars, are you asking if the guys will want you to enjoy sexy times with them without me there?"

"It's not happening," he mutters.

"Fair enough," I reply, snuggling in next to his massive frame. His hand traces soft circles against my skin. "You'll walk your own path, Mars. If you only want to be with me, that's fine."

His hand stills, his breathing slow and steady in his chest. "Do you want me, Rakas?" he murmurs, not looking at me. "Beyond this night . . . do you want me in your life? In your bed?"

I can't help but think back to our dinner tonight, hearing him admit to being all alone. No father. No mother. No siblings. Just a demanding job that requires endless travel. He left everything behind in Finland. His home, his surrogate family. Mars Kinnunen is all alone.

Not anymore.

My heart thrums as the words echo down to my very bones. No one deserves to walk through life alone, especially not someone as wonderful as the man lying naked in my arms. "Yes," I say, cupping his face. "Ilmari, yes." I kiss the tip of his nose, both his cheeks. "Yes, I want you," I whisper, trailing my kisses down his neck. "Yes, I need you."

"Then you have me," he replies, his fingers digging into my hair.

"Say it," I tease, slinging a leg over his hip as I press myself against him, leaning up for a kiss.

"Oon sun, Rakas," he murmurs, his mouth brushing against mine.

"Damn straight," I reply, pushing on his shoulder as I roll on top of him, straddling him. "Now, get your fine Finnish ass in that shower. I'm not done with you yet."

67
JAKE

"Oh, yeah," I grunt, tipping my head back, eyes closed. "Yeah, right there. Feels so fuckin' good. Don't stop—"

Caleb lifts the massager wand away from my calf and clicks it off. "Dude, you have to stop."

I blink my eyes open, glancing down the length of my body to where Cay is sitting, my legs propped in his lap on a pillow. Sy is curled up on his other side, watching us.

I just got back from a brutal early morning workout, and Caleb agreed to use the wand on my legs. Of course, I had to bribe him first. And Caleb Sanford isn't cheap. I'm making a home-cooked steak dinner tonight and doing his laundry for a week. But it's worth it.

Was worth it. Now he's stopped, and I'm about to threaten that I won't make my world-famous Cajun rub grilled shrimp skewers.

"What the hell?" I whine.

"You were making sex noises," he replies, glaring at me. "Shut up while I do this, or I'll make that mouth earn it's moans."

I bottle up quick, eyes wide.

We haven't discussed it since, you know, *it* happened. The dick sucking. That night was fucking amazing. By the time we all stumbled into my shower at 3:00am, we could all barely stand. I was so tired the next morning, I slept through my alarm and missed strength and conditioning. Totally worth it.

Rachel is perfect for me. For us. The *us* being me and Caleb. Because the scary truth is that I think there is an *us*. The guys have always teased us about it, and Caleb has always just shrugged it off. He never lets the chirping get to him, even when he played.

DLP is a label that used to haunt me. When my last team first teased me with it, I wanted to prove how not gay I was. I screwed bunnies left and right. I made some stupid choices in the name of my bullshit no-homo agenda. I know I hurt some girls. And now the truth is clear to me: I hurt Cay too.

I was the first one he technically came out to, and I threw myself into being his supportive straight friend. I cut the toxic crap and backed him one hundred percent. I even bought an 'I'm an Ally' rainbow heart sticker for the water bottle I take to the gym. The other guys can laugh, but I'm gonna be on the right side of history.

More importantly, I want to be on the right side of my friendship with Cay. He's never asked me for anything. Never really mentions it at all. He's not the type of guy who dates. For the last few years, I think he's survived solely on super-secret hookups.

Enter Rachel.

She's twisted us both up and now we're inside out and upside down. A few months ago, my life was so easy. I had everything planned out: career, marry a hot wife, kids, retire and coach. It's the playbook for so many guys. It's comfortable. Pro athletes like routine.

Now I'm sitting here with my legs in Caleb's lap, waiting for Rachel to get home. Because we live together. The three of us. And we fuck like gods. The *three* of us. And this is *not* what I had in mind for my short list of totally obtainable life goals. It feels like I went to Seattle to meet Amy, met Rachel instead, and then she promptly snatched my Etch-a-Sketch from my hand and shook it all to hell.

Apparently, I'm making a new list of life goals: play professional hockey, bind my soul to Rachel Price, mouth-fuck my best friend and love it, and convert my house into a four-person sex den, marriage and kids optional.

Who am I, and what have I done with Jake Compton?

Rachel is on her way home right now. With Mars Kinnunen. Apparently, they worked out their drama last night. We didn't get all the details of the surprise daddy reveal, but I know this much: they fucked. Caleb and I expected it. We sorta told her to do it. But it still hits different knowing it happened.

"Hey," Caleb mutters, his dark gaze locked on me, reading my every thought. "You good?"

Am I good? I can't quite tell. I feel like I swallowed a pin ball, and now it's just trapped inside me, pinging around. I want her back. I feel unsettled with her gone. I just want her to walk through that door and hope that this weight on my chest lifts away.

"Think she'll actually get him in the door?" Caleb muses.

I shrug. "She got you on your knees. I bet she can handle one broody Finn."

"My guess is he did most of the handling last night."

I roll my eyes at him. "Shut up and massage my legs, or I'm giving your shrimp skewers to Poseidon."

He smirks, clicking the massager back on. The rounded head pulses as he presses it to my leg and I sink back against the cushions of the sofa, letting my DLP take care of me.

I think I must fall asleep on top of Caleb, because when the front door alarm chirps, I suck in a breath, jolting awake. Poseidon bolts off the couch with a bark, racing to the door. I'm instantly on edge. There's only three other people with the code to my front door. One is on the couch with me and one is in Japan. My heart leaps in my chest knowing this must be—

"Puppy!" Rachel cries and the dog goes nuts, bouncing and whining like an idiot. That girl is gaga for Poseidon. All dogs really. We walk him on the beach in the evenings, and when we pass another dog, she's just as embarrassing.

And it's not just dogs. Sometimes we see crabs in the sand or dolphins out in the surf, the occasional gopher tortoise. Whenever that happens, our calm, collected doctor totally loses her cool. It's goddamn adorable. The other day, Caleb had to forcibly remove her from a pair of ladies and their horses doing a sunset ride.

My memories of her jogging down the beach wearing cheeky swimsuit bottoms fizzle from my brain as reality comes crashing back to me. If Rachel is home, that means . . .

"Oh shit, here we go," I murmur, slipping my legs off Caleb's lap.

Sitting at this angle on the couch, we're hidden from view, but I can hear her talking by the door. A deep voice responds. Unless Poseidon has learned the power of speech in the last two minutes, Mars Kinnunen is in my house.

Cay must have fallen asleep too, because he's rolling his shoulder and cracking his neck, his mouth set in a deep frown. Right, game faces on. This is *our* turf. Show no fear. Mars Kinnunen is gonna come in here and show his damn face. He's gonna say more than three words to me, or so fucking help me—

"Easy," Caleb mutters, sensing the way I'm spiraling out.

Fuck, I'm terrible at this. I just want to bounce off the couch like Poseidon and wrap Rachel in my arms. I want to drag her upstairs and bury myself in her sweet pussy and tell her how much I missed her. She was only gone 32 hours. I have got to chill.

"Hey!" she calls out. "I'm home!"

"In here," I reply.

Shit, do I sound casual enough? Meeting your lover's lover for the first time is not a casual moment . . . but then I already know Mars. I mean, no one really *knows* Mars Kinnunen. But we're teammates. I see him every day. We play together. Travel together.

He came to the beach the other day. We had our longest non-hockey related conversation over by the grill. I asked him what kind of beach food they eat in Finland, and he actually answered me. It was at least five sentences.

"Be cool," Caleb mutters darkly as Rachel comes around the corner.

Fuck, just seeing her face has me relaxing. "Hey, baby," I call, holding out my hand over the back of the couch.

She comes right to me, and I take in Mars for the first time standing behind her. He's never been in my house before. He's standing there, framed in the entryway, his gaze moving slowly around the open living space. Rachel blocks my view of him as she takes my hand and curls herself over the top of the couch.

"Hey, angel," she says, smiling at me.

My senses fill with her as she leans down, kissing me. I weave my fingers into her hair, staking my claim. Mars better be watching. This girl is mine, and I'll kiss her whenever I want. She smells like her—all floral and soft. But she smells like him too. It makes my cock twitch and my hindbrain growl. I want to drag her over the top of the couch and wrap her in my arms, holding her against me until his scent fades. Or at least until mine mingles back in.

She pulls away with a soft laugh and gazes down at me, brushing my hair off my forehead.

I chase her hand like the pussy-whipped fool I am.

"Hard work out this morning? You seem sleepy."

"It fucking sucked," I mutter. "I got home and passed out."

She hums, glancing down the couch to look at Cay. "Did you boys behave while I was gone?"

"Better than you," he replies, his gaze darting over her shoulder to where Mars is still just standing there like a giant statue.

She straightens, her hand taking Caleb's on the back of the couch and giving it a squeeze. Fuck, she already knows us so well. She knows I need the instant reconnection, the affirmation. While Caleb is still lost in emotional no-man's land. When he's ready to warm up, she'll be there, but she's not gonna push him.

"Mars, you want something to drink?" she calls over her shoulder, moving past him towards the kitchen.

"No, thank you," he replies in that deep voice.

Rachel pulls open the door to the fridge. "Jake, Cay, you want anything?"

"Grapes," I call, as Caleb says, "Water."

I feel like a volcano ready to blow. I don't do awkward silences, but Mars and Caleb could be gold and silver medalists in the sport. This is so fucking unfair. I'm gonna come off as the panicked, needy one when I can't stand the heavy silence any longer.

Rachel shuts the door and turns, balancing several drinks and the bowl of grapes in her hands. "Here," she murmurs, offering Mars the bottle of water clutched in the curve of her elbow. "Come say hello."

He takes it wordlessly, following behind her into the living room.

She hands Caleb a can of sparkling water before offering me the grapes with another soft smile. She knows this is weird for me. At least she's a talker too. Thank fucking god.

Caleb and I are sitting at the short end of the "L" shaped sectional. I'm tucked into the corner, and he's flopped at the other end. Rachel comes around the long end and sits next to me, curling her legs under herself as she cracks open her own can of shitty sparkling water.

Like the weirdo he is, Mars doesn't sit next to her. No, he sits in the oversized chair, his bottle of normal person water untouched in his hand. Poseidon hops up next to her instead, his face all up in her business looking for pets.

"You know we know, right?" I call, unable to stand the silence a moment longer.

Mars pulls his broody gaze away from her and the dog. "What?"

"I said you know we know . . . right? He knows we know?" I add at Rachel.

"He knows you know, Jake," she replies, taking a sip of her water, one hand scratching between Sy's ears.

"He wouldn't be here if he didn't know," Caleb adds, his own dark gaze locked on the Finn. Caleb is always so good at reading people. "He's curious. He wants her, but he wants us to curl up and die so he can have her. He wants his path clear of all obstructions—"

"Cay, don't be a jerk," Rachel warns.

"Then let him tell us I'm wrong," he replies, his gaze shifting slowly back to the Finn. "Am I wrong, Mars?"

I watch him too, waiting.

Mars says nothing.

"Fucking perfect," Caleb mutters.

"Wait, so how is this gonna work then?" I say, shifting to stretch out my legs as I pop a grape into my mouth. "Mars, are you moving in here?"

"No," he and Caleb say at the same time.

"So . . . what then?" I say, glancing around. "You're with Rachel, and we're with Rachel and never the two shall meet? You gonna keep being weird at practices? You gonna avoid us in the group chats? Total Great Wall of Kinnunen? Because I gotta say, that's not really gonna work for me."

Ever the peacemaker, Rachel takes my hand and gives it a squeeze. "What would work for you, Jake?"

My gaze locks on the bear in my living room. "Well, I mean . . . Mars, you gotta try harder, man. Be part of the team. And I don't just mean this team," I add, gesturing around at the four of us. "And we *are* a team."

"Explain," he says, his blue eyes narrowed at me.

"Seriously? That wasn't clear enough? Okay . . . umm . . . well, you gotta talk to me more. I want full sentences and like, facial expressions and stuff. And you gotta be in the group chat. Use emojis and GIFs if you don't wanna talk. But leaving me on read is the fastest way to piss me off. Ask these two," I say, jabbing a thumb at Rachel and Cay, the bowl of grapes balanced in my lap.

He makes a face like he just sucked on something sour, but slowly he nods.

"I'm not saying change your whole personality," I add quickly. "I'm just sayin like . . . let us *see* your personality. You must show it to Rachel. She wouldn't be interested in a total dud of a dude. Just . . . I want more," I finish with a shrug.

Mars glances to Rachel and she gives him a nod. Sighing, he turns back to me. "I don't like red meat and I prefer reading to watching television. And I have a labral tear in my right hip."

I take a deep breath. This isn't groundbreaking information, but it's a start. "How bad is it?"

"Painful enough that I'm compensating in the net. But it's on the mend."

"How long have you been playing injured?"

"And keeping it secret," Caleb adds with a glare.

"All season," he replies. "I first noticed it over the summer."

I shake my head, my frustration rising. A lot of traumatic shit I keep bottled up tight is threatening to come out and now is not the time or the place. I take a deep breath. "Man, you gotta tell us shit like that. I get not telling coach, but you gotta tell me. I'm your D."

"I know," he mutters, his gaze dropping to the bottle of water in his hands.

"I'm protecting you out there. I would have changed my game to hold back, guard your right side better—"

"No," he growls. "You shouldn't have to compensate for me. We play our own positions."

"We play as a *team*, asshole," I reply, sensing Caleb tense next to me. "You're hurting, you tell your D-line, and we protect you with everything we've got. That's how it works. You're not alone, Mars. Not on that ice, and not in this house. You don't get to work alone anymore."

"It's a difficult habit to break," he admits.

"Yeah well . . . our Rays shit will work itself out on the ice," I reply. "But if you're with Rachel now, you're with *us* too. Me and Cay. You gotta trust us. No more secrets. You're gonna tell us when you're injured, and you gotta let us help you. Agreed?"

Slowly, he nods.

"Decide here and now, Mars. Get all in with us or get all the way out." My speech over, I point over my shoulder towards my front door.

He glances sharply at Rachel before looking back at me. "What does 'all in' mean to you, Compton?"

Next to me, Caleb shifts. I can't help but smirk. "Well, for starters, you gotta let me sleep with my thumb in your ass. And you know about Naked Thursdays, right?"

"Ohmygod," Rachel mutters as Caleb snorts.

"This is a joke, yes?" Mars glances to Rachel, one brow raised. "He's joking?"

"Yeah, Mars. I'm just fucking with you. Well . . . I mean, that'll be up to you," I add with a wink. "Say the word, and we'll commence with the fucking right here, right now. Cay and I can't wait to see you make use of that torpedo between your legs. Are you sore, Seattle?" I add, throwing her a teasing grin. "Not gonna lie, it gets me hard picturing the two of you together. I really hope you're into sharing, Mars. Cause Cay and I flipped a coin, and I get to tag-team her with you first."

Rachel groans again as Mars looks at me like I've grown a second head.

"You're serious?" he asks again.

And now I'm laughing. I slip off the couch, giving Poseidon a pat as he trots at my side around Caleb's end of the couch. "Actually, yeah. About the coin flipping thing. We got bored last night watching *Great British Bake Off*. But I don't think you're really up for a tag-team right now," I add, sizing him up. "And if I know my Seattle Girl, she didn't stop until your dick all but killed her last night. Am I right, baby girl? Does your sweet pussy need time to recover before we double-team you again?"

She just rolls her eyes at me, letting me lean over the back of the couch to kiss her upside down. "Are you having fun?" she murmurs.

"Hey, if he can't take it, he can leave," I say loud enough for him to hear.

"How about we ease into the chaos a little," she replies, her fingers brushing lightly down my arm. "Start with something a little more casual than a four-way."

"How about we start with dinner?" I look over at the giant Finn. "Mars, you're staying for dinner."

68
CALEB

Mars Kinnunen is still here. He's standing at the sink with Rachel while they clean up from dinner. Jake is outside taking care of his precious grill. He's a total snob when it comes to his grills. I don't care so long as I get to enjoy the meats of his labor. Tonight, it was steaks and grilled shrimp. Inside, Rachel prepped wild rice and a salad. Since the guys are in season, they also ate their weight in broccoli.

Now Mars is washing plates as she sets them aside. Her music plays over the surround system, something soft and girly. It's been on all evening. They murmur to each other as she takes a sip of wine. She says something, her dark eyes glancing up towards him and he smiles. She bumps him with her hip, laughing as he nearly drops a dish. It plops back into the soapy water.

Watching them in this moment I know the truth: she's worked her magic on him too.

Fuck, he's not going anywhere.

Not that I thought he would. I've watched this building between them for weeks. The explosive sexual tension between them may be gone, but the simmering need remains. He's crazy about her. And she's crazy about him. It's new. It's exciting.

But this isn't going to work for all of us if he thinks he gets to keep his relationship with her totally separate from ours. Jake may have been joking about the sharing thing, but I'm not. I'm not going to hide away just to make him more comfortable. This is my house too. My girl. My life.

Setting my ice water down on the island, I snatch up the bread-basket and the butter dish from the table, bringing them around to the sink.

"Thanks, babe," Rachel says, flashing me a smile.

The butter dish goes rattling down as I reach for her with both hands. Cupping her face, I pull her to me, sealing our mouths with a hungry kiss. She gasps against me, her lips parting. Then her hands come up, gripping to my elbows as she kisses me back.

My entire body lights up, loving the feel of having her in my arms. She's so yielding, brazenly kissing me back in front of Mars. My hands brush across her shoulders, down her sides, to her waist, as I pull her to me.

She comes willingly, her soapy hands dragging through my hair before they drop between us, pressing against my chest. We break our kiss, foreheads pressed together, and she lets out a soft laugh. Her wet hands are splayed across my ratty Minnesota Hockey t-shirt.

"Look who finally decided to come out of his shell," she teases.

"Hey, baby." She cups my cheek, tilting her head back to look at me. "Wanna help him finish up the dishes?" She glances over her shoulder at Mars.

He's standing there, arms crossed over his barrel chest, his sporty man bun, blond beard, and fierce cheekbones giving him that GQ Viking look. He glares at me, tugging the dish towel off his shoulder and tossing it down. "Say what you need to say, Sanford."

I turn my gaze back to Rachel, brushing my thumb along her soft cheek. "I want to fuck you, Hurricane. Right here. Right now. And I want him to watch."

She sucks in a breath, eyes wide. "Cay—"

"We can't move forward until we all know he can handle sharing. And currently he's not sure," I say, pointing over her shoulder at him. I lift my gaze to look at him. "Are you?"

She turns in my arms to look up at him with those pretty brown eyes. "Mars?"

A muscle in his jaw twitches as he stares at me. I don't dare adjust my hold on her. If my touching her is enough to coil him like a spring, what will my fucking her in front of him do? We have to know.

And screw Jake and our stupid coin toss last night. He's much more valuable than me. We're not going to open this door only to have Mars barrel through it and knock Jake's lights out. If someone has to take the hit, it's going to be me. My defenseman deserves to have someone put him first for once.

"Tell her the truth, Mars," I say.

All three of us already know it.

"No," he admits, letting out a low breath. "I'm not sure. Sanford, I need you to take your hands off her." He says it so damn politely, but his meaning is clear. He wants to rip my fucking head off.

"Mars," she whispers, going tense in my arms.

"Easy, Hurricane." I brush both hands down her arms. "He's not going to do anything to me, and we're not going to stop. We'll call this exposure therapy. It's one thing for Mars to say he wants you. But he doesn't get to take you away from us. And he doesn't get a nice, sterile version of our life where the only one who touches you in his presence is him."

As I speak, I skate my hands over her shoulders and around to cup her breasts. She arches slightly into me, her body responding to the heat of Mars' gaze and the teasing of my hands. Fuck, our girl loves to be shared. Loves to be watched. She's insatiable. Is he willing to set his damn pride aside and help me? Or is this over for him before it begins?

"You love it when we fuck, don't you Hurricane?" I whisper, one hand trailing down her front to slip inside her leggings. "You're always so wet for us. Such a good girl. This perfect pussy is so smooth. Should we show him?" I tease, nipping her earlobe.

When she just whimpers, I jerk her leggings down enough to expose her bare pussy. Then I give it a slap that has her gasping, her ass pressing against me.

"Cay—" She closes her eyes, tipping her head back against my shoulder.

I lift a hand to her jaw and hold her tight. "Don't you dare close your eyes. You look right at Mars. You let him know when I do something you like."

Two feet away, Mars stands there, horrified and mesmerized in one, his lips parted as he watches my hand slip under her t-shirt to cup her bare breast. Meanwhile, the fingers of my right hand are parting her pussy lips, letting my middle finger glide through her wetness.

"She's tight, isn't she, Mars?" I tease as she squirms in my hold.

"Her cunt is heaven. Have you had her ass yet? You strike me as an ass man—"

"Stop talking" he growls.

"No."

Fuck, I'm totally getting punched in the face. It's worth it to feel her pressed against me. I shove two fingers in her, and she winces. I drop my hand away immediately as Mars take a protective step closer, his gaze a blue-eyed inferno.

"Jake was right," I tease, letting my finger circle her wet clit. "Mars wore your pussy out last night, didn't he, Hurricane?"

She just sighs in my hold, letting me tease her clit.

"Did he take your ass too, baby? *Tell me*," I growl, my free hand wrapping around her throat. That has Mars tensing, his muscles tight across his shoulders.

"Yes," she whispers, breathless as I work her over.

"Did you ride him, Hurricane? Did you take him to the hilt?"

"Yes."

"Did you suck him off?"

"No," she replies on a moan. I know she's close, teetering on that edge.

I glance over at him, a smile in my voice as I say, "You didn't suck him off? But that's your specialty. Should we show him how good you take a cock down your throat? You look so beautiful on your knees. And we both know how much you love to gag on me."

I slap her pussy again and she cries out, her body strung so tight with the need to come. "Please, Cay," she whispers, trying to turn in my arms. "Please, don't tease me."

I let her turn away from Mars, cupping her cheek with a steady hand. "Get on your knees and take out my cock," I command, holding her walnut brown gaze. "You're gonna suck me off while the goalie watches. Only after you've choked on my cum will I put you on this counter and hold you down so he can tongue-fuck you. We don't stop until you come all over his stupidly handsome face. Agreed?"

She nods, her eyes glassy with need.

"Agreed?" I say over her shoulder at Mars.

He's fighting his every urge to step in, but slowly, he nods. He's curious enough not to kill me . . . yet.

With a grateful sigh, Rachel drops to her knees in front of me. She tugs up on my ratty shirt, but I'm already ahead of her, jerking it off one handed and tossing it on the island. Then both my hands are in her hair, pulling it up until I fist it one-handed on her crown.

She presses her face against my crotch, breathing me in before she gives my grey sweats a sharp tug. I'm not wearing underwear, so my cock bobs free in her face, hard and ready to fucking go.

"Mitä vittua," Mars curses, his voice low and gravelly. "Sanford— your cock." His eyes are wide as he stares down at my pierced dick.

I chuckle as Rachel wraps her hand around my base. I tug her hair, tipping her head back. "You didn't tell your new boyfriend about me?"

She shakes her head, her mouth curling into a lusty smile.

"Do you think he wants to see it up close?" My gaze darts over her head to Mars. He towers almost five inches taller than me. "Have you never seen a pierced dick before, Kinnunen?"

"No," he mutters. "Never. Mitä helvettiä . . . does it hurt?"

"Right now, my only pain is blue balls," I reply. "Our girl was in the middle of something." I give her hair a soft tug. "Show him, Hurricane. Let him watch."

She wraps her mouth back around me, teasing me with her tongue.

"Why did you do it?" Mars mutters, watching her suck me. "Why go through such mutilation?"

I huff a laugh that comes out part groan. Fuck, she's good at this. "Ask Rachel if it was a good investment of time and pain." I pull her off me. "Hurricane, do you like my pierced dick?"

She nods, gazing up at me. "You know I do. But it's not enough to have the piercings," she adds, flicking her tongue over my tip like a fucking siren. "You have to know what to do with them. But you guys all know that. It's not about the stick, it's about the handling," she teases, her free hand dropping from my hip to cup my balls.

I groan, my hand in her hair softening as I let her get back to work.

"What does it feel like for the man?" asks Mars.

"Jeezus," I pant. "If you're so curious, go get it done and find out.

Or find a different pierced man willing to fuck you in the ass. Then you'll know."

Rachel looks up between us with a smile. "Do you want to come down here with me?" she says at him, batting her lashes.

He deadpans her. "The man has four metal bars through his cock, Rakas. I don't have to be gay to find that fascinating." He looks over her at me. "Can I touch it?"

Well, kill me dead.

Those are four words I never expected to escape from the mouth of Mars Kinnunen.

"You want to touch my hard dick, Mars?"

"Only if you're amenable," he replies.

Holy fuck, this guy is totally serious right now. I can't help the laugh that escapes me as I drag a hand through my hair, the other still holding Rachel's hair up on top of her head. One minute we were fucking. Now, I guess it's show-and-tell hour. "Be my fucking guest, Mars. Her dick is your dick, apparently."

He steps forward, bending slightly to look at it from a lower angle. "I can see how the placement would bring women added pleasure."

"Oh, you have no idea," Rachel teases, still on her knees.

And now I've stepped into some alternate reality where Mars Kinnunen is reaching out his hand, his calloused thumb stroking the underside of my cock, rubbing along my piercings while Rachel holds me still at the base.

"It feels quite strange," Mars murmurs, his tone almost academic.

Behind me, the door slams shut. Mars drops his hand away from my dick and we all turn. Jake is standing there, eyes wide, dirty grill tongs in hand. He goes from surprised to serious in 2.5 seconds.

"What the *fuck* is going on?"

69
JAKE

I think my brain just exploded. I'm pretty sure that if I turned around, I'll find it splattered all over the sliding glass door.

Mars was just touching Caleb's dick. *My* Caleb. And Caleb was letting him! That's what has me feeling like my brain just burst. Has Caleb been holding out this whole time? Has he been harboring a secret crush on Mars? Was this all a ploy to get to him in the group?

Before I can follow that bread crumb trail to my heart's demise, Rachel pops up from behind the island, eyes wide as she takes me in. I stare right back, trying to weave this new reality together.

Okay . . . so Rachel was on her knees. Between them. Facing Cay. Something sexual was definitely about to happen, but Rachel was in the middle . . .

So then why the fuck was Mars touching my Cay? He was definitely touching his dick when I walked in here!

The three of them blink at me like a trio of guilty owls. Then Rachel gives a nervous laugh, pulling up her leggings. Caleb does the same with his shorts, tucking his ribbed dick away.

Unfreezing my feet from the floor, I hurry over, rattling down my tray of dirty grill tools. My heart is beating a mile a minute. My mouth feels dry. I'm clammy. I'm sweating. What the fuck is wrong with me?

"I go outside for two fucking minutes, and I come back to see Mars giving you a handy?" I cry, staring daggers at Caleb.

The asshole just shrugs at me. I want to punch him in the goddamn face, almost as much as I want to drag him into the open door of the pantry and put him on his knees. If he thinks he's gonna become fuck buddies with Mars Kinnunen, and I'll have no fucking comment, he is dead wrong.

I spin to face the broody Finn. This is all his damn fault. He was the one doing the touching. "Are you bi?"

"No," he and Rachel say at the same time.

My gaze darts between them, my stare leveling on the Finn. "Well then why were you touching Cay's cock?"

"Jealous, angel?" Caleb teases.

Oh, fuck him. He's about to be feeling the palm of my hand on his ass. "You fucking know I am," I snap. "At no fucking point did we *ever* discuss that bringing Mars into this meant he'd be jerking you off in my goddamn kitchen!"

"That's not what was happening," Rachel says. "Mars was just . . ." She glances over her shoulder at him, clearly looking for help.

"Curious," Mars replies.

"Yeah, he's never seen a guy with a pierced dick before," Caleb adds, arms crossed as he keeps smirking at me. He's fucking loving this. He knows he's under my skin worse than a goddamn splinter. "You came in when things were just getting good," he adds with a wink.

"Getting *good*? I repeat. "Was he about to drop to his knees too?" At the look of worried surprise on Rachel's face I suck in a deep breath, dragging both hands through my hair. "Oh my god, I'm spinning out," I mutter.

"Just a little," Rachel replies. "Angel . . . try using your words—"

"I'm jealous!"

Rachel's eyes go wide. "Jake, what—"

"I'm jealous of you, and I'm jealous of them, and I want more," I go on, spilling my guts all over the kitchen floor.

"More?" Her voice is so gentle, her gaze so open.

"Yes," I say quickly, taking a step closer. "I don't think I can just sit around and wait to have my turn with you," I admit, one hand still mussing with my hair.

"Can you explain better?" She replies.

"No," I say. And it's true. I don't even know what I've said. In all this panic, I've already forgotten.

"Try," she urges. "Kitchen, remember? Sudden death rules still apply."

I take a deep breath, filling my whole chest with air and puffing it out as I glance from Caleb back to Rachel. "I want more," I say again.

"More what?" Rachel inches closer to Caleb's side.

For a second, I'm sure she's going to take his hand. My gaze narrows on that spot between their hands. She wants to touch him, but she knows he doesn't want it. Fuck, she knows him so well. Does she know me too? Does she know what I'm trying to say without saying it?

Meanwhile, Mars just stands there like a stone giant, watching me spin out. His presence unnerves me, even as it makes me bolder. I'm not going to hide away from him. This is my life. My house. And Rachel and Cay are *mine*. I was here first. I'm not gonna be afraid of him or threatened by him. If he wants Rachel, he's gonna have to fit into *our* life, not the other way around. And if he doesn't like what I say or what I do, he can show himself to the door.

With that fire burning in my bones, I move around the island, coming to stand between Rachel and Cay. "More everything," I admit. I turn to Rachel, taking in those gorgeous dark eyes. I so rarely use her name, but the moment calls for it. "Rachel . . ." I let myself feel the music of the sound. "I love you, baby girl. And I want you," I say, cupping her face with both hands.

"Every hour of the fucking day. I'm thinking about you," I go on. "I'm obsessed. I'm possessed. On the ice, off it. You're it for me. Rachel, you're the fucking one. There's not a doubt in my mind."

"I know," she murmurs, tears in her eyes. Her hands lift, wrapping gently around my wrists. Then her gaze trails down my face to settle on my lips. "But?"

Fuck . . . *but*. It kills me that there's a *but*.

"But being with you," I begin, searching for the right words. "Watching the way you love Cay . . . watching you fall for Ilmari the way you have . . . I think I'm jealous."

"Why are you jealous, Jake?" she murmurs. Her touch roots me, calming the storm of my swirling thoughts and emotions.

"Because you're free," I admit. "You love with your whole heart. You're all in three times over. I never thought something like that was possible. But I see you . . . I see you with them," I add, gesturing to the guys. "And I know it's real."

Taking a deep breath, I drop my hands down to her shoulders. "And I want it too. I want to be free too."

Holy fucking shit. What is with this kitchen? This place must have truth serum pumping out of the air vents, because I'm spilling all my deepest secrets. I want more, and that's the truth. I want Rachel. All day. Every day. But more than that, I want what Rachel has. I want to be free to live and love out loud. What feels this fucking right can't possibly be wrong . . . right?

Her hands drift down, resting on my chest as she breathes deep, her gaze locked on me. "And . . . how do you be free, Jake? What do you want?"

And now I can't breathe. She wants me to say it out loud? Can't she just use our weird telepathy? I swallow, focusing all my attention on her mouth as I say, "I want more."

"What is more?" she presses.

Fuck, she really is gonna make me say it. I know Mars didn't sign up for confession hour, but I don't care. I'm fighting for what I want. And what I want is standing in this room.

Slowly, I turn, heart in my throat. My every breath lifts my chest as I face Cay. "I want more," I admit, speaking the words out loud. "I'm tired of crawling out of my damn skin pretending that I don't. I have no idea what the fuck I'm doing here, but that's how I feel," I finish with an awkward shrug.

I know he already knows this. Rachel knows too. Why else was she being so cagey during our last sudden death match? All her talk of me finding someone else to love. She stood in this kitchen, right next to Cay, and told me to find my happiness with someone other than her. She wants this for me too . . . right?

Caleb's dark gaze goes volcanic. "Say it," he mutters.

"I want more," I repeat.

Caleb's tattooed arm stretches out, his hand banding around my throat as he squeezes, pulling me closer.

I gasp, my neck arching in his hold as I let him reel me in. My dick twitches in my shorts. Fuck, I'm a goner. All he has to do is look down and he'll see how hard I am for him.

He holds me right before him, the pressure of his hand still at my throat. "Say it, Jake."

I groan, fighting the urge to tremble as my body responds to the sound of his dominating tone. Never in a million years would I have guessed that I'd sub for Caleb Sanford. But the memory of being on my knees with his cock in my mouth has me squirming. I liked it. I fucking *loved* it. I've been riding the high of that moment for two days straight.

And I want more.

I lean into his hand, wordlessly daring him to increase his pressure. He does, and my cock hardens still further. I swallow against his hand. "I want more, Cay," I rasp out.

"Say it."

"I want you."

My gaze drops from his face, down his chest, to the top of his shorts. I can clearly see the bulge of his erection. I breathe a little sigh of relief against the pressure of his hand. He wants me too.

Thank fucking god.

"You want me?" he murmurs, his hand softening slightly at my throat.

"I want you," I say again, not an ounce of shame in my words.

The corner of his mouth quirks into a smile and my stomach flips. *Oh shit, here we go.*

Caleb leans in, his lips so close to mine, as he breathes my air. With that half-smile still on his face, he drops his hand away from my throat and steps back, leaving me reeling. "Then beg for me."

My whole body feels like it's on fire, tiny little flames licking every inch of my skin. "Please," I whisper, my voice breaking. "Please, Cay . . ."

"You beg so well," he teases, those dark eyes piercing me. "Do it again. On your knees this time."

I don't even hesitate. I just drop to my knees, gazing up at him. Rachel stands right next to us, watching. I want her to watch. I want her to see how much I'm in this. I need her to know what I want this dynamic to be. They all need to know. Because I'm done fighting this. Done pretending I don't want what Caleb can offer me.

"Please, Cay," I say again. Reaching out with both hands, I grab hold of his hips. "I want you so bad. Want a taste. Want more. Please—"

Caleb's hand brushes lightly over my hair and I fight a groan. "Then be my good fucking boy and take me out," he orders, his soft hold turning into a vice grip as I wince.

I tug on his shorts, dropping them to his ankles. His hard, pierced, cock bobs free right in my face. The tip is already wet and waiting for me. I groan, my gaze feasting on the metal rods on the underside of his shaft. They fascinate me. I'm not surprised Mars was curious too. But I'll be damned if he's gonna touch Cay again without my fucking permission. I never thought I'd say this, but this dick is mine.

I glance up, unsure of what comes next. Can I taste it? I want it in my mouth. But I don't know the rules. Do I wait?

As if he can read my mind, his hand softens in my hair again. "What are you waiting for? Hurricane can't help you this time. She's got her own dick to suck. Now, open that sweet mouth, and take me deep."

If I think too hard about what I'm doing right now, I may just lose my nerve. I'm on my knees in my kitchen, Caleb's cock inches from my lips. Rachel and Mars Fucking Kinnunen are right behind me. They're gonna watch me suck this dick.

Fuck, why is that turning me on even harder? Who am I? What happened to Jake Compton? Is this who I always was . . . or is this who I'm meant to become? I decide I don't fucking care.

I grab his cock around the base with one hand, loving the sound of his sigh. I hold tight to his hip with the other. Last time the asshole tried to choke me with his fancy hip thrusts. But I'm running this show now. Opening my mouth, I lean forward and lick his rounded head. That first taste of him on my tongue has me groaning.

The pain is sharp in my knees as I lean forward, opening my mouth to tease him a little more. I have literally no idea what I'm doing. This is only the second time I've had a dick in my mouth. Caleb's dick. Only this dick. The thought of any other dick makes me wanna gag. But Cay?

I groan again, sinking around him, my own dick hardening in my pants as I swallow him deep. I work him with my tongue, tensing as I feel the ribbed roll of his piercings. I start sucking, not caring if it's loud or if I make a mess.

"Such a good boy," he croons, both hands soft in my hair. He's moving his hips a bit, matching my rhythm as I suck. I like it. I like the feel of us being in sync.

Honestly that's what I crave most from him. I want his damn walls down, and I want us totally in tune. Rachel gets me. It's our twin thing. No, it's the Rachel and Jake thing. We just breathe in sync. We have from the beginning.

Cay and I can get there too, but I have to work for it. And he has to surrender to it. We'll find each other through sex if that's what he needs. Hopefully, as his walls stay down more and for longer, he'll just keep them down. He'll stay with us just like this. He'll let us love him and need him. It's all I want.

"You're so perfect," Cay murmurs, his hands smoothing over my shoulders, almost like a massage. It makes my dick ache with longing. "You were made to suck my dick. So beautiful on your knees. So powerful."

He's right. This *is* powerful. Every word out of his mouth lowers his walls. I want him to keep talking, keep pretending like he's owning this moment. But I'm in total control. I think, deep down, we both know it.

I grab tight to his hips with both hands and open my mouth wide, taking him deep. I don't even care that I'm choking, saliva dripping down my chin. My nose brushes the soft bristles of his dark hair and I breathe him in. Fuck, my dick is weeping. He smells so good. I want to curl up against his skin and breathe him in.

Rachel says the same thing about me. She calls my body wash her pussynip. Well, this smell on Cay is my dicknip. I need to come. I need some goddamn relief. But he's gonna blow first. In my mouth. Down my throat. I'm taking him all in. He's fucking mine. They all are.

I glance over my shoulder to see Rachel trembling in Mars' arms as they kiss, his hand working her clit as she whimpers.

"Back on your knees, Hurricane," Cay orders. "Take care of Mars. Right here in front of me. I wanna watch him come down your throat. Finish him while Jake finishes me, and you'll get that tongue-fucking we promised."

Caleb wraps his hand possessively around the back of my head, pulling my attention back to him as he moves his hips. Behind me, I sense Rachel dropping to her knees. Fuck, this has me turned all the way on. She's choking on Mars while I suck Caleb. We're all in this. Mars isn't running scared.

Riding the high of this moment, I wrap my hands around Caleb's ass, squeezing his firm cheeks, as I bury his cock down my throat. I suck long and slow, holding him to me as he curses and groans.

"I'm gonna—"

He doesn't get the rest of his words out before I drop a hand between his legs and cup his balls. That finishes him. He groans deep, hips hitching as he releases, his warm cum filling my mouth. I'm a mess as I pull back, his cum mixing with my saliva on my chin. I can't swallow it all.

I lift away, huffing for breath through my nose. My hard cock is tented in my shorts. I'm aching with the need for him to touch me. But I feel sated too. I took care of Caleb. He *let* me take care of him.

His thumb sweeps over the mess on my chin. When he presses in at my lips, I open, sucking his thumb into my mouth, savoring more of his taste.

"So beautiful," he murmurs again, his gaze softer, his walls lowered.

He pulls me to my feet and I stand there, swaying slightly. His hand on my shoulder steadies me. Then he turns me, making me watch as Rachel takes Mars in her mouth. She's gazing up at him so lovingly. And yet, I know she hasn't forgotten about us standing here. Neither has he. The energy between the four of us is charged.

Rachel whimpers, her free hand working her clit as she finishes Mars. The huge Finn grunts out his release and Rachel swallows, making it look effortless. Meanwhile, I still feel like a mess.

Caleb steps in behind me, his hand slinking around my hip to smooth itself over my hard cock. I groan, pressing into his hip with my ass, even as my cock wants to chase more pressure. He stills as Rachel stumbles to her feet.

As we watch, Rachel shimmies her leggings all the way off. She tugs off her tank top, leaving her naked in my kitchen. Fuck, she's so beautiful. She glances between the three of us before hopping her bare ass right up onto my kitchen island. Spreading her legs slightly, she works her clit with two fingers. "I was promised a tongue-fucking," she says, our goddess incarnate.

I practically use Cay as a springboard to get to her first, my hands smoothing over her bare shoulders. She catches my chin with her hand, tipping my face up to hold her gaze. I look in her brown eyes, not quite so dark as Cay's. She wants to know that I'm okay with Mars being here. That I want this. That I'm all in.

The way I see it, fair is fair. She can have Mars so long as I get Cay. Mirroring her smile, I call over my shoulder. "Mars, get over. Hold our girl open for me."

Rachel smiles with relief, whimpering as my hand drops to tease her wet pussy. Fuck, we're gonna make a mess of our girl. I want her squirming on this counter before we're done. And then someone is getting on their knees to finish me. So much sexual tension in one house all the time? I'm honestly scared for my dick health.

Mars steps in beside me, hesitant but willing.

"Hold her," I direct, moving my hand off her thigh.

He replaces my hand with his, and I take it as a win. Cay is already on my other side, holding her left thigh. Our girl is spread before us, panting with need as she lies back on her elbows, gazing up at us like we're her beginning, middle, and end. Oh yeah, this doesn't stop until she screams all our names.

70
RACHEL

"**O**h god," I pant. "I'm done. No more." I never thought I'd say this, but there's such a thing as too much sex. Mars Kinnunen is an animal. The man doesn't tire. We've been at it for hours, and I'm officially ready to wave the white flag. This is a first in Rachel Price history. I roll onto my side and crawl away towards the end of the bed.

"Where do you think you're going?"

"Away," I huff, sweaty and breathless. "Far, far away."

With a growl he grabs my ankles and drags me back, flipping me over.

"Ilmari!" I cry, kicking my legs. It's no use. I'm trapped in his iron grip. "Come at me with that monster cock again, and you'll be paying for my vaginal reconstruction."

"Money well spent." He drops down to his elbows, spreads my thighs, and lets his mouth feast on my battered pussy. I'm dripping with his cum, but he doesn't care, his tongue teasing me from ass to clit.

"Oh my god, you're insatiable," I cry, my thighs squeezing his head as I squirm under him.

"You started this," he says, lifting his mouth away.

"What?" I push on his head with both hands but it's like trying to shift a boulder. "You were supposed to be driving me home from work, remember? Little did I know you actually meant to kidnap me and drive me to *your* home."

Not that I complained. The heat of our sexual tension was hot enough to fry an egg during the whole car ride. We barely made it inside his little waterfront bungalow before we were ripping off our clothes. We were ravenous for each other, fucking on his kitchen table, down the hall, all the way to his bedroom.

That was hours ago. Now his clean linens smell like sex and sweat and utter debauchery.

"I said you couldn't handle me," he warns. "I offered you an out on our first night together."

I prop myself up on my elbows as I hold his gaze. "Oh, is that what you think? You think I can't handle you, Kinnunen?"

He smirks, rocking back on his knees, his proud cock on display. The cut lines of his muscles are so sharp you could chip a tooth. His hair is down and wild around his shoulders. He looks utterly sinful. "You're the one crawling away," he replies in a total deadpan.

I take a deep breath and let it out in a huff. *Oh, this is so not happening.* Rachel Price is not going to lose in a battle of wills against Mars Kinnunen. Not so long as there is breath in my body. I swing my legs over the side of the bed. "Okay, big guy. You still wanna play? Fine. Grand finale. Get over here."

I scoot down the side of his bed towards the bedside table, snatching up the bottle of lube. I've learned quick that it's a must with Mars. He's just too damn big to play safely without it.

"What are you doing?" he mutters, still on his knees in the middle of the bed.

"Get over here," I say again. "Stand up."

He moves off the other side of the bed and walks around the end. His massive frame looms over me as he brushes my hair back from my face with a gentle hand. "What are you doing, Rakas?"

Judging our size difference at this angle, I pop up onto my knees on the edge of the bed and flip the cap off the top of the lube. Squirting some on my chest, I grin up at him, tossing the bottle aside. "Come here," I say, grabbing him by the hips.

"What is this?"

"You're gonna fuck my tits and blow on my face."

His expression flickers like a broken TV, changing so quick I can't tell what he's thinking. Cupping my face, he leans down, his gaze molten. "Mennään naimisiin."

I laugh, one hand smearing the lube down between my breasts. The heat of his gaze is enough to set me on fire. I will never get enough of this man. He's going to be the death of me.

RIP Rachel Price, dead from too much amazing sex.

I don't know what time it is. I don't care. Our sexathon is finally over, and Mars is sated. His head rests on a pillow on my lap as I gently stroke his hair back from his face. One of his heavy arms lays over my thighs, his fingers brushing lightly against my skin.

"Tell me about this one," I murmur, my finger stroking the tattoo on his shoulder.

He hums low, clearing his throat. "The bear?"

I turn my head a little, looking down at it. I suppose it's a bear. It's demonic looking, with a skull face and flaming eyes, exaggerated claws. But now I see the pattern of feathered pine trees. "Mhmm."

"That's Otso," he says, his deep voice muffled by the pillow. "He is the spirit of Bear, king of the forest. Sacred to Finns."

"And the skull demon wearing the crown?" I say, my hand brushing lower toward the middle of his back.

"That's Tuoni, god of death, lord of the underworld."

"This tattoo is important to you," I murmur, my hand smoothing over his blackened skin. He doesn't respond. Of course, it is. "When did you get it?"

"When my mother died," he replies, his body still.

"You were seventeen."

He nods. Pushing off my lap, he sits up, his massive frame dwarfing mine as he leans against the headboard.

"How did she die? You said cancer at dinner . . ."

"Yes. It was a rare brain cancer. She went quickly, for which I'm grateful."

"And your stepfather kept you?"

He huffs, shaking his head. "Juhani was never my stepfather. Mother never married after Halla."

"Then—"

"He was her neighbor," he replies before I can ask my question. "My mother grew up in the house next to the Kinnunen's. She and Juhani were the same age, they went to school together before he started his junior hockey career. They were friends."

I lean against his shoulder, letting my fingers brush down his bare chest. "Were they sweethearts?"

He glances down at me, his arm going around me with his hand on my head, fingers stroking my hair. "They never discussed it with me openly . . . but I think not."

"Why?"

He shrugs. "I believe Juhani has no interest in women. Even now, he has never married. He was at mother's funeral. He was already playing for the Liiga at the time. He helped me sell mother's house. I moved in with the Kinnunen's that summer. Just before I began with the Liiga, I took Juhani's name. I haven't looked back."

"You call him your father? He raised you?"

"Not quite," he mutters. "I knew him through my youth, certainly. We saw each other at holidays and family events. But he didn't raise me."

"But . . . you told Halla he did," I say gently, my fingers now stroking his arm.

He goes still. "I don't want to talk about Halla."

But I'm not ready to let this drop. It's so rare that Ilmari opens up. And I need to know. Need to understand. "He abandoned you. In the divorce, he left?"

"Yes."

"Did you never see him again?"

"I never wanted to," he replies, shifting away from me.

"Mars—"

"He began reaching out in earnest after I joined the Liiga," he says, getting off the bed. "He wanted to know why the money he sent every month was no longer being accepted. Mother took care of it, you see. I never knew he sent money."

I roll onto my knees facing him. "But surely, the fact that he never stopped supporting you financially—the fact that he's reaching out now—"

He turns sharply around to face me, still gloriously naked. "Is he?"

Shit. "Mars—"

"Is he reaching out, Rachel?" he presses. "He's certainly not reaching out to me. So, I must assume he is reaching out to *you*. Is Halla asking about me?"

Letting my shoulders drop, I shrug. "He just wants an update—"

"I do *not* want a relationship with that man," he growls, snatching his boxer briefs off the floor and slipping them on.

"I haven't told him anything," I quickly assure him. "I wouldn't do that without your permission, Mars. Never—"

"But you want to," he huffs. "You want to tell him of my progress."

"My parents split too," I say. "Divorce is always awful. And parents can make terrible choices. But I know that if I never gave my dad a second chance—if I didn't learn to forgive—"

"You want me to forgive Halla for abandoning me?" he growls. "He deprived me of ever having a father."

"And he will carry that shame and that pain to his death," I say quickly, tears in my eyes. "But Mars, I *know* him. I've worked closely with him for two years. I'm not saying you have to forgive him, or let him in. All I'm saying is that life is long . . . and the hate you carry is a heavy burden. Maybe there's hope for a future where you learn to put it down."

"You want me to forgive him," he says again, his face a mask of frustration.

"No," I say, crawling to the edge of the bed and holding out my hands to him.

He stays back, glaring down at them.

"I care about *you*, Ilmari. Your happiness, your future, your peace of mind. Hating him hurts you. It's a wound you carry. And I'm a doctor. I can't help but want to heal a wound when I see it," I add with a shrug.

His shoulders relax a little as he steps in, taking my hands in both of his. Slowly, he lifts them up, placing kisses on my knuckles. "I have lived so long with this hate," he admits, his voice soft.

I nod, lifting one hand away to stroke his face. "I know. But that doesn't mean you have to live with it forever. And I'm here for you. I've got strong shoulders too. I can help you carry it . . . if you want," I add softly.

He cups my face, his gaze tender as he looks down at me. Slowly, he nods. The wound isn't healed. Not by far . . . but it's a start.

IT turns out Ilmari is something of a skin care snob. I've been in his bathroom for the last half hour, treating myself to some kind of Nordic charcoal face mask. I peek around the corner of the open bathroom doorway and see his bare legs stretched out on the bed. Last I checked, he was reading his e-book and popping raspberries like candy.

As I rinse the mask off my face, the doorbell rings.

"Are you expecting someone?" he calls from the other room.

"No," I garble back, my face sudsy as I scrub off the charcoal mask.

I'm about to pop the cap off a fancy European toner product when I hear him shouting.

"Rakas!" There's a sense of urgency to his tone.

I hurry out of his bedroom into the main living area. Mars is standing shirtless at his front door, not the back, arms crossed over his muscled chest. I peek past him to see Jake, Caleb, and the dog on the other side of the door. Poseidon presses his nose against the glass, yipping as he sees me. I can't help but smile.

"How do they know where I live?" Mars mutters.

"We can hear you, asshole!" Jake huffs. "Seattle, make him open the door."

"For the record, I had nothing to do with this," Caleb calls.

"Yeah, it was all Sy's idea," Jake adds.

Poseidon yips again, whining as he dances at their feet.

"How do they know, Rakas?" Mars says again.

"Because I told them, obviously," I reply. "Mars, just open the door."

"Come on," Jake calls. "The ice cream is melting!"

With a heavy sigh, Mars unlocks the door and stands back. Poseidon comes blasting in, desperate to get to me.

"Hi, my angel puppy," I coo. "Who's the bestest boy in the whole world?"

"That would be me," Jake teases. "I brought ice cream." He holds up a bulging plastic grocery bag. "Mars grab the spoons."

"Why are you here, Compton?" Mars mutters, his arms once again crossed.

"Coach just sent over the tapes for review for Tuesday's game," he replies, helping himself to Ilmari's kitchen as he digs out the spoons. "We figured we'd watch it with you." He glances around the living area. "You do have a TV, right?"

With another sigh, Mars walks over to the living room and picks up a remote. Giving it a click, a TV magically emerges from within a piece of furniture.

"Cool," Jake says, watching the TV go up.

Meanwhile, Caleb fishes the ice creams out of the bag. "Come grab yours, Hurricane—"

"No way," Jake growls. "Not so fast. Mars, get over here."

Caleb groans, shaking his head with laugh.

"What's wrong?" I say.

"Cay's just trying to steal my thunder," Jake replies. "He doesn't believe in my superpower."

"It's not a superpower," Caleb huffs.

"It is! Stop trying to take this away from me."

"What's going on?" I say, my gaze darting between them.

Jake turns to me. "Oh, he's just mad because he doesn't believe me when I say I have the magic ability to match every person to their favorite ice cream flavor on a look. It's like a sixth sense," he says with a shrug. "So, Mars, get over here and prove me right so I can rub it in Caleb's face."

Mars looks to me for help, but I just gesture him forward with a grin.

Jake snatches up the four pints of ice cream and lines them up in a row on the island bar. "Okay, Mars, pick one."

I step up next to Mars, my arm around his waist, as I lean in to read the labels: chocolate peanut butter, lemon sorbet, pistachio, and mint chocolate chip. There's utter silence in the kitchen as Mars deliberates. With a shrug, he reaches out and picks up the pistachio ice cream.

"Fuck," Caleb mutters.

"Ha—yes! I fucking *told* you," Jake cheers.

"That is the stupidest superpower ever," he jabs, snatching up his mint chocolate chip. With his free hand he holds out the sorbet for me, leaving Jake his chocolate peanut butter.

"You're just mad because you don't have one," Jake teases, snatching up a spoon.

"Are they always like this?" Mars mutters, his ice cream forgotten in his hand as he watches them make themselves entirely at home in his living room, moving the ottoman and rearranging pillows.

"Yes," I reply.

He looks utterly defeated as he takes his ice cream and joins them. I'm not in the mood for my sorbet just yet, so I slip it into the freezer, grabbing a glass of water instead.

"Come on, Seattle Girl," Jake calls, flipping a pillow down on his lap and patting it.

Smiling like a loon, I take in my guys all sitting in Ilmari's living room eating their ice cream. Poseidon has already helped himself to a stretch of the rug, lying flat out on the floor. Stepping over the dog, I drop down onto the couch between Jake and Ilmari.

Jake pats the pillow in his lap again. "Come here, baby."

With a grateful sigh, I lay on my side, letting my freshly blow-dried hair fan out across the pillow on Jake's lap. I curl my legs up too, nestling my feet in against Ilmari's thigh. Ilmari works the TV remote, connecting it to his laptop so he can stream the game footage on the big screen.

I lay with my head in Jake's lap, smiling as he pauses every couple bites to stroke my hair. The guys all watch the game footage, quickly absorbed in pointing out plays to each other and talking strategy. All the while, Jake reassures us both with soft touches. I know it was his idea to come over. He just needs to be where I am. The feeling is mutual. Caleb may not say anything, but I know he feels the same.

I need Ilmari to want this too. I need him to want *us*. This feeling. This sense of family. My lost and lonely boy. He doesn't have to be alone anymore. None of us do. A beautiful future rests right in front of us, if only we're all brave enough to reach out and take it.

11
RACHEL

"**W**ait—you're gonna have to say that again," Tess squeals, her voice echoing all around the inside of my Toyota RAV4.

When Jake learned I was terrified to drive my pickup truck, he drove it straight back to the Rays offices and handed the keys over to Vicki. He came home in this cute little SUV. It's small enough that I don't feel like I'm driving a spaceship, but big enough for me to fit all three massive hockey guys and still have room for Poseidon, beach chairs, and a cooler in the back for beach day.

Which is the plan for today. I'm currently driving halfway across town to pick up Ilmari. His truck is in the shop this week, so he's missing a set of wheels. I only agreed to take him to the grocery store if he suffered through beach day with me and the guys.

Is this emotional extortion? I mean, yeah. But I want them all to get to know each other better. After our ice cream night, Mars said he would try. And I intend to facilitate that at every opportunity.

And I could strangle Caleb and Jake right now. They're being so weird. I'm pretty sure Caleb means to avoid his feelings with his dying breath. It's been so hard not to just slam open the door while Jake is in the shower and shout out, "Caleb is in love with you, you idiot!"

Meanwhile, Ilmari is using his no car bullshit as an excuse to stay away. They're all running scared. From their feelings, from each other. Well, it stops today. Poseidon and I have a plan. Operation Beach Day will give us all a chance to just relax. And the public venue means there's no chance of feelings boiling over into action. I may be a horny little horndog after three men at once, but I draw the line at public indecency.

Speaking of horny . . .

"Hellooooo," Tess sings into the phone. "Earth to Rachel. You there?

You were in the middle of telling me how you've added a third freaking man to your hockey harem!"

I snort. Tess is the only one who knows about the guys. I've been hiding it from everyone. I've all but iced out Harrison. I'm pretending we're playing the world's longest, most unsatisfying game of phone tag, but really I'm hiding. I'm not ready to pop the pretty pink bubble of my new, very fragile polyam relationship.

"Rachel, I swear to god—"

"I'm here," I say with a laugh, checking traffic as I make a turn at a red light.

"So . . . what's the deal? You went to Cincinnati with the goalie—stood me up, by the way," she adds. "I had an expensive bottle of wine and a $70 cheese board waiting for you, bitch."

I snort. "Yeah, well I had a 6'5" blond Viking saying 'bend over.' You tell me what you would've done in my position, Tess."

"Ooooohmygod," she squeals. "He did *not* say that!"

"He did," I reply, my chest feeling all warm and fuzzy.

"So . . . what is this then? The boys and you are all one big happy family? You're taking dicks three at a time, living the dream in the beach house with the dog and the four-person income? When's the wedding? Am I invited?"

I groan, hands gripping tight to the wheel.

"Uh-oh. Trouble in paradise? It's been like a week, Rach. What happened?"

"I don't know. There's something they're not saying. Something holding them back. Caleb and Jake, at least. I feel like the vibe between us can't settle until they let their secrets out."

"Rach, this whole thing is one big messy secret," she replies. "You've all but made me swear in blood to stay silent. They've got secrets, you've got secrets, and you're keeping it all a secret. I don't know how you're doing it, honestly. And I don't know how they're cool with it."

"What do you mean?"

"I mean that guys like that . . . rich guys, confident guys, guys used to showing off their girls and being super public with their relationships . . . asking them to shut up and hide out in the corner with you while you work through your trauma has got to be tough on them."

I sigh. "Tess—"

"I know, I know," she says quickly. "I didn't live through it with you. And I know how hard you've worked to rehab your image. But . . ." She sighs, falling silent.

"But what?" I urge.

"Well . . . at least part of you has to know what you're doing here, right?"

"What do you mean?"

She huffs. "Come on, Rach. You *know* the press heat you'll get for this when it comes out. 'Hal Price's wild daughter dating three men.' The headlines will write themselves. You've got two NHL players and their equipment manager wrapped around your sexy little finger. When this blows up in your face—and it *will* blow up in your face, because secrets like this *always* do—you'll leave a Rachel-sized crater in their lives. They'll never recover, babe. Their careers, their hearts. You'll blow them wide open, and leave them for dead."

My heart is pounding as I check my mirrors, switching lanes. "What do you mean 'leave them for dead?'"

"Well . . ."

"Tess," I hiss into the phone.

"Fine," she huffs. "I'll just say it, okay? I'm saying it. You've got priors. You never stick around, Rach. The moment things get tough, you bail. The moment things get too public, you bail. If you think there will be a nanosecond of press scrutiny on your life or your decisions, you bail. You've perfected the art of living like a mouse in the wall."

"This is different," I say quickly.

"*How* is this different? All I've heard is that you're living in a mousey little nest of secrets. You're living with two men, involved with a third. They all live very high-profile lives and yet you're managing to keep it all under wraps. But that won't last, Rach. Listen to Tess. You *will* get caught. What's your game plan when you do? You gonna break up with them all and bail again? You going to pick one and yeet the others? Or are you gonna put on your big girl panties and march out into your own dang spotlight and live your life boldly on your terms?"

"But it's not just my life," I say, pulling over at the front of Ilmari's neighborhood. "They didn't sign up for my mess—"

"They *did*," she presses. "By choosing you, they chose your baggage too. That's how grown-up relationships work, Rach. They don't get the girl without the drama. If all three of them are sticking, and you want them to stick, you gotta let them stick, babe. But you have to come up with a plan. Sit down with them, ask them what they want, and plan it out. I love you, and I don't want you hurt, and I *really* don't want to see you live with the pain of having hurt them."

I sigh, dropping my forehead down to my knuckles on the steering wheel. "You're right."

"Of course, I'm right. I'm a freaking genius . . . also this is a straightforward relationship problem with a super easy solution, so . . ."

I laugh. "Super easy?"

"Yep," she replies. "It's called communication, Rachel. That's the beginning and the end of your problems. They need to communicate with each other, and you need to communicate with them. I won't pretend to be the queen of polyam relationships. But I *do* know something about failed relationships and toxic relationships . . . and one-sided relationships. And I *definitely* know about staying in a relationship long after it's ended. The missing link in all of them? Open communication. Talk to your boys. Make them talk to each other."

I sigh again, glancing in my rearview mirror to see Poseidon standing, his nose poking over the top of the back seat, smiling at me with those pretty blue eyes. Maybe Operation Beach Day is coming at just the right time.

"Tess, I gotta go," I say, quickly spinning out a new plan.

"Okay. Well, let me know how it goes!"

We hang up and I drive down to the back of the little neighborhood, pulling up outside Ilmari's house. "Come, Sy," I say. He pops through the front seats and shoots like a rocket out of the car, rushing for Ilmari's front door. He yips in excitement, jumping up and down as Ilmari opens his door.

As I walk up the little stone path, I hear him cooing at the dog in Finnish, petting him. I can't help but smile. He's wearing a pair of board shorts and a tank top, his hair pulled up in his characteristic bun, a beach towel tucked under his arm.

"Hey, Rakas," he says at me, holding out a hand.

I take it and he reels me in, Sy dancing at our feet as we kiss. "Hey," I say, my nerves settling at his mere touch.

"What's wrong?" he says, sensing my mood.

Big girl panties, Rach. You can do this.

"Do you mind if we come in for a minute?" I say.

Without hesitation he steps back, gesturing me inside. Poseidon darts in first, eager to explore. I follow him in.

Ilmari shuts the door behind me. "What's wrong, Rakas? What happened?"

I take a deep breath, turning to face him. "Get your phone out, Mars."

He narrows his eyes at me. "Why?"

"Because I want you to google me. There's some stuff you deserve to know before this goes any further."

72
CALEB

"What are you saying, Hurricane?" I glance at her from over the top of my aviators.

She's looking like a snack wearing a pink bikini, a big sunhat, and oversized sunglasses. She takes a sip of her Diet Coke, glancing back at me. "Exactly what I just said. I think we all need better communication. And I think we need to start by talking about the big stuff. The dreaded 'R' word stuff," she adds, giving me a pointed look.

"God, do we *have* to talk about radishes right now?" says Jake from my other side. "Come on, Seattle, it's beach day."

"That's not the 'R' word I meant, and you know it," she deadpans.

"Yeah, Jake. She clearly means refrigeration," I reply, leaning back in my chair, eyes closed as I soak up the sun.

The little sea siren dragged us all to the beach today. It's the only shared day off for all four of us for the next three weeks. The guys are about to head into a major sprint: one week of four games, two weeks of three. It's gonna be brutal.

So today we're lined up in a row of beach chairs, Poseidon running and jumping in the surf after the tennis ball Jake keeps throwing for him.

"I'm not following," says Mars from his spot on her other side, hiding under the shade of the big rainbow beach umbrella with his sensitive Finnish skin. "What is this 'R' word?"

Jake and I both snort. "Radiation poisoning," I say, as Jake says, "Racquetball."

"Will you stop?" Rachel huffs at us. "Relationship, Ilmari. I'm saying we need to talk more about relationships."

"Our relationship?" he replies.

"It doesn't have to be *our* relationship as in you and me or even about us," she replies, gesturing at the four of us. "I just think there are questions we need to be asking. I've never done this before—"

"None of us have, Seattle," Jake says, tossing the tennis ball again. Poseidon goes speeding after it, barking like an idiot.

"Right, so it won't hurt us to just be open and honest about a few things," she says.

I sigh, knowing it comes out more like a groan. "Like what, Hurricane?"

"Like . . . kids," she says, and now all three of us are frozen solid. "Hey, protest all you want, but this conversation is happening." She leans forward in her chair, which does amazing things for her breasts. "Jake, do you want kids?"

His mouth opens in surprise. "With you, Seattle? Fuck yeah, sign me up. I love kids."

Mars and I both tense.

"I wasn't necessarily implying with me," she adds quickly, hiding behind the brim of her sunhat.

"Is this like a weird hypothetical then? Like, am I designing my super woman to have these fictional kids? Can our house be on top of a waterfall? That game isn't as fun as me just picturing you under me, Seattle. Fucking you until you get pregnant with my—"

"Enough," Mars growls, throwing a flipflop at his head.

"Hey—she *asked*, asshole," Jake huffs, throwing it back. Now Poseidon thinks it's a game and chases after it.

"Ilmari, what about you?" Rachel turns to him. "Do you ever see yourself wanting kids?"

"No," he replies, wrestling the flipflop from the dog and shoving it on his foot.

"Like it's a hard line for you? Kids are totally out of the picture? You can't be with someone who wants kids?"

Slowly, he turns to stare at her. "This will go faster if you just tell us your position, Rakas. Do *you* want children?"

"This isn't about me," she says again.

"Don't even try it, Hurricane," I say, tugging her hat off and tossing it to Jake. "We all know what this is about. You're measuring us all up. Any guy who doesn't check all the boxes on your list is getting cut loose, right?"

She huffs. "You're so far off base, Cay."

"Am I?"

"Yes."

I lean over in my chair, matching her glare for glare. "*Am* I?"

"Yes!"

"Then answer the damn question. Do you want kids, Rachel?"

She huffs again, crossing her arms under her boobs. "Okay, fine. *Yes*. I think I'd like to have a kid. I'm not sold on the idea of kids plural. But twins run in my family, so there's a pretty good chance I'll get a two-for-one deal."

"Oh, here's where I take one for the team," Jake says with a laugh, tossing her hat back to her. "Put me in, Coach, and we'll double those odds."

Mars leans over. "You're a twin too, Compton?"

"Yep. My twin sister Amy lives in Japan. She's a total brain. Big time robotics engineer. That's actually how Seattle and I met. Does he know the story?" he adds, glancing at Rachel.

"The CliffsNotes version," she replies.

"Does he know we did it six times that night?" Jake teases. "I feel like it's the most important detail of the story. Hey Mars—did you know it was *six* times? We did it that last time up against this window and, I swear to god, my soul left my body for a full minute."

"Please shut him up," Mars mutters, staring out at the waves.

"If only that were possible," I reply, shaking my head.

Jake punches my arm.

"Ask Mars your question again, Hurricane," I say, rubbing the spot on my arm.

She goes still, her can of Diet Coke halfway to her lips. "What?"

"Kids, Mars. Yes or no? Well, kid singular, with the serious risk of twin action happening," I add.

He grunts. "Fine."

"See? Done. Next question. This time, Rachel answers first."

"Nuh-uh," she huffs. "No way. We are *not* playing the game this way—"

"Marriage—yes or no, Jake?" I say over her.

"To Rachel? Fuck yes. In Seattle I was ready to call down to the front desk for an Elvis minister," he adds.

This pulls a laugh from her. "Where were you planning to find an Elvis minister in Seattle?"

"Baby girl, I'm a millionaire NHL star," he says, tipping his sunglasses up off his face. "That's not me bragging, it's just a fact. If I want an Elvis minister, I'll find one. Better be on high alert, or I'll have him jump out from behind a bush and make you say your vows."

"I swear to god, Jake Compton, if you shotgun marry me with an Elvis minister, I will kill you on the honeymoon," she replies.

Now we're all laughing as Jake settles back down in his beach chair.

"Noted. So, it's not a matter of *if* you'll marry me. It's a matter of formality," he reasons. "Spontaneity is clearly out. And no Elvis. I take it you're strictly a lace invitations and four-tiered wedding cake kinda girl?"

"I don't mind a little spontaneity," she murmurs. "But I'm definitely not a lace invitations girl."

"She's a barefoot at the beach, close friends and family only, champagne toasting down the aisle kind of girl," I reply, stretching my legs out in the warm sand. "And she wants a backless dress to show off her toned muscles. She's worked hard for them, and she wants to remember how great she looks when she's old and grey . . . right, Hurricane?" I say, tipping a smile her way.

She purses her lips, crossing her arms again. "Don't pretend like you know me, Cay."

"I *do* know you," I reply with smirk. "Plus, you may have left your tablet open on the couch yesterday and I sat on it. My ass accidentally pulled up your Pinterest app." I glance over at Jake. "She's into Christmas. Like, it's bad. Worse than you and Amy."

"Oh, *yes*," he says, pumping his fist. "Hey Mars, you like Christmas? They celebrate that in Finland, right?"

The three of us snort.

"Yes, Compton. We have Christmas in Finland," Mars replies patiently.

"You can't be so nice to him about everything," I say at Mars over Rachel's head. "You gotta punch him, or he doesn't get the message that he's being annoying."

"I get it fine, asshole," Jake huffs. "I was just trying to be nice to the new guy. But hey, you want me to sit here and shut up? I can do that too."

Rachel and Mars both laugh.

"No, you really can't," I reply. "But she's gonna make a big deal about it, so just be ready. She's already pinned a bunch of Finnish Christmas recipes to her Pinterest—"

"God, Cay! Stalk much?" she cries, pouting in her chair.

"Rach, just ask the question you really want to ask so we can move on from the twenty questions portion of beach day," I press.

"You're one to talk," she snaps, narrowing her eyes at me behind her designer shades.

"You want to know where this is going," I reply. "You don't care about whatever vague visions of the future we saw for ourselves with some faceless hot wife and bratty kids. You want to know whether we see *you*. Whether we see *this* . . . whatever this is," I add, gesturing to Jake and Mars.

"I'm terrified I'll ruin all your lives," she admits. "There's too much baggage . . . too much scrutiny. And this is too . . ."

"Unique?" I offer with a shrug.

"Weird," says Jake. "But cool. Like, I'm cool with it," he adds quickly.

"It is wholly unexpected," says Mars.

We all glance his way.

"Not one person sitting here ever expected this," he says. "It is fitting, I think, that we have this conversation at the beach," he adds, turning to gaze at the three of us. "All our lives now rest on shifting sands. This arrangement between us is fragile. The most perilous part is that we all come wielding hammers for hands. One strike, and it will all come crashing down. I can't control your swing of the hammer just as you cannot control mine," he adds, looking right at me and Jake. Then he turns to Rachel, taking her hand. "All we require from you, Rakas, is time. Building firm foundations on sand takes patience and time."

She nods, covering his hand with hers, giving it a squeeze.

"Aaaaand *that* is a new fucking record!" Jake says, clapping his hands. "Mars, that was amazing! Seriously, it was inspirational."

"Don't be a dick," I mutter.

"Who's being a dick?" he says. "I'm one hundred percent serious right now. That's the most I've ever heard him talk. Dude, you're like the wise old owl from a cartoon movie."

"You're such an idiot," I laugh, knocking his hat off his head.

"Come on," Mars mutters, grabbing Rachel's hand and pulling her out of her chair.

"Where are we going?"

"This is a beach, is it not?" he replies, tugging off his shirt and tossing it aside, showing off that wicked cool back tattoo. "We're going swimming."

"Fuck, *finally*," says Jake, jumping out of his chair. "Come on, Cay. Get your floaties on and come swim with us!"

I take a spray of sand to the crotch as he runs off, Poseidon chasing after them. As I watch, Mars scoops Rachel up with one arm and drags her into the water. Jake holds out his arms and Mars tosses her. She and Jake both go under, smashed by a wave. Poseidon stands in the surf barking his head off, furious at being left out.

Meanwhile, my stupid Grinch heart pounds, threatening to grow two sizes as one word echoes around in the empty space of my hollow chest. *Family*. I could have a family. A real one, not just the people who birthed me and raised me that I see out of obligation once every few years.

But Rachel is afraid we won't stick. She's afraid the world is going to find out about us—the team, the fans, the media. She's afraid it'll all come crashing down. What will we do when the storm strikes our house built on sand? Will we stand together and brave it? Will we hold on for dear life? Or will we let it tear us apart?

The terrifying answer is that I don't know. Not yet. This is all too new. Mars is right, we need time. We need this bubble of privacy to last a little longer.

"Cay, come on!" Jake yells. "Bring the football!"

Digging in Rachel's beach bag, I pull out the football and stand. There's time for me to contemplate the shifting sands of time later. For now, I just want to be where they are.

13
RACHEL

As soon as we get back to the house, we all split off in different directions. I order enough Mexican food to feed a whole hockey team and it'll be here in an hour. Meanwhile, Jake and Cay are wrestling the beach stuff out of the car and Ilmari wandered upstairs to take a shower.

We're all thoroughly covered in sand and crusty seawater. I pat my messy bun, watching my sun-kissed reflection in the entry mirror do the same. Jogging up the stairs, I pad down the hall into Jake's room and drop my sticky beach clothes to the floor of the bathroom, turning on the double shower heads.

The room slowly fills with steam as I step under the deliciously hot spray, the jet of water stinging my sunburned shoulders. I make quick work of scrubbing the worst of the sand off my body. The little green loofah does the best he can to rid me of all remnants of the sea.

I dip my head under the spray, dragging my nails across my scalp as I work in a clarifying shampoo. My eyes are closed, rinsing out the shampoo, when the bathroom door opens.

"Room for one more?" Caleb calls.

"Mhmm," I say, turning towards the spray to wash the soap out of my eyes.

"I think I have half the beach lodged in my ass crack," he mutters, reaching around me for the tired loofah.

I smile, handing him the bottle of body wash. "Where's Jake?"

"He drew the short straw," he replies, working the loofah into a lather and dragging it down his sandy legs.

"What does that mean?"

"Means he's stuck outside giving Sy a bath."

I snort. "You can talk tough like you don't love that dog all you want," I tease. "But we all know you're a smitten kitten."

He raises a dark brow at me, pouty lips pursed. "A smitten kitten?"

"Yeah," I reply, wiping a dollop of suds off his chin. He's working a whole five o'clock shadow look that just does it for me. I trail both my hands up, resting them on his shoulders. "I've decided I think you're a cat."

"A cat?"

"Yeah . . . moody, temperamental, aloof, judgmental—"

"This is great, Hurricane. Really making a guy feel good here."

I laugh, pulling him closer until his sudsy body glides against my wet skin. "And clever, confident, independent." I kiss a different part of his face with each word. "Loyal to a fault."

He drops the loofah, his hands banding around my waist.

Taking my shot, I gaze up at him. "You need to tell Jake you're in love with him."

"I already did," he replies leaning in to kiss my wet neck.

"You said you love him," I correct. "He already knows that. He doesn't know you're *in* love with him."

He stills in my arms. "Rachel—"

"He deserves to know. Whatever it is keeping you silent, you deserve to have a voice too," I press. "Tell him how you feel."

"It's too much too fast," he mutters.

"He's talking marriage here, Cay," I counter. "Babies and holidays and forever. He's all in, but he doesn't know what he's *in* for. You could be so good together, Cay. Good to him, good *for* him. And we both know he'd light up your life in ways I can't—"

"Rachel—"

"I'm not being self-deprecating here," I add quickly. "My heart didn't feel complete with Mars missing. And yours doesn't feel complete without *him*. It doesn't hurt my feelings to know with total clarity that I'm not enough for you, Cay. We are complex, emotional beings that live such full and beautiful lives. To think that one singular person can provide us with everything we need to best live out that life is . . . well, silly," I add with a shrug.

"You make it sound so easy," he mutters.

"So long as you're not being honest with him, you're not being honest. *Period.* Mars talked about swinging hammers at our house of glass? House, meet Caleb Sanford and his paralyzing fear of letting someone requite his love."

"You wanna talk about hammers and glass houses?" he challenges. "Mars."

"What about him?"

"Everything about him," he huffs. "He's a total mystery to us. Is he in this? Is he willing to share you? And I don't just mean in a 'we're all separately having sex with you' kind of way. Jake and I want a unit, Rachel. We want a fucking team. He's gotta get in or get out."

I swallow my nerves. "You've been talking about him?"

"All the fucking time. And Jake and I are on the same page with this. Ask him if you think I'm lying."

"I don't think you're lying, Cay," I reply gently. "What do you need him to do?"

"Prove that he's in this for real. We should all be together in *this* house. We don't care that you fuck him, but he doesn't get to keep you all night halfway across town. And he needs to get on board with sharing you," he adds, giving me a level look. "We're sick of walking around on eggshells with him."

"I really think he'll get there," I reply. "He wants this too. He wants a family. He's just a slow mover."

"Well, help him along."

I puff out my chest, meeting him stare for stare. "Alright, Mr. Bossy. Let's make it interesting. I handle the Mars situation, and you confess your undying love to Jake. First one to hear them say, 'I love you too' wins."

He raises a dark brow at me and smirks. "You think it'll be so easy to reel Mars in?"

I smile back, patting his cheek like the competitive little shit I am. "Oh, sweet Cay. I'm afraid you're just a house cat. And this is a lion fight."

He huffs a laugh. "What are you gonna do, Hurricane?"

I tip up on my toes and kiss him. "What do hurricanes do best?"

He groans, his hands trailing down to cup my ass. "They spin shit up."

I smile against his mouth. "Damn right. Now, you're gonna press me up against the wall and pretend like you're fucking me—"

"Pretend?" he growls, both brows shooting up in indignation.

"Trust me, baby. You don't want to be in me for what comes next. I can't guarantee your safety."

His smile falls. "Oh, what the fuck are you gonna do?"

I shrug with a smile. "I've just been practicing something, and I want to see if it works."

"Practicing? What the—"

"Mars!" I call out, my voice echoing around the bathroom. "Ilmariiii!"

Caleb grunts, glancing over his shoulder. "What is this, the call of the kraken?"

"Get on your knees, Cay. Tease my pussy."

"You're fucking psycho," he mutters, dropping down to his good knee.

I drag my fingers through his wet hair, lifting a leg over his shoulder. Tipping my head back, I let out a little moan as Caleb wastes no time tonguing my clit. God, all my boys are great with their tongues.

"Rakas?" comes Ilmari's deep voice from the bedroom. "Are you in here?"

Taking a deep breath, I say the little phrase I've been practicing. "Kulta," I call in my best siren's voice. "Tule tänne."

He barges into the bathroom and I let out a little moan of excitement. I know the moment he sees Cay through the steam because I can hear his feral growl over the sound of the dual shower heads.

"Kulta," I say again. "Mä haluun sut. Tule tänne."

The door to the shower flings open as Mars comes barging in fully dressed in jeans and a t-shirt. He lunges for Caleb, pulling him off by the shoulder, leaving me scrambling to right myself, both hands pressed against the tiled wall.

He flings Caleb away, his back slamming the glass of the shower with a muttered curse. Then Mars is boxing me in, his noses inches from mine, water raining down his face, soaking his shirt. "What did you just say?"

I smile up at him, tugging on the hem of his wet shirt. "You heard me," I tease.

He jerks his shirt off, letting it drop to the shower floor. "Say it again."

"Mä haluun sut," I murmur, my hand stroking down the middle of his bare chest. "I want you, Ilmari."

"No, the other thing," he growls.

"Kulta," I repeat with a smile, my hands lifting to tangle in his golden hair. "Kultaseni—"

The words have barely passed my lips and he's kissing me, wrapping me in his arms. We both fight to get his pants off. The jeans are slicked to his massive tree trunk legs. We peel them down until they're trapped around his ankles.

His proud cock juts out between us, and I wrap both my hands around it, stroking him tight. He curses in Finnish, moving his hips against my hands. Then he wraps both hands firmly around my waist. "Jump," he mutters.

With a gasp, I push off the ground as he lifts me. His hips slam me against the tiles of the wall as he notches his cock at my pussy and lets me sink down. My back arches as he pulls on my hips, burying himself in me.

"Ohmygod—" I cry out, my head tipping back as he pumps his hips against me.

Remembering my goal, I open my eyes, reaching out my hand. "Cay," I cry. "Cay, baby please. Mars, I want him too," I pant with each slam of his hips. "Kulta, please. I need him too. Need you both. Fill me. Fuck me. Please—"

Caleb stands three feet back, leaning against the shower glass. "What do you say, Mars? You were curious about my dick before. How about I shove it in our girl's ass and let you feel all four of these barbells up close and personal?"

I pant, holding still in his arms, waiting for him to decide.

"Yes," he growls. "Sanford, come."

"This isn't the Rays locker room," he replies, not moving. "You want my cock, you call me by my name. And you look at me when you ask," he adds.

I hold my breath, watching as Mars turns to look at Cay.

"Caleb," he says in that deep voice. "Come."

With a wolfish smile, Caleb pushes off the glass wall and steps around to the other side of us. He reaches up to the top shelf for the bottle of lube. "Turn her for me."

I wrap my arms and legs more tightly around Mars as he pulls me off the wall, my whole weight balanced in his arms, his cock impaling me. Oh god, I didn't think this through. This will be too tight a fit. It'll be—

"Oh—*fuck*—" I whimper, my muscles tightening as Caleb shoves two lubed up fingers into my ass.

"Easy, baby," Caleb soothes. "Relax for us. You're already so tight with Mars inside you. How does he feel?"

I calm at the tone of his voice. "So good," I whisper, my voice all but lost over the pounding of the shower heads.

"But you're not satisfied are you, Hurricane?" Caleb teases. "You love to get fucked. Love to be shared. Love being watched."

"Yes," I sigh, my body relaxing as he stretches me out.

It's all Mars can do to hold still and let Cay work.

"You want all your men, don't you?" Caleb says, brushing his wet lips over my shoulder. "You want to be filled three times over. Mars in your tight pussy, me in your ass, Jake pounding that smart mouth. God, you'd look like a queen. You'd drip with our cum from every hole."

At his dirty words, Mars groans. "Hurry the fuck up, San—Caleb."

Caleb chuckles. "Hear something you like, Mars? You want to see our girl filled with three cocks?"

"Stop teasing her, and do it," he growls.

"Am I only teasing *her* now?" he replies, my eternal shit-stirrer. "You seem pretty interested, Mars. Is it the cum? You like the mental image of our girl dripping from every hole?"

Mars twitches inside me and Caleb pulls his fingers out of my ass. "Oh shit . . ." he murmurs. "You do, don't you? Mars, do you like cum play? Shit, we can have so much fun if you're down to get our girl a little messy. You should have said something sooner."

"Shut up and get in her ass," Mars orders.

"Yes, sir," Caleb replies, squirting the lube down his dick and slathering it. "Breathe in, baby," he says, the tip of his cock tapping at my tight hole. "Breathe out like a good fucking girl. Let's show your goalie why three is more fun. Mars, bend your knees a bit. We're not all giants," he teases.

The guys maneuver themselves so that Ilmari is pressed against the wall, using it for balance as he bends his knees. Caleb steps in close. I moan as I feel him push his way inside me. He teases, moving his tip in and out, those barbells rubbing me so good. I'm a panting mess when he slams forward, his cock sliding in deep.

"No niin," Ilmari groans, his head arching back as he feels the first glide of Caleb's pierced cock along his shaft. "Fuck—I can't—"

"Hold on, man," Caleb huffs. "Don't fucking move. Hold her still, and I'll have you both seeing stars." He grips tight to my hips and goes to work, pounding up and in, sliding almost all the way out before he buries himself to the hilt again and again.

Mars is muttering curses and I'm about to scream.

"I'm coming," I cry out. "Cay—baby—" But I can't hold on, can't stave it off. The orgasm comes crashing through me and then I'm pulsing around my guys, strangling their cocks, my core humming as it contracts over and over. I'm boneless, my body melting against Mars as he cries out his release, his hot seed pumping into my greedy cunt.

"Almost—fucking—there—" Caleb pants, jerking his hips against me until he's crying out, his cum filling my ass.

I moan as I chase that perfect feeling of being so full. The high of my orgasm is at its peak. The only thing left is to come floating down. Caleb pulls out of me and staggers back against the tiled wall, his chest heaving as he recovers his breath.

"Help me," Mars mutters. He's such a mess, he can't safely get me down.

Caleb steps forward, hands on my hips, and they both lift me as they set me on my feet. I sway like a seagrass, feeling such heat and emptiness throbbing between my legs. They clean me up, Caleb turning off the water, as Mars wraps me in a bathrobe. Picking me up in his arms, he carries me to Jake's big bed. We all fall into it, Mars and Caleb naked to either side of me, my wet hair fanning out against the pillow that smells like Jake.

"Well, Mars?" Caleb says on a breath. "You done pretending you don't like sharing her?"

A sleepy smile tips my lips as I glance up, gazing into Ilmari's handsome face.

"Yes," he mutters.

My heart flutters and I curl up against him, my face pressed against his warm skin.

"Good," Caleb replies on a tired sigh. "Stick with us, Kinnunen. Your place is here now."

I don't know if Ilmari responds. I'm too tired and blissed out to stay awake a moment longer.

Game day and I'm on fucking fire! Home barn advantage means the Jacksonville crowd is roaring. Chants of "Duuuuuval" fill the air as the Rays slice up the ice.

I've already made one goal and one assist. As a defenseman known for grinding guys into the boards, shots on goal are rare for me. But I saw an opening in the second period and I took it all the way to the net. My assist was a lucky open shot to Sully at the top of the third. He put it right through the five-hole. The Panthers goalie didn't even know what hit him.

Two minutes left in this game and we're up by two. The Panthers are giving it everything, but our offense is playing stronger than ever. All the action is down at their zone. Which is great for us because Mars is still out of the net. His big return game is Friday night.

Focus. Pass the puck. Keep bringing the heat.

Novy and I are a great pair. He's a fast skater and hard as nails. He pounds number 15 into the boards, shooting the puck across to me. I work fast, shooting it down the ice to Langley. But then a huge, Panthers D-man comes slamming into him, checking him down to the ice with a brutal crunch.

Seeing red, I surge forward off my line, taking the fight to him. We lock shoulders, grunting as we bat at the puck between our feet. I bite down on my mouth guard, groaning as I give him an almighty shove, working myself and the puck free.

Just as I'm about to pass the puck up to Sully, their other D-man covers him, forcing him back. Making an instinctual decision, I dart left towards center, taking the puck with me. I'm looking for someone—anyone—to pass it to. But the tables have turned, and all my forwards have turned into defensemen, battling the Panthers back to clear my way.

It happens in seconds. I skate right down the slot, the ice beneath my feet turning blue. Any closer and I'll be giving the goalie a kiss. I feel the rush of guys surging behind me. I'm gonna get checked into this goalie. And then I'll have a pile of Panthers on me, gloves off, punching me bloody.

Rule number one in Hockey: never touch the goalie.

In a panic, I spray ice to stop and fake right, darting left to clear the net. With a flick of my stick, I send the puck into the corner of the net just as the Panthers D-man slams into his own goalie, skating too fast to stop in time.

The cherry lights up, the sirens blast, and the arena erupts in cheers as I hear Bruno Mars singing "Uptown Funk" over the surround sound for the second time tonight. That's my song. The song they play when I score a goal.

The team skates in, surrounding me. They're all talking at once, slamming my pads and cheering me on. I'm so high on adrenaline, I'm shaking like a leaf. But I've got to focus. One minute left in this game.

The coach calls for the last shift change, and I dart off the ice with Novy, dropping down to the bench to the cheers of the crowd pounding on the plexiglass behind me. The other defensemen on the bench all pat my back and congratulate me. It's rare to have such an offense-forward game. I'm not used to the attention.

I watch the last thirty seconds play out, the Panthers scrapping for one more shot on goal. But it won't matter. We've won. I take my helmet off and grab a water bottle, squeezing it over my head, letting the ice-cold water cool the fire in my blood.

Glancing down the bench, I see Caleb standing in the corner, his arms crossed, grinning at me. I know he's impressed. Hell, I've impressed myself.

The buzzer goes off to end the game, and the Rays fans erupt. I ride my high all the way to the locker room as the guys spray me with beer and Sully gives me the game puck. Coach Johnson drags me out of the showers to do press and I'm still humming.

All the while, I'm looking everywhere for *her*.

Rachel wasn't on the bench tonight. Did she see any of the game? God, I hope she did. I can't help it. I'm that guy who wants his girl in the stands, wearing his jersey, cheering him on, making heart eyes through the plexiglass.

I make my escape from the press area. As I head towards the locker room, I pass Avery. "Hey man, you seen Doctor Price around?"

"Do I look like her keeper?" he replies, stalking off.

I shake my head. That guy always has a burr up his ass about something. Some of the guys are starting to complain. Langley won't even use him anymore. Shrugging it off, I turn down another hallway and that's when I see her. Rachel is coming out a doorway at the end of the hall with a box of supplies in her hands.

"Hey," I call out.

Her tired expression vanishes as she sees me, her face lighting up. "Hey! You played so amazing tonight, Jake. Really—"

I silence her with a kiss, wrapping both my arms around her as I crunch whatever she's holding between us.

"Jake—" she gasps against my lips. "Someone will see."

"I don't care," I growl. "I'm tired of hiding. Tired of pretending I'm not with you when I am."

"Jake," she sighs. "We've talked about this—"

"No talking," I grunt, pressing my lips to hers again. "Not now. Kiss me like I just single-handedly won an NHL game."

She laughs against my lips. "You feeling pretty good? Are you the big man tonight?"

My hands rove, one slipping inside the back of her pants as the other cups her face. "Seattle, I need you," I say, dropping my face to her neck and breathing her in. God, she smells so good. We do our laundry together now, so our clothes have begun to smell the same. Whatever detergent we use, now I smell it every time I pull on a t-shirt. It's her, it's me. It's *us*. And I'll never get enough.

"We're at work," she chastises, balancing her little box of tape and bandages.

"I don't fucking care. Baby, I need you. Need to be inside you." I press her against me so she can feel just how serious I am.

"Jake . . ." She says my name like a sigh and a prayer, and I need to hear it again. I need to be inside her when she says it.

Things have been so crazy this week with all our conflicting schedules and games. We're out of sync and I hate it. I need her. I need us to be in sync again.

She pushes against my shoulders. "We're in a hallway."

"Then think fast, because I'm not stopping," I growl, my hand diving up under her shirt to cup her breast over her bra.

She gasps, her box of supplies dropping to the floor. The bandages rattle as the tapes roll away. "Jake—"

"I want you so goddamn much," I groan. "I need you, Seattle. Miss you. Need to fuck you. *Now*."

"Oh god," she gasps. "Come on."

Grabbing my hand, she pulls me back down the little hallway to the door that leads through into a storage room. Several rows of metal shelves house all kinds of equipment from first aid to cleaning supplies to boxes and boxes of skate laces and stick tape. A pile of old sticks is stacked in the corner, and a few rows of goalie nets are stacked up, some missing the netting.

The door shuts behind us and she's turning in my arms, her hands going up around my neck. "You feeling good tonight?"

"So fucking good," I mutter, my lips chasing hers.

"Yeah? You want to ride your adrenaline high a little longer?" she teases, her hand dipping into my shorts to cup my rock-hard dick. "Wanna fuck me, angel?"

"Every hour of every day," I groan, shoving my hand up under her shirt to unhook her bra. That gives me a bit more wiggle room to cup her breasts. Flipping her Rays polo shirt up with her bra, I expose her peaked nipple and sink my mouth around it with a groan, flicking and teasing her the way I know she likes.

"Take me, Jake," she pants, shimmying her pants halfway down her thighs and putting my hand between her legs. "Fucking own me. Show me why I'm yours."

"Fuck," I growl, my fingers sliding through her wetness. I slow down, taking a breath with my eyes closed as I just let myself feel her. Her presence, her warm breath on my cheek, the heat of her core. From the first moment we met in Seattle, it hasn't faded for me, this feeling of rightness, this feeling of wanting to be where she is.

She's my girl. *Mine*. And I'm hers. And I'm done hiding.

"Come here." I take her by the shoulders and walk her backwards until she's bumping into the stack of old nets. "Turn around," I growl. "Hands on the crossbar."

She turns, bending herself over the top of the crossbar as I tug her pants further down, smoothing my rough hands over the round curves of her ass. She hums her need, pressing against me.

Desperate for that moment of connection, I free my rock-hard cock. Palming it roughly, I step in closer to her. "Spread wider, baby girl," I pant, bending my knees to get at the right angle. I love taking her from behind. I get deeper and she feels tighter. We work as a team to get into position, my cock right there at her entrance, pressing in.

"Yes," she hisses, her face falling forward onto her elbows as I slam all the way in.

We both groan, our bodies humming with that first feeling of connection. I pant, holding her hips as I work myself in and out, her wetness coating my hard shaft. "Baby, you feel so good," I mutter, rocking into her. "I love you so much. Need you so bad. I want everyone to know."

"Jake—" Her words are cut short as a noise behind us has us both gasping.

The door to the storage room squeaks opens to reveal Mars standing there in his pre-game warmup clothes. Rachel's discarded box of medical supplies is balanced in his hand. She gasps, her whole body going tense against me. I'm still buried to the hilt inside her pussy while I've got her pressed up against a stack of goalie nets.

Oh shit . . .

The door clicks shut behind Mars and then he's moving, his heated gaze locked on us. He drops the box to the floor, uncaring as the pieces rattle away.

"Not the face," I grunt, unsure of what will happen next.

But then he's stepping right past me to her, cupping her face as he bends down to kiss her senseless. I stand there, watching as she pours her heat into him. He's fierce, gripping her hair and jerking her head back. She moans against his mouth, arching up against the crossbar as she slams her hips against me, working her pussy over my hard shaft.

Oh fuck, she wants me to keep going.

I missed out on the shower threesome, which earned Cay salty eggs and burned bacon the next morning. Since then I've seen Mars kissing Rachel and there was a playful moment on the couch where we passed her around for a hot and heavy make out session, but we were all too tired to do more.

He hasn't shared her with me yet. Not like this. Not a full-on double team. Testing his limits, I slam into her, and she moans, her pussy clenching me tighter. "Good girl," I groan. "You take me so fucking well."

He tenses, a low growl in his throat. Hey, if he's gonna learn to share with me, he better get use to an audio track, because I'm a talker.

She breaks her kiss with Mars, and he straightens himself upright, his gaze dark as he watches me fuck her against the net. She arches into me, loving every second.

I smooth my hand up her back under her polo shirt. "You love to be watched. Don't you, baby girl?"

"Yes," she hums, her pussy squeezing me tighter.

"Such a good fucking girl. This pussy is heaven. So tight and warm. Isn't it, Mars?" I add, glancing over at him. I know how badly she wants this, and I want to make it happen for her. She wants the four of us to be together. "I think our girl might need more," I say. "She loves to be filled."

I pound her with each statement, and I know she's close. He better fucking decide what he's doing. "You just wanna watch this time, big guy? Wanna watch me show you how to use these nets?"

With a growl, he fists her hair, tipping her face back to look at him. "You want more, Rakas?"

"Yes. Please, Mars. Oh god, *please*—"

I slow my pace as he steps in, pulling her off the top of the crossbar. We have to shuffle and then he's dropping his shorts just enough to release the beast. I groan, loving this angle as I watch my girl take him in her mouth. Mars holds her by the shoulders, rocking against her. I work my hips too, matching his pace until we're owning her from both ends.

I never thought I'd want to share my girl with another man, but there's something about seeing her like this that just does it for me. Rachel is a moaning mess, sucking and gagging on his huge dick as she takes me so well, her warm pussy squeezing me, bringing me right to that edge.

"Baby, I'm gonna come," I groan. My hips jerk once, twice, and then I'm filling her as she squeezes me so tight, chasing her own orgasm.

Mars follows us, his hips stilling as he unleashes. I watch as she chokes and gags, swallowing him down. After a moment, he releases her, and she gasps for breath. One of her shaky hands goes up to clutch the crossbar.

I slip out of her, leaving my hands on her hips to steady her. I work quickly to right myself then her, slipping her pants up over her bare ass with my mess between her legs. Mars does the same. At least if someone comes in, they won't see us all mid-fuck. But Rachel is still folded over the net, delirious as she gathers her senses.

Now that the heat of release is burned out of me, a cooler head is prevailing. Fuck, this was reckless. Anyone could have come in. Someone *did* come in. We're just lucky it was Mars. It could have been Avery. That asshole would have gone stomping around the whole arena ratting us out.

Mars leans over her, whispering something I can't hear as he brushes her hair back from her face. She nods and he kisses her brow. Then he steps away. "You played well tonight," he says at me, dropping to one knee to gather the medical supplies. He hands the box out towards me.

"Thanks," I say, still feeling breathless as I take the box.

He holds onto it, looking in my eyes. "I like you, Compton."

I blink, glancing down at Rachel and back to the giant Finn. "I like you too, Mars."

"I like you for Rachel," he adds.

"Same," I reply, unsure of where this is going.

"Good," he says in that deep voice. "Please take this as the only warning I will give: Fuck our girl against one of my nets again, and I'll cut off your pretty little cock. Understood?"

Aaaand, there he is.

"Sure thing, Mars," I reply with a cheeky salute.

He rolls his eyes and turns away.

"Hey, does that rule apply to your stall in the locker room too?"

He growls, not turning around.

"Okay, wait. Hear me out," I say, knowing I'm gonna get punched. "What about on the ice mid-game? Do you think we could work around it? Or have like, some kind of hand signal for you to scoot over?"

The door slams shut behind him.

Rachel snorts, pushing up off the crossbar. "You're so ridiculous. He's going to punch you if you don't cool it with the teasing."

"Worth it," I reply with a grin, stepping forward to wrap her in my arms again. "Don't pretend like you don't love my stupid ass."

"I do," she replies, her gaze sobering a bit as she brushes my hair off my brow with a flick of her fingers. "Jake, I really do."

75
RACHEL

I'm a nervous wreck. This is the first time I've been off for a game since the season started. It feels so strange not to be down in the tunnels with the guys, running around like a crazy lady shouting for more tape and bandages.

For a hip and knee specialist, I sure have spent a lot of time performing basic first aid. You'd think some of these guys were made of glass for how quickly they bruise and bleed. And the old stereotype about hockey players and their missing teeth? Yeah, not just a stereotype. Between practice and games, I've had to personally deal with no less than four chipped teeth and three knocked straight out.

"Hey, honey," Poppy calls with a wave. She's pushing through the crowd carrying a big tub of popcorn and a soda. "Oh, girl, you look amazing! Kinnunen is just gonna die that you're wearing his jersey tonight."

I can't help but smile. It's meant to be a little surprise for him for his first night back on the ice. Jake is probably going to pout for a month when he finds out, but it's not every day you have Olympic scouts come to watch you play. Ilmari has worked hard for this. He's earned himself a piece of eye candy tonight.

"This is so exciting," Poppy says. "You know, this is my first game I've gotten to watch as a spectator? I've been running myself ragged this season."

"Same," I reply, snagging a few pieces of popcorn off the top of her bucket.

"I felt like I wanted the whole game day experience," she explains. "So, after popcorn and soda, we'll switch to hotdogs and beer!"

I laugh. "Sounds good."

"You ready? Leo in the ticket office snagged us some great seats right on the ice."

"Yeah, hold on," I reply. "We're just waiting for one more." I pop up on my toes, glancing all around. He's late, of course. I bet anything he got dragged below to deal with a crisis. A familiar shout from behind me has me turning. When I see him, I can't help but smile wider.

Caleb comes weaving through the crowd balancing a tray of nachos and a big soda. He looks like any other Rays fan—backwards cap, Rays jersey, jeans, flip-flops. He catches sight of me and stills, his gaze sweeping down from my curled hair to my Kinnunen jersey to my tight jeans and knee-high boots. His mouth opens slightly in shock.

I can't help but do the same, seeing as there are big 42's emblazoned on his shoulders. If he thinks I won't tease him for wearing Jake's jersey, he's got another thing coming.

Recovering his wits, he hurries over to us.

"Hey, Caleb," Poppy calls in greeting. "Ooo, nachos! Why didn't I think of that?"

Call me a food snob, but my twin is a Michelin-rated chef. I'm not eating congealed cheese on salted cardboard. I could, however, be persuaded to buy some German roasted almonds. That delicious, roasted cinnamon smell wafts down the halls, drawing me in like a siren's call.

"Rach, do you wanna split some nachos when we get our hot-dogs?" Poppy asks.

I laugh again. "Girl, you're like ninety pounds soaking wet, where are you gonna put all this away?"

"Oh, don't you worry about me," she replies. "We St. James' are professional eaters. Caleb here will tag out before I've even gotten started. Now come on, I don't wanna miss any of the pregame show! Do you have any idea how much time and energy I put into our home game production?" Like the loose cannon she is, Poppy goes racing off, leaving us in the dust.

"Jake's gonna flip when he sees you in that," Caleb mutters, stepping in beside me.

"He'll flip right back when he sees *you* in that," I tease, my eyes tracing him up and down.

He drops a hand from his tray of nachos, his fingers brushing against my palm as we weave through the busy crowd. In the weeks I've been living with him, I've learned to treat him like a cat. He's picky about where he sits, what he eats. If he doesn't want affection or closeness, he lets you know, which is most of the time. He's not a snuggler unless he's asleep, and he's definitely not into PDA. In that sense, he and Jake are night and day.

Even Ilmari is more physically affectionate than Caleb. Mars likes eye contact. And he likes when I feel him watching me. When I'm at work and he spots me, he'll stop and wait for me to notice him, casually moving on as if nothing happened when our eyes meet. It's like something out of a damn Austen novel. It gets me so fucking hot every time.

But Caleb never seems to want physical reassurance outside of sex. So, the fact that he's offering now means I practically leap to reciprocate, weaving my fingers in with his as we move towards our section. He gives my hand a squeeze. "You good, Hurricane?"

I nod. Just as I'm about to speak, Poppy darts out from around the corner and Caleb drops my hand like a hot potato.

"Hurry up, you two!"

We both take deep breaths, following along after her to find our seats.

ame night. Rays vs Kraken. Home game. It's my first game in
three weeks. The cortisone shot helped reduce inflammation
and Rachel added a gel shot last week. The joint lube has improved
my range of motion significantly. The two treatments, combined with
rest, have me feeling like I'm back up at eighty percent. It's enough.
It'll have to be because the FIHA reps are finally here.

Warm-ups are done and everyone is getting ready to hit the ice.
In the stall next to me, Morrow curses. "Fuckin' stupid piece of shit."
He gets up and hobbles across to the other side of the locker room,
complaining about a frayed skate lace.

As soon as he's gone, Compton slides down the bench, nudging
my elbow. "Hey. How you feeling tonight?"

"Fine." I focus on adjusting the straps of my pads.

"Anything I need to know?" he presses, voice low. "You know,
before we get out there . . . anything I need to do or not do?"

I glare at him. He's breaking my concentration. I don't like to
engage in conversation before the game. And I really don't like him
doubting my readiness to play. I gesture to my pads. "You want me to
take these off, Compton? You want to wear them, is that it? You think
you can play my position better than me?"

"Hey, man, don't get defensive. I'm just tryna help you out. I know
this is a big game for you with the scouts here. You just tell me how I
can help show you off—"

"Just do your job," I mutter.

He huffs, clearly upset by my rudeness. "Yeah, you know what, I
think I will just do my fucking job." Just when I think he's about to
slide away, he leans in closer, his voice lowering. "Is this about the
other day in the storage room? You still pissed about the whole goalie

net thing? Because if you're not cool with sharing, that's really something we gotta know."

I go still. The last thing I need to be thinking about right now is Rachel. Or me and Rachel. Or me and Rachel and Jake Compton fucking like champions against my damn nets.

In no version of my future did I ever imagine I might be considering sharing a wife and a life with a teammate. Certainly not an optimistic, fun-loving, sushi-eating, obnoxious defenseman.

This is why I had reservations about Rachel. Maybe part of me always knew she would complicate my life beyond my medical care. Now she has Jake Compton trying to treat me like more than a teammate. He's trying to be my friend.

But I'm no good at this. I'm quiet and awkward. I live in my head. Rachel doesn't try to pull me out. She just climbs inside with me. She's in and I can't get her out. Even Caleb seems to understand me. We get along. We did even before Rachel. We share a mutual fondness for silence and order.

But Jake Compton is loud and outgoing and messy. He makes friends with anyone and everyone. He's always laughing, always teasing, always fucking smiling. This can't work. He'll get sick of my moods and my melancholy, and he'll force me out.

Not that Caleb is any less moody, but he's Compton's DLP. He's not going anywhere. Compton can't possibly tolerate a second man in his life who is so difficult to live with. So, I'll be out. This can't last. Compton won't want it to last, and I won't blame him. There's no way, with our clashing personalities, that he'll ever let me stay.

"Move away from me, Compton," I mutter.

"Jeez," he huffs. "Good fucking luck, asshole."

I close my eyes, taking a deep breath. I can't think about him right now. I can't think about Rachel . . . about losing her to him. Tonight, I have a job to do.

"You ready, boys?" our captain calls across the locker room. "Let's go kick some Kraken ass!"

As one, the team gets to our feet. It's time to play.

77
RACHEL

"**W**hat if he doesn't like that I'm here?" I murmur, standing in our spots two rows up behind the plexiglass. We're slightly diagonal from the goal. If Ilmari turns his head to the left, he'll likely spot us. "What if I distract him? Maybe I should go—"

"Don't you fucking dare," Caleb growls, grabbing my elbow. "You're staying right here, Hurricane. We want both our boys to see you just like this."

I glance to my left, but Poppy's not paying attention. She's in full social butterfly mode, laughing and chatting it up with the season ticket holders seated behind us. I swear, this woman could make friends with a parking meter.

"Why do you want them to see me like this?"

"Because they need the motivation," he replies.

I laugh, taking a sip of his drink. Regular Coke, of course. Full sugar. "Oh, yeah?"

He rolls his eyes at me. "Cut the shit, Hurricane. You know you look like a hockey wife. You look like *his* wife," he adds, his eye darting down to the number 31 on my shoulder.

I swallow, feeling suddenly breathless. I hand his soda back over to him. "Why do you think it matters that I'm wearing Ilmari's number and not Jake's tonight?"

"Because Mars will be motivated to win," he replies. "He's gonna be thinking about you all game. Every shot on goal, every save. He'll be thinking about stripping you out of that jersey and fucking you senseless. If we try and lay a hand on you tonight, he'll bite it off bear-man style."

"Wearing a jersey is that big a deal?" I say with a raised brow.

"It's that big a deal," he replies solemnly. "If I still had a jersey, I'd want to see you in it too," he admits. "Seeing you in another man's jersey? Well, it's a rare kind of torture. One look at you, and Jake is gonna play his best game of the season."

Hidden in the press of other standing fans, I take his hand, giving it a gentle squeeze. "Yeah?"

He smirks. "You think our pampered little Taurus is all sweet and spoiled? Just wait until he doesn't get what he wants. The Kraken forwards better have matador training."

"Oh, god," I mutter, just as the lights go out.

Next to me, Poppy is jumping up and down, grabbing my hand as she screams. The opening music starts and the lights come up, creating a super cool tropical reef look across the ice. It's totally mesmerizing as the lights and the video displays work together to make a visual experience for the arena. It's like we're racing through a coral reef, darting like fish. The colors of rippling water dances across all our faces.

"This is so fuckin' cool," Cay mutters at my side, reluctantly impressed. Neither of us have ever gotten to see the pregame show from this angle.

I take his hand with a grin, bouncing on the balls of my feet.

By the time the intense music crescendos and the smoke machine starts, they have the crowd going wild as each player is announced. The Rays come shooting out onto the ice as their names are called, starting with the forwards. Langley, then Karlsson, then our captain, Sully. All three of us are losing our minds cheering as they announce Novikov and Compton on defense. Last to hit the ice is Ilmari. The crowd goes craziest for him as he skates slowly towards his goal, totally in the zone.

The lights come up and the Kraken skate out to a horde of 'boos' as both sides do their last moments of warmup before the puck drops.

"Let's get their attention," Caleb jeers. God, he is such a pot-stirrer! Why does he get off on this so much? His enthusiasm should be dissuading me, right?

Jake and Novy skate past and Caleb calls out.

"Don't," I cry, tugging on his arm. "I've changed my mind—"

"Hey, 42—you suck!" he shouts as loud as he can, his hands wrapped around his mouth.

Two things happen at once. The two guys standing in front of us duck down to grab their beers. At the same time, Jake's head jerks around, triggered by the sound of Caleb's voice. I stand there like a deer in the headlights as he slides to an effortless stop and takes us both in. The glare of the lights off his clear visor means I can't quite make out his eyes, but I sure as heck can see the set of his jaw clench tight.

"Oh, shit," Cay mutters, bracing a hand around my waist as Jake comes darting forward.

"Make it stop, make it stop," I rasp, tugging on his arm.

He just laughs, holding me still.

Jake skates right up to the boards, slamming both hands against the plexiglass. The guys in front of us cry out in surprise as one spills his beer all down his front while his friend laughs.

"What the *fuck*, Seattle?" Jake shouts as he glares at me.

Next to me, Poppy shrieks. "Compton, what are you doing—"

"Take it off!" he barks at me.

The crowd around us is noticing, all eyes drawn to us. Oh, this is bad, bad. Such a bad idea. *Stupid, Rachel!*

"Maybe if you play *really* well tonight, she'll wear your jersey on Saturday," Caleb teases, living for this moment of supreme assholery.

The group around us laughs as Jake gives us a look like he just popped his spleen.

"I'm sorry," I call through the glass, suddenly regretting every single decision of my stupid life. The look of torture on his pretty face is that gutting for me. I want to climb the plexiglass and make him hold me.

But Caleb's having none of it. "She's totally not sorry," he jabs. "Go skate, douche canoe! Try not to embarrass her!"

If it were possible for Jake to spontaneously combust, this would be the moment. Instead, he slowly turns and skates away, shoulders set in determination.

"I'm going to murder you," I hiss in Caleb's ear, elbowing him in the side.

"Not yet you won't," he says, clearly living for this moment. "Smile for the goalie."

I gasp, turning my attention to the net where Ilmari is standing.

He's staring right at me through the cage in his mask, his eyes lost to the shadows. Slowly, he lifts it up and back, wanting to see me without any impediment.

The guys in front of us laugh and point at me, ducking away so he gets a clean shot. They might not know exactly what they've stumbled into here, but they're more than happy to help Caleb stir this big ole pot of shit.

The look on Ilmari's face has me ready to turn into a puddle. "Oh, god," I whisper breathlessly.

That's when Caleb raises his arm from my waist to my shoulders, tugging me closer into his side to give me a big sloppy kiss on the cheek. Mars watches the whole thing, slowly lowering the mask back over his face, burying himself deep inside his armor.

"You really *do* wanna get murdered tonight, don't you?" I mutter.

"Worth it," he replies.

The guys in front of us laugh as I push him off and Poppy shrieks. "Oh my goodness, what is happening right now? We don't want our boys upset before a big game!"

Caleb laughs too, dropping his hand away from me. "Don't worry, Pop. It's just a little team-building exercise." He gives me a wink, his hand dropping back down between us to take mine. We're the only two who know the truth: the Rays aren't the *team* he's talking about. Not at all.

I'm gonna kill him. Caleb Sanford is a dead man. He put her up
to this, I know it. I bet he bought her the damn jersey. With *my*
damn credit card! He thinks he's so fucking funny, spinning me up
like this. I can hardly see straight as I skate into position.

I was already in a shit mood because of Mars. Right when I think
I'm making progress with that asshole, he shoves me away hard.
I know Rachel loves the guy, but if he doesn't cool it with his Mr.
Freeze routine, I'm gonna have to stage an intervention.

We'll see if he can maintain the freeze-out after a week-long Amy
Compton hot yoga retreat. I don't even care anymore. I'm that ready
to force him open. I'll fly us all out to Japan and trap us at an onsen
for a week. We won't leave the damn steam room until Mars learns
to unclench those stupid buns of steel. Sake, stretching, and steam.
That's the magic combo to uncork this surly Finn.

I can't believe she's wearing *his* jersey! I mean, I know they trau-
ma-bonded over his injury. And now the Finnish Olympic scouts are
here. But *I* was here first. She should be in *my* jersey!

I swear to fuck, Caleb is behind this. And shit, why does he look
so good in my jersey? He's who I saw first, and I swear to god, my dick
twitched a little in my jock. He's never worn one of my jerseys before.
Never.

He's up to something. Well, that sneaky shit is gonna get what's
coming to him. But it'll have to wait. Right now, there's a job to do.
And since I can't rip that jersey off Seattle—or punch Cay in the
nuts—every Kraken on this ice better watch the fuck out. I intend to
make someone bleed.

79
RACHEL

"Ohmygod!" I cry out, clutching Caleb's arm. My voice is echoed by the gasps and cheers of half the arena as Jake makes another brutal check of a Kraken forward, sending him spinning down onto the ice.

Caleb is grinning like its Christmas. We're only eight minutes into the first period, and already the Rays have scored a goal. The offense is skating like a real line tonight, and Jake and the defense are sending Krakens into the boards left and right. Usually, this level of aggression is saved for a bit later in the game, but the other defense pairings are feeding off Jake's chaotic energy.

As the Krakens try to bring the puck down into our zone, he makes a brutal check against the boards right in front of us, the fans all around us pounding on the glass as he fights with the forward for control of the puck. Their grunts and the sound of their pads slamming the plexiglass filling the air.

Poppy nearly loses control of her bucket of popcorn. "Why is he so angry?"

Caleb just laughs, nudging me in the ribs with a knowing wink.

"Get it out!"

"Fight!"

"FIGHT!!"

The fans around us are rabid, jeering Jake on in his mania. With an almighty shove of his shoulder, he crunches the guy against the plexiglass before shooting off, moving the puck with his stick, and passing it down to Langley.

We settle back in our seats, the crowd around us cursing and moaning that there was no fight.

"See?" Cay says with a grin, "He's on fire tonight. They'll win, and they'll owe it all to you, Hurricane."

I fold my arms tight over my Kinnunen jersey. This was a huge mistake.

THIRD period has officially started and I'm an emotional wreck. The score is stuck at 1-0, with the Rays holding onto their lead. This game is quickly devolving into a brawl. The Kraken have had enough of Jake's pound and grind. They've pulled a big scary guy off their bench. He must be a fourth line guy. He's not even trying to work the puck. He's out there to work Jake. He's all too pleased to chase him around the ice, meeting him check for check.

If I have to swallow one more scream, I swear I'm gonna choke on my tongue. I don't know how Jake still has the energy. Every shift he's leaving it all on the ice and when he gets back to the bench he stays dialed in, watching the action, waiting to rejoin the fray.

And Ilmari has been a machine. The Kraken brought the heat late in the second period, hungry for a point before the intermission. He was at the far end goal for all that action. It was all I could do to just scream and hold to Caleb's hand as we watched him battle it out on his knees, using his body as a wall to stop that puck again and again.

Now he's back at our end of the rink for the final period, and the Kraken's center is on a breakaway after a nasty steal. The man is small and fast like a bullet, darting away from Karlsson. Jake and Novy scramble to untangle from their blockers and get to Ilmari's aid. Jake cuts down the ice. The sound of his blades slicing echoes in my ears as he pushes for more speed.

"He's not gonna make it," Caleb shouts, gripping my hand. "Mars is on his own—come on, Mars! Come on!"

"Block it!"

Everyone around us is screaming and I'm just frozen in time, watching as Ilmari faces off against this fleet-footed forward. The man gets fancy, distracting Mars with his combination of footwork and puck handling as he races down the ice. It all happens in seconds as the forward shoots left while slinging his stick out behind him, trying for a hook shot into the right corner of Ilmari's net.

But Ilmari didn't fake with him. His instincts are honed to

perfection as he stays still, his glove hand darting out to fill the hole the forward expected him to make.

Heart in my chest, I forget to breathe as I stand there with the crowd, eyes locked on Ilmari. We all seemed to have blinked and missed it. Casual as can be, Ilmari tips his glove down, dropping the puck at his feet.

Saved.

Effortless. A god on ice.

Sully squares off for the puck drop and wins the fight, sending it behind to a waiting Jake. He barrels forward with it, over the red line, heading straight towards the goal. I swear I'm gonna die from this stress as Caleb all but strangles me, shouting at Jake to pass it.

Jake moves the puck, shooting it past a Kraken to a waiting Langley, who tips it into the back of the net.

Goal.

Rays 2. Kraken 0.

And just like that, our furious grinder earned himself an assist. The crowd goes wild. To either side of me, Caleb and Poppy jump up and down.

"God, I fucking love hockey!" Caleb shouts, wrapping an arm around my shoulders and kissing my cheek.

I can't help but smile, lost in the euphoria of an arena of eager Rays fans. But then I go still, a presence pulling at me. My gaze darts right to where a lonely Ilmari stands, guarding his posts. He's looking right at me. He's watching me, waiting for me to notice him. My goalie wants to be seen. He wants *me* to see him.

The Rays all skate back down to their end of the ice and Ilmari moves out, ready to congratulate Langley for his goal. Langley taps his helmet against Ilmari's as they pat shoulders. I watch, pulse thrumming, as Mars reaches for Jake next, their helmets touching. They hold longer than Mars and Langley. Slowly, Jake nods. Then he's skating off towards the bench and Ilmari shifts back into position, ready to guard his net.

It's in that moment that the most delicious little idea slips into my head. What's the old saying? Two hockey players, one puck?

I reach for Cay, looping my arm in his. "When the game ends, trade jerseys with me."

"What?"

"You heard me," I say with a grin.

He glances down at me, those dark brows narrowed. He works through my angle in his mind, the gears churning fast. His carefree smile turns to a matching grin as he leans in. "Oh, you really are out here fixing to get me killed tonight."

"Don't worry," I sing. "The boys might just let you beg for mercy."

80
ILMARI

A shutout. Rays win 3-0. The win was hard earned, which is just how I like it. We all had to work together tonight to keep the Kraken from gaining any points. I know I played a great game, but when my team looks good, it makes me look even better.

By the end of the third, the Kraken were rabid dogs. Penalties flew on both sides. They pulled their goalie to gain an extra man, but it didn't help. Sully scored on the open net with less than a minute left in the game. The buzzer hadn't even sounded before our fans were already celebrating.

Getting back to the locker room is a blur. Showering is a blur. Somehow, I've found myself being shuffled down the hallway towards the press table. The FIHA scouts will be waiting there, the Finnish press. They want to see me, speak to me.

Compton walks just ahead of me, still grinding nails in frustration that Rachel wore my jersey. I'm just as angry. I had to spend the game knowing she was watching my every move. And Caleb was right by her side, taunting me. He kept touching her, his hands brushing over my number at her shoulders, as if he hoped it might rub off.

Impossible. She's *mine*.

I don't know if this is a game they're playing, but it's not funny. The last thing I need right now is Compton finding a reason to push me out faster. Petty revenge because Rachel wore my jersey seems like enough of a reason.

But I can't think about that now. The lights flash and pop as we take our places at the table, me on the end, him in the middle, Coach Johnson on his other side.

Jake is in no mood for press, but he's a professional, answering the first question that asks him about his cutthroat performance. "Yeah, you know, it was about bringing the heat from the first drop of the puck. We wanted the Kraken to fight for it."

I stop listening, my gaze catching on a few familiar faces in the crowd. Torben Korhonen is standing at my end of the table with a press pass around his neck. He works for the Finnish Liiga. He's covered me for years here in the U.S. Behind him stand a group of men in European suits. The FIHA reps. They stand so quietly, watching the press event unfold.

Korhonen's voice hooks my gaze back to him. "This is a question for Kinnunen," he calls. "May I ask it in Finnish?"

I lean forward, giving him my full attention. "Joo."

He switches to Finnish, and I feel like I can breathe. "This is your first game in three weeks. Information from the Rays coaching and medical staff has been sparse. Should your fans have concerns about your health?"

Holding his gaze, I answer the question clearly fed to him through the FIHA reps. "If I wasn't fit to play, I wouldn't be on the ice. The Rays coaching and medical staff take a deep interest in the overall health and wellness of all their players," I reply. "I'm grateful to play for a team that puts my health first, focusing on my longevity of play, not merely that I play every game."

Korhonen nods and the person next to him jumps at the chance to ask her question. Coach leans into his mic, ready to answer. As I sit there, listening to his complicated answer about a possible conference win, Compton goes still as stone next to me. Then he backhands my arm, his gaze locked on something in the crowd. I follow the direction of his gaze.

That's when I see them. They've slipped into the back of the press area using their team IDs. Rachel and Caleb stand together, his arm around her shoulders. My heart races faster as I take her in, my gaze dropping from her gorgeous face down to her shoulders to—

I freeze.

Not my number. The little witch is wearing 42 on her shoulders now. My gaze darts over to Caleb and I see the 31's on his shoulders. They switched jerseys. The asshole has the gall to blow me a kiss and wave. Rachel slaps his hand down.

I'm going to kill him. I jerk in my chair like I'm about to get up, but Compton's hand on my arm stills me. *Not here*, he says wordlessly. Not now. Not in front of the FIHA scouts. I just have to sit and let them tease me.

Why does Compton seem just as upset? He got what he wanted. Rachel is in his jersey now. I glance at him, noting the way he fumes. But his eyes aren't on her anymore. They're on Caleb.

I sigh with realization, sitting back in my chair. This is about my jersey. He doesn't want either of them wearing it. He wants them both for himself. As we watch, the pair of them wave, grins on their faces, and dart away. Compton and I both crane our necks, watching as they disappear. If we weren't trapped at this press table, we'd be charging after them. Or at least, he would. I don't know that I'd be welcome to interfere.

The press event drags on, with Compton and I both managing to answer two more questions each. Then our PR rep calls an end to the event and Compton launches to his feet, grabbing me by the arm. "Come on," he growls.

Korhonen steps forward like he's about to steal another question, but I don't even hesitate. Spinning on my heel, I let myself be dragged by Compton back into the tunnels.

"He thinks he's so fucking funny," Compton mutters, marching past the security towards our locker room. "I know he put her up to this."

"She didn't seem to be protesting," I add darkly.

"Oh, she *will* protest," he huffs. "When I rip them out of those fucking jerseys and spank their asses raw. Come on."

I go still, eyes wide as I look at his retreating form. I don't understand what's happening here. Why is he inviting me to come along? Why isn't he pushing me away?

When he realizes I'm not following, he spins around. "You broken, Mars? I said let's go!"

"Go where?"

"Home. I swear to fuck—you gotta drive, man. I'm too big of a mess. I'll crash the car."

Home. He wants me to drive him home.

We grab our bags from the locker room and duck out the team entrance into the parking garage. Compton follows at my side, helping himself to the back of my truck as he tosses his gear bag in the back. I do the same, unlocking the doors. We both climb in, engine roaring as I pull out and head towards the exit.

"This was all his idea!" His arms are crossed as his knee bounces in agitation. "I swear to fuck, when we get home, we're gonna tie him down and blindfold him while we tag team Rachel until she begs for mercy."

I focus on the road, my hands tight on the wheel. "Blindfold him?"

"Yeah, Cay likes to watch," he mutters. "Well, let's see how he likes being in the room and not seeing a damn thing. Add a gag too. I don't want to hear his dirty talk tonight. I want him on his fucking knees!"

I drive us onto the interstate and Compton pulls out his buzzing phone.

"Oh shit," he hisses.

"What?"

"It's Cay. He's trying to video call me. Fuck!"

We both know there's only one reason Caleb wants to call using video. "Answer it," I growl.

The bright lights of downtown fade behind us as we head out the stretch of road towards the beach. Compton presses the green button on his screen and the call connects. "Cay, what the fuck?"

"Hiya!" comes Caleb's falsely bright voice. "You guys almost home? We've been waiting here forever."

Bullshit. They only had a twenty-minute head start on us at best.

"Cay, don't fucking do it," Compton growls.

"Don't what? Start without you? Too late, pretty boy."

"Where is he?" I say, trying to keep my eyes on the road. "What's happening?"

"I think he's on the stairs."

"Yep! Just needed to get a few things from downstairs," comes Caleb's voice. "Ice, candle, chocolate sauce. I can't decide what I want to start with. I'm thinking the ice. I bet our girl loves a little temperature play. Gonna rub a cube over her clit and then suck it, warm her right back up, make her moan my name—"

"Fuck!" Compton yells, slamming the door with his fist. "When we get home, your ass is getting tied up in the fucking shower, water on *cold*!"

Caleb just laughs, because apparently, he has a death wish.

"Oh, no you fucking don't," Compton yells. "Cay! That's *my* fucking room!"

"Yeah, Hurricane says your bed is the most comfortable. You comfortable, baby?"

I hear her muffled voice and my heart hammers in my chest. I need her like I need air. Need to get to her. I press down on the accelerator, the truck roaring as we drive up and over the long bridge crossing the intercostal waterway.

"Touch her in my bed, and I'll kick your ass!" Compton shouts. He's losing control. "Oh—*fuck*—" His voice is suddenly breathless as he sinks back against the seat.

"What? Compton, what's happening?"

Slowly, he turns the phone, showing me the screen. My gaze darts right as I look at it, then back to the road. My heart drops from my chest and I have to look again. Rachel is stretched out naked in the middle of his bed, blindfolded, her arms and legs tied down to the four corners.

"Voi helvetti," I mutter, breathing hard through my nose as I navigate traffic.

"Listen to me, asshole," Compton barks into the phone. "We're almost home, and when we get there, you better fuckin' hide. Either that or be waiting on your knees to choke on my dick, because I am *done* getting teased tonight. *Fucking done.*" He doesn't let Caleb respond before he hangs up.

"Are you alright?" I say after a moment.

"Just drive."

I focus on the road, both of us seething. As I make the turn onto the A1A, I glance over at him. "You love them both."

He looks at me like I've grown two heads. "Of course, I do. What kind of fucking question is that?"

I rephrase. "You love him like you love her."

His looks back out the windshield, dark brows lowered. "Yes."

"You want them both."

"Yes."

"You want them to want you."

"Yes," he breathes, his voice deep with barely checked emotion.

"And me?"

He glances my way again. "What about you, Mars?"

"What do you want from me? Where do I fit in to this love triangle?"

He scoffs, shaking his head. "Seriously? Is that why you've been such a dick this week? You're over there thinking this is a love triangle and you just, what? Visit sometimes? Occasionally we all form a square?"

"Compton—"

"You've been calling the shots here, Mars. Not us," he shouts. "I'm the one being a team fucking player. *I* wanted you to move in. I said it day fucking one. If you're in this, you gotta be all the way in. There's no other way I see this working."

"You want me in?"

He huffs, arms crossed. "Rachel wants you in, Mars. And I will do fucking anything for that girl. She's mine. She's *ours*. I invited you to move in. And Caleb was wearing your jersey tonight if you didn't notice. We're all over here tryna build a pyramid, and you're still stuck with pencil and paper asking where you fit in the triangle!"

I look sharply over at him. "You never invited me to move in—"

"Yes, I *did*!" he cries. "Day one I said, and I quote, 'Mars, are you moving in here?' And you said no."

I blink at him, slowing the truck to a stop at a red light. "That's not an invitation to move in."

"Well, I'm sorry I didn't have flowers and a box of chocolates, Mars," he says, rolling his eyes. "I thought on beach day it was all settled with your big, fancy speech about building foundations on shifting sands," he adds. "That's why we need the pyramid. A triangle on sand falls right over. A pyramid doesn't. Ask Egypt. *You* pushed us to make a pyramid, and now you're playing dumb, and I'm fucking sick of it."

I'm reeling, heart racing. He wants me in. Compton wants me all the way in. I glance over at him again. "I don't want to fuck you, Compton. If that's what you mean by 'all in' then . . ."

He stares at me, his face utterly unreadable. "You're shitting me right now. This is a joke."

"No," I reply. "I don't want to upset you or—"

"I don't wanna fuck you, Mars!" he shouts. "God, you are so one hundred percent shitting me right now. This is a prank. You're all in on it, and I'm being pranked." He groans, dragging both hands through his hair, as he drops his elbows to his knees, holding his head in his hands.

"It's not a prank," I murmur.

He jerks his head up, glaring at me. "Mars, I have *zero* interest in fucking you or getting fucked by you. Are you kidding? The idea of your monster cock coming anywhere near me is literally terrifying. Honestly, I don't know how Rachel does it. I don't have the courage to bottom for you, and I totally lack the death wish to try and top you." He gestures between us with a frantic hand wave. "So, are we good? We done here? You need this super weird conversation to go on any longer?"

I smirk, my gaze locked out the windshield as we pull up at the end of his street. "No. We're good."

He's already unbuckling his seatbelt. "Good, because I need you with me on this. Caleb pays, agreed? That little shit gets his mouth stuffed with a gag, and then he watches us take our girl over and over again. We don't stop til she's dripping from every hole."

I pull up in front of his garage, and he's got his door open before I even get the truck into park.

Grabbing our gear bags from the back, he tosses mine to me, slinging his own over his shoulder. "Let's get this fucking done."

81

RACHEL

I moan, back arching off the bed, as I grip tighter to my wrist restraints. "Yes—Cay baby, I'm gonna come—"

Caleb lifts his mouth away from my pussy, letting the spiral of my orgasm fizzle and fade, leaving me panting on the bed. He's been edging me for the last ten minutes, ever since he hung up the call with Jake.

"Please," I say on a sigh, unable to see him through my blindfold. I love the sensory deprivation, as every other sense is heightened. The taste of him on my tongue, warm and inviting. The feel of his hands on my body as he explores me, the softness of Jake's high thread count sheets. The man is a snob when it comes to bedding. I swear, it's like sleeping on a cloud. Right now, strapped down to the mattress, I feel like a debauched angel. And I love it.

The security unit on the wall chirps and we both go still. Moments later, the front door slams shut.

"Uh-oh," I tease. "Somebody's in trouble now—*ah*—"

His tongue in my cunt shuts me up. I'm gasping as he spears me, his hands rough as he forces my thighs apart a little wider, my ankles straining against their ties. I sink into the feeling of his mouth on me, devouring me.

"CALEB!"

Jake's voice echoes through the house as, down the hall, Poseidon whines, scratching at the door of Caleb's room. He's far too innocent to witness what's happening in here.

"You better be hiding or on your fucking knees," Jake shouts, his voice coming from the stairs now.

Mouth on my pussy, Caleb laughs. God, this man is fearless. He wants to get caught, wants to get punished. Meanwhile, my heart races, pulse hammering in my throat. I know the moment Jake can see us stretched out on his bed.

"Cay!" he bellows.

Caleb lifts his mouth off me, peppering my thigh with quick kisses. "It was nice knowing you, Hurricane," he laughs.

I can't see anything as Jake and Ilmari burst into the room, but I feel their feral energy as the weight of Caleb's body leaves the bed.

"Finally," Caleb calls out. "Sorry we didn't—whoa—*fuck*—"

I shriek as I hear the unmistakable sounds of a fight. "Guys, stop," I cry, knowing there's nothing I can do.

"You're fucking dead," Jake growls, his voice muffled as they wrestle each other to the floor.

"Ouch—*shit*—you punch like a golf pro," Caleb teases.

"Get his—his arm—"

"*Ow*—"

"Paska—"

"No—not the face," Caleb grunts.

Oh my god, they're gonna kill him. He finally let that smart mouth take a joke one step too far. There's a continued scuffle as it sounds like they wrestle him to the floor.

"Hold him," Jake mutters as Caleb laughs.

Ilmari mutters darkly in Finnish.

"Think that was funny, asshole?" Jake shouts, his voice moving as he heads over to his closet. "Your little jersey switching game is gonna cost you big time. You'll be lucky if you're not sleeping out on the dunes tonight."

I go still, waiting for Caleb to give up the truth that switching the jerseys was all my idea. But I know he won't say anything. He's having too much fun. And he *did* agree to switch rather quickly.

"No one wears my number but Rachel," Ilmari growls. "The only way you wear it again is if we tattoo in on your forehead. Agreed?"

Caleb groans and I can only imagine he's being pressed into the floor, Ilmari's heavy weight on top of him. "*Ungh*—agreed."

"Get him up," Jake calls from his closet. "We're gonna tie him up."

"Ooo, getting kinky, angel?" Caleb teases.

"Shut him up."

More scuffling.

"Guys, don't," I plead, ready to turn myself in and offer myself up to their mercy.

"Oh, come on man. Not the sock," Caleb grunts. "Not the—*nuuuungh*—"

I arch up, trying desperately to see something through my blindfold. Someone gagged Caleb, and now he's grunting as they get him up. The dresser rattles. Oh god, they're tying him to the dresser?

"Blindfold him," Ilmari growls.

When Caleb wordlessly protests, I hear Ilmari laugh. The sound sends a chill though me. These men are not playing any more games tonight.

"You wanna know what happens next, Cay?" Jake teases. "Just listen close and use that colorful imagination."

Caleb grunts and I know they must be blindfolding him with something too. It's a rare kind of torture for a man who likes to watch, likes to tease with his words. Now he gets to stand there, his only intact sense his hearing as he audibly witnesses the circus they're about to make of my body.

As if I need any reminder, Jake calls out. "Don't think we didn't see you flitting around in our jerseys tonight, spinning us up with your flirty smiles. You're fucking next, Seattle!"

"We're *fucking* you next," Ilmari corrects.

My entire body lights up in anticipation. We're all here. We're all in. The four of us. I suck in air through my heaving lungs as I hear them dropping their clothes to the floor. Whatever the punishment is, I want it.

"I'll take her first," says Jake. "Stretch her out before you attack her with that anaconda. We need her to last tonight. All fucking night. Wait—do you guys have snakes in Finland?"

"No talking," Ilmari growls, and I can't help but smile.

"You gonna fuck me, angel?" I call. "Gonna teach me a lesson for being a brat?"

Weight sinks down at the end of the bed as I feel something brush along the skin of my shins. "Jake—"

"Feel this, baby?" he says, that deep, velvety voice doing unspeakable things to my insides. "What do I have in my hands?"

I gasp, knowing full well what was left on the floor in my rush to undress earlier with Cay. My mouth tips into a smile as he trails the fabric up my thighs. "Your jersey," I whisper.

"That's fucking right," he growls, dropping his body over me as he shoves two fingers deep inside my cunt.

I cry out, trying to arch my hips into his seeking fingers, but my ankles are restrained, the jersey caught between us. The leather straps tug at my skin, chafing. It's the best possible kind of pain. "Jake—"

But he silences me with his mouth, stealing all my air as he kisses me like it's the first and the last time I'll ever be kissed. I moan into him, body on fire from head to toe as he keeps working his fingers in me, our kiss messy as we try to devour each other.

He pulls back, panting, his breath warm on my face. "If a girl wears my number, that girl is mine. Are you mine, Rachel?"

"Jake—"

"And I don't just mean that I get to fuck you and hold you and orbit you like a satellite," he adds. "I mean that you're all fucking mine. You're *my* Seattle Girl." He grips tight to my jaw, holding me still as I pant. "Wear my jersey, you better be ready to wear my ring and my name, because that's where this is going for me. Don't fucking tease me again unless you're all the way there too."

I gasp, but he silences the sound with another kiss, his fingers still working me, his thumb pressing down on my clit until I'm moaning, desperate to come. Jake loves me. He wants to marry me. He's teased me about the Elvis minister, but this is different. He's all in.

He pushes off me with a groan, sitting back on his knees between my spread legs. "Mars, anything to add about the jersey business before we get down to business?"

"Yeah, I will throw that one away," he says quietly.

I go still, my head slowly turning in the direction of his voice. "Why?" I whisper.

"Because my woman doesn't wear a store-bought costume bearing my number," he replies. "She wears *my* jersey. That is what you wear, Rakas."

"Fucking agreed," says Jake. "It's settled then. We'll burn these in the fire pit and make s'mores," he adds, tossing the jersey to the floor. "Now, back to business. We're going to take this body and make it ours, baby," he growls, one hand cupping my pussy again as the other palms my breast. "You are all fucking ours, Rachel. Cay doesn't get to touch. He doesn't get to look. Not until we say."

Using the wetness between my legs, he rubs it on my peaked nipple. "Mars, taste," he orders.

Heart in my throat, I wait for that perfect feeling of Ilmari's closeness, of him joining in fully. The bed sinks on my left side and my senses fill with the smell of his cologne.

He brushes his nose along my jaw, his beard prickling. "Tell me to stop, Rakas."

"Don't stop," I whisper. "Never stop. Love me."

His mouth closes around my nipple, and I sigh into him, my arms bristling with goose bumps as Jake drops to his knees and buries his face in my pussy. They work me together, Ilmari's massive hand palming my other breast as he teases me. The feeling of two men pouring their hearts and souls into my skin, teasing me, cherishing me. It's almost more than I can bear.

Tears sting my eyes behind the blindfold as I squirm, desperate to touch them, to reciprocate with my hands, my mouth. I want them everywhere.

"Free her legs," Jake orders, taking his mouth off my clit before I can come.

Mars shifts his weight, dropping off the bed to do as he's told. I don't know what happened between them that Jake is taking on this dominant role, but I don't mind one bit. I love a bossy Jake. My pussy clearly does too because I'm quivering with the need for him to take control.

Ilmari's hands are tender as he releases the restraints from my ankles one at a time, kissing the inside of each ankle reverently as he lets me go.

Meanwhile, Jake keeps teasing me with his fingers and his mouth, working me right up to that edge. "Has she come yet?" he calls at Caleb.

"*Ngho,*" Caleb says through his makeshift gag.

"You okay?" I call, my voice whiny and breathless.

He grunts again, rattling his fists against the dresser drawers. I guess if he really wanted to, he could Hulk-out and jerk the drawers loose from the frame. I can't help but smile, picturing him standing naked, tied up in a web of his own making. I don't intend to leave him there all night, but this is an important lesson for him that actions have consequences. The jersey switch may have been my idea, but he's always stirring the shit and dancing away like my little naughty devil. Besides, the guys have to know they can check each other, and I won't interfere.

As soon as both my legs are free, Jake tips my hips back, his weight hovering over me as he seeks my mouth again. I open for him, kissing him back as I sigh at the feeling of being so in sync. This man is part of me. I was unraveled in Seattle, and his threads wove me back together. We're part of the same tapestry now, making a new, beautiful picture.

"Please, angel," I beg. "I need you."

"You need me?" he pants against my lips.

"So much."

"You mine, Rachel?"

"Yours," I say, gripping my wrist restraints. Feet flat on the bed, I tip my hips, notching his cock at my wet center. "Please, Jake. Come find me. I need you. Find me. Find—*ah*—"

He slams into me, his cock sliding in deep. The cradle of my hips catches him as we rock together, riding out our pleasure. I wrap my legs around him. He helps, shifting his weight as he comes down on top of me. Then we're both sighing, breathing through our mouths as we work our hips together.

"No waiting, baby," he says against my lips. "Come with me. Come now. Again and Again," he breathes. "All night. Come for us. Be with us, baby girl."

It feels so easy with the blindfold on to sink into my bliss, letting him wind me up as he slips a hand between us and works my clit. The heat spreads through my whole body, tingling across my chest, down to my fingertips. My breath catches, and then I'm flying and falling, spiraling through the air. My pussy clenches tight as the orgasm catches fire, spreading across the whole of my core, rocking me deep.

"Yes," Jake groans, his face buried in my neck as he slams deep with his hips and holds me there, letting my core pulse around him as he comes too. The moment of our shared euphoria cascades down around us like the rain that first painted the sky on our night in Seattle.

"I love you," I whisper, breathless and spent. "Jake, I love you."

"I love you," he repeats, kissing my neck, my shoulder, his hand lovingly cupping my face to turn it so he can claim my lips. "I love you, Rachel. Never let me go."

I nod, knowing in my heart that I can't. It would take ripping at the fabric of my soul to do it, something that now feels unthinkable.

He pulls out of me and rolls to the side, his arm still draped over my middle as he catches his breath. "Mars," he calls. "She's all yours."

The end of the bed sinks low as my goalie drops to his knees between my spread legs. His hands press to the mattress just above my hips on either side, sinking us down. I shiver at the feel of his bristly beard on the sensitive skin of my thighs as he kisses my hips. First one, then the other. His fingers sink deep inside me, and he groans as he pushes Jake's cum back in.

"Release her hands," he says, and I feel Jake roll to his side and crawl up the bed.

As Jake works to free me, Ilmari studies me with his hands, his face, his tongue. He alternates between brushing against me with the tip of his nose and tracing a line with his tongue—across my hip bone, under my navel, above my clit.

I whimper, dropping my left hand to Ilmari's head as Jake releases my wrist from the restraint. My fingers feel tingly as I stroke his bearded face.

Ilmari arches into my touch, chasing it. My thumb brushes the shaved side of his scalp above his ear. When my right hand comes free, I drop it down too, both hands smoothing along the grain of his hair.

"Kulta," I say on a sigh, my hands cupping his bearded cheeks. "Kultaseni. Please. Mä haluun sut. Oon sun." It's the only Finnish I know, but it's effective as his body covers me, his lips claiming mine.

I wrap myself around him fully, feeling so small in his arms. Small, but strong. He's the biggest of my guys, but he doesn't treat me like a tender flower. He takes hold of me, sinking his body against mine until he's dropped to his elbows, letting me bear his weight. I love the press of him on top of me.

"Mä kuulun sulle," he murmurs, his lips against my lips. "Say it, Rakas."

"Mä kuulun sulle," I repeat. "What does it mean?"

His thumb hooks under the edge of my blindfold as he tugs it gently free.

I open my eyes, blinking up at him, his handsome face swarming my vision. I smile at the look of love and longing in his eyes. My quiet one. The one who needs to be seen the most. "What does it mean?" I say again.

He gazes down at me with those deep blue eyes. "I belong to you." As he says the words, he notches his cock between my legs and presses in.

I arch into him, widening my hips to take him. "Say it again."

"Mä kuulun sulle," he repeats. "Mä rakastan sua." He works his hips, sinking in deeper than before. My body works to accommodate his size. He slides a hand over my hip, tipping my thigh open so he can sink all the way into the hilt and we both groan.

I'm lost in this new feeling of fullness as his words continue. He pours his heart out in Finnish, speaking softly to me as we kiss and move together. A tear slips down my temple as I arch my head back, my flesh pressed against his, his cock moving so deep inside me.

Then suddenly he's growling, his arms wrapping around me as he rears back. I cry out, holding on as he balances me on the lap of his splayed knees. I'm fully impaled on him, my legs wrapped around him as he holds my weight on his thighs. When he moves again, I drop my head back, eyes shut, crying out.

He's so deep. Gravity is pulling me down so that I practically feel him in my chest. We rock together, his strong arms around me as our hips move in sync. His power is on full display like this, holding me as if I weigh nothing. I arch back, my breasts bouncing as I ride him. It feels fucking amazing.

"Ohmygod," I cry out, my orgasm building deep and low. Usually, I need some kind of clitoral stimulation to get me all the way there. This angle makes that impossible, but I feel it all the same. It's looming, just within reach.

"Kulta," I whimper, my hands sliding over his inked shoulders to cup his cheeks. "Teach me how to say it." I know he knows what I mean. I think he's been saying it. I hold his gaze as we move together. "Ilmari, please—"

Those deep blue eyes gaze into my soul as he stills inside me, his cock buried so deep. "Mä rakastan sua," he murmurs, his hands holding tight to my hips, thumbs brushing my sensitive skin. "Mä rakastan sua," he says again, slower.

"Mä rakastan sua," I repeat.

"En voi elää ilman sua," he says, shoving against me with his hips. "Oon sun," he pants.

"Vain sun," I echo, arching back.

I fight a scream as my body gives over to the sensation of being split in half by this man who loves me. Then he's crying out too, his hips bucking against me as he comes. The feel of his warm release triggers mine, and suddenly I'm caught in the throes of another orgasm, my core squeezing him with everything I have.

By the time the waves of my release fade, we're both shaking, bodies sweating. He gently folds forward with excellent core control, placing me gently down onto the bed. Then he pulls out. I feel the warm mixture of their releases between my legs. I'm so full of them both, but I want more. I want Caleb.

I let my gaze go to him at last. They've tied him to Jake's dresser at the wrists with what looks like neckties. Another tie holds the sock in his mouth, while someone draped Ilmari's discarded jersey over his head. He looks ridiculous.

"Let him go," I say at Jake. "Please, angel. Let him come to us."

Jake rolls off the bed to free Caleb as I turn my attention back to Ilmari. He gently moves my legs to the side, lying next to me. His massive frame makes me feel so sheltered and loved. He turns my face towards him, his large fingers light against my skin. His fingertip brushes my septum ring and he smiles. "Mä rakastan sua," he says again, voice low. "You understand me?"

I nod, my hand brushing along his forearm. "You know I love you too, right? I'm theirs. They've claimed me and there's no letting go. But you're mine. I claim *you*, Ilmari. No letting go," I whisper with a shake of my head.

He catches my hand as I stroke his chest, bringing it to his lips as he nods.

Jake leads a darkly brooding Caleb over to the bed by the meat of his shoulder. "Doesn't our girl look beautiful, Cay? She's full of our cum. It's dripping out of her. A sign that she's claimed. Loved. She's *mine*. You want to be mine too, troublemaker?"

Caleb's dark gaze roves my body, taking me in from my sweaty brow down to the sticky mess between my legs. Slowly, he nods.

Jake slings an arm around his bare chest, pulling him back against him as he whispers in his ear loud enough for us all to hear, "Then get on your knees and lick her clean . . . while I fuck this tight ass."

I gasp, heart in my throat, as I watch Caleb go still in Jake's arms. I have no idea what the bounds of his sexuality are. He likes to dominate, likes to control. Does he have it in him to cede that control?

Slowly, Caleb turns in Jake's hold to look him in the eye. "Is that what you want, Jake?"

It's a masterful deflect, forcing Jake to take another step out of the closet. I watch Jake's chest rise and fall as he nods.

A small smile spreads across Caleb's face. "I've never done this before. You really want to be my first?"

Then Jake is gripping his face with both hands. They're so close they're practically sharing breath. A thousand unspoken words stretch between them. I can't breathe, can't blink, waiting to see if Jake will do the thing he's so clearly longing to do. His gaze drops from Caleb's eyes to his mouth, and I swallow a whine. I want them to kiss. Want them to stop denying what they both want. What they *need*.

Jake leans in a little closer, his thumb brushing over Caleb's perfect, pouty lips. "I intend to be your first and your fucking last." Their noses brush and Jake's eyes shut tight as he rasps, "Now, get on your goddamn knees." Then he shoves Caleb away.

Caleb melts out of Jake's hold, moving onto the bed. Ilmari shifts up, keeping his hands on me. He helps me move with him, making more room for both of them at the end of the bed.

Caleb drops to his knees, folding over me with a hungry groan as he kisses my breasts, down my stomach to my hips. "How do you feel, Hurricane?"

I smile, lifting my hand to brush his cheek. "Ready," I whisper.

Jake moves to stand at the end of the bed, lube in hand. "Get your ass over here," he growls, reaching for Caleb's hips.

Holding my gaze, Caleb shifts down the bed, wincing slightly as he puts pressure on his bad knee.

Behind him, Jake works lube down his hard shaft. "Nothing happens until you take care of our girl," he declares, his free hand resting on Caleb's hip.

With a groan, Caleb drops to his elbows between my spread legs, brushing kisses up my inner thigh as he works his way to the mess between my legs. If he didn't want to do this, he'd say something. Caleb Sanford doesn't do anything he doesn't want to do.

I take a deep breath as he makes his first pass over my clit. He hums, his lips teasing me as he flicks with his tongue. His whole body stills, and he sucks in a sharp breath against my pussy. I glance over him to see why. Jake has just pressed a finger into his ass.

"You've done anal enough to know how this goes," Jake teases, swatting his ass. "You gotta relax, Cay. Breathe it out. Come on, be my good fucking boy. You want me to own this ass, you gotta show me how much you want it."

Caleb groans, his mouth savoring my pussy as Jake starts teasing him open, working his fingers in and out. Tipping my head back, I look for Ilmari. He's watching it all unfold, a hungry look on his face. I knew he would like sharing once he gave it a try. I reach for him with my free hand, my other hand settled on Caleb's dark auburn hair.

Ilmari leans over me, covering my mouth with his, kissing me deep. His hand roves from my neck, down the line of my sternum to cup my breast.

"Fuck, I need more," Caleb groans, face lifting from between my legs. "Mars, how much time do you need?"

Ilmari narrows his blue eyes. "Time for what?"

"To fuck her," Jake supplies. "He wants you to fuck her again. How much time before you can?"

I snort.

"What?" says Caleb. "What is that face?"

I glance up at Ilmari. "Do you want to tell them, or should I?"

"Tell us what?" says Jake, his gaze darting between us.

"Mars has basically no refractory period," I reply.

"He—what?" Jake cries.

"Of course," Caleb mutters shaking his head.

Jake is less diplomatic. "Are you fucking kidding me, Mars? You've got the height and the looks *and* the accent . . . *and* you can fuck all night long?"

"Yes," Mars replies, wholly nonchalant.

"Fuck, I even bragged to you about the night of six times," Jake cries. "You didn't say anything!"

"Are we really going to complain about this?" I say quickly. "Caleb asked when he's ready and he's ready now."

"It's just not fucking fair," Jake mutters.

"You do just fine, angel," I tease.

"Right, here's what's gonna happen," says Caleb, up on his knees as he gestures between us. "Mars is gonna lie down. Hurricane, you'll ride him. I'll take your ass while Jake takes mine. Agreed?"

I glance quickly from Caleb to Jake and watch as Jake's expression changes from one of confusion to interest to excitement.

"That is the kinkiest fucking thing I've ever heard," he says with a grin. "Mars, *please* say you're in. I'm gonna die if you don't. We gotta try it."

Mars glances between them. "I'm fucking Rachel, yes? No one is fucking me?"

Caleb laughs again as Jake says, "I mean, we could probably put some peanut butter on your toes and get Poseidon in here if you're feeling like you need it to get a little freaky—"

"No," Mars growls as Caleb and I laugh.

"Well then get ready," Jake orders.

I crawl to my knees, folding myself against Caleb. My hands loop around his neck as I kiss him, peppering along his jaw to reach his ear. "You're good?" I murmur. When he nods, I drop my face to his chest, breathing him in.

"Come here, Rakas," Ilmari calls.

I glance over my shoulder to see him reclined against the headboard, fisting his hard cock.

"Better you than me," Caleb teases, giving my ass a swat.

I hiss, turning in his arms as I crawl over to Ilmari. He scoots down the bed, reaching for me with both hands. He grips me by the hips, helping me swing up onto his lap. His big cock is nestled in front of me. I reach down with a free hand, stroking him from root to tip. Seeing him on his back for me, I feel like a queen.

He makes me feel like one. He looks at me like I hung the moon and all the stars, both hands sliding up from my hips to palm my breasts. Taking a breath, I arch up on my knees, slipping his cock between my thighs to notch him at my entrance. I hold there, teasing his tip. The feeling of waiting stretches between us as we both know the sensation that will jolt us to our cores.

"Do it," he growls. "Sit down, Rakas."

I shudder, my breath shaky as I sink down on his length, his thick girth filling me so tight. I'll never get tired of this feeling. Each time is a little claiming. I'm claiming him and he's claiming me. He's mine and I'm his. This is where we fit, where we find our home. We both exhale together as I start to move my hips, working him inside me. His hands drop to my hips, his body relaxed as he watches me move on top of him, my breasts swaying.

"Oot kaunis, Rakas," he murmurs, lifting a hand to trace a finger down my chest tattoo.

I lean over him, my palms flat against his chest as I ride him. "What does that mean?"

"You're beautiful," he replies, his right hand shifting its hold of my hip until he's strumming my clit with his thumb.

I moan, biting my bottom lip as my back arches, loving the feel of having him so hard inside me.

And then Caleb is behind me, one hand on my shoulder. "Lean forward, Hurricane," he says. "All the way down."

My excitement spikes as I drop down to my hands on either side of Ilmari's head. We hold each other's gaze as Caleb starts prepping me, working the lube inside with first one finger, then two. We both pant, sharing breath as Caleb takes hold of my hip, controlling my movements.

"You feel ready?" he says, his hand smoothing up my back.

I nod.

"Words, Rachel—"

"Yes," I breathe. "Take me, Cay."

Caleb presses in closer between Ilmari's spread legs, working his cock in my ass. I groan, relaxing for him, ready to let him in. Letting more of my weight fall onto Ilmari, I relax my hips and sigh on a long exhale as Caleb presses in.

"Saatana," Ilmari curses below me. "So tight—Rakas, are you hurting?"

"No," I say on a breath.

"Fuck—I forgot about his cock," Ilmari grunts.

"You like that, Mars," Caleb says, thrusting in hard and fast so his piercings tease my inner walls at the same time that they tease Ilmari. He gets the full effect, the muscles in his neck going tight as he closes his eyes, his breath frozen in his chest.

"Want Jake to fuck me into you, Hurricane?"

I whimper, arms already shaking.

"He'll pound me, and I'll pound you, which will set fireworks off for Mars. You both ready?"

"Do it," Mars replies. "Rakas, lie down on me."

He helps me get the weight off my hands, folding me over against his chest. I'm pressed completely against him as Caleb curls over the top of me from behind, seated to the hilt in my ass. The pressure is overwhelming as their two cocks fill me so full. I breathe through it, waiting for Jake to join us.

Caleb grunts, cursing under his breath. "Come on, Jake. Fuckin' do it."

"You gotta relax," Jake replies, his voice soothing.

"Oh, fuck," Caleb groans. "Holy fuck—"

I moan as Jake presses into him, which moves him into me.

"Who would have thought that for being such a smart ass, you'd have such a tight ass," Jake teases. "Cay, you feel like heaven, man."

Caleb just groans, still adjusting to the feel of a cock in his ass.

"You ready for more?" Jake calls. "Cay, wake the fuck up and help me. You move when I move, yeah?"

"Yeah," Caleb groans, one hand on my hip and the other pressed flat to the mattress.

Under me, Ilmari curses softly in Finnish.

"Remember, this was your idea," Jake teases.

"Just fucking—*ah*—fuck—" Caleb's curse ends on a strangled cry as Jake unleashes on us all. He pounds into Caleb, holding to his hips as he rocks forward.

Caleb is a swearing mess as he finds a rhythm, working with Jake to thrust in tandem, moving inside me. The piercings glide up and down my inner walls, moving tight against Ilmari's girth and sending him into a storm of breathless Finnish cursing. Mars throws his hands up behind him, bracing against the headboard as two huge hockey players move above us.

Meanwhile, my soul quietly ascends to a higher plane. I'm gone. Deceased. Dead from too much overwhelming euphoria. My body is sandwiched between three men I love who love me. We all found our path to each other in the most surprising of ways. They're working together to bring all of us pleasure. A unit. A team.

I can hardly draw breath as I let my men love me, tearing me open as they drive themselves deeper into every part of me—my heart, my psyche, my soul. Something in this moment marks a new change. For the second time, I'm experiencing an unraveling of my being. The first happened when I met Jake in Seattle. This is the second.

The Great Unraveling of Rachel Price.

Jake threatened to do it the day we met in the Rays parking garage. He doesn't even realize that he's managed to do it twice over. I am myself no longer. I am whatever *we* are. I'm in this. And I don't want to hide anymore. I want to claim these men before the world.

Unable to hold it back a moment longer, I cry out my release, the orgasm tearing through me. The heat builds in my core, expanding in a torrent of energy that has me seeing stars, my whole body rocked by the force of it. I'm the first domino to fall. Then the guys all start to fall apart.

Beneath me, Mars pushes up with his hips, his hot seed spilling inside me, filling my pussy with more cum. Caleb unleashes in my ass, his weight dropping on top of us as he moans and trembles, overcome with new sensations as Jake finishes inside him.

We all lie in a tangle of sweaty arms and legs, waiting for our souls to drift back down into our bodies. Jake is the first to finally move, sliding off Caleb and dropping to the bed alongside Mars. He wears a look of bliss, one arm slung up over his head as he takes deep breaths.

Caleb holds to my hips, gently pulling out of me. Then he flops down on the other side of Mars, finally quiet and sated. With nowhere left to go on the bed, I stay on top of Ilmari, his half-hard cock still nestled inside me.

"Shower," Jake grunts. "Change sheets. Ice cream in bed."

"This bed is too small for four people," Mars mutters.

"I'll sleep in my room," comes Caleb's sleepy voice.

"No," I say, my hand flopping listlessly at my side, searching for Caleb. "I want us all together."

"Shower first," says Mars, giving my bare ass a gentle tap. "I have an idea."

Somehow, we stumble into Jake's shower, taking turns under the dual shower heads. The guys place me in the middle, helping me work shampoo into my hair and washing me gently between my legs. I lean against Jake as the water shuts off. Then Ilmari is handing me a towel.

Once I'm in my bathrobe, my wet hair knotted up on top of my head, Ilmari takes my hand, giving it a kiss. "Go get the ice cream. We'll deal with this."

I wander down the hall, leaving my three shirtless guys in the bedroom. Passing Caleb's room, I free Sy from his prison. He dances around my feet in greeting.

"And bring up some water," Jake calls.

"And my phone," Cay adds. "Shit—and my phone charger!"

I snort, shaking my head. Sy races down the stairs with me and helps me get all the stuff together. I use a tray to carry it all, as well as the pockets of my bathrobe. I'm loaded down with four bottles of water, two phones and two chargers, four bowls, four spoons, and three pints of ice cream. The bowls and spoons rattle as I work my way up the stairs.

I pause in the hallway, eyes wide as I look into the explosion that has suddenly hit Jake's room. Before my eyes, Mars and Caleb stand together on one side of a mattress. They must have just carried it in from one of the other bedrooms. Giving it a push, it topples to the ground with a loud thud.

I step into Jake's room to see they've taken his mattress out of the frame too and plopped it on the floor near the wall of glass leading out to his balcony. The other mattress is slightly thinner, but it rests up against the first, creating a floor of mattresses wide enough for all four of us plus Poseidon to sleep without crushing each other or sweating ourselves to death.

Jake is already making the first mattress into a respectable bed with pillows and a blanket. Ilmari and Cay aren't trying as hard with the second one.

Heart overflowing, tears in my eyes, I clear my throat.

All three of them look up at me standing in the doorway holding the tray. Jake is on his feet in moments, taking it from me.

Behind him, Ilmari studies my face. "Are you . . . you hate this, yes? You are hating it?"

"It won't look like this forever," Jake says quickly. "We just didn't want to bother with a drill tonight to get the bed frame apart. This was the easiest fix," he adds with a shrug. "Wait—you seriously hate it?"

Caleb just huffs, dropping to his back on the second mattress. "She doesn't hate it, assholes. She fucking loves it. She's trying not to cry, she loves it so much. I bet if you hug her right now, she *will* cry."

"Shut up," I say with a sniff, crossing my arms inside my fuzzy bathrobe. "Was that on my Pinterest too, Cay?"

"No," he replies with a smug smile. "I just know you."

Dropping to my knees at the end of the mattress, I tug off my robe and crawl over to him in my little sleep cami and silky shorts.

"What are you doing?" he mutters.

"Snuggling with you," I reply, climbing over his legs to curl up at his side.

His body goes stiff. "I don't snuggle."

"Here, kitty kitty," I tease, stretching out next to him and slinging a leg over him.

He groans. "Hurricane, I just want to sleep."

"I thought you wanted ice cream."

"No, Jake wants ice cream. *You* want ice cream. I never know what Mars wants. And *I* want to go to sleep. Since my mattress is now in here, I have to sleep in here."

I wiggle closer to him. "I don't want ice cream anymore. I just want this."

"I never wanted ice cream," Ilmari adds with a shrug.

Jake sighs, still holding the tray. "So, I guess *I'm* bringing this back downstairs."

"Leave the phone and the charger," Cay mutters, eyes still closed.

Jake turns and leaves with a huff, Poseidon racing off behind him.

Ilmari drops down on the stretch of empty mattress and rolls to his side, curling himself in close behind me.

"Someone needs to turn the light off," Caleb mutters.

"Jake will do it when he gets back," I say with a sleepy yawn. I shift on the bed until I can slip under the makeshift covers. There's a sheet and a blanket, which is good enough for me. Behind me, Ilmari does the same, eager for us to be skin-on-skin. I reach a hand back to brush his hip and find bare skin. "Kulta . . . are you naked?"

He hums low. "I sleep naked."

I smile, eyes closed. I knew that already, but I wasn't sure if the same rules applied around the guys.

"Perfect," Caleb mutters. "A naked Finn, a hairy dog, and Jake, who snores."

"Don't forget me," I tease.

"And what's your cursed trait?"

"How is that not obvious? I'm a snuggler," I reply, pressing myself closer to kiss his bare chest.

He groans.

"Hey, you comfortable over there, Mars?" Jake calls as he enters the room and flips out the lights.

"Yes," Mars replies.

"Good, cause it's your last fucking night on my mattress," he growls, dropping down to the free spot on the other side of Caleb. "I'll call it a 'welcome home' gift, but it's the only one you'll get. New house rule: no one steals Jake's mattress. Trust me, you do *not* want to live with me if I'm not getting a solid eight hours of sleep."

"Listen to the man," Caleb mutters, already halfway to dream land.

"I'll trade with you, angel," I offer.

He just snorts. "And wake up with a Finnish sausage up my ass? I don't think so."

"Everyone shut up now," Caleb grunts.

"Hey Mars, how do you say 'good night' in Finnish—*ouch*—shit, Cay," Jake pouts.

Showing mercy on Caleb, I scoot back, reducing my snuggling from a full-on squid assault to a respectable hand hold.

Taking a deep breath, I speak into the silence of the room. "I love you." I don't qualify it. I don't need to. They know. And now, after tonight, I know too. They love me.

Jake says it back, rolling to his other side. Caleb mutters something that sounds close enough, and Ilmari scoots closer to me, fitting me to him, my big Finnish bear spoon. The only missing piece is Poseidon, who takes his sweet time deciding where he wants to sit down before curling up with his head resting on my ankle, my own little furry ball and chain.

But I don't mind. Sleeping on the floor on our mattress pile with room for all five of us, I breathe deep, filling my lungs with the peace of knowing that, in this moment at least, we're safe and happy. What we have is sacred.

But we need a plan. We need a way out of the safety of the shadows and into the harsh light of day. All of us. Together.

83
RACHEL

"**I**'m just asking if she's said anything about me," Langley says lying on his back on the massage table.

The Rays gym is pumping out the rock tunes as players swarm everywhere. It's a recovery day, with another game tomorrow, meaning workouts are light. Most guys are just doing a bit of cardio.

I jiggle Langley's legs, working to release the lactic acid buildup from his strength and conditioning session. "Uh-huh. And I already told you, I haven't talked to her in like a week."

"So, she hasn't said *anything*?" he presses.

I huff, dropping his legs down. "Why would she say something about you, Langley? You really think getting whacked in the head with a soccer ball left that big of an impression?"

"I—" He swallows his words, biting his bottom lip. "Well . . . no," he admits softly.

I offer him my hand, helping him sit up. "Look, it's sweet that you liked her, okay? But Tess is . . . complicated."

He narrows his pretty green eyes at me. "What do you mean?"

"Well . . . she's still married for one," I say. "It's been the divorce from hell, and her ex is literally the devil, but—"

"She's married?" he says, his sweet, tender heart breaking.

"I mean, they're separated," I repeat. "Have been. And she's *never* going back to that piece of shit. But it just complicates things."

His softness forms an edge as he glares at me. "Did he hurt her?"

"I'm really not comfortable discussing her business with you, Langley."

He sighs, nodding his head as he looks down at his trainers.

I take hold of his arm, helping him through some stretches to loosen up his shoulders. "Besides, the last thing you want right now is a long-distance relationship, right? You're young. You're focused on your career. You don't want that hassle."

He nods, knowing I'm talking sense.

"And I mean . . . you're not really her type," I add, moving over to his other arm.

He looks sharply at me. "What do you mean? I could be her type."

I look him up and down, taking in his pro athlete body. That she can work with easily. Tess Owens loves a well-muscled man. It's his All-American, preppy baby face. His sweet as pie personality. And he's too young. Too uncomplicated. A total puppy. He would bore her in the end.

"Well, I've known her for a while now, and she has exactly two types," I explain, ready to let him down easy. "Zoë Kravitz in *Big Little Lies,* and that actor who plays Jax Teller . . . playing the role of Jax Teller," I add. "We tried to watch his other stuff, and she pitched a fit. That's it. You gotta be a Kravitz or a Teller, and you're neither," I finish with a shrug.

"I can be a Teller," he says, puffing his chest out. "I could grow a beard, I think."

I snort. "Oh, honey. That's literally the *least* interesting thing about Jax Teller. You gonna buy a motorcycle too? Treat her like an old lady? Start stashing guns and drugs in the Zamboni?"

"Well . . . no," he says, his brain clearly chewing on the puzzle of how to appeal to Tess, a woman he'll likely never see again.

My spidey senses tingle as I watch him. "Langley . . . did something happen between you two while she was down here?"

"No," he says quickly. Too quickly.

"Langley," I say in my best, most adult mothering tone.

Before he can respond, Poppy comes breezing across the gym. "Rachel! Rach! Girl, I need to talk to you!" She sings out the last sentence as she darts between the equipment like a blonde squirrel.

"What's up?"

She's always so perfectly polished. Her blonde ponytail looks effortless, all her flyway pieces specifically chosen to be let loose. Meanwhile, my hair is up in the same old messy knot. She's matched the coral on her lips to the coral of her yoga pants, sparkling white Gucci tennis shoes on her feet. She's finished the look with a Rays t-shirt that she's artfully cut to be a scoop-necked crop top with just the barest little strip of her tummy showing. Honestly, it's cute, and I'm stealing the idea.

"What do you need?" I say again, still working my fingers over Langley's shoulder.

She huffs, glancing at him. "Get lost for a minute, honey."

His eyes go wide. "But we're in the middle of—"

"Yeah, that's great," she says over him, taking his hand and tugging him off the table. "Tell your story walkin. We'll let you know when we're done talkin."

He huffs, stomping off as Poppy grabs me by the arm and pulls me away from the massage area back towards my office.

"Poppy, what—"

"Not here," she says, breathless as she all but pushes me into my office and shuts the door. As soon as it closes, she spins around, dropping her purse to the floor. "My phone has been ringing off the hook all morning."

I glance at the clock on the wall. "Pop, it's barely 7:30—"

"You don't think I know that?" she cries. "The calls started coming at 5:00am. It was all I could do to make myself presentable and get in here to find you!" She tugs her phone out of the side pocket of her leggings and taps the screen, showing me her call history. She swipes with her finger, showing me the list of red missed calls.

An ominous feeling of doom sinks into the pit of my stomach. "Just tell me."

"They're all about you. Asking about last night."

I let out a deep breath. I logged out of all my social media apps years ago. And I never really check the news. "Show me."

Shaking her head, she steps over, showing me her phone. Apparently, I was a trending topic on the hockey sites, the Ferrymen sites, and the celebrity gossip sites. There's footage from several different angles—the official game footage, personal cell phones. All show the same thing. It's the moment Jake skates up to the plexiglass, pounding on it, shouting at me and Caleb. Some of the montages are cut to make Caleb and I look much more touchy-feely than we were. Some show me giving him moon eyes. A few have the cheek kiss. The way we lean in so casually. Caleb looks calm. He looks happy. My soft heart hardens, wanting to protect him from the scrutiny.

"And these are just the short video clips that went viral," Poppy explains. "People have questions, Rachel. They think they know what they're seeing. I'm tryna stay ahead of it for you, but I need to know if what I know is the thing I think I know."

I glance at her, trying to piece together what she just said. "The thing you—what?"

She huffs, tossing her phone down on the counter to put both hands on her size 4 hips. "Rachel Price, did you spurn Jake Compton and take Caleb Sanford as your lover?"

"What—*no*—no spurning," I say quickly.

"Did you spurn Jake Compton and take Mars Kinnunen as your lover?" she presses.

I shake my head. "I haven't spurned Jake, Poppy."

She gasps, her eyes narrowing like a terrier hunting a mouse. "So, you *are* with Jake Compton. Why, you sneaky little minx. I didn't suspect a darn thing! How long?"

"Poppy," I say with a sigh, shaking my head. I thought we could stave off the unraveling longer than this, but apparently, it's already started.

"Well, what was this then?" she says in a huff. "You were just teasing him? Wearing Kinnunen's jersey to get a rise out of him? And what was Caleb doing involved? I thought they were friends."

"They *are* friends, Pop. It's—god, it's complicated—"

"Oh my good gravy, is it a love triangle?" She gasps again, hand to mouth. "Is *Caleb* the spurned lover? Are they trying to make you choose? Have you decided—"

I groan, grabbing Poppy by the shoulders, lowering my face to hers. "Girl, pull yourself together. No one, and I mean *no one* is getting spurned here. I wouldn't even know how to spurn something. Last night was an inside joke between friends, okay? We all work together, and it was a joke. That's the official story, alright? No romance, no spurning, no broken hearts."

"An inside joke between friends?" she repeats.

"Between *colleagues*," I correct, slipping into PR crisis manager mode. "We're all working on the same team, and the three of us had a fun night out in the stands, right? We ate our weight in junk food and we got to watch our friends play. Caleb and I played a little prank on the players where we wore their jerseys. Good clean fun, alright?"

She nods. "Yeah . . . good clean fun."

I don't need to offer up a single detail of how Caleb and I actually paid for that good clean fun. I'm wearing long sleeves to work today because of the marks on my wrists. And my poor pussy still has her own heartbeat. So fucking worth it.

I take a deep breath. This isn't unmanageable. There was no kissing, no sex tape, no secret footage from last night floating on the dark web. If anything, maybe it's good it happened this way to start. If the rumors are given a little air, a little room to germinate and grow . . .

I glance back at Poppy, furiously focused on her phone as her thumbs tap tap tap away. "What can I do to help?"

"Hmm?" She doesn't look up.

She's quiet for another minute and I clear my throat. "Pop?"

"Yeah—what?" She looks up at last.

"How can I help? My family has PR people too." I take a breath, hating that the words are about to slip from my lips. "I could . . . talk to my dad."

I've tried so hard to rehab my image on my own. Old Rachel is gone. I left her in California along with my Jimmy Choo collection. I'm not that partying celebrity girl anymore. I'm a sports medicine doctor. A highly educated, professional woman.

With three boyfriends . . . on the same NHL team.

And I think two of my boyfriends might be boyfriends.

And my other boyfriend wants to play in the Olympics. As in, he's *actively* being recruited for a coveted spot on a National Olympic Team. Now. This weekend. Scouts are here to watch him play again tomorrow.

And here I thought it would be cute to play a game of jersey-switch in front of the cameras.

Yeah, this is a PR disaster waiting to happen. I will not apologize to anyone for loving three men, but I am in so far over my head. And I'm breaking the cardinal rule of the Price Family. I'm flying solo. I have been for months. We've learned through hard experience that the only way we survive is together.

I love my boys, but they're not Prices. They have their own names to protect, their own families, their own reputations. My protective instincts flare as I think of the press hounding them the way they've hounded my family. The salacious stories, paparazzi outside my house day and night, going through my trash. The barrage of personal questions that constantly overshadow all attempts to promote your work, your art, your career.

Just the thought of their lives being inconvenienced in any way makes me see red. I want to take every gossip paper and burn it to ash. I want us all to hide out in Jake's beach house for the rest of our days, four little turtles in our sandy shell.

It hurts because I woke up feeling so hopeful. Now, watching as Poppy St. James goes into PR crisis mode, the truth is glaringly obvious: there was never any hope that this would ever be anything but bad. *Really* bad. Apocalyptic bad.

Jake and Ilmari will be reduced from star NHL player status to benched oddities. The Rays owners won't want the constant bad press they bring to every game, every interview. They'll get traded to different teams. That'll be step one, as their agents and the League attempt to cool the heat of the press. They're still great players. Someone will want them enough to scoop them up. Ilmari will end up in Winnipeg or back with the Liiga while Jake gets transferred out to Texas.

Then the PR rehab will really begin. They'll fly under the radar, go on coordinated dates so they're photographed with nice women, uncomplicated women. Women who aren't me. My heart breaks at the thought.

And I can't even begin to think what will happen to Caleb as they rehab Jake's image away from him too. The 'just friends' bullshit parade will march boldly across every corner of the hockey internet. Because a man can't possibly be a damn fine defenseman, checking players into the boards every day, only to go home to another man at night. Jake's agent will give him a doomed offer: our salacious relationship, or his starting position.

Ilmari will be just the same: your lover and her lovers, or the Olympics. Choose.

"Rach? You okay, hon?"

I glance up to see Poppy looking at me, her head tipped to the side in quiet curiosity. I shake my head. "No. I'm not okay."

She steps forward, putting an arm around my shoulder. "Oh, honey, it's okay. This is no big deal. I know I came in all gloom and doom. You can just call me Lil Miss Storm Cloud," she teases with a laugh. "I get in my head and go deep into 'manage it' mode. I'm sure you get it."

"Yeah, I do," I murmur. I really do. If she's the queen of managing crises, I'm the empress, the goddess, the all-powerful genie. I'm going to manage the shit out of this situation, protecting my guys at all costs. I don't care if I take the fall. I'm not dragging them down with me.

"You leave this with me," Poppy soothes. "Nothing a lil polish can't make shine."

"You'll let me know if there's anything I can do?" I say, still going through the motions with her. I need her to leave. I can't breathe until she leaves. Can't scream. Can't cry.

"Just do your job, Doc," she replies with a smile. "You leave the PR to me and Clairy B."

She leaves, letting the pulsing beat of the gym music filter inside this small room, thumping in my chest. In this moment, my office has never felt smaller. I look around the four white walls, devoid of decoration save for a pair of health inspection certificates in cheap gold frames. I feel a panic attack coming on. Shit, I haven't had one of these in years. My breath is short and tight in my chest. I need help. I need to lift this crushing weight off my chest before I pass out. I need *him*.

Raising a fluttering hand to my chest, I open my phone and tap my contacts. It's far too early, but I don't care. Finding his name, I hold my phone to my ear and wait, the call ringing. On the third ring, he answers.

"Thank fucking god. Where the hell are you?"

"Harrison," I whimper into the phone, tears coming. "I need you."

"I know. I've been wandering this damn arena for fifteen minutes trying to find you. Where *are* you?"

84
CALEB

"**H**ey, Sanny?" Novy calls with a wave, popping his head inside the laundry room.

"Aww, what happened to Snuffy?" says Morrow. "I liked that nickname."

I just roll my eyes as the guys both laugh. I'm standing at the big folding table, ironing jerseys for tomorrow's game. This is only the third in a whole pile. And this is only task one of like twenty I have to complete today. "What do you need, Nov?"

"Not a thing," he replies, leaning against the table, his eyes on my hands as he watches me work, crunching on his homemade granola. "Compton still around?"

"How should I know?"

Novy and Morrow exchange an incredulous look. "Uh . . . maybe because you *live* together," Novy replies with a laugh.

"And you carpool in to work all the time," Morrow adds.

"And you've got your weird DLP-ESP," Novy finishes.

"That hasn't been officially diagnosed yet," I tease back, setting the iron aside to flip the jersey over. "We're still on the waitlist for that study at Mayo."

The guys laugh as Morrow snags the bag of granola out of Novy's hands and races around the table behind me with it, shoving some of the crunchy mix in his mouth.

"Asshole," Novy growls, hands flat on the table. "Give it back."

Morrow steals another handful and zips the bag shut, tossing it back at Novy.

"I've been down here since I got in," I explain, moving the iron over the back of Sully's jersey, ignoring their antics. "I don't know anything happening outside this room."

They exchange a look, and Novy shakes his head.

I narrow my eyes at him. "What is it?"

Novy's a good guy, even if he's a bit rough around the edges. He's the wild stallion type, always balancing a bevy of puck bunnies. Stays out too late. Parties too hard. Never really serious about anything but hockey. But he's a good player and a loyal teammate.

Right now, he's got a sober look in his eye. Something's up. He needs to talk. He shares another glance with Morrow, still munching his granola.

"What?" I say again. "Come on, guys. I got a shit ton to do, so if you're not gonna—"

"Are you with him?" Morrow blurts out.

My gaze tracks to him as Novy groans. "Dude, come on," he says. "You're not supposed to just ask a guy if he's gay like that. That's like, breaking the rules. Right?"

Now they're both looking at me.

My stomach drops. *Oh shit.* "What are you assholes talking about?"

"You haven't seen it then?" Novy asks with a raised brow.

"You haven't heard?"

I groan, dragging both hands through my hair. "Fuck, guys. Drop the suspense, before I go looking for Colonel Mustard holding a candlestick. Now, what the *hell* are you talking about?"

"Aw, shit. It's everywhere, man," Novy says with a shake of his head. "The guys are all chirping with it online."

"Chirping with what?"

"That you and Compton are together," says Morrow. "You know, like . . . *together*. Like a gay thing."

"Yeah, I get what 'together' means."

"There's all this footage from the game last night," Novy adds. "Compton skating up to you on the ice, and you're wearing his jersey and, like, smiling and shit."

I know exactly what they're talking about. God, it felt good in the moment. Rachel was by my side, and we were laughing, having fun. I had my girl and my . . . fuck—well, he's not really my guy, is he? We fool around a bit with Rachel, but he's given me no indication he wants anything outside the comfort her presence provides, the inhibitions she helps us all lower.

Visions of last night fill my senses, making my heart race and my palms sweat. I've been trying so hard not to think about it. Jake's face so close to mine, his thumb on my lips, the smell of his cologne invading my lungs, filling me up. I wanted him to kiss me . . . but he didn't. He pulled away.

But then he put me on my knees and popped my fucking cherry in the middle of an orgasmic four-way. I've never been filled like that before. Not even by a toy. I may love sticking my dick in asses, but I've never once considered having a dick in mine. Turns out it wasn't even a question. He offered, and I couldn't bend over fast enough.

And I want more. I want his cum in my mouth, my ass. I want to lay that man out and feast on him till he begs me to stop. I want Rachel to hold him down while I fuck his tight ass, riding him hard and long, edging him to within an inch of his sanity.

And I want kissing. More than sex, I want him to want me. I want the intimacy of my lips on his and I want it to be *his* idea. Until then, Jake's not queer for me. He's just a straight man having his cake and eating it too.

I clear my throat, snatching up the iron again and putting my eyes on my work. "So, all of this chirping is based on me wearing Jake's jersey to the game last night and the fact that he skated up to the boards?" I move the iron down the sleeve, glancing up between the guys. "You know I was with Doctor Price and Poppy too, right? Did the footage catch that? Pretty sure Doc was in a jersey. Is she getting dragged too?"

My heart is silent in my chest, unwilling to beat. What the fuck am I doing? I don't want to draw attention to Rachel, but I also need to try to deflect this for Jake's sake. Her image with the guys is spotless right now. So is Poppy's. This could work. I can buy us time and get Novy and Morrow to help me spread the 'nothing to see here' message far and wide.

"Yeah, some of the noise is tryna say you and Hot Doc are a thing," says Morrow with a shrug. "But that's just the celebrity news and stuff the bunnies spread around."

"Only some of the noise, huh?" I say, setting the iron aside as I slip Sully's jersey back on its hanger and hang it up. "What does most of the noise say . . ."

Novy sighs, leaning against the table, arms crossed over his barrel chest. "Inside the League, the news is that you and Compton are finally out."

I let out a breath, trying to control this sick feeling in my gut. Distracting my hands, I reach for the next jersey. Fuck, it's Jake's. "Finally? What, like we've been trapped in the closet lookin' for a key to unlock the door?"

The guys offer me weak smiles. They're not buying my deflection.

"Come on, man," Morrow mutters. "You gotta know you guys have a reputation from the other teams, right?"

I say nothing, eyes on my work as I smooth out Jake's jersey.

Novy clears his throat. "Yeah, apparently some of the guys from the Pens and the Kings are chirping about it. And some of *our* guys share chats with them. They were all talking about it up in the PT room just now. Avery goaded them on—"

"Which is totally not cool," Morrow says, voice firm.

"Yeah, we're not gonna tolerate any Rays chirping about our guys," says Novy with a reassuring nod. "The jerks talking about it upstairs got their asses handed to them, so don't even worry about it."

I glance up sharply from my work. "Wait—by who?"

"Kinnunen," Morrow replies.

"Who knew Mars was such an ally, huh?" Novy laughs. "Most I've heard him talk all season. He told Perry what he could do with the weight he was lifting."

"Yeah, but then he switched to Finnish," Morrow adds.

"Made the poor kid cry. I never want him to yell at me in Finnish," Novy said, eyes wide as he shakes his head in horror.

"And I don't know what the deal is with Avery," Morrow mutters.

"Yeah, that guy is such an asshole," Novy huffs, arms crossed. "I don't know why they hired him, honestly. I wish they'd can him and just hire Price."

I glance between them. Rachel hasn't said anything, but I know Avery's reputation. And I've seen them interact a bit at games. He's always putting her down and leaving her hanging. I think he might feel threatened by her. "Wait—was he chirping too?" I say, eyes narrowed at the guys.

"Nothing Mars couldn't handle," Novy replies with a shrug.

"He needs to learn his place, or the guys are gonna turn on him,"

Morrow adds. "I don't want my head of PT ribbing my teammates in front of me. That's not gonna fly."

"And hey—Sanford," Novy mutters, stepping around the table to stand by me.

I glance over at him, trying to control my breathing, giving nothing away.

"The point here is that if you ever *do* want to tell us anything . . . you can. You or Compton. Because this is a team. It might be a new team, but the way we see it, we'd like to stick around a while."

"Yeah, totally," Morrow adds. "Team means family."

"We want a good atmosphere here," Novy goes on. "We don't want bullshit and drama. Jokes is one thing. We all love jokes. Chirping on a guy for being gay is another," he adds, his face solemn. "You just tell us which end is up, and we'll make sure the next guy who chirps you is the last guy."

I nod, surprisingly touched by this unexpected show of support.

"So . . . you telling us anything right now?" Novy asks, one dark brow raised.

I shake my head. "No," I mutter, trying not to let disappointment lace my words. "There's nothing. Jake and I are just friends."

"Best friends, right?" Morrow adds with a grin. "Live-in best friends who sleep in separate beds but finish each other's sentences. Total Bert and Ernie situation, right?"

I roll my eyes as he laughs.

"And if Jake ever pulls his head out of his ass and realizes you're a catch and a half?" Novy teases. "You still gonna be just friends then, Bert?"

I shake my head. "Listen, assholes. If Jake and I ever become more than live-in best friends, you two will be the first to know, okay? For now, I'll be sucking my own dick. But only if I get through with ironing all these first, and you're both distracting me."

Novy steps forward, slinging an arm around my shoulders. "As long as you're distracted, come help us find Compton. We're gonna lay the heavy on him too over breakfast."

"And make sure he gets the tab," Morrow adds.

Flipping the iron off, I follow after them. I won't be able to focus until I deal with this. I need to talk to Jake. But first I want to find

Rachel. She's the one with the unparalleled experience handling online gossip. She'll know what to do.

"Hey," I call. "Have either of you seen Doctor Price this morning? I uhh . . . need to ask her something about an order shipment."

"Yeah, we saw her when we came down," Novy replies, leading the way out of the room.

"She was at the coffee cart looking cozy with some guy," Morrow adds, his eyes on his phone as we walk towards the stairs.

I halt in the middle of the hallway. "What guy?"

Morrow just shrugs, eyes still on his phone. "I don't know, some hunky guy."

"He was a hunk, huh?" Novy says with a laugh. "God, not you too. Am I the only straight man left on the Rays D-line?"

"What? He was all tatted and cool." At my blank stare Morrow quickly adds, "I mean, you're tatted and cool too, Sanny. Don't think we're out here tryna replace you."

"Yeah, Snuffy. You're the coolest guy we know," Novy teases. "Hot Doc wishes her arm candy was as cool as you."

Well, if I thought I had no jealousy where Rachel was concerned, that just went out the goddamn window. A tatted cool hunky guy is acting as my girl's arm candy? Forget Jake. He can take care of himself. I'm officially tracking a hurricane.

85
RACHEL

"**H**arrison!" I run down the length of the stands in front of the practice ice, not caring when I startle a pair of figure skaters working on a lift.

My brother and I have been circling each other like mice in a maze for almost ten minutes. I finally just told him to stand still and wait. So, there he stands, with his colorfully tatted forearms in the pockets of his jeans. He's not a big, hulking athlete like my guys. He's my height and build, with my same dark hair and brown eyes.

I rush to him, throwing my arms around his neck as I bury my face against his shoulder. "I'm so glad you're here," I say. The warm, woodsy scent of his Tom Ford cologne acts like a security blanket, instantly easing my worries and fears.

It will be okay. Everything will be okay. Harrison is here.

He hugs me back, his arms wrapped tight around my waist, as his face turns slightly to kiss my cheek. "Hey, Lem."

I sigh at his use of my family nickname. Daddy came up with it when we were ten. Rachel became Rachello, which became Limoncello, which somehow morphed into Lemonhead. Now it's just Lem.

I pull back, holding on to his brightly tatted forearms. "You wanna tell me what the heck you're doing here?"

He stares daggers at me. "You really gonna stand here and ask me that?"

"Harrison—"

"Oh, we're doing this," he growls. "My twin is not gonna fall off the face of the fucking earth, dodging my calls for *weeks*—did you know Somchai adopted another goddamn cat?"

"What?" I gasp. "But you hate cats—"

"I know I fucking hate cats. And *he* knows that too. But his auntie came by last week with another sob story about finding kittens in a box outside the back of her restaurant. Apparently, she found homes for all but one. So now I have a peaches and cream kitten named Apricot and she sleeps on my Hermès house shoes."

"How is Oreo taking it?" I murmur eyes wide.

"He's fine—wait—fuck." He drops his hands sharply away from me. "No way. You are *not* turning this around on me you sneaky little weasel."

Damn. I had him on the ropes. One more well-placed gasp and he was about to unload two months of life details at me while I nodded and hummed. That would have bought me at least another thirty minutes before he turned the interrogation lamp back around on me.

I'm not ready to come clean, not even to Harrison. It still feels too soon. The guys and I, we're not ready for people to know our business. What even are we? What do I call them? Are they my boy-friends? My partners? What do they call each other? Is this a united front yet? Without knowing the answers to these questions, it feels like a betrayal to share our business with outsiders.

Not that Harrison is an outsider. He's a Price. He'll take my secrets to the grave and beyond. But he's not one of *us*. He's not one of my guys.

And that's when the startling truth hits me . . . they're my guys now. Ilmari, Jake, and Caleb. Not Harrison. Not dad. For the first time in my life, my inner circle has shifted. Tears stinging my eyes. Harrison isn't my guy anymore. It hurts me more than I ever thought it could. I feel like I'm being cleaved. He's my twin and my brother and my best friend in the world, but he's not my person anymore.

I sniff back my tears, shaking my head. "Harrison," I whimper.

Slowly he nods, his hand lifting to gently cup my cheek. "It's okay, Lem. You know you can tell me anything." I cover my face with both my hands, and he sighs, stepping in to rub my back with a gentle hand. "Let's start with his name."

I choke on a laugh. "God, I'm a mess. I don't know why I'm so emo-tional about this."

He gives me a sympathetic look. "Maybe because you're in love with him and you're afraid of my disapproval. That's why you've been hiding out, right? You fell for a player? We all saw the footage from the game. Dad got alerts last night from Steve and the PR team. They've been in overdrive covering your crazy ass."

I sigh. So that's why Poppy knew, and I didn't. My number is untraceable. All press contact with the family goes through daddy's PR team. If the press is trying to get to me, they'll have to go through him . . . and now Poppy.

"Daddy knows?"

"Why do you think he put me on a chartered plane at the ass crack of dawn?"

"You flew out from Seattle?" I say with a confused frown.

"No, I was up in New York City again. See, you've been such a little hermit crab you didn't even know where I was. What if the apocalypse hit and we had to find each other, huh? You'd go get yourself lost somewhere out in Oklahoma not knowing I was in the opposite direction."

I huff a weak laugh. "So, daddy sent you down here to chastise me?"

"*I* sent me down here to *check* on you," he corrects. "I just used dad's plane," he adds. "Come on, Lem. You know how this works. Price family first. We stick together. Your shit is about to hit the fan and the Prices have to get organized. We need to have the story straight. And I wanna meet the guy . . . or is it guys," he adds with a smirk. "The gossip sites have been having fun speculating wildly. Are you down here juggling two guys, Lemon Cake?"

He's right. Price family first. Or at least, Price family *came* first. It's not fair to leave them in the dark, trying to clean up one more mess they didn't make. "Actually, it's three."

"Three o'clock?" Harrison says, checking his watch.

"Three guys."

He stills, glancing up slowly. "You wanna say that again?"

I hold his gaze. "I've fallen for three guys, Harrison. I'm in love with them, and they're in love with me . . . and two of them are in love with each other. It's . . ." I shrug, unable to come up with the right words to describe what we are. Perfect seems trite, even though it fits. We're a perfect mess of messy perfection. I love what we are. I want to protect it, keep it hidden and safe. But the sexy, hockey-playing cats are out of the bag now. Harrison knows.

"Oh . . . shit," he murmurs, eyes wide as saucers. "Okay, so umm . . . fuck." He lets out a heavy exhale. "Right, then. Let's start with their names."

"Let's start with coffee," I counter.

He nods, dragging a hand through his dark hair. "Yeah . . . coffee. Good idea."

86
CALEB

"**M**ars!" I bark, crossing the gym towards the row of exercise bikes.

He's sitting on the bike at the end, phone in hand, sweat pouring down his face. He glances up sharply at the sound of my voice. "What?"

"Where's Jake?" I say, trying to control the hint of panic in my voice. I haven't found Rachel and her mystery man either.

"No idea," he mutters, eyes back on his phone.

"Well, where's Rachel then?"

"Office," he replies.

"No, the fuck she isn't. Apparently, she's been spotted around the facility arm-in-arm with a handsome, dark-haired, tattooed man."

The asshole has the audacity to smirk, his gaze dropping from my face to my tatted arm. "Is it not possible they're gossiping about *you*? They're all talking about your jersey trick from last night—"

"How can I be the hot guy she's hanging on when I'm right *here*, trapped in this time loop of a conversation with *you*," I growl. "Are you not the least bit curious to know why our girl is flirting with another guy?"

His brows lower over his blue eyes as he glares at me. "Why don't you speak louder. I don't think they heard you at the beach."

"Fine. I'll go find her myself!" I stomp off, determined to do another circuit of the practice facility when he calls out.

"Caleb, wait!"

I turn to see him unfolding himself from his exercise bike, grabbing a sweat towel to dab at his face. "You're coming?"

"Only to keep you from trouble," he replies. "I'm sure there's a perfectly reasonable explanation for what Rachel is doing. And she won't like this jealousy," he adds, looking me solemnly up and down. "Pack it away."

I take a deep breath, my frustration simmering. But fuck, he's right. I know he's right. I don't like this feeling. I'm not this guy. I don't get jealous. I take another breath.

"Better?"

Slowly, I nod.

"I would check the coffee cart," he says, slinging the sweat towel over his shoulder.

"She was already spotted there," I reply, turning on my heel to head for the doors. It's an odd sensation, but my limp suddenly feels worse, as if my body is betraying me, trying to slow me down before I make a total ass of myself.

But I'm not worried. I have Mars to hold me back. He'll keep me from doing anything truly embarrassing, like dropping to my bad knee and begging Rachel not to leave us for a broodier, sexier man.

We make our way through the practice facility, out of the Rays-only area into the large, glass-walled atrium. The coffee cart is hopping with a long line of figure skating moms all sporting their matching hairdos, little puffy vests zipped over their designer sweaters.

I may as well be invisible as all eyes focus on Mars. A few eager kids come rushing over. He runs interference, saying hello and shaking some hands as I peer around the room. I don't see her anywhere. And we've got to get out of here before we get swarmed by fans all wanting a piece of Mars.

"She likes to watch the figure skating," he says over the heads of the kids. "She'll take breaks and sit up in the stands with a coffee."

"How do you know that?" I say with a raised brow.

"Because I like to watch her," he replies with a shrug.

I laugh, grabbing him by the arm. "Okay, Mr. Kinnunen, time to go. It's time for your Swedish seaweed wrap and hot stone massage. Say bye, kids. Wish him luck against Toronto."

"Bye, Mr. Kinnunen!" they call.

"Later, Mars!"

He lets me pull him away, both of us moving towards the open doors that lead into the main practice arena. The rink is packed. Kids run drills while a few adults with whistles try to control the chaos.

"She's not here," Mars says before I even get the chance to look.

"You're sure?"

"Do you see her?" he replies with a frown.

"Well, not yet, but—"

"Do you feel her?"

I blink up at him. "What—*feel* her? Like telekinesis or something?"

With a sigh, he grabs me by the shoulders and turns me to face him.

"Mars, what—"

"Close your eyes and breathe," he mutters. "*Do it.*"

I close my eyes, but my breath sits like a rock in my chest.

"Stop overthinking all the time," he soothes. "Stop thinking. Just *stop* . . . and breathe." He exaggerates a big inhale letting it out.

I take a shallow breath, letting it out.

"Again."

I take another deeper breath.

"Good. Now, open your eyes."

I open them, looking up into his serious face.

"You know Rachel," he mutters. "You love Rachel. She's part of you, yes?"

I nod.

"Yes?" he presses.

"Yes," I repeat.

"Then tell me if you feel her here. Don't think. Don't look. Just feel. Is she here?"

I keep my eyes on him as I take another breath, letting myself sink into a quieter headspace. I think of how I feel in those lazy moments on the couch and she's in my arms, the way I feel when she enters the kitchen. I'm not a touchy person, but I try for her. I want her touches. I think of the way my body lights up where she looks at me. It's pulled to her.

I huff a laugh, shaking my head. "Well, that's a neat little magic trick."

"Is she here?" he repeats.

I roll my eyes. "No, Mars. She's not here."

"Then we keep looking," he says, turning on his heel. "The figure skaters are at the next rink anyway."

Now he's in the lead, moving down the hall to the smaller rink.

This one doesn't have the plexiglass up. The moment I step into the room, my gaze turns sharply left, drawn to her.

And there she is, sitting in the stands about a third of the way down, snuggled in next to a dark-haired guy in a black t-shirt and jeans with tatted forearms. They're sipping on coffees, their bodies turned in towards one another, wholly oblivious to the pair of teenagers skating on the ice.

Yeah, this guy has to go. I growl low in my throat, stomping forward.

"Caleb," Mars says in that warning voice.

As if she can sense us too, Rachel's head pops up. Her eyes look pink and puffy, like she's been crying.

Oh, what the fuck. Whoever this guy is, he's fucking dead.

She murmurs something to him, and he sits back on the bench with a cocky smirk, watching us approach. And because he has a death wish, he slings his arm over her shoulder and gives me a wink.

"Rachel, who the fuck is this guy?"

Well, shit. The words are apparently out of my mouth before I've even had a chance to finish thinking them. And she's already turned to him, shoving him off, saying something I can't hear. Mars is right behind me, his big hand on my shoulder.

The cooler, slimmer version of me has the nerve to laugh, elbowing her in the side as he leans forward and says, "I'm her husband. Who the fuck are you?"

87
RACHEL

"*H*arrison!" I cry, slapping him in the chest. God, he's such a little instigator. Between him and Caleb, I don't know who is worse. At least we're alone, which is why I dragged Harrison in here in the first place. The next closest person to us is the figure skating coach standing down at the far end of the rink messing with the Bluetooth speakers.

My idiot twin cracks himself up, laughing at Caleb's expense. Mars stands behind Cay, one hand on his shoulder, as if he needs physical restraining. Before I can choose between going to soothe Caleb or pushing Harrison from the top of the bleachers, a new voice enters the fray.

"Oh, hooooly shit! Is it twin o'clock up in here?"

All four of us turn to see Jake walking down the rink from the opposite direction, a huge smile on his face. He climbs up the bleachers, holding out a hand to my brother. "Harrison, right? So great to meet you, man."

Taken slightly aback, Harrison holds out his hand and lets Jake shake it.

"How did you know we were here?" says Caleb.

"Mars texted me," Jake replies. "Not a moment too soon. Novy and Morrow were being super weird tryna get me to buy them breakfast."

Caleb goes still, his expression carefully veiled.

Jake turns all his attention back to my brother. "God, you know, I bet you get this a lot, but you look *just* like your dad," he says, glancing between us. "You're right, Seattle. You make a very handsome dude," he adds at Harrison with a wink.

"I'm happily married," Harrison replies, extracting his hand from Jake's grip.

"You're her twin," Caleb mutters.

Recovering his snark, Harrison smirks at him. "Yeah. And you must be the Tweedle Dumbass of the group."

Jake snorts as he plops down on the bleachers a row down from us. "Tweedle Dumbass . . ." He glances over at Caleb. "I think I might like that more than Snuffy—"

"Don't you fucking dare," Caleb mutters, crossing his arms over his chest.

"And you must be the Swede," says Harrison, his eyes now on Ilmari.

"Finn," Mars and I say at the same time.

"What did I say?" Harrison says, glancing at me.

"You said Swede," I reply. "That's a whole other country, H."

"Right," he laughs. "Well . . . these are the guys, right? What are you calling them—your boyfriends? Your squad? Your pussy posse?"

Jake snorts, his mouth open like he's about to speak.

"Don't," I snap. "The first of you to refer to our relationship as the 'pussy posse' will be the first voted off the island. Agreed?"

"Agreed," Jake replies quickly.

Caleb nods.

Ilmari does nothing. But hell will literally freeze over before he says the words 'pussy' and 'posse' in the same sentence.

"So . . . you're the one-night stand in Seattle," Harrison says, pointing at Jake.

Jake laughs. "Guilty. But I had nothing to do with her leaving your fancy brunch—oh, and hey—happy wedding," he says, tapping Harrison's leg with his fist.

"And you're the dildo at the airport guy," Harrison adds, pointing at Caleb.

Jake chokes on another laugh as Ilmari glances down at Caleb. "You're what guy?"

"It's a long story," I say at the same time that Caleb looks right back at him and says, "Hurricane has a foot long squid tentacle dildo. Ask nicely, and she'll put it in your ass."

Ilmari's eyes go wide as the other three laugh.

"And we've already established you're the Swede," Harrison says.

"Finn," Ilmari, Jake, and I say at once.

"Harrison, stop teasing them, or I'll call Som right now and tell him to rescue three more cats," I threaten, giving him my best hard stare.

"Fine," he mutters.

I hadn't gotten very far into my story before the guys walked up, so

Harrison is still flying a bit blind. He knows the basics, which is that we all sort of stumbled our way into this twisty pretzel of a relationship.

"How long are you in town?" Jake asks him.

"That remains to be seen," Harrison replies. "The jet is on standby."

Jake snorts. "The jet? What, like your family has a private jet you keep fueled?"

Harrison and I just look at him.

"Well . . . fuck," he mutters. "Your family has a private jet."

"Kinda," I reply with a shrug. "H was worried about me. I've been flying solo since I moved down here, which is breaking major rules."

"You haven't been solo, babe," Jake replies, sitting forward on the bench to take my hand. "I know you've missed your brother, but I hope you haven't felt alone—"

"Jake, *no*," I soothe. "It's just . . . Price Family rules, you know? For so long now, we've only had each other. They sensed trouble brewing with me and Harrison knew it was time to regroup. The Prices stick together. Always."

"Are we the trouble brewing?" says Caleb, still glancing warily at my twin.

I know trusting people is tough for him. He'll do his best because Harrison is my brother, but for as much as H talks a big game about hating cats, he practically is one himself. And so is Caleb. I have a feeling they'll get along like oil and water . . . like cats in a bag. At least for the first little while.

But I can just imagine them a few Christmases from now, thick as thieves as they plot out a devious plan to make all the coffee mint flavored. Harrison will tolerate Jake. He'll be clinically polite to Ilmari. But he'll love Caleb. They'll text incessantly, even as they pretend they barely know each other. Harrison will help Caleb put together a grilling cookbook for Jake for Christmas. He'll pretend like it's no big deal and Caleb will shrug when Jake thanks him for it. Meanwhile, I'll be a blubbering mess.

My breath catches as that beautiful vision of our shared future pops like a soap bubble, leaving my heart pounding. God, I want to stay in the vision longer. I want to see the boys up at my family's ranch in Montana. I want to know that my parents love and accept them, accept *us*. I want to see them laughing as we open presents,

Somchai and my mom busy in the kitchen making French toast for breakfast. Jake will finally wear daddy down and convince him to give him guitar lessons. He'll learn four chords and give up. Then the guys will all drag me out ice skating on the frozen lake.

"Rakas?" Ilmari is looking at me, his blue eyes soft.

I blink, swallowing the ball of emotion in my throat, and glance around at all of them. I missed something. They're all looking to me. "What?"

"Your brother asked what time you finish with work today," Ilmari replies.

I clear my throat. "Um, I'm finished now. I was just waiting to get a ride home."

Harrison snorts. "Still a little chicken shit behind the wheel?"

"I'm finished," says Ilmari. "I will take you."

I glance to Jake and Cay.

"I've got hours yet," Caleb mutters. "Longer the longer I stand here."

"I'll give you my keys before we go," Jake says. "I'll ride back with Mars and Rach."

Caleb looks to me, giving me a nod before he walks off.

I turn to Harrison. "Will you stay the night?"

"Of course, he will," says Jake, getting to his feet. "He's coming out to the house. I was already texting a grocery delivery order as we've been sitting here. You like seafood, Harrison?"

"Yeah," Harrison says, his tone hesitant.

"Great, I'm making a low country seafood boil tonight—shrimp and andouille sausage, corn, onion, potatoes—the works. It'll be delicious."

"Jake is a great cook," I add.

"Oh, shit—that's right," Jake says with a laugh. "You're a chef. Well, I don't have a Michelin star, but I do okay."

"I'm sure it will be fine," Harrison replies.

I stand up, taking a deep breath. This is fine. My twin is unexpectedly here and he's coming out to the beach house where I live with two and a half men and a dog. The internet is speculating wildly about the status of my relationships, I have an NHL public relations manager in 'manage it' mode, and the fate of four people's careers now hang in the balance.

This is totally fine. That's what the cartoon animals always say right before the anvil falls from the sky, right? This is all going to be just fine.

88
RACHEL

"**A**re you well?" Ilmari murmurs, one hand brushing my hip as we stand at the sink washing dishes.

I nod, my hands in the soapy water scrubbing a plate before I hand it over to him.

He takes it silently. "You're worried."

"Of course, I am," I reply, not daring to look at him. "This is unsustainable. We all know it."

As soon as Harrison stepped out onto the back patio to take a call with his restaurant, Caleb filled us all in with the CliffsNotes version of what happened in the laundry room this morning with Novikov and Morrow. And I let the guys know what happened with Poppy in my office.

Jake whipped out his phone, instantly going online to check out the gossip for himself. He's been in 'minimize it' mode ever since. 'This is fine, babe,' he's said at least ten times. 'It's no big deal.' He said it all the way out the door, determined to go get us all ice cream, which apparently is his cure for any crisis or malady.

No big deal. Right. NHL players are spreading the rumor that Jake and Caleb are finally out as gay. Meanwhile, the celebrity tabloids are saying we're in a tragic love triangle. The gossip is only finding fuel with the puck bunnies, no doubt thanks to delightful creatures like Aspen Albright. In less than 24 hours, they've apparently spread the rumor that I spurned Jake's proposal in favor of Caleb. They're calling me crazy for ditching a player for an equipment manager, saying all kinds of horrible, disparaging things about Caleb and his position.

The only one who seems to have escaped the fray so far is Ilmari—thank god. He doesn't need this attention now. Not when the FIHA scouts are still here.

"I think you need to get some distance," I murmur, still not looking at him.

"What does that mean?"

Letting out a shaky breath, I glance up. "You haven't been dragged down in this yet. You can still break away."

"Break away?"

"Please, Mars," I press, holding his gaze. "I know how hard you've worked to keep your privacy intact. But nothing about me is private. I wish to god that it were," I add with all the sincerity I can muster. "But I never had that luxury."

He's quiet for a minute before saying, "What does distance mean, Rachel?"

I flinch, hating his use of my real name. "Mars, this doesn't have to be your fight," I say. "You've got a career to think about. Not just your NHL contract, but the Olympics, remember? If this blows up any bigger, if you get pulled into it . . ." I shake my head, tears in my eyes.

"I'm not afraid of celebrity magazines," he mutters.

"It's not the tabloids that should worry you, Mars. It's the NHL press. There's a whole world of hockey fans out there that won't understand us. They'll get vicious and cruel and seek to tear us down. Ask Harrison if you don't believe me," I say, pointing out the glass doors to where we can see him pacing on his phone. "It's already started with Jake and Cay—all these rumors about them being gay. And it's not just blogs and media hacks, Mars. It's other players. You heard the gossip this morning. You had to shut it down."

"The rookies need to learn to keep their mouths shut," he mutters darkly.

"This is bigger than a few chirping rookies and you know it. If the gossip gets bad enough, the FIHA will pass on you, Mars. They'll pick a safer option, someone not tied to an unstoppable human storm of bad press."

"So . . . are you telling me to leave?"

His tone is tearing me apart. "I'm not telling you to do anything. And I don't want you to leave I—*god*—" I turn away from him, shoving my hands back into the soapy water, scrubbing furiously at the next plate.

I can feel his eyes on me, daring me to look at him.

I'm saved by the front door. The alarm chirps as the door opens and closes.

"Hey, babe, they didn't have the sorbet you like, but we found this almond milk stuff!" Jake calls from the entryway. "It's got cookie dough bites and I thought—whoa—what the hell is going on?" He steps into the kitchen, Caleb following just behind, with Poseidon hot on their heels. Their worried gazes dart between me and Ilmari.

Caleb drops the bag of ice creams on the island. "What happened?"

"Rachel would like for me to leave," Ilmari mutters.

"What the fuck?" Jake gasp. "Rach—"

"Kulta, *no*," I say, grabbing his arm. "I'm trying to *protect* you—"

"You're trying to manage me," he growls, pulling away. "You're trying to make decisions for me. I make my *own* decisions, Rachel."

"But I can't bear it," I whisper, shaking my head. "I cannot *bear* the idea of ruining your life. Of stripping something from you that you've spent a lifetime protecting. You want privacy, Ilmari. You want hockey to be the story of your life, not who you're dating. You want to play in the Olympics—"

"I want *you*," he counters, grabbing me by the shoulders. The heat of his anger crackles like a fire. We're both panting, my head tipped back as I gaze into his stormy blue eyes.

"Mars," I whisper, trying to put everything I feel into the word.

"Don't call me that again," he growls. "*You* don't call me that ever again. They can, but not you."

I gasp, confused. "Mars, what—"

"That is *not* my name," he shouts. "My partner will call me by *my* name. Say it."

I jolt in his arms, heart pounding. "Ilmari," I say on a breath.

"Say it again."

"Ilmari."

"Who am I to you, Rakas?" he asks, his voice lowering, deepening with such great feeling. "When people ask you who I am, what will you say?"

I lift my arms, pressing my hands against his chest, my right hand splaying over his heart. It pounds furiously beneath my hand. "You want control? You want a say in what happens next? Then tell me what *you* want. Who do you want to be to me—"

"I want you to stop being so damn afraid all the time," he shouts, both hands cupping my face, holding me captive. "You can't hide away all your life, Rakas. You can't stop the bad things from happening—to yourself, to your brother, to any of us. I know because I've lived the same as you, trying to keep my life small. Really all I did was build myself a cage. And then I trapped myself inside that cage and told myself the bars weren't real."

His words split me open, digging down to the hidden truths I keep buried so deep. Because he's right. I've let my fears become a cage. Fear of failure. Fear of losing control—of myself, of the narrative around me, of my success. Fear of the unknown. Fear of disappointing my family. Fear of always being known as the worthless, talentless Price.

"I am afraid," I admit, tears slipping down my cheeks. "I think I've been afraid all my life."

He nods, raising a large thumb to brush away my tears. "Then that is what I want, Rakas. I want to be the one to carry the burden of your fears. Your doubt, your worry, your insecurity—lay them all on my shoulders. I am strong enough. I will not bend. I will not break. I will carry them for you so you can be free, mun leijona."

More tears fall as I wrap a hand around his wrist, leaning into his touch. "What does that mean?"

"It means 'my lioness,'" he replies. "For that is what you are to me, and have always been: a fearless, dark-haired lioness. Look at yourself through my eyes, Rakas. Through Jake's eyes. Through Caleb's eyes."

I shake my head. I want to be strong enough. I want to believe I could be this person they all see.

"I see you, mun leijona. They see you too," he adds, gesturing at Caleb and Jake. "You would brave any danger for those you love. Climb any mountain, leap from any clifftop. A love like yours is wild and dangerous. You need men who will not seek to harness you or break your spirit. You need men who will *protect* you. Who will provide a safe space for you to love as freely as your heart will allow. We are those men."

Jake and Caleb step around the island, coming to stand beside him. I'm fully crying now, ugly tears streaming down my face as I reach for them both, my hands clinging to their t-shirts. Caleb's hand goes to my shoulder, while Jake cups my face, gazing down at me so tenderly.

"Place yourself in our care, and we will *never* stop fighting for you," Ilmari says. "We will never stray, never waver. We will seek no exit. Love us and watch how we love you in return. One family. One unit. Unbreakable."

I look to Jake, waiting for him to speak.

His hands brush gently against the soft skin of my cheeks. "You know I love you, Rachel. I may not say it as fancily as Mr. European Accent over here—which, thanks for that, by the way," he adds at Ilmari with a glare. "You don't speak ten words together for weeks. But then the two times you *do* speak, you make speeches that should be printed out and sold with a free at-home pregnancy test—"

"Focus, Jake," Caleb mutters with a shake of his head

"Right—shit—" He turns back to me, and I can't help but smile at his antics. "Baby, I love you," he says, sobering the mood. "You're my whole fucking world. But keeping this quiet is killing me. I'm so done. I wanna be public with you—them too," he adds. "I'm all in. I wanna own this story and run with it. I want to get out ahead of it and show all the doubters that this *can* work."

But then he's glancing warily at Caleb. "What do you think? You're the most private one of all of us. What we're doing here might get pretty intense. It'll drag you into a harsh spotlight . . ."

I face Caleb, taking his hand. "Jake is way underselling it," I say. "The press will get worse before it ever gets better," I explain. "Since we'll be such a novelty, the scrutiny will last twice as long too. They'll hunt down ghosts from our pasts—exes, family, friends, former teammates. They'll tell wild stories. It'll be awful," I admit, heart in my throat.

"You'd all be risking your jobs every day," I go on. "Family might turn on you, friends will distance themselves. Teammates, coaches, owners—hell the whole League might turn on you." I hold my gaze on Ilmari and Jake. "Everything you worked a lifetime to achieve . . . they can take it from you. With enough bad press, they'll bury us alive."

"Our jobs are ours to risk," Ilmari replies. "If we say it's worth the risk, you have to put your trust in us that we will handle it."

"I'm not worth it," I whisper, tears stinging my eyes again. "I'm not worth this—"

Caleb steps in, grabbing me by the shoulders. "Enough. Alright? Don't you dare fucking say that again. Rachel, this is not just about you, or haven't you realized that yet? We're not risking it all for you. We're risking it for *this*," he says gesturing around. "*Us*. We may call you a queen when you're riding our cocks, and god knows we'll treat you like one every day for the rest of your fucking life if you'll just shut up and let us, but this is a democracy. We're all in this for our own reasons." He glances at the guys. "I say we vote."

I gasp. "Vote?"

"Yeah. We vote on going public," he explains. "No more hiding out. No more secrets," he adds, holding my gaze, his double meaning clear. Oh god, he's going to do it. He's ready to tell Jake how he feels.

"You know my vote," says Jake. "I've been all in since Seattle. I'll go on all my social media platforms right now and shout it from the rooftops—"

"No," Caleb says quickly. "We get through tomorrow's game. The Finnish scouts are still here for Mars. And tomorrow is Toronto," he adds.

Jake's gaze darkens. "Don't fucking remind me."

"We get through tomorrow," Caleb says again. "Then we make a plan." He glances around at all of us. "Agreed? No one says a word until after tomorrow."

Ilmari nods, his arms crossed over his chest.

"Fine," says Jake.

Caleb looks to me. "Hurricane?"

I nod, taking a deep breath. After tomorrow. Meaning this is our last night of peace and quiet. The calm before the storm. "Let's all go to the beach," I say. "Let's walk under the full moon, just us and the ocean."

"And Harrison?" Jake asks, glancing over his shoulder to where my brother is still outside, gesticulating wildly while he shouts into the phone, no doubt making a chef cry.

I smile. "He can watch Sy til we get back. Right now, I just wanna be with my guys."

89
JAKE

Game day. We're playing the Toronto Maple Leafs and I'm a goddamn mess. I'm always a mess when I play Toronto. It's psychological. What the fuck ever, I'm not in the mood to lie down on a couch and spill all my trauma. There's a job to do, and I'm going to do it.

Harrison is leaving town. Rachel's on the way over to the airport with him to say goodbye before he hops on their daddy's private jet. I'm trying not to be jealous of her. Amy had to cancel her holiday plans, meaning it might be summer before I see her again. It's too fucking long.

Unable to resist, I pull my phone from my pocket and call her. As if she was waiting for it, she answers on the first ring. "Hey, bro."

"Hey, Am." I don't know what else to say. I just need to hear her voice.

"You play Toronto today," she says into my silence.

"Yeah. On my way to the arena now."

"How's Cay?"

How the fuck should I know? He's impossible to read. Meanwhile, I'm an open book that wears everything right on my sleeve. He's already told me to relax three times this morning. "He's fine," I say.

Amy sighs into the phone. "Does it ever get any easier?"

I check my lane as I move over. "No."

"Wanna talk about it? Or we could talk about your new girl—"

"Am, I think I might be bi," I blurt, cutting her off. "Or like . . . I don't even fucking know. Queer maybe. I hate labels. And I don't like dudes."

"Okay," she says gently. "So, you don't feel bi, but you think you might be? Why?"

I huff, making another turn one-handed, my left hand holding the phone. "You know why."

"Caleb," she replies. "It's always been Cay. He's your lobster."

I shake my head. Everything with Amy is either a *Friends* reference or a movie quote. "I'm not gay," I say again.

"But the news is saying you are," she murmurs. "My phone notifications went crazy the other day."

"Yeah," I mutter. "And there'll be a whole lot more where that came from soon."

"What do you mean? Jake, is everything okay? Is this about the girl? The rock star's daughter?"

"Amy, she's Seattle Girl."

She gasps. "Oh my god . . . why didn't you *say* anything?" she cries. "God, how did Caleb take it? I can't even imagine how upset he was. Oh god—is that what you mean? Is this an Edward-Jacob-Bella situation? Am I gonna have to get on a plane and come tit punch a rocker chick for breaking my brother's heart—"

"Amy, no," I say over her. "No, it's not like that. It's . . ." I take a deep breath. "Okay, are you sitting down?"

"Jake, you're scaring me . . ."

"We're together," I say. "The three of us. We—she—it's not a love triangle, and it's not doomed or scary. It's fucking perfect. Amy, I've never been happier."

"You're together," she repeats. "The three of you? Like you're with her and you're with him and—"

"He's with her," I add. "Yeah, and there's a third guy. You know Mars Kinnunen, the goalie?"

"You're with your goalie too?"

"No," I say on a laugh. "I mean, he's with her, but he's not with us. I mean—he's with us in the sense that we all live together but . . . I feel like I'm not explaining this well."

"He's your metamour," she replies.

"My meta-what?"

"Metamour," she repeats with a laugh. "It's the polyamorous term for the platonic partner of your partner."

"And how the hell do you know about metamours?"

"Because I'm a cultured and culturally sensitive globe-trotting scientist," she replies. "And I've been known to dabble in polyam too."

I sit up straight as an arrow, nearly dropping my phone. "What the fuck, Amy. You serious? Be so freaking for real right now."

"Don't pop a lung," she laughs. "Remember you have a game to play tonight."

"Amy . . ."

She huffs. "I don't tell you everything about me, Jake. I experimented in college, and I've done some dating around recently. You know, filling that lonely void in my life. Nothing too crazy," she adds. "Not like moving in with my goalie, my equipment manager, and my sports medicine doctor. How's the sex, by the way? I bet it's unreal," she teases.

I fight to suppress the memories so my dick doesn't get hard while I'm on the phone with my sister. "Amy, the scream that I could scream in this fucking car right now."

She giggles. "That good, huh?"

I groan, fighting off the image of Rachel's tits bouncing in my face as she rides my cock, Mars taking her from behind. "Best sex of my life. They slay me dead every time. I'm never going back. Never. They're it for me."

"I'm happy for you, Jake. And I can't wait to meet your Seattle Girl." I sense the hesitation in her voice. I'm ready for it when she says, "But . . . how will all this work? I can't imagine your fans will be enlightened enough to appreciate the nuances of your sudden conversion to queer polyamory."

"We're working on it," I reply.

"You're working on it? What does that mean?"

"It means we have a plan, and we're gonna come out, and it's gonna be fine."

"Wait, come out as in like . . . *you're* coming out?"

"Well, I can't very well let them go public without me," I say. "We're living in *my* house, Amy."

"Do you want them to go public without you?"

"Fuck no," I growl. "I'm in this. All the way in. Til death do us part in, you feel me?"

"Yeah . . . but is that just with Rachel? You're all in with Rachel and you approve of her having other lovers and you all cohabitate . . . or you're all in with Cay and your goalie too?"

"Mars is straight," I say quickly. "And he's not my type. I told you; I don't like guys."

She sighs. "So where does that leave Caleb?"

"He's mine." The words come out on instinct, and I find there's nothing left to be said. It's the truth. Caleb Sanford is mine. I want him to be mine in all ways. But I'm afraid. I'm holding back. This weight I carry, this fucking trauma that eats at me, it'll suffocate me if I let it.

"You need to talk to him, Jake."

"No. Not on Toronto day. I can't."

"Maybe today is the best day," she counters. "At some point, you've gotta let this go. I'm sure if you'd just talk to Caleb, he'd say the same."

I sit in silence, the only sound the clicking of my turn signal. "I'm afraid," I admit.

"Afraid of what?"

"Afraid I won't be enough. Afraid they won't need me like I need them. I can't tell Cay how I feel. I can't carve out another piece of my fucking heart and hand it to him to hold. Not when she's already got a piece."

"Why can't you give him a piece too?"

Fuck, now tears are stinging my eyes. I fight them back, admitting my deep dark truths to my twin. "What if he doesn't love me the way I love him? What if he just wants to be my friend—"

"He loves you, Jake."

I shake my head. "No, he's so damn hard to read."

"Jake, *listen* to me," she says, voice firm. "Caleb Sanford is in love with you. Ask him and he'll tell you."

"I don't deserve it," I whisper. "I don't deserve the good things that happen to me—"

"Jake, *stop*—"

"He deserved it more," I say at last, one tear falling as my deepest truth spills out. "He was better, faster, stronger—"

"Jake—"

"I don't get to have it all, Amy. That's not the way life fucking works. We're not meant to have all our dreams come true. It's too easy. Too unfair."

"So . . . what?" she huffs, clearly fed up with my bullshit pity party.

"You're just going to punish yourself, and Caleb in the process? One shitty thing happens, and now you're going to resign yourself to a lifetime of almost-happiness? That's idiotic, Jake. And it's wholly unfair to Caleb. *Talk* to him. Do it today. Put a period at the end of this awful chapter and turn the page."

I sigh, pulling into my assigned spot in the parking garage, and cut the engine. I sit there, staring at the grey concrete pylon in front of my car. "Why are you so fucking smart?"

"Because I resorbed half your brain cells in the womb."

I snort, shaking my head. "That's not how science works."

"How would you know, dummy? You whack a piece of rubber with a stick for a living."

I laugh. "Yeah, big robot brain scientist girl can't even heat up a Hot Pocket."

"That happened exactly once and that microwave was on the fritz," she counters with an indignant huff.

We sit in silence for another minute, just sharing the call waves.

"I love you, Amy," I murmur. "I miss you."

"Jake, you have no idea. Send me pictures more often, yeah? And I want to video chat with your new girl soon. And I want to meet the goalie properly too."

"Come home," I say, sitting forward, one arm folded over top of my steering wheel. "I'll buy the tickets. Do whatever you need to do on your end, just . . . I need to see you. I need you to meet Rachel."

"Jake," she sighs, ready to tell me no.

"What we're about to do is really fucking scary, Amy," I say. "Mom and dad won't get it and—fuck—" I sigh, dropping my forehead to my arm. "I'm afraid. I'm talking a big game, but I don't want things to change with the people I care about. Please don't shut me out."

"Jake, *never*," she says. "Are you listening to me? There is nothing you could do that would ever have me walk away from you. Not least of which is love the people you were destined to love. If they're your family now, then they're my family too."

I smile, feeling a little lightness in my chest. "She's a fraternal twin too."

Amy laughs. "Oh god, of course, she is. Am I gonna hate her?"

I consider for a minute. "Hmm . . . I mean, you're both scientists . . . you both like dogs and yoga."

"All sounds good so far."

I huff, remembering the night we met. "She's a zodiac girl."

"Well, shit," Amy mutters. "It's not a capital offense, I guess. But if she goes trying to compare our moon signs, I'm reserving the right to tit punch her."

"I can't let you harm the tits," I say with a soft smile. "They're too fucking perfect. Besides, she's scrappy as hell. Don't start something you can't finish."

"Noted," she replies. "Hey, Jake?"

"Yeah?"

"You deserve every good thing in life. Don't wait for it to come to you. Go out and get it."

Tears sting my eyes again. "I'm buying you a ticket. You're coming home."

"I'm too busy."

"You're always too busy. You're coming anyway."

"If I come home, I may never leave again," she admits, her own voice catching now.

"Good," I say on a breath. "Bye, Amy."

"Bye, Jake. Skate well tonight. And stay safe."

Stay safe.

Easier said than done when you play professional hockey. There's a risk of injury with every practice, every game. As a D-man, I make the hits more than I take them, but either way involves potential harm. And with Brett Durand on the ice tonight, no one is safe.

The puck drops in thirty minutes, and it's all I can do to keep my shit together. My palms feel clammy as my pulse hums erratically. The sound echoes in my ears as I stand in this empty hallway.

Technically, I'm not the problem. It's fucking Jake. I can't stand watching him play Toronto. In years past, I just skipped those games. Pretending it's not happening isn't an option tonight, because now I'm his damn equipment manager. I have to be here. I have to do my job.

I've already arranged it with Jerry that he's taking point on the bench tonight. I may have to be in the barn, but I can't be down on that ice. No, I'll be the runner tonight. I'll just stay busy in the locker room and avoid looking at the TVs.

"Yo, Caleb! Need some black two-inch, man. Can you help me out?" The new guy Nate comes jogging over. He's a good kid with a clear love of hockey, but he's only just learning the ropes of a busy game day routine.

My knee twinges as I crouch down, digging in the box at my feet. Cursing, I snatch up a handful of black two-inch stick tape rolls, handing them off to Nate.

"Cool. Thanks, man."

"Tell Jerry I'm coming up with the blade box in ten!" I call after him.

I step around the corner to where the blade sharpening machine sits alone. Flipping the switch, the machine whirrs to life. I put on my safety goggles and take a deep breath.

"Hey," a voice calls behind me.

I jump, flipping the off switch and glancing over my shoulder. Rachel is standing there in her matching Rays uniform. She's got her glasses on tonight, minimal makeup, her hair pulled up in a ponytail.

I love to see that she's over her aversion to wearing the septum ring. Now she pretty much never takes it off.

Glancing up and down the hallway, a mischievous smile on her face, she tips up on her toes and kisses me. Just a peck, quick like it's a habit.

"What was that for?" I mutter, soaking in the feel of her closeness.

"Because I love you," she replies. "Do I need another reason?"

I let out a breath, shaking my head. Her presence helps. Having her this close is calming me down. Damn it, I'm as bad as Jake. I'm within an inch of asking her for a damn hug.

"You about ready? Puck drops soon," she says, still smiling. She doesn't know anything is wrong. We haven't told her. I don't want her to know.

"Almost done," I say, turning my attention to the blade box.

The pregame show has started, the pulsing beat of the music making the walls vibrate. I feel it in my chest, like the pounding of a hundred hammers against my bones.

"You benching tonight?" she says, leaning against the wall, arms crossed.

"No," I mutter. "You?"

"Yeah, Tyler just asked me to take point tonight. He's dealing with Davidson and his possible broken finger."

I set Morrow's blade back in the box. "Davidson broke his finger? When—is Mars okay—"

"He's fine," she says quickly. "They've got Kelso changing now. Ilmari's good. He's in the zone. I usually just try to avoid him pregame," she says with a shrug. "Honestly, I'm avoiding them both tonight. Jake is in a major mood. Did something happen?"

"Leave him alone," I mutter, my attention focused back on the blades in my hand as I try to remember how to breathe. Fuck, she's got those eyes and that face. She'll press with questions. I can't talk about this now.

"Why?" she says. "Cay, what's wrong—"

"Drop it," I say, cutting her off.

She balks, leaning away in surprise at my harsh words. "Caleb . . ."

"Look, he's got bad blood with Toronto, okay? Just—the sooner this game is over, the better."

She looks up at me, those dark eyes so open and honest. I don't even realize her fingers are brushing down the tatted sleeve of my forearm. I have to shut her down, or she'll tear me open.

"Do you need to talk about it?"

Fuck, I'm in love with this woman. She's not pressing, not forcing. She's asking. She's offering me her hand. She's making it my choice. She's always giving me the choice to do more, take more, have more.

I shake my head. "Just leave it. Please—" I don't even know what I'm pleading for.

Please go away. Please stay. Please hold me. Please make it stop hurting.

"What do you need from me?" she says. Again, with the support, the unquestioned loyalty. She's shredding me without trying.

"Nothing. Look, I've gotta finish these," I say, gesturing at the box.

"Okay." She drops her hand away, stepping back. She's giving me the space I'm clearly asking for but fuck if I don't also want her to jump me like she did that first night we met. I want to feel her everywhere—her scent, her warmth, the soft silken texture of her hair. I want the essence of her to blot out the stain of this stressful night.

As she steps away, I call out for her. "Hey, Hurricane . . ."

She turns, glancing over her shoulder. "Hmm?"

"Wanna fuck like animals in the shower later?" I say, finding the will to give her the smile I know she originally came looking for.

She snorts, smiling back at me and damn it if it doesn't make it a little easier for me to breathe. "I thought you'd never ask. See you around, Sanford."

I nod, watching her go before I turn my attention back to the blade sharpener. Flipping the switch, it hums to life. The sound helps drown out the hammering of my heart in my chest.

An NHL game is sixty minutes. Three periods of twenty minutes each. With three pairs of D-men in constant rotation, that's about twenty minutes of active play for Jake—more if he and J-Lo skate well tonight. Twenty minutes in sixty that he'll be out on that ice. Twenty minutes in sixty, during which time my heart will cease to beat.

Twenty minutes . . . my own life was changed in just over seven.

91
ILMARI

*S*omething's wrong with Jake. Usually he's the life of the party in the dressing room. He's always distracting me—asking questions, stealing my tape. Before Rachel, we kept our conversations limited to hockey. Now he asks me whatever the hell comes to his mind.

How do you say hippopotamus in Finnish?

What's your favorite kind of sushi?

Not tonight. He was silent as the grave tonight, quietly going about his pregame prep—wrapping his sticks, gearing up, stretching, taping his shin guards. Now he's out on the ice, circling like a hungry shark.

I like to watch horror movies. This is the moment in the film where the audience gets the inkling that the hero may have been possessed by some dark force. As I go through my stretching routine down on the ice, I keep glancing over at him, expecting to see the whites of his eyes.

I know Rachel has noticed too. She's standing in the corner of the bench, tablet in hand, watching him skate with a worried look on her face. I wish there was something I could do to ease her fears.

But I can't think about them right now. I have to focus on my game. There's a reason the FIHA scouts wanted to come to this game. Toronto has a Finnish player too: Timo Mäkinen. He's a right winger, and they're scouting him as well. They want to see how he plays against me. They want to see him score on the Bear.

I like Mäkinen, he's a good player. But hell will freeze over before I give him a point tonight. I see him now at the other end of the ice. No. 27. He's fast. Great footwork, good puck handling. Coach Tomlin and I reviewed all his recent footage. He likes to set up his shots. If my defense can make him rush, he'll get sloppy.

"Compton!" I shout from my spot on the ice, stretched out in a full split. "Compton!"

Jake skates over, sliding to a stop in front of me. "What?" The storm cloud brewing over his head looks ready to unleash havoc.

I roll forward onto the ice, sliding my legs back until I'm up in a kneeling position. "You see No. 27?"

He glances down the ice, eyes narrowed. "Yeah. Mäkinen. He's Finnish too, right?"

I nod. "He doesn't score tonight."

Jake's dark gaze darts down to me. "You got beef with him?"

"No. But the scouts want him to score on me tonight. You're not going to let that happen. Rush him into making sloppy shots. Tell the others."

He nods, still all business.

I get to my feet just as he turns, ready to skate away. "Hey—"

He turns back and I skate up, my blocker going to his shoulder as I step in. "I don't know what's wrong. I won't ask. I only have one question: are you here?"

He looks sharply at me, dark brows narrowed as he scowls. "What the hell does that mean?"

"Are you *here*?" I repeat. "Are you on this ice tonight? Because if you're not, I will go to Coach right now and have you benched."

He shrugs away from me. "I'm here, Mars. I'm right fucking here."

Against his will. I see it all over his face. He doesn't want to be here. He's angry and he's scared. Something is definitely wrong.

"Why don't you play your game and I'll play mine," he mutters. "That's what you're always telling me, right?"

"Jake—"

The whistle blows. Our time is up. We have to get into position. He skates off and I watch him go.

Taking a deep breath, I push off with my skate, gliding along the ice into the crease. I do my ritual of scuffing the ice, tapping each side of the goal with my stick when I'm done. Then I look down to my left, my gaze locked on that two-inch-thick red line. The goal line. Taking a deep inhale, I let it out, the heat of my breath filling my mask. Nothing is crossing that line tonight.

92
JAKE

I skate into my starting position. Left defense. Parallel to me, J-Lo skates to a halt. We meet eyes and nod. He's dialed in, ready for the puck drop. In front of us, Langley, Sully, and Karlsson are in position too.

I look down the ice to the Toronto defenseman across from me and my blood runs cold. No. 60, Brett Durand. He's a big fucker, built like a rugby player—broad shoulders, thick neck. And he hits like a truck.

I've played against him twice a year for years. It would have been more if I played for an Atlantic Division team. Thank god the Rays were placed in the Metro Division. After tonight, I won't have to see this asshole again until the end of the season.

The crowd is going wild, on their feet for the start of the game. The puck drops and it's like all my senses zap into laser focus.

Do your job.

Fuck, Toronto is a great team. They win control of the puck, and the forwards fly down the ice. J-Lo and I spring into action. I know Mars is behind me, waiting in the crease, a giant among men. To get to him, this center has to get through me.

Hard check. I slam him with my shoulder, working him off the puck. I send it rocketing down the ice towards a waiting Langley. The kid skates off, flying faster than a bullet. He reminds me so much of Caleb, it's scary.

The crowd boos as Langley tries to make a pass that is intercepted by Durand. He does his job, passing it forward. He's the definition of a grinder. He'll leave the fancy puck handling to the forwards.

The Toronto offense push us hard, bringing the puck back across center line. J-Lo stays forward, and I hold back.

"Eyes sharp!" Mars calls at me. "Watch 27!"

As he says it, the puck is passed to Mäkinen and the Finnish winger blasts forward, trying to fake me out like he's going for the center approach. He darts right instead, ready to skate along the wall. I'm right on top of him, closing off his shot window. He grunts, passing the puck back instead.

I stay on him, skating backwards as we both move in on Mars and the goal. His forwards are in a brawl with Sully and J-Lo, fighting for control of the puck.

"Clear it!" Mars bellows.

I hold my position at the top of the crease, ready to block any approach.

"He's coming down the middle!"

I'm ready, giving their center a full-frontal smash and crash, working the puck away from him and sending it flying down the ice feet ahead of Karlsson. He races after it, feet slicing the ice.

"Good clear," Mars calls behind me.

I nod, watching for J-Lo before we make our move. He gives the signal and we both fly towards the bench. Morrow and Novy are ready for the shift change, leaping over the boards to take our place.

"Hey, watch 27!" I call at Morrow. "Mars says he doesn't score tonight."

Morrow nods, racing off to fill my spot as Karlsson loses his fight with Durand and the pucks goes blasting down the ice towards the Rays goal.

Less than two minutes in, and this already feels like a goddamn dog fight.

SWEAT pours from my forehead, drenching my undershirt, stinging my eyes. Start of the second period and I feel like I've been on this ice for three fucking hours. Score is 2-1. We're up by one. Mars is pissed, but at least Mäkinen didn't score the Toronto goal.

The Bear has officially come out to play. He's ruthless, calling shots and working us ragged as we pick up the slack from our tired forwards. But we're still fifteen minutes to intermission.

Mars is playing offensively tonight, leaving the net more than I've seen him do in recent games. He surges forward, meeting Mäkinen at the crease. Mäkinen wasn't expecting it. He fumbles his shot and Mars bats the puck away just in time, sending it over to Langley.

But Langley is too far ahead of it. He turns to chase after it but Durand is there like a freight train, plowing through him. Langley goes spinning down to the ice and I swallow a scream of rage. I can't breathe as I wait for him to scramble to his feet, dazed but unharmed. He's racing after Durand, trying to stop him before he shoots to pass.

I've got Mäkinen covered, leaving J-Lo to take point at the crease with Mars. I want him back. I don't like him playing out like this, not with Durand on the ice.

"Mars, get in the box," I shout, my panic getting the better of me.

I shove Mäkinen harder than I need to, but it's enough to have him reeling back. It buys me a few precious seconds to move in towards the goal.

"Mars, get back, I got it!"

He needs to get back in the goal. I want him safe in the net. I can't fucking breathe with him out like this. But he's determined to play out, ready to push back against these fierce forwards. It's a good strategy. The man is a giant. He's fucking terrifying. He's keeping them on their toes, making them take their shots from farther back.

Just when I think Sully and J-Lo have the puck cleared, a few things happen at once. Sully takes a hard shove from behind. Then J-Lo gets tripped up and nearly loses his balance as his skate catches on the end of No. 34's stick. It sends him slipping to the side of the goal, leaving the path to Mars open.

He's out too far. I can see it from here.

"Mars, get back!" But my shouting can't help him.

Making a bold choice, Mars leaps, throwing himself backwards and flat, dropping to the ice with his feet at one end of the goal, arms stretched out to the other, stick clattering down.

He takes a spray of snow right in the grill of his mask as the Toronto forward does a pirouette, his shot blocked by Mars' full-body defense. The forward trips over J-Lo, sending them both down to the ice.

The shot was blocked, but now Mars has to recover for the rebound. He scrambles, his body curling in so he can get back up on his knees. He can't protect the goal like that. Can't see what's coming from the left.

But I can.

"Mars!" I cry out. I'm tearing up the ice, Mäkinen forgotten in my wake. But it's too late. I'm too slow.

Durand goes skating in too fast, straight into the crease, puck on the end of his stick, and slams into Mars. The puck follows Mars over the red line as he goes backwards inside his own net. I hear his cry of pain, that deep voice piercing through me, rattling my very bones.

My goalie is hurt.

Mars is hurt.

Rule number fucking one in hockey? *Never* touch the goalie.

With a roar of rage, I fling my stick aside, dropping my gloves. I'm gonna make this man bleed if it's the last thing I do. I barrel right into Durand, tackling him down to the ice. And then I'm an animal. I see only red as I punch every part of him I can reach. My fists crunch against his helmet as he cries out, wrestling with me.

I'm not alone for long. Every Ray on the ice has dropped his gloves. Never touch the fucking goalie. They descend like hounds on the scrap of rotten meat that is Durand. The ref and linesmen finally descend, blowing their whistles and grabbing for anyone they can reach.

I'm the last one at the bottom of the pile, straddling Durand as I punch him in the fucking teeth.

"That's enough," Sully yells, his arms around me as he pulls me off. It takes him and a lineman to do it. I resist them both, cursing and jerking my arms.

"Five for fighting!" the ref yells at me. "Get in the box, 42!"

"Fuckin' pussy ass bitch," Durand mutters, spitting blood onto the ice. Then he looks up at me, a big, laughing smile on his face.

"You're fucking dead!" I shout, busting free from the hold Sully had on me.

"No—Compton—" He scrambles after me, Langley lunges too, grabbing me before I can drop back down on Durand.

"That's it, 42! You're out!" The ref shouts. "Get off the ice!"

The fans are going nuts, the sound of whistles shrill in my ears, and then it's like I suddenly remember where I am. "Mars!" I cry out, my head swiveling around as Sully and J-Lo drag me over to the bench.

"He's fine," J-Lo mutters.

I can't leave this ice until I know. "Mars!" I call out again. "Mars!"

He's on his knees, his mask flipped up, talking to the lineman. At the sound of my shouts, he looks my way and nods once.

Thank fucking god.

Meanwhile, Durand is skating to the penalty box, blood streaming out of his nose onto his white Maple Leafs jersey. The Rays fans boo him, while on this side of the ice they scream and cheer for me. It's a hollow victory. No victory at all, really. He'll be in the box for five minutes and then back on the ice, while I'm out of the game. I can't protect Mars anymore. Can't protect my team. I'm a worthless fucking piece of shit who can't keep anyone safe.

"Jake!"

I close my eyes, unwilling to turn my head. I can't face her. Can't see the disappointment in her eyes. She watched it all. She watched Mars take the hit. She watched me fail to protect him. She watched the fight.

"What the hell do you think you're doing, Compton?" Coach bellows. "Get off the damn ice. Now!"

Sully and J-Lo let me go, and I step through the open hatch onto the bench. Morrow has already hopped the boards, ready to take my place.

"Get back out there and refocus," Coach calls. "Everyone get your heads out of your asses, and let's play some damn hockey!" He rounds on me, finger in my face. "I don't know what the hell has gotten into you tonight, but if that fight didn't put you on the bench, I was gonna do it myself. You're a goddamn mess, Compton. Get back in that locker room and take care of your face. Price!"

I wince, closing my eyes.

"Yes, sir?" she calls, moving down the bench behind the guys.

"Go with Compton," Coach barks. "Make sure he hasn't broken any bones in his seven-million-dollar-a-year hands!"

"Yes, sir." She looks up at me with such a face of shock and confusion.

I can't fucking stand it. Spinning away from her, I stomp down the hall towards the locker room.

93
RACHEL

"Jake!" I call, running after him. "Jake, what just happened out there? What's wrong—"

"Go away, Rachel," he growls.

I nearly run into him as he stops cold in the doorway to the locker room. "Jake, what—"

"What the hell did you do?"

I peer around Jake's shoulder to see Caleb standing in the middle of the empty locker room, looking at Jake with tears rimming his eyes.

"I had to," Jake croaks. "Cay—"

But Caleb doesn't wait. He spins on his heel and limps out of the room.

"Jake," I say, my hand on his arm.

He jerks out of my hold. "I'm fine, Rachel. Go back out there. The team needs you."

"Coach told me to check you out—"

"I'm fine." He jerks his helmet off and slams it into his stall.

I put my hands on my hips, watching him tug off his gloves and throw them down too. "You're not fine. You're so angry, your hands are shaking. What happened out there? You just went feral on that guy—"

"He fucking deserved it!" he shouts, spinning around to glare at me.

With his helmet off, the cut on his brow is more pronounced. It's bleeding down his temple. My gaze drops to his knuckles. They'll swell up something awful, but I doubt anything is broken. He'd be making a much bigger fuss if he had broken fingers.

"Come with me," I say, holding out my hand.

"I need to change."

"You need your forehead to stop bleeding first," I say, dropping my hand to my side. "You change now, you'll just be giving the EMs double the bloody laundry to wash."

He lifts a shaking hand, wincing as he dabs at the cut. "It's nothing." *Damn bull-headed Taurus.*

"Are you a medical professional?" I say, one dark brow raised. "No. *I am.* And Coach sent me back here to take care of you, so that's what I'm gonna do. Now, get your ass across the hall into the exam room so I can clean that cut."

With a growl, he stomps off. This isn't my Jake. He's been body snatched by aliens, I swear to god. He marches across the hall into the small room we use for first aid. Balanced on his skates, he leans against the exam table, arms crossed.

I turn away from him, washing my hands at the sink and slipping on a pair of blue surgical gloves. Then I grab the first aid box. Stepping over to Jake, I set it down on the exam table next to him and start cleaning the wound.

"Take whatever time you need to collect yourself," I murmur, dabbing away the blood. "But you *will* tell me what happened out there tonight. As you love me, and I love you, you will tell me what's wrong with you, Jake . . . and Caleb."

"Rachel," he says on an exhale.

As if speaking his name is a summons, Caleb reappears in the doorway, arms folded tightly over his chest. He glares at Jake. "I told you not to fucking do anything."

"I had to," Jake mutters, not looking at him.

"No, you didn't—"

"First rule in hockey!" Jake barks, brushing my hand away from his brow. "He hit my goalie. You want me to just let that go unanswered? I'm his D, Cay. I have to have his back out there!"

Caleb shakes his head. "You were gunning for Durand all game. Making nasty checks, pissing him off. You goaded him—"

"I wanted to *kill* him!"

"Compton!"

We all turn, Caleb slipping just inside the room as Assistant Coach Andrews comes storming around the corner. "What the hell was that?" he barks.

Jake drops his gaze the floor, saying nothing.

Coach Andrews huffs, turning to me. "Is anything broken, Doc?"

I'm still holding the bloody gauze in my hand. "I don't think so, sir. But I was starting with the head lac."

"I'm fine," Jake mutters. "I don't need to be babied—"

"Shut up and let the doctor work," Andrews orders. "So, what the hell happened out there, huh? What did Durand do to you? Cause I was watching you all first period, and you had that guy on your shit list from the word jump."

"Just an old beef," Jake mutters.

"An old beef? Judging by the way you were gunning for him out there, you'd think he stole all your damn cattle! Is that it? Did he steal your girl, Compton? Did he fuck your sister and kick your dog? I'm not putting you on the ice again until I know what the hell is going on."

Simmering with rage, Jake says nothing.

"Did he make fun of your mama?"

"No," Jake mutters.

"Did he beat you in the draft?"

"No—"

"Then what—"

"He crippled Caleb!" Jake shouts.

An echoing silence follows his words.

"What?" I whisper, heart in my throat.

Jake crosses his arms over his chest. "First game of our rookie season, seven minutes into the first period, Durand checked Cay into the boards from behind, took him down to the ice and broke his fucking leg. He's the reason Cay can't play anymore."

I suck in a breath. I've heard the story, obviously. I just never thought to memorize the name of Caleb's assailant. I use that term because that's what he is. The hit was made after play had stopped. He got a major fine for it.

I spin to face Caleb. He's standing there by the doorway looking white as a sheet, seconds away from a panic attack. "Oh . . . Cay," I murmur.

The fire in Coach Andrews cools instantly. "Is that true, Sanford? Durand made the dirty hit on you?"

Slowly, Caleb nods.

"Well . . . fucking hell," Andrews mutters, dragging a hand over his close-cropped scalp. "Alright, look—I gotta get back out there. Compton, I . . ." He shakes his head. "There's nothing I can do about the fine."

"I know," Jakes replies.

"And we won't know yet if you're suspended for any more games . . ."

"I know," he says again.

"What do you two need from me right now?" Andrews glances between them.

"Nothing," Caleb says quickly. "I'm fine."

But I know my Cay. He's not fine. He's drowning inside. I want to go to him. Want to hold him. I need Andrews to leave. I need to be alone with my guys.

"Compton?" Andrews says, one brow raised.

Jake just shakes his head. "Nothing, sir. Sorry I got booted. Caleb being in the barn was messing with me. I thought I had it handled."

"It's understandable," Andrews replies. "That kind of shit is hard to live with. Hard to carry. You're both good guys," he adds, nodding at Caleb too.

"Watch him close, Coach," Jake says. "If Durand is on the ice, no one is safe. Caleb isn't the only player he's sent to the hospital. He's dangerous. He shouldn't be starting. He shouldn't even be in the League."

"Well, that's not our call, right?" Andrews says gently. "And plenty of guys get sent to the hospital. It's the game. All we can do is play our best. Play smart. Protect each other. I know that's what you were doing. You were just protecting Kinnunen, right?"

Slowly, Jake nods.

"Right, I gotta go back out there. Doc, you good here?" Andrews says.

"Yeah, I got it," I murmur.

Andrews turns on his heel and walks out, leaving me alone with my guys.

"Cay," I murmur, stepping over to him.

He goes stiff, flinching away from me. "Don't."

I drop my hands, tears in my eyes as I gaze up at his beautiful, tortured face. "Why didn't you say anything?" I glance back over my shoulder at Jake.

He huffs a laugh. "And what were we gonna tell you, huh? That we're both still messes over something that happened six fucking years ago? That I can't fucking *breathe* when I step on that ice and I know Durand is on it? That I still have nightmares about that night? Is that what you want to hear, Rachel? You wanna hear how I failed him? How I couldn't protect him? How I let him down and cost him everything?"

Caleb shakes his head. "Jake—"

"Don't you fucking dare," Jake growls at him, tears brimming in his hazel eyes. "I was right *fucking* there! He had to push past me to get to you! He shouldered me out of the way to make that hit—"

"You didn't know what he was planning—"

"I was right *there!*" Jake shouts, a sob caught in his throat.

It tears me apart. I'm open and bleeding with them. I turn, ready to go to Jake, but Caleb beats me to it. He pushes off the wall, crossing the tiny room to stand in front of him. Lifting both hands, he cups Jake's sweaty face. "It's not your fault," he murmurs.

Jake shakes his head, eyes shut tight, as one tear slips down his cheek.

Caleb wipes it away with his thumb. "You couldn't have done anything. You weren't close enough. And you didn't know. The play was over. It's not your fault, Jake."

Jake sucks in a breath as he lifts his hands, wrapping them around Caleb's wrists. "I'm sorry—"

"It's time to let it go," Caleb murmurs.

"I can't," Jake says on a moan. "I—*oh god*—can't breathe—"

Caleb drops his hands to the pads of Jake's shoulders, stepping in closer, their foreheads all but touching. "Hey—*hey*—look at me."

Jake shakes his head, eyes shut tight.

"Look at me, Jake."

Jake groans, opening his eyes to gaze down at Caleb.

"It's not your fault," says Caleb. "I forgive you, because it's not your fault. There's nothing to forgive."

"Cay," Jake whimpers, dropping his forehead down to touch Caleb's.

"Forgive yourself, Jake. We have to move on."

And then Jake crumbles, wrapping himself around Caleb, his sweaty, bleeding face buried at Caleb's neck. "I watched the hit on Mars in slow fucking motion," he whimpers into Caleb's shoulder.

"I know," Caleb, soothes, his arms around his hulking frame.

"I saw Durand skate in. I saw the hit. I couldn't stop it—wasn't fast enough—"

"I know. I was trying not to watch, but I couldn't bear it," Caleb murmurs. "Couldn't keep my eyes off you on that ice."

"I heard Mars yell," Jake says, his hands fisting tight to the back of Caleb's polo shirt. "He cried out in pain, and I heard you in my head," he sobs. "I was right fucking there all over again. I watched your hit, Cay. I watched your bones break. I heard it. Oh god—I heard the snap like the cracking of a tree branch—"

"Shh," Caleb soothes, tears streaming down his face too. "There was nothing you could do."

I'm crying too, standing back helplessly, as they both fall apart before me.

"You lost everything," Jake cries, his heart shredding into pieces. "And you deserved the fucking world, Cay. You were the better player. Faster, stronger, smarter on the ice—"

"Stop," Caleb murmurs, his voice twisted with pain. He brushes his hand through Jake's sweaty hair, still trying to soothe him. "Baby, stop—"

"It should have been me," Jake cries. "God—it should have been me taking that hit—"

"*No*," Caleb growls, grabbing him by the jersey and shoving him back. He's right in Jake's face, his own beautiful face a mask of rage. "Never fucking say that again."

"Cay—"

"*Never* say it again. I took the hit, alright? That's all there is to it. We can't wish it any different. So, you are gonna let this fucking go. We are done reliving that one shitty moment and sharing the awful weight of pain and regret, Jake. I'm so fucking done. No more. Move on with me. Move on *with* me," he whispers again, his voice softer. It's a wish, a plea and a prayer.

Jake's battered hand cups Caleb's face as they gaze into each other's eyes, hazel green meeting brownest black. Jake breathes through parted lips, chest heaving, his face wet with his sweat and tears. "I'm with you, Cay."

"Jake—"

Before Caleb can get another word out, Jake's hand snakes around to hold him at the nape as he presses in, kissing Caleb with parted lips. Caleb goes still as stone, his body stunned. Seconds pass before he recovers, his arms going around Jake, kissing him back with the pent-up passion of all his long years of waiting.

I stand back, dazed, heart overflowing, as I watch them find their way to each other at last. Jake is ravenous, groaning his need into Caleb's mouth as Caleb lets him lead. They're awkward with their hands, encumbered by Jake's gear. And their height difference is pronounced because he's still in his skates. But none of that matters—

"Doc!"

I jolt, watching the guys break apart, as seconds later the new equipment guy comes running down the hall.

"Hey, Doc. They need you up on the bench."

I spin to face him, heart in my throat. "Why—what happened?"

"Novy just took a skate to the face. He's bleeding like crazy."

"Oh shit," I breathe, glancing over my shoulder to look at Jake and Cay.

"Go," Caleb says. "I got this."

Breaking myself away, I rush out into the hall and follow Nate back out to the bench.

Rachel runs off after the new kid and I'm left alone with Caleb. He's standing there, my blood on the collar of his shirt, looking at me like I'm the answer to life's great unanswered question. My heart races a mile a minute.

I just kissed Caleb. I just kissed a man. I kissed my best friend . . . in front of my girlfriend. And I liked it. Loved it. I want to kiss him again.

Okay, I'm officially freaking out.

Caleb's eyes go wide as he watches me spin out. He knows me too well. Knows I'm a goddamn mess. He takes a step back. "Jake, it's okay—"

"I don't know what the fuck I'm doing!"

"I know," he murmurs.

I drag my throbbing hands through my sweaty hair. "I'm freaking the fuck out, Cay."

"I know," he says again. "Jake, there's no reason—"

"You're my best fucking friend!"

My voice sounds oddly strangled. God, I was so sure when this finally happened, I'd be so much cooler about it. I'd say some cheesy line like, 'Baby, you can manage my equipment any time.' Then I'd wink just to make him laugh and we'd fall into each other—not that I've given it much thought.

Instead, Caleb is shrinking back, looking at me like I'm a cornered animal ready to strike. "Jake, we don't have to—"

"I want more," I squawk, stumbling forward on my skates. "I want more, Cay. I want *you*. But I'm fucking terrified to want you at the same time."

I reach forward slapping my hands down on his shoulders, elbows locked. He can't keep pulling away from me, but fuck if I'm ready to let myself get closer. I have to say this. Have to get it out before it eats me alive.

"Rachel's my girl," I say on a breath, chest heaving like I've just run a marathon. "I want her to love me and marry me and have my huge hockey babies. But I think you might be my guy, Cay. And I *never* thought I'd be the kind of guy to have a guy, you know what I mean? But you're here, and you're you, and you know me better than anyone," I say with a surprised shake of my head. "You might know me better than Amy at this point."

"Likely," he mutters, slipping his hands in his pockets, unwilling to take a step closer or reciprocate my touch.

I have to keep going. I have to get it out. He deserves this. I scramble to think of the right words. "I tell everyone my favorite movie is *The Hangover* but it's not. You know the real answer, Cay."

He huffs a laugh. "Oh god, really? *Practical Magic*? Still?"

"Fucking of course that's my favorite movie!" I say, pushing off him with both hands. "Amy made me watch it like a thousand times growing up. It's amazing. I want that house, Cay."

"I know."

"And that's the only reason I learned to flip pancakes in the air," I add. "Girls go crazy for that shit. It's like pussy magic to them."

"I know. I've seen you in action," he replies.

"I don't want to mess this up," I admit, my gaze locked on him. He's still in arm's reach but I'm afraid to touch him. Afraid to break this.

He holds my gaze, his own expression softening.

I've never been attracted to men. Not once in my life can I remember sitting there thinking, 'Hey, that guy's so handsome, I'd let him spoon me.' Even looking at Caleb now, I'm not struck senseless by his beauty. I'm not drawn to the allure of his rippling pectorals or his fancy pierced cock.

Fuck, I'm the worst lover ever, right? This is why I hate labels. I hate the performance. The expectation. I hate that I'm standing here thinking about how I'm not attracted to my guy.

But I am.

The truth hits me, and I feel like I'm spinning out all over again. I'm so attracted to Caleb, it's not even funny. I'm just not attracted to the way he looks. Don't get me wrong, he's objectively a ten. But I'm attracted to . . . *him*. His unwavering loyalty, his patience, his sense of humor. I'm attracted to the way he pretends to be full when we go out for sushi so I can finish what's on his plate. I love the way he sets up the TV to record my favorite cooking shows when we're gone for away games.

"Nothing has to change, Jake," he says. "We can go on just as before. We can just be with Rachel and not each other. I have no expectations—"

"Kiss me again," I hear myself say.

"What?"

I hold his dark gaze, heart hammering in my chest. "You fucking heard me, Cay. Shut that door. Then get over here, and kiss me like I'm the last man you'll ever kiss for the rest of your lucky fucking life."

The energy in the room turns on a dime as Cay goes still as a statue. His entire body morphs from passive to possessive. Tearing his gaze from me, he spins around and moves to the door, shutting it with a sharp snap. The sound rattles my bones.

Oh, it is so fucking on.

But then he just stands there, one palm pressed flat against the wood of the door, not moving. For the briefest of moments, I lose my nerve.

I misread him. He doesn't want this. He doesn't want me. Why would he—

Then he spins around, his eyes like black coals as he crosses the room in two strides, both hands coming up to cup my face as he drags me down. I barely have time to suck in a breath before his mouth is on mine and he's claiming all my air in a fevered kiss.

I groan, loving the press of his body so close to mine. This kiss is even better than the first one. I feel his strength with each press of his lips, his need to dominate buried just beneath the surface of his iron self-control. I want him unraveled. I want him undone.

With one hand gripping his shoulder, I drop my other hand between us and cup his hard cock. He groans, pressing his hips into my hand. He can't help himself. I feel desperate to do the same.

"This is mine," I growl. "Do anything you want with Rachel. Please god, if you're listening, let me witness it. Let me be there," I tease, my lips against Caleb's mouth, sharing his air. "But no other men. This is my cock, Caleb. I ride it. I suck it. I fuck it. It's *mine*. Promise me that, and I'll give you anything."

He leans back, looking into my eyes, his parted lips wet with my kisses. Then he drops his hands to my hips and jerks me forward. "I want everything, Jake. Every piece of you."

We fall back together, kissing like two men dying of hunger. As we kiss, my hand slips inside the top of his pants with barely enough room to wrap around his dick. I don't have the space to jerk it, so I just hold on and squeeze, letting him move his hips in search of some friction.

Then he shoves my shoulders, sending me stumbling back until I hit the exam table with my hip. I slip my hand out of his pants, both hands gripping to the table's edge as I steady myself.

Cay tugs up my jersey with one hand, his other dropping to my hockey pants, fingers finding the buckle of my belt. The sound of that soft click fills my senses as I feel the pants loosen. Then he drops his fingers down to the tie.

"Here, let me," I murmur, trying to take over for him. Fuck, I feel like a fifteen-year-old virgin, fingers fumbling. This is crazy. Why am I so nervous? I've sucked his cock; I've fucked his ass. But here I am, hands shaking, like this is my first time.

He catches me by the wrist and holds me still as he gazes up at me. "Let me," he murmurs.

"It's complicated," I say, thinking of all the layers trapping me—jock and garter, hockey pants, shin pads, socks, chest protector, jersey. I'm taped into my damn socks from the outside. I'm still wearing my skates—

"Jake . . ."

I look down at him, chest fluttering with nerves.

"I know how to undress you," he says with half a smile.

Fuck, of course he does. He played hockey for twenty years. He's my damn equipment manager. I huff a nervous laugh and nod.

"I only want one thing," he murmurs, his fingers working lose the laces of my pants as he tips up on his toes, kissing me.

I groan, my hands gripping his shoulders as I let him work me open. Both his hands slip inside my padded pants, fingers snagging the top of my jock. He sucks my bottom lip, teasing with his teeth as he tugs on the elastic waistband with his left hand, his right diving inside to fist my hard cock.

We both groan, my body going limp as he works his fist slowly up and down my shaft. His hand is rough, but I don't fucking care. It's Caleb and he's touching me and he's kissing me, and I never want him to stop.

"Keep kissing me," he pants against my lips. "That's all I want. Jake, *please*—"

I grab his face with both hands, drowning him in my kisses. I give him everything, holding nothing back. My sweat is drying on my face, leaving our kisses tasting salty. I'm grimy and bloody and if I don't get out of this kit, I'll start to fucking stink, but I don't care. Caleb just said 'kiss me' and no force on earth will stop me.

There's not much he can do other than work my cock one-handed, but it's enough. Fuck, is it enough. I'm wound so tight from the game, from the fight, from this emotional release a decade in the making. Caleb is mine. He *wants* to be mine.

"Cay," I pant, breaking our kiss. My hips press back against the table as I hold still, his thumb brushing over the tip of my dick, smearing my precum. I bite my lip with a groan, eyes shut tight. As I open them, he's still standing there. "I love you," I whisper.

His hand stills on my dick. "Jake—"

"I love you," I say again, more confidence in my voice this time. "I'm in love with you, Cay."

He sighs, his shoulders relaxing as he leans in, cupping my sweaty, bleeding face with his free hand. "Fucking finally. A guy can only hold out for so long."

We both laugh, our lips finding each other as he presses in, his fist working my cock again.

The rattle of the doorknob is the only warning we have before the door swings open. "Hey Sanford, you in here—"

Caleb does his best to shove off me and step back, his hand slipping from my pants. He doesn't turn around, so he can't see the look on Jerry's face as he stands there in the doorway, taking in the scene.

He can't, but I can. Good ole Jerry's mouth opens wide like he's a damn cartoon character. There's nothing to see as we're both fully clothed, but there's everything to know. And fuck, but he knows.

"I—I'll just come back," he squawks, turning on his heel and rushing away.

"Jer, wait!" Caleb calls. "Fuck," he mutters. His gaze darts to me, worry in his eyes as he shakes his head. "He's a fucking sieve, Jake. He'll tell everyone—"

"Hey," I soothe, hand on his shoulder. "It's okay—"

"It's not fucking okay," he snaps, slapping my arm away. "The whole team will know—"

"Good."

"What?" he says on a breath, dark eyes wide.

I just shrug. "We want this, right? We all want out. You, me, Rach, Mars. We want to go public. So let him tell the guys."

"No." He shakes his head. "No, we were going public about us all dating Rachel. We're not doing this, Jake. You're not coming out. Being polyamorous will be more than enough of a publicity nightmare."

I study his face. "Do you not want people to know about us too?"

"Jake," he sighs with a shake of his head.

I'm trying really hard to pretend I'll be cool either way, but I'm totally not. I need him to want me out loud. I can't fucking stand the idea of more secrets, more hiding. Jake Compton is coming out. I'm bi and I'm poly and I've never been happier in my life. That's gotta mean something, right?

"Is it your job?" I say. "Are you worried they'll can you? We'll sign the disclosure forms. We can do this totally above board. And everyone on the team already calls us DLPs. It's not like they'll be that surprised," I add with a nervous laugh. "But . . . if you're worried—"

"You think I'm worried about *me*," he says, cutting me off. "Jake, I don't give a fuck about my job or my reputation or fucking any of it. I'd quit right now." He steps forward, hands on my shoulder pads. "But you've been bi for all of two seconds. I've been out for years. It's not easy—"

"But it *is* easy," I say. "Loving you, loving Rach, it's the easiest thing I've ever done, Cay. Even having Mars around just feels . . . right. Am I right? Tell me you feel it too."

"Of course, I do," he says quickly. "But Jake, us feeling right together—"

"Is the *only* thing that matters," I say, cutting him off. "Your approval, your love, Rachel's love—they are the only things that matter to me, Caleb."

He lets out a shaky breath, panic still lacing his features.

"Besides, it's not like I'm coming out as bi and open for business," I add. "My business is firmly closed. In fact, I'm about to be the worst openly bi player in pro sports history because my gayness begins and ends with you. You're it for me, Cay. You're the only guy for me. She's my girl, and you're my guy, and Mars is . . . Mars," I add with a shrug. "Please don't make me hide this. If I say I'm willing to risk it, let me make that choice."

Caleb steps back, shaking his head. "This is so fucking crazy. What the hell are we doing?"

I drop my hands to my hockey pants, buckling them shut and flipping my jersey down with a smile. "Just you wait. I'm gonna love you so fucking hard, Cay. And I'm gonna do it out loud . . . whether the hockey world likes it or not."

95
ILMARI

The buzzer sounds the end of the game and I breathe a huge sigh of relief. What a goddamn mess. Jake ejected in the second period for fighting. Novikov took a skate to the face and is probably still off getting stitches. Midway through the third period, Toronto's goalie left the net to the scream of the fans, skated over to the bench, folded himself over the boards, and puked his guts out. Play stopped as they got him off the ice and the backup took over.

Rays won, but it doesn't feel like a victory. We all survived something out here tonight. Something horrible. The teams form a line to shake hands. I see Mäkinen and he sees me. He laughs and shakes his head, calling out in Finnish, "Did we just fall out of a tree?"

I can't help but laugh too. That's definitely what this feels like. I'm dazed and confused, sitting at the bottom of this tree of a game wondering how I managed to hit every limb on the way down. "You played like shit," I say back.

"Speak for yourself, Kinnunen. You let in three goals."

"None from you," I reply. "And at least I kept down my lunch."

He laughs again. "What a mess. The scouts will likely pass on us both."

"They won't. You'll wear the blue and white," I say, cuffing his shoulder.

"As will you, my friend," he says before skating off.

I work my way back to the locker room, unsurprised that Rachel is still missing. She left with Novikov and didn't come back to the bench. Doctor Tyler took her place. Jake isn't in the locker room either. His stall is cleared out.

I go through all my routines, stripping out of my gear, before hitting the shower. As I'm in there, Coach Tomlin pops his head in. "Hey Mars, hurry up! The FIHA guys are out here waiting."

My hands still in my hair, shampoo rinsing down the drain as I exhale. The hot spray of the water hits my face. I'm disappointed. This game is not the image I wanted them to have of me. But I can't control it. I played my hardest while missing two of my best defenders. I let in three goals, but they were good shots. Toronto earned each one.

I shut off the water, staring at the tiled wall. This is my last chance at an Olympics. The scouts know it and so do I. Whatever happens will happen. Taking a deep breath, I turn, ready to face my fate.

"THANK you so much for agreeing to see us tonight." Elias Laakso sits at the table across from me. He's one of the top FIHA reps based here in North America. Next to him sits Harri Järvinen, part of the defensive coaching staff for the Leijonat, the Finnish Men's National Team.

"My pleasure," I say.

We're seated in one of the arena offices up near the boxes. It's a conference style room with a large table and wheeled chairs. Pictures of arena events frame the wall behind the men's heads.

"That was a difficult game," says Järvinen, while Laakso helps himself to the pitcher of ice water on the table. "The Rays lost two good defenders, but you played your hardest, Kinnunen."

"Toronto earned their goals," I reply.

"You've had some health issues this season," says Laakso. "You've missed quite a few games. Away from the eyes of the agents and the coaches, can you tell us honestly: should we be concerned about your fitness?"

I take a breath, letting it out. Jake is right, no more hiding. "I have a minor labral tear in my hip," I explain. "I'm rehabilitating it under the guidance of my team's Barkley Fellow. She's a specialist in hip injuries. She benched me as a precaution. I've been receiving treatment from the Cincinnati Sport Clinic. Between the cortisone shots and the joint gel, combined with a new physical therapy regime, I feel stronger than before. There is no reason to believe it will get worse. That being said," I add, "none of us can guarantee our health from one day to the next."

Järvinen is glancing down, swiping his finger across his tablet. "I see nothing here from the Cincinnati Sport Clinic."

"An oversight," I reply. "I'll have Doctor Price email you everything again tonight."

"Welcome, but unnecessary," Laakso replies. "The starting spot is yours, Kinnunen. You've more than earned it. You're the third highest ranking goalie in the NHL. You were first in the Liiga. You've been a rising star since your days on the junior league."

"Add to that the fact that your record is utterly spotless," Järvinen adds with a pleased nod. "You live and breathe for the game."

"You do the Kinnunen family proud," says Laakso. "You do Finland and the FIHA proud. The Leijonat jersey is yours . . . if you want it."

"Well done, Kinnunen," Järvinen adds with a smile. "It's an honor well-earned."

Their words flow around me like a morning mist. I breathe in, feeling empty. Did I hear them correctly? I'm on the team. I'll wear the blue and white of Finland. I'll play in the Olympics.

But my mind catches on Järvinen's words. My record is utterly spotless. My personal record, he means. I have no record because, before Rachel, I had no life. I lived to play hockey. Nothing else mattered. But she blasted into my life with all the subtlety of an avalanche, and now I live for so much more.

"Needless to say, there will be need to be some coordination with the Rays as we move forward," says Laakso. "But that will be a matter for your agent to arrange . . . assuming you accept our offer," he adds with a raised brow.

I swallow, looking up from my folded hands to face the gentlemen across from me. "Before I make my answer, I feel I must warn you about something. You may even wish to rescind your offer."

"Warn us?" says Laakso.

"Sounds ominous," Järvinen adds with a level gaze.

I nod, slowly piecing together the words in my mind. None of this matters if I can't share it with Rachel. I want her at my side for every step of this journey. Jake and Caleb too. I will not hide what we are. I chose the Kinnunens as my family. Now I choose again. I choose Rachel. Even if it costs me this chance, I will choose her.

"As you both know, I am a private person. I have a spotless record because I don't share my life with the world. I am not reckless. I live well within my means. I give generously to charities, never attaching my name."

"Yes, we know," Laakso murmurs, his fair brows raised in curiosity.

"The Kinnunen name is synonymous with hockey the world over," I go on. "I've worked hard to keep it that way. I have never been involved in a scandal."

"You are Finnish," Laakso reasons with a nod.

"These Americans all care about the drama," Järvinen scoffs with a wave of his hand. "Everything is an opportunity to aggrandize oneself."

I nod, clearing my throat. "All that to say . . . it is likely you will soon hear my name quite a lot in the press. I assure you now that there is no scandal."

"He's right, this does sound ominous," Järvinen teases.

"Speak your mind, Kinnunen," Laakso offers gently. "We promise to listen and reserve judgement."

I lean forward, elbows on the table. "Do either of you know of the rock band The Ferrymen?"

96
RACHEL

"This is the last one," I say with a tired sigh, snapping the buckle closed on one of our wheeling medical boxes. Moving a hockey team isn't all that different from moving a rock band. It's an elaborate dance, with everyone knowing their roles. I release the brakes on the box and wheel it forward. Two of the assistant EMs step forward and grab it, adding it to the line of boxes being loaded onto the truck.

What a disaster of a game. Between Jake getting himself booted out, and Novy opening his face on the ice, I'm ready for the world's largest glass of chardonnay. Poor Novy. It was a total freak accident. He got dropped to the ice and a Toronto player tripped over him. Only problem is that they all have sharpened metal knives for feet.

One look at Novy's gushing face, and I sent him straight to the ER. It's a gnarly cut, following the line of his jaw up under his ear. I'm a glorified physical therapist, so I wasn't about to do stitches. And Novy is a playboy millionaire with a string of fashion brand endorsements. Leave it to a plastic surgeon to fix him up nice and pretty.

Poor Langley looked like he was going to be sick at the sight of all the blood. And Poppy was a shrieking mess, tears streaming down her face as she all but shoved me into the back of the ambulance, shouting that someone had to go with him.

By the time one of the cops at the hospital brought me back to the arena, the game was over. To add to the drama, all my guys seem to be missing.

I pack up the last of my odds and ends, shoving them into my backpack. "Hey, Teddy," I call as he walks past. "You seen Compton around anywhere?"

He shakes his head. "Nah. Sorry, Doc."

With a sigh, I sling my backpack onto my shoulder and start

walking in the direction of the locker room. We only took two cars here today and I have no keys. Unless I can find one of my guys or steal their keys, I'm stuck here. I can't imagine they left without me.

I turn the corner and a deep voice calls from the far end of the hallway.

"Rakas!"

I spin around with a relieved sigh to see Ilmari marching towards me, a wide smile on his face. My stomach does a little flip. Damn, he's so handsome. Brooding Ilmari makes my pussy purr with excitement. But a beaming Ilmari? I may as well be pregnant. And with the way he's looking at me now, with that devastating smile that reaches all the way to his eyes—

"Ohmygod," I gasp, my heart suddenly fit to burst. I know why he's so happy. In the chaos of tonight I forgot all about the scouts. "Oh my god!" I cry, dropping my bag to the floor and rushing forward.

We collide, my hands going to his shoulders as his drop to my waist. My senses fill with the comforting scent of him, freshly washed from the showers. His hair is still in a wet knot on his head, his pre-game Rays shorts and hoodie tight against his bulging frame.

"Kulta, what—"

He silences me with a kiss, groaning out his need for me as he glides his hands over my ass, pulling me closer. I know what he wants. On instinct I jump, and he lifts me, growling into our kiss as he turns me into the wall. My legs wrap around his waist, and I let him feast, my fatigue utterly forgotten.

"Kulta—baby—" I pant between kisses. "Tell me."

"I got it," he says on a breath. "It's mine."

"Oh, thank god," I cry, trying to hold him closer, wanting to share his skin. "I'm so proud of you, Ilmari."

"Mä rakastan sua," he mutters. "En voi elää ilman sua. Mennään naimisiin." He pulls back, his hips holding me pressed against the wall as his large hand lifts to frame my face. Those beautiful dark blue eyes stare into me, unraveling me. "Mennään naimisiin," he repeats, his voice gravelly. "Sano joo, Rakas."

Tears in my eyes, I shake my head with a smile. "I only caught maybe half of that. You know I love you too, right? I love you so much." I kiss him again, slower this time, savoring each one.

"Oh, what the hell is this?" comes a deep voice.

We break our kiss and Ilmari and I both turn our heads to see Doctor Avery standing there with his backpack slung over his shoulder. He scoffs, shaking his head. "You riding the players now, Doc? Is tonsil check a new service we're offering?"

Ilmari loosens his hold on me as I shimmy down to the floor. He keeps his body pressed in close against mine, like he's trying to block me from Avery's view.

Shit. This does look bad. But I really don't care. I'm not going to let Avery ruin this moment for Ilmari. Putting a smile on my face, I place a soothing hand on his arm. "Ilmari was just offered the starting spot on the Finnish Olympic Team," I call down the hall. "We got a little carried away celebrating."

Avery huffs, grabbing my discarded backpack by the handle and walking towards us. "And what does he get if he makes the medal stand?"

I tense, hating his smug fucking tone. He thinks he's catching us. He thinks this is a dirty secret and he means to use it if he can. I square my shoulders at him. "Hmm, I hadn't thought," I say, tapping my chin with a finger. "I'll probably offer to sit on his face. I know how much he likes that. Gold medal will definitely have to be something special. Maybe I'll finally let him get me pregnant."

"Rakas . . ." Ilmari mutters low in warning, his hand wrapping around to grip my hip.

Avery stills, his gaze darting between us. "Wait—you guys are together? Like, for real?"

"Not that it's any of your goddamn business, but yes," I reply. "Ilmari and I are together. So, you can take whatever shitty ideas you have about holding it over on us and forget it."

He huffs a laugh. "Oh, this is rich. I was coming to find you, Doc. Coach is looking for you. Apparently, your *other* boyfriend finally got himself caught with his pants down tonight."

I go very still, trying to school my features.

Avery smirks. "Judging by your expression right now, he wasn't caught with you. Good to know. That just won me a bet." He turns to Ilmari. "Oh wait—did you not know, Mars? About the other guy? Or maybe *you're* the other guy."

"Don't," I murmur, holding tighter to his arm. "He's not worth it."

Avery just huffs again. "Just one guy's opinion, but I'd hold off on knocking her up, Kinnunen. Sounds like she may already be pregnant . . . with another dude's baby." With that, he drops my backpack to the floor at my feet and saunters off back down the hall.

"I hate that man," Ilmari growls.

"Forget him," I say.

"He won't stay quiet. He'll tell everyone."

"Sounds like it may already be too late." Dropping my hand to my side, I take his, weaving our fingers together. With my free hand, I duck down and grab the strap of my backpack. "Come on. We need to find the guys."

"Doctor Price!"

Ilmari and I both spin around, hands held fast.

Coach Johnson is standing at the opposite end of the hall. He waves us down. "We've been looking for you! Come on. You too, Kinnunen."

"Oh shit," I murmur. "Off the ice, and into the fire we go, huh?"

Ilmari gives my hand a squeeze. "Lead the way, Rakas."

Taking a deep breath, I hold Ilmari's hand and walk us down the hall towards our fate.

"**I**s someone gonna tell me what the hell is going on here?"

Coach Johnson stands in the middle of the locker room, hands on his hips. He's a big man, with broad shoulders and a barrel chest. Next to him stands Assistant Coach Andrews. Near the door, Vicki and Poppy huddle together, looking extremely confused.

The only other two people in the room are Jake and Caleb . . . and they're holding hands. My eyes go wide, shocked by their brazen public display of affection. Caleb doesn't even like holding my hand in the privacy of the living room. What the hell did I miss tonight?

Ilmari and I join Jake and Caleb in the middle of the room.

"Did you get it?" Jake says, a wide smile on his face.

Ilmari nods.

"Oh, fuck yes!" He drops Caleb's hand and holds his up, waiting for Ilmari to give him a high-five.

With a sigh, Ilmari does.

"Congrats, man," Caleb adds.

"We are so fucking celebrating tonight. Cedar plank salmon fillets and steamed broccoli for everyone," Jake teases. "We'll pop the cork on some aged cucumber water."

I try to hide my smile.

"What the hell is he talking about?" Coach Johnson says at Ilmari, while behind him, Andrews says, "Oh shit," eyes wide.

"I'm going to the Olympics," Ilmari announces to the room. "Starting goalie for the Finnish National Team."

Behind us, Vicki and Poppy squeal with excitement, calling out their congratulations. Andrews steps forward to shake Ilmari's hand. "Amazing," he says. "So well deserved."

"Oh my goodness," says Poppy. "We'll have to get started on the press releases pronto. And we'll do a photo shoot, interviews—"

"Wait just a goddamn minute," Coach Johnson says, holding up a hand. "Mars, we're happy for you. But that isn't the reason I'm delayed getting home to my wife and kids tonight. Now, we're gonna get to the bottom of this right now. I've got Andrews here, the PR rep, Vicki from the team manager's office. We're all standing here looking at the four of you. What the hell is going on?" He glances between us, his gaze landing on me. "Price? Wanna enlighten us?"

I glance at Jake and Caleb, unsure of what to say. "I . . ."

"Okay, how about I start?" says Coach. "Just before you came in here, Compton was in the middle of telling us that he's in a romantic relationship with our equipment manager."

Ilmari and I both glance sharply over at the guys. This was never part of the discussion. We only ever discussed them coming out as all dating me. I definitely missed something big when I went to go take care of Novy.

"Is it true?" I say, tears in my eyes as I glance between them.

"Yeah, Seattle," Jake replies with a smile, nudging Caleb with his shoulder. "The asshole finally wore me down."

I bit my lip to keep from smiling as Caleb curses under his breath. "Can you try not to make a joke of everything?" he mutters. "This is serious."

"Thank you, Sanford," Coach replies. "This *is* serious. Compton are you telling us you want to come out? Is this a gay pride thing?"

"I mean . . . no one is really gonna be all that surprised, sir. Caleb and I already live together. The rumors have circled us since college. We're just . . . not denying them anymore," Jake says with a shrug.

Coach turns to the ladies by the door. "What are the rules here, Vicki?"

Vicki glances between us. "So long as they declare the relationship with HR, and they go through the proper briefings, technically speaking there's no issue."

"And the PR angle?" Coach adds at Poppy.

"Oh, goodness," she says, flipping her sleek blonde ponytail off her shoulder. "Well, coming out is still a pretty significant thing in the sports world. It'll cause quite a splash . . . if that's what you want," she adds, looking at Jake. "Are you wanting to come out to just the team and ask for a gag order on press? Because there's only so much we can do . . ."

"No, it's fine," Jake says. "I want this to be public. I want everyone to know I'm with Caleb."

"I sure hope you know what you're doing wanting to go public with this," Coach warns.

"I'm confused though, honey," says Vicki. She points between Jake and I, her dark eyes narrowed. "Are you not together anymore?"

"We are," I say.

Poppy's eyes go wide, her mouth open as she glances between us. "What—I don't—"

"Oh, hell," Coach mutters. "Is this a love triangle thing?"

"It's more like a pyramid," Jake replies.

"Explain yourselves," says Vicki, arms crossed.

"We're together," I say, glancing at the guys. "The four of us. Well, Jake and Caleb and I are together," I clarify. "And Ilmari and I . . . but he's not with them."

They all stare at us with confused looks on their faces.

"I'm too old for this," Coach says at last, shaking his head.

"You're—is it like a swingers thing?" says Andrews, clearly trying to be hip enough to understand.

"No, it's polyamory," replies Poppy with an excited grin. "You're polyamorous. Right, Rachel?"

I nod. "But I swear to you, I never—*we* never planned on this. It just kind of happened," I admit. "I met Jake first, before I ever joined the Rays. We met in Seattle during the off season. And when I got here, we started things back up again. Through him, I met Caleb. And Ilmari found his way to us," I add with a smile, squeezing his hand. "We all live together. We're together, sir. We're a family. And we'd like to go public. But it's complicated because of my family and my history. And the guys have their NHL careers to think about," I add, glancing from Ilmari to Jake.

"We never meant to hide anything, sir," Jake adds. "We've just been cautious as we considered how best to do this. Mars and I don't want to hurt the team or bring anyone bad press. But we can't live a lie either. It'll just get worse if we do. We don't want the guys chirping at us or feeling like we have secrets in the locker room."

"And the guys are ready to know," Caleb adds. "Novy and Morrow came to me last week saying the team will support us. The press outside the Rays will eat it up because of Rachel and her family, but inside our team, the guys seem cool. They just don't want secrets."

"What is all this about your family, Price?" Coach says, his sharp eyes glaring at me.

"I umm . . . my dad—"

"Her dad is world famous rock star Hal Price!" Poppy squeals. "You know, front man for The Ferrymen?"

"Christ, why do I keep forgetting that?" Coach mutters, rubbing his face with a tired hand.

"You're saying the guys know you're in a four-way sharing relationship with the team doctor and they're cool with it?" says Andrews, one brow raised.

"Well, they don't know *all* the details," Caleb admits. "But they know pieces. Like, Jerry caught Jake and I tonight."

"And Avery just caught Mars and me," I add.

"And the guys have been guessing I'm with Rach for months," says Jake. "We had the form signed and everything. We were just keeping it quiet."

"Damn," Coach huffs. "Right, well here's order number one: stop fucking around in the goddamn barn. I should fire you all for that alone. There will be no funny business on the job. You understand me, Compton?" he says, pointing a finger in his face. "I get even a whiff of you making eyes at Sanford at work, I'll send you both packing. Same goes for you, Kinnunen. We keep that shit at home."

"Yes, sir," Jake mutters. Caleb echoes him.

Coach sighs, glancing at me. "There's a bigger issue here, Price."

I go still, holding his gaze. "Sir?"

"Based on what I've heard, it sounds like you've been engaged in a romantic relationship with—not one—but *two* of my players this season."

I nod again. "Yes, sir."

He sighs. "Well, Vicki, correct me if I'm wrong, but she only had clearance from HR with Compton, correct?"

"That's correct, sir," Vicki replies.

"No," Ilmari mutters next to me.

"Don't," I whisper, squeezing his hand.

"So, you've been romantically involved with Kinnunen, *and* you've been his primary care provider, yes? You've been actively treating him for a groin pull?" Coach asks.

I let out a breath as I nod. "Yes, sir."

He sighs again, shaking his head. "So, you see our problem. Right, Doctor Price?"

"Yes, sir," I say again, not daring to let tears sting my eyes.

"Rakas, don't," Ilmari growls, lowering his face towards me.

"I'm not going to lie, Ilmari," I reply, trying to keep my voice calm. "We knew what we were doing. I knew. Jake and Caleb pressed me on it, but I ignored them because I wanted to make sure you got the level of care you deserved—"

"This is all Avery's fault," Ilmari snaps, turning his gaze back to the coaches.

"Avery? What did he do?" asks Andrews.

"He's the fucking worst," Jake mutters. "Excuse my language, sir," he adds at Coach.

"The guys all hate him," Caleb adds. "Some of them won't even work with him anymore. They all prefer Rachel. Which just pisses him off even more. He's always riding Rachel's case and making life harder for her at practice and games."

Andrews looks to me. "Is this true, Price?"

"If the guys have a problem with Doctor Avery, they haven't mentioned it to me," I admit. "But I do treat several of them in the capacity of a PT. Langley and Sully, J-Lo, Karlsson . . . Kinnunen—"

Ilmari steps forward. "The only reason I even approached Doctor Price is because I didn't trust Avery. I went to him twice in the off season to discuss my pain and *twice* he shut me down. He told me I needed a better stretching routine. And then he said I was too old. His official recommendation was that I retire."

I gasp, turning to face him. "He did *not* say that."

"He did," Ilmari mutters. "Why do you think I was so reluctant to have you help me?" He turns back to the coaches. "She helped me when I felt abandoned by the medical staff here. She used her own resources to get me up to Cincinnati for treatment when I refused to go through Avery. Doctor Price has never once done anything to jeopardize my health or my safety. And if you fire her—"

"Stop right there, Kinnunen," Coach barks. "You may be a fantastic player, but you are not in charge here. The fact remains that she knowingly broke the rules, and you helped her do it. She knew what she was doing was unethical—"

"Is it unethical to provide the level of care a player deserves?" Jake counters. "Just because this team employs subpar medical professionals, doesn't mean we should suffer for it. Mars was right to get treatment from her—"

"I'm not contesting that fact," Coach shouts over him. "But Doctor Price still engaged in a sexual relationship with her patient! It sounds like she's been doing *everything* in the shadows since she got here. How are we to know what she did and didn't do with Kinnunen? Where are the records of this Cincinnati trip? Why wasn't I informed that my star goalie left the state for clandestine medical procedures?"

He turns his stormy gaze on me. "I don't begrudge you your servant's heart, Doctor Price. I even thank you for the care you've so clearly shown my players. But you've got a lot to learn about working as part of a team. Secrets and lies and operating on your own without any oversight is not the kind of teamwork I expect. It's not conduct I can condone either," he says, a note of finality in his voice.

"What are you saying?" says Jake, one arm looping protectively around my waist.

"I'm saying this is out of my hands," Coach admits. "I may be the Head Coach, but I'm not the ultimate shot-caller here. My personal recommendation is that Doctor Price be fired, effectively immediately—"

"Coach, no!" Jake cries.

"Oh my goodness," Poppy gasps, tears in her eyes.

"This is wrong," says Ilmari.

"So fucking wrong," Caleb echoes.

"*As I said*," Coach calls over them, "it's not my decision. This has to go up to the General Manager. With all these accusations about Avery—to say absolutely *nothing* about the rat's nest that is your complicated romantic lives. Then there's Compton and his coming out, Kinnunen and his Olympic announcement—I mean, what the *hell* are you thinking?" he barks, eyes on Ilmari. "They're gonna pull your offer, son."

"They won't," he replies.

"They *won't*?" Coach echoes, his tone incredulous. "How the hell can you—"

"Because I already told them everything," he explains.

"Ilmari," I murmur, tears now burning my eyes.

"I told them to be prepared that the news of my relationship with Doctor Price would make the American press," he goes on. "Luckily, Finns are more amenable to the idea that people can dare to have personal lives. And it is no scandal to be a man in love with a smart, talented woman. It is no scandal for that man to cohabitate with two men he sees as closer than friends. They are family to me. Finns who know my history will be happy that I have a family to call my own. My agent is already working on the press releases. I have the full support of the FIHA."

"Kulta," I whisper, taking his hand. Relief floods me, mingling with my shame and embarrassment. I've made such a mess of everything. To still have his support means the world to me.

"Right," Coach says on a tired sigh. "I can't possibly make this decision. Not without input from the GM. What I *can* do is say that, effectively immediately, Doctor Price is suspended—"

"No," Jake barks.

"Shut up," Caleb says, grabbing his arm. "Suspended isn't fired. It's a fucking win."

Jake grumbles, shaking his head. Next to me, Ilmari is silent as the grave. Jake and Ilmari inch closer to my left and right, buttressing me.

Coach holds my gaze. "You're suspended until further notice, Doctor Price. Give us time to unravel this mess, and we'll decide what to do with your fellowship. But I have to warn you," he adds. "It doesn't look promising."

"Yes, sir," I murmur. "I understand."

He sighs again. "Fine. I can't deal with any more of this tonight. All of you go home. And Compton, Kinnunen, you let this affect your play or your attitudes out on that ice, and I'll suspend you too. Understood?"

"Yes, sir," Jake grits out.

I squeeze Ilmari's hand, and he mutters out a, "Yes."

"Good. Now, everyone get out of here. We're back at it bright and early. Well . . . except for you, Price," he adds at me. "While the suspension is in place, you'll need to hand over your ID and keycards. You're banned from access to the team until further notice."

I give him a stiff nod. "Yes, sir."

Operating on autopilot, I sling my backpack around to my front and open the smallest pocket. With shaking hands, I pull out my lanyard that contains my Rays ID and door access keys. Stepping forward, I hand the entire lanyard over to Vicki.

She accepts it wordlessly, tears brimming in her eyes.

Not waiting to see if the guys follow me, I walk right out the door of the locker room and don't look back.

"*S*he still in the bathroom d'you think?" Jake whispers, coming to stand in my doorway.

He's been an anxious mess since we got home. It's understandable. We're all a mess. Rachel was practically a zombie as we got her out of the arena. And then she made the excuse about needing to use the bathroom as soon as we got home and disappeared into her room, shutting the door behind her.

That was an hour ago.

"I very much doubt it," I mutter, turning my attention back to my laptop. Her room is right across from mine, so I've been casually camped out at my desk, pretending to be on my computer, just waiting for any signs of life behind her closed door.

Usually, when she's in there, she's cranking music or talking to Tess or her brother on the phone. Now she's silent as a mouse.

"We should check on her," Jake says.

"If you want," I say with a shrug.

He leaps across the hall, knocking on her door. "Babe? Can I come in?"

When she doesn't respond, he glances over his shoulder at me. Then he drops his hand down to the handle and gives it a wiggle. She didn't lock it. I'm not sure if that's a good sign or not, but Jake swings it open.

"Hey, baby—*what*—Seattle, what are you doing?" he cries, disappearing into her room.

I launch from my desk chair, stumbling across the hall into her room. I step around Jake to see Rachel moving from the dresser back to her bed, stacking clothes inside an open suitcase. My heart drops out of my fucking chest. "Hurricane . . ."

"Baby, *no*," Jake cries. "What are you doing?" He crosses the room, snapping the lid of her suitcase closed before she can drop another pile of clothes inside. "Rachel, stop!"

"Jake," she sighs, tears streaming down her face. "Please, don't do this—"

"Don't do *what*?" he cries. "Let the love of my fucking life pack a bag to leave me?"

"I can't stay here," she pants, tossing the pile into the other suitcase instead.

"What the hell are you talking about? You *live* here!"

"How can I keep living here? I don't have a job. I don't have a reference. I can't even return to Cincinnati, because Doctor Halla already gave my spot away for the year."

She keeps packing as she talks, rushing into her ensuite bathroom. "I can't stay here and ruin all your lives. I can't drag you further down into my mess. I can't make this any worse—god, I make everything fucking worse. You all deserve so much better. I don't know what I was thinking, risking your jobs, your reputations—I can't—I don't—oh *god*—"

She drops the bag of toiletries to the floor, sinking onto the end of the bed between her two half-packed suitcases, burying her face in her hands.

"Mars, get the fuck in here!" Jake shouts before dropping to his knees at Rachel's feet, his hands wrapping around her wrists as he starts murmuring softly to her. "Please, don't do this, baby girl. Don't lose hope. Don't give up on us—on the Rays. This is a mess, but we'll sort it out. Together, we'll figure it out—"

She shakes her head. "No, Coach was right. I've been running around, making all these decisions, hurting everyone I come into contact with, jeopardizing everything. You've worked so hard to build all this, Jake," she says, gesturing around. "I can't be the one to tear it down."

Jake looks around, incredulous. "What—this fucking house? *I'll* tear it down. I don't give a fuck about this house, Rachel. I care about the *people* in it. You and Cay and Mars and the dog—and yes, I really love my coffee maker—shit, and my home gym," he adds. "But I can get a new coffee maker," he says quickly. "I can't get a new *you*."

Mars steps into the room behind me, looking sharply around. "No," he says tonelessly.

Rachel looks up, seeing him standing there. "Ilmari," she sighs, shaking her head.

"Wait," I say. "Everybody fucking stop. Rachel, we're not gonna play this game with you. At least, I know I'm not. I will not spend a single moment of my time convincing you to stay—"

"Don't be an asshole," Jake growls at me.

"I'm not being an asshole," I counter. "I'm knowing my own self-worth. I don't beg the people I love to love me back. Jake, get off your fucking knees, and stop being a pussy. If she wants to go, let her go. If she wants to stay, let her stay. We don't try to convince her either way."

"Agreed," says Mars, crossing his arms over his bare chest.

Jake is at literal war with himself, the soft marshmallow side of him wanting to melt for her and stay on his knees. Then there's the obstinate, confident, god of a man who rules a hockey rink. He wants to flip her over and spank her ass raw for daring to even think of leaving us. With a groan, he stumbles to his feet and steps back, his body tense as he comes over to stand by me.

"Good boy," I say.

"Shut the fuck up," he mutters, his face a mask of agony.

Rachel sits on the end of the bed she never sleeps in wearing nothing but her blue silk cami and a matching pair of sleep shorts. Her tousled hair frames her face, half of it up, half down.

"You wanna go, Rachel? Keep packing. Mars here will drive you to the airport, the bus depot, the cruise dock. Just tell him where, and he'll take you. You wanna stay? We'll be downstairs."

I have to physically turn Jake around, pushing him out the door first, but the three of us walk out in silence, leaving the door open behind us, and troop down the stairs to the living room. I give Jake's shoulder a nudge, and he sinks like a rock onto the couch.

"If she leaves us, I'll never forgive you," he mutters darkly, his gaze unfixed as he stares in the direction of the TV.

"Yes, you will," I reply, sinking onto the couch next to him.

"Oh, you fucking think so?"

"I do."

"Why?"

"Because, if she leaves us, she didn't love us enough to stay, respect us enough to let us make our own decisions, or want us enough to fight through this storm," I reply. "My Hurricane *is* the fucking storm. When she remembers that fact, she'll come down those stairs and stir us all up. Until then, give me the fucking remote. We're watching *Great British Bake Off*."

99
RACHEL

*H*ow did everything get so messed up? Five months ago, I was sitting at a bar in Seattle, wallowing in my professional failure, day drinking by myself . . . well, almost by myself. I *wished* I was by myself.

Then in walked my Mystery Boy.

Now here I am, five months later, feeling like nothing has changed. I'm still alone. Still wallowing over a professional failure.

Only *everything* has changed. I've changed. They've changed me. Jake, Caleb, Ilmari. They each took a piece of me and unraveled the threads, weaving their own threads back in with mine. The result is something entirely new. Something stronger. Something more beautiful than I could have ever made on my own.

I've been sitting in this room for the last hour, spiraling out of control. Like a skydiver without a parachute who takes their jump in the dark, I've been spinning, looking for anything to orient myself. Which way is up? Which way is down? How do I stop this feeling of free fall?

And then my Caleb gave me the anchor I needed.

Choice.

We all have a choice in this world. Stay or go. Love or hate. Fight or flee. I get to choose what happens next. I may not be able to control whether the Rays let me keep my job, but I can control how I respond to it.

Stay or go, Rachel?

Do I want to stay here? Do I want to stay with my guys? *Yes*, comes the deep voice of longing, echoing out from the very center of being. I want to stay. I want to belong here with them. My guys. My family.

Love or hate?

Do I love Jake Compton?

I smile, closing my eyes as my mind floods with the memories of our first night together. That man claimed me on that perfect night.

Our souls entwined. It was fate. It was nature in poetic motion. He's mine and I'm his. Loving him is easier than breathing. My joy and my happiness, he brings sweetness to my life. He centers me and makes me feel whole. Yes, I love Jake Compton.

But do I love Caleb Sanford?

Moody, temperamental, aloof. He wears a hard shell. Some of it hides his very real pain. He's been hurt in this life. He knows loss and tragedy. But he also knows the resilient hope that comes from healing. He knows how to weather a storm, even one that strips you to nothing. He knows how to rebuild. He's a survivor. He's the strong center that holds. He is the place where we all find strength.

And that's the secret to Caleb. His shell hides his pain. But it also hides his hopeful heart. He's an optimist, though he'll never admit it. He's a dreamer. I want to see the world through his eyes. I want to see his dreams and make them real. My strength, my heart. I love him so madly.

And what of Ilmari? Do I love Mars Kinnunen?

I close my eyes again, breathing deep, searching for that feeling of utter peace and quiet I can only chase in his arms. Ilmari is like the trees in the forest, rooted deep and stretching high. He is soft, yet unyielding. Stalwart. He contains multitudes. He makes me believe that home isn't a place. It's a feeling. Home is being in his arms. It's feeling his eyes on me. It's having him buried deep, moving together like one being, sharing flesh and breath and soul. Yes, I am in love with Ilmari Kinnunen.

My breath comes out in a shaky pant as I feel like my heart is overflowing with love for these men that have so completely captured me. I love them all. I want to stay. I want to be theirs. Only one question remains.

Fight or Flight?

Do I have the strength to stay? Do I have the strength to love them as they deserve to be loved? Unashamed, unafraid, and wholly out loud. God, I fucking hope so.

I scramble to my feet, heart pounding, as I rush to my open door. I move into the hallway, running on bare feet towards the stairs. I hurry down, my hand ghosting along the cool metal of the banister.

I spin around the bottom stair, marching down the short entry hall until the walls give way to the great room. All three of my guys are right where they said they'd be, sitting on the couch in a row, waiting for me.

Tears of gratitude pour down my cheeks as I practically stumble into the room, sweeping around the back of the sectional. All eyes are on me as I drop myself on Caleb's lap. I bury my face against his bare chest, my hands brushing through his hair to circle his nape as I sob.

"I'm sorry. Cay, please—I'm so sorry. I want to stay. Please let me stay. Love me, and fight with me, and let me stay."

Slowly, his arms lift and come around me. His hands smooth up and down my back before one goes to my hair. Gently, he weaves his fingers in and pulls my head back until he can look me in the eye. "You're staying?"

I nod.

"You're fighting?"

I nod again.

"Words, Rachel," he growls.

"Yes," I say on a breath. "I want to stay and fight and love you. All of you. I can't promise perfection. Frankly, I have no idea what the hell I'm doing—what I *will* do. But I know from the bottom of my heart that we are stronger together than I could ever dream of being apart."

I glance from Jake to Ilmari, back to Caleb. "I know I've made mistakes. I've doubted and manipulated. I've sought to control everything. In my fear, I thought I had to. I've been so alone for so long. So used to surviving on my own—"

"Well, that stops now," Caleb says. "You're dealing with three hockey players, Rachel. We don't work alone. Team first. Team always."

I nod, trying to center my breath. "Team first," I repeat.

"I know your family carries a lot of weight for you," he goes on. "Price Family against the world and all that. But this will only work if you make *this* your family. The Price-Compton-Sanford-Kinnunen Family."

"I swear to fuck, we are not hyphenating our names like that," Jake mutters.

I bite my lip to keep from smiling. Closing my eyes, I take another breath and nod.

"You done threatening to leave us?" Caleb says, his gaze imperious as he keeps his heart locked deep inside his shell.

I nod. "Yes."

"Good," he mutters. "Because you scared him half to fucking death," he says, pointing at Jake. "If you've got something to say to him, now might be a good time."

The last vestiges of my walls come crumbling down at I look to my Jake and see the tears in his eyes. I practically throw myself at him, crawling off Caleb's lap and onto Jake's. "I'm sorry," I cry. "Angel, I'm so sorry. I was so messed up."

Jake has none of Caleb's cool aloofness. He wraps himself around me, peppering me with kisses on my shoulder, my neck, my cheek. Each one feels like a gift, like a spark of his life soaks into my skin and lights me up from the inside, warming me and giving me strength.

"I love you, Jake," I murmur, kissing him back. "Angel, I love you. I love you so much."

"Never let me go," he pants, his hands in my hair. "Rach, please. Never let me go. Marry me." He pulls away, hands cupping my face. "Marry us."

My eyes go wide. "What?"

"We can't make it official," he says, shaking his head. "I googled it. There are laws that say we can't be official, but I want you to marry us anyway. No Elvis, no churches, no paperwork. Just your promise linked with mine."

I glance from him to the others, eyes wide. "How would that—you don't want that," I whisper, looking to Ilmari. "You would want that?"

He scowls at me. "What do you think 'mennään naimisiin' means?"

I blink back at him. "I don't know. I don't speak Finnish!"

"It means 'marry me,'" he huffs. "I say it all the goddamn time."

"Well how am I supposed to—"

"Enough," Caleb says. "Hurricane, do you want to be illegally married to Mars based on nothing more than a verbal agreement spoken here in this living room?"

I fight a laugh as I nod. Sitting on another man's lap, feeling his hard cock against my thigh, I hear myself saying, "Hell, yes. I marry you, Ilmari."

He nods, lips pursed like he can't decide if he's pleased or still annoyed.

"And Cay, baby?" Jake teases, brushing a hand through my messy hair. "You wanna be illegally married to Cay and live in dirty fucking sin with him? You want to be his good girl and ride his weird, ribbed cock for the rest of your life?"

I snort. It's quite a set of vows. The kind you most definitely immortalize in song form so that your children and their children can never escape it. I'll put daddy to work on it as a birthday present for Cay. "Yes," I say, my gaze locked on Cay's gorgeous, dark eyes. "I marry you, Caleb. You're mine."

He smirks, ever the cool customer.

"And me, baby?" says Jake, both hands cupping my face. "I loved you from the moment I saw you. You stole my breath away, and I've been living on borrowed time ever since. Be my life support. Keep my heart beating. Marry the fuck outta me."

I grin, my own hands cupping his cheeks. "I love you so much, Jake. You walked into that bar, and I never stood a chance. I am so irrevocably yours. Be mine forever."

"Forever," he murmurs, his lips brushing mine. "Forever and forever and forever."

We kiss, pouring our need into each other. I fight him for dominance until I'm squirming, breaking our kiss, his hands on my breasts, kneading me through the silk of my cami.

"Fuck," I pant, slapping his hands down so I can jerk my cami off up over my head. I throw it behind me, not caring where it lands. "I need you all. Need to have you."

Three pairs of eyes watch me, but it's Caleb who speaks. "Say what you want, Hurricane."

Pushing off Jake's lap, I stand and take a step back, dropping my silky shorts to the floor, leaving me naked. "I want all three of you. All at once. I want to be dripping with your cum. Make a mess of me. Claim me so there's no more doubt where I belong."

100
RACHEL

All three of my guys are staring at me wide-eyed. *Good.* I want all their attention. All their love. But I also want to play. I want to break the curse of this awful night and bring us back together. I want joy again. Laughter and love.

And I want some really amazing sex.

"I'm going upstairs now," I say, ready to poke my three stupidly hot men into action. "I want three cocks inside me. Either join in, or I'll get creative with my toy collection."

Turning on my heel, I get exactly three steps before they all give chase. Ilmari is the fastest, slinging me over his shirtless shoulder and carrying me up the stairs like a sack of flour. I grin like a loon as Caleb and Jake follow, taking the stairs two at a time.

Ilmari marches me down the long hall into Jake's room and tosses me down at the foot of the bed. The old frame is gone. Instead, the guys have rigged up a double king bed on a low-rise platform. Ilmari bought a copy of Jake's precious mattress, so there would be no arguing over spots.

My breath leaves me in a puff of air as I scoot towards the middle. But then I gasp, laughing out loud, as he grabs me by the ankles and drags me down the bed, spreading me open. Muttering something I don't catch in Finnish, he drops to his knees on the floor and covers my pussy with his mouth.

"*Oh*—" My back arches as he pins me down with his firm grip, his tongue teasing me from pussy to clit. I curl forward with a moan, my hands going to his hair.

Behind him, Caleb and Jake make quick work of shedding their clothes. All three of them were shirtless to begin with, so a drop of the pants has them naked and ready to go. The room is lit only by the soft light of the bathroom and the hallway, making everything feel dark and close and comfortable.

"Lie back," Caleb commands, climbing onto the bed next to me. Jake drops down on my other side. They each take a shoulder, pressing me into the mattress. Then they take my arms, stretching them up above my head. Jake keeps his fingers woven with mine, holding me down, as he descends on my breast, his eager tongue flicking my nipple as he sucks.

I sigh into the blissful feeling of two men loving me at once, and then Caleb is kissing me. All three of them are here and the feeling is indescribable. I'm fevered. I'm flying. Falling, sinking, glowing.

I close my eyes and let myself feel it all, crying out in ecstasy as my first release tears through me. The moment it starts, spreading out from my center, Ilmari shoves two fingers inside my pussy, his tongue teasing my clit.

"Fuck—" I fight against the weight of my three men holding me down. My body wants to curl forward. My core wants to bear down on Ilmari's fingers. "More," I plead. "I want more."

Ilmari works me until I'm a squirming mess. Then he sits back on his heels, a smirk on his face. I gaze down my body at him, chest heaving, the peaked tips of my nipples glistening with Jake's kisses. Then I turn my head to the side looking at Caleb. "Angel, you feel like helping me drive Cay wild?"

Caleb's gaze darkens.

"Fuck, yes." Jake grins, peppering a few more kisses up my chest before he nips my chin. "What did you have in mind?"

I smile, rolling onto to my side and then up on my knees. "I thought I might ride his face while you suck his cock," I tease, brushing one finger down Caleb's stubbled jaw.

His gaze hardens. "Don't fucking tease me," he mutters, his hand gripping my chin.

"Who's teasing?" I reply. "Lie down."

We hold each other's gaze for a few more seconds before he drops his hand away from me with a breathless, "Fuck." Then he shifts above me towards the middle of the bed, flopping across it horizontally.

"That's it," Jake teases, spreading Caleb's legs and crawling between them. "What a good boy—"

"Don't you fucking start unless you want me in that ass," Caleb growls, still propped up on his elbows, his pierced cock hard and ready.

"If you expect me to sit on your face, you better lie down," I say.

"Try not to come," Jake adds, his hands grazing up Caleb's thighs. "See how long you can last." As I watch, he wraps a hand around Caleb's base. Then he descends, sinking his mouth around Caleb's cock. Both men groan, Caleb's hands fisting tight to the sheets as he closes his eyes.

Ilmari slips off the bed, finally losing his pants as he moves around to the side. "Come, Rakas." He has himself in position at Caleb's head and I know exactly what they both want.

With a smile, I inch forward, holding out my hands to Ilmari. He helps me straddle Caleb, holding my weight as my bare pussy rests on Caleb's chest. I glance down to see his dark eyes watching me.

"You gonna sit or not, Hurricane?" His hands give my ass a squeeze. "I'm fucking starving."

I glance up at Ilmari and he nods, helping me into position over Caleb's face. Caleb holds me by the hips, pulling me down, and then I'm crying out, body locked in a spasm as he sucks on my clit.

"Oh my god," I whimper, my hands braced on Ilmari's hips as he steps in.

He fists my hair. "Take me, Rakas."

I lean forward, holding onto Ilmari's hips as I drag my tongue over his tip, savoring the salty taste of his precum. Meanwhile, Caleb fists my ass with both hands as he teases my pussy lips, my clit, my cunt. He spears me with his tongue, holding me still as he works two fingers inside me, curling them along my inner wall.

I groan around Ilmari's cock, his hand fisting tighter in my hair. "Come for us again," he says. "Fill Caleb's mouth. Make him drown."

As he speaks, Jake surprises me by crawling up Cay's chest. His hands go to my shoulders as he curls in close against me.

I gasp, glancing over my shoulder. "Jake—what—"

"Hold still." His hand drops between us as he slides his cock between my legs from behind, his tip teasing my entrance as we straddle Caleb's face together.

"Fuck," Caleb pants. "Oh, fuck—"

Jake does a few practice thrusts, his cock notching at my entrance. Then Caleb's mouth is there and he's teasing us both. It's messy and dirty and I fucking love it. I groan, head tipping back to rest against Jake's shoulder.

Then Ilmari drops down, hands in my hair, and kisses me senseless.

The pressure in my core builds as Jake wraps both hands around me, holding me tight to him as he thrusts with his hips, his tip teasing my entrance without penetrating me.

I'm shaking as I feel my orgasm ready to break like waves against the rocky shore. "I'm so close," I cry, my mouth sharing air with Ilmari.

"Mars, get on the bed," Jake pants, hauling me backwards with a force of strength, my orgasm popping like a soap bubble.

"No," I whine, that shaky, disorienting feeling of a delayed release making me feel dizzy. "I was right there," I pant.

Behind me, Jake chuckles, kissing my neck, my shoulder. "Don't get greedy," he teases, giving my ass a swat. "You know we'll keep you coming all night long. Suck his cock again, baby. I'm taking this cunt. This time, make our guy see stars."

Caleb rolls over with a groan, slipping off the side of the bed as Mars moves higher up on the bed, sitting propped at the head, his thick tree trunk legs spread wide. "Come, Rakas."

I drop away from Jake's grasp and crawl forward on hands and knees, kissing up Ilmari's thighs and over the soft skin of his hips. I breathe him in, loving that masculine smell.

"Mä rakastan sua," he murmurs, brushing my hair back as I lower my mouth around him, taking him to the back of my throat.

Behind me, Jake taps my hip. I adjust my stance, widening my legs. His hands smooth up my thighs, over the round curve of my ass as he inches forward on his knees, ready to notch himself at my entrance.

"Wait," Caleb calls.

I stop sucking Ilmari long enough to glance over my shoulder. Caleb walks up to the bed holding something in his hand. "What is that?" I murmur.

"What does it look like?" he says with a smile.

I narrow my eyes at the thing in his hand. "It looks like a butt plug."

"That's because it is." He's holding a bright pink butt plug glistening with lube. Reaching between me and Jake, he presses the tip in at my ass. "You want it, Hurricane?"

I nod. He and Jake smile, hungry gazes dropping down to my ass as he presses the toy in. I gasp, fighting the urge to clench.

"That's it," he soothes. "Breath it out like my good girl. Did I mention it vibrates?"

"No—*ahh*—fuck—" I cry out, my ass suddenly humming with the vibrations of the toy.

"Oh, yes," Jake laughs. "Bend over, baby girl. I'm taking this pussy—"

"Not so fast," Caleb calls.

Jake and I both glance over our shoulders.

"Oh, what the fuck is that?" Jake mutters.

"You didn't think I'd leave you out, did you, *angel*?" Caleb teases.

My eyes go wide as I see he's holding another slightly larger butt plug. This one in black.

"Bend over," Caleb orders, his free hand smoothing down the curve of Jake's ass.

"Oh, fuck," Jake moans, bending over me.

The buzzing in my ass is making me feel so full, bringing my orgasm right back to the edge. "Hurry," I beg. "Please."

"Fuck—shit—" Jake pants, his eyes wide as Caleb inserts the plug.

"Now, be my good pets, and come." As Caleb says the word, he turns on Jake's plug.

Jake groans, his body going slack behind me as his every sense is diverted to the strange new feeling of the plug in his ass. I hear the soft buzz, humming in time with mine.

"Fuck her, Jake," Caleb orders. "Fuck her, or I turn it up."

"Oh god," I whimper.

Ilmari has been silent this whole time, watching us like we're an interesting nature documentary. Now he has one hand slowly fisting his cock, a smile tipping his lips. "Look at me, Rakas," he says in that deep voice. "Keep your eyes on me. I want to watch him take you."

I'm fluttering like I have a thousand butterflies loose inside me. The heat of Ilmari's gaze is enough to burn me to ash. Between his gaze and the buzzing, I'm already a goner.

Then Jake reaches between my legs, his fingers sinking into my pussy with a groan. "Fuck, I can feel it buzzing in your ass." Then he's pressing in with his cock. The toy makes it a tight fit. "Holy god," he moans.

"Feel good?" Caleb murmurs, standing at the side of the bed, watching us.

"So fucking good," Jake pants. He starts moving his hips, but the movement is erratic. "I can't—can't last—can't focus—"

"Try harder," Caleb teases. "Or . . . maybe we should make it harder."

"Turn it up," Ilmari orders, his eyes still locked on me.

We both cry out as the buzzing intensifies. I'm a moaning mess. Jake does everything he can to pound into me. The buzzing steals all our sanity as we both come, our bodies rocked by waves of euphoria.

Just as I'm about to beg for mercy, the buzzing stops, and I can breathe again. Behind me, Jake groans, his cock still buried in me.

Caleb drops the remotes onto the bed and leans down, kissing us both. First Jake, then me. "What a beautiful sight," he murmurs, his fingers brushing the bare skin of my shoulder. "Hurricane, now that you're good and stretched out, you'll take Mars in the ass while I fuck your cunt."

I whimper as I nod, letting my men move me into position. Ilmari stays at the top of the bed, rolling forward to his knees. They turn me around, helping me onto my hands and knees as well until I'm facing the end of the bed.

Jake flops down beside us, the butt plug still in his ass, while Caleb pulls mine out, handing Ilmari the lube.

"Down lower," Ilmari orders.

I hurry to obey, my body still humming from my release. I drop down to my elbows, leaving my ass in the air. His left hand smooths down my back to my hips, while his right begins working more lube into my ass. By the time he's pressing three fingers in, I'm a whimpering mess, begging him to take me.

He works his way in, murmuring softly in Finnish. Sinking to the hilt, the curve of his thighs presses against the roundness of my ass. That perfect feeling of fullness centers me, warming me from the inside out. My heart pounds in my chest as my mouth goes dry. Holding tight to the sheets with both hands, I glance over my shoulder. "You're mine," I murmur.

"Yours," he replies, rocking his hips against me. He's gentle for such a giant of a man. But even gentle anal with Ilmari is a full body experience. I'm groaning, sweat beading on my brow, as I push up on my hands, looking for Caleb.

He's standing next to the bed, watching us fuck.

"Come," I say. "Be with us."

He steps forward, sinking back down onto the bed. It takes a second to maneuver him under me. He slides down the length of my body and nestles himself at the cradle of my hips. He slips his hand between us, his fingers teasing at my entrance, pulling away, he brings them to his lips, tasting the mix of Jake and mine's release.

"So perfect," he murmurs, a smile in his eyes. "Sit down, Hurricane."

With a deep breath, I drop my hips, riding Ilmari and Cay in one, letting Caleb's pierced cock fill me so tight and full.

"No niin," Ilmari groans, muttering other soft curses in Finnish as he and Cay quickly find their rhythm. Cay's piercings give us that perfect ribbed pressure. Between that and Ilmari's size, I don't stand a chance. I never did. Death by too much dick. And this is a death I mean to die over and over and over again.

"Please—god, don't stop," I cry out. "I'm right there—right—*there*—"

Behind me, Ilmari cries out, his body going stiff against me as he comes, his release filling my ass. I shatter, my core clenching around Caleb, strangling him so tight. My pussy pulses, threatening to pull him in deeper. Beneath me, he groans, his warm cum filling me too, mixing with Jake's release.

I drop down onto his chest, our breathing erratic as we recover. Ilmari pulls out of me first, slipping off the bed and disappearing into the bathroom. Caleb rolls me onto my side, his cock slipping out as I flop boneless onto my back.

Jake is there on my other side, turning my face with a gentle hand. He leans in, kissing me. "I love you," he murmurs against my lips. "I love you, baby."

"I love you," I reply, tears stinging my eyes. I turn my head to look back at Caleb, cupping his cheek. "I love you, Cay."

"I love you, Hurricane."

"And me?" Jake says with a huff, lifting up on one elbow to glare over me at Caleb. "You know, you never said it earlier. You let me say it, but *you* never said it."

Caleb rolls his eyes, flopping onto his back.

"Hey, you know I'm a needy fucking asshole," Jake growls. "Unless you want another emotional wreck on your hands, you better be ready to tell me something right the fuck now, even if all you can muster is feelings of fond regard."

Caleb smirks, tucking both his hands behind his head, saying nothing.

"Cay," I sigh with a shake of my head.

"You mother fucker," Jake growls, slipping off the bottom of the bed. At some point he ditched the butt plug. He marches naked around the bed, his half-hard cock flopping in the breeze as he climbs on Caleb's side of the bed and straddles him, pinning him down.

I rush to scoot out of their way as Caleb laughs, curling forward like he's ready to wrestle. But Jake is bigger and stronger. He's at his peak NHL fitness level. He pins Caleb down at the elbows, holding him with his hips as he glares down at him. "Say it."

Caleb laughs again. "A confession under duress is inadmissible—"

"Say it before I take mine back—"

Caleb rocks his hips against Jake and Jake gasps into silence. He does it again and Jake's eyes flash from anger to lust, back to anger.

"Don't you fucking dare," Jake growls.

But Caleb does it again, shifting his hips until his hard cock is brushing up against Jake's.

Heart in my throat, I watch as Jake groans, eyes shutting tight.

"Oh god," he mutters. Distracted, he lets Caleb slip his hold.

Caleb drops a hand between them, wrapping their cocks together in his fist. "Hurricane, get me the lube."

I roll to my knees, searching the bed for the bottle. Flipping open the cap, I drizzle the lube over Caleb's fist. He strokes them together and they both shiver, groaning with need.

"Kiss me." Caleb's thumb sweeps over the tip of Jake's cock.

"Say it," Jake counters.

"Kiss me like I'm the last man you'll ever fucking kiss," Caleb orders. "Because I am. You're mine, Jake Compton. Have been mine. Will be mine." With each confession, he works them together with a tight stroke of his fist.

Jake's eyes shut tight. "Please just fucking say it," he whimpers, lowering his face until his breath is fanning over Caleb's parted lips. "Baby, please—"

"I love you," Caleb says. "Jake, I love you. I'm in love with you. I am so fucking in love with you. Do anything, be anything, only love me too."

Jake goes still, gazing down at him. Slowly he nods. Then they're kissing, pouring out their desperate need for one another as they grind their hips together.

My heart overflows for them, watching them finally smash their walls to dust. I intend to love them and make them each so happy, but their truest happiness will come from sharing this love with each other too.

Slipping off the end of the bed, I pad across the room towards the bathroom. The feel of their sticky release rests warm between my thighs. As I reach for the door, Ilmari pulls it open. His eyes go wide as he takes in the scene over my shoulder. I glance back too, just in time to see Caleb flip Jake down to the mattress. Their kisses are ravenous as Caleb wraps a hand under Jake's thigh and spreads him wide.

"Oh fuck—*oh fuck*—fucking do it," Jake cries out.

Caleb presses in and Jake arches off the bed on a shout.

I gasp as a sharp tug jerks me backwards into the bathroom. The door snaps shut and Ilmari picks me up, plopping me on the sink. I hiss, the sting of the cold counter a shock to my bare ass cheeks.

"Let's leave them to their moment, Rakas," he murmurs, stepping between my spread legs. His hands gently brush my hair back from my face. "You are pleased for them?"

I nod, tears stinging my eyes. "So pleased. They're in love."

"And do you doubt their love for you?"

"No," I say on a breath. "Of course not. Do you doubt my love for *you* when you see me loving them?"

"No," he replies, his thumb brushing over my lips. "Your love is boundless, Rakas. I am learning from you what it means to love. And from them," he adds without a hint of shame. "I've never belonged anywhere—"

"You belong *here*," I say fiercely, cupping his bearded cheeks. "You belong with me. With *us*. Never doubt that. I know I was upset earlier. Hiding is my default. I hide when things get hard. But I'm learning about love from you too. You and Cay and Jake. The way you all love me . . . I don't want to hide anymore. I want to stand. I want to fight. Every night you put on your gear, and you fight. You take every hit, block every shot."

His fingers brush down the column of my neck, down my sternum, over my tattoo. His gaze follows the path of his fingers. "No more hiding, Rakas. No more fear. Promise me."

I nod, raising a hand to brush down his forearm. "I promise I'll try. Is that enough for now?"

He nods.

"Kulta?" I murmur, gazing up at him.

His deep blue eyes peer through me. "What?"

"My ass is freezing," I admit, biting my lip to keep from smiling.

He snorts, glancing down at how I'm spread naked on the counter. I squeal as he scoops me into his arms, hauling me into the shower. He flips on the double nozzles, and I shriek as a double blast of icy cold water hits us.

"Ilmari!"

He just laughs, holding me as I squirm. "If you're going to be married to a Finn, we have to toughen you up, Rakas. Hot saunas and cold showers."

"Never," I groan, relaxing under the spray as the water warms.

He sets me down on my feet, but I don't want to lose the feel of him so close. I turn in his arms, my wet skin brushing against his. As we stand under the hot spray, kissing and exploring each other, the bathroom door slams open. Caleb and Jake come barging in naked, drunk on too much sex as they kiss and stumble their way into the shower too.

Ilmari and I make room, his arms staying around me as we give them space under the second shower head.

They keep kissing, laughing and jostling each other, as Jake spins Cay around, shoving him up against the tiled wall. Caleb grunts, hands flat. Jake presses in with his hips, his hard cock nestled between Caleb's ass cheeks as he starts to grind.

"Aren't you tired yet?" I tease, heart pattering at the look of joy on their faces.

"God, I fucking love polyamory," Jake pants, holding Cay pinned to the wall with one hand as he leans over to give me a quick kiss. "Mars, the team needs you, man. Fuck our girl. Right here next to me. Let me hear her shatter while I take Cay for everything he has."

I glance up at Ilmari, waiting to see his reaction.

With a low groan, he glides his hands down my sides to my hips. His steely blue gaze locks on me and he smiles. "Up, Rakas."

I swear, I have never climbed a man so fast in my life.

101
JAKE

Is there such a thing as too much sex? Can it actually impair function? Cause I think I might have the sex sickness. I feel hungover
when I didn't drink. All my muscles hurt . . . in the best possible way.
Cay had to give me the 411 on bottoming aftercare, and let me tell you
that was an awkward conversation to have at three am.

Oh yeah, apparently, I'm a bottom now. Add that to the 'about me'
section of the Rays team roster website. Caleb says the proper term
is 'vers.' I'm learning all kinds of new words. I'm a bisexual polyamorous vers. Whatever. Cay can throw all the fancy new words at me
that he wants. I'm still Jake Compton. I don't feel any different.

At the same time though, I woke up this morning knowing nothing will ever be the same.

I move robotically down the stairs in search of breakfast and
the coffee maker. Stretching both arms over my head with a yawn, I
almost miss the large blue bag perched next to the front door. That's
Seattle's bag. Oh, what the ever-loving fuck—

"Rachel!" I bellow.

Stomping through the entry hall, I pause to find Rachel and
Caleb sitting at the kitchen island. Mars is at the stove, cooking something that smells amazing. Rachel and Cay both turn, eyes wide as
they take me in.

"Jake? You okay?" she says.

"Why the fuck is your bag by the door?" I say, pointing over my
shoulder. "I thought we dealt with that last night."

Caleb snorts, turning his attention back to his breakfast. "Told
you he wouldn't remember."

"Remember what?" I say, my gaze darting between them. Why
do the guys look totally unbothered by Rachel's packed suitcase?
Clearly, I'm missing something . . .

"I told you all last night after the shower," she says gently. "I think you were kind of out of it."

"We sexed him to death," Cay teases, spearing a piece of fruit with his fork.

She ignores him, eyes on me. "I'm going to LA for a few days. I already bought the ticket when I did my little panic spiral last night, but now it has a return date," she adds quickly, slipping off her stool to come take my hand.

"Why are you going to LA?"

She looks dressed and ready to leave—clothes on, hair washed, makeup done. I bet if I slept in any longer, I'd wake to find her gone. She tips up on her toes and gives me a quick kiss. She tastes like bacon and strawberries and fresh coffee.

"My parents are out in LA," she explains, leading me over to the island.

There's a small spread of breakfast—fresh juice, sliced berries and bananas, a big plate of bacon, and it smells like Mars is cooking something with eggs.

"Rakas, was this one mine?" he calls, leaning away from the stove to reach for a coffee mug.

"Hmm?" She glances over her shoulder. "No—"

"Mitä vittua," he curses, spitting the coffee out into the sink and slamming the mug down. "Why is it mint?"

Rachel snorts. "Kulta, the blue mug was Caleb's. Red was yours."

"Yeah, thanks a lot, asshole," Caleb mutters. "You owe me a new cup of coffee."

"Why was it mint?" Mars says again.

"Caleb likes peppermint mochas because he's fucking psychotic," I say in a huff, snatching up a piece of bacon. "But don't change the subject. *Why* are you going to LA?"

"Because my parents are there," she repeats. "And because I owe them an explanation in person. And because if I have to sit here for a week stewing in the fallout of my suspension, I'm gonna climb the freaking walls," she adds. "Jake, I can't just be trapped here while you three go into work. I'll be a mess. And my parents deserve to hear from me in person what's going on."

I glance from Cay to Mars. They seem fine with this. I shouldn't be freaked, right? "And you have a return ticket?"

She nods. "I come home Sunday."

"Hey—we play in LA this week, don't we? Isn't our Saturday game against the LA Kings?"

"Yeah," Caleb replies, taking a bite of his crunchy buttered toast.

"Cool," I say, brightening up as I snag a handful of blueberries. "So, we'll get to see you out there. And we can formally meet the parents. This'll be great!"

Rachel and Caleb both go still.

"What? Marrying a girl means we meet her parents, right?" I say, popping a couple berries in my mouth. "Isn't that how this works?"

"I . . . hadn't thought of that," she murmurs.

Slowly, we all turn as one to gape at her.

"What do you mean you hadn't thought of it?" Caleb replies.

"I mean I quite literally never thought of the first 'hey mom, meet my boyfriends' conversation," she squawks, hopping off her stool again.

"How is that possible?" I say.

"Well—I don't know! I guess, in my mind I've played out all these visions of us together—Christmas and vacations and games—but in all those scenarios, they already knew you," she explains. "I never once considered needing to have the awkward intro moment."

Caleb huffs a laugh. "What's the big deal? Have you never introduced your parents to a boyfriend before?"

The deafening silence in the room is broken only by the sizzle of eggs as all three of us stare at her.

"You gotta be shitting me, Seattle," I mutter. "You've *never* introduced your parents to a boyfriend before?"

"Of course, not," she cries. "My early twenties were a who's who of human trash. There was never a moment I wanted to waste my parents' time with an introduction of some guy that was only going to be around for the length of a—"

"Dooooon't you dare finish that sentence," I say. "Look, I know you had guys before us, but here's the new house rule: frisbee golf rules apply to all past relationships."

They all exchange a confused glance. "Frisbee golf rules?" she asks.

"Yeah, you know like, do I know that frisbee golf is a thing? Yeah, of course, I do. But do I want to learn a single other detail about it no matter how big or small? Hell to the fucking no. Your past relationships are frisbee golf to me, Seattle. And I will happily extend you the same courtesy."

She snorts, rolling her eyes. "That is the stupidest—"

"Smartest idea you've ever had," Caleb says over her. "I'm with Jake on this. Frisbee golf rules. Mars, you agree?"

"I'm not even pretending to listen," he mutters, turning with the skillet in hand. "Fetch your plate, Jake."

I snatch a plate from the island and hold it out as he slips some kind of egg scramble onto it. "Hey, thanks," I say with a grin. "Who knew this whole sex team thing could come with so many perks? I can't remember the last time someone made me breakfast."

"I make you breakfast all the time," Caleb mutters.

"Yeah, calling up the stairs to ask if I want the milk left out for cereal is *not* making me breakfast," I reply, digging in the drawer for a fork.

"Okay," says Rachel, getting to her feet. "I'm gonna go brush my teeth and grab my laptop. Kulta, you'll be ready in five?"

"Joo," he replies, his back turned again at the stove.

"You're leaving now?" I say, fork paused halfway to my lips.

"Mhmm. Ilmari is taking me to the airport on his way into the gym." She leans over me to kiss my forehead. Turning she gives Cay a kiss too. Then she flits around the kitchen island, her arm slinking around Mars' waist as they mutter something in Finnish, and she pecks him on the cheek. Poseidon follows her everywhere at this point, racing after her as she jogs for the stairs.

"So, you're really fine with her going?" Cay mutters the moment she's out of earshot.

"Yeah, why wouldn't I be?" I say with a shrug. "It makes sense that she wants to tell her family about us in person. And how cool will it be to get to meet Hal Price?"

"Easy," he mutters. "You know how weird she gets about him. When you meet him, you gotta be cool, okay? Don't embarrass her. More importantly, don't embarrass *me*."

"Hey, I'm not the one you need to worry about," I say defensively.

"Sure, I've seen The Ferrymen in concert once or twice. But ask our giant Finnish friend here how many times he's seen them live." I turn to face him, smirking.

Mars just shrugs.

"Yeah, I'm not worried about Mars losing his cool," Caleb replies.

"I'm not gonna lose my cool!"

"Both of you shut up," Mars mutters, glancing towards the stairs. "We have more important matters to discuss. I'm not going to the gym. I'll take her to the airport, then I'm coming straight back here. We have much to plan."

"I agree," Caleb replies. "I've been up since six. I have a list going already."

"Me as well," says Mars with a nod.

I glance between them. "Is this about Operation Coming Out Day? Because I've got a bunch of ideas too."

"No, I'm talking about our plan for getting Rachel her job back," Caleb replies.

"Same," says Mars.

I glance between them. "Okay . . . yeah, that's super important. But you know what's even *more* important? Going public with our relationship."

"I don't know if she'll still want to do that if this suspension is final," Caleb says with a grimace. "I mean, her whole thing is that the press only reports on her scandals and her failures. We might have to give this time to all blow over."

Mars is nodding his head and I swear to fuck, my heart drops from my chest.

"No. No fucking way," I snap. "We are not going backwards. Look at me right now and tell me that we're *not* going backwards."

Both guys look at me but say nothing.

"Alright, listen," I say, lowering my voice. "We have a chance here. A *real* chance. This trip to LA could be the perfect timing. Let's get her safely out of the way, and then it's grand gesture time."

Mars raises a brow at me. "Grand gesture time?"

"Yeah, I think we can deal with both pieces of this at once," I explain. "We can get Rachel her job back *and* we can come out to the public as the Fearsome Foursome, official name TBD."

Caleb just huffs. "You think in five days we can get Rachel her job back and coordinate an entire public relations campaign? Not to mention we have jobs. You both have to play hockey, remember?"

"Of course, I do," I reply. "Which is why we're gonna need some help. We're gonna call in every favor we collectively have. That's the point of a grand gesture, right? It takes a group effort. The press will be expecting a spectacle with this, so let's give it to them. Go big or go fucking home. Are you both with me?"

Caleb sighs. "Tell me your idea first before I say yes."

I grin at him. "Oh, you're gonna fucking love it."

102
RACHEL

Four days without my guys and I'm a mess. Not that I've gone cold turkey. That's not possible when you're unofficially married to Jake Compton. He texts me as much as ever. The time change makes it fun, since he's typically up at 6:00am east coast time, and now I'm on the west coast.

I've been trying to just lie low, spending quality time with my mom, relaxing by her pool. She's enforcing a strict media ban. Dad's team is still dealing with the smattering of press requests, keeping me out of it, and the Price houses are a no TV, no news, no gossip safe haven. We listen to music, cook, and ignore the outside world. It's perfect. An emotional battery recharge.

It turns out that my fear of coming out to my parents as polyamorous was wholly unnecessary . . . because Harrison came out for me. He did a great job of coaching them into acting natural, but I saw through their weird, forced smiles in a second. The little fink ratted me out.

"Don't be mad at Harri, Lem," Daddy said, wrapping his arm around my shoulders and giving me a squeeze. "He was just playing the overprotective twin card. If we didn't swear on our lives that we'd be cool when you told us, he threatened to withhold grandchildren."

So that was it. That was the big reveal. As far as daddy is concerned, if I'm happy, he's happy for me. He wants them to come over for dinner after their game to officially meet them.

Mom has been the harder sell, but then she asks the harder questions. She wants details, backstories, dates. She wants to know things like 'If you have children, who will be the father? Or do none of you care?' You know, casual poolside chats.

Is it strange to say I'm not worried? I'm not worried about the big unanswered questions in our relationship. The essential things are there. I love them and they love me. We want a life together. We're willing to fight for it. The rest is just details.

At this point, I'm more concerned about my suspension. My career aspirations have never been about needing money. I know that's an incredibly privileged thing to say, but it's true. I've never had to work. I choose to work. I wanted to go to med school and become a doctor. I wanted the long hours in the lab, thankless night shifts at the clinic. And I love the sweat and stress of game day. I love feeling like part of the team. I may not be a player, but I earn a little piece of every win too.

This suspension is my fault. I'll accept it if they choose to terminate me. But damn will it hurt. It doesn't matter if I think I did the right thing by Ilmari. I broke the rules. We're not supposed to let emotion cloud our judgement.

I understand . . . but I also disagree. Humans are complicated. We're emotional. Our stories are so rarely linear, our health journeys dynamic. If I didn't have the emotion of Ilmari's story fueling me, I might have made different choices regarding his care. Maybe I would have chosen the path of Avery and dismissed him out of hand.

I just wish I could do more to fight for my job. I want to stand before Doctor Tyler and the General Manager and state my case. But in four long days, the only thing Tyler has asked for are the scans from Cincinnati. Other than that, it's been radio silence on all fronts.

It's been almost eerily quiet. Nothing from Poppy. Nothing from dad's PR team. Just peace . . . and quiet . . . and text updates from Jake regarding pelican watch.

The guys say they don't have any updates, but I've been part of the team for months now. The Rays all gossip worse than a ladies' knitting circle. They know something. They're just keeping it from me. Which is stressing me the fuck out.

Their plane touched down super early this morning. Since I'm on suspension, I don't have pass privileges to see them at the arena or the hotel. Not that I would try. I'm not doing anything to risk my suspension getting worse. I don't even want to go to the game tonight. Though Jake has made it crystal clear they expect to see me there. Last night, he forwarded me four tickets. Rays family area, right on the ice.

I'm trying not to think about it. We're all meeting for a quick lunch in an hour. Everything will look brighter once I'm back in their arms.

"ARE you sure this is the place?" I say, peering through the dark glass of the SUV.

Daddy keeps a few drivers on staff, and he assigned Carl to me for the week. He's a great guy. I've known him since I was fourteen. "That's the name you gave me, honey," he says from the front seat. "GPS says it's right here."

I peer out the window again. When Jake sent me the name of the café, I just forwarded it to Carl and finished getting ready. I was expecting it to be a little hole in the wall. Caleb likes finding quirky places with sandwiches named after celebrities. Otherwise, Jake drags us out for expensive sushi.

This is neither. It looks like the restaurant of a swanky hotel.

"You staying, or going, honey?" says Carl. "I gotta move this beast."

"I'm . . . staying," I say, my hand dropping to the door handle. This is unexpected, but who am I to judge? Maybe it has a $60 club sandwich with shaved turkey and applewood smoked bacon called 'The Kevin Bacon.'

"Just call when you're ready to go!" Carl says from the front seat.

"Thanks, Carl," I say, slipping out the back, phone in hand. I dial Jake as I shut the door and cross the sidewalk into the hotel lobby.

"Hey, babe!" he says brightly.

"Hey, I'm at this weird hotel restaurant. Is this right?" I say, glancing around. "It's a cloth napkin, fine china place and I'm in jeans. The waiters are wearing tails."

"Yeah, we're on the way. We're running late. Blame Cay—"

"Do *not* blame Cay," I hear Caleb say near the phone.

I smile, feeling better knowing they're near. "How far out are you?"

"Maybe like ten minutes," Jake replies. "We put in a rez. It's under Compton. Just grab the table and we'll be right there."

"Okay," I say, stepping through the double glass doors into the swanky restaurant.

The hostess smiles at me, her ebony skin dewy and perfect in the light streaming in through the windows. "Good afternoon," she says in a sing-song voice. "Do you have a reservation?"

"Hey—babe," Jake says in my ear, pulling my focus.

"Yeah?"

"We love you, Rachel."

My heart flutters as I smile. "Yeah, I love you too, angel."

"Great, be there in ten!" He hangs up.

I drop my phone down to my side.

"Miss, did you have a reservation?" the hostess says again.

"Yes," I say, slipping my phone into my pocket. "Name is Compton."

"Yes, of course. The other member of your party is already here. Right this way, Miss."

I go still. "Other member?"

"Yes, he arrived just before you," she replies. "I'll show you to the table."

"No—they're not here yet."

I just talked to Jake. We literally just hung up, and he's not here. So . . . who *is* here? Who am I meeting? The poor hostess looks just as confused as me. My curiosity gets the better of me.

"Show me to the table."

"Of course," she sings with a twirl of her finger. "Right this way."

We move around the fancy glass dividing wall and enter the main dining area. It's packed with late afternoon lunch-goers. I see small portions of fancy food on large plates. Yeah, no hockey player in the universe would pick this place.

She shows me to a corner table by the window where a man in a suit sits on his phone, glass of iced tea sweating on the white tablecloth in front of him. He's an older man, salt and pepper hair, serious eyes under thick dark brows. He oozes wealth and sophistication. He picked this restaurant; I'd bet any money.

My heart drops from my chest as I clutch to my bag like it's a life saver ring. I know this man well, though I've only met him a few times. He's Mark Talbot, General Manager of the Jacksonville Rays.

He glances up as the hostess approaches, his gaze shifting from her to me. His expression is impossible to read as he stands, setting his phone down on a stack of files perched on the edge of the table. "Doctor Price, glad you found the place." He holds out his hand and I robotically step forward and shake it.

"I'll send your waiter over to you now," the hostess chimes as she waltzes away.

I stand there at the corner of the table, watching as Mr. Talbot reclaims his seat. He glances up at me, dropping his napkin back in his lap. "Won't you sit?" He gestures to the open chair. "I hope you like tuna tartare."

103
RACHEL

Heart in my throat, I take the seat opposite Mr. Talbot. Glancing around, the truth sinks in. This is a table for four with places set for two. My guys aren't coming. They lied to me. I have a feeling Mr. Talbot is about to tell me why.

"Have you been here before?" he says, taking a sip of his iced tea.

"No," I reply.

"Well, I ordered a few things. We can graze as we chat."

As if on cue, the handsome waiter comes forward and presents an artfully arranged plate of tuna tartare. The marinated pieces of fish are balanced atop a bed of diced avocado, garnished with green onions and sesame seeds.

"Can I get you something to drink, Miss?"

"Just water," I murmur.

"You can order anything you want," says Talbot. "Wine? Cocktail?"

"Water will be fine," I repeat.

The waiter floats away, leaving us alone at the table.

"Well, let's dig in," says Talbot, helping himself to the tartare. "Do you not want any—"

"I want to know what's going on," I reply. "Sir, I came here expecting to meet . . . someone else."

"You . . . oh, hell." He huffs a laugh, setting his fork down with a rattle. "Those sneaky assholes. Did Compton trick you into coming here? God, that explains why you're being so damn weird." He sighs, shaking his head with another laugh and I relax a little.

I say nothing, waiting.

"Well, then let's forget about the damn tartare for a minute," he says, shoving his plate to the side. "I can see from the haunted look on your face that you're not going to eat a bite until you know why the hell I'm here."

I nod, hands clasped tightly in my lap.

"Well, Doctor Price. The long and short of it is that my house is on fire, and I'm ready to do anything to put it out."

"Fire, sir?"

"Yes," he replies, those dark eyes glued on me. "My team. My organization. In the past five days, we've been rocked from top to bottom. Ever tried putting out a house fire, Price? I can tell you now that it's not any damn fun."

"I don't understand."

"Don't you? This all started with you, Doctor Price. I think you're the only one who can end it."

"End what?"

"The madness that has taken hold of my team," he says with a wave of his hand. "In the last five days, I've had over half my players in my office threatening to quit on me. The other half are asking to be traded. They're making demands, holding my feet to the goddamn coals. I'm ready to cry uncle. So here I am, talking to you." He taps the table between us.

This is about me? The whole team is involved? That doesn't make any sense. "Ask me anything, and I'll tell you, sir," I say.

"I really only have one question for you, Doctor Price," he replies. "Do you like working for the Rays?"

"I . . . yes, sir," I murmur. "I love it. I love the team. I love the support staff, the camaraderie. I loved the idea of being part of something new, of building something lasting from the ground up."

He nods slowly. "And what's your five-year plan, Price?"

I let out a shaky breath. "Umm . . . I always hoped that, if I won the Barkley Fellowship, it would lead to a full-time position. Not that I ever expected it," I say quickly. "I just know that Barkley Fellows often transition into permanent roles. And that's what I want . . . wanted," I correct.

"From what I've gathered, you didn't actually pick the Rays though," he replies. "The fellowship was all set up for some other doctor."

I nod, clearing my throat. "Yeah, from what I understand, he fought a white-water raft and the raft won. The position became vacant, so I filled it."

"So, you didn't pick the Rays," he presses. "You settled for the only open option."

"I guess I don't see it like that," I reply. "I took an opportunity. A door opened, and I leapt through it. And, at least in my life, the best things to ever happen to me were always the things I never planned for. Did I ever see myself as a sports medicine doctor for an NHL team? No. Frankly, when I arrived in Jacksonville, I couldn't even tell you the names of all the positions. But I quickly fell in love with this city and this team. I wouldn't change my placement for anything."

He nods, pensive as he takes another sip of his iced tea.

My eye drops to the stack of manilla folders by his elbow. "What are those?" I dare to ask.

"These?" He places his hand over the stack. "These are your files, Price."

"My files?"

"Yeah, this top one is all your professional records," he says, lifting the top file. "Courtesy of Doctor Tyler. It's your resume, transcripts, your application to the Barkley Fellowship, including letters of recommendation from doctors at the LA Galaxy, the Lakers, and the Cincinnati Sport Clinic."

"And the others?"

He picks up the second file. "Well, these have been flooding into my office for the past five days. It's letters of support from pretty much every high-profile patient you've ever worked with."

"Oh my god," I murmur, tears stinging my eyes.

Talbot flips open the file, thumbing through the pages. "I've got letters here from golf pros, an Olympic bronze medalist high diver, and what looks like half the Cincinnati Bengals. All glowing in their praise. To a one, they all say I'm an idiot if I don't hire you immediately."

I'm floored. This was my guys. It had to be. How did they get this all in motion so quickly? "Mr. Talbot—"

"And then there's these," he says, holding up the last folder.

I bite my lip trying to stop the tears from brimming over.

"Letters of support from every single player on my team. Every Ray, including most of the farm team guys. The support staff wrote too. The equipment managers all rave about how nice you are, how easy you are to work with. There's even a letter in here from the coffee cart lady at the practice complex. Apparently, Candy says you're generously paying for her son's trombone lessons this year because she can't afford them. He made first chair in his middle school orchestra thanks to you. And George on the janitorial staff said you bought him a new moped with a matching helmet when his broke last month."

They even tracked down George? Yep, I'm officially crying. I snatch my napkin off the table, dabbing under my eyes.

"If nothing else, all this drama shined a light on a festering wound," he goes on.

"Oh?"

"Yeah. It turns out most of the guys were dissatisfied with the level of care they were getting under Doctor Avery. They were just all suffering in silence. But they're not silent anymore. I've had over half the team in my office this week threatening to quit if I didn't can him. The other half has been banging down my door telling me to hire *you* in his place."

I shake my head. This is too much. I didn't want to earn a spot this way. "Sir, I never meant to cause you this much trouble," I say, leaning over the table. "I just wanted to do my job. I like to help people, and I'm in a position to do so. Money is nothing to me, sir. I think you might understand that better than most," I add.

He says nothing.

"I work hard because I want to," I go on. "I help people because I can. And I swear to you, I would *never* jeopardize a player's health. Everything I did with Kinnunen was to keep him safe. I pulled him from the ice, even when he didn't want me to. I got him scans. I worked in all the PT with him that I could. Yes, we fell in love," I admit. "But if anything, that made me *more* committed to his care, not less. And if that makes me a terrible doctor because I get emotionally invested in patient care, well . . . I guess I don't care," I say with a wave of my hand. "Sir, I don't care. I'm a double Cancer, which means I'm an emotional fucking wreck of a human who cares too deeply and tries too hard. Maybe they shouldn't let double Cancers go to med school. But I did, and I'm here, and I stand by my choices. I would make them again."

My speech sucks all the wind from my sails, and I slump back in the chair, snatching up my water to take a sip.

Talbot goes on as if I didn't just spill my guts. "Langley's letter is four pages long. He has a real gift for writing, as it turns out. He says he hasn't felt so good on the ice in years, and that it's all down to your regime of physical therapies."

His smirk falls into a decided frown when he lifts out the top paper. "This one is from Kinnunen." He flashes it at me and I can see the brevity. The whole letter barely covers half the page. He really had so little to say about something as important as this?

"Want me to read it to you?" He looks down at the page and clears his throat. "Dear Mr. Talbot, Give Dr. Rachel Price back her job, or I'll leave the Rays, effectively immediately. And I'll take Jake Compton with me. And this—" He hefts out a stack of papers held together with a binder clip. "These are all the offers they've both farmed in a matter of days from other teams willing to take them both. Five NHL teams, three Finnish Liiga teams, a Swedish team. And I got a text from my secretary as I sat down that she has trade offers pending on four other players too."

My heart drops out of my chest. "Sir, I'll talk to them. They won't do this to you, I promise—"

"Oh, they're not the only ones threatening to leave the team," he replies with a huff. "I already told you, Price. I've got half a dozen more letters echoing a similar threat—Novikov, Sullivan, Langley, Morrow, Gerard. How the hell am I supposed to replace my entire starting lineup? You tell me."

"I'll . . . talk to them," I say, still shaking my head. "This isn't how I wanted this to go, sir. This isn't right. This isn't how I wanted to earn back my place on the Rays—with threats and avarice and—"

"Friendship," he corrects. "Concern, outrage. That's what all this is, Price," he says, holding up the thick stack of files. "This is what teamwork looks like. This is what respect looks like. These are the files of someone who is honorable, someone who engenders loyalty. These men are ready to burn down the Rays for you, and I'm not just talking about Compton and Kinnunen."

I'm crying again, trying to hold myself together and failing miserably.

"When my whole team is telling me something, it behooves me as their manager to listen. And what they're telling me is that they like you, Price. They trust you. They want you on this team. You can't buy loyalty like this," he says, tapping the top of the files. "You've earned a second chance. I'm here to see that you get it."

"Sir—"

"So, here's my deal," he says over me. "Finish out one more week of suspension without pay so Coach Johnson is satisfied. He needs to see that actions have consequences. So do the players. Set the example and do your time in the penalty box without complaint."

"Yes, sir," I murmur, nodding my head.

"Good." He's quiet for a moment before adding, "Then I want you to come back and finish out the rest of your fellowship."

I gasp, looking up. "Sir—"

"Let me finish, Price," he says, raising his hand. "This isn't official yet, but the Rays are parting ways with Doctor Avery. As I said, when my team talks, I listen. They've spoken in one clear voice. Avery is out. That means I have a hole in my roster. I'm going to move that the board of directors approve the creation of three new PT positions—director and two assistant directors. One assistant will work exclusively with our injured players. The other will be a joint hire with the strength and conditioning team."

I nod, not sure what I'm supposed to say. He's dangling something that is starting to look decidedly like a carrot. But I'm afraid to trust it, afraid to hope.

"Consider your fellowship a trial period, Price," he goes on. "Keep your nose clean. No more going rogue. No more pissing off Coach Johnson. And for the love of god, no more falling in love with any more of my Rays. At the end of the fellowship, you can take your pick of the assistant director positions."

All the air leaves my chest in a huff. "Sir, I don't—" I shake my head.

"You say 'thank you,' Price," he teases. "And you say, 'Yes, Mark, I accept.' Because if I have to go over to those guys and tell them I couldn't close the deal with you, I'm legitimately concerned for my safety. You're saving my life with your answer, Price. Say 'yes,' and we can all leave here happy."

"All?" I say, confused by his phrasing.

"Yeah, your three demons have been haunting the corner of the restaurant for the last five minutes," he adds, pointing over my shoulder.

I spin around, eyes wide, to see Jake, Caleb, and Ilmari sitting at a table at the far corner of the room, watching us like hawks. And they're not alone. Seated next to Ilmari is a curvaceous woman with a head of fiery auburn curls twisted up in a messy bun. Her red-painted lips split into a grin as she smiles and waves. Tess is here.

104
RACHEL

Before I can think to leave my chair, my guys are already up and moving this way. All eyes in the restaurant watch them approach. They're hard to miss, making the space between the tables their own sporty GQ runway.

Mr. Talbot and I stand.

"I should have requested a bigger table," he says in greeting, shaking Jake's hand.

"We can't stay," Jake replies. "Got a game to play, remember?"

Ilmari has eyes only for me, wrapping me in his arms. I fight the urge to cry all over again as I breathe in deep, my face pressed to his chest. He's doing the same, his large hand stroking down the back of my hair as he rests his face at my temple.

He murmurs softly in Finnish things I don't understand, but I feel. Then he cups my cheek, searching my eyes. "You are well?"

I nod, too overcome for words just yet.

"It's like I told you guys back in Jax," Talbot says at the guys. "I'm a firm believer in second chances when they're earned. Doctor Price has clearly earned the team's trust and their loyalty. They want her on this team, so I want the same. I want my team happy and healthy and whole."

"He's going to let me finish my fellowship," I say, finding my voice at last.

"Oh, that's so great, baby," Jake says, leaning in to kiss me while I'm still in Ilmari's arms. "The guys are gonna be jazzed. They really came through this week—"

"Yeah, and now I need you to call the dogs off," Talbot warns. "Spread the word far and wide: Doctor Price is still a Ray. She'll be back on the job in time for our trip out to Texas."

"Thank you, sir," Jake says, shaking his hand again.

"Don't thank me," Talbot replies. "It was the right thing to do. Now, seeing as my life is no longer in mortal danger, I'm going to sit back down and finish this tartare . . . and maybe order a steak. I imagine at least three of you have more important places to be right now."

"Shit, yeah," Jake says, checking the time on his phone. "We've gotta get back to the hotel." He looks to me and back down to Talbot.

Mr. Talbot just snorts. "All of you go. I didn't want to share this anyway," he adds, dragging the plate of tartare in front of him.

"Thank you, sir," I murmur.

He's smirking as he looks up at me. "Just see that those three get back to the hotel and loaded on the bus in time."

I turn, taking Ilmari and Jake's hands as the five of us weave through the tables of the restaurant and out into the lobby of the hotel. As soon as we're out the doors, my guys explode into talking all at once, jostling for position as they hug me and kiss me and ask me what happened.

"Umm—hellooo!" Tess waves frantically. "The best friend is standing right here, and I've gotten literally nothing. Girl, I flew across the country for this. Put your boy toys down and give me a damn hug."

I turn in Jake's arms with a laugh, throwing my arms around Tess instead. "What the hell are you doing here?" I cry.

"Caleb invited me," she replies.

I glance over my shoulder at him, one brow raised. "Why?"

"If things went bad with Talbot, we didn't want you to be alone," he replies with a shrug.

"Yep, just call me Ms. Moral Support," Tess adds with a laugh. "But now that things are all good, we can go to the game together! You know I've been dying to see the Rays in action. Mama loves a powerful man on skates. And Jake said he sent you enough tickets to share."

"Yeah, I sent over four," he replies. "But Poppy can get you more," he adds. "No problem. Just shoot her a text, Seattle."

I force a smile, feeling suddenly awkward. "I don't know . . . it won't be weird? I'm still technically suspended. I don't want to overstep or—"

Jake presses in, kissing me senseless. Breaking our kiss, we both suck in air, "You're coming to the game," he says. "And Mars and I flipped for it. You're wearing my jersey tonight. I already gave it to Tess."

"Yep," she says, patting the side of her massive purse. "All good to go! Hey, maybe if you wear his jersey, I'll wear Ilmari's—"

"No," all three guys growl at once, turning three dark stares on my best friend.

I fight the urge to laugh as Tess leans away, eyes wide. Her face slowly shifts from shock to mirth. "Jeez. Touchy subject."

Ilmari's hands go around my waist as me pulls me in closer. "You wear mine next game," he murmurs, kissing my cheek. His soft beard tickles my skin.

"Guys, we gotta go," says Caleb, checking the time on his watch.

"We'll see you at the game, baby," Jake says, giving me another quick kiss. "Take care of our girl, Tess!"

"You got it," she calls with a wave.

"Mä rakastan sua," Ilmari murmurs, his lips brushing against my temple.

"Niin mäkin sua," I reply, practicing my new phrase.

He smiles down at me with such joy and my insides light up like a lantern. He kisses my forehead, passing me off to Caleb.

Cay surprises me when he cups my cheek and kisses me too. "See you later, Hurricane."

With that, my guys troop out the front doors of the hotel, leaving me with Tess.

"Girl, you won the man candy lottery," she teases. "Triple cherries. Those guys are head over heels in love with you."

I smile. I can't help myself. For only like the fourth time today, I'm about to cry. "Yeah," I say, heart overflowing.

"Come on," she laughs, wrapping an arm around my shoulders. "We've got a few hours before the game and, if I remember right, Mama Price makes a mean pitcher of sangrias."

"RACHEL Diane Price, get your booty down here or we're gonna be late!" Tess shouts up the stairs.

I ignore her. I'm on my knees in my room, tearing my bag apart looking for my Rays tech t-shirt. "God, where is it?"

"Rachel!" Tess calls, stomping down the hall. "Girl, why do I feel like I'm always hollerin' for you?" She stands in the doorway, hands on her hips. Apparently, she came prepared because she's wearing a super cute Rays t-shirt cut in a "V" that does wonderful things for her cleavage. She's paired the t-shirt with a pair of black leggings and sparkly tennis shoes. Her wild hair is up in a messy pony and a winged cat eye lines her hazel eyes.

"Tess, you look hot," I say, eyes wide. "Hubba-hubba. Who are you trying to impress tonight?"

"Nobody," she says with a flick of her hair. "I look good because it makes *me* feel good. And you can't wear that," she adds, pointing at my white bra. "As your emotional support friend, I can't let you go to a packed hockey arena with your girls flopping out."

"I know," I say, turning back to my bag. "I'm looking for my Rays shirt."

"Umm, no you're not. You're wearing the jersey."

I glance over to where the No. 42 jersey is laid flat on the bed. "I'm not wearing that."

"Oh yes, you are." She stalks over to the bed and snatches it up. "Jake said they flipped a coin. It's fine."

"Yeah, no offense, but I don't believe them. If you knew what happened last time . . ." I smile, falling quiet.

"Why, what happened last time?" she says. Then her eyes go wide. "Oh god, it's a sex thing, isn't it? I don't want to know. Yes—no. I do, but I don't." She groans. "Damn, I'm not drunk enough for this!"

"Tess, I'm not going to kiss and tell," I say with a laugh.

"Not yet, you won't. We're both stone cold sober. Just wait till we've had a few of those cans of wine. Now, arms up. You're putting this on." She stands right in front of me, scrunching up the jersey.

"Tess," I say with a roll of my eyes.

"Arms up, Rach. Don't make me wipe your booty too."

With a huff, I lift my arms and she slips the jersey on over my head. It's huge on me. It's a real jersey, meant to be worn over Jake's pads. The big Rays logo is sewn onto the front with a 42 on each shoulder. I have to double-roll the sleeves to free my hands.

Tess is losing her patience as she taps her foot by the door. "Okay, grab your wallet and your chapstick and let's gooo!"

WE pull up to the arena to see crowds of people surging outside, waiting to get in. More than the fans, what surprises me is all the press. Paparazzi crews are jostling, hurrying like ants with their cameras and mics.

"This is crazy," I murmur, peering through the dark glass of the SUV window. "I've never seen it like this before."

"Well, it's LA," says my mom from the front seat. She decided at the last minute to join us. Daddy said he didn't want to draw attention.

"I suppose that's true," I reply. It's not uncommon for celebrities to attend NHL games, especially in New York and LA. "I bet we just missed someone famous," I laugh.

"Yeah. Like, ooo maybe its Harry and Meghan," Tess says on a sigh.

"You really think Harry and Meghan dropped everything to come to an NHL game on a Saturday night?"

"You don't know," she replies.

"I kind of do," I tease back.

"Let's go, ladies," mom calls from the front seat. "Rachel, eyes forward, and straight inside, honey."

"What—"

Before I can get the rest of my question out, the SUV rolls around the corner, and I realize we're driving right up to the press scrum. The police have put up barriers to keep the crowds back. The cameras line each barrier. Behind them, people press in on both sides, shouting and waving posters, screaming as our car rolls to a stop.

I gasp, eyes wide, as I see two of the posters. On one, PRICE = LOVE is written in all the colors of the rainbow. Another sign covered in glitter reads LOVE AT ANY PRICE.

"What the—"

"Rach, *go!*" Tess shouts from behind me.

A police officer opens my door, and the shouting intensifies tenfold. Mom is already down on the pavement, holding out her hand to me. I take it, letting her pull me from the car. As soon as I step out, all the bulbs of the cameras flash, blinding me as the press start shouting and the people behind start screaming.

I'm delirious, blinking in the harsh light of the flash bulbs, as mom pulls me forward. Tess steps in at my back, and the three of us rush through the middle of the scrum, not stopping as all around us people shout.

"Hot doc spotted!"

"Rachel!"

"Price means love!"

"We love you, Rachel!"

The arena security are ready to open the doors for us, letting us inside. The doors shut and I spin around, eyes wide, taking in the surge of people outside. "What the fuck was that?" I cry.

I glance from my mom to Tess. Both of them are suddenly looking decidedly guilty. I shake my head in shocked disbelief. Whatever is happening right now, they're both in on it. "Oh, what in the name of ever-loving *fuck* is going on?"

"**H**oney, don't get mad," mom says.

"Don't get mad?" I cry. "Too late! What the hell was that? Where did all those people come from? What are they doing here?"

"They're here to see you," Tess replies. "To support you, Rach. You and the guys."

"Support me?"

"Yeah—look, we *really* need to let Caleb explain," she says, nodding at my mom.

"Caleb?" I squawk. I feel like the world's worst trained parrot, only able to echo every fourth word they're saying.

"Come on, honey," mom says, taking my arm. "Everything will make sense in a minute."

The security guard scans our tickets and then mom and Tess lead me through the maze of the lower level towards our seat section. As soon as we enter the throngs of people, all hell breaks loose again.

From left and right, people start shouting my name. They surge to get closer. Mom and Tess stay to either side, holding my hands. Fans wave posters when they see me, cheering and screaming our names. Not just mine. I hear a lot of shouts for Jake and Ilmari, even Caleb. Most of the posters sport the numbers 31 and 42. And two words are on almost every single one.

PRICE IS LOVE

LOVE IS LOVE

FALL IN LOVE AT ANY PRICE

"We love you guys, Rachel!" one young woman calls out.

"Love the jersey!" comes a shout from the other direction.

"We're here for you, Rachel!"

"Love is love!"

Suddenly, wearing this jersey feels like I've got a big target painted on my back. This is crazy. "I need to go to the bathroom," I pant. I don't need to go; I just need to get out of these throngs of people.

Mom glances over her shoulder. "But we're almost to our section—"

"Now," I cry, tugging us out of the flow of traffic towards the women's restroom. I go in first. Rushing around the corner, I find the edge of the sink and hold on for dear life. I look up at my reflection in the mirror and take a deep breath.

Mom and Tess come in to flank either side of me, mom putting her hand on my shoulder. We look so much alike. Except where my eyes are dark brown, hers are blue.

"Oh, honey," she murmurs. "I'm sorry. I warned them this would be a lot for you to take. Harrison likes the spotlight, but you were always my little snuggle bunny. You prefer the calm and the quiet."

I hold her gaze in the mirror, the tears in her eyes reflecting the tears in mine.

"This was never going to be easy," she goes on, brushing my hair back behind my ear. "In choosing them, you've chosen a difficult path for yourself. A path that will mean leaving the comfort of your burrow . . . at least for a little while. But if you love them as you say you do, you need to understand what this means to them. You need to see how much they need it. How much they need *you*," she adds gently.

"Mom," I whimper, the tears threatening to fall.

"I was worried when you first told me about them," she admits. "Not about the polyamory," she adds quickly. "We're Prices. We've seen and done it all already."

I sigh, shaking my head as next to me Tess laughs. Understatement of the decade.

"I was worried that they wouldn't understand you," mom goes on. "I was worried they would take from you. And you're such a giver, honey. You'd give the clothes off your back. But they *do* know you, Rachel. They see you. They know what you need. Let them give it to you now. Let them show the world how much they love you. Let them have this moment. Ride it out with them, and they'll be yours forever."

"They did this," I whisper, already knowing it to be true. Who else could?

Mom and Tess both nod.

"And you both knew? Of course, you did," I answer for them. "That's why you're really here, isn't it," I say at Tess's reflection.

"We all love you, Rach," she says with a watery smile. "You deserve your happily ever after. You've got three knights in shining skates out there, waiting to show the world what your love means to them." She holds out a hand. "Come on. Let's go find them."

I nod, sniffing back my tears as I turn. My focus catches on something in the mirror and I glance back. "Umm . . . Tess?"

She looks back at me. "Hmm?"

"What am I wearing?"

She flashes a grin at my mom. "Yeah, I totally can't believe you let me get away with that."

I look in the mirror again. I'm wearing a Rays jersey. Jake's jersey. The front has the Rays logo, and the top shoulders have Jake's 42s. But the back is Ilmari's 31. And instead of either of their names at the top, the jersey reads PRICE.

"What am I wearing?" I say again.

"We reeeeeally need to find Caleb," Tess says, grabbing my hand.

My determination hardens into stone as I set my fear and confusion aside. Oh yeah, we are going to find Caleb. And then I'm getting answers.

RUSHING down the stairs of our section, mom calls out our seat numbers again.

"AA, seats one through four!"

All around us, people shout when they see me. I hear more people screaming my name, waving signs. Why the heck are they screaming *my* name? That's what I'm not understanding. Why Price?

As we near the bottom of the stairs, I stop dead in my tracks. Standing there in the BB row, just behind our seats, are two faces I know as well as my own: Harrison and Somchai. They're both looking over their shoulders, smiling up at me.

My gaze catches on the face of a pretty woman standing next to Harrison. Something about her is familiar. She's young, maybe late

20s. Her dark hair is pulled up in a ponytail and she's holding a beer as she smiles up at me . . . and she's wearing a Compton jersey.

An explosion goes off in my mind and now I'm crying again. "Amy," I say, hurrying down the last four stairs to my row.

She laughs, holding out one arm, sticking her beer out to the side. "Hey, Rachel! So nice to finally meet you. My brother hasn't shut up about you for months."

I'm laughing and I'm crying as I hug her.

"And you'll notice her twin, the man who shared a womb with her, gets ignored," Harrison says with a huff.

Amy lets me go, and then we're all laughing as I hug Som first. He rocks a whole Thai mob boss vibe, with tattoos covering most of his body, even up his neck and a few on his scalp. His hair is growing in a bit, long on top like Ilmari's. He looks tough, but inside he's a big softie.

"Hey, sissy," he says, giving my cheek a kiss.

"What the heck are you guys doing here?" I cry, finally giving Harrison his hug.

"Price Family always comes first," Harrison says, kissing my other cheek.

Mom, Tess, and I shift into our row. As soon as I'm standing in front of the plexiglass, I turn, looking up into the stands. All around us people are wearing 31 and 42 jerseys. A woman moves to the side, and I do a double take. The back of her jersey reads PRICE.

My heart starts to race as I read more of the signs. This can't be happening. This isn't real—

"Finally!" Tess cries.

I turn around to see Caleb jogging down the stairs of the section, favoring his good leg. Behind him, people scream and cheer. He comes down to the bottom of the row, stopping to shake hands with Harrison and Somchai. Amy throws her arms around him, and they hug. Then he slips past mom, and she hugs him too. Tess just squeezes back in the row saying, "Boy, you better work your magic before she bolts!"

And then Caleb is standing before me, his dark gaze rooting me to the bleachers. "Hey, Hurricane," he says with a smile. He takes my hand, weaving our fingers together.

"Cay, what is going on?" I murmur.

"You hadn't noticed? We figured if the press was going to make us into a spectacle, we'd just beat them to it." He gestures behind us to the sea of people waving posters.

"I don't understand," I say with a shake of my head. "What did you do?"

"We came out," he replies. "Well, Jake and I came out. We've been photographed every night this week in public being . . . out," he says with a smirk. "He's been doing interviews, podcasts, a few TV spots."

"What?" I say on a breath.

"Yep, Jake Compton is officially very out as a bisexual NHL player. Poppy is calling him the new face of queerness in pro sports," he adds with a roll of his eyes.

"And . . . you're okay?" I murmur, squeezing his hand.

"More than okay," he replies. "It had to happen. To get what we all want, he and I had to come out."

"But you're not the only ones, are you?" I say with a raised brow.

He smiles. "Baby, the three of us have been doing press for five days coming out in every way possible. Mars has even been doing it in two languages."

"What?" I cry. "How did I miss this? My phone has been radio silent," I say as I tug it from my pocket.

He dares to look a little sheepish. "Yeah . . . babe, that's not your phone." He pulls a matching phone from his pocket. Same case and everything. "*This* is your phone."

I gasp. "Oh, what the fuck?"

"Turns out Mars could be a spy," he says. "He mirrored them and swapped them when he took you to the airport. That's just a burner. No one has been able to contact you because no one has that number. And Poppy and your dad have been running major interference. It's getting gnarly, to be honest."

I gasp, snatching the phone from his hand and unlocking the screen. I've got hundreds of alerts and notifications. Even as I hold the phone, it's buzzing with more. "Oh, I am going to *murder* you!" I hiss. "Is that why all these people are here?"

"Yeah, they all know our story now," he replies. "They know how you and Jake met in Seattle. They know how we met at the airport. They know how you cared for Ilmari."

Sensing my panic, Caleb cups my cheek and leans in. "Baby, breathe. This is good, okay? It's all good."

"What do you mean?" I cry, my brain already going into overdrive thinking of all the ways this will blow up.

"You've been taught to think that the press is wholly bad," he says. "That people knowing your story can only be bad. That they only want to tear you down."

I can't help but scoff. "Well, duh—"

"But look around," he says, gesturing up to the stands. "For every one troll who has something negative to say about us, there will be a thousand more people ready to wish us well. That's what we wanted to show you tonight, Rach. We just wanted you to step out of your own way and let us show you that people *can* be good. They can be kind. They can be understanding. We are not alone. And this is not going to be bad."

"Caleb," I breathe, not knowing what else to say.

"Jake and Ilmari ran a contest," he goes on. "First fifty people to buy Rays season tickets would get flown out to this game with comped airline tickets, hotel, the works. They're footing the bill together. Rach, within the first hour, Poppy had to shut the website down."

"Oh my god."

"Season ticket sales have doubled," he adds. "Our next six home games are sold out."

"Stop," I whisper, shaking my head. It's all too good to be true.

But he just smiles. "Our story is out there now. It's trending all over social media. Poppy had to hire help to deal with the overflow, and I think your dad is ready to kill us, but it's working," he adds quickly. "They're on our side. They love our story. They love *you*."

I glance over and see my mom trying to pretend she's not listening with tears in her eyes. Yeah, she's been helping them. Her media ban was effective, keeping me in the dark. Always protecting me.

"Why do the jerseys say Price?" I whisper, needing Caleb to say it out loud.

His smile softens as he cups my face again, his thumb brushing along my cheek. "That was my idea. You're always saying that it's the

Price Family against the world, right? We just figured you could use a deeper bench."

And now I'm ugly crying, pressing my face against his chest, clinging to him.

"Mars is gonna say he can't legally change his name unless you marry him first," he says in my ear, his voice getting louder as the music crescendos. "But I googled it, and cohabitation also works, so don't let him trick you. He just may have to wait five years," he adds with a shrug.

"Wait—legally," I cry, pulling back from him.

Caleb nods. "I submitted all the paperwork on Monday. Within the next two to four weeks, it'll be official. I'll be Caleb Price."

I shake my head, heart overflowing, unwilling to believe this is all real. "And Jake and Ilmari?"

Before Caleb can respond, the announcer's voice comes blaring over the speakers.

"Get on your feet, Rays fans! It's time to bring out the starting lineup!"

All around us, the Rays fans cheer and stomp.

"At forward, number 19, Josh O'Sullivan!"

The Rays fans go wild as Sully shoots out onto the ice, skating around in a sharp circle.

"At forward, number 20, Ryan Langley! At forward, number 17, Henrik Karlsson!"

Langley and Karlsson come skating out one after the other and the guys start shooting pucks into the empty net.

"And at defense for the Rays, number 3, Cole Morrow! At defense number 42, Jake Price!"

The Rays fans go wild as Jake skates on to the ice with Morrow. Jake looks great in his white away game jersey. The 42's mark his shoulders and back, but stitched across the top is my name.

"And starting in the goal for the Rays is number 31, Ilmariiiii Priiiiice!"

Even many of the Kings fans go wild cheering for Ilmari. Meanwhile the Rays fans lose their ever-loving minds.

Ilmari steps out onto the ice in his full goalie kit, his mask already pulled down, looking every inch the Bear. But he doesn't skate to his goal. He doesn't even look at it. I can feel his eyes on me as he skates straight across the ice. The fans behind us go nuts as he skates right up to the glass and tips his helmet back, his steely blue eyes gazing into my soul. Tugging his blocker off, he presses his hand flat against the glass.

Without hesitation, I reach out and place my hand in the imprint of his. "Oon sun," I call through the glass.

He smiles and I feel it everywhere. "Vain sun, Rakas."

As the crowd screams behind us, Jake skates up too, tugging off his glove, a wide smile on his face. He presses his hand against the glass next to Ilmari's. "Hey, Seattle Girl." His smile melts me inside. "How mad are you on a scale of one to ten?" he shouts through the glass.

I can't help but laugh, shaking my head as Caleb leans in to kiss my temple. "Ten," I call back.

"Yes," he teases. "Angry make-up sex is the best."

"Oh god," Harrison says behind me.

"Cover your ears, Mama Price," says Tess as the others laugh.

"Hey—and my sister is here!" Jake calls, pointing at Amy. "I brought her all the way from Japan, so I win first dibs tonight."

"Shut up and go skate!" Caleb barks.

Everyone around us laughs as Jake blows Caleb and I a kiss and skates off, shamelessly sporting my name on his back.

Ilmari drops his hand away from the glass, replacing his blocker as he lowers his mask down over his face. With a nod, he turns and skates away. Seeing the name Price on his back settles everything home for me. This is the second time he's remade himself, claiming the family he wants, choosing his life. I have a choice too.

I lean in closer, both hands pressed against the plexiglass. "Ilmari Price!" I call, my warm breath fogging the chilled glass.

He pauses, glancing over his shoulder.

"Win this game, and I'll marry you!"

All around me, our friends and family shriek with surprise.

Ilmari skates back over to me, flipping his mask up, his eyes on fire. "Say it again," he growls.

"No way in hell am I waiting five years to make that name change legal," I say, pointing at his jersey. "You wanna be a Price?"

Glancing to Caleb, he gives a curt nod.

"Then you're going to be a Price," I say. "Win this game, and I'll marry you. Make it a shutout, and we'll do it tonight."

"And if we lose?" he says.

"You won't," I reply, giving him a knowing look.

His face is set in determination as he lowers his mask and skates off again to the cheer of the crowd.

"Jake is gonna lose his fucking mind when he finds out," Caleb says next to me.

"He'll be fine," I murmur, taking his hand and bringing it to my lips.

"Oh, you think so?"

"I know so," I reply.

"How?"

Turning to face him, I smile. "Because if I marry Ilmari, that means *you* get to marry Jake. And he truly couldn't find a better man."

His eyes go wide as he gazes down at me, a smile tipping the corner of his lips.

"Yeah, I thought you'd like that," I tease. "But they win first. We don't cave unless they win. Stay strong with me."

"Fuck," he mutters under his breath, watching as Jake skates past looking like our every dream.

"Oh, and there's one more surprise left tonight!" Harrison calls from behind us.

I glance over my shoulder with a groan. I'm honestly not sure how many more surprises I can take. "What is it?"

Harrison points down to the rink where a team of people are rolling out a carpet onto center ice. A pair of men hurry onto the ice wheeling an amp and a microphone. Then a third man brings out an electric guitar on a stand.

"Oh my god," I gasp, eyes wide. "You did *not* rope him into this," I say, turning to gape at Caleb.

He raises both hands in mock surrender. "Hurricane, I swear to god, he volunteered."

"Apparently they booted a children's choir for him," Harrison says with a grin, poking his face down between us.

"Ohmygod," I groan, burying my face in my hands.

"Come on, it's not that bad," Caleb teases. Wrapping me in his arms, he rests his chin on the top of my head.

"Please rise for the playing of our National Anthem!" comes the announcer's booming voice. "Performed tonight by one of rock and roll's biggest legends . . ."

The whole arena goes feral as my dad steps through the plexiglass, the cameras zooming in on him. His smiling face appears up on the jumbotron. He looks effortlessly cool in his ripped t-shirt and leather jacket, jeans, and a pair of scuffed motorcycle boots. He waves to the crowd as he walks down the carpet towards his waiting guitar.

"Hockey fans, please welcome to the ice the lead guitarist of The Ferrymen, LA's own native son, Hallllll Priiiiice!!"

Content in Caleb's arms, I smile and watch as Jake and Ilmari skate up to the carpet's edge and each remove a glove to shake my dad's hand. The crowd goes wild as he picks up his guitar. The moment he strums that first note, a hush falls. Then, closing his eyes, he leans back and begins to play.

Epilogue
ONE YEAR LATER

"Easy, Hurricane," Caleb mutters, taking his hand and covering mine, giving it a gentle squeeze.

I take a deep breath, letting my hands go still. Whenever I'm nervous during a game, I spin the guys' wedding rings round and round on my thumb, focusing my energy on the feel of the cool metal brushing against my skin. They all have the same band—white gold, inset with four small diamonds.

It's our little ritual. The guys can't wear jewelry on the ice, so at the start of each game they hand their wedding bands to me. I hand them back when they finish. Taking it off made Jake so depressed, he finally popped his tattoo cherry. Now he has a thin, inked band around his finger that stays hidden under the ring.

Tonight, I'm only holding one ring because Jake is standing next to me. Decked out in a blue and white Finland jersey, he's fighting with Harrison for control of the popcorn bucket.

The arena buzzes with excitement as dance music pumps up the crowd. My gaze is locked on center ice where the Olympic rings are painted. This is it. The gold medal game. Finland vs. Canada . . . *in* Canada. Everywhere I look is the red and white of the Canadian flag—jerseys, scarfs, hats, signs, painted faces.

My heart feels like it's going to burst with excitement . . . and gratitude. All around me, our friends and family are here to cheer for Ilmari. Harrison and Somchai stand next to Jake, both wearing Suomi sweatshirts. Som looks ridiculous in a Suomi beanie with a big blue and white knit puff ball on top.

On the other side of Caleb, the Kinnunens are singing all the cheers. Juhani is a Finnish hockey star in his own right, so he's been swarmed by the fans at every game. His sister Laura and her daughter Helena stand to his right. They've been so kind and welcoming, letting the three of us into their lives as we show them how much we love Ilmari.

We spent part of last summer with them in Finland, and it was so fun to see a different side of Ilmari. I'm now officially a convert to Finnish saunas and cold baths. We even installed a sauna at the house that Ilmari uses after every game. I smile, cheeks warming. We've had some serious fun in that thing.

I'm distracted as a baby lets out a loud squeal. Mäkinen's wife Kristina bounces their toddler on her hip in the row in front of us. He's a little cherub, with bright blond curls and pink cheeks. He's wearing baby-sized noise-cancelling headphones, bundled up in a lion costume. The moment I saw him, I think my ovaries exploded. Jake has already had to physically remove him from my arms once tonight.

Caleb snakes his arm around my waist. "He's gonna do great, babe. He's feeling good. Feeling strong."

I nod, trying to swallow my nerves. The last game was a disaster. Finland vs. Sweden. Ilmari took a gnarly hit that had my soul threatening to escape my body. An elbow to his mask tipped him back, shoving him into his net. He hit the crossbar as he fell, knocking the goal loose.

The scream I screamed. As the lineman escorted the Swedish player over to the penalty box, the guys were physically holding me back from climbing the plexiglass and ripping his heart out. Those are the two hardest parts about being a hockey wife: the waiting and the hits. And I'm a hockey wife twice over.

I have no one to blame but myself.

"Hey, Seattle—look," says Jake, giving me a nudge, his fist full of popcorn "He's here."

I follow the line of his point to see Doctor Halla standing at the far end of the row in the aisle, glancing at his ticket. He's decked out in Suomi gear too, including a t-shirt and scarf. I smirk. I don't know that I've ever seen him in anything but scrubs or a suit. It's weird. Like seeing a dog ride a skateboard.

"He came," Caleb murmurs next to me.

I smile, giving both their hands a squeeze as I brush past Jake to go greet him.

It turns out no one can hold a grudge quite like a Finn. And my husband is the most Finnish Finn I've ever met. So, we're taking it slow. Halla came to a Rays game in the spring. He also came down at the end of the summer to celebrate the launch of Ilmari's sea turtle conservation organization.

On the night of the gala, it turns out Ilmari donated half a million dollars to a non-profit run by three overenthusiastic, but rather hapless do-gooders. His additional money and oversight provided a total overhaul of their organization. Now, Out of the Net is a proper non-profit with a board and a CFO and a growing volunteer base.

Halla made a sizable donation too, all but matching Ilmari's contribution. Sea turtles up and down the coast of North Florida are going to sleep well at night knowing a pair of Finns are determined to keep them safe.

I slip past Harrison and Som, waving Halla down. "Hey! Halla, over here!"

He waves in greeting, his gaze trailing down our row. He settles on Juhani and Laura and nods. Juhani has been supportive of my mission to help father and son mend their fences. I think it was Juhani's interference more than anything that earned Halla a ticket to this game.

"Hello, Rachel."

"Hey," I say, feeling breathless. "Glad you could make it."

Som scoots down a bit to make room for us on the end.

"Did you get to watch the other games," I say.

"Oh yes," he replies. "I recorded them all."

"What did you think of the last game?"

His gaze darkens. "The Swedes played dirty."

"Yeah, I was gonna kill No. 12," I say.

"Get in line," he mutters.

We stand there for a minute, the excitement of the crowd pulsing all around us.

"Well," I say, feeling nervous. "I should head back to my seat—"

"Price, I—Rachel," he corrects, his hand on my elbow. "I've never thanked you. For any of this—I never—"

"Hey," I say, patting his hand. "It's okay—"

"No. I should thank you," he presses. "You're the only reason this is happening. You're the reason he's letting me get closer. My own attempts have been feeble at best. When you spend so long living in the cloud of your mistakes, it's difficult to see your way out of the fog."

"I know what you mean."

And I really do. I spent so long lost and searching too, wondering if I'd ever amount to anything. Hal Price's wild daughter. The party girl. The mess. The spoiled brat. I was so bitter and angry and just plain scared.

"We all deserve a second chance," I say. Feeling like this is a moment of truth, I lean in. "But just know that, if Ilmari is a lion, I'm his lioness. Hurt my husband, and I'll rip out your fucking throat. Agreed?"

He smirks, giving me a nod. "Joo."

I still, that simple one-word answer sparking something in my memory. I slip in front of Som to go back to my seat, but then I'm glancing over my shoulder. "What did you ask him?"

He glances my way. "Hmm?"

"That night," I say, inching closer. "At dinner in Cincinnati . . . you asked him something. I know enough Finnish now to know his answer was 'yes.' What did you ask?"

He huffs a laugh, his mouth tipping into a smile. Raising a hand, he cups my cheek. The tenderness feels strange, but I don't pull away. "I asked him if he was in love with you."

I suck in a sharp breath, eyes wide.

He drops his hand away, still smiling.

My heart hammers in my chest. He asked then? He asked in Cincinnati . . . and Ilmari's answer was already yes.

Halla gives me a nod, his own eyes teary. "Take care of him?"

It's not really a question. We both know I will. Ilmari is *mine*. I will love him and fight for him with my last breath. Slowly, I nod. "Joo."

"OHMYGOD!" I cry, my hands clinging to Jake and Caleb's arms as we all jump up and down. This game has been out of control. The Canadians want it bad. A gold medal win on their home ice? It's what dreams are made of. They're playing fierce and dirty, pumped up by the wild crowd.

Ilmari has been a brick wall, blocking shot after shot. And the Finnish offense has been amazing, led by Mäkinen. The score has been locked at 1-0 since the end of the second period. Finland is winning. And we're almost down to the last two minutes of the final period. Canada is ready to try anything to even the score.

"Oh fuck—they're doing it!" Caleb shouts. "The goalie's on the move!"

"Ohmygod," I scream again, watching as the Canadian goalie books it over to the bench. The second his skates are off the ice, their fastest forward goes blasting out. Now their sixth man is an NHL top-scoring speed skater, famous for his slap shot.

"Oh, holy shit! I'm freaking the fuck out!" Right now, Jake couldn't find his cool with a GPS. He's a howling maniac, screaming at the Finnish defenders to check and block.

All the action is down in the Finnish defense zone. I can practically feel the concentration surging off Ilmari, even from here. I hate that he's at the opposite end of the ice. I feel so helpless, but there's nothing any of us can do. This is his game to win or lose.

The Finns fight dirty, trying to wrestle the puck away from the Canadians. If they can just get the puck loose and down ice, they can score again on the open net. The Canadians know it's a risk. This is their Hail Mary chance to tie this game.

"Get it out!"

"Come oooon!!!"

The whole arena is going wild. The Finnish fans are trying to match the volume of the Canadians, even though we're outnumbered 50-1. Mäkinen digs in along the boards, fighting a forward for control. He's able to slap the puck out, sending it towards the center line.

The heat is off Ilmari as the clock ticks down. Then Canada's number 10 makes a sloppy shot, and the puck goes spinning towards the corner.

"Holy—goalie goal!" Caleb screams. "Goalie goal! Goalie goal!"

"Oh my god, he's gonna do it!" Jake practically strangles me as he reaches around to grab Caleb's shoulder, and now they're both jumping, jostling me between them.

I hardly know what I'm seeing as Ilmari races after the puck, leaving his net. His defenders hold back the Canadians for all of two seconds as Ilmari turns, lining up the shot on his paddle. With a whack, he sends the puck flying over the heads of the players.

I watch in slow motion, Caleb and Jake screaming to either side of me, as the tiny black puck sails down the length of the ice. It lands in the Canadian defense zone and glides over the ice, straight into the back of the empty net. There's a moment of suspended animation as the whole arena registers what just happened. Then the cherry lights up, the siren wails, and the score board changes. 2-0.

And then the Finns absolutely erupt. Our section of the stands becomes like a human volcano as we explode with screaming, crying, hugging, and chanting.

"Best game ever!" Jake shouts.

Down on the ice, the Finnish team crowds Ilmari. A goalie goal in the last minutes of a gold medal match? Yeah, there's no way the Canadians are coming back now. It's over. Finland wins. Ilmari just guaranteed the team the gold medal.

Tears are pouring down my face as I hug everyone around me, my heart racing. I clench my fist tight, loving the press of Ilmari's heavy wedding ring against my skin. His ring is safely tucked on my thumb. Tilting my hand, I look down at the stack of three diamond rings I wear as my wedding bands. They twinkle under the bright arena lights.

The guys each picked one. Ilmari's is at the bottom of the stack, a mirror to theirs in a slimmer style. Caleb's is in the middle, a thin band of diamonds, nothing flashy. It's perfect. Jake's rests on top, four rectangular cut diamonds, dotted with emeralds—green for his eyes. I squeeze my fist tighter, heart overflowing with happiness.

Next to me, Jake pouts.

"Angel?" I say, wrapping my arm around his waist. "What's wrong?"

He just shakes his head and sighs. "There'll be no living with him after this."

I just smile. I think we're all going to live together just fine.

"GOD, this is taking forever," Jake groans, his eyes on his phone.

I roll my eyes, ignoring him. Caleb does the same. Ilmari texted us an hour ago that he was finally free and on his way over to the hotel.

"He'll get here when he gets here," I say, shifting against Caleb's side. As I say the words, there's a knock at the door.

Jake launches off the other king bed wearing nothing but his athletic shorts, and hurries over to the door. "Fucking finally!"

Caleb and I both laugh. I slip off the side of the bed, snatching up Ilmari's ring from the bedside table.

"There he is!" Jake shouts, flinging open the door. "Oh—fuck, man—seriously? Like I don't have enough of a complex already?"

I don't hear what Ilmari says as I step around the end of the bed, but I see him standing there in the doorway, hugging Jake. It's new for them. Jake insisted. He may not want sexual contact with Mars, but our Jake is a hugger. Ilmari just lets it happen now, his hands patting awkwardly at Jake's shoulders. But his gaze is all on me.

Tears sting my eyes as I watch him pull away from Jake. He's standing there with his gold medal around his neck, looking every inch the hockey god. We were all at the medal ceremony earlier. I bawled my eyes out when they put it around his neck. And we've already all said our congratulations. We took a thousand pictures, posting them to social media at Poppy's insistence.

But here he is at last, in the privacy of our hotel room, and we can celebrate how we want. No cameras. No press. No 'Team Price' media circus.

It's been a year of major adjustments for all of us, letting the press and the hockey community get over the shock of our unorthodox relationship. But my guys were right—for every one asshole internet troll who wants to tell us we're going to hell, a thousand more people are always there to wish us well.

Ilmari's gaze heats hotter than a fire as he brushes past Jake, sweeping me into his arms. I melt against him, desperate for his every touch. "How does it feel?" I say, mid-kiss, my hands smoothing down the strap of his medal.

His hands are all over me, holding me tight to him. "Amazing," he mutters.

I smile up at him, raising my hand to stroke his cheek.

His eye catches the glint on my thumb and he's snatching for my wrist. "Give it back."

I let him slip his wedding ring off my thumb and watch as he slides it back onto his finger. It's almost like a weight lifts off him as it slips into place, like he's not complete without that ring around his finger reminding him of who he is and where he belongs.

I cup his face with both hands. "I'm so proud of you, kulta. You were amazing."

He kisses me again and I let myself get lost in this feeling of his power, his joy. Our kissing heats up, and soon he's breaking away with a soft curse.

"What do you want?" I say. "Our gold medal Olympian gets whatever he wants tonight."

"Yeah, but only for tonight," Jake warns from the edge of the bed. "Tomorrow it's back to me calling all the shots."

Ilmari growls, casting him a glare as behind him Caleb huffs an incredulous laugh.

"What do you want?" I say again.

"You know what I want," he replies, his voice fevered with need.

Taking a deep breath, I nod. "Then, I'm saying yes."

"Yes?"

"Joo."

"Yes, Rakas." His joy is infectious as he grabs me, hauling me up against him. He turns us, dropping me onto the bed next to Jake. "Get lost, Jake," he growls.

"What? Ouch—" Jake gasps indignantly as Ilmari swats his hand away from me.

I'm wholly at Ilmari's mercy as he jerks my cami off up over my head and tosses it to the floor, leaving me topless.

"Go play with Caleb," he orders. "Right now, she's mine."

Jake scoffs, pushing himself off the bed. "Just so you know, scoring a goalie goal to clinch the Olympic gold medal is literally the *only* set of circumstances I can accept that mean you get your way right now. Come tomorrow, you slap my hand away from my wife, I'll bite it off."

"Noted," he mutters, eyes on me as he takes the gold medal off and drops it to the floor, his shirt following.

Caleb steps around behind him to stand by Jake. As Ilmari strips off my silky shorts, I glance over to them, watching as Caleb slings an arm around Jake's shoulder and cups his cock. "Do you wanna watch with me, angel? Or I can put you on your knees and pound your sweet ass."

Jake groans, leaning into him, but it's Ilmari who replies, dropping his athletic pants to the floor and fisting his hard cock. "No ass play tonight. And neither of you better fucking come."

Caleb blinks at him. "What?"

"We can't touch Rachel, and we can't come? Cool," Jake deadpans. He turns to Caleb. "Wanna just play checkers or something?"

I snort a laugh, but I'm quickly silenced by Ilmari grabbing me by the calves and dragging me down the bed. He drops to his knees, flinging my legs over his broad shoulders as he descends, his mouth claiming my needy pussy.

"Oh god—" I gasp, arching my back as both hands go to his head. I dig my heels into his back, holding him close as he devours me. I can't control my moans as his tongue licks and teases. He hums against me, knowing how I love it. My human vibrator. This man eats pussy like a god. All my guys are talented. And they're always ravenous. Enthusiasm alone can get you a long way.

I open my eyes, seeking out my other guys. Jake watches, transfixed, while Caleb teases him with kisses, his hand now inside Jake's shorts, stroking him from root to tip. I lick my lips, wanting to taste them while Mars tastes me, but he gets what he wants tonight and, in this moment, he wants me to himself.

With a groan, Jake turns in Caleb's arms, his free hand cupping Caleb's face as they kiss. Cay keeps his hand in Jake's shorts, working him slowly as they taste each other. Seeing them love each other takes me over the edge. I cry out, my orgasm battering me as Ilmari works me with his tongue and fingers, drinking in my release with a hungry groan. He likes to warm me up with at least one orgasm before he enters me. It's easier with his size if I'm slick and ready. *Done.* I am literally desperate for this man.

I sling my legs off his shoulders, panting for breath, as I crawl up the bed away from him. "Tule tänne," I pant. "Kulta, tule."

With a growl he's on his feet, climbing on the bed over top of me. He sinks down into the cradle of my thighs. It takes nothing for him to notch his cock at my entrance and press in.

I exhale on a long moan, relaxing my body as he fills me so full, settling at my center. Tears sting my eyes as I hold onto his shoulders, rocking with him, my heart overflowing. "I love you," I murmur. "Ilmari—so proud of you—"

He silences me with a kiss, his body claiming me as he mutters against my lips in Finnish, pouring out his love for me. He curls a hand under my thigh, spreading me wider and pressing in deeper.

"Oh—" My neck arches back as I feel the exquisite spiraling of a G-spot orgasm building deep in my core. My whole body is heating and my brain feels fuzzy. The tightness is exquisite. "Yes—*there*—"

"Tell them," he growls, slamming into me with his hips. "Rakas—tell them."

Panting, I turn my gaze away from him, holding to his shoulders. Caleb and Jake are still standing at the end of the bed, their clothing shed. Caleb has both their cocks fisted in his hand. Jake's head is tipped back, eyes closed, as Caleb sucks on his neck.

"Guys," I call out. "Jake—Cay—"

They break apart, their heads turning our way. Ilmari slows his thrusts, dropping his face to kiss my neck. I hum with pleasure, reaching out a hand for them. "Come here."

They step forward, Jake taking my hand.

"I took out my IUD," I say. "Last week. I took it out."

Their eyes go wide as they both register my full meaning. We've been talking about it for months. Jake wanted us to start trying the night we all got married. Luckily, the other two were on my side that we should delay. Weather the media storm, find our new normal. But now feels like the time. We're happy. We're ready. I want the next phase of our life to start.

"Hooooly fucking shit," Jake cries, his expression euphoric. "You serious right now, Seattle?"

I nod, biting my lip as Ilmari starts to move again.

"Oh, fuck yes," Jake says, dropping to his knees at the side of the bed. He takes my hand and holds it, kissing my knuckles as Ilmari worships me with his body.

Caleb stands behind Jake, eyes wide. Of all the guys, he's been the most anxious about the idea of kids. But Caleb always does best with action. He'll learn by doing and grow his confidence, I have no doubt.

Jake looks on in wonder as Ilmari shifts his hold on me, burying himself deep with each thrust. I sink back, eyes closed, as I let his passion meld with mine. Stronger together. Never to be parted. Ilmari Price is my husband. My lover, my friend.

I moan as my orgasm spirals tighter.

"Come," Ilmari begs. "Come again, Rakas. Come with me—*please*—"

Hearing my husband beg sends me shattering. His hips slam in and hold as his warm release fills me. My pussy holds him tight. I'm panting, sweating, seeing stars. I sag back against the bed as he slips out. Breathless, he rolls to my side, his hand going down to my pussy. He swipes a finger over my entrance, bringing it to my lips. I suck his finger into my mouth with an eager groan, tasting the mix of our releases on my tongue.

"Caleb, come," Ilmari orders. "Take her. Take our wife. Fill her."

Suddenly, Caleb looks almost afraid. I hold out my hand to him, shifting up to my elbows. "Come here, baby."

He steps forward, sinking to his knees on the edge of the bed with a soft wince. He's out of his element here. No games, no kinks. This is sex and intimacy on a whole other level. Knowing what we both need, I take charge, rolling up to my knees. "Lie down," I say, voice firm.

"Hurricane—"

"Lie down, Caleb," I say, wrapping my hand around his nape. "I'm going to ride your cock like a fucking queen. You're *mine*. My husband. This is all of us or none of us. Are you all in?"

Nodding, he shifts closer, wrapping his arms around me. We kiss as I flip him down to the bed. Dropping onto my elbows to suck his pierced cock into my mouth. He groans, hands in my hair as I work him hard. I'm ravenous as I climb onto his lap, shifting my hips until his cock is pressed against my clit. I shiver, smiling down at him as I lift my hips and notch him at my entrance.

He has eyes only for me as his gaze darkens. "Do it," he growls.

I sink down hard and fast, and we both cry out. His piercings rub me so perfect as I start to move, finding my rhythm as I fuck myself on his perfect cock. He holds on for dear life, hands on my hips, watching in awe as my breasts bounce with each thrust.

"Baby, I'm already close," I cry, my greedy cunt already squeezing him so tight.

"Me too—" He groans, his head arching back as he holds me still, his hips slamming up into me.

I cry out, the power of his thrusts sending me free-falling. I'm gasping and moaning, rocked by an orgasm that has me practically convulsing. I squeeze him so tight, wave after wave hitting me. And then his warm cum fills me, dripping out of me back onto him.

I'm a shaking mess as we both come down off our high. Then he's curling forward into a sitting position, his cock still buried inside me. I don't even realize I'm crying when he wipes my tears and kisses me.

"I love you, Rachel. Baby, I love you so much," he murmurs. He's the least vocal of my guys, showing his devotion with action rather than words. To hear them now, I'm like a flower seeking sunlight, clinging to him, showering him with kisses.

"I love you," I whimper. "Cay, I love you."

"I love you, Hurricane," he says, breaking our kiss as he looks for Jake.

Knowing it's his turn at last, Jake drops onto the bed at our side, wrapping his arms around both of us as he kisses first me, then Caleb, then me again. "I love you both so much," he murmurs. "I love you. My girl and my guy. I'm the luckiest guy in the world. I even love you, Mars," he adds over our shoulders at Ilmari.

I turn to see Ilmari sitting on the ottoman by the side of the bed, still naked. Slowly, he nods, which we all know by now is Ilmari for 'I love you too, but I'm too emotionally guarded to say it. So, I'm just going to stare at you and hope that's enough.'

I smile, heart overflowing as I turn to Jake, Caleb's cock still nestled in my pussy. "Angel please," I say, cupping his face. "You know how much I need you."

He grabs me under the arms, lifting me clean off Caleb and turning, dropping me onto the other bed. "Hands and knees, baby girl. I wanna go deep."

I roll eagerly to my knees, facing the end of the bed. But Jake doesn't immediately follow me. I turn my head to see him pushing back on Caleb's shoulder, laying him out on the opposite bed. Bending over, he sucks Caleb's half-hard dick into his mouth, licking him clean with a hungry moan. Caleb fists Jake's hair with both hands, his gaze volcanic as he moves his hips, willing himself to stay hard enough to choke Jake.

I whimper as, from across the room, Ilmari groans, his hard dick in his hands. He's loving this as much as I am. His breeding kink is on full blast knowing it's now possible to get me pregnant. "That's enough," he orders. "Jake, fuck our wife. Now. She takes all our cum tonight."

Jake pops off Caleb with a groan, shifting up quickly to kiss him. Then he sinks onto the mattress behind me, his hands tracing up my sides, over my shoulders, as his hard cock nestles between my ass cheeks. He folds himself over me. "Kiss me."

I turn, dropping my shoulder enough that we can kiss. It's sloppy and quick, but we don't care. Then his hand is slipping between my legs, seeking out my entrance. "Fuck, baby," he groans. "You're so fucking wet. They made a mess of you. You're dripping in their cum."

I whimper at his words, feeling him plunge in with his fingers, moving the mess around, putting it back in.

"I never thought I had a breeding kink, but this is turning me all the way the fuck on," he says on another groan. "Mars, come feel," he calls.

"Just finish her," Ilmari replies.

"Jake, please," I beg, starting to feel desperate from this waiting. "I need you, angel. Need your cum." The words come out between panted breaths as he grabs hold of me, notching himself at my entrance.

"You're mine, Seattle," he says, slamming himself home.

We both cry out and I drop down to my elbows, changing the angle. I give him free rein. I want him to use me and fill me, pounding as hard as he wants.

"My wife," he groans as he claims me. "My lover. Mother of my children. My fucking soulmate. That's what you are. You took something from me the night we met, and I'll never get it back. I don't *want* it back. You changed me, baby."

"You changed me too," I cry, my body lost to the euphoria of being so perfectly filled.

"You're my everything," he says. "My whole fucking world. You and Cay and Mars. You're my world. Full stop. Nothing else matters."

"Yes," I beg. If the universe is benevolent, she'll let me keep them forever.

Sharing a wavelength as always, he bends himself over me, cupping my breasts as he thrusts into me. "Never let me go. Rachel, please."

I arch back until we're both on our knees and I'm pressing my hips against him, rocking with him, my hands holding to his on my breasts. "Never," I say with all the power I can muster. "Never, Jake. Mine forever."

Then he's crying out, coming inside me. His release triggers mine. This one slower and deeper than the others. It's a kind of pulsing ache that builds and devours, like my entire body has suddenly turned to liquid gold.

We drop down to the bed and he rolls to my side, pulling out of me. Ilmari is there in a heartbeat, turning me onto my back. He drops his hand between my legs, cupping the mess spilling out between my legs. "Take it all," he growls. "Keep us inside you, Rakas. Make us a family. Make us whole."

I nod, tears in my eyes as all three of my guys come to the bed. Jake stays on my left side, Ilmari my right. Caleb slips onto the bed behind Jake, his arm banding over him to splay flat across my stomach. We lay there, all four of us, in a bed too small, and hold each other.

We may have built this foundation on shifting sands, but together we're holding stronger than ever. I have three bonds, unbreakable. They have their own bonds too—bonds of friendship, teamwork, and love. No matter what the future holds, I know who I am now, and I know where I belong.

"Anyone want room service?" Jake mumbles. "I'm ordering an ice cream sundae."

Ilmari just groans. I think Caleb might already be asleep. Meanwhile, I can't help but smile. This all started in a hotel room with the man at my side. My Mystery Boy. Now here we are, living a life neither of us could have ever dreamed.

I snuggle in closer, closing my eyes. I don't need to celebrate this moment with ice cream. Life is already so sweet.

THE END

EVER *wish you'd been a fly on the wall during that infamous ESPN interview? Keep reading to find out how it went down in this exclusive bonus scene!*

Love & Hockey: At Home with the Jacksonville Rays

Janine Marsh | Dec 17, 2022, 3:00 PM ET
This ESPN exclusive interview took place at the home of Jake Compton, starting defenseman for the NHL's Jacksonville Rays. Present for the interview were: Janine Marsh, ESPN Special Correspondent; Jake Compton, Defenseman (#42); Ilmari Kinnunen, Goalie (#31); and Caleb Sanford, Assistant Equipment Manager.

Janine: It's a sunny Wednesday morning here in North Florida, and I'm sitting out on the private lanai of one of the top-performing defensemen in the NHL. Jake Compton, you were a first-round draft pick, NCAA standout, and most recently you skated with the LA Kings. Now you're one of the first players in League history to wear a Rays jersey. How does it feel?

Jake: You know, Janine, it feels pretty great. Honestly, it feels like I've come home. We've got a great team we're building here in Jax. It's a great group of guys, and I'm just excited to see what the future will bring.

Janine: The NHL last saw an expansion back in 2021, when the Seattle Kraken joined the League. Now the Jacksonville Rays are the new team on the block. Any hiccups or headaches so far?

Jake: Well, expansion years are always rough on the whole League. A lot of trades happen that can ruffle some feathers, and building a team from scratch is no easy job. It's not just the guys that have to learn a new rhythm, a new shorthand—it's the whole team, support staff and back office too.

Janine: It must help that you're being coached by such a legend. Hodge Johnson is a two-time gold medalist with Team Canada, and a fearsome defenseman in his own time playing for the NHL....

Jake: Yeah, Coach J is great. But honestly, our whole coaching staff is excellent. The GM spared no expense in finding the best.

Janine: And speaking of support staff, we have someone else here with us today. Caleb Sanford, former NHL forward, nicknamed "the Lightning" at the University of Michigan—you're currently an Assistant Equipment Manager for the Jacksonville Rays. How has the transition felt behind the scenes?

Caleb: Like Jake said, building out a new team from scratch can be difficult. We're lucky that all the guys seem to get along . . . for the most part.

Janine: Any divas we should worry about? Any prickly personalities?

Caleb: Yeah, I'm sitting right next to him.

Jake: Hey, careful—

Caleb: I wasn't talking about you.

(long silence)

Ilmari: You cannot possibly mean me.

Caleb: Only if the imported European skate with memory foam tongue and thermoformable core fits.

Jake: *(laughs)* Yeah, dude, just admit it. You're high maintenance.

Ilmari: I fail to see how my skate preference makes me high maintenance.

Jake: Tell us, how's the view from seat 20A?

Ilmari: You always sit in the same seat too—

Caleb: Yeah, 'cause we want to sit by Rachel, but you always make her sit by you, and you won't sit anywhere except seat 20A.

Jake: Not to mention you took over my bathroom with all your skincare products. Seriously, why does a man need three different facial toners? Half your face is covered with hair anyway.

Janine: *(laughs)* I should mention that we're joined in this interview by two-time Stanley Cup-winning goalie, Ilmari Kinnunen, who currently starts with the Rays. And by "Rachel"—I assume you're referring to Dr. Rachel Price, your team's first Barkley Fellow?

Caleb: Yes.

Janine: For readers who may not know, Dr. Rachel Price is the daughter of legendary rocker Hal Price of The Ferrymen. Compton, if I'm not mistaken, you're currently dating Dr. Price. It's been something of a whirlwind romance, right?

Jake: Oh, definitely. Rachel and I are dating—wait, no, scratch that. We're not—dating sounds weird to say, right?

Caleb: Yeah, it's weird.

Jake: We sort of skipped right past dating if I'm honest. I've been teasing her since the night we met that I was going to find an Elvis minister and marry her on the spot. That girl is it for me.

Janine: Since the night you met? Wow, that sounds a little . . .

Ilmari: Impetuous.

Caleb: Dramatic?

Jake: Shut up, a**holes. It's romantic.

Janine Marsh: Walk us through it, Compton. How did you two meet?

Jake: Earlier this summer, I met Rachel out in Seattle, and it was a total lightning-in-a-bottle, you-jump-I-jump kind of situation. I swear all she had to do was turn around on that barstool and I knew I'd found my girl.

Janine: Wow, so it was love at first sight, huh?

Jake: For me? Totally.

Caleb: He's a Taurus. He can't help himself.

Janine: *(laughs)* You say it was love at first sight for you. . . . I assume Rachel was slower to feel the sting of Cupid's arrow?

Jake: I wouldn't say that. We both knew from the beginning that this was something special, but we parted ways after Seattle. I didn't even get her name—

Janine: Wait—you didn't ask for her name?

Jake: *(laughs)* Nope. And before you go judging me, I should make it clear that she didn't ask for mine either. We had an agreement—no names, no real life. We were like a pair of magnets from that first moment though. I wanted to tell her my name. Hell, I wanted to propose over our morning coffee. But I woke up and she was gone. I thought I'd never see her again. It was truly one of the worst moments of my life, feeling like I missed a shot I was meant to take.

Janine: But you *did* see her again . . . and it sounds like you took your shot?

Jake: Yep. Two months later, I was walking into the practice rink, minding my own business, and there she was, looking like my every dream. There was some last-minute cancelation with her fellowship—something about a guy falling out of a white-water raft. Anyway, he was out, and she was in. She had less than twenty-four hours to up and move to Jacksonville. She didn't know I was on the team until she saw me standing there. I would have proposed right then too. She held me off for about two weeks before I got her to move in with us.

Janine: *(laughs)* Only two weeks? Doesn't sound like she put up much of a fight.

Jake: Like I said, when you know, you know. The four of us are meant to be together. We figured we could

get busy living the life we want to live and actually be happy, or we could keep fighting this thing and all be separately miserable. We chose to be happy.

Janine: Wait, did you just say "the four of us"? What do you mean by that?

Jake: Well, Cay and I have been best friends since college. We've lived together on and off ever since. Somewhere along the line, we got nicknamed the "DLPs." I never really thought much about it but—

Janine: DLPs?

Caleb: It means domestic life partners.

Jake: Yeah, strictly platonic. Well . . . I mean there were a few times in college when we—

Caleb: *(mutters)* Stop.

Jake: Yeah, we'll go with mostly platonic. But then Rachel showed up like a hurricane and spun everything around.

Janine: Uh-oh. . . . Did she come between you?

(long silence)

Jake: Umm, I don't . . .

Caleb: Jake, I swear to god—

Jake: Can you clarify the question, Janine?

Janine: Did Rachel Price cause a rift in your friendship? Was there an awkward love triangle?

Caleb: No.

Jake: For all of two seconds. But that was over as soon as I saw them together—

Caleb: Jake—

Jake: What—*ouch*—I wasn't talking about like that, a**hole. I meant to say that I saw how *happy* she made you. How happy you make each other. It was honestly a no-brainer for me. Especially once I realized I was jealous for all the wrong reasons.

Janine: So, you're saying that, while you were pursuing a romantic relationship with Rachel Price . . . she was pursuing a romantic relationship with your equipment manager? And that made you jealous?

Jake: Yeah, like I said, for all of two seconds. But I wasn't jealous that they were together. I was jealous that I wasn't with them too, even though I was. Does that make sense? I saw the way she loved Cay and the way she made him happy, and I don't know . . . something just clicked for me, I guess. It was like, all my life, I thought I was this one person, you know? And I thought I knew what I wanted, what I was working toward. But it only takes that one thing to change everything. Rachel was that one thing for me—for us.

Caleb: *(nods)* She's a catalyst.

Janine: A catalyst? What do you mean by that?

Caleb: A catalyst is a substance that increases that rate of change in a chemical reaction. It speeds things up. Rachel was the catalyst we needed to speed up the rate of change within our separate relationships.

Jake: Dude, we're not all chemistry majors—

Caleb: I'm saying she took the paths we were already on and accelerated the speed at which we were walking them. Jake, you and I were already on our way to each other. I didn't need Rachel to show up to know I'd loved you for ten years. If I wasn't such a f**king coward, terrified of your rejection, I would have made you mine a long time ago. Rachel swept in and showed us both how great it could be if we gave this thing a real try. No more DLPs. No more hiding. She freed us from our fear. I wasn't walking to you anymore—I was running. That's a catalyst.

Janine: So . . . you're together? You and Compton are in a romantic relationship too?

Jake: Yeah, we're together. Caleb is mine. So is Rachel. I love them both. I'd marry them both if I could. I'm new to all this, so I don't really know the rules. I don't think I can marry them both though—

Caleb: You can't. Not legally.

Jake: Well, I'm marrying one of you, so flip a coin or something. 'Cause I'll be damned if I never get to stand at the head of an aisle and see at least one of you walking toward me.

Caleb: Wait—are you serious?

Jake: I mean, it doesn't have to be as casual as flipping a coin. Knowing you, you'll want to make a pro-con list but—

Caleb: But you'd marry me? If I asked . . . you'd say "yes"?

Jake: Who do you think you're talking to right now? If you don't ask me at least once, I'll punch you in the f**king head. And then I'll ask you. And if you say "no," I swear to god, I'll punch you harder. Just try and get out of this without wearing my ring. You're stuck with me, Cay. Deal with it.

Janine: *(laughs)* Marriage is that important to you then, Compton?

Jake: Totally. I'm a romantic, remember? The marriage, the kids, the house, and the dog. I want it all. Whether I marry Rach or I marry Cay, we're all together. They're mine. Mars too.

Janine: Wait . . . Kinnunen, where do you fit inside this not-a-love-triangle?

Ilmari: Rachel is mine.

(long silence)

Jake: Wow, I'm really feeling the love right now. You know I do like ninety percent of the cooking, right? I learned to make lohikeitto for you, a**hole. I'm the only one who will watch sci-fi movies with you. I let you use my foot massager. And do you wanna know what I was doing just before ESPN came over? I was folding your laundry. Care to try again?

(long silence)

Ilmari: Jake is mine too.

Jake: And . . . ?

Ilmari: And his lohikeitto really is very good.

Jake: But we don't f**k—if that was your next question, Janine.

Janine: I was not going to ask that. I would never—

Jake: It's okay. We want to be an open book about this. Rachel has dealt with a lot of really awful and heavy shit in her life. The press has been terrible to her family. She can't help who her dad is, and she's allowed to feel like you're all a bunch of vultures ready to pick her bones—no offense, Janine.

Janine: None taken.

Jake: Ask us anything you want about our relationship, and we'll tell you. We want our story out there.

Caleb: The *true* story. Not bullshit gossip and tabloid fodder.

Janine: Well, how do you feel about going public with this somewhat nonconventional relationship in the middle of a new season on a new team? Are you worried about the added press scrutiny?

Jake: It's only natural that people will be curious. As you say, it's not the traditional family, but it works for us and we're happy. We're not hurting anyone, and we're not asking for anything other than privacy. . . . You know, after we finish this very public interview.

Caleb: He's saying we don't want any special treatment, and we don't want to live under a microscope either. We want to get the truth out there, then we want to move on.

Ilmari: We want to focus on hockey, on building out this new team and our careers.

Janine: You have to admit, it's a daring career move. There's only been one other openly gay player in the NHL. And this is coming at a time when the League is publicly rolling back support of LGBTQ+ causes. Do you fear any reprisals from fans or the League? What about the team—

Jake: Our teammates have been nothing short of amazing. Seriously, I've never played with a group of guys that feel so much like family. The Rays support us one hundred percent.

Caleb: And luckily, Rachel comes from a very different world than us. Hockey may still be in the Dark Ages when it comes to diversity issues, but thankfully the music industry is a little more enlightened. We hope we can count on The Ferrymen fans to lead the way in showing the hockey world that love is love and families come in as many colors and flavors as a Baskin-Robbins ice cream cone.

Jake: Damn, that was really poetic, Cay. Also, now I want ice cream.

Janine: Can I ask on behalf of the readers—what's your favorite flavor of ice cream?

Ilmari: No.

Jake: Yes—or wait, no. Let me guess yours—

Caleb : Change the subject, Janine.

Janine: *(laughs)* Okay, fine. Speaking of The Ferrymen, how does Hal feel about his daughter dating three professional hockey players?

Caleb: We'll leave it to Hal to make his own statement.

Jake: But like any good father, we hope he wants his daughter to be happy, whether she finds that happiness with one handsome hockey player or three.

Ilmari: Her happiness is our only concern.

Janine: Is there a reason you're doing this interview without her?

Jake: She's actually out in L.A. as we speak, visiting her family. The team plays the Kings this weekend and we'll finally get to meet Hal and Julia in person.

Janine: Meeting the parents sounds intimidating, especially given who her parents are.

Caleb: That's honestly the reason we wanted to speak to you. For how famous her father is, Rachel is a very private person. She avoids the press at all costs, and we intent to keep it that way.

Ilmari: We're *all* private people.

Jake: But we also understand that media scrutiny comes with the game. I just can't stand the idea of living in constant fear that some reporter might catch me kissing Cay or holding Rachel's hand and "out" us to the world. And we really don't want any bullshit stories about her stringing us all along or some sexist crap like that. This is a loving, committed relationship between four consenting adults.

Caleb: So, we're outing ourselves and praying the world will hear us, respect us, and leave us in peace. I'm in love with Rachel Price *and* Jake Compton. I share my life with them and we're very happy.

Jake: I'm in love with Rachel Price too. She's my—she's the most amazing woman I've ever met. She's . . . everything. She's everything to us. She showed me how easy it is to love Cay. She brought me Mars. Cay called her a catalyst, but I'm calling her the glue. She's the thing holding us together, making us a family, and we're so damn lucky. All three of us. Right, Mars?

Ilmari: *(nods)*

(long silence)

Jake: Mars . . .

Ilmari Hmm?

Caleb: We're "outing" ourselves.

Jake: Yeah, it's your turn.

Ilmari: But you both just said everything that needs saying.

Caleb: Yeah, but this is our official public statement.

Ilmari: Yes, and you both just stated—

Jake: God—will you just f**king out yourself already so we can finish this and go get some ice cream?

Ilmari: What else needs to be said that hasn't already been said? How can Ms. Marsh be in any doubt as to our positions? We live together, we work together, we share in the trials and joys of life together. We are one family. As you are mine, I am yours. Your burdens are mine to share and your victories are mine to celebrate. There is nothing extraordinary in this. We are just four people living a life. We love Rachel, we protect Rachel, and we will do anything to make her happy. What else does Ms. Marsh need to know?

Janine: Nothing. I understand, Kinnunen. It's beautiful, truly. I can see how deeply you care for each other, how you care for Rachel. She's one lucky woman.

Jake: And you don't have any more questions for us? You don't want, like, more details—who walks the dog, who does the dishes, who gives the best back massages?

Janine: Do you want to give us more details?

Caleb and Ilmari: No.

Janine: Then I think we're done here.

Jake: Awesome. Hey, want to walk down the block with us and go get some ice cream? They have coffee chip and it's pretty good.

Janine Sure. Wait—how did you— coffee chip is my favorite flavor.

Caleb: *(sighs)* He knows.